"Chekhov's early stories are his springtime: touching, stormy, full of joie de vivre, with flashes of sunlight, mischievous breezes and an ironic kaleidoscope of Russian faces. His grey, twilit, heart-wrenching autumn is still ahead, so rejoice in Chekhov's springtime!"

—*Vladimir Sorokin, author*

"Absurd, zany, mordant and melodramatic—these stories are full of surprises, and are the perfect antidote for anyone who still thinks of Chekhov as gloomy."

—*Geraldine James, actress*

"This international, invigorating, and in many ways utopian translation project brings a wealth of voices, tones and nuances to Chekhov's early stories."

—*Sasha Dugdale, poet, playwright and translator*

"In this groundbreaking edition of Chekhov's earliest publications (1880–1882), Rosamund Bartlett and Elena Michajlowska make available in English the full complement of stories, sketches, and humoresques included in volume 1 of the definitive scholarly edition of his work. Given that most English-language collections of Chekhov's prose feature his later, more widely known stories, this volume provides an invaluable resource for scholars, writers, and general readers alike.

This alone would have been enough. But in her astute introduction Bartlett also provides a riveting discussion of how the history of publication and republication of individual works, combined with the serial revisions and rewritings undertaken by Chekhov himself and compounded by the eventual compilation and recompilation of an authorized *Collected Works*, which grew (in the years after Chekhov's death) from the original ten to an eventual twenty-two volumes, vastly complicate the matter of dating and chronology. Add to the proliferation of versions in Russian the further complications introduced by serial translations of this or that story in this or that version tagged with this or that date—and, as it turns out, even the scholarly thirty-volume edition contributes to this chronological jumble. In this context, earliness itself merits scrutiny.

The volume's fifty-eight stories have been brought into English by a collaborative of eighty-three translators from nine countries. Each began working on a single text, then went on to participate in a recursive process of crowd translation. The work proceeded so collaboratively and the process ultimately proved so productive that the results are credited to the collective as a whole. The English versions are thus beautifully coherent—yet they are also stylistically divergent, as demanded by Chekhov's take-offs on a stunning range of speech acts and genres: letters, testimony, statistical tables, speeches, catalogues, excerpts, almanacs, and more. The stories themselves are quite wonderful, and these new translations represent a tremendous achievement.

Finally, Bartlett's editorial apparatus deftly makes sense when clarification is required or a private joke needs explaining. She has shrewdly placed immediate sense-making notes at the bottom of the page, with more extensive background information at the end of the volume; the format itself makes the book both maximally accessible and a great pleasure to read."

—*Cathy Popkin, Jesse and George Siegel Professor in the Humanities, Department of Slavic Languages, Columbia University*

"What a gift to readers of Chekhov: the most comprehensive edition of his earliest fiction in English! Assembled through the collaborative efforts of more than eighty translators, this remarkable volume is an outstanding collective achievement. Chekhov's early creations reveal a side that may surprise those who know only his mature works: irreverent, versatile, brimming with raw energy, and often uproariously funny. Read together, they offer a fresh insight into how the future master of subtle understatement was finding his voice. Kudos to the indefatigable Rosamund Bartlett and her tireless team of translators for bringing this treasure to light. For any lover of Chekhov, this book overflows with delights, discoveries, and revelations. A second volume, please!"

—*Radislav Lapushin, Associate Professor, University of North Carolina at Chapel Hill*

"*Chekhov's Earliest Stories: Stories, Novellas, Humoresques 1880–1882*, edited by Rosamund Bartlett and Elena Michajlowska, is a landmark publication. The perennial, deep engagement with Chekhov has burgeoned in recent decades: adaptations of his works abound. Is there any other writer, except perhaps Shakespeare, who continuously reinvents the world the way Chekhov does? Yet many of his early works have never been translated into English, and this is the first complete translation of all his very earliest stores, accompanied by helpful annotations. Bartlett, a foremost English translator-scholar worldwide, has written a groundbreaking introduction brimming with vital new information and insight. She and her distinguished colleague Michajlowska have assembled a dazzling international team of 83 translators to give us this uniquely precious collection. Chekhov virtually leaps off the pages in these often absurd, edgy, funny but always keenly observed earliest works."

—*Robin Feuer Miller, Edytha Macy Gross Professor of Humanities, Professor of Russian and Comparative Literature, Brandeis University*

"This is the definitive English text of Chekhov's beginnings, the best window we have into the first three years of his career. If Chekhov had known, in his early twenties, that the half-baked pieces he was sending out to cheap periodicals would one day be treated with such consummate editorial care, in a volume culled from the collective international work of almost a hundred translators and scholars, he would likely have been delighted, amused, and mortified. And so are we, reading him at his most unguarded."

—*Yuri Corrigan, Associate Professor of Russian and Comparative Literature, Boston University*

Anton Chekhov

EARLIEST STORIES

Stories, Novellas, Humoresques, 1880–1882

Edited by Rosamund Bartlett
and Elena Michajlowska

CHERRY ORCHARD BOOKS

2025

Cherry
Orchard
Books

Anton Chekhov
Earliest Stories

————————————————————

Stories, Novellas, Humoresques, 1880–1882

Edited by
Rosamund Bartlett and Elena Michajlowska

Translated by
Dina Akhmadeeva, Olga Akroyd, Carol Apollonio, Judith Armstrong,
Claire Atwood, Rosamund Bartlett, Adam Bartley, Maria Bloshteyn,
Katherine Bowers, Philip Chadwick, Sarah Chatta, Tung Chan, Oliver Clark,
Elena Dimov, Polina Dimova, Rachel Patricia Dixon, Rob Myatt, Katherine Dye,
Luka Fisher, Alex Fleming, Mercedes Flowers, Philip Franco, Jean-Paul Gilbert,
Michael Gluck, Jessica Gokhberg, Walker Griggs, Jackson Gzehoviak, Helen Hagon,
Louise Hardiman, George Hargreaves, Julia Hon, Matthew Horowitz, Sally Ivanova,
Hannah Jackson, Anne Marie Jackson, Anna Krushelnitskaya, Tamar Koplatadze,
Maria Khotimsky, Thomas Kitson, Rupert Kettle, Katherine Lane, Anna Li,
Marina Matushenko, Anna Mazhirov, Neil McCallum, Charles McCloy,
Bridget Menkins, Ronald Meyer, Elena Michajlowska, Piers Murphy, Lana Nadj,
Oliver Okun, Dominika Pasterska, Marianka Pencheva, Tatiana Peshkova,
Natalie Pierson, Elena Polevaya, Lillian Posner, Melissa Purkiss, Ronan Quinn,
Rollo Quinault, Stephen Rich, Olga Rich, Elizabeth Rattley, Angus Robinson,
Sofia Reimchen, Margarita Shalina, Anastasia Shteyn, Erica Siegel, Eric Spoerl,
Tom Stableford, Mark Swift, Cheryl Tan, Nina Tchernova,
Tselmegtsetseg Tsetsendelger, Hannah Tyburski, Alexander Walsh, Isobel Walsh,
William Watkins, Timothy Dwight Williams, Alex Wordley, Valeriya Yermishova,
Josephine von Zitzewitz

Library of Congress Cataloging-in-Publication Data

Names: Chekhov, Anton Pavlovich, 1860-1904, author. | Bartlett, Rosamund,
  editor. | Michajlowska, Elena, editor. | Akhmadeeva, Dina, translator. |
  Chekhov, Anton Pavlovich, 1860-1904. Works. English. 2025 ; vol. 1.
Title: Anton Chekhov earliest stories : stories, novellas, humoresques,
  1880-1882 / Anton Chekhov ; edited by Rosamund Bartlett and Elena
  Michajlowska ; translated by Dina Akhmadeeva [and eighty two others].
Description: Boston : Cherry Orchard Books, an imprint of Academic Studies
  Press, 2025. | Phrase "Chekhov's complete collected works, vol .1" on
  title page, per editors of the book, refers to Chekhov's Polnoe sobranie
  sochineniĭ i pisem v tridtsati tomakh (Moskva : Nauka, 1974-1983).
Identifiers: LCCN 2025002252 (print) | LCCN 2025002253 (ebook) |
  ISBN 9798887198088 (hardback) | ISBN 9798887198095 (paperback) |
  ISBN 9798887198101 (adobe pdf) | ISBN 9798887198118 (epub)
Subjects: LCSH: Chekhov, Anton Pavlovich, 1860-1904—Translations into
  English. | LCGFT: Short stories.
Classification: LCC PG3456.A13 B38 2025 (print) | LCC PG3456.A13 (ebook)
  | DDC 891.73/3—dc23/eng/20250227
LC record available at https://lccn.loc.gov/2025002252
LC ebook record available at https://lccn.loc.gov/2025002253

ISBN 9798887198088 (hardback)
ISBN 9798887198095 (paperback)
ISBN 9798887198101 (adobe pdf)
ISBN 9798887198118 (epub)

Book design by Tatiana Vernikov
Cover design by Ivan Grave

Published by Cherry Orchard Books, an imprint of Academic Studies Press
1007 Chestnut Street
Newton, MA 02464, USA
press@academicstudiespress.com
www.academicstudiespress.com

Contents

Introduction

1. Chekhov's Juvenilia and Its Afterlife

This volume brings together in English translation Anton Chekhov's fifty-eight earliest pieces of fiction, exactly as they appear in the authoritative Academy of Sciences *Complete Collected Works and Letters in Thirty Volumes*.[1] Beginning with his first publication in March 1880, and ending with the story he wrote in December 1882, they are arranged in chronological order and comprise the first of the edition's ten turquoise volumes devoted to Chekhov's short prose. Of those ten volumes, the last four contain the sixty short stories which brought Chekhov greatest renown, and which have been most frequently anthologised. These are the stories dating from "The Steppe" in 1888, when he began to write for literary journals, and culminating with "The Betrothed" in 1903, shortly before he died. The assortment of over five hundred stories, novellas, comic sketches, literary parodies, and vignettes which fill the first six volumes of the *Complete Collected Works*, by contrast, are less well known, at least in English. Chekhov became famous in Russia after he began publishing stories under his own name in national newspapers from 1886 onwards. But that still leaves the best part of four volumes of stories signed with a variety of different pseudonyms and published in lowbrow comic magazines. These stories project an authorial image which is often quite at odds with the received view of Chekhov as a mature and sober writer complete with pince-nez. The earliest of them, in particular, introduce us to an irreverent young comic writer trying his hand at different genres, with the sole aim of entertaining his readers. They show us Chekhov at his most irrepressible and unselfconscious, and hence offer a unique insight into his creative processes at their earliest stage of development, long before anyone, least of all their author, took them seriously.

No other celebrated Russian writer before Chekhov launched their career by contributing frivolous stories to comic magazines chiefly for mercenary reasons. When he published his first story in the spring of 1880, Chekhov had

---

1   A. P. Chekhov, *Polnoe sobranie sochinenii i pisem v tridtsati tomakh* [Complete collected works and letters in thirty volumes], ed. A. F. Bel'chikov et al. (Moscow: Nauka, 1974-1983). Henceforth *PSS*.

recently turned twenty, and was a first-year medical student at Moscow University. He had no intention at that point of becoming a professional writer, and from the outset published under various different noms de plume, partly in order to preserve his real name for all the serious articles he might submit to scientific periodicals in the future. It was chiefly on account of his family's dire poverty that he initially followed his elder brother Alexander into print. Chekhov fervently believed he would principally work as a doctor during his student years, while continuing to turn out a mixture of humorous stories, frivolous parodies, reviews, and reportage with ever greater facility. If he had difficulty placing stories to begin with, he was a sought-after author by 1884, when he graduated. That year he published over a hundred stories and began to vacillate about his vocation.

In 1885 Chekhov received his first invitation to contribute to a major St. Petersburg newspaper. The increased visibility and prestige motivated him to invest more in the stories he wrote, rather than simply dash them off, and this in turn brought him attention from Russia's most prominent newspaper editor. Alexey Suvorin commissioned his first story from Chekhov in February 1886, and, crucially, insisted the author sign it with his real name. Abandoning the camouflage of "Antosha Chekhonte" and all his other light-hearted pseudonyms was a life-changing moment. "I have been writing for six years," Chekhov remarked in his first letter to his new editor, "but you are the first person who has gone to the trouble of making suggestions and explaining the reasons for them. My pen-name of A. Chekhonte probably does seem strange and contrived. But since I first dreamed it up 'at the dawn of my misty youth' I've grown used to it and don't notice its oddity."[2] Equally momentous was the letter Chekhov received a month later from the celebrated writer Dmitry Grigorovich, who exhorted him to honour his literary talent. It struck him "like a bolt of lightning," he wrote in his reply: "I almost burst into tears I was so overcome with emotion, and now I feel it has left a deep imprint in my soul."[3] Henceforth, Chekhov took his writing seriously, but he also retained his commitment to medicine. He began to quip in letters about having "a mistress—literature" in addition to his "lawful wedded wife of medicine," and about how

---

2   Letter from Anton Chekhov to Alexey Suvorin, 21 February 1886, *Anton Chekhov: A Life in Letters*, ed. Rosamund Bartlett, trans. Rosamund Bartlett and Anthony Phillips (London: Penguin Books, 2004), 54.

3   *Anton Chekhov: A Life in Letters*, 55.

"having two trades" and chasing after two hares at once made him happier and more at ease with himself: "When I've had enough of one, I can go and spend the night with the other."[4]

Eight years after making his wholly unremarkable debut as a prose writer, Chekhov was elevated to the lofty heights of Russia's literary magazines—the so-called "thick journals" where all the country's greatest writers first published their work. After the constraints of filing copy for the "thin" illustrated weeklies and daily newspapers printed on cheap paper, it was a daunting prospect to be given free rein and write for a prestigious publication which appeared monthly. Being invited to write for a "thick journal" was a sure sign that Chekhov had received the imprimatur of the literary establishment. In a country whose elite writers historically emanated from the landowning nobility, and where there was little social mobility, this was a remarkable achievement for the son of a bankrupt shopkeeper who had been born a serf. The democratically minded Chekhov refused to let his newfound success go to his head while completing his story "The Steppe" for *The Northern Herald*, however. As he wrote to the poet Yakov Polonsky in January 1888: "Isn't it the same whether a nightingale sings in a big tree or a bush? The requirement that talented people should only publish in thick journals is small-minded, smacks of servility and is harmful, like all prejudices."[5] Even when he won a literary prize towards the end of that momentous year, wry humour mingled with pride in his achievement in making such an unlikely leap. "Second and third-rate magazine writers should put up a statue to me, or at the very least present me with a silver cigarette case; I have paved their way to the thick journals and into the hearts and approval of respectable people," he wrote to Suvorin with his tongue in his cheek. And it was with typical self-deprecation that he maintained with confidence in the same letter that nothing he had previously written would "survive in people's memory for even a decade."[6]

As time went on and he refined his craft, Chekhov inevitably developed a more critical attitude to the short prose he had dashed off in his early twenties, when he had to adhere to deadlines and stringent word counts, cater to

---

4   Letter from Anton Chekhov to Alexander Chekhov, 17 January 1887; letter from Anton Chekhov to Alexey Suvorin, 11 September 1888, *Anton Chekhov: A Life in Letters*, 82, 149.

5   I. P. Viduetskaya, *A. P. Chekhov i ego izdatel' A. F. Marks* [A. P. Chekhov and his publisher A. F. Marks] (Moscow: Nauka, 1977), 122.

6   Viduetskaya, *A. P. Chekhov i ego izdatel' A. F. Marks*, 159.

the demands of mass-market publications, and make his readers laugh. "Oh, how good it is that no one knows how I began to write," he confided to his sister Maria in 1900.[7] Chekhov was at this point living in Yalta and reviewing his early output for the first time in almost twenty years. Gravely ill with tuberculosis, concerned for her and their mother's financial future, and desperately short of cash, he had sold the rights to an edition of his collected writings—far too cheaply, as it later turned out. He reserved the right to decide which stories to include from the period before he wrote for literary journals, but his Petersburg publisher Adolf Marks drove a hard bargain and demanded delivery of fair copies of his selections for the first volume within six months. In a nod to the German political philosopher, Chekhov joked that he had now become a "Marksist," but this was no laughing matter, as he had few of his earliest publications to hand. Writing to a friend, he compared the challenge of tracking them all down to hard labour. It was as if he had been asked by his publisher, he lamented, to think back to the more than a thousand occasions when he had sat on a riverbank with a rod and provide exact times and locations for every single fish he had ever caught.[8]

What made the task harder was that Chekhov was a writer who routinely covered his tracks by disposing of his manuscripts. Naturally it is intriguing to be able to study textual variants in those few cases where autograph drafts have survived from his early period. Such is the case with the novella "Late-Blooming Flowers" in the present volume, which was serialised over four issues between October and November 1882 by a short-lived Moscow weekly magazine. Chekhov first chose the surname Zebrov for his protagonists the Priklonskys, for example, and in a later draft had second thoughts about his atmospheric lengthy opening:

> Outside was a grey, tearful autumn...
> Dark-grey clouds, smeared as if with mud, completely shrouded the sky, their stillness inducing a feeling of melancholy. It seemed that the sun did not exist; it had not cast a single glance on the earth for an entire week, as though fearing to soil its rays in the slush pretending to be pavements. Large raindrops cut through the grey air, knocking endlessly on the darkened windows. Spleen, melancholy and apathy could

---

7   Anton Chekhov, letter to Maria Chekhova, 15 January, 1900, *PSS, Pis'ma v dvenadtsati tomakh* [Letters in twelve volumes], 9:14.

8   *PSS, Pis'ma*, 8:61.

be seen in everyone's faces... There was not a single face evident on which one could not read desperate boredom... There was also boredom at the house of the princes Priklonsky.

One dark afternoon, when the raindrops were drumming on the windows with particular force, and the wind was howling and sobbing in the chimney, it was not just boredom glimmering in the faces of the inhabitants of this house. Sadness and desperation took pride of place.[9]

In the final draft, Chekhov transferred this opening, with a few amendments, to the beginning of the third chapter and replaced it with the terse sentence: "It was a dark autumn afternoon at the house of the princes Priklonsky."[10] It was an inspired decision, revealing his innate feeling for composition already at this early stage.

Since it had never occurred to Chekhov to keep for posterity the items he had published in ephemeral comic magazines at the beginning of his career, let alone compile a bibliography, the process of preparing a selection of his early stories for the Marks edition of his collected works proved tortuous. The texts of several hundred early stories had first to be located in metropolitan libraries by helpful friends and associates, and then laboriously copied from the original magazine issues. Chekhov compiled detailed lists of these early stories, planning to include a broad selection,[11] but he ended up summarily discarding half of them. Finally, only about a third of his stories were included in the first ten volumes of the Marks edition of the collected works, which also embraced his plays and *The Island of Sakhalin*, the nonfictional account of his 1890 visit to a notorious Siberian penal colony.

"The Distorting Mirror," one of the very last stories Chekhov wrote in 1882 (the penultimate tale in the present volume), was the only one to make the final cut from his earliest period. Re-reading the story in Yalta seventeen years later, Chekhov could not stop himself from wanting to revise it. Not only did he change the subtitle from "A Fantastic Christmas Story" to "A Christmas Story," but he removed words and phrases which now seemed to him too obviously jejune or narrowly topical. This was the fate meted out to the original last line of the story, for example, which refers to a prolific Russian writer of moderate talent known for his grandiloquence: "Oh women, women!"

---

9   *PSS*, 1:522.

10   *PSS*, 1:592.

11   *PSS*, 1:550.

I exclaim now, and I exclaim the truth, even though I am not Shakespeare or even Averkiev." The text which appeared in the first volume of the Marks edition of the collected works in 1899 differs in dozens of small ways from the version initially published in January 1883 in *The Spectator*.[12] Bearing in mind the state of his health in 1899, and the extent of the task before him in preparing such a large number of stories for publication in his collected works, it seems Chekhov reconsidered his initial wish to include a large number of his earliest stories when he grasped how much work would be involved. He also revised two other pre-1883 stories which feature in the current volume, "The Trial" and "An Unfortunate Run-In," in 1899. Both were earmarked for his collected works, but neither went further than the proof stage.

The fact that Chekhov eventually selected only one pre-1883 story for his collected works could on one level be interpreted as his verdict on the literary qualities of his juvenilia. He certainly must have regarded some of his early stories as clichéd hack work, but in truth his feelings were mixed. In addition to not having the full complement of his early stories to choose from, he needed to steer a tricky course between the interests of his publisher and the exigencies of the censor when deciding which of them to include in 1899. And then there were the expectations of his colleagues in the literary community and his readers, who had next to no knowledge of the decidedly lowbrow comic stories he had published under pseudonyms. Chekhov himself must have quickly realised that it would have been quite incongruous with his status as a celebrated author, and a shock for his fellow writers, if his collected works were to begin with his earliest scribblings: he had to show some respect. The executive decision he made to put all his stories written before "The Distorting Mirror" to one side also probably stemmed from his realisation that he would inevitably want to revise them, and that his time and his limited energies could be better spent.

The national outpouring of grief in Russia following Chekhov's death in 1904 stimulated the clamour for further volumes to be added posthumously to the ten-volume Marks edition of his collected works. Everything Chekhov had ever written now suddenly became of interest, including all those obscure early magazine publications which still remained inaccessible to the general reading public. Some critics were opposed to what they felt would be the besmirching of Chekhov's literary reputation with the publication of work they

---

12   *PSS*, 1:538-542, 597-598.

dismissed as his early "rubbish," but further volumes were nevertheless published, beginning with the eleventh which appeared in 1906. In his preface to the posthumous twelfth volume, the poet and critic Pyotr Bykov stoutly defended the value of publishing Chekhov's juvenilia on the grounds that the early stories allowed the possibility of following the development and unusual blossoming of his "subtle and versatile talent." If the exuberant humour, poetic imagery, and pensive air of melancholy in the "forgotten" stories, exhibited much that was already typically "Chekhovian," he argued, the stories were also valuable as vivid snapshots of Russian life in the early 1880s.[13] By the time a second Marks edition of the collected works was completed in 1916, it contained twenty-two volumes and included 350 stories written between 1880 and 1888, most of which Chekhov had collated before he died. Some critics now began to assert that Chekhov had not suddenly changed from an untalented into a brilliant writer, and that the early and late periods were interrelated.[14]

Despite this advocacy for the early stories, when the inaugural Soviet edition of the complete collected works in twenty volumes was launched in 1944, the editors continued to separate those early stories which Chekhov himself chose for the Marks edition of his collected works from those reissued posthumously.[15] There was yet another storm of protest about his juvenilia in the 1960s when the Academy of Sciences announced an authoritative critical edition, the *Complete Collected Works and Letters in Thirty Volumes*. The prospect of all of Chekhov's stories now being subjected to the same scholarly scrutiny and published in chronological order was an unpalatable one for some members of the Soviet literary establishment. For the venerable writer and critic Korney Chukovsky, for example, who was then in his eighties, the casual sexism and crude stereotyping found in many of the early stories was not only "unbearably tasteless" but incompatible with the work and outlook of the mature writer, and therefore actually "anti-Chekhovian."[16]

---

13   *A. P. Chekhov i ego izdatel' A. F. Marks*, 91, 157.

14   *A. P. Chekhov i ego izdatel' A. F. Marks*, 93–94.

15   A. P. Chekhov, *Polnoe sobranie sochinenii i pisem v dvadtsati tomakh* [Complete works and letters in twenty volumes], ed. S. D. Balukhatyi et al. (Moscow: Gos. izdatel'stvo khudozhestvennoi literatury, 1944–51).

16   *A. P. Chekhov i ego izdatel' A. F. Marks*, 92–93.

2. Will the Real Young Chekhov Stand Up?

While the first English translations of Chekhov's mature stories began to appear in 1903, when their author was still alive, his very earliest stories reached an international readership much later, for the obvious reason of their relative inaccessibility. Constance Garnett included the 1882 story "A Living Chattel" (called "Live Goods" in this volume) in the thirteenth and last volume of her pioneering *Tales of Tchehov*, published between 1916 and 1922, when the French transliteration of Chekhov's name was still common. It is the sole example of a pre-1883 story, however, as no others were at her disposal at the time. Garnett's English Chekhov remained the benchmark for decades, with translations of other very early stories only appearing sporadically.[17] That situation began to change in the 1950s, following publication of the inaugural Soviet edition of Chekhov's complete collected works.[18] Nora Gottlieb produced the first English-language anthology devoted to the "young Chekhov" in 1960.[19] Her fourteen selected stories include one from 1882 ("Two Scandals"), with the rest first published between 1883 and 1886. Harvey Pitcher and Patrick Miles were able to draw on the expanded Academy of Sciences edition of Chekhov's complete collected works for the anthology of twenty-seven stories they published as *Early Stories* in 1982. Their selection, which does not include any of Chekhov's fiction published between 1880 and 1882, ranges from 1883 to 1888.[20]

A major step in bringing the young Chekhov to an English-language audience came in 1998, when Peter Constantine published his anthology *The Undiscovered Chekhov: Thirty-Eight New Stories*. Its purview extends from 1881 to

---

17   See, for example, Anton Chekhov, *Selected Stories*, trans. E. Chamot (London: n.p., 1941), which includes "Belated Blossoms" and "The Mistress," both dating from 1882.

18   See, for example, Anton Chekhov, *"Wife for Sale* (aka Live Goods)," trans. David Tutaev (London: John Calder Ltd., 1959); *The Unknown Chekhov: Stories and Other Writings*, trans. Avrahm Yarmolinsky (New York: Noonday Press, 1954) ("Because of Little Apples"); Anton Chekhov, *The Image of Chekhov: Forty Stories by Anton Chekhov*, trans. Robert Payne (New York: Alfred A. Knopf, 1963) ("The Little Apples," "St Peter's Day," "Green Scythe" [*sic*]); Anton Chekhov, *The Crooked Mirror and Other Stories*, trans. Arnold Hinchcliffe (New York: Kensington, 1972) ("The Crooked Mirror," "He and She," "Two Scandals").

19   Anton Chekhov, *Early Stories*, trans. Nora Gottlieb (London: The Bodley Head, 1960).

20   Anton Chekhov, *Early Stories*, trans. Patrick Miles and Harvey Pitcher (Oxford: Oxford University Press, 1982).

1887, and six stories coincide with the present volume.[21] In his Introduction, Constantine relates his excitement at stumbling on Chekhov's earliest fiction when browsing through issues of *The Alarm Clock* and other Russian pre-revolutionary comic magazines in the New York Public Library—all bibliographical rarities. Although many of the stories he chose to translate were new to anglophone readers, none were strictly speaking "undiscovered," having long been available in Russian in the Academy of Sciences edition of Chekhov's complete collected works. The Italian Slavist Giuseppe Ghini went on to point out in a 2017 review article, moreover, that eleven stories in the first edition of *The Undiscovered Chekhov* were actually translated not from the original magazine texts but from the versions revised for the Marks edition of Chekhov's collected works (and reproduced as the main texts in the Academy of Sciences *Complete Collected Works and Letters*). Far from prefiguring Chekhov's later work, as claimed by a prominent scholar of Russian literature reviewing the collection at the time of publication, Ghini explains, they actually *are* his later works "in their range of characters, tones and settings."[22] This is the case with "The Trial," for example, translated from the revised version completed a full eighteen years later, which Chekhov ultimately decided against including in the Marks edition of his collected works. As Ghini painstakingly demonstrates, the discrepancies between the 1881 and 1899 versions are quite significant.

"The Trial," by "Antosha Chekhonte," originally appeared in the "illustrated literary, artistic and humorous magazine" *The Spectator* (*Zritel'*). Entitled "Village Scenes. a: The Trial," it was planned as the first in a series which was never in fact continued. Comparison of the openings of the original and later revised versions of the story is revealing. The twenty-one-year-old neophyte author includes copious detail in the original 1881 version:

> A large suburban village. The hut of the medical orderly Kuzma Ye-gorov. It is stuffy, hot. Vicious mosquitoes and flies crowd around eyes and ears being an incredible nuisance... Clouds of tobacco smoke

---

21   Two amplified editions have since appeared: Anton Chekhov, *The Undiscovered Chekhov. Forty-Three New Stories*, trans. Peter Constantine (New York: Seven Stories Press, 2000); Anton Chekhov, *The Undiscovered Chekhov. Fifty-One New Stories*, trans. Peter Constantine (London: Seven Stories Press, 2001).

22   Giuseppe Ghini, "The Still Undiscovered Chekhov, or It Is Highly Recommended That Translators Get a Background in Philology," *Toronto Slavic Quarterly* 59 (Winter 2017), http://sites.utoronto.ca/tsq/59/index_59.shtml.

hang in the sweltering air, which is saturated with all kinds of smells... There is enough tedium in the air, in people's faces, in the whining of the mosquitoes, to make you want to hang yourself... And it stinks of carbolic too...[23]

The literary skills of the thirty-nine-year-old celebrated writer, on the other hand, are evidenced in the revised version's greater economy and its effective scene-setting by means of a few carefully constructed sentences of varying lengths, not to mention judicious use of punctuation:

The shopkeeper Kuzma Yegorov's hut. It is stuffy, hot. Vicious mosquitoes and flies swarm round eyes and ears being a nuisance... There are clouds of tobacco smoke, though the smell is not of tobacco, but of salted fish. A sense of tedium is in the air, in people's faces, in the whining of the mosquitoes.

On "trial" is Kuzma Yegorov's son, accused of stealing twenty-five roubles from his father. In the original 1881 version he is described as Mitrofan the clerk, complete with blue nose, pink tie, prickly collar, and shiny boots, nervously pulling on his small moustache. In the 1899 revision he still pulls at his moustache, but is simply introduced as Serapion who works at the barber's in town. In the original story, Chekhov has a motley assortment of eleven clerical and military figures, tradesmen, medical orderlies, and policemen sitting around a table in judgement. The round dozen is made up by the splendidly named village constable Grandioznov, who at the beginning of the proceedings is depicted lolling on a trunk by the door reading a newspaper. As a representative of the younger post-reform generation, Mitrofan is more educated than all of them, and his contemptuous attitude only increases the ferocity of the corporal punishment meted out to him after the guilty verdict is passed. Four members of the ramshackle "jury" take part in thrashing him: Kuzma and the junior medical orderly Ivanov, the non-commissioned officer Ferapontov and the policeman Fortunatov, who has come from town to visit his auntie Anisya. After Kuzma has administered thirty lashes and declared it enough, Ferapontov whispers: "More!.. I've got all worked up... Forty... Fifty..." Ferapontov mutters "More! Let me at him!" again even after Kuzma's wife has

---

23   *PSS*, 1:512-513.

found the money safe and sound in her husband's pocket and their son has been exonerated.[24]

Only seven "jury" members remain in the revised version of "The Trial," and Kuzma Yegorov alone takes off his belt to administer the sentence of corporal punishment. Chekhov now notably makes a state official, the policeman Fortunatov, the personification of brutality and violence, so that the story is transformed from a "village scene" into a "direct criticism of Tsarist Russia," as Giuseppe Ghini points out.[25] "'More!' whispers policeman Fortunatov. 'More! More! Have at him!'" we now read after Kuzma announces the thrashing should stop. And then when the money has been found, there is a pointed refrain: "'More!' Fortunatov mumbles. 'Thump him! Have at him!'" Finally, and most importantly, Chekhov changes the story's conclusion so that it ends with an image of aggression rather than a positive note of vindication for Kuzma's unjustly punished son. In both cases the latter downs a shot, presumably of vodka, before leaving the hut "like a mighty warrior, with his blue nose held aloft." In the revised version, however, Chekhov then adds a final decisive sentence which both reinforces the suggestion of indiscriminate state-sponsored violence and enhances the story's artistic structure by reprising the earlier refrain: "As for policeman Fortunatov, he paces the yard for a long time afterwards, red in the face, eyes bulging, muttering: 'More! More! Have at him!'" When revising the story, the mature Chekhov systematically removed superfluous detail, shaped sentences in a more rhythmical way, and used punctuation more creatively.

It is on the basis of these sorts of discrepancies that Giuseppe Ghini justifiably questions whether Peter Constantine's anthology *The Undiscovered Chekhov* can really be considered an accurate representation of Chekhov's early work from the 1880s. As he points out, "many expressions are different, the heroes are different, the end is different, the perspective is different." His close reading of both the earlier and later printed versions of "The Trial" reveals, furthermore, that the work of the literary scholars in the first volume of the

---

24 *PSS*, 1:514-515.

25 Giuseppe Ghini, "Perevodchik ne mozhet ne byt' tekstologom. Po povodu rasskazov yunogo Chekhova," *Yazyk i tekst* 4, no. 3 (2017): 12-19, https://psyjournals.ru/journals/langt/archive/2017_n3/Ghini. For an Italian version of this article, see "Dolori del giovane Čechov. Considerazioni filologiche sui racconti giovanili," *Biblioteca di Studi Slavistici* 43 (2019), https://library.oapen.org/handle/20.500.12657/58247.

Academy of Sciences edition of Chekhov's complete collected works is not always reliable. Nikolay Belchikov and Mikhail Gromov, who clearly applied themselves to the momentous task of preparing the texts, notes, and appendices assiduously, and with zeal, nevertheless failed to document the textual variations faithfully. It transpires that they not only omitted several words from the original story when detailing the discrepancies with the revised version in the relevant editorial pages, but added or changed a number of others. They also misspelled Grandioznov as "Grandiozov," and on one occasion mixed up Ferapontov with Fortunatov.[26] The surprisingly tricky question of what constitutes the authentic "young Chekhov" is thus an issue which needs careful consideration.

The fact is that Chekhov revised several of his earliest stories long before signing his contract with Adolf Marks. In late 1881, for example, nearly two years after his literary debut, he made dozens of mostly small alterations to his story "Artists' Wives." First published in December 1880 under the rubric "Sunday Sketches" as "A Portuguese Legend in the Russian Manner about Artists' Wives," it was one of his first successes, and was chosen for inclusion in the *Alarm Clock Almanac*, which appeared in early 1882.[27] Further textual amendments came in the spring of 1882, when Chekhov selected "Artists' Wives" along with eleven other stories for his first anthology, *Mischief* (*Shalost'*). His revisions were not always minor. For example, the original text of his story "Before the Wedding," first published in October 1880, begins with an excitable and garrulous narrator introducing the annual autumn "wedding season" in Moscow. "We men are an unfortunate species," he laments; "nature treats us badly in spring, we are hot in summer, married off in autumn, and cold in the winter. It's just frightful!" Chekhov decided to cut the original lengthy opening paragraph in its entirety when revising the story for inclusion in *Mischief*. Conversely, he also added new text, for instance, to the breathless homily Mrs. Podzatylkina delivers to her newly betrothed daughter. Just before sending her off to receive words of wisdom from her husband, Mrs. Podzatylkina instructs her on no account to repeat all the nasty things she has just said about him: "Otherwise that sorry excuse for a human being will start pestering me, and to hell with him! Off you go, before I give myself a heart attack!.. You're all

---

26   See Antosha Chekhonte, Sel'skie kartinki. a) Sud, *Zritel'*, no. 14, 23 October 1881, 2-3; Ghini, op. cit.

27   *PSS*, 1:565.

out to get me! When I am dead, you'll remember my words though! Oh, you tormentors!"[28]

Chekhov introduced revisions when he began anthologizing his work both for stylistic reasons, and in order to circumvent possible objections by the censor. In the highly repressive conditions of imperial Russia immediately following the assassination of Alexander II in 1881, even innocuous comic stories by obscure writers hiding behind pseudonyms could be deemed subversive. Chekhov's first book reached the printers, but for pusillanimous censorship reasons *Mischief* was never published.[29] In 1884, when censorship was less severe, he was more successful in publishing revised versions of six of his early stories with a thespian theme in an anthology he entitled *Tales of Melpomene*.[30] When it came to the story "The Baron," first published in December 1882, Chekhov cut two long passages from the original magazine publication detailing the earlier life of the central character, who is an ageing and impoverished prompter in a theatre. In the first version of the story, the "baron" is elegant, handsome, and wealthy, an authentic former aristocrat fond of cantering on his fine English racehorse through "grass which had received nourishment from his own ancestral land." He is renowned furthermore for his numerous romantic conquests, and for his all-engulfing passion for the theatre, but the vast sums he has invested in supporting dramatic talent over the years have led him into debt and then penury. All this colourful background is gone from the revised version. The "baron" still loves theatre more than life, but he is now a decidedly more pathetic and abject figure whose title is just an ironic nickname.[31] *Tales of Melpomene* appeared under Chekhov's alter ego "A. Chekhonte," and featured one story dating from 1880, four from 1882 (including the third and final revision of "Artists' Wives"), and one from 1883.[32]

---

28 *PSS*, 1:48, 500.

29 Anton Chekhov, *The Prank: The Best of Young Chekhov*, trans. Maria Bloshteyn (New York: Review Books Classics, 2015), represents the first full English translation of this anthology, and includes original illustrations by Chekhov's artist brother Nikolay.

30 "Artists' Wives," "He and She," "Two Scandals," "The Baron," "Revenge," plus "The Tragedian" ("Tragik"), dating from 1883.

31 *PSS*, 1:532-534, 595.

32 Chekhov included the following stories in the volume: "Letter to a Learned Neighbour," "Chase Two Hares and You Will Lose Them Both," "Papasha," "A Thousand and One Passions, or A Terrible Night," "Before the Wedding," "Artists' Wives," "St Peter's Day,"

Apart from the fact that these revisions shed light on Chekhov's literary technique as it evolved, it is important to take note of them because it was the later versions of all the early stories, as well as those he amended for the Marks edition of his collected works, which were deemed definitive in both the Stalinist-era Soviet edition of Chekhov's complete collected works and the later and more comprehensive Academy of Sciences edition. A partially distorted and misleading picture of the "young Chekhov" has inevitably resulted. The only parts of the original magazine publications included in the Academy of Sciences edition are words and phrases which differ from the later versions. These are listed by page number and relegated to the small print in the editorial apparatus at the back of each volume. The original published versions are thus effectively excluded from the canon, and it is difficult to gain a sense of them as complete stories. If an exception is made for "A Little Joke," Chekhov's tobogganing story of March 1886, whose original text is printed in full in the appendices, it is because the changes he introduced in 1899 were so extreme. Chekhov made his previously loquacious narrator far more reticent and self-doubting, and, in a similar vein to his revisions to "The Trial," replaced the original happy ending, so that the story ends instead inconclusively on a melancholy, ironic note far more consonant with his mature style.[33] Just as the revised version of "The Trial" sits alongside unrevised stories in the first volume of the Academy of Sciences edition of Chekhov's complete collected works, it is the 1899 version of "The Joke" which is misleadingly juxtaposed with unrevised stories from 1886 in the fifth volume.[34]

Giuseppe Ghini is not exaggerating when describing the widespread misunderstanding this situation has produced. Not only have distinguished Chekhov scholars often referred to the later revised texts when discussing the early stories, but recent Russian publishers have unthinkingly reproduced some of Chekhov's 1899 revised versions when supposedly issuing anthologies of his humorous stories from the early 1880s.[35] Needless to say,

---

"Personality Types," "On the Train," "The Sinner from Toledo," "Confession," and "Flying Islands."

33 Both the 1886 and later version, published in 1900 in the second volume of the Marks edition of the *Collected Works*, are included in Anton Chekhov, *The Exclamation Mark and Other Stories*, trans. R. Bartlett (London: Hesperus Classics, second edition, 2024)—the anthology features stories published between December 1885 and June 1886.

34 See *PSS*, 5:21-24, 489-492, 612-613.

35 Giuseppe Ghini, op. cit.

translators worldwide, who cannot be expected to be trained philologists, have also unwittingly compounded the problem by quite reasonably assuming that the texts in the first volumes of the collected works correspond fully with the dates indicated on their title pages (vol. 1: 1880–1882, vol. 2: 1883–1884, etc.) Convinced that the authentic young Chekhov has been unfairly forgotten, Giuseppe Ghini scoured libraries in Moscow, Helsinki and Munich to track down copies of a number of early stories as originally published (including "The Trial"). In 2018 he published a pioneering collection of twenty-five of them written between 1881 and 1887 in Italian translation.[36]

It should be noted that Chekhov revised his very earliest stories least, because he chose so few of them for inclusion in the Marks edition of his collected works. The majority of the fifty-eight stories in this volume thus appear in the form in which they were originally published in the humorous magazines which launched Chekhov's career as a writer. It is the most comprehensive anglophone edition of his earliest fiction. Nineteen stories appear here in their revised form, as per the Academy of Sciences edition of the complete collected works. In the case of the sixteen stories earmarked for inclusion by Chekhov in his anthologies *Mischief* and *Tales of Melpomene*, the revisions were completed very soon after original publication in the early 1880s, and are slight. Chekhov introduced more substantial changes to two of the three stories he selected for the Marks edition of his collected works in 1899, of which "The Trial" and "The Distorting Mirror" have already been discussed. In the case of the story "An Unfortunate Run-In," first published in the St. Petersburg magazine *Fragments* in November 1882, Chekhov removed the subtitle "From the Chronicle of the Chernorechensky Bank," which had given the story a quasi-journalistic character, and uncharacteristically added the four lines of dialogue indicated in italics below:

> "Gentlemen!" I shouted in an imploring voice. "This is plain rudeness! I have asked you! I'm not well and I want to sleep."
> *"You talking to us?"*
> *"Yes."*
> *"What do you want?"*
> *"Stop shouting, please! I want to sleep!"*

---

36   Anton Čechov, *Il primo amore e altri racconti inediti* [First Love and other unpublished stories], trans. Giuseppe Ghini (Milan: Edizioni Ares, 2018).

"Sleep then, no one is stopping you; and if you are not well, go to a doctor!"

3. Young Chekhov's Fictional World

The "Stories, Novellas, Humoresques," which make up the first volume of Chekhov's *Complete Collected Works,* bring us into direct contact with the vibrant creative imagination of their gregarious novice author. They also plunge us, thrillingly, straight into the daily life of pre-revolutionary Moscow and provincial Russia in the early 1880s: one moment we are mingling with the inebriated clientele at a seedy Salon de Variétés, or accompanying a brow-beaten husband on a visit to bribe his son's maths teacher, the next we are ensconced in a troika with a pompous retired general heading out to shoot quail on a summer's day or sitting in a doctor's surgery. Chekhov's first experiments in fiction in 1880 were written expressly to entertain the burgeoning lower middle-class readership of the new weekly magazines which had begun to spring up as Russia belatedly embraced industrialisation, peasants migrated to the city and then learned to read and write. He turned out to have an innate talent for spinning a good yarn, not to mention making his readers laugh, so he very quickly became a regular contributor to St. Petersburg publications such as *The Dragonfly* and *The Alarm Clock,* which billed itself as a "satirical journal with drawings and caricatures." Soon Chekhov was also writing for a brand-new magazine in Moscow, *The Spectator,* founded in 1881, as well as an assortment of other short-lived metropolitan weeklies. At the end of 1882, he was then solicited by Nikolay Leikin, the publisher and editor of *Fragments.* Founded in St. Petersburg a year earlier, it had already become the most popular comic magazine in Russia.

There is astonishing variety in Chekhov's first fifty-eight pieces of prose. Writing under different pseudonyms certainly allowed him to assume multiple identities as a writer, but he was also clearly keen to experiment with all kinds of genres and styles. They include an epistolary parody, a list of all the most cliched ingredients of popular Russian novels (such as an auntie in Tambov, a faithful retainer, pineapples and oysters), and the hilarious spoof homework of an illiterate schoolgirl. Chekhov tried his hand at monologues, pages of comic classified advertisements, absurd supplementary census questions ("Does your wife *beat* you or *not*? Do you *beat* her or *not*?"), and ridiculous problems set by a "mad mathematician." There is a lengthy imitation of a turgid almanac complete with outrageous daily menus ("stuffed sperm whale," "stewed Adam's apples"), a story composed of comic letters and telegrams relating to performances by the celebrated actress Sarah Bernhardt, and an account of life consisting entirely of questions and exclamations for each stage ("*Youth.* You are too young to drink vodka! Tell me about the sequence of tenses!").

Having grown up as a die-hard fan of *Don Quixote* and the stories of Nikolay Gogol, Chekhov was drawn to parody and irony from the start. Writing as Don Antonio Chekhonte, he posed as a Portuguese novelist when writing the racy "Artists' Wives," set in Lisbon (even though at that point he had not even set foot in St. Petersburg, let alone travelled abroad). He also penned a pseudo-Spanish medieval thriller ("The Sinner from Toledo"). "One Thousand and One Passions, Or a Terrible Night *(A Novel in One Chapter with an Epilogue),*" is dedicated to Victor Hugo. The seemingly interminable novella "A Hollow Victory," meanwhile, was the result of a bet Chekhov made with an editor—that he could hoodwink his readers into believing it was the work of the Hungarian novelist Mór Jókai. In "Flying Islands," which follows the adventures in outer space led by an eccentric English scientist (author of *Did the Moon Exist before the Flood? If It Did, Why Was It Not Submerged Too?*), Antosha Chekhonte poses as the translator of Jules Verne. He also experimented with the gothic in his supernatural tale "The Distorting Mirror." Most of Chekhov's earliest stories are short, some even less than a page: having to adhere to strict word counts provided him with an excellent training in concision. It comes as a surprise, therefore, to encounter novellas in this volume. Unlike "A Hollow Victory," which Chekhov tried to spin out as long as he could, well aware it was not going anywhere, "Live Goods" and "Late-Blooming Flowers" appear to show him limbering up to attempt a full-length novel. The story "Green Point," set on a country estate in time-honoured manner, is actually subtitled "a small novel," and composed of two miniature chapters.

Readers might also be surprised to discover that not all Chekhov's early fiction is humorous or shallow. "At the Wolf-Baiting," for example, is a sketch which delivers a serious message about cruelty to animals:

> Finally they release the last wolf. This wolf is slaughtered, and the crowd heads off home debating which dogs were good or bad.

> By way of conclusion we have to ask: what is the point of this whole puppet-show? It cannot be about showing off dogs because it is such a small space and there is also nowhere to demonstrate prowess. What is the moral?
> The moral is of the worst kind. It is just about giving the ladies a thrill and nothing else!

"The Mistress," a devastating and unusual exploration of exploitation and sexual harassment, is similarly forthright, and could be read allegorically as a veiled indictment of the injustices and iniquities of the tsarist regime. Chekhov tells a gripping story about the tortured experiences of a handsome but impoverished young married peasant. Stepan is employed as a coachman, but is expected by his aristocratic female employer to perform other more personal services. His refusal provokes extreme violence. It is not customary to see artistic value in anything Chekhov wrote at the very beginning of his career, but "The Mistress" is an accomplished and atmospheric work with finely drawn characters and lyrical qualities more commonly found in his later fiction:

> Outside, a quiet and serene Russian summer's night had begun. The moon was rising from behind the distant kurgans. Ragged little clouds with silvery edges floated towards it. The horizon became paler, and pleasant pale greenery spilled right across its entire breadth. The stars grew fainter and, as if frightened by the moon, drew in their tiny rays. A nocturnal, cheek-caressing dampness began to spread in all directions from the river. When the clock in Father Grigory's log house struck nine, the chime reverberated throughout the whole village.

Another story from Chekhov's early period which belies his later avowals that he had not taken this writing seriously is "Late Blooming Flowers," in which he already evinces a clear ability to evoke an elegiac autumnal mood:

> The long-fallen yellow leaves, patiently awaiting the first snow and trodden underfoot, gleam in the sun like gold ten-rouble coins. Nature is sinking quietly and submissively into slumber. There is no wind, nor any sound. Motionless and mute, as if exhausted by spring and summer, nature basks in the sun's gentle, warming rays, and as you gaze at this incipient repose, you want to become still yourself...

Having grown up in the claustrophobic world of the provincial Russian merchantry, Chekhov's school education and then his medical studies brought him into contact with a much wider social spectrum, which he reflected in his stories. Much of his early fiction is about young people of his own age in straitened circumstances, but his characters range widely, from schoolboys and old women, to landowners and peasants. Chekhov had become obsessed with the stage as a teenager in his native Taganrog, so it was natural that several of his early stories should feature theatrical types, and that his first anthology should be entitled *Tales of Melpomene*. The inherently dramatic qualities of stories such as "On Account of The Apples" and "Rural Aesculapiuses" bear direct witness to his playwriting talent.

Naturally, not all the stories of Chekhov's juvenilia succeed. In the early 1880s he was living in cramped circumstances, and moonlighting while focusing most of his energies on his medical studies. There were late nights, strict deadlines, and only a few kopecks a line as remuneration. Nevertheless, the experience of reading all his early stories together gives us a remarkable feeling for the lives of ordinary Muscovites as they fretted about their professional aspirations or romantic failures. We can sense Chekhov's own wry identification with his characters' endurance of endless cold winters and their longing for the summer and escape from the city to the dacha. The stories taken together also reveal Chekhov's sheer adaptability and gift for invention. Magazine editors expected their authors to follow the seasons and produce stories for their Christmas and Easter issues. Whether it was a question of deft caricature, lampooning florid prose, or sending up melodrama, even at the very beginning of his career Chekhov was nothing if not versatile.

Rosamund Bartlett

About the Translations

This volume is the result of a unique international collaboration between eighty-three volunteer translators from nine countries, and represents the culmination of a project inaugurated in 2014 under the auspices of the Anton Chekhov Foundation (www.antonchekhovfoundation.org). Established in London in 2008 in order to help with the restoration of Chekhov's house in Yalta, the Foundation is a UK-based charity. Its goal is to honour Chekhov's literary and humanitarian legacy through a variety of charitable projects. As Trustees of the Anton Chekhov Foundation, we had many aims when we conceived the idea of publishing translations of all fifty-eight stories in the first volume of the *Complete Collected Works*. First of all, we wanted to make Chekhov's earliest stories accessible to a wider reading public and illuminate a relatively little-known chapter of his literary career. We believed that closer acquaintance with Chekhov's fictional beginnings could provide an insight into the unique nature of his artistic talent which would be useful for writers and scholars alike. The inherently dramatic qualities of many of the earliest stories, meanwhile, have something to offer all those with an interest in Chekhov's work for the theatre.

When we launched the Early Chekhov Translation Project, we also sought to encourage the study and appreciation of the Russian language, so another goal was to make it as inclusive as possible. This is therefore a "crowd-translated" publication completed by an international community of volunteers who, like us editors, freely donated their time. Accordingly, we invited not only professional, but aspiring translators of all ages and backgrounds to participate. We asked that our volunteers choose one story to work on, either individually, or in collaboration with others, and were delighted by the enthusiastic response: the entire volume was assigned within a few days. Based in countries as far flung as Australia, New Zealand, the United States, Canada, the Netherlands, Sweden, Poland, Bulgaria, and Mongolia, as well as Great Britain and Ireland, our volunteers ranged from pupils studying Russian in secondary schools to university undergraduates and postgraduates, as well as literary translators, retired academics, professionals from many other walks of life, and native Russian speakers fluent in English.

All our volunteer translators worked from the texts in the Academy of Sciences edition of Chekhov's complete collected works published in Moscow between 1974 and 1983. As with everything else Chekhov wrote, his early stories have been digitised and so are freely available via scholarly sites such as the Fundamental Digital Library of Russian Literature and Folklore (Fundamental'naya Elektronnaya Biblioteka Russkoi Literatury i Fol'klora). This valuable repository of primary and secondary texts was established in 2002 to "provide the global scholarly community and any interested individuals free and unfettered access" to the major works of Russian literature, as well as provide a resource for education in the humanities at all levels.

Work on preparing this volume for publication has been collaborative throughout. Several of our volunteers, based in different continents, kindly gave us help at the earliest stages of the project in ensuring our call for translators was disseminated as widely as possible across different parts of the world. Lana Nadj, a writer, solicitor, and translator from Sydney, Australia, with a Belarusian background and expertise in animal rights law, was indispensable as a consultant at the project's earliest stages. Dr. Inna Birchenko, an evolutionary biologist and conservationist from Ternopil in Ukraine who had earlier made an important contribution to our Anton Chekhov's Garden project, provided invaluable assistance in managing communications with our many translators. Once first drafts had been completed and submitted, the editorial process began democratically with a peer-review forum. Translators were invited to read through drafts of other stories in the volume and contribute suggestions for revision, at the same receiving suggestions for revising their own draft from others. The next stage was undertaken by Amanda Calvert, a professional translator from the UK who generously volunteered to read through all the draft translations. She brought her experience of living and working in Moscow for thirty years to the thoughtful suggestions she made for further revision. These were passed on to our translators who were asked to consider them before submitting a final draft. We editors then slowly reviewed the entire manuscript, with the aim of producing accurate and idiomatic English versions which would be consistent with the rest of the volume and reflect Chekhov's prose style as it developed. After first reviewing each translation independently, with reference to previous drafts, we worked closely together, reading every word aloud and discussing linguistic and stylistic issues in detail. Translators were asked to review our suggested revisions and discuss any issues with us, either by correspondence or through conversations online. We were thus able to incorporate further refinements and agree on a final text. Since each story received input at several different stages in this way from translators, readers, and editors involved in the project, it was decided to make the translation of the entire volume collective.

Many friends and colleagues have generously given advice and support on our journey towards publication, and we would particularly like to thank Rebecca Abrams, Marina Boroditskaya, Georgia de Chamberet, Michael Earley, Giuseppe Ghini, and Robin Miller for their input and wise counsel.

Note on Transliteration and Russian Names

We have adopted a simplified transliteration system for Russian names in the stories, preferring "Maxim" to "Maksim," "Yegor" to "Egor," "Alexander" to "Aleksandr," and "Sofia" to "Sof'ya," for example, and commonly accepted spellings such as "Tchaikovsky" and "Bolshoi." We have also clarified names which are clearly of foreign origin, opting, for example, for "Joachim" in "Letter to a Learned Neighbour" and "Zwiebusch" in "A Hollow Victory," rather than "Ioakim" and "Zvibush." In cases where proper names and place names are spelled with an "ë" in Russian, we have reflected actual pronunciation by preferring "Pyotr" and "Oryol" to "Petr" and "Orel." While some translators of Chekhov's early stories have opted to find equivalents of his invented comic names in English, we have chosen to transliterate them and provide explanations as to their meanings in footnotes where appropriate. Firstly, this is because the humour of these names sometimes derives from their visual appearance. Take, for example, the absurdly long and convoluted surname of a young schoolgirl in "Holiday Assignments": "Peshemoreperekhodyashchenskaya" (Пешеморепереходященская in Russian). One is inclined to laugh even without knowing it implies someone walking across the sea on foot. Sometimes Chekhov's comic surnames have no obvious meaning, but nevertheless possess delightful onomatopoeic qualities which require no translation, such as that of Second Lieutenant "Zyumbumbunchikov" in "Before the Wedding." Annotated transliteration also allows us to see Chekhov inventing spurious foreign names, such as "Tarakanchio" in "Antosha Chekhonte's Classified Ads Bureau," which combines the Russian word for "cockroach" with a supposedly Spanish suffix.

A few exceptions have been made, such as for the names of the two hunting dogs in "St. Peter's Day," which have been translated rather than transliterated as "Futile" and "Musician." The parodic miniature novel "Flying Islands," which "A. Chekhonte" purports to have "translated" from an original work by

Jules Verne, is set in London (a city Chekhov never visited), and features a central character who is Scottish. "Sir John Lund" has been preferred to "Ser Dzhon Lund." Chekhov gives his elderly servant "Tom" a surname which means "snipe," so he appears as "Tom Snipe" in this volume. "Vil'yam Bolvanius," the seven feet, one inch bald astronomer with four pairs of spectacles on his nose who takes them into space, has spent two years living off crayfish, slime, and crocodile eggs in the Australian bulrushes and bears a pseudo-Latin surname which implies he is actually a "bolvan," meaning "blockhead" or "dimwit." He appears as "William Doltius" in this volume.

The cities of Kyiv, Odesa, and Kharkiv are referred to by the pre-revolutionary names they were known by when Chekhov was writing and Ukraine was part of the Russian Empire (Kiev, Odessa, Kharkov). We have transliterated other place names, but in the opening story, "Letter to a Learned Neighbour," we have provided a straightforward translation of the invented name of the village of "Bliny-S'edeny". "Eaten Pancakes" in fact sounds almost as if it could be the ancient name of a rural English village. Similarly, we have sought to find humorous equivalents for the comic names of the railway stations in "On the Train," hence "Crash, Bang, Wallop," "Run for Your Life!," "Swindler Town," and "Knackers-on-the-Hill."

About the Translators

Olga Akroyd studied English and Russian at Queen Mary, University of London, and completed a master's degree at Oxford. Her doctorate from the University of Kent examines the works of Melville and Dostoevsky from a cross-cultural, comparative perspective. In 2023 she published *Presidents and Place: America's Favorite Sons*, a volume co-edited with Tom Cobb, to which she contributed an article about the St. Petersburg activities of John Randolph, American Ambassador to Russia during the reign of Nicholas I. She is currently an independent scholar, translator and EFL tutor.

Carol Apollonio is a Research Professor at Duke University. Author of books and articles about Russian literature, including *Simply Chekhov* and *Dostoevsky's Secrets*, and the blog *Chekhov's Footprints*, she holds a Chekhov centennial medal from the Russian Ministry of Culture. She is an Honorary President of the International Dostoevsky Society. Her recent translations from Russian include novels by Alisa Ganieva.

Judith Armstrong has an MA and PhD from the University of Melbourne, where she later became Reader and Head of the Department of Russian and served as a member of the university council. As well as teaching a range of courses on the literature, history, and culture of pre- and postrevolutionary Russia, she has published five academic books. She has gone on to publish several more books of fiction and nonfiction since becoming a full-time writer in 1996, as well as articles and reviews for newspapers, magazines, and opera programmes.

Claire Atwood was a student in the seminar on Chekhov's stories and plays in the Slavic Department at Harvard University in 2015 when she participated in the Early Chekhov Translation Project. She worked under the supervision of Maria Khotimsky.

Rosamund Bartlett launched a campaign to preserve the Chekhov House-Museum in Yalta in 2008, and became a Trustee of the resulting Anton Chekhov Foundation, a UK-registered charity. She is the author of *Chekhov: Scenes from a Life* (Free Press), editor and co-translator of *Chekhov: A Life in Letters* (Penguin Classics), and translator of two anthologies of Chekhov's stories, of which *About Love and Other Stories* (Oxford World's Classics) was shortlisted for the Oxford-Weidenfeld Translation Prize. A new edition of her anthology *The Exclamation Mark and Other Stories* was issued by Hesperus Press in 2025.

Adam Bartley is a former university lecturer in Latin and Ancient Greek. He has been a professional translator of Russian, German, Dutch and, sometimes, Latin and Ancient Greek since 2014. He has also translated nineteenth-century observations of new Britain by the Danish traveller Richard Parkinson, medieval Latin texts on emperor Frederick II and a Dutch short story by Remco Campert.

Maria Bloshteyn is a Leningrad-born, Toronto-raised editor, translator, and scholar. She is the author of *The Making of a Counter-Culture Icon: Henry Miller's Dostoevsky* (University of Toronto press, 2007), translator of Chekhov's *The Prank* (NYRB Press, 2015), a censored anthology of twelve early short stories illustrated by Nikolay Chekhov, and the editor and main translator of *Russia is Burning: Poems of the Great Patriotic War* (Smokestack books, 2020). She is a part of the international group of editors and translators involved with the Kopilka project, a repository of Russophone poems about the war with Ukraine.

Katherine Bowers is an Associate Professor of Slavic Studies at the University of British Columbia. She is the author of *Writing Fear: Russian Realism and the Gothic*, as well as a number of other works on Russian literature and culture of the long nineteenth century.

Philip Chadwick is a teacher at Manchester Grammar School.

Sarah Chatta was an undergraduate at Oberlin College, studying Russian and creative writing, when she participated in the Early Chekhov Translation Project under the supervision of Polina Dimova.

Tung Chan was a sixth-form pupil studying Russian at Winchester College, when he participated in the Early Chekhov Translation Project under the supervision of Stephen and Olga Rich

Oliver Clark was a sixth-form pupil studying Russian at Winchester College, when he participated in the Early Chekhov Translation Project under the supervision of Stephen and Olga Rich

Elena Dimov is a translator of Russian poetry originally from Vladivostok. She has a master's degree in oriental studies from the Far Eastern Federal University and a PhD from the Russian Academy of Sciences. Her translation of Maria Rybakov's novel-in-verse *Gnedich* was published by Glagoslav. Her translations have also appeared in Boston University's *Arion* journal and the *Cardinal Points* literary journal. She now resides in Charlottesville, Virginia, where she has taught courses in Russian language and culture, and edits the website Contemporary Russian Literature.

Polina Dimova is an Associate Professor of Russian at the University of Denver and was a Visiting Assistant Professor at Oberlin College in Russian language and Comparative Literature. She has published on European modernism, the relations of literature to music and art, and intermedial translation. She is the author of *At the Crossroads of the Senses: The Synaesthetic Metaphor across the Arts in European Modernism* (Pennsylvania State University Press, 2024).

Rachel Patricia Dixon began learning Russian in her first year at the University of St. Andrews, and has since then studied, worked, and travelled in Russia and Ukraine. She recently completed her master's in translation and professional language skills at the University of Bath and is looking forward to starting her career as a translator.

Katherine Dye was an undergraduate at Oberlin College, studying comparative literature and French, when she participated in the Early Chekhov Translation Project under the supervision of Polina Dimova.

Luka Fisher is a queer woman of the trans experience. She is an artist, composer, cultural producer, and Russian translator. She holds an MFA in photo/media from CalArts and a BA in International Relations and Russian Literature from George Washington University. She served as an associate producer and actress in Lyle Kash's majority trans cast and crew feature film *Death and Bowling*. Together with Kyler O'Neal she wrote music for Invertigo Dance Company's interdisciplinary trans performance *Walk the Walk* in 2023. She is currently pursuing an MA in curatorial studies and public practices from USC Roski.

Alex Fleming is a literary translator from Russian and Swedish into English. Her published translations include works by Maxim Osipov, Katrine Kielos-Marçal, and Andrés Stoopendaal, and they have featured in *Granta, Asymptote, Literary Hub,* and *Image Journal,* among other publications. She is also the editor of *Swedish Book Review,* a journal of new Swedish writing.

Mercedes Flowers was a student in the seminar on Chekhov's stories and plays in the Slavic Department at Harvard University in 2015 when she participated in the Early Chekhov Translation Project. She worked under the supervision of Maria Khotimsky.

Philip Franco was an undergraduate at Oberlin College, studying Theatre and Russian, when he participated in the Early Chekhov Translation Project under the supervision of Polina Dimova.

Jean-Paul Gilbert was an undergraduate at Oberlin College, studying Russian, when he participated in the Early Chekhov Translation Project under the supervision of Polina Dimova.

Michael Gluck is a translator of Russophone literature. He is the recipient of a PEN/Heim Translation Fund Grant and has a PhD in Slavic languages and literature from Columbia University.

Jessica Gokhberg received her PhD in literature from Duke University, specialising in Cold War literary history. She has published on the topics of socialist realism and transnational feminist movements. She is currently a high school English teacher in Minnesota.

Walker Griggs was an undergraduate at Oberlin College, studying Russian and Biology, when he participated in the Early Chekhov Translation Project under the supervision of Polina Dimova.

Jackson Gzehoviak was a student in the seminar on Chekhov's stories and plays in the Slavic Department at Harvard University in 2015 when he participated in the Early Chekhov Translation Project. He worked under the supervision of Maria Khotimsky.

Helen Hagon studied Russian and French at the University of Nottingham and later gained an MA in translation studies from the University of Portsmouth. Based in Lincolnshire, UK, she now works as a freelance translator, tutor, and writer.

Louise Hardiman is a historian specialising in Russian, Ukrainian, and Soviet art. She has edited and translated folk tales by the Russian Arts and Crafts artist Elena Polenova, and her latest book is the edited volume *Courtly Gifts and Cultural Diplomacy: Art, Material Culture and British-Russian Relations* (Brill, 2023).

George Hargreaves has been learning Russian for over twenty years, having fallen in love with the language as soon as he discovered it. He worked as a professional translator for almost a decade, predominantly in the field of experimental contemporary fiction and video games. He still works on small projects for fun when the opportunity comes up.

Julia Hon resides in Washington, DC. She began studying Russian in Wisconsin and has since lived in Moscow, St. Petersburg, Ufa, and Tbilisi. This is her first published translation.

Sally Ivanova is a self-confessed grammar geek and has been a lover of languages since childhood. She completed both an undergraduate degree in Spanish and Russian and a master's degree in translation at the University of Bristol. During her postgraduate studies, she became particularly fascinated by audiovisual translation and now works as a subtitle editor for a London-based media company

Anne Marie Jackson has translated works by Daniil Kharms, Alexei Nikitin, Maxim Osipov, and Teffi, among others. She was once shot dead by Chechen rebels in a Russian film.

Hannah Jackson first began learning Russian at school at the age of twelve, and participated in the Early Chekhov Translation Project while studying Russian and French at Oxford University. As part of her degree, she spent four months living in Russia, studying at St. Petersburg State University. After graduating in 2016, she worked briefly as a translator before joining a London-based education charity. She has worked in education since then, and currently supports schools in England with community engagement. She continues to enjoy learning languages and reading Russian literature in her spare time.

Anna Krushelnitskaya is a translator and educator based in Ann Arbor, Michigan. Her publications include *Cold War Casual* (Front Edge, 2019)—a bilingual collection of interviews about propaganda on both sides of the Iron Curtain, *Babi Yar and Other Poems* by Ilya Ehrenburg (Smokestack, 2024), and (as co-editor) *Dislocation: An Anthology of Poetic Response to Russia's War in Ukraine* (Slavica, 2024). Her translations have also featured in *Disbelief: 100 Russian Anti-War Poems* (Smokestack, 2022) and in publications such as *South Florida Poetry Journal, Russian Free Verse, Articulation, View.Point, East West Literary Forum* and *Russian Life*.

Tamar Koplatadze is an associate professor in Slavonic studies at the University of Oxford. When participating in the Early Chekhov Translation Project, she was a student at the University of Bristol. She has continued to pursue her interest in Chekhov's fiction with a recent academic article, "Anxieties of Modern Love in Chekhov's Short Stories." Aside from the nineteenth century, her research focuses on Russian postcolonial studies. Her book *Postcolonial Identities in Central Asian and Caucasian Literature* (Oxford University Press, forthcoming) is the first major study of its kind. She also enjoys sharing her research on various public platforms, including the BBC.

Maria Khotimsky supervised the seminar on Chekhov's stories and plays at the Slavic Department, Harvard University, in spring 2015, and the group of four students who participated in the Early Chekhov Translation Project.

Thomas J. Kitson holds a PhD in Russian literature from Columbia University. His translation of Iliazd's *Rapture* won a Read Russia Prize Special Mention. He received a 2019 NEA Translation Fellowship for Iliazd's *PhiloSophia*, recently excerpted in Rab-Rab Press's bie bao series. More translations from Iliazd, Veniamin Kaverin, Alexis Gritchenko, Ilia Surguchev, and Vasily Shulgin are forthcoming in *In the Ruins of Empires: Constantinople's Russian Moment (1919-1923)*.

Rupert Kettle was a sixth-form pupil of Russian at Winchester College, working under the supervision of Stephen and Olga Rich, when he participated in the Early Chekhov Translation Project.

Katherine Lane received her MA in Slavic and East European languages and cultures from the Ohio State University and went on to earn an MLIS from Rutgers University. She now works as a librarian in Philadelphia with special interests in foreign languages and visual literacy.

Marina Matushenko was born and raised in Vladivostok, Russia, but moved to Australia to complete her law degree in 1998. She has since been practising as an immigration lawyer in Sydney. Marina provides translations as part of the service to her clients who hail from Russia and former USSR.

Anna Mazhirov is a fiction writer and translator born in Ukraine and raised in New York. After studying acting at the St. Petersburg State Theatre Arts Academy, she graduated with a BA in English and Russian from Duke University and an MFA in creative writing from Syracuse University. Her short stories have been published in *AGNI* and *Witness*. She has also translated filmed theatre performances of Chekhov's plays and stories for Stage Russia, including *The Seagull*, *The Black Monk*, and *The Lady with a Lapdog*. She is at work on her first novel.

Neil McCallum is a translator from European and Asian languages who has lived between Chester and Chengdu and is currently residing in London. He has previously won the Susanna Roth prize for translation from Czech, as well as Russian and Czech scholarships, and grants from Santander Bank for work in Spanish.

Charles McCloy studied Russian at the University of Bristol and has lived and worked in Moscow, Tyumen, and Kyiv. He works in commercial real estate and has a specialist focus on the Russian-speaking world, in particular the logistics sector in Central Asia. He enjoys engaging in Russian cultural events and undertakes small-scale translation projects in his free time.

Bridget Menkis was a student at Oberlin College, studying Russian and computer science, when she participated in the Early Chekhov Translation Project under the supervision of Polina Dimova.

Ronald Meyer taught the seminar on Russian Literary Translation at Columbia University for over two decades. His translations include Anna Akhmatova's *My Half-Century: Selected Prose,* Fyodor Dostoevsky's *The Gambler and Other Stories,* and three works for the Norton Critical Edition of *Anton Chekhov's Selected Stories.*

Elena Michajlowska joined Rosamund Bartlett's campaign to preserve the Chekhov House-Museum in Yalta in 2008 as a project manager, and is a Trustee of the Anton Chekhov Foundation. She completed an MA in Screenwriting and Production at the University of Westminster and has worked on numerous film, art, and tech projects. She is the co-author of PUTSCHYOURSELF, an interactive documentary project that explores state violence, traumas of transition, and collective memory prompted by the Soviet coup d'état of 1991.

Piers Murphy was a sixth-form pupil studying Russian at Winchester College and working under the supervision of Stephen and Olga Rich when he participated in the Early Chekhov Translation Project.

Rob Myatt graduated from the University of Bristol in 2014 with a First-Class Honours BA in Russian and German. He has been working as a professional translator ever since, translating from Russian, German, Polish, Danish, Swedish, and Norwegian into English. He has published several short fiction and nonfiction translations, and one full-length nonfiction translation.

Lana Nadj holds accreditation as a professional Russian-to-English translator from Australia's National Accreditation Authority for Translators and Interpreters. She is a writer and a practising lawyer.

Oliver Okun was an undergraduate at Oberlin College, studying Russian, when he participated in the Early Chekhov Translation Project under the supervision of Polina Dimova.

Dominika Pasterska has a BA and MSc from the universities of London and Edinburgh. She studied Russian language and literature as a postgraduate at the University of St. Petersburg and later at Moscow State University whilst living and working in Moscow from 2000 to 2006. Dominika currently works as a freelance editor, researcher, and translator based in Warsaw, Poland.

Marianka Pencheva graduated from Plovdiv University Paisiy Hilendasky in Russian philology in 1981 and in English philology in 1993, before taking Harvard University's educational management course. She has taught Russian from beginners to advanced level and translated technical Russian for the aviation industry. She is an NHS translator and has worked as a professional guide for Russian tourists. She lives in London and currently works in adult education.

Tatiana Peshkova graduated from Perm Drama School and from the Department of Foreign Languages at Perm Pedagogical University before building a career in both acting and translation. She has translated into Russian plays by Georges Feydeau, Enda Walsh, and Martin McDonagh, and worked in Russia with a number of outstanding theatre directors, including Michael Hunt, Robert Wilson, Romeo Castellucci, Peter Sellars, and Theodoros Terzopoulos. She is keen to develop further her abilities in translating English-speaking playwrights.

Natalie Pierson was an undergraduate at Oberlin College, studying biology and Russian, when she participated in the Early Chekhov Translation Project under the supervision of Polina Dimova.

Elena Polevaya is a musician, opera singer, composer, teacher, and translator of Russian and Ukrainian. Born into a Russian Ukrainian family, she has lived in eastern Ukraine, Siberia, and Moscow, where she studied cello, piano, musicology, and opera singing. Her passion for the art of translation was inspired early on by her father who read her children's books in English, translating them phrase by phrase into Russian. Since moving to Australia in 1992 she has been able to realise her two passions of singing opera and earning a living as a professional translator of Russian.

Lillian Posner was an undergraduate at Oberlin College, studying Russian and East European studies, when she participated in the Early Chekhov Translation Project under the supervision of Polina Dimova.

Melissa Purkiss completed the first draft of her translation in this volume while studying for her MA in Russian literature at the University of Oxford. She has since completed a DPhil, also at Oxford, and currently works in publishing.

Rollo Quinault was a sixth-form pupil of Russian at Winchester College, working under the supervision of Stephen and Olga Rich, while participating in the Early Chekhov Translation Project.

Ronan Quinn was a journalist at the *Irish Times*. He has translated novels such as *Prisoner* by Anna Nemzer, detective stories for Emil Costa, and works by Vladimir Kernerman, including *Daniel Stein, a translation without a translator*. He has also translated poetry, including Ida Nappelbaum's *My House*, and political and economic books by Boris Guberman. He is himself a poet and has published in a variety of different venues in Ireland, Britain, and the United States.

Stephen Rich is a teacher at Oundle School. He previously taught at Winchester College, where seven sixth-form pupils of Russian participated in the Early Chekhov Translation project under his guidance.

Olga Rich previously taught at Winchester College, where seven sixth-form pupils of Russian participated in the Early Chekhov Translation project under her guidance.

Elizabeth Rattley was a final-year university student when she participated in the Early Chekhov Translation Project. She is now working in international education.

Angus Robinson was a sixth-form pupil of Russian at Winchester College, working under the supervision of Stephen and Olga Rich, when he participated in the Early Chekhov Translation Project.

Margarita Shalina is the translator of Chekhov's *The Duel* (Melville House). She provided the literal translation to Annie Baker's critically acclaimed adaptation of Chekhov's *Uncle Vanya* (Soho Rep.), and has contributed translations to *Food Chain* by Slava Mogutin (ITNA Press), *Pussy Riot: A Punk Prayer for Freedom* (Feminist Press), *St. Petersburg Noir* (Akashic), and the journal *Animal Shelter* (Semiotexte).

Anastasia Shteyn was born in Moscow and holds a literature degree from the University of Toronto. She currently manages research programmes at The Alan Turing Institute in the UK.

Erica Siegel received her PhD in Slavic languages and literatures from Columbia University in 2010. She is still at Columbia, now serving as assistant dean of communications and outreach at the James H. and Christine Turk Berick Center for Student Advising at Columbia College and the School of Engineering and Applied Science.

Anastasia Snetkova was a student in the seminar on Chekhov's stories and plays in the Slavic Department at Harvard University in 2015 when she participated in the Early Chekhov Translation Project. She worked under the supervision of Maria Khotimsky.

Eric Spoerl was an undergraduate at Oberlin College, studying English and History when he participated in the Early Chekhov Translation Project under the supervision of Polina Dimova.

Tom Stableford is a translator from, and writer on, Russian, Czech, Ancient Egyptian, Hindi, and Japanese.

Mark Swift earned a BA in Russian at the University of Iowa in 1979 and a PhD at Bryn Mawr College in 1996. He has published journal articles, book chapters, and a monograph on Chekhov: *Biblical Subtexts and Religious Themes in Works of Anton Chekhov* (2004). In 2019 he retired from the University of Auckland in New Zealand after twenty-two years as a senior lecturer in Russian and European studies.

Nina Tchernova is a translator, editor, and lecturer who moved to Australia from Russia over twenty years ago, having trained at the Moscow State Linguistic University. On top of running a Russian translation agency, she teaches English, interpreting, and Russian in Australian colleges.

Yi Lin Cheryl Tan is a culinary enthusiast with a potato allergy. This detail was perhaps overlooked when she chose to study Russian at university, a decision heavily influenced by her admiration for bliny.

Tselmegtsetseg Tsetsendelger grew up in Mongolia and Russia speaking both languages, memorising poems, and reading literature. She studied Russian and International Studies at Kenyon College in Ohio and currently resides in New York.

Hannah Tyburski was a student of Russian at Oberlin College, working under the supervision of Polina Dimova, when she participated in the Early Chekhov Translation Project.

Alexander Walsh is a lawyer living in London. He spent time studying cello at the St. Petersburg Conservatory and learnt Russian there. He has an MA in history and Russian in addition to a diploma in law from City University and is a Trustee of the Anton Chekhov Foundation.

Isobel Walsh is a family lawyer living in Herefordshire and London, and is a Trustee of the Anton Chekhov Foundation.

William Watkins is a graduate of Oberlin College and Conservatory, where he studied Russian and violin performance. He has previously spent time in St. Petersburg working as a freelance translator and ESL teacher and currently works as a software engineer in Seattle.

Timothy Dwight Williams is a senior lecturer in the Faculty of English at Adam Mickiewicz University in Poznań and translator of articles and books from Polish and Russian. He lives in Poznań with his wife, the artist Joanna Arent-Williams, and their dog Kierkegaard.

Alex Wordley was a sixth-form pupil of Russian at Winchester College, working under the supervision of Stephen and Olga Rich, when he participated in the Early Chekhov Translation Project.

Valeriya Yermishova is a literary translator and conference interpreter. She served as president and president-elect of the New York Circle of Translators between 2014 and early 2017, and teaches at City University of New York, Hunter College. She has translated Viktor Shklovsky and Sergey Kuznetsov.

Josephine von Zitzewitz has held research and teaching positions at the universities of Oxford, Bristol, Cambridge, and UiT—The Arctic University of Norway. She has written two monographs on Soviet samizdat—*The Culture of Samizdat: Literature and Underground Networks in the Late Soviet Union* (Bloomsbury Routledge, 2020) and *Poetry and the Leningrad Religious-Philosophical Seminar 1976–1980: Music for a Deaf Age* (Routledge, 2016)—and numerous articles on Russian-language poetry. Her translations have appeared in UK and US journals, as well as in several anthologies, including *Dislocation*, a bilingual volume of anti-war poetry (Slavica, 2024).

Anton Chekhov

Earliest Stories

Letter to a Learned Neighbour

Village of Eaten-Pancakes

My dear neighbour.

Maxim... (I have forgotten your patronymic, exquse me kindly!) Exquse and forgive this old codger* and ridiculous human soul for daring to trouble you with my pathetic written blabbering. A whole year has passed since you deigned to settle in our part of the world, as neighbour to me, insignificant person that I am but I still do not know you, nor have you met the pitiful dragonfly that is myself. So, allow me, dear esteemed neighbour, by way at least of these doddering hieroglyphs to make your acquaintance and shake, in my mind, your learned hand and congratulate you on your arrival from St. Petersburg in our unworthy native soil, inhabited by simple folk and peasants i.e. plebeian elements. I have long searched, thirsted even, for a chance to make your acquaintance, for Science, in certain respects is like our own mother, same as cilivisation and because I sincerely respect those people, the famous names and titles, whose celebrated name and rank, crowned with the halo of popular fame, laurels, cymbals, decorations, ribbons and diplomas, boom like thunder and lightning around all parts of our universe, both visible and invisible i.e. the sublunar. I ardently adore astronomers, poets, metaphysicians, part-time lecturers, chemists and other high-priests of Science, of whom you are a member by way of your clever facts and branches of Science i.e. its fruits and rewards. People say you have had many books published during your mental sessions with tubes, thermometers and heaps of foreign books filled with enticing illustrations. The other day, our local maximus pontifex, Father Gerasim, called in at my pitiful premises, my ruins and rubble, and with his customary fanaticism cursed and scolded your thinking and ideas regarding the origins of humankind and other phenomena of the visible world and he also got angry and steamed up about your intellectual world and mental horizons adorned with luminaries and hieroglyphs. I don't agree with Father Gerasim with regards to your intellectual ideas, as I live and breathe only Science, which Providence has given the human race for excavating from the bowels of the visible and invisible earth precious metals, metalloids and gems, but all the same, please forgive me old fellow, if I, a barely visible insect, dare to refute some of your ideas regarding the essence of nature in my crusty way. Father Gerasim told me you have supposedly composed a composition in which you deigned to recount some not completely substantial ideas rigarding humans, their primordial state and antediluvian existence. You have deigned to compose the idea that humans originated from monkey tribes of marmosets, orangutans and other such. Forgive me as an old man, but on this important point I do not agree with you and I have some bones to pick with you. For if man, ruler of the world, cleverest of all respiring beings, came from a simple, ignorant monkey, he would have a tail and a savage voice. If we came from monkeys, we would be put on display and led around town by Gypsies and we would be paying to look at one another, dancing to the command of Gypsies or sitting behind bars in a menagerie. Are we covered in fur? Do we not wear raiments of which monkeys are deprived? Would we really love and not despise women if they smelled even a little of the monkey which we see every Tuesday at the Marshal of the Nobility's. If our ancestors had come from monkeys, they would not be laid to rest in a Christian cemetery; my great grandfather Ambrosy for example, who lived in the days of the Kingdom of Poland, was buried not as a monkey, but next to the Catholic abot Joachim Shostak,* whose notes on a moderate climate and the immoderate consumption of hot drinks are still kept by my brother Ivan (he's a Majer). Abot means Catholic priest. Exquse a nitwit like me for interfering in your learned affairs and yattering on like an old man and imposing on you my wild and rather crude notions, which learned and cilivised persons are more likely to have in their stomachs than in their heads. But I can't keep quiet and can't bear it when scientists think wrongly in their heads and can't not tackle you. Father Gerasim informed me of your misguided thinking about the lunar body i.e. the moon, which replaces the sun in the hours of gloom and darkness, when people are sleeping and you are conducting electricity from place to place and fantasising. Don't mock an old man for his foolish words. You write that people and tribes live on the moon i.e. the lunar body. This is simply impossible, for if there were people living on the moon they would block its magical and enchanting light with their houses and verdant pastures. Moreover, people can't live without a bit of rain, and rain falls down to the earth, not upwards to the moon. People living on the moon would fall to the ground and this does not happen. Sewage and slops would fall on our land from an inhabited moon. And can people live on the moon if it exists only at night and disappears during the day. And governments can't allow anyone to live on the moon as its distance and inaccessibility mean that people could very easily hide there from their civic duties. You have made a bit of a mistake. You have composed and printed in your clever composition, as Father Gerasim tells me, that on our greatest luminary, the sun, there are some black spots. This can't be, as this simply could never be true. How could you see spots on the sun, if we can't look at the sun with the naked eye, and why would there be spots if it is possible to live perfectly well without them? And from what sort of wet substance are these spots made if they don't burn away? Maybe you think even fish live on the sun? Exquse me being such a poisernous devil's trumpet and making such stupid jokes! I am most frightfully devoted to science! That billowing sail of the nineteenth century the rouble has no value for me, as science has eclipsed it in my eyes with her far-reaching wings. Every new discovery torments me like a little nail in my back. Though I'm an ignoramus and an old-world landowner, I'm still an old scoundrel engaged in science and discoveries which I produce with my own hands, filling my ridiculous little head and crude skull with thoughts and an array of great knowledge. Mother Nature is a book which needs to be seen and read. I have made many discoveries with my own brain, the sort of discoveries which no reformer has ever invented. I can tell you without bragging that I'm not at the bottom of the heap when it comes to education, acquired through hard graft and not the wealth of parents i.e a father or mother, or guardians, who often ruin their children with wealth, luxury and six-storey dwellings with slaves and electric service bells. Here's what my worthless brain has discovered. I have discovered that on Easter Sunday, in the early morning, our great, fiery, radiant mantle, the sun, sparkles playfully and picturesquely with its rainbow colours and makes a glittering impression with its wonderful twinkle. Another discovery. Why are days short and nights long in winter and the opposite in the summer? Days are short in winter because they shrink from the cold like all other visible and invisible objects, and because the sun sets early, while nights expand from the lumination of lamps and streetlights, because they warm up. Then I also discovered that dogs eat grass in spring like sheep, and that coffee is bad for full-blooded people, because it makes your head spin, blears your vision and so on and so on. I've made a good many discoveries, although I don't have any certificates or diplomas mind you. You must come over and see me, dear neighbour, for heaven's sake. Let's discover something together and study literature, and you can teach lousy old me some calculations.

I recently read something by a French scientist who said that a lion's muzzle is not at all like a human visage, as scientists think. We can confab about that too. Do me the onner, come over. You could even come tomorrow. We are currently fasting for Lent but we will cook meat for you. My daughter Natashenka asks that you bring along some clever books. She is emancipay, you know, so she thinks everybody's a fool, and only she is clever. Young people are getting their opinions out there now, I can tell you. God bless them! I am expecting my brother Ivan (the Majer) to come in a week, a good person, though between you and me he is a dyed-in-the-wool bourbon who does not care for science. My steward Trofim should deliver this letter to you at exactly 8 o'clock this evening. If he brings it later than that, use your professorial authority and slap him about the cheeks, no point beating about the bush with his kind. If he delivers it later, that means the devil stopped by the tavern. The custom of visiting neighbours was not invented by us nor will it end with us, so be sure to come with your contraptions and books. I would come to you myself, but I am awfully bashful and lack the courage. Exquse me for bothering you like a scoundrel.

I remain, yours respectfully, retired non-commissioned officer of the nobility in the Don Cossack army, your neighbour

Vasily Semi-Bulatov[1]

---

1   The letter writer's invented surname is close to that of Chekhov's school friend Vasily Zembulatov, a fellow liberal-minded medical student at Moscow University. 'Semi-Bulatov' could mean 'seven swords' (*bulat* means "Damascus steel") and implies toughness.

What Does One Usually Encounter in Novels, Tales, etc?

A count, a countess with traces of a former beauty, a neighbouring baron, a liberal-leaning writer, an impoverished nobleman, a foreign musician, dim-witted lackeys, nannies, governesses, a German bailiff, a squire, and an heir from America. Faces which are not handsome, but pleasant and appealing. A hero who saves the heroine from a rabid horse, who is of stern mettle, and ready to demonstrate the strength of his fists at any opportunity.

Celestial heights, a boundless, impenetrable, incomprehensible far horizon, in a word: nature!!!

Fair-haired friends and red-haired foes.

A rich uncle, liberal or conservative, depending on the circumstances. His counsel does not enrich the hero as much as his death.

A dear old aunt in Tambov.

A doctor with a concerned expression who brings hope in a crisis; often has a cane with a knob and usually has a bald patch. And wherever there is a doctor, rheumatism from righteous labours, a migraine, brain fever, care for a wounded dueller, and the inevitable advice to visit a spa.

A servant who worked for the old masters, ready to go anywhere for them, even across hot coals. A great wit.

A dog that has mastered all but the task of speaking, a parrot and a nightingale.

A dacha just outside Moscow and a mortgaged property somewhere in the south.

Electricity, mostly connected for no apparent reason.

A briefcase made of Russian leather, Chinese porcelain, an English saddle, a revolver that never misfires, a medal in a buttonhole, pineapples, champagne, truffles and oysters.

Inadvertent eavesdropping leading to great revelations.

Countless interjections and attempts to employ some technical term in the right place.

Delicate references to rather indelicate circumstances.

Very often, the absence of an ending.

Seven deadly sins to start off with and a wedding to tie up loose ends.

An ending.

Chase Two Hares
and You Will Lose Them Both

The clock struck twelve in the afternoon, and Major Shchelkolobov,[1] the owner of two and a half acres of land and a young wife, stuck his bald head out from
under a calico blanket and swore loudly. Yesterday, walking past the summer
house, he had heard his young wife, the 'Majoress,' Karolina Karlovna, having
a more than amicable conversation with her visiting cousin; she had called
her husband, Major Shchelkolobov, a muttonhead, and had argued with her
feminine frivolousness that she did not love her husband, that she never had
and never would, because of his (Shchelkolobov's) thick-headedness, peasant
manners, propensity for mental derangement and chronic drunkenness. This
attitude from his wife had shocked and infuriated the Major, filling him with
the greatest possible indignation. He had not slept the entire night or morning.
His head seethed with unusual activity, his face smouldered and was redder
than a boiled lobster, his fists clenched convulsively, and in his breast there
took place such a commotion and clamour such as he had not seen or experienced even at the Siege of Kars.* Glancing from under the blanket at God's
green earth and swearing, he jumped out of bed and started to walk around the
room shaking his fists.

"Hey, blockheads!" he shouted.

The door creaked, and the Major saw his valet, 'coiffeur,' and floor-scrub-
ber Panteley, wearing his old cast-offs, with a puppy under his arm. He leant
against the doorpost and blinked respectfully.

"Listen, Panteley," began the Major, "I want to speak with you candidly,
man to man, in a humane fashion. Stand up straight! Let go of that fistful of

---

1   The major's humorous surname connotes the aggressive gesture of flicking (shchelkat')
someone's forehead (lob), while his wife Karolina Karlovna first name and patronymic
allude to her German origins. Later on in the story when she addresses him by the diminutive Apollosha, we learn that his incongruous first name is that of the Greek god "Apol-
lo(n)."

flies and listen! That's it! Are you going to give me a frank answer, straight from the heart, or not?"

"Yes, sir."

"Don't look at me with such astonishment. Looking at your master with astonishment is not allowed. Shut your mouth! What a brute you are, old man! You don't know how to behave in my presence. Answer me directly, without humming and hawing! Do you beat your wife, or not?"

Panteley covered his mouth with his hand and gave a very stupid grin.

"Ev'ry Tuesday, your Honour," he murmured, and began to giggle.

"Very good. What are you laughing at? It's no laughing matter. Shut your mouth! Don't scratch yourself in front of me; I don't like it." The Major thought for a moment. "I suspect, old fellow, that peasants are not the only people who punish their better halves. What are your thoughts on this score?"

"Not the only ones, your Honour!"

"For instance?"

"There's a judge in town, Pyotr Ivanych... Do you want me to tell you about him, Sir? I worked for him as caretaker ten or so years ago. A fine master, in a manner of speaking, that is... but once he starts drinking, watch out! He used to come home after he'd had a few and start walloping the mistress. God strike me dead if I'm lying! And all of a sudden, I'd get a whack in the side too, to round things out. He'd beat the mistress and say: You, he'd say, are a fool, you don't love me, so, he'd say, for that reason I wish to kill you and put an end to your life..."

"And what would she do?"

"Forgive me, she'd say."

"Really? By God, that's magnificent!"

And the Major rubbed his hands together in delight.

"It's the honest truth, your Honour! What else can you do with 'em, your Honour? My missus, for example... She needs a good beating now and then! She stepped on my accordion and broke it, and ate the master's pies... Can you believe it? Hm!.."

"Stop your argy-bargy, you blockhead! What are you on about? You'll never manage to say anything intelligent! Mind your own business! What is the mistress doing?"

"Sleeping."

"Well, what will be will be. Go and tell Marya to wake her and say that I wish to see her... Wait!.. What do you think? Do I look like a peasant?"

"What should you look like a peasant for, your Honour? Who ever heard of a master looking like a peasant? You don't at all!"

Panteley shrugged his shoulders, the door creaked once again, and he went out; with a preoccupied expression on his face, the Major began to wash and dress himself.

His pretty little twenty-year-old wife entered while he was dressing. "Darling!" said the Major in the snidest tone possible, "I don't suppose you could spare an hour or so of your ever-so valuable time?"

"With pleasure, dear!" the Majoress answered, as she placed her forehead to the Major's lips.

"Darling, I'd like to go for a walk, or maybe a boat ride on the lake... I don't suppose you would be willing to keep me company with your oh-so pleasant personage?"

"Won't it be hot? But all right, my dear, I'd love to. You can row, and I can steer. Shouldn't we take a bite to eat with us? I'm so terribly hungry..."

"I've thought of that, already" he answered, fingering the whip in his pocket.

Half an hour after this conversation, the Major and the Majoress rowed out towards the middle of the lake. The Major pulled at the oars, and Karolina Karlovna worked the rudder. "What a little..." muttered the Major, directing furious glances at his day-dreaming wife and burning with impatience. "Stop!" he said in a deep voice when they reached the middle of the lake. The boat came to a stop. The Major's physiognomy grew crimson, and his knees began to shake.

"What's the matter, Apollosha?" asked the Majoress, looking at her husband with astonishment.

"So," he began to mutter, "I'm a muuuttonhead, am I? So I... I... What am I? So I'm thick-headed? So you never loved me and never will? So you... I..."

The Major roared, raised his hands up to the heavens, brandished his whip in the air, and in the boat... *o tempora, o mores!..*[2] there ensued a terrible uproar, an uproar such that not only to describe it, but even to imagine it, is barely possible. To depict what now occurred would be beyond the ability of even an artist who has been to Italy and who possesses the most vivid imagination... Things moved so fast that Major Shchelkolobov did not have

---

2   "Oh, the times! Oh, the customs!" (Latin).

time to come to terms with the new-found lack of hair on his head, nor did the Majoress manage to make use of the whip she had snatched from her husband's hands, when the boat overturned and...

Meanwhile, Ivan Pavlovich, formerly the Major's steward and now the district clerk was sauntering round the edge of the lake in expectation of that blessed hour when the village's young married women would go for a swim; he whistled from time to time, took a puff at his cigarette, and meditated upon the aim of his stroll. Suddenly he heard a terrible scream, in which he recognised the voices of his former masters. "Help!" cried the Major and the Majoress. Without thinking twice, the clerk cast off his coat, trousers and boots, and began swimming to the middle of the lake after crossing himself three times. He could swim better than he could read or write, which is why after some three minutes he was already alongside the distressed parties. Ivan Pavlovich swam up to the drowning couple and was at his wit's end as to know what to do.

"Who should I save?" he asked himself. "The devil take them!" It was totally beyond his strength to save both of them; one was already more than enough. He made a face that expressed his utter bewilderment, and began to reach first for the Major, then for the Majoress. "Just one," he said. "I can't manage both of you? What am I, a whale?"

"Vanya, my dear, save me," squealed the trembling Majoress, holding on to the Major's coat tail, "save me! If you save me, I'll marry you! I swear by everything sacred to me! Ah, ah, I'm drowning!"

"Ivan! Ivan Pavlovich! Be a gentleman... bah!" said the Major in his deep voice, gasping for air. "Save me, brother! I'll give you a rouble for vodka! Help a fellow man, don't let me die in my prime... I'll cover you in riches from head to toe... save me, I say! Come on, what kind of a man are you... I'll marry your sister Marya... I'll marry her, by God! She's such a beauty. Don't save the Majoress, to hell with her! If you don't save me, I'll kill you, I won't allow you to live!"

Ivan Pavlovich's head began to spin, and he very nearly sank like a stone. Both promises seemed to him equally favourable—each was better than the last. Which to choose? Time was running out! "I'll save them both," he decided. "I'll get more with both of them than with just one. That's it, by God! The Lord is merciful, he won't forsake me. God bless!" Ivan Pavlovich crossed himself, grabbed the Majoress with his right hand and the Major's tie with the index finger of the same hand and, grunting, began swimming to the bank.

"Kick with your legs," he ordered, paddling with his left hand and dreaming of his bright future.

"The mistress will be my wife, and the Major my brother-in-law... Very neat! Go for it, Vanya! Now we can eat all the cakes we want and smoke expensive cigars! Thank you, Lord!" It was difficult for Ivan Pavlovich to pull a double load and swim against the wind, but the thought of his bright future kept him going. Smiling and giggling with glee, he delivered the Major and the Majoress to dry land. Great was his happiness. But upon seeing the Major and Majoress clinging affectionately to each other... he suddenly grew pale, struck his forehead with his fist and let out a sob, paying no attention to the girls who, climbing out of the water, crowded around the Major and the Majoress, gazing every now and then with astonishment at the brave clerk.

The next day, as a result of the Major's machinations, Ivan Pavlovich was dismissed from the district administration, and the Majoress banished Marya from her apartments with the order that she go "to her darling brother."

"Oh, people, people," Ivan Pavlovich uttered aloud, strolling along the bank of the fatal pond, "is this what you call gratitude?"

Holiday Assignments

Completed by Boarding School Student Miss Nadya N.

Russian language

a) Five examples of "Sentence Composition"

1) Recently Rusia was at war with Abroad, More Over many Turks were killed.*
2) The railway hisses, carries people and is made off iron and materials.
3) Beef is made from bulls and cows, mutton from lambs and rams.
4) Daddy was passed over for promotion at work and not given a medal, so he got angry and retired for family reasons.
5) I adore my friend Dunya Peshemoreperekhodyashchenskaya[1] because she is diligent and attentive in class and can mimic Nikolay Spiridonych the hussar.

b) Examples of "Grammatical Agreement"

1) During Lent priests and deacons do not want to marry newlyweds.
2) Peasants live at the dacha winter and summer and beat horses, but they are awfully unclean, because they are smeared with tar and do not hire maids or porters.
3) Parents give their daughters in marriage to military men who have an income and their own house.
4) Boy, respect your Papa and Mama—and for that you will be considered a darling and loved by all the people in the world.
5) He had not even breathed a sound before the bear hurled him to the ground.*

---

1   An absurdly long invented surname suggesting a person "crossing the sea by foot."

c) Essay

How I Spent My Holidays

As soon as I passed my exams, I went with Mama, the furniture and my brother Johann, a 3rd year high school student, to the dacha. We were visited by: Katya Kuzevich with her Mama and Papa, Zina, little Yegorushka, Natasha and many other friends of mine, who went for walks and embroidered with me in the fresh air. There were many men, but we, young ladies, kept away from them and paid them no attention whatsoever. I read many books including by Meshchersky, Maykov, Dumas, Livanov, Turgenev and Lomonosov.*

The countryside was magnificent. The young trees grew very close together, no axe had as yet touched their slender trunks, a slender but almost unbroken shadow from the small leaves lay on the soft and delicate grass, all dappled with the golden heads of buttercups, the white specks of woodland harebells and the crimson crosses of wild pinks* (stolen from Turgenev's *A Quiet Backwater*). The sun rose then set. A flock of birds flew in the place where the dawn had been. Somewhere a shepherd was tending his flock and some kind of clouds were floating a bit below the sky. I adore nature. My Papa was preoccupied all summer: the good-for-nothing bank suddenly wanted to sell our house, and Mama followed Papa about all the time and feared he would do himself some harm. So if I had a good holiday, it was because I studied a lot and behaved well. The End.

Arithmetic

Problem: Three merchants invested capital into a business, which a year later made a profit of 8000 roubles. *Question*: how much did each of them receive, if the first merchant invested 35 000, the second merchant-50 000, and the third merchant-70 000?

Answer: To solve this problem, we must first find out which of the merchants invested the most, and to do that, we must subtract all three numbers from each other, and we will then see that it was the third merchant who invested the most, as he invested not 35 000 or 50 000, but 70 000. Good. Now let us find out how much profit each of them received, and to do that we must divide 8000 into three so that the third merchant gets the biggest share. 3 divides into 8 2 times. 3×2=6. Good. Let us subtract 6 from eight and we get 2. Add zero. Subtract 18 from 20 and we get 2 again. Add another zero, and so on, until the end. The answer will be 2666 $^2/_3$, and so we have solved the problem, i.e., each merchant received $2666^2/_3$ roubles, and the third one probably a little more."

*Authenticity confirmed by Chekhonte**

Papasha

Thin-as-a-Dutch-herring Mamasha came into the study of fat-and-round-as-a-beetle Papasha[1] and coughed. As she entered, the maid fluttered off Papasha's knee and slipped behind the door-curtain. Mamasha did not pay the slightest attention to this, because she had already succeeded in adjusting to Papasha's little weaknesses, her attitude that of an intelligent wife who understood her sophisticated husband.

"Pampushka," she said, seating herself on Papasha's knee, "I've come to you for advice, my dear. Wipe your lips, I want to kiss you."

Papasha blinked and wiped his lips with his sleeve.

"What do you want?" he asked.

"It's this, Papochka... What are we going to do with our son?"

"You really don't know? Heavens above! None of you fathers care about anything! It's shocking! Pampushka, at least be a father, even if you don't want—can't be—a husband!"

"There you go again! I've heard this a thousand times if not more."

Papasha made an impatient gesture and Mamasha nearly fell off Papasha's knee.

"You husbands are all the same, you don't like hearing the truth."

"Did you come to talk about truth or about our son?"

"All right, all right, I won't... Pampusha: our son, yet again, has come back from school with bad marks."

"Well, what of it?"

"What do you mean, what of it? They won't let him do the exam! He won't get into the fourth year!"

"What if he doesn't? It's no great matter. As long as he studies and doesn't fool around at home."

---

1   *Mamasha* and *Papasha*, stressed on the second syllable, are diminutives of "Mama" and "Papa" in Russian but can often carry a slightly patronizing connotation. *Papochka*, another diminutive, is stressed on the first syllable. *Pampushka* is a Ukrainian garlic bun.

"But Papochka, he's fifteen years old! How can he be in the third year at that age? Imagine, that horrible arithmetic teacher gave him a D again... Have you ever heard anything like it?"

"He needs a good thrashing, that's what I'm hearing."

Mamasha ran her little finger over Papasha's plump lips and felt she was flirtatiously knitting her brows.

"No, Pampushka, don't talk to me about punishments. It's not our son's fault... It's all a plot... Our son—no need to be modest—is so advanced, it's unbelievable that he couldn't do stupid arithmetic. He knows everything perfectly well, I'm sure."

"He's a charlatan, that's what he is. If he didn't fool around, and did more work... Sit down on that chair, my love... I don't think you're comfortable sitting on my lap."

Mamasha fluttered off Papasha's knee and went over to the armchair as gracefully as a swan, or so it seemed to her.

"Lord, how callous!" she murmured, settling down and shutting her eyes. "No, you don't love your son. Our son is so good, and clever, and handsome... It's a plot, a plot! No, he must not stay down for another year, I won't allow it!"

"But if the rascal is a bad student... Oh, you, mothers! Now, off you go, I have got things to get on with..."

Papasha turned back to his desk, hunched over some papers, and looked sideways at the door-curtain, like a dog eyeing his bowl.

"Papochka, I'm not going—I'm not! I can see I'm tiring you, but do be patient... Papochka, you must go to the arithmetic teacher and order him to give our son a good mark... You must tell him that our son is good at arithmetic, but his health is poor, and that's why he can't please everyone. You must put pressure on the teacher. Can a grown man sit in the third year? Do try, Pampusha! Imagine, Sofia Nikolayevna thought our son as handsome as Paris!"

"That's very flattering to know, but I'm not going! I don't have time for loafing around."

"No, you will go, Papochka!"

"I'm not going—that's my last word... Now, be off with you, darling—I have work to do here..."

"You will go!"

Mamasha had stood up and raised her voice.

"I'm not going!"

"You will go!" shrieked Mamasha. "But if you don't, if you don't feel like taking pity on your only son, then..."

Mamasha screamed and pointed to the door-curtain with the gesture of an enraged tragic actress... Papasha, disconcerted, lost his head and for no reason at all, throwing off his frock-coat, began to sing a song... He always became flustered and turned into a complete idiot whenever Mamasha pointed out the door-curtain to him. He gave in. They summoned their son and demanded that he explain himself. The son got angry, scowled and frowned, and said that he was even better at arithmetic than the teacher, and that it was not his fault if it was only schoolgirls, rich pupils, and those who sucked up who got As in this world. He burst out sobbing and supplied the full address of the arithmetic teacher. Papasha shaved, drew a comb over his bald spot, dressed as smartly as possible, and set off to "take pity on his only son."

Like most Papashas, he arrived at the teacher's house unannounced. What things you see and hear when you arrive unannounced! He heard the teacher say to his wife: "You cost me dearly, Ariadne! There's no limit to your whims!" And he saw the teacher's wife throw herself round the teacher's neck and say, "I'm sorry! You don't cost me dearly, but I value you highly!" Papasha determined the teacher's wife to be very pretty, but that she would not be so delightful if she were fully dressed.

"Hello," he said, approaching the couple casually and clicking his heels. The teacher was for a minute taken aback, while the teacher's wife blushed and as quick as lightning darted into the next room.

"Excuse me," began Papasha, smiling, "perhaps I have somewhat disturbed you... I completely understand... Are you well, sir? Let me introduce myself... I am not a nobody, as you see. I am also in the public service... Ha, ha, ha! Don't worry!"

The teacher smiled faintly for the sake of decorum and politely indicated a chair. Papasha turned on one foot and sat down.

"I have come to talk to you," he continued, displaying his gold watch to the teacher. "Mm, yes... You will of course excuse me, I'm not skilled at expressing myself in a scholarly way. With our lot, you know, it's all off the cuff... Ha, ha, ha. Did you go to university?"

"I did."

"There you are then... So yes, well... It's warm today... Ivan Fyodorych, you've given my boy a D... Mm... yes... It's not a problem, you know... Just desserts and all that. If he deserves praise, praise him, and if it's a lesson he needs, give him a lesson... He, he, he! But it's not very nice, you know. Can my son really have such a poor understanding of arithmetic?"

"How shall I put it? It's not so much that he is bad, it's that he doesn't do any work, you know. And he doesn't know anything."

"Why doesn't he know anything?"

The teacher's eyes widened.

"What do you mean, why?" he asked. "He doesn't know anything and he doesn't study."

"For heaven's sake, Ivan Fyodorych! My son is a superb student. I myself study with him... He sits up all night... He has an exceptional grasp of everything!.. So what if he does play up a bit... that's just youth... Weren't we all young once? I'm not disturbing you, am I?"

"Good heavens, of course not!.. I'm actually very grateful to you... You fathers visit us teachers so rarely... However, this shows how much trust you place in us, and the main thing in everything is trust."

"Of course... The main thing is not to interfere... So my son is not going into the fourth year?"

"No, he's not. Arithmetic after all was not the only subject in which he got a D, was it?"

"I can go and see the other teachers. But about the arithmetic... He, he, he!.. You will amend it?"

"I can't!" (The teacher smiled.) "I really can't!.. I wanted your son to move up, I did my very best, but your son does no work, and he's quite rude... On more than one occasion there has been some unpleasantness between us."

"He's y-young... What do you expect? Surely you can change it to a C!"

"I cannot!"

"Come on, it's a trifle!.. What are you trying to tell me? As if I didn't know what's possible and what you can't get away with. It is possible, Ivan Fyodorych!"

"I can't! What would all the others who got a D say? It's not fair, however you look at it. I can't do it!"

Papasha winked with one eye.

"You can, Ivan Fyodorych! We are not going to spend ages discussing this, Ivan Fyodorych! This is not the sort of thing one can chatter idly about for three hours... Will you tell me what in your academic opinion you consider fair? But we know what your idea of fairness is. He, he he! You should just be straight, Ivan Fyodorych, and call a spade a spade. You deliberately gave him a D, didn't you? What's fair about that?"

The teacher's eyes widened and... that was all. Why he did not take offence will forever remain the secret of a teacher's heart for me.

"Deliberately!" continued Papasha. "You were expecting my visit... Ha, ha, ha... Well, of course!.. Fine with me... He gets his just desserts... I understand employment, as you see... And all the progress that's been made... but all the same, you know... mmm... yes... the old ways are best of all, more useful... What's mine is yours."

Breathing heavily, Papasha extracted his wallet from his pocket and a twenty-five rouble note unfurled itself in the direction of the teacher's fist.

"Please!"

The teacher blushed, recoiled, and... that was all. Why he did not show Papasha the door will forever remain for me the secret of a teacher's heart...

"Don't be embarrassed," continued Papasha. "'I understand. The person who says he's not on the take is the one who is. Who isn't, these days? It's impossible not to, old chap... So you haven't got used to it yet? Please, Sir!"

"No, for heaven's sake..."

"Is it too little? But I can't give you any more... You won't take it?"

"For goodness sake!"

"As you wish... But you'll amend the D, won't you?... It's not me asking as much as his mother... She's in tears, you know... She has palpitations and that sort of thing..."

"I am very sorry for your wife, but I can't do it."

"If our son doesn't go up into the fourth year... what will happen? Hmm... No, you must let him go up!"

"I would love to, but I can't... Would you like a cigarette?"

"Merci beaucoup...[2] Putting him up wouldn't stop you... What rank are you?"

"Titular Councillor.* However, it should be the 8th grade in terms of my post. Ahem!"

"I see... Now, you and I understand each other? On the same page, so to speak? Agreed? He, he!"

"I can't, sir, for the life of me, I cannot!"

---

2   *Merci beaucoup*: "thank you very much" (French).

Papasha paused for a minute, and pondered, before setting upon the teacher again. The offensive continued for a long time. The teacher was obliged to repeat his invariable 'I cannot, sir' about twenty times. Finally, the teacher got fed up with Papasha who was becoming even more intolerable. He tried to exchange kisses, asked that he be examined in arithmetic, cracked a few racy jokes and started becoming very familiar. It made the teacher sick.

"Vanya, it's time for you to go!" the teacher's wife called from the other room. Papasha understood what was going on and blocked the teacher from the door with his large frame. The teacher was worn out and began to whimper. Finally, he thought he had hit upon a brilliant solution.

"Look here," he said to Papasha, "I'll revise your son's mark, but only if my other colleagues also give him a C in their subjects."

"Promise?"

"Yes, I'll change it if they do too."

"It's a deal! Give me your hand! You're not a man, but a star! I'll tell them you've already revised the mark. It'll go like clockwork! A bottle of champagne on me. When is the best time to find them at home?"

"Right now."

"And we of course will be friends? Will you drop round some time for an hour or two?"

"It would be a pleasure. Goodbye!"

"Au revoir[3]! He, he he!.. Ah, young man, young man!.. Goodbye!.. Obviously you send your regards to your colleagues? I'll pass them on. And my best compliments to your wife. Do call on us!"

Papasha clicked his heels, put on his hat, and vanished.

"A fine fellow," mused the teacher, looking after the departing Papasha. "A fine fellow. Speaks his mind. He's simple but kind-hearted, that's clear... I love people like him."

The evening of that same day Mamasha was again sitting on Papasha's lap (and after her, the maid). Papasha assured her that "our son" would go up to the next class, and that you could talk scholarly people round not so much with the help of money, as with pleasant approaches and some polite pressure to the throat.

---

3   *Au Revoir:* "goodbye" (French).

My Jubilee

Young men and maidens!

Three years ago, I felt the presence of that heavenly fire for which Prometheus was chained to a rock... And lo and behold, for three years, I have liberally despatched my work, which has passed through the purgatory of the above-mentioned flame, to the furthest corners of my extensive fatherland. I have written prose, I have written poetry, I have written in all measures, manners, and forms for nothing and for money, I have written to all the journals but... alas!!!.. my envious rivals have found it necessary not to publish my works and, if they have published them, then without fail in the "rejections" column. I sowed about fifty stamps in *The Cornfield*, drowned a hundred in the *Neva*, burned dozens in *Little Fire*, and blew five hundred on *The Dragonfly.** In short: since the start of my literary activities up to the present time, I have received exactly *two thousand* responses from editors! Yesterday, I received the last of these, which, in content, was like all the rest. There was not so much as a hint of "yes" in any of these responses. Young men and maidens! Each of my packages to editors cost me at least 10 kopecks; consequently, I have squandered 200 roubles on these literary activities. You can buy a horse for 200 roubles! My yearly income amounts to only 800 francs per annum... You see what I'm getting at!!! And I've had to starve for celebrating nature, love, women's eyes, for shooting poisonous arrows at haughty Albion's avarice; for having shared my fire with... the gentlemen writing me responses... Two thousand responses-over two hundred roubles and not a single "yes!" Pah! And edifying matter with them! Young men and maidens! I am today celebrating the milestone of receiving my two thousandth response, raising my glass to the conclusion of my literary activities and resting on my laurels. Show me someone else who in three years has received as many "No's," or place me on an unshakeable pedestal!

A Prose Poet

One Thousand and One Passions, or a Terrible Night

(A Novel in One Chapter with an Epilogue)

Dedicated to Victor Hugo

The bells in the tower of the Church of One Hundred and Forty-Six Martyrs struck midnight. I shuddered. The time had come. I convulsively grabbed Theodore by the hand and went outside with him. The sky was as dark as printer's ink. It was as dark as the inside of a hat on a head. A dark night is like a day stuffed into a nutshell. We wrapped ourselves in raincoats and headed off. A strong wind blew right through us. Rain and snow, those wet brothers, lashed at our physiognomies. Lightning, despite the winter season, ploughed the sky in all directions. Thunder, lightning's fearsome, majestic companion, lovely as a wink of blue eyes and swift as thought, shook the air horrifically. Theodore's ears began to glow with electricity. St. Elmo's fire flew, crackling, over our heads. I looked up. I trembled. Who does not tremble in the face of nature's grandeur? Several dazzling meteors flew across the sky. I started counting them and counted 28. I pointed them out to Theodore.

"A bad omen!" he muttered, pale as a Carrara marble statue.

The wind moaned, howled, sobbed... The wind's moans are the moans of a conscience mired in horrific crime. Near us, the thunder toppled an eight-story building and set it on fire. I heard screams flying out of it. We walked past. What did I care about a burning building when one hundred and fifty buildings were burning in my chest? Somewhere out there a bell was ringing, mournfully, slowly, monotonously. A battle of the elements was underway. Some unknown forces, it appeared, were labouring over the terrible harmony of the elements. What are these forces? Will man ever know them?

A timid yet daring dream!!!

We hailed a *cocher*.[1] We got into the carriage and sped off. A cocher is a brother to the wind. We hurtled along like a bold thought hurtles along the mysterious convolutions of the brain. I slipped a purse full of gold into the cocher's hand. The gold helped the whip double the speed of the horse's legs.

"Antonio, where are you taking me?" moaned Theodore. "You look demonic... Hell flickers in your black eyes... I am beginning to be afraid..."

Pitiful coward!! I remained silent. He loved *her*. *She* loved him passionately... I had to kill him because I loved her more than life itself. I loved *her* and hated him. He had to die on this terrible night to pay for his love with his death. Love and hate were boiling inside me. They were my second life. These two sisters, living in one skin, wreak havoc: they are spiritual vandals.

"Stop!" I said to the cocher when the carriage arrived at its destination.

Theodore and I jumped out. From behind the clouds the moon gazed at us coldly. The moon is a dispassionate, silent witness to sweet moments of love and revenge. It had to witness one of us dying. An abyss lay before us, an abyss as bottomless as a barrel of felonious Danaids. We were standing on the edge of the crater of an extinguished volcano. People tell terrifying tales about this volcano. I made a movement with my knee and Theodore plummeted into the horrifying abyss. The crater of a volcano is the maw of the earth.

"Curses!!!" he screamed in response to my curses.

A powerful man, casting his enemy into the crater of a volcano on account of the beautiful eyes of a woman, is a majestic and edifying sight! The only thing missing was lava!

The cocher. The cocher was a statue, erected by fate to commemorate ignorance. Away with routine existence! The cocher followed Theodore. I felt that only love remained inside my chest. I fell face down on the ground and wept with ecstasy. Tears of ecstasy are the result of a heavenly reaction, occurring in the depths of a loving heart. The horses whinnied merrily. How distressing it must be not to be human! I released them from their bestial, tortured lives. I killed them. Death is both the shackles and the release from shackles.

I dropped by the Purple Hippopotamus Hotel and drank five glasses of good wine.

Three hours after my act of revenge I was at the door to her apartment. A dagger, that friend of death, helped me via corpses make my way to her door.

---

1   *Cocher*: "Coachman" (French).

I listened out. She was not asleep. She was dreaming. I was listening. She was silent. The silence lasted about four hours. Four hours, for a lover, are four entire centuries! At last she called her maid. The maid walked past me. I threw a demonic glance at her. She divined my intention. Sanity left her. I killed her. Better to die than to live without sanity.

"Aneta!" *she* cried. "Why isn't Theodore here? Anguish is gnawing at my heart. I am suffocated by a sinister premonition. Oh Aneta! Go fetch him. He is probably carousing now with the godless, horrible Antonio!.. Oh Lord, who is it that I see?! Antonio!"

I entered her room. She went pale.

"Get out!" she screamed, and terror distorted her beautiful, noble features.

I looked at her. A look is the sword of the soul. She staggered. In my eyes she saw everything: Theodore's death, diabolical passion, and a thousand human desires... My pose was—majesty itself. My eyes were glowing with electricity. My hair was vibrating and standing on end. She saw before her a demon in earthly form. I saw that she was beginning to admire me. Four hours it lasted, the graveyard silence and the contemplation of each other. Thunder struck, and she fell on my chest. A man's chest is a woman's fortress. I embraced her. We both screamed. Her bones cracked. A galvanizing current ran through our bodies. A passionate kiss...

She fell in love with the demon in me. I wanted her to love the angel in me. "I'm giving a million and a half francs to the poor!" I said. She fell in love with the angel in me and started crying. I started crying too. What tears those were!!! A month later, at the Church of St. Titus and Hortense, a formal wedding was held. I wedded *her. She* wedded me. The poor gave us their blessing! *She* begged me to forgive my enemies whom I had killed earlier. I forgave them. I went to America with my young wife. My young, loving wife was an angel in the virginal forests of America, an angel before whom lions and tigers bowed their heads. I was a young tiger. Three years after our wedding Old Sam was already carrying a little curly haired boy around. The boy looked more like his mother than me. This angered me. Yesterday my second son was born... and I hanged myself from joy... My second boy is reaching out his little arms to the readers and asking them not to believe his Papa, because his Papa not only never had children, but never even had a wife. His Papa is scared stiff of marriage. My little boy is not lying. He is an infant. Believe him. Childhood is the time of purity. None of this ever happened... Good Night!

On Account of the Apples

The small-time landowner Trifon Semyonovich has lived on his patch of black soil on a corresponding line of longitude and latitude between the Pontus Euxinus[1] in the south and the Solovetsky Islands in the north for a long time. Trifon Semyonovich's surname is long, like the word 'entomologist,' and it comes from a very sonorous Latin word indicating one out of a multitude of human virtues. His black soil extends to 8000 acres. His estate, because it is an estate, and he is a landowner, is mortgaged and up for sale. The sale began before Trifon Semyonovich developed a bald patch, it is still dragging on, and, thanks to the bank's gullibility and Trifon Semyonovich's cunning, it is not going well. Sooner or later, the bank will crash, because Trifon Semyonovich, like his own kind, the name of which is legion, borrows roubles and does not pay interest, and if he does pay from time to time, then he pays with a kind of ceremony with which good folk donate a kopeck for the repose of their soul and for church construction. If this world were not this world, and called things by their real names, then Trifon Semyonovich would not be called Trifon Semyonovich but something else, people would bestow on him names usually reserved for swine. To be frank, Trifon Semyonovich is a proper swine. I invite him to agree with this assessment. Should this invitation come to his notice (he reads *The Dragonfly* now and then), he most probably will not get angry, and as an understanding person, will actually completely agree with me, indeed he may also be generous enough to send me a dozen lovely Antonovka apples* this autumn for not broadcasting his long surname, but limiting myself on this occasion to his first name and patronymic. I do not intend to describe all Trifon Semyonovich's virtues: there is a long list of them. In order to capture Trifon Semyonovich from top to toe, one would have to spend as long writing about him as Eugène Sue spent on his magnum opus *The Wandering Jew.** I will not touch on his cheating at cards, nor his politics, as a result of which he does not pay either his debts or the interest he owes, nor his dirty tricks involving a priest and a sexton, nor his horse-back rides through the village in a costume

---

1   *Pontus Euxinus*: Latin name for the Black Sea.

dating back to the time of Cain and Abel; rather I will limit myself to just one little scene, which characterises his treatment of people. It was in order to celebrate the latter that he drew on his experiences of three-quarters of a century to compose the following tongue twister: "Dimwit, nitwit, dumb-bell, dummy lost at Rummy."*

One thoroughly fine morning (the incident occurred at the end of summer), Trifon Semyonovich was strolling down the long and short avenues of his magnificent garden. All the usual stuff that poets find inspiring was scattered around him in huge quantities with a generous hand, and seemed to be saying and singing: "Take it my good man, enjoy and make the best of it before autumn gets here!" But Trifon Semyonovich was not enjoying it, because he was anything but a poet and also because that morning his soul was partaking with a particular ardour in cold slumber,* as it always did when its master felt he was out of pocket. Behind Trifon Semyonovich marched his trusty retainer, Karpushka, an old codger of about sixty, who was keeping a watchful eye on their surroundings. This Karpushka almost outdoes Trifon Semyonovich himself in terms of virtues. He cleans boots beautifully, is even better at hanging surplus dogs, robs all and sundry, and is unmatched at spying. Following the scribe, the whole village calls him the "oprichnik."[2] Rarely a day goes by without the peasants and neighbours complaining to Trifon Semyonovich about Karpushka's behaviour and habits. But their complaints are in vain because Karpushka is an irreplaceable member of Trifon Semyonovich's household. When he goes walking, Trifon Semyonovich always takes his faithful Karp with him; it is both safer and more fun that way. Karpushka has an inexhaustible supply of cock and bull stories, humorous catchphrases and jokes and is simply incapable of keeping his mouth shut. He talks non-stop and is silent only when he hears something which arouses his interest. On the morning in question he was walking behind his master and telling him a long story about how a couple of high school boys in white caps and with rifles on their shoulders were riding past the garden and imploring him (Karpushka) to let them into the garden to hunt, tempting him with a fifty-kopeck piece, and how he, knowing full well whom he served, had rejected the half rouble with indignation and had set Kashtan and Serka on to them. Having finished this story, he was about to launch into a lurid description about the outrageous way of

---

2   *oprichnik*—member of a ruthless guard unit set up by Ivan the Terrible in 1565 to consolidate his power. The unit answered only to him.

life of the village medical orderly when he heard a suspicious rustle from the apple and pear tree groves. Karpushka bit his tongue, pricked up his ears and started to listen carefully. Convinced that there was a rustle and that this rustle was suspicious, he tugged at his Master's coat-flap, and hurried in the direction of the rustle. Trifon Semyonovich, anticipating a scandal, roused himself and, scampering along on his old legs, ran after Karpushka. There was good reason to run...

On the edge of the orchard, under an old apple tree with a lot of branches, a peasant girl stood chewing something; near her a young, broad-shouldered lad was scrabbling on his knees, collecting the windfalls from the ground; he threw the unripe apples into the bushes but the ripe ones he carried lovingly in his broad, grubby palm to his Dulcinea. Dulcinea, evidently, was not worried about her stomach and was munching the apples one after the other and with much enjoyment, while the lad, crawling over the ground and picking up the apples, had totally forgotten about himself and only had his Dulcinea in his thoughts.

"Pull them off the tree!" the girl whispered, egging him on.

"No, I'm scared!"

"Why are you scared? I bet the oprichnik is in the tavern..."

The lad got to his feet, leapt into the air, broke off an apple from the tree and gave it to the girl. But the lad and his girl, as with Adam and Eve in times gone by, were unlucky with this apple. Hardly had the girl bitten off a piece of the apple and handed it to the boy, hardly had they both felt on their tongues its sharp sourness, when their faces contorted, then drooped and paled... not because the apple was sour, but because they saw in front of them Trifon Semyonovich's stern features and Karpushka's gloating little mug.

"Hello, my friends!" said Trifon Semyonovich, approaching them. "So you are eating apples, are you? I hope I am not disturbing you?"

The lad took off his hat and lowered his head. The girl began to study her apron.

"Well, how is your health, Grigory?" Trifon Semyonovich asked, turning to the lad. "How are you getting along, my fine fellow?"

"I only took one," the lad muttered, "and it was a windfall..."

"And how are you, sweetheart?" Trifon Semyonovich asked the girl.

The girl started studying her apron even harder.

"You haven't had your wedding yet, have you?"

"Not yet... Honest to God, sir, we only took one, and that..."

"All right, all right. Well done. Can you read?"

"Nope... Honest to God, sir, we only took one, and that was a windfall."

"You can't read, but you can steal. Well, thank God for that at least. Knowledge is not a burden. Did you begin stealing a long time ago?"

"I wasn't stealing, was I?"

"And what about your sweetheart," Karpushka asked, turning to the lad. "Why is she looking so miserable? Perhaps you don't love her enough?"

"Shut up, Karp!" said Trifon Semyonovich. "Well now, Grigory, tell us a fairy tale..."

Grigory coughed and smiled.

"I don't know any fairy tales, sir," he said, "and anyway, do you think I need your apples? If I want one I can buy one."

"I am very happy, my dear, that you have plenty of money. Come on, tell us a fairy tale. I am listening, Karp is listening, your beautiful sweetheart is listening. Don't be embarrassed, be bolder! A thief's soul should be bold. Is that not the case, my friend?"

And Trifon Semyonovich fixed his malicious eyes on the lad who had been caught red-handed... Sweat started to pour from the lad's forehead.

"You'd do better to make him sing a song, sir! How can you expect a fool like him to tell us a fairy tale?" Karpushka piped up in his nasty tenor voice.

"Shut up, Karp. Let him first tell us a fairy tale. Well, get on with it, my friend!"

"I don't know any."

"You don't know any? But you know how to steal? How does the Eighth Commandment go?"

"What on earth are you asking me? How should I know? And honest to God, sir, we only ate one apple and that was a windfall..."

"Tell us a fairy story!"

Karpushka began to tear up some nettles. The lad knew very well what the nettles were for. Trifon Semyonovich, like people of his kind, is an adept hand at exercising arbitrary rule. Either he locks a thief away for a day in a cellar, or he flogs him with nettles, or he lets him go, but not before stripping him naked... Is this news for you? But there are people for whom (and indeed places where) this sort of behaviour is a well-established routine and as old as the hills. Grigory took a sideways look at the nettles, hummed and hawed for a while, coughed, and, instead of telling a fairy tale, began gibbering away. Groaning, sweating, coughing, constantly blowing his nose, he began to describe how, during the time of Russia's ancient warriors, they used to pummel the misers and marry the beautiful maidens. Trifon Semyonovich stood and listened, without taking his eyes off the storyteller.

"That's enough," he said when towards the end the lad started spouting utter nonsense.

"You tell stories splendidly but you steal even better. Well now, my beauty," he turned to the girl. "Let's have the Lord's Prayer!"

The beautiful girl blushed and recited the Lord's Prayer in a breathless, barely audible voice.

"Well, and how about the Eighth Commandment?"

"Do you think we took a lot of apples, is that it?" asked the lad, with a desperate wave of his hand. "Here's my cross if you don't believe me!.."

"It is bad that you don't know the Commandments, my dears. You must be taught. Was it him who taught you to steal, my beauty? Why are you silent, my little cherub? You have to answer. Come on, out with it! Silence is a sign of agreement. Well, my beautiful one, hit your handsome boy because he taught you how to steal!"

"I won't," the girl whispered.

"Go on, hit him a little. Fools must be taught. Hit him, sweetheart! You don't want to? All right then, I'll tell Karp and Matvey to take the nettle to you... You still don't want to?"

"I won't."

"Karp, come here!"

The girl flew at the lad and slapped him. The lad smiled stupidly and began to cry.

"Well done, my lovely! Now get hold of him by his hair! Come on, darling! You don't want to? Karp, come here!"

The girl took her betrothed by the hair.

"Don't hold like that, it's more painful for him! You've got to tug!"

The girl began to tug. Karpushka went crazy with delight, he whooped and tittered.

"That's enough," said Trifon Semyonovich. "Thank you, sweetheart, for punishing the wicked. Well," he turned to the lad; "now it's time for you to teach your young lady a lesson... She punished you and now it's your turn to punish her..."

"The things you think up, sir, really... Why should I hit her?"

"What do you mean why? Didn't she just hit you? So now you'll hit her! It's for her own good. You don't want to? Your decision. Karp, call for Matvey!"

The lad spat, grunted, took his betrothed's long braid in his fists and began to beat her hard. In beating her hard, he became ecstatic without realising it and got carried away, forgetting that he was not hitting Trifon Semyonovich but his own betrothed. The girl wailed. He hit her for a long time. I don't know how this story would have ended if Trifon Semyonovich's pretty young daughter Sashenka had not jumped out from behind the bushes.

"It's tea-time, Papa!" shouted Sashenka and, seeing what her Papa was up to, burst out laughing.

"Enough!" said Trifon Semyonovich. "You can go now, my dears. Farewell! I will send you some apples for your wedding."

And Trifon Semyonovich bowed low to the offenders he had punished.

The lad and the girl straightened themselves up and went on their way. The lad went to the right, the girl to the left, and... to this day they have not met again. Had Sashenka not appeared on the scene, they might well have had to try the nettles too... This is how Trifon Semyonovich amuses himself in his old age. And the apple also does not fall too far from the tree in his family. His daughters are in the habit of sewing strings of onions on to the hats of guests of "low rank," and as for guests of the same rank who are drunk, they write 'ass' or 'fool' on their backs in big letters with chalk. His son, the retired Second Lieutenant Mitya, meanwhile, even outdid his father one winter: in league with Karpushka, he smeared tar on the gate of a retired soldier because this soldier refused to make a present of a wolf cub to him, and because this same soldier allegedly armed his daughters against the retired Second Lieutenant's gingerbread and sweets.

After this you can hardly call Trifon Semyonovich by his first name and patronymic!

Before the Wedding

Last Thursday, in the home of her esteemed parents, it was announced that little Miss Podzatylkina[1] was now engaged to Collegiate Registrar* Nazarev. The betrothal could not have gone better: two bottles of Lanin champagne* and one and a half buckets of vodka were downed, while the ladies drank a bottle of Chateau Lafite. The parents of the bride and groom cried at the right time, the happy couple kissed each other enthusiastically, while a schoolboy from the eighth grade toasted the young couple with the words "O tempora, o mores!" and pronounced "Salvete, boni futuri conjunges"[2] with quite a flourish. At just the right moment, the red-haired Vanka Smyslomalov, who had been doing nothing while waiting for the lots to be drawn, right on cue struck a note of terrible tragedy, tore at the hair on his large head, pounded his knee with his fist and exclaimed: "Goddamit, I loved her and I still love her!" These words afforded the young ladies inexpressible delight.

Miss Podzatylkina is remarkable solely for being completely unremarkable. No one has ever noted any sign of intelligence in her, therefore there is nothing to say about it. Her appearance is thoroughly ordinary: she has her father's nose, her mother's chin, cat-like eyes and a breast no better than average. She can play the piano, but is unable to read music; she helps her Mama in the kitchen, always wears a corset, she cannot eat Lenten fare, thinks that a correct use of the mysterious letter *yat** is the source of all wisdom, and above all else on earth loves well-built gentlemen and the name "Roland."

Mr Nazarev is a man of average height with a pasty, expressionless face, curly hair and a flat nape. He works in an office somewhere and receives a tiny salary that is barely enough to cover his tobacco; he always smells of egg-white soap and carbolic acid, considers himself a formidable ladies' man, talks loudly, and is in a constant state of amazement; when he speaks, he splutters.

---

1   The name Podzatylkina implies she has been slapped on the back of the head. The surname of her previous admirer Vanka (diminutive of Ivan) Smyslomalov, mentioned in the same paragraph, suggests he has little sense.

2   "Oh, the times, oh, the customs!"; "Long live this good future couple!" (Latin).

He plays the dandy, looks down on his parents, and will not let a single young lady pass him by without availing himself of the opportunity to tell her: "How naive you are! You'd do well to read some literature!" More than anything else in the world, he loves his own handwriting, the magazine *Entertainment,** and squeaky boots, but most of all he loves himself, particularly when he sits in the company of unmarried girls, drinking tea with sugar and frenziedly denying the existence of demons.

So now you know what Miss Podzatylkina and Mr Nazarev are like!

The morning after the betrothal, Miss Podzatylkina woke up and was summoned to her Mama by the cook. Lying on her bed, her Mama proceeded to deliver the following lecture:

"Why on earth have you got dressed up in your woollen frock? You could have put on your barège dress today. I've got the most awful headache! Yesterday that bald ugly mug, by which I mean your father, decided he'd play a joke on me. I could do without his stupid jokes! He brings me something in a glass... "Drink it," he says. I thought it was wine, so I drank it, and in the glass was the oil and vinegar dressing for the herring. That is what he calls a joke, the drunken ugly mug! He only knows how to cause embarrassment, the drivelling idiot. I have to say, I am extremely surprised and astonished that you were so happy yesterday and didn't cry. What was there to be happy about? Have you come into money or something? I'm astonished! Anyone would have thought that you were glad to be leaving your parental home. And, indeed, perhaps that is the case. What's that? Love? What's love got to do with it? And it's not as if you're marrying the man out of love. You're just after his status! Well, isn't that true? You know it is. And, if you want to know my opinion, I don't like him. He's awfully arrogant and haughty. You'll have to put him in his place... What's that you say? Don't even think about it! After a month you'll be at each other's throats: he's that kind of man, and you're that kind of girl. Only unmarried girls like marriage, but there's nothing good about it, you mark my words. I should know—I've been through it. You'll find out for yourself, all in good time. Don't keep twirling around like that, my head is spinning enough as it is. Men are all idiots, and living with them isn't a bed of roses. Your man is an idiot too, even if he does give himself airs. Don't listen to him too much, don't indulge him, and don't go out of your way to show him respect; he's not worth it. Consult your mother on all things. Straight away anything happens, you come to me. Don't do anything without your mother, heaven forbid! Your husband won't give you good advice, won't teach you anything worthwhile, and he'll try to work everything out to his own advantage. Bear that in mind! Don't listen too much to your father either. Don't invite him to stay with you, lest you foolishly blurt something out. You never know! He'll try to filch something from you. He'll sit around your house for days on end, and what on earth would you want him to do that for? He'll ask you for vodka and smoke your husband's tobacco. He's a nasty, dangerous man, even if he is your father. The rogue has a kind face, but there is such malicious passion in his soul! He'll start to borrow money—don't give it to him! He's a swindler, even if he is a Titular Councillor. There he is now, shouting, and calling for you! Go to him, but don't tell him what I've just told you about him. Otherwise that sorry excuse for a human being will start pestering me, and to hell with him! Off you go, before I give myself a heart attack!.. You're all out to get me! When I am dead, you'll remember my words though! Oh, you tormentors!"

Leaving her mother, Miss Podzatylkina went off to see her papa, who was sitting on his bed and sprinkling his pillow with powder to keep the bedbugs at bay.

"My dear daughter!" her papa said, "I'm very glad that you are intending to enter matrimony with such a clever gentleman as Mr. Nazarev. I'm very glad and fully approve of the marriage. Get married, my girl, and be not afraid! Marriage is such a solemn affair that... well, what can I tell you? Live, be fruitful and multiply! May God bless you. I... I... I'm going to cry. But tears don't get you anywhere. What are human tears? Just a bit of half-cocked psychiatry, that's all! You should listen to my advice, my girl! Don't forget your parents! A husband is not going to be as good for you as your parents, that's for sure! Your husband only likes your material beauty, but we love everything about you. What will your husband love you for? Your character? Your kindness? Your feelings? Oh no! He'll love you for your dowry. After all, we're not giving you away with just a few kopecks, my darling, but with a whole thousand roubles! You have to understand that! Mr. Nazarev is a thoroughly decent man, but you shouldn't respect him more than your father. He'll stick by you, but he won't be a true friend to you. There'll be moments when he... No, best for me to remain silent, my girl! Listen to your mother, darling, but be careful. She's a good woman, but she is a two-faced free-thinker, she's frivolous and affected. She's a noble, honest person, but... never mind her! She won't be able to offer you good advice, not like your father, the author of your existence. Don't take her into your home. Husbands don't exactly adore their mothers-in-law. I did not like my own mother-in-law, in fact, I disliked her so intensely that on more than one occasion I sprinkled burnt cork into her coffee, which led to some quite delectable denouements. Second Lieutenant Zyumbumbunchi-kov[3] took his mother-in-law to the military court. Don't you remember that? Actually, you weren't born then. Just remember, the most important person in your life is always your father. Remember that and obey no one but him. Then, my girl... European civilisation has planted the idea among the female section of society that the more children they have, as it were, the worse off they'll be. That's a lie! Stuff and nonsense! The more children parents have, the better. Hang on, no, that's not right! It's the other way round. I've got it wrong, my darling. The fewer the children, the better. I read that yesterday in one of our periodicals. Some fellow called Malthus* thought that up. So there you are, then. Someone's just driven up... Hah! It's your fiancé! How suave he is, the swindler, the swine! What a man! A real Walter Scott! Go and receive him, sweetheart, while I get dressed."

Mr. Nazarev came rolling in. His betrothed greeted him and said:

"Sit down and make yourself at home!"

He clicked his right heel a few times and sat down next to his fiancée.

"How are things?" he began in his usual overly familiar way. "How did you sleep? You know, I didn't sleep a wink all night. I was reading Zola and dreaming of you. Have you read Zola? You haven't? Goodness, gracious me! That's a crime! There was this official who gave me a copy. Fabulous writer! I'll lend it to you. Ah! Then you would be able to understand! There are some feelings I feel that you've never felt! Allow me to give you a smacker!"

Mr. Nazarev stood up and kissed little Miss Podzatylkina on her lower lip.

"Where are your folks?" he continued with even greater familiarity. "I've got to see them. To tell the truth, I'm a bit angry with them. They've really taken me for a ride. Pay attention... Your Papa told me that he was a Court Councillor,* but now it turns out he's only a Titular Councillor.* Hmm! What-ever next? And then... He promised he'd give you away with a dowry of one and a half thousand, but yesterday your dear Mama told me that I won't get more than a thousand. A dirty trick, wouldn't you say? Even the bloodthirsty Circassians wouldn't go as far as that! I won't allow myself to be swindled. Do what you like, but don't touch my pride or my selflessness. That's no way to

---

3   This absurd invented name sounds as comic in English as it does in Russian (in his 1885 story "Both Are Better," Chekhov will have his male narrator use *zyumbumbunchik* as a term of endearment).

treat a man! It's irrational! I'm an honest man, and therefore I dislike dishonest people! I'm easy-going, but don't try your cunning or casuistry on me; let everything be done in accordance with the human conscience! So there! They even have ignorant-looking faces. What kind of faces are they? They are not proper faces at all! You'll have to excuse me, but I don't feel any filial feelings for them. Once we're married we'll have to put them in their place. I don't like impudence and philistinism! I might not be a sceptic or a cynic, but all the same, I'm familiar with the basics of education. We'll put them in their place! My parents have been out of the picture a long time. Have you already had coffee? No? Well then, I'll have a cup with you. Go and fetch me a cigarette, would you, as I've left my tobacco at home."

His fiancée left the room.

This was before the wedding... I dare say that it is not only prophets and somnambulists who know what will happen after the wedding.

The American Way

Having the strongest of inclinations to enter into the most legal of marriages, and bearing in mind there can be no marriage without the participation of a member of the female sex, I have the honour, happiness, and pleasure humbly to request widows and spinsters to give their gracious attention to the following:

First and foremost, I am a man. And this is very important, of course, to a woman. I am 5 feet and 8 inches tall. I'm young. My old age is as far off as St. Peter's Day* is to the sandpiper. I'm distinguished. Not handsome, but not bad-looking either, and I'm so not bad-looking that I have been mistakenly taken for handsome on more than one occasion in the dark. My eyes are hazel. My cheeks (alas!) are minus dimples. I have two rotten molars. I cannot boast of having elegant manners, but I allow no one to harbour any doubts as to the strength of my muscles. I wear size 7 ¾ gloves. Other than poor, though noble, parents, I have nothing. But I do have a brilliant future. I am a great admirer of pretty girls in general, and maids in particular. I believe in everything. I dabble in literature and so successful am I in this endeavour that I seldom shed tears over the Rejections Column* in the *Dragonfly*.* I have plans in the future to write a novel, in which the main character (a beautiful sinner) will be my wife. I sleep 12 hours per day. I have a gargantuan appetite. I drink vodka only in company. I have good acquaintances. I know two men of literature, a versifier and two spongers, who preach to mankind on the pages of the *Russian Newspaper*.* My favourite poets are Pushkarev* and sometimes myself. I am amorous and not jealous. I want to get married for reasons known only to myself and my creditors. That, in a nutshell, is who I am! And now for the sort of person my intended should be:

A widow or a spinster (the choice is hers) who is not older than 30 and not younger than 15. Not Catholic, i.e., aware no one is immaculate in this world, and certainly not a Jew. A Jewish wife is bound to ask "What do you charge per line? And why didn't you go to Papa? He would have taught you how to make money,"* and I don't like that sort of talk. A blonde with blue eyes and (if possible, please) black eyebrows. Not pale, not red-faced, not thin, not fat, not tall, not short, attractive, not possessed by demons, not with short-cropped hair, not chatty, and a home-bird. She should:

Have good handwriting, because I need a copyist. There is not much copying to do.

Love the journals I contribute to, and share their views in real life.

Not read *Entertainment*,* *New Times Weekly*,* *Nana*,* not be moved by the leading articles in *The Moscow Gazette*,* nor swoon from articles of the same sort in *The Shore*.*

Be able to: sing, dance, read, write, cook, fry, sauté, cuddle, bake (but not scold), lend her husband money, dress with taste in clothes bought *with her own means* (NB) and live in absolute obedience.

Be unable to: nag, hiss, squeak, scream, bite, bare her teeth, break the dishes, and make eyes at friends invited home.

Remember that a cuckold's horns do not embellish a person and that the shorter they are, the better and safer for the person who will have to pay the price for them.

Not be called Matryona, Akulina, Avdotya and other such vulgar names, but have a more noble name (for example, Olya, Lenochka, Maruska, Katya, Lipa, etc.)

Make sure that her mama, that is to say my profoundly respected mother-in-law, lives at the other end of the earth (otherwise I cannot answer for my actions) and

Have a minimum of 200,000 roubles in silver.

Actually, this last point can be changed, at the discretion of my creditors.

Artists' Wives

(Translation from the Portuguese)

Alfonso Zinzaga, the freest of citizens of the capital city of Lisbon, and a young novelist, quite well known (at least, so he thought himself), and with great promise (again, in his own opinion), returned home, worn out from a long day of walking along the boulevards and visiting editorial offices, and as hungry as the hungriest dog. He lived in room 147 of a hotel he had described in one of his novels under the name *The Poisonous Swan*. Having entered his room, he surveyed his small, narrow, low-ceilinged living quarters, wrinkled his nose and lit the lamp, at which point a touching picture met his gaze. Amidst the piles of paper, books, last year's newspapers, decrepit chairs, boots, dressing gowns, daggers, and caps, slept his lovely wife Amaranta on a little, blue-grey calico couch. The tenderly affectionate Zinzaga approached her and, after some reflection, tugged at her arm. She didn't wake up. He tugged at her other arm. She sighed deeply, but didn't wake up. He patted her on the shoulder, tapped on her marble forehead with his finger, touched her shoe, yanked at her dress, sneezed loud enough for the whole hotel to hear, but still she didn't stir.

"That's sleeping for you!" thought Zinzaga. "What the devil? Has she taken poison? The failure of my last novel might have deeply affected her..."

So Zinzaga, wide eyed, shook the couch. A book slowly slipped off Amaranta and landed on the floor, its pages rustling. The novelist picked up the book, opened it, took a look at the title page and turned pale. This wasn't just any old book, and certainly not some book or other, but his latest novel, printed under the patronage of Count Don Barabanta-Alimonda, entitled *The Torture in Saint Moskovsk of the Forty-four Men with Twenty Wives*, a novel, as you can see, about Russian life, thus exceedingly interesting—and suddenly...

"She fell asleep reading my novel!?!" Zinzaga whispered. "What disrespect to a Count Barabanta-Alimonda publication and to the efforts of Alfonso Zinzaga, who has given her the glorious name of Zinzaga!"

"Woman!" barked Zinzaga at the top of his Portuguese lungs. He pounded his fist on the edge of the couch.

Amaranta sighed deeply, opened her dark eyes and smiled. "Is that you, Alfonso?" she said, reaching for him.

"Yes it's me!.. You're sleeping? You're... sleeping?..." muttered Alfonso, sitting down on a decrepit chair. What were you doing before you fell asleep?"

"I went to my mother's to ask for money."

"And then?"

"I read your novel."

"And you fell asleep! Say it! You fell asleep?"

"I fell asleep... Why are you getting angry, Alfonso?"

"I'm not angry, but I'm offended at your frivolous attitude to something which, if it hasn't yet, will surely bring me fame! You fell asleep because you were reading my novel! Is that it?"

"Enough, Alfonso! I was really enjoying your novel... I was riveted by it. I... I... I especially liked the scene in which the young writer, Alfonso Zenzega, shoots himself with a pistol..."

"That scene isn't in this novel, it was in *One Thousand Flames*!"

"Really? Then what was the scene that I found so moving in this novel? Oh yes—I cried when the Russian Marquis, Ivan Ivanovitsh,[1] throws himself out of her window into the river... the river... Volga."

"Aaahh... Hmm!"

"And drowns, while blessing the Viscountess Ksenia Petrovna... It made a great impression on me..."

"In that case, why did you fall asleep?"

"I was so tired! I didn't sleep a wink last night. You were so sweet, you read me your lovely new novel all night long, and I couldn't trade the pleasure of hearing you for sleep..."

"Aaahh... Hmm... I see! Give me something to eat!"

"You haven't eaten yet?"

"No."

"But as you were leaving this morning you told me that you would be lunching with the editor of the *Lisbon Regional Gazette*?"

"Yes, I thought they would publish my poem in the *Gazette*, damn them!"

"And you mean they didn't?"

"No..."

---

1   By writing "Ivanovitsh" instead of the correct "Ivanovich" Chekhov suggests pronunciation by a non-Russian speaker.

"That's bad luck! Ever since we met I have hated editors with my whole being! So you are hungry?"

"Yes."

"Poor Alfonso! And you have no money?"

"Hmm... That's an odd question?! Is there nothing to eat?"

"No, my friend. My mother fed me, but she didn't give me any money."

"Hmm..."

The chair creaked. Zinzaga got up and started to pace up and down... Having walked about and thought for a bit, he did his best to convince himself, for whatever it was worth, that hunger is cowardice, that man is born to battle with nature, that man does not live by bread alone, that he who is not hungry is no artist, and so on and so forth, and probably would have convinced himself of this, had he not remembered that in room number 148 next door in *The Poisonous Swan* lived the Italian genre painter Francesco Butrontsa, a talented man with a bit of a reputation, and, something of some consequence in this world, an ability Zinzaga had never possessed, to have dinner every day.

"I will pay him a visit!" Zinzaga decided, and he went next door.

When he went into room 148, Zinzaga was presented with a scene that enthralled him as a novelist and lacerated his heart as a hungry man. The hope he might dine in Francesco Butrontsa's company was dashed when the novelist caught sight of his friend amidst frames, stretchers, armless dummies, easels and stools, which were strewn with faded costumes of all kinds and ages. Clad in a hat à la Van Dyck and a Peter the Hermit costume, Francesco Butrontsa was standing, violently waving a maulstick and roaring at the top of his voice. He was more than formidable. One foot was on the stool, the other on the table. His face was aflame, his eyes were flashing, his goatee was trembling, his hair was standing on end, and he seemed to be about to lift his hat into the air at any moment. In the corner, clinging to a statue of an armless, noseless Apollo with a big jagged hole in its chest, stood the wife of the seething Francesco Butrontsa, a German woman named Karolina, who was looking at the lamp in horror. She was pale and her whole body was shaking.

"Barbarians!" thundered Butrontsa. "You don't love art, you strangle it, and you can go to hell! How could I have married you, you cold-blooded German! How could I have stupidly bound myself, a person as free as the wind, as an eagle, an antelope, an artist, to this piece of ice, woven out of prejudice and trivialities... Diablo! You are ice! You are a wooden, stone slab of beef! You... you are a fool! Cry your eyes out, you pathetic, overcooked German sausage. Your husband is an artist, not a shopkeeper! Cry, beer bottle! Is that you, Zinzaga? Don't go! Wait! I'm glad you're here... Look at this woman!"

Butrontsa indicated Karolina with his left foot. Karolina started to cry.

"That's enough!" began Zinzaga. "What are you arguing about, Don Butrontsa? What has Donna Butrontsa done to you? Why are you making her cry? Think of your great motherland, Don Butrontsa, your motherland, a country in which adoration of beauty is closely linked to adoration of women! Remember that!"

"I'm exasperated!" cried Butrontsa. "Put yourself in my shoes! As you know, at the request of Count Barabanta-Alimonda, I have started on a grandiose painting... The Count asked me to paint the Old Testament Susanna... I asked her, this fat German woman, to get undressed and pose for me, I've been asking since first thing this morning, I've got down on my knees, I've lost patience, but she flatly refuses! Put yourself in my shoes! How can I paint without a model?"

"I can't do it!" Karolina sobbed. "It is indecent!"

"You see? You see? Talk about lame excuses, dammit!"

"I can't! I honestly can't. He orders me to get undressed and, of all things, stand at the window..."

"That's how I visualise it! I want to paint Susanna in the moonlight! The light of the moon falls on her breast... The light from the torches of the Pharisees who have come running up illuminates her back... It's a play of colours! It cannot be otherwise!"

"For the sake of art, Donna Butrontsa," said Zinzaga, "You must forget not only modesty, but all... other feelings too!"

"There is no way I can force myself to do it, Don Zinzaga! I simply cannot stand at the window on display!"

"On display... Anyone might think, Donna Butrontsa, that you are afraid of the eyes of the crowd which, so to speak, if you were to look at it... The point of view of art and reason, Donna, is such that..."

And Zinzaga said something that an intelligent man would never utter whether in a fairy tale or written down on paper—something totally decent, but extremely incomprehensible.

Karolina threw up her hands and started to run about the room, as if she feared they were going to undress her by force.

"I wash his brushes, palettes and rags, my dresses are smudged from his paintings, I give lessons to feed him, I sew his clothes, I tolerate the smell of hempseed oil, I pose for art classes for days at a time, I do everything, but... naked? Naked? I can't!!!"

"I will divorce you, you red-haired harpy!" shouted Butrontsa.

"Where on earth am I to go?" moaned Karolina. "Give me money so I can get to Berlin, from where you brought me, then you can divorce me!"

"Agreed! I'll finish Susanna and send you back to your Prussia, a country of cockroaches, rotten sausage and pork worms!" shouted Butrontsa, not noticing that he was elbowing Zinzaga in the chest. "You cannot be my wife if you can't sacrifice yourself for art! Vvvv... Rrrr... Diablo!"

Karolina began to sob, her head in her hands, and sank into a chair.

"What are you doing?" yelled Butrontsa. "You've sat on my palette!"

Karolina got to her feet. She had indeed been sitting on her husband's palette, with its freshly mixed paints... O ye Gods! Why am I not an artist? If I were a painter I would present Portugal with a magnificent picture! Washing his hands of it all, Zinzaga hurried out of room 148, rejoicing in the fact that he wasn't a painter but also grieving with his whole heart that he was a novelist who hadn't succeeded in dining with a painter.

At the door of room 147 he met the pale, alarmed, trembling inhabitant of room 113, the wife of the future Royal Theatres opera singer, Pyotr Petruchenets-Petrurio.[2]

"What's wrong?" Zinzaga asked her.

"Oh, Don Zinzaga! We have such a misfortune! What am I to do! My Pyotr has injured himself!"

"How did he injure himself?"

"He was practising how to fall on stage and he hit his temple on a trunk."

"The unfortunate fellow!"

"He is dying! What am I to do?"

"Get him to the doctor, Donna!"

"But he doesn't want to go to the doctor. He doesn't believe in medicine. And anyway... he owes all of them money."

"In that case go to the apothecary and buy some lead ointment. It really helps with injuries."

"But how much does it cost?"

"It's cheap, Donna. Very cheap."

---

2   A comic name in which both parts of the surname are variations on Pyotr (Peter).

"I thank you. You always were a good friend to my Pyotr! We still have a bit of money that he made from an amateur production at Count Baraban-ta-Alimonda's... I don't know if it will be enough. Could you possibly give me a small loan for that pewter ointment?"

"Lead ointment, Donna."

"We would pay you back right away."

"I can't, Donna. I spent the last of my money on three reams of paper."

"Farewell!"

"The best of luck!" said Zinzaga, with a bow.

The wife of the Royal Theatres' future opera singer had barely had time to take a step away from him when Zinzaga saw before him the inhabitant of room 101, the spouse of Ferdinand Lai,[3] the operetta singer, cellist and flautist who was said to be the future Portuguese Offenbach.

"What can I do for you?" he asked her.

"Don Zinzaga," said the wife of the operetta singer and musician, wringing her hands, "would you be so kind as to calm my ruffian down! You are his friend... Maybe you'll be able to stop him. The shameless man has been straining his throat since crack of dawn and I'm sick to death of his singing! The baby can't sleep and he's just tearing me to pieces with his baritone! For God's sake, Don Zinzaga! I'm even embarrassed in front of the neighbours... Can you believe this? Even their children can't sleep thanks to him. Please let's go! Maybe you'll be able to calm him down somehow."

"At your service, Donna!"

Zinzaga proffered the wife of the singer and musician his arm and set off for room 101. In room 101, between the bed that occupied half of the space and the cradle that occupied a quarter of it, there was a music stand. On the stand were yellowish sheets of music which the future Portuguese Offenbach was looking at as he sang. It was difficult to make out at first what and how he was singing. One could only guess from his sweaty, red face and from the effect that it had on his own ears and those of other people, that his singing was excruciatingly awful, and that he was in a frenzy. It was clear that he suffered as he sang. He was stomping out the rhythm with his right foot and fist, at the same time lifting his leg and arm high into the air and continually knocking his notes off his music-stand, craning his neck, screwing up his eyes, twisting his mouth,

---

3   *Lai* in Russian means (a dog's) "barking."

and punching himself in the stomach... In the cradle lay a tiny little person, who accompanied his insuppressible father with screams, squeals and squeaks.

"Don Lai, don't you think you should take a break?" asked Zinzaga, on entering the room.

Lai did not hear him.

"Don Lai, don't you think you should take a break?" repeated Zinzaga.

"Take him out of here!" sang Lai, gesturing at the cradle with his chin.

"What are you rehearsing?" asked Zinzaga, trying to make himself heard. "What are you re-hear-sing?"

Lai seemed to choke on something, then fell silent and fixed his eyes on Zinzaga.

"What do you want?" he asked.

"Me? Um... I... I mean... don't you think it's time for a break?"

"It is none of your business!"

"You'll burn yourself out, Don Lai! What are you rehearsing?"

"A cantata dedicated to Her Highness Countess Barabanta-Alimonda. Anyway, what's it got to do with you?"

"But it's already night time... It's time, in a certain sense, to sleep..."

"I have to sing until ten o'clock tomorrow morning. Sleep won't help us. Those who want to sleep, but I, for the good of Portugal, perhaps for the whole world, must not sleep."

"But the baby and I want to sleep, my dear!" interjected his wife. You are yelling so loudly that not only can we not sleep, we can't even sit in the room!"

"You will fall asleep if you want to!"

After saying this, Lai stomped out the rhythm with his foot and started singing.

Zinzaga blocked his ears and ran out of room 101 like a madman. When he got back to his own room, he saw a touching scene. His Amaranta was sitting at the table, making a clean copy of one of his novellas. Big tears were falling from her large eyes onto the notebook.

"Amaranta!" he cried, seizing his wife's hand. "Could it be that the wretched hero of my wretched novella has reduced you to tears? Could it be, Amaranta?"

"No, I'm not crying for your hero..."

"Well what for then?" asked Zinzaga, disappointed.

"My friend Sofia Ferdrabantero-Nerakruts-Rozga,[4] the wife of your friend the sculptor, broke the statue her husband was preparing to present to Count Barabanta-Alimonda, and... she couldn't bear his grief... She's poisoned herself with matches!"

"The poor... statue! Oh wives, the devil take you all, along with your dresses with long trains that get caught on everything! She poisoned herself? God damn it, it is a subject for a novel!!! Actually, it's too trivial!.. Everything is mortal on this earth, my friend... If not today, then tomorrow, if not tomorrow, then the day after, your friend was bound to die all the same... Wipe away your eyes and, rather than cry, listen to me..."

"You've got a subject for a new novel?" Amaranta asked quietly.

"Yes..."

"Don't you think it would be better, my dear, if I heard it tomorrow morning? My brain is somewhat fresher in the mornings..."

"No, you've got to listen today. Tomorrow I'll have no time. The Russian writer Derzhavin* has arrived in Lisbon and I'll have to pay him a visit tomorrow. He's arrived with your favourite... regrettably favourite... writer Victor Hugo."

"Really?"

"Yes... So, hear me out!"

Zinzaga sat down opposite Amaranta, threw his head back, and began: "Place of action: the whole world... Portugal, Spain, France, Russia, Brazil, etcetera. In Lisbon, the hero learns from the newspapers that misfortune has overtaken the heroine in New York. He sets off for New York. He is captured by pirates who have been bribed by agents of Bismarck. The heroine is a French secret agent. In the papers there are hints... of English involvement. There is a network of Poles in Austria and gypsies in India. There are intrigues. The hero is in prison. They want to bribe him. Do you get it? Then..."

Zinzaga spoke ardently and passionately, his arms waving, his eyes flashing... he spoke for a long, long time... a terribly long time!

Amaranta fell asleep twice and woke up twice; outside, they had put out the streetlamps and the sun had come up, and he was still talking. The clock struck six, Amaranta's stomach was desperately longing for a cup of morning tea, but he was still talking.

---

4   A comic invented triple-barrelled name in which the last part means "rod" in Russian (*rozga*).

"Bismarck tenders his resignation, and the hero, no longer wishing to hide his identity, reveals himself as Alfonso Zunzuga and dies in terrible agony. A quiet angel carries his quiet soul up into the blue sky..."

And so Zinzaga got to the end, as the clock struck seven.

"Well?" He asked Amaranta. "What do you think? Do you reckon that the scene between Alfonso and Maria won't make it past the censors? Eh?"

"No, that little scene is sweet!"

"Is it generally good? Be frank. You are a woman, and the majority of my readers are women, so I need to know your opinion."

"How can I put it? I feel as if I have come across your hero somewhere before, I just can't remember where exactly..."

"You can't have done!"

"I have. I encountered your hero in a novel, a ridiculously stupid novel, I have to tell you! As I was reading that novel I was amazed how they could print such rubbish, and when I finished it I decided that the author must be unbelievably dumb, to put it mildly. They print rubbish, yet they don't publish you. It's astonishing!"

"I don't suppose you remember at least the title of that novel?"

"I don't remember the title, but I do remember the name of the hero. It's etched into my memory because it contained four "r's" in a row... Such a stupid name... Karrrro!"

"It wasn't in the novel *Sonnambula in the Ocean*, was it?"

"Yes, yes, yes, that was the one. You know our literature so well. That was the one... Your hero is very like Karrrro, except that he is much more intelligent, of course. What's the matter, Alfonso?"

Alfonso had leapt to his feet. "*Sonnambula in the Ocean* is my novel!!!" he shouted.

Amaranta turned red.

"So you think my novel is unbelievably dumb?" he shouted, so loudly that even Amaranta's throat hurt. "Oh you brainless duck! So that's how you view my *oeuvre*, madam? Do you, you donkey? You've spoken your mind? You will never see me again! Farewell! Hmmm... brrr... you idiot! My novel is unbelievably dumb?! Count Barabanta-Alimonda knew what he was publishing!"

Throwing a contemptuous look at his wife and pulling his hat down over his eyes, Zinzaga left room 147, slamming the door.

Amaranta sighed, but she didn't burst into tears nor did she faint. She knew that Alfonso Zinzaga would return to room 147, however furiously angry he was. Leaving room 147 forever would amount to the novelist having to live, and consequently write without a free copyist on Lisbon boulevards under the blue Portuguese sky. Amaranta knew this and was not too worried by her husband's exit. She just sighed and set about comforting herself. Usually after these frequent arguments with her husband she would take comfort in reading an old newspaper page, which she kept next to a tiny bottle of perfume in a tin box that had once contained fruit drops. Among the advertisements, telegrams, political news, daily events and other man-made affairs, the old newspaper page included a pearl known in journalistic jargon as *Miscellanea*. In *Miscellanea*, beneath a story about how one American outsmarted another American and how the famous singer Miss Dubadolla Svist[5] ate a barrel of oysters and crossed the Andes without even getting her feet wet, was a little piece that was quite suitable to the consolation of Amaranta and other artists' wives. I will relay it below word for word:

"For the attention of the Portuguese and their daughters: in one of the cities of America, discovered by Christopher Columbus, a man of extreme energy and courage, there lived a certain Dr. Tanner. This Dr. Tanner was more of an artist in his way than a scientist and was therefore known to the world and Portugal not as a scientist, but as an artist of a sort. Being American, he was at the same time also human, and since he was human, then sooner or later he was going to fall in love, which one day, of course, he did. He fell in love with a beautiful American woman, he fell madly in love like an artist, fell so much in love that he once prescribed *argentum nitricum*[6] instead of *aquae distillatae*[7]—he fell in love, proposed, and got married. He lived with his beautiful American wife at first extremely happily, so happily, in fact, that the honeymoon was extended beyond its usual period of one month to six months. There is no doubt that Dr. Tanner, being a learned man and, consequently, very easy to get on with, would have lived happily with his wife until the very grave, had he not detected in her one terrible flaw. Madame Tanner's flaw was that she ate like a human being. This flaw in his wife was like a knife in Dr. Tanner's heart. "I will re-educate her!" he decided, and set himself the task of training Madame Tanner to eat less. At first, he weaned her off breakfast and supper, and then also drinking tea. Within one year of the wedding

---

5 A comic double-barrelled name implying "kick the bucket" and "whistle" in Russian.

6 *argentum nitricum*: "silver nitrate" (Latin).

7 *aquae distillatae*: "distilled water" (Latin).

Mme Tanner was no longer preparing four dishes for lunch, but just one, while within two years after signing the marriage contract she could already satisfy herself with an unreal quantity of food. Specifically, in a course of a day she ate and drank the following quantities of nutritional substances:

1 gr. salt
5 gr. protein
2 gr. fat
7 gr. water (distilled)
1/23 gr. Hungarian wine.

———————————————————

Total 15 1/23 grams

We don't count gases, because science is not yet capable of determining the quantities of gases we require. Dr. Tanner was triumphant, but not for long. In the fourth year of his married life the thought that Mme Tanner was eating too much protein began to torment him. He turned to his training regime with even greater energy and would have brought the 5 grams down to one or zero if he had not started to feel that he had fallen out of love with his wife. As an aesthete, he could not but fall out of love with his wife. Instead of remaining an American beauty into ripe old age, Mme Tanner for no apparent reason took it into her head to become as thin as an American rake, and lose her beautiful figure and mental capabilities, thereby showing that while she seemed fit for further training, she had become utterly unfit for conjugal life. Dr. Tanner demanded a divorce. Learned experts appeared at his home, examined Mme Tanner from every point of view, advised her to take the waters, do gymnastics, prescribed her a diet, and found the demands of their respected colleague to be completely legitimate. Dr. Tanner gave his expert colleagues a dollar each, treated them to a good breakfast and... since then Tanner has lived in one place and his wife in another. A sad story! Women, how often you cause the unhappiness of great men! Women, are you not to blame for the fact that great men often do not leave heirs? People of Portugal, it is up to you to bring up your daughters in the right way! Do not turn your daughters into destroyers of homes and family nests! We will finish here. Tomorrow's edition will not be printed because it is the editor's birthday. People of Portugal! Those of you who have not paid for your subscription in full, please hurry up and pay!"

"Poor Mme Tanner!" whispered Amaranta, after she had skimmed through that little story. "The poor thing! How unhappy she was! Oh, how happy I am compared to her! How happy I am!"

Amaranta, delighted that there were people in this world more unhappy than she was, carefully folded up the newspaper page, put it in the box, got undressed and went to bed, all the time revelling in the fact that she was not Mme Tanner.

She slept until she was awoken by the most horrible hunger in the person of Alfonso Zinzaga.

"I am hungry!" said Zinzaga. "Get dressed, my dear, and go over to your *madre* for some money. *Apropos*: I ask your forgiveness. I was wrong. I have just found out from the Russian writer Derzhavin,* who came here together with Lermantoff,* another Russian writer, that there are two novels, totally different to one another but both with the same name: *Sonambula in the Ocean*. Off you go my dear!"

While she was getting dressed Zinzaga told Amaranta about an incident he was planning to describe, adding in passing that the description of this incident, which touched body and soul, would require some sacrifice on her part.

"The sacrifice won't be great, my dear!" he said. "You will have to write out this description under my dictation, which will not take you more than seven or eight hours, and make a fresh copy, and, by the way, as you are doing it jot down your opinion regarding all my works... You are a woman, and the majority of my readers are women..."

Here Zinzaga was being somewhat untruthful. It was not the majority as all his readers amounted to just one woman, because Amaranta was not "women," but just one "woman."

"Will you agree?"

"Yes," Amaranta said quietly, and then she turned pale and fell senseless on to the tattered, dusty encyclopaedia that was forever lying about the room...

"These women are an amazing breed!" exclaimed Zinzaga. "I was right when I called woman a creature of eternal mysteries and surprises for the human race in *One Thousand Flames*! The tiniest happiness knocks them to the ground! Oh women's nerves!"

And the happy Zinzaga dropped to his knees before the unfortunate Amaranta and kissed her on the forehead...

That is how it is, female readers!

Do you know what, maidens and widows? Do not get married to these artists. "To hell with all those artists," as the Ukrainians say.* It would be better, all you maidens and widows, to live in some tobacco shop or sell geese at the market, than to live in the very best room of *The Poisonous Swan*, with the very best protégé of Count Barabanta-Alimonda.

Truly, it would be better!

St. Peter's Day

The yearned-for morning of the long-dreamed of day has arrived; hurrah, gentlemen hunters!!—the 29th of June* has arrived... The day has come when all debts, bugs, expensive grub, mothers-in-law, and even young wives are forgotten—a day on which one can cock twenty snooks at the village constable who forbids shooting...

The stars paled and misted over... Here and there voices could be heard... Grey-blue, acrid smoke poured from the village chimneys. A still not fully awake sexton appeared on the grey belfry and rang the bell for morning mass... The snoring of the night watchman stretched out under a tree could be heard. Pine grosbeaks woke up, began to stir, and started flying from one end of the garden to the other, commencing their unbearable, tiresome chirping... In the blackthorn an oriole broke into song... Starlings and hoopoes began bustling above the servant's kitchen... A free morning concert started up...

Two troikas drove up to the house of the retired cornet of the guards Yegor Yegorych Obtemperansky[1] with its ramshackle porch, picturesquely overgrown with prickly nettles. There was a great hubbub going on in both the house and the yard. Every living thing around Yegor Yegorych was galvanised into action: clattering up and down staircases, running in and out of barns and stables... One of the shaft-horses was replaced. Caps flew off the heads of the coachmen, a red lantern was glowing under the nose of the servant, Katka's toady, the cooks were called "witches," the cursed names of Satan and his fallen angels were invoked... Within five minutes, the tarantasses* had been filled with carpets, travelling rugs, bags of provisions, and gun cases.

"Ready, sir!" boomed Avvakum.*

"If you please, we are ready!" Yegor Yegorych shouted in a cloying voice, and a lot of people appeared on the porch. The first to jump into the tarantass was the young doctor. He was followed by the lower-class Kuzma

---

1   The retired cornet's surname is a nod to his temperamental character.

Bolva[2] from Arkhangelsk, an old man in heel-less boots and a rusty-red top hat, with a twenty-five pound two-barrel shotgun, and yellowish-green marks on his neck. Bolva is a pleb, but the landowners, out of respect for his advanced years (he was born at the end of the last century), and his ability to shoot a twenty-kopeck coin when it is tossed up in the air, are not squeamish about his plebeian origins and take him with them when they go hunting.

"This way, Your Excellency!" Yegor Yegorych addressed a short, grey-haired, plump man in a white jacket with bright buttons, and a St. Anna's Cross* round his neck. "Move up, doctor!"

The retired General grunted, put one foot on the step, and, supported by Yegor Yegorych, shoved the doctor in the stomach and sat down heavily next to Bolva. The General's puppy Futile and Yegor Yegorych's pointer Musician[3] leapt in after him.

"Mmm...Vanya, old chap!" the General addressed his nephew, a high-school student with a long single-barrelled rifle over his shoulder. "You can sit here, next to me. Come here! Mmm yes... Right here. Don't joke around, my friend! The horse might take fright!"

After exhaling another puff of tobacco smoke into the shaft-horse's nostrils, Vanya leapt into the carriage, moved Bolva away from the General and sat down. Yegor Yegorych crossed himself and sat down next to the doctor. Perched on the box, next to Avvakum, was the tall, skinny instructor of maths and physics from Vanya's high-school, Mr. Manger.[4]

The first tarantass was full. Now the loading of the second began.

"Ready!" yelled Yegor Yegorych, when the remaining eight men and three dogs had settled into the second tarantass after long arguments and scuttling to and fro.

"Ready!" yelled the guests.

"Well? So, shall we get going, Your Excellency? Lord, give us thy blessing. Let's be off, Avvakum!"

The first tarantass lurched and moved off. The second, containing the most ardent hunters, swayed, creaked ominously, lurched to one side and

---

2   Like Avvakum, Kuzma is a common old-fashioned, lower-class first name. "Bolva" is not far from the Russian word *bolvan*, meaning "blockhead" or "dimwit."

3   The dogs' names in Russian are "Tshchetnyi" and "Muzykant."

4   The name in Russian is Manzhe, a transliteration in Cyrillic of *manger*, meaning "to eat" or "dish" (as in *blanc-manger*, literally "white dish") in French.

rolled up to the gates, having overtaken the first tarantass. The hunters broke out into a simultaneous smile and clapped their hands in delight. They were on cloud nine, but... malicious fate!.. a scandal broke out before they even left the yard...

"Stop! Wait! Stop!!!" came a shrill tenor voice from behind the troikas.

The hunters looked round and paled. The most insufferable person in the world was chasing after the troikas, a person known throughout the whole province as a trouble-maker, retired Captain of second rank Mikhey Yegorych, Yegor Yegorych's brother... He was waving desperately. The troikas came to a halt.

"What do you want?" asked Yegor Yegorych.

Mikhey Yegorych ran up to the carriage, stepped on to the footboard, and took a swing at Yegor Yegorych. The hunters started making a commotion.

"What is going on?" asked the red-faced Yegor Yegorych.

"What is going on," yelled Mikhey Yegorych, "is that you are a Judas, a beast, a swine!.. A swine, Your Excellency! Why didn't you wake me up? I'm asking you, why didn't you wake me up, you ass, you scoundrel? Excuse me, gentlemen... It's nothing... I just want to teach him a lesson! Why didn't you wake me up? You don't want to take me with you, is that it? I get in your way? You plied me with drink on purpose last night and thought that I would oversleep, and not wake up till midday! Oh, what a fine fellow you are! Excuse me, Your Excellency... I shall just bash him... once... Excuse me!"

"Where do you think you are going?" shouted the General, flinging his arms wide. "Don't you see there is no room? You're one too many... excuse me..."

"You're cursing in vain, Mikhey," Yegor Yegorych said. "I didn't wake you because there's no point in you coming with us... You don't know how to shoot. Why do you want to come? To get in the way? You know you don't know how to shoot!"

"I don't know how to shoot?" shouted Mikhey Yegorych, so loudly that even Bolva blocked his ears. "Well, in that case, why the devil is the doctor going? He doesn't know how to shoot either! Is he a better shot than I am?"

"He's right, gentlemen," said the doctor. "I don't know how to shoot, I don't even know how to hold a gun... I can't stand shooting... I don't know why you're taking me with you... Why the devil are you taking me? Let him have my place! I'll stay behind!.. There's room for you, Mikhey Yegorych!"

"Do you hear? Do you hear? Why *are* you taking him?"

The doctor got to his feet with the obvious intention of getting out of the tarantass. Yegor Yegorych grabbed the doctor by his coat-tails and pulled him down.

"Hey... don't tear my coat! It cost thirty roubles... Let go! And anyway, gentlemen, I would ask you not to talk to me today... I'm out of sorts and might cause a scene without meaning to. Let go, Yegor Yegorych! Sit down in my place, Mikhey Yegorych! I'm going to get some sleep!"

"You have to come, doctor!" said Yegor Yegorych, not letting go of the doctor's coat-tails. "You gave your word of honour that you would go!"

"That word of honour was forced out of me. Well, what is the point of me going?"

"The point" squeaked Mikhey Yegorych, "is that you won't be left with his wife! That's the point! He's jealous of you, doctor. Don't go, my dear fellow! Don't go to spite him! He's jealous, by God, he's jealous!"

Yegor Yegorych turned scarlet and clenched his fists.

"Hey, you!" someone yelled from the other carriage. "Mikhey Yegorych, stop horsing around! Come here, we've found a place for you here!"

Mikhey Yegorych smiled maliciously.

"Well, shark?" he said. "Who has got the upper hand now? Did you hear? They've found room for me! I'll go to spite you! I'll go and I'll get in the way! I promise, I will get in the way! You won't kill a damned thing! And as for you, doctor, don't go. Let him burst from jealousy."

Yegor Yegorych got to his feet and shook his fists. His eyes were bloodshot.

"You wretch!" he said, addressing his brother. "You're no brother to me! No wonder our late mother cursed you! Father died in the prime of his life because of your reprobate behaviour!"

"Gentlemen..." the General intervened. "It seems to me... that's quite enough. You are brothers, family!"

"He's the family ass, Your Excellency, not a brother! Don't go, doctor! Don't go!"

"Let's go, to hell with you... Argh... What the hell! Let's go!" yelled the General, hitting Avvakum on the back with his fist. "Let's go!"

Avvakum whipped the horses, and the troika moved off. In the second tarantass, the writer, Captain Kardamonov,[5] lifted the two dogs up onto his lap and the determined Mikhey Yegorych settled himself down in their place.

---

5   A comic name suggestive of cardamom (*kardamon* in Russian).

"It's lucky for him you managed to find a space for me," said Mikhey Yegorych, "or I would have had him... You've got to expose the blackguard, Kardamonov!"

Last year Kardamonov submitted an article to *The Cornfield** under the title "An interesting case of multiple pregnancy among the peasant population," read in the Rejections Column* a response that was damaging to his authorial self-esteem, complained to his neighbours, and passed as a writer.

According to the plan of action that had been sketched out, it was decided they would go first to the peasant's hayfield located five miles from Yegor Yegorych's estate, and hunt for quails. Having arrived at the hayfield, the hunters climbed out of the tarantasses and divided themselves into two groups. One group, led by the General and Yegor Yegorych, went to the right; the other, headed by Kardamonov, to the left. Bolva fell behind and went off on his own. What he loved about hunting was the peace and quiet. Musician ran ahead, barking, and within a minute had flushed out a quail. Vanya shot and missed.

"Damn, too high!" he grumbled.

Having been taken hunting 'to be trained,' the puppy Futile, hearing a gunshot for the first time in his life, barked, and, tail between his legs, ran back to the tarantass. Manger shot at a lark and hit it.

"I like this bird!" he said, showing the lark to the doctor.

"Get lost..." said the latter. "I would ask you not to chat with me... I'm out of sorts today. Leave me alone!"

"You're a sceptic, doctor!"

"Me? Hmm... what is a sceptic?"

Manger thought about it.

"A sceptic is a misanth... a misanth... an ungracious person," he said.

"You're lying. Don't employ words that you don't understand. Leave me alone! I might cause a scene without meaning to... I'm out of sorts..."

Musician pricked up his ears. The General and Yegor Yegorych turned pale and held their breath.

"I'll shoot!" the General whispered. "I'll... I'll... Excuse me! You've already had two goes..."

But nothing came of Musician's pricked ears. Standing idle, with nothing to do, the doctor threw a pebble at Musician and hit him between the ears... Musician yelped and jumped. The General and Yegor Yegorych looked round. A rustling was heard in the grass and out flew a large bustard.

The second group began to whisper and point at the bustard. The General, Manger, and Vanya took aim. Vanya took a shot, Manger's gun misfired... But it was too late! The bustard had flown behind the kurgan* and landed in the rye.

"I believe, doctor, that... this is no time for jokes!" the General turned to the doctor.

"What?"

"This isn't the time for joking."

"I'm not joking."

"You spoilt our fun, doctor!" noted Yegor Yegorych.

"You shouldn't have brought me along... Who asked you to? But anyway... I don't want to get into a discussion about it... I'm out of sorts today..."

Manger killed another lark. Vanya flushed out a young rook, shot, and missed.

"Damn, too high!" he muttered.

Two shots were heard in succession: Bolva killed two quails behind the kurgan with his heavy two-barrelled shotgun and stuffed them into his pocket. Yegor Yegorych flushed out a quail and shot. The wounded quail fell into the grass. A triumphant Yegor Yegorych picked it up and brought it over to the General.

"I winged it, Your Excellency! It's still alive!"

"Well, yes... Alive... It must be put out of its misery."

Having said which, the General lifted the quail to his mouth and gnawed through its throat with his fangs. Manger killed a third lark. Musician pricked his ears again. The General threw off his cap, and raised his gun... "After it!" A big quail flew out, but... the scoundrel of a doctor stood right in the line of fire, almost in front of the General's muzzle!

"Get out of the way!" yelled the General.

The doctor jumped aside, the General fired, but the shot, of course, was too late.

"That was mean of you, young man!" yelled the General.

"What's wrong?" asked the doctor.

"You're getting in the way! Why the devil did you get in my way?! I missed thanks to you! What a God-awful mess!

"But why are you shouting? Pff... I'm not afraid of generals, Your Excellency, and especially not retired ones. Calm down, please!"

"What an extraordinary person! He just goes round, getting in the way—even an angel would lose its patience!"

"Don't shout please, General! Shout at Manger here! He, by the way, is afraid of generals. No one can get in the way of a good hunter. Can it be that you don't know how to shoot?!"

"Enough! You're given one word—you send back ten... Vanechka, give me the powder flask!" the General said turning to Vanya.

"Why did you invite this lout on the hunt?" the doctor asked Yegor Yegorych.

"It was impossible not to, brother!" answered Yegor Yegorych. "I had to invite him! After all, I'm in debt to him to the tune of... eight thousand... That's the bottom line, old man! If it weren't for these damned debts..."

Yegor Yegorych did not finish his sentence and waved his hand dismissively.

"Is it true that you're jealous?"

Yegor Yegorych turned his back on the doctor and took aim at a high-flying hawk.

"You've lost it, you greenhorn!" came the General's booming voice. "You've lost it! It's worth one hundred roubles, you little pig!"

Yegor Yegorych walked up to the General and asked what the matter was. It appeared that Vanya had lost the General's ammunition belt. A search for the ammunition belt began, and the hunt was interrupted.

The search lasted an hour and a quarter and resulted in success. Having found the ammunition belt, the hunters sat down for a rest.

The second group was having just as little luck in quail hunting as the first. In this group, Mikhey Yegorych behaved just like the doctor, if not worse. He knocked guns out of hands, swore, beat the dogs, spilled gunpowder, in short—he caused chaos... After unsuccessful attempts at shooting quails, Kardamonov chased after a young hawk with his dogs.

They shot the hawk but couldn't find it. The second-rank Captain killed a gopher with a stone.

"Gentlemen, let's dissect the gopher!" suggested Nekrichikhvostov,[6] clerk to the marshal of the nobility.

---

6   An invented name containing the Russian words "do not shout" and "tail," perhaps implying the clerk is required to keep quiet and follow his superior.

The hunters sat on the grass, took out their penknives, and began the dissection.

"I'm not finding anything in this gopher," said Nekrichikhvostov, when the gopher was cut up into small pieces. "There isn't even a heart. Although here are the guts. You know what, gentlemen? Let's go to the marshes! What can we kill here? Quails aren't proper game; not like woodcocks, snipe... What do you think? Let's go!"

The hunters got up and ambled over to the tarantasses. Having reached the tarantasses, they let off a salvo at the common pigeons and killed one.

"Your Excelle... Yegorygorch! Your... Yegorch..." cried the second group, catching sight of the first group who were taking a break. "Hey, hello!"

The General and Yegor Yegorych looked round. The second group waved their caps.

"What is it?" yelled Yegor Yegorych.

"There are things happening! We've killed a great bustard! Get over here!"

The first group did not believe the story about the bustard, but went over to the tarantasses. Having got into the tarantasses, the hunters decided to leave the quails in peace and to drive three more miles to the marshes, in keeping with the plan.

"I get terribly hot-tempered when I'm hunting," the General said to the doctor, when the troikas had driven about a mile away from the hayfield. "Terrible! I wouldn't even spare my own father. You have to... forgive an old man!"

"Hmm..."

"How generous-hearted that scoundrel has become!" Yegor Yegorych whispered in the doctor's ear. "A result, no doubt, of the fashion to give one's daughters away in marriage to doctors! His Excellency is a sly one. Hee-hee-hee..."

"There is more space now!" noted Vanya.

"Yes."

"I wonder why? We suddenly got a lot more space..."

"Gentlemen, where is Bolva?" Manger suddenly caught on.

The hunters looked at one another.

"Where's Bolva?" Manger repeated.

"He must be in the other troika. Gentlemen," Yegor Yegorych shouted, "is Bolva with you?"

"No, he isn't!" shouted Kardamonov.

The hunters considered the matter.

"Well, to hell with him!" the General decided. "Don't turn back on his account!"

"We ought to, Your Excellency. He's frail! He'll die without water. He won't make it."

"If he wants to, he'll make it."

"The old man will die. He is ninety, after all!"

"Rubbish."

Having arrived at the marshes, our hunters' faces fell a mile... The marshes were crowded with hunters, so there was no point in clambering out of the tarantasses. Having thought the matter over, the hunters decided to ride another three miles to the state-owned forests.

"What are you going to shoot there?" asked the doctor.

"Blackbirds, eagles... Well, grouse."

"I see. Well, what will my unfortunate patients do now? Why *did* you take me with you, Yegor Yegorych? Ah!"

The doctor sighed and scratched his head. Arriving at the first wooded area they came across, the hunters got out of the tarantasses and began to deliberate amongst themselves: who should go to the right and who to the left?

"You know what, gentlemen?" Nekrichikhvostov proposed. "That old, you know, law of nature, you know, that says that game won't escape us... Hmm... The game won't escape us, gentlemen! Let us first fortify ourselves!"

A bit of wine, some nice vodka, caviar... smoked sturgeon... Right here, on the grass! What's your opinion, doctor? You know best: you're a doctor. One should fortify oneself, no?"

Nekrichikhvostov's proposal was accepted. Avvakum and Firs laid out two rugs and unpacked bags and bundles with foodstuffs and bottles. Yegor Yegorych sliced the sausage, cheese, smoked sturgeon, Nekrichikhvostov uncorked the bottles, Manger cut the bread... The hunters licked their lips and reclined.

"Well then, Your Excellency! Here's to..."

The hunters downed their glasses and ate. The doctor immediately poured himself a second and downed it. Vanya followed suit.

"There must be wolves here too, I presume," Kardamonov remarked philosophically, giving the woods a sideward glance.

The hunters considered the matter, discussed it, and after about ten minutes decided that one could presume there were no wolves.

"Well? Another one? Let's do it! Yegor Yegorych, what are you looking at?"

They downed another shot.

"Young man!" Yegor Yegorych turned to Vanya. "What do you think?"

Vanya shook his head.

"You can have a drink with me," said the General. "Don't drink without me, but with me... Have a tipple!"

Vanya poured a shot and drank.

"Well? What about a third round? Your Excellency..."

They drank a third. The doctor drank his sixth.

"Young man!"

Vanya shook his head.

"Drink, Amphiteatrov!" said Manger in a patronising tone.

"With me you can, but without me... Have a tipple!"

Vanya drank.

"Why is the sky so blue today?" asked Kardamonov.

The hunters pondered the question, analysed it, and after about a quarter of an hour decided they did not know why the sky was so blue.

"Hare... hare... hare!!! Go for it!!!"

A hare appeared from behind a hillock. Two mongrels chased after it. The hunters jumped up and seized their guns. The hare flew past and shot into the woods, with the mongrels, Musician and the other dogs on its heels. Futile thought about it, looked suspiciously at the General, and also dashed after the hare.

"A big 'un! Should have... How did we... miss it?"

"Yes. What is this bottle doing here..? Why aren't you drinking, Your Excellency? Tut, tut... So that's how it is? All-right!"

They drank a fourth shot. The doctor drank his ninth, issued a wild groan and set for the woods. Having chosen the widest patch of shade, he lay down on the grass, put his coat under his head, and immediately began to snore. Vanya was done for. He downed another shot, started in on the beer, and his heart soared. He got on his knees and recited twenty verses from Ovid.

The General noted that Latin is very similar to French... Yegor Yegorych agreed with him and added that when learning French, it is imperative to know Latin, which resembles it. Manger did not agree with Yegor Yegorych, remarking that this was not the place to pontificate on languages, what with a physicist and mathematician sitting right there, and with so many bottles standing about, adding that his gun had cost him a lot when he had bought it, that now it was impossible to find a good gun, that...

"An eighth, gentlemen?"

"Wouldn't that be too many?"

"Good God! You think eight is too many? You evidently have never drunk before then!"

They drank an eighth shot.

"Young man!"

Vanya shook his head.

"Enough of this! Come on, like in the army! After all, you shoot so well..."

"Drink up, Amphiteatrov!" said Manger.

"Drink with me, but not without me... have a little tipple!"

Vanya set down his beer and took another shot.

"A ninth, gentlemen, eh? What thoughts have you on the matter? I can't stand the number eight. My father died on the eighth... Fyodor... I mean, Ivan... Yegor Yegorych! Pour the drinks!"

They drank a ninth shot.

"Goodness, it's hot."

"Yes, it's hot, but that won't get in the way of our drinking a tenth!"

"But..."

"Screw the heat! We'll show the elements, gentlemen, that we don't fear them! Young man! Set an example... Put your uncle to shame! We fear neither cold nor heat..."

Vanya downed a shot. The hunters yelled "hoorah" and followed his example.

"There is a risk of sunstroke," said the General.

"No, there isn't."

"There isn't... with our climate? Hmm..."

"But there have been cases... My godfather died of sunstroke..."

"What do you think, doctor? Is it possible in our climate to get sunstroke? Doctor!"

There was no answer.

"Have you ever had to treat a case? We're talking about sunstr... Doctor, where *is* the doctor?"

"Where's the doctor? Doctor!"

The hunters looked around: there was no doctor.

"Where *is* the doctor? Has he disappeared? As wax melteth before the fire! Ha-ha-ha."

"He's gone after Yegor's wife!" Mikhey Yegorych blurted out.

Yegor Yegorych paled and dropped the bottle.

"He's gone after his wife!" Mikhey Yegorych continued, chomping on some smoked sturgeon.

"Why are you lying?" Manger asked. "Did you see him?"

"I saw him. There was a peasant going by in a cart... well, and he got in and off they went. I swear to God. An eleventh, gentlemen?"

Yegor Yegorych got up and shook his fists.

"Where are you going?" I asked him, Mikhey Yegorych continued. "I'm going for dessert, he says. I have already cuckolded the old husband, he says, and now I'm off to polish his horns. Farewell, he says, dear Mikhey Yegorych! My respect to your brother Yegor Yegorych! And then he did this with his eye. Cheers... hee-hee-hee."

"Let's go!!" shouted Yegor Yegorych, and, swaying somewhat, ran to the tarantass.

"Quickly, or you'll be too late!" shouted Mikhey Yegorych.

Yegor Yegorych pulled Avvakum onto the driver's seat, jumped into the tarantass, and, threatening the hunters with his fists, drove off home...

"What is the meaning of all this, gentlemen?" asked the General when Yegor Yegorych's white cap was no longer visible. "He's left... So how the hell am I supposed to get home? He left in my tarantass! That's to say, not in mine, but the one I should have left in... How strange... Hmm... That's pretty audacious on his part..."

Vanya started to feel ill. The vodka, mixed with beer, acted like an emetic... Vanya needed to be taken home. After the fifteenth round the hunters decided to give the troika to the General on condition that, upon arriving home, he would send out fresh horses for the rest of the party right away.

The General began to take his leave.

"Tell him, gentlemen," he said, "that... that only a swine would act like that."

"You must call him out on his promissory notes, Your Excellency!" advised Mikhey Yegorych.

"Huh? Promissory notes? Well, yes... It's about time he... Enough is enough... I've waited and waited, and now I am fed up waiting... Tell him he's got to pay up... I bid you farewell, gentlemen! Do call on me! But, as for him, he's a swine!"

The hunters said goodbye to the General and helped him into the tarantass, next to Vanya who was feeling somewhat the worse for wear.

"Let's go!"

Vanya and the General drove off.

After the eighteenth round, the hunters set off for the woods, and after taking a few shots, they lay down and had a sleep. The General's horses arrived for them before nightfall. Firs handed Mikhey Yegorych a letter addressed 'To my brother'. The letter contained a request, non-compliance with which would result in an official complaint lodged with the court bailiff. After the third shot (having woken up, the hunters had begun the count again), the General's coachmen packed the hunters into the tarantasses and delivered them to their homes.

When he arrived home, Yegor Yegorych was greeted by Musician and Futile, for whom the hare had just been an excuse to bolt off home. Giving his wife a threatening look, Yegor Yegorych began his search. All the storerooms, cupboards, wardrobes, trunks, and chests of drawers were searched, but Yegor Yegorych did not find the doctor. He did find someone else: the parish clerk Fortunatov under his wife's bed...

It was already dark when the doctor woke up... Having wandered round the wood for a bit, and having remembered that he was on a shoot, the doctor swore loudly and began to holler. There was, of course, no answer, and so he decided to walk home. The road was good, safe, and well-lit. He covered sixteen miles in some four hours and by morning he was already at the district hospital. After letting off steam by cursing the orderlies, the midwife, and the patients, he began to compose an extremely long letter to Yegor Yegorych. In this letter he demanded "an explanation for recent unseemly conduct," cursed jealous husbands, and swore that he would never, ever, go hunting again, not even on the twenty-ninth of June!

Personality Types

(According to the Latest Scientific Findings)

Sanguine. This type reacts easily and quickly to all impressions, Hufeland* says, which results in frivolousness... In his youth he's a *bébé* and a *Spitzbube.*[1] He is rude to his teachers, doesn't cut his hair or shave, wears glasses, and soils walls with graffiti. He's a lousy student, but manages to complete his course of study. He doesn't honour his parents. If rich, he plays the dandy, and if poor he lives like a pig. He sleeps until noon and goes to bed at odd times. His writing is riddled with mistakes. Nature brought him into this world for love alone: he only does things he loves. He's never averse to drinking himself senseless; if he gets hellishly drunk in the evening, he wakes the next morning dishevelled, with a slight fog in his head and in no need of "similia similibus curantur." He marries by accident. He constantly quarrels with his mother-in-law. He doesn't get on with his relatives. He's an all-out liar. He's mad about scandals and amateur performances. In an orchestra he plays first violin. Being frivolous, he's a liberal. He either never reads at all or devours books. He likes newspapers and is not opposed to dabbling in journalism himself. The rejection columns of humorous journals were invented exclusively for the sanguine type. He is consistent in his inconsistency. If in government service, he's a bureaucrat in charge of special commissions or some such. If employed at a high school, he teaches literature. He rarely attains the rank of Active Councillor of State, and if he does, he becomes phlegmatic or sometimes choleric. Idlers, scoundrels, and non-entity are all sanguine types. Sharing a room with a sanguine person is not recommended: he tells jokes all night, and when he runs out of jokes, he finds fault with his nearest and dearest or lies. He typically dies from diseases of the digestive tract and premature exhaustion.

A sanguine female, if not stupid, is the most tolerable of women.

---

1   *Spitzbube:* "scoundrel" (German).

Choleric. Bilious type with a yellow-grey face. Nose somewhat crooked, and eyes which roll in their sockets like hungry wolves in a small cage. Irritable. Ready to tear the whole world to pieces over a flea bite or pin prick. When he speaks he splutters and shows his brown or very white teeth. He's utterly convinced that in winter, "it's far too damned cold," and in summer, "it's far too damned hot." Changes his cook every week. Feels lousy when he eats because everything is overcooked and too salty... A choleric is typically a bachelor, and if married, he keeps his wife locked up. He's insanely jealous. He doesn't get jokes. He finds everything intolerable. He reads newspapers only to curse journalists. Already in his mother's womb he was convinced that all newspapers lie. As a husband or friend, a choleric is insufferable; as a subordinate—unthinkable; as a boss—unbearable and highly undesirable. Unfortunately, he is often a pedagogue, teaching maths and Greek. I don't recommend sharing a room with a choleric: all night long he coughs and spits and loudly curses the bedbugs. When he hears cats or cockerels singing at night, he coughs, and with a trembling voice he dispatches his lackey onto the roof to do whatever it takes to catch and strangle the singer. He dies from consumption or liver disease.

A female choleric is a devil in a skirt, a crocodile.

Phlegmatic. A phlegmatic is a dear person (I speak, of course, not of an Englishman, but of a Russian phlegmatic). His appearance is utterly ordinary and unsophisticated. He's always serious because he's too lazy to laugh. He eats when and what he pleases; he doesn't drink for fear of an apoplectic stroke, and sleeps twenty hours a day. An indispensable member of all possible commissions, boards, and emergency sessions, where he doesn't understand a thing, shamelessly nods off, and patiently awaits the end of proceedings. With the help of aunties and uncles he marries at thirty years of age. He's the most convenient candidate for marriage because he doesn't grumble, is compliant and obliging. He calls his wife darling. He likes roast piglet with horseradish, songbirds, anything sour and asparagus. The expression "Vanitas vanitatum et omnia vanitas" (Nonsense of nonsenses and all kinds of nonsense), was thought up by a phlegmatic. He falls ill only when selected for jury duty. At the sight of a fat woman, he grunts, waggles his fingers and tries to smile. He subscribes to *The Cornfield** and is angry it has no colour illustrations or humorous content. He considers writers to be the most intelligent and, at the same time, lethal people. He regrets that his children are not caned at school and he is not averse to caning them himself on occasion. He is happy with his office job. In an orchestra he plays the double-bass, bassoon or trombone. In a theatre he's the cashier, lackey, prompter, and sometimes, to make ends meet, an actor. He dies of paralysis or dropsy.

A female phlegmatic is a tearful, goggle-eyed, plump, fine and luscious German woman. Like a bag of flour. She was born to become a mother-in-law. To be a mother-in-law is her ideal.

Melancholic. Grey-blue eyes on the verge of shedding tears. Wrinkles on the forehead and around the nose. A somewhat crooked mouth. Black teeth. Inclined to hypochondria. Always complaining about a pain in the pit of his stomach, a stabbing sensation in his side and poor digestion. Favourite pastime—to stand in front of the mirror and examine his flabby tongue. He thinks he has a weak chest and is suffering from nerves, so every day drinks a decoction instead of tea, and a vital elixir instead of vodka. With deep regret and a sob in his voice, he informs his loved ones that laurel and valerian drops no longer help... He reckons it doesn't hurt to take a laxative once a week. He's long been convinced that doctors don't understand him. His foremost benefactors are healers, witch-doctors, drunken medical assistants and sometimes village midwives. From September to May he wears a fur coat. He suspects every dog of having rabies, and since a friend told him that a cat can strangle a person who is asleep, he regards cats as irreconcilable enemies of humanity. His last will and testament has long been prepared. He vows and swears that he never drinks. Occasionally he imbibes warm beer. He marries an orphan. If he has a mother-in-law, he calls her a most wonderful and wise human being. He silently hears out her exhortations, head cocked to one side; he believes his most sacred duty is to kiss her plump, sweaty hand smelling of gherkin brine. He maintains an active correspondence with his aunties and uncles, godmother, and childhood friends. He does not read newspapers. At one time, he read the *Moscow Gazette*, but this caused him chest pain, heart palpitations and blurred vision, so he gave it up.* He surreptitiously reads works by Debay and Jozan.* During the Vetlyanka plague* he fasted five times. He suffers from watery eyes and nightmares. He's not particularly happy at work and will advance no higher than assistant to head of desk in the civil service. He loves the folk song *Luchinushka.** In an orchestra he plays flute or cello. He sighs day and night, therefore I don't recommend sharing a room with him. He has constant premonitions of floods, earthquakes, war, the final collapse of morality, and of his own death from some horrid disease. He dies of heart defects, his witch-doctors' cures, and partly hypochondria.

A female melancholic is the most unbearable and restless creature. As a wife she drives her husband to a state of stupor, despair, and suicide. The only good thing about her is that she is easy to get rid of: just give her money and send her off on a pilgrimage.

Choleric-melancholic. In the days of his youth he was a sanguine type. A black cat crossed his path, a devil knocked him on the back of the head and he turned into a choleric-melancholic. I refer to the most famous and immortal neighbour of the editorial office of the *Spectator.** Ninety-nine percent of Slavophiles are choleric-melancholics. He is an unrecognised poet, an unrecognised *pater patriae*, an unrecognised Jupiter and Demosthenes... and so on... A cuckolded husband, too. In general, any loud-mouthed weakling.

On the Train

Mail train number such-and-such is tearing along at a rate of knots from "Crash, Bang, Wallop" station to "Run for Your Life!" station. The engine is whistling, hissing, huffing, puffing... The carriages are shuddering, their ungreased wheels making them howl like wolves and shriek like owls. Up above, down below, and inside the carriages there is darkness... "Something's afoot! Something's afoot!" rattle the doddering old carriages... "Trouble and doom, trouble and doom!" chimes the engine... Draughts and pickpockets are roaming the carriages hand in hand. It's all a bit scary... I stick my head out of the window and gaze aimlessly at the distant horizon. The lights are all green, which means the scandal we are heading for is still some way off. The signal and the station lights can't be seen... Darkness, depression, thoughts of death, memories of childhood crowd in... Heavens!

"I've sinned!!" I whisper. "Oh, how I've sinned!"

Someone reaches into my back pocket. There is nothing in my pocket, but it's still awful... I turn round. In front of me is a stranger. He is wearing a straw hat and a dark grey shirt.

"What can I do for you?" I ask him, feeling my pockets.

"Nothing, sir. Just looking out the window, sir!" he replies, swiftly withdrawing his hand and leaning into my back.

A raucous whistle pierces the air... The train begins to go slower and slower and eventually comes to a stop. I get out of the carriage and head to the buffet for some liquid courage. The buffet is besieged by passengers and train crew.

"Hmm... There's vodka here, and it's not bitter!" says the stout chief conductor, addressing a portly gentleman. The portly gentleman wants to say something, but can't: a year-old sandwich has got stuck in his throat.

"Plice!!! Plice!!!" bellows someone on the platform, in the kind of voice hungry mammoths, ichthyosauruses and plesiosauruses used to bellow in ancient times before the Flood... I go over to see what is going on... A gentleman with a cockade is standing outside one of the first-class carriages and showing people his feet. Someone walked off with his boots and stockings while he was asleep...

"What am I going to travel in now?" he shouts. "I've got to get to Reval!* It's your job to keep order!"

The policeman stands in front of him and assures him there is "no need to shout here"... I go into my carriage, No. 224. In my carriage it's the same as before: darkness, snoring, and the smell of tobacco and cheap vodka—it whiffs of the Russian spirit. Snoring next to me is a red-haired coroner travelling to Kiev from Ryazan... Two or three feet away from the coroner a pretty girl is dozing... The peasant in the straw hat is huffing and puffing and tossing from side to side, not knowing where to put his long legs... Someone in the corner is having a snack and chomping away for all to hear... And there are people sleeping soundly under the seats. The door squeaks. Two wizened little old women with bundles on their backs come in...

"Let's sit down here, my dear!" says one of them. "It's so dark! Lord have mercy on me! It seems I have stepped on someone... But where is Pakhom?"

"Pakhom? Gracious! Where can he have got to? Gracious!"

The little old woman bustles about, opens the window and scours the platform.

"Pakh-om!" she rasps. "Where are you? Pakhom! We're over here!"

"I'm in trouble," cries a voice outside the window. "They won't let me on the machine."

"Not letting you on? Who is it who is not letting you on? That doesn't matter! They can't not let you on if you have a real ticket!"

"They've stopped selling tickets! The ticket office is locked up!"

Someone is leading a horse along the platform. Hoofbeats and snorting.

"Step back!" shouts the policeman. "Where do you think you are going? Why are you creating a disturbance?"

"Petrovna!" groans Pakhom.

Petrovna throws off her bundle, grabs a big tin kettle and scuttles out of the carriage. The bell rings for the second time. A small conductor with a thin black moustache comes in.

"You should have got a ticket!" he says to the old man sitting opposite me. "The ticket inspector is here!"

"Really? Hmm... That's not good... Which one is he?.. The prince?"

"Oh no... You'd never be able to herd the prince in here, even with sticks"

"Which one is he then? The one with the beard?"

"Yes, that one..."

"Well, if it's him, then there is nothing to worry about. He is a good sort."

"On your head be it."

"Have a lot of hares hopped on board?"

"About forty."

"Really? Well done them! Good businessmen!"

I freeze. I am also a hare. I'm always a hare when I travel. Hares are what they call railway passengers who bother the conductors for change rather than the ticket clerks. It's great being a hare, dear reader! Hares get a 75% discount on a tariff which hasn't been advertised anywhere, and they don't need to crowd round the ticket office, or be obliged to take their ticket out of their pocket continually, while the conductors are more polite to them and... it's a good deal, basically!

"Do you really think I am ever going to pay for anything?" the old man mutters. "Not on your life! I pay the conductor. The conductor has got less money than that railway baron Polyakov!"*

The third bell jangles.

"Oh Lord!" exclaims the old woman as she fidgets. "Where has Petrovna got to? That was the third bell already after all! It's God's punishment... She's got left behind! Poor thing, she's got left behind... But her things are here... What'll I do with her things, with her bag? Oh dear, she's got left behind!"

The old woman pauses for a moment to think.

"She should have her things if she is going to be left behind!" she says, and throws Petrovna's bag out of the window.

We are heading towards Swindler Town station, which is on the "Frum to Common Grave" line according to the guide. The ticket inspector and the chief conductor come in with a candle.

"Tickets please!" barks the chief conductor.

"Ticket please!" says the ticket inspector, turning to me and the old man.

We cower and squirm, hiding our hands, eyes glued to the chief conductor's encouraging face.

"All yours!" says the ticket inspector to his companion and walks off. We are saved.

"Ticket please! Hey, you! Ticket please!" the chief conductor prods a lad who is asleep. The lad wakes up and takes a small yellow ticket out of his hat.

"Where are you headed?" says the ticket inspector, twiddling the ticket between his fingers. "You are going the wrong way!"

"You are going the wrong way, you oaf!" says the chief conductor. "What a genius—you've got on the wrong train! You need to go to Knackers-On-the Hill, and we are heading for Swindler Town! Here, take it! One should never be a fool!"

The lad blinks hard, stares blankly at the smiling people around him and starts rubbing his eyes with his sleeve.

"Come on, don't cry!" people advise him. "It's always better to ask. A great big chump like you, and you're bawling! You've probably got a wife and kids too."

"Ticket please..." says the chief conductor to a farm-hand wearing a top hat.
"Eh?"

"Ticket please! Turn round!"

"A ticket? Do I need one?"

"Your ticket!!!"

"I see... Well, if that's what's needed, why not hand it over? I'll hand it over, don't you worry!" The farm-hand in the top hat reaches under his shirt, takes about an hour to extract a greasy scrap of paper, and hands it to the inspector.

"What are you giving me? This is a passport! Give me your ticket!"

"I don't have any other ticket," says the mower, clearly alarmed.

"Well, how can you be travelling if you don't have a ticket?"

"But I've paid."

"Who did you pay? Don't lie!"

"The conductor."

"Which one?"

"I don't know which one! The conductor, that's all I know... Don't get a ticket, he said, we'll take you without one... So, I didn't get one..."

"We'll have a word with you at the station! Madam, your ticket please!"

The door squeaks open, and to our great surprise Petrovna comes in.

"Gracious, it was hard finding my carriage... Don't know how anyone can work it out, they're all the same... And they still wouldn't let Pakhom on, the vipers... Where's my bag?"

"Hmm... An evil spirit... I threw it out the window to you! I thought you had been left behind!"

"Where did you throw it?"

"Out the window... Who knew you were going to be back?"

"Well, thank you... Who asked you to do that? Lord forgive me, but what a witch! What am I to do now? You didn't throw yours out, you old crow... You should've thrown your snout out! Oh... darn you!"

"You'll have to wire from the next station," advise people in the carriage, laughing.

Petrovna begins to wail and blaspheme. Her friend holds on to her bag and also cries. The conductor comes in.

"Whose things are these?" he yells, holding up Petrovna's things.

"She is pretty!" whispers the old man sitting next to me, nodding at the pretty girl. "Mmm... very pretty... Damn it, I don't have any chloroform! Otherwise I'd give her some to sniff, and lightning quick I'd be kissing her! Good thing everyone's asleep!.."

The straw hat tosses about and rails out loud about his disobedient legs.

"Scientists..." he mutters. "Scientists... Bet you can't go against the natural order of things! Scientists... hmm... Bet they won't ever come up with a way for you to unscrew your legs and screw them back on again!"

"It's nothing to do with me... Ask the public prosecutor!" raves the coroner sitting next to me.

In the far corner, two high school pupils, a junior officer and a young man in blue-tinted glasses are playing a furious game of cards by the light of their four cigarettes.

A tall lady of the "it goes without saying" type is sitting on my right. She reeks of face powder and patchouli.

"Ah, vot a vonderful sing zis railway is!" some creep whispers into her ear in a disgustingly pretentious way, speaking with a fake French accent. "Nowhere does one become intimate so queekly and so pleasantly as on ze railway. Railway, 'ow I love you!"

A kiss... Another kiss... Whatever next! The pretty girl wakes up, surveys everyone, and unconsciously puts her little head on the shoulder of her neighbour, the high-priest of Themis... but he, the fool, is asleep!!

The train stops. A halt.

"The train is stopping for two minutes..." rumbles a hoarse cracked bass voice outside the carriage. Two minutes go by, then two more... Five, ten, twenty minutes go by, and the train is still standing. What on earth is going on? I get out of the carriage and walk up to the engine.

"Ivan Matveyevich! Are you going to be finished soon? Damn it!" shouts the chief conductor under the engine.

The driver, all red, sopping wet and with soot on his nose, crawls out on his belly from under the engine...

"Do you have a God?" he says to the chief conductor. "Are you a human being? Why are you rushing me? Can't you see? Aagh... darn the whole lot of you! Do you call this an engine? It's not an engine, it's a piece of rubbish! I can't drive this."

"What is to be done?"

"Do what you want! Give me another one, but I won't go on this one! Just put yourself in my shoes..."

The train driver's assistants are running around the broken-down engine, banging and shouting... The station manager in his red cap is standing nearby, telling jolly Jewish jokes to his assistant... It's raining... I head back into the carriage... The stranger in the straw hat and dark grey shirt darts past... He is carrying a suitcase. It's my suitcase. Heavens!

Salon des Variétés*

"Driver! Wake up, damn it! Salon des Variétés!"

"The Saucy Virility? Thirty kopecks."

The entrance and a lone policeman, loitering outside the entrance, are lit up by streetlamps. It costs about one rouble twenty to get in, and twenty kopecks for coats (the latter is actually optional). You have barely stepped inside when you are already overwhelmed by extremely powerful smells from the cheap boudoir and changing room. Slightly tipsy customers... A propos: don't visit the Salon if you are not the worse for wear... Being slightly sozzled is not just required, it is a matter of principle. If the customer is smiling and his glazed eyes are blinking when he comes in, that's a good sign: he won't die of boredom, and might even attain bliss. Woe betide him if he is sober! He certainly will not approve of the Salon des Variétés and once back home, will thrash his kids to ensure that they don't visit the Salon when they are older... Tipsy customers hobble up the stairs, hand their tickets to the doorman, enter a room adorned with portraits of the great and the good, then draw themselves up and boldly plunge into circulation. Hungry for powerful impressions, they dash back and forth, through all the rooms, from door to door, scurrying about and prowling from corner to corner, as if looking for something... What an assortment of tribes, faces, colours and smells! Ladies come in all colours—red, blue, green, black, multi-coloured, speckled, just like those three kopeck coloured prints...

We saw these ladies here last year and the year before that. You will certainly see them next year too. None can flaunt a décolleté, nor a decent dress... or even a bosom. But what wonderful names they have: Blanche, Mimi, Fanny, Emma, Isabella... not a single Matryona, Mavra or Pelageya! The dust is frightful! Particles of rouge and powder, alcohol fumes hang in the air... It's hard to breathe, one wants to sneeze...

* * *

"How rude you are, sir!"

"Who, me? Oh... hmm... well! Allow me to tell you in plain language that we are only too well acquainted with your female ideas! Allow me to offer you a hand!"

"What for? You've got to introduce yourself properly first... First you've got to treat me to something!!"

An officer speeds over to the lady, takes her by the shoulder and makes her turn her back to the young man... The latter does not like this... After brief consideration he decides that he is offended, takes the lady by the shoulder and turns her back towards him...

* * *

A gargantuan German with a drunk, dumb physiognomy belches for all to hear as he makes his way through the crowd; a pockmarked little man minces behind him and shakes his hand...

"Bbuurrrp... hic!"

"Sincerely grateful for the generous belch!" says the little man.

"You're vilkom... h...hic!"

A crowd has gathered round the entrance to the hall. In the crowd, two young merchants are frantically gesticulating with their arms and expressing mutual hatred for each other. One is as red as a lobster, the other is pallid. Both are as drunk as a lord, of course...

"What about a smack in the ffface?"

"You ass!!"

"What if you're... an ass yourself! Philanthropist!!"

"Bastard! What are you waving your hands around for? Hit me! Go on, hit me!"

"Gentlemen!" a woman's voice is heard in the crowd. "How can you quarrel like this in the presence of ladies?"

"To hell with the ladies! I don't give a damn for your ladies! I feed thousands of them! You, Katka... stay out of it! Why did he have to insult me? I didn't even touch him!"

A fop wearing an enormous tie flies up to the pallid merchant and grabs him by the hand.

"Mitya! Daddy's here!"

"Sssso what?.."

"For God's sake! He's sitting at the table with Sonya! He all but caught sight of me! The old devil... We must leave! Right away!!"

Mitya throws one last piercing gaze at his enemy, threatens him with his fist, and retires...

* * *

"Tsvirintelkin! Go over there! Raisa's looking for you!"

"To hell with her! Don't want to! She's got a face like a door latch... I've picked myself another madame... Luise!"

"You can't be serious? Who, that big cannon?"

"That's the whole point, my friend, that she is like a cannon... A woman through and through! You can't even get your arms round her!"

Fräulein Luise is sitting at the table. She is tall, fat, sweaty and as sluggish as a snail... Standing on the table in front of her are a bottle of beer and Tsvirintelkin's fur hat... The contours of her corset are crudely etched on her massive back. How sensible of her to hide her legs and hands! Her hands are huge, red and calloused. Only a year ago she lived in Prussia where she mopped floors, cooked *Biersuppe** for the Pastor and nursed little Schmidts, Millers and Schultzs... But Fate chose to disturb her peace: she fell in love with Fritz, and Fritz fell in love with her... But Fritz cannot marry a poor woman, he'll call himself a fool if he marries a poor woman! Luise swore eternal love to Fritz and departed from her dear *Vaterland*[1] to earn her dowry in the cold Russian steppes... And now every night she comes to the Salon. During the day, she makes little boxes and knits tablecloths. Once she has collected the necessary sum of money, she will return to Prussia and marry Fritz...

* * *

Si vous n'avez rien à me dire[2] is heard from the hall...

Uproar in the hall... Anyone who comes on stage is applauded... The cancan is pathetic and hopeless, but people sitting in the front rows are drooling with pleasure... Just take a look at the audience when the dancers cry "Down with men!" Give the audience a lever right now and they would turn the world upside down! They scream, shout, howl...

"Ss-hhh-hh..." a paltry officer in the front rows hushes some girl...

The audience protests furiously against this hushing, and their applause shakes the whole of Bolshaya Dmitrovka Street. The paltry officer gets to his

---

1   "Fatherland" (German).

2   "*Si vous n'avez rien à me dire*": "If you have nothing to say to me" (French).

feet, holds his head high and, assuming an air of importance, leaves the hall, noisily and theatrically... In this way he maintains his dignity, you see!

A Hungarian orchestra is in full swing. Such dumpy little people these Hungarians, and how badly they play! They put Hungary to shame!

None other than Mr. Kuznetsov* himself is standing behind the bar with a black-browed madame. Mr. Kuznetsov provides the drinks and madame takes the money. The drinks are taken by storm.

"A ssshot of vodka. You hear me? Vvodka!"

"Kolya, shall we scratch our throats? Drink, Mukhtar!*"

A man with a cropped head looks dumbly at the shot-glass, shrugs his shoulders and downs the vodka in a frenzy.

"I can't, Ivan Ivanych! I have a heart defect!"

"To hell with that! Drinking won't hurt your heart!"

The young man with a heart defect drinks.

"Another shot!"

"No... I have a heart defect. I have drunk seven shots as it is."

"To hell with that!"

The young man downs another drink...

* * *

"Sir!" pleads a girl with a pointy chin and little rabbit eyes, "buy me dinner!"

The man wavers...

"I'm hungry! Just one dish..."

"You don't give up, do you?... Hey, waiter!"

A piece of meat is served... The girl eats... my, how she eats! She eats with her mouth, her eyes, her nose...

There is intense firing at the shooting stall... Tyrolean women are loading guns non-stop... Two of them are not too bad-looking... An artist standing to one side is drawing one of the Tyrolean women on his cuff.

"Gutbye... fahrevell!" the Tyroleans cry.

The clock strikes two... There is dancing in the hall. There is noise, brouhaha, shouts, squeals, the cancan... Awful stuffiness... Customers already loaded with alcohol top up at the bar, and by three o'clock, there is total chaos.

In the private rooms...

Actually, let's get out of here! How pleasant it is to leave! If I were the owner of the Salon des Variétés, I would charge for leaving, not for entry...

The Trial

The shopkeeper Kuzma Yegorov's hut. It is stuffy, hot. Vicious mosquitoes and flies swarm round eyes and ears being a nuisance... There are clouds of tobacco smoke, though the smell is not of tobacco, but of salted fish. A sense of tedium is in the air, in people's faces, in the whining of the mosquitoes.

There is a large table; on it sits a saucer with some nutshells, a pair of scissors, a small jar containing green ointment, cartridges, empty bottles. Assembled round the table are: the village elder, Kuzma Yegorov himself, the medical orderly Ivanov, the deacon Feofan Manafuilov, the bass singer Mikhailo, Parfenty Ivanych the godfather, and the policeman Fortunatov, who has come from the city to visit his auntie Anisya. Standing at a respectful distance from the table is Kuzma Yegorov's son Serapion, who works at a barber's shop in the city and has come to visit his father for the holidays. He feels very uneasy and keeps tugging at his little moustache with a trembling hand. Kuzma Yegorov's hut has been hired as a temporary first aid post and in the entrance hall the infirm are waiting. A peasant woman with a broken rib has just been brought in... She is lying on the floor, groaning and waiting until, at long last, the medical orderly gives her the benefit of his attention. Outside, beneath the windows, a crowd is gathering—they have come to watch Kuzma Yegorov thrash his son.

"You keep on saying that I'm lying," says Serapion, "so I do not intend to speak with you at length. Words, Papa, do not prove anything in the nineteenth century because, as you yourself are well aware, a theory cannot exist without practice."

"Hold your tongue!" Kuzma Yegorov replies sternly. "Stop beating about the bush and keep to the point: what have you done with my money?"

"Money? Hmm... You're such a clever man, you should understand yourself that I have not touched your money. It is not for me you're hoarding your lucre... There is nothing to scold me for..."

"You've got to be open with us, Serapion Kuzmich," says the deacon. "After all, why are we asking you about this? We wish to prevail on you and put you on the path of righteousness... Your dear Papa only wants the best for you... And so he has asked us... Tell us plainly... Who has not sinned? Did you take the twenty-five roubles which were lying in your Papa's chest of drawers, or not?"

Serapion spits to one side and says nothing.

"Tell us!" shouts Kuzma Yegorov, pounding the table with his fist. "Tell us, was it you or not?"

"As you wish... Suppose we say..."

"Suppose I say," the policeman corrects him.

"Suppose I say I did take them... Suppose I say I did! Shouting at me won't achieve anything, Papa, nor will banging your fists. Hard as you may try, the earth will not swallow up that table. I have never taken money from you and if I ever have, then it was out of necessity... I am a human being, an animated proper noun, and I need cash. I am not a stone!.."

"If you are short of cash, go and earn it, but don't fleece me. You aren't the only one, I have seven of you to support!"

"I'm aware of that, without you lecturing me, but I suffer from poor health, as well you know, consequently I cannot earn a living. So why begrudge me a crust of bread? You'll be called to answer for that before our Lord..."

"Poor health!.. You haven't got a hard job, all you have to do is keep clipping, and yet even that sort of work you shy away from."

"Call that a job? That is not a job, it is no more than keeping one's head above water. And I don't have the training to be able to live off such a job."

"You're wrong about that, Serapion Kuzmich," says the deacon. "Yours is an honourable, intellectually demanding job, and that is why you work in the main town of our province, shearing and shaving intelligent, distinguished people. Even generals do not scorn your trade."

"I could tell you a thing or two about generals, if you wished."

The medical orderly Ivanov is slightly tipsy.

"According to my medical judgement," he says, "you are nothing more than turpentine."

"I know all about your medical judgement... Who, may I ask, last year all but dissected a drunk carpenter instead of a corpse? If he hadn't woken up, you would have torn his stomach open. And who mixes up castor oil with hemp-seed oil?"

"There is no way round that in medicine."

"And who sent Malanya to the other side? You gave her a laxative, then an anti-laxative, then another laxative, and it was too much for her... It is not human beings you should be tending to but, beg my pardon, dogs."

"May Malanya rest in peace," says Kuzma Yegorov. "May she rest in peace. But it was not her who took the money and it is not her we are talking about... So tell us... Did you take it to Alyona?"

"Hmm... Alyona! Shame on you for even mentioning her in front of a clergyman and a gentleman of the police."

"But tell us: did you take the money or not?"

The village elder edges out from behind the table, lights a match on his knee and applies it deferentially to the policeman's pipe.

"Pff..." the policeman says angrily. "You've filled my nose with sulphur!"

Having lit his pipe, the policeman gets up from behind the table, approaches Serapion and, fixing him with a furious stare, shouts in a shrill voice:

"Who do you think you are? What is this? What's it about? Eh? What does this mean? Why don't you answer? Insubordination? Stealing people's money? Hold your tongue! Answer! Speak! Answer!"

"If..."

"Be silent!"

"If... *You* be quiet! If... I am not afraid! You think very highly of yourself! But you... you are a fool and nothing more! If Papa wishes to throw me to the wolves, then I am ready... Tear me apart! Beat me!"

"Be quiet! Stop ja-a-abbering! I know your type. You're a thief, right? Be quiet! Who do you think you're talking to? Stop bandying words about!"

"He should be punished," says the deacon, sighing. "If they do not wish to unburden themselves of their guilt with a confession, Kuzma Yegorych, then a good hiding is in order. A good hiding—that's my view!"

"Thump him!" says Mikhailo, the bass singer, in a voice so deep it frightens all those present.

"For the last time: was it you, or not?" asks Kuzma Yegorov.

"As you wish... Suppose I say I did... Torment me! I am ready..."

"A thrashing!" Kuzma Yegorov decides and, turning crimson, he gets out from behind the table.

There are people pressed against the windows. The infirm crowd round the doors, lifting their heads. Even the peasant woman with the broken rib raises her head...

"Lie down!" Kuzma Yegorov says. Serapion slips off his jacket, crosses himself and, resigned to his fate, lies down on the bench.

"Tear me into pieces," he says.

Kuzma Yegorov takes off his belt, stares for some time at the audience that has gathered, as if waiting for someone to help, then he begins...

"One! Two! Three!" Mikhailo counts in his low bass voice. "Eight! Nine!"

The deacon stands in a corner and, lowering his eyes, begins to leaf through his book...

"Twenty! Twenty-one!"

"Enough!" says Kuzma Yegorov.

"More!" whispers policeman Fortunatov. "More! More! Have at him!"

"I think a little more is required!" says the deacon, lifting his head from his book.

"And not a squeal out of him!" exclaims the crowd in astonishment.

The infirm make way as Kuzma Yegorov's wife comes into the room, her starched skirts crackling.

"Kuzma!" she says to her husband. "What's this money I found in your pocket? Isn't this the money you were looking for a while back?"

"Indeed it is... Get up, Serapion! The money has been found! I put it in my pocket yesterday and forgot all about it..."

"More!" Fortunatov mutters. "Thump him! Have at him!"

"The money has been found. Get up!"

Serapion gets to his feet, puts on his jacket and sits down at the table. There is a prolonged silence. The deacon is embarrassed and blows his nose into a handkerchief.

"Forgive me," Kuzma Yegorov mutters, turning to his son. "Don't... I'll be damned if I thought we'd ever find the money. Forgive me..."

"Forget it. It's hardly the first time... Don't worry about it. I'm always ready for any torment."

"Have a drink... You'll get over it..."

Serapion downs a shot, then leaves the hut like a mighty warrior with his blue nose held aloft. As for policeman Fortunatov, he walks around the yard for a long time afterwards red in the face, eyes bulging, muttering:

"More! More! Have at him!"

Antosha Chekhonte's Classified Ads Bureau

for the convenience of advertisers, **Antosha Chekhonte's Classified Ads Bureau** *has taken a lease on the section for advertisements and miscellaneous notices in the "Spectator"* for the whole of 1881.*

Theatrical Touts Cooperative

hereby announces that, for the convenience of the public, it has chosen a tavern *close to the theatre* as its base. In view of the forthcoming tour of the well-known Sarah Bernhardt,* it has entered into agreement with the relevant personages and offers its services.

Dr. Chertolobov[1]

Specialist in female, male, children's, chest, back, neck, head and many other illnesses. Patients seen daily from seven in the morning to twelve at night. Poor patients treated for free on 30th February, 31st April, 31st June and, on 29th February, at a generous discount. Private house, Gavrikov Lane, Molchanovka, Moscow.

New Times Bookshop

Now offers the following titles for sale:

---

1   "Chertolobov"—comic invented name containing the Russian words for "devil" and "forehead."

In an Interesting Condition, novel in 4 parts by N. Morskoy.* Price: 5 roubles 23 kopecks.

In Memory of Dr. Auguste Debay, author of *Hygiene and Marital Physiology* (78th edition, Paris, 1874), brochure by the aforementioned Morskoy.

The Pigsty, Its Organisation, And Its Inhabitants, by the rhetorician Evgeny Lvov.*

I Was Not At The Anniversary Celebration, lyrical poem by the aforementioned Lvov.

Good Riddance! Ode by the Jesuit Tarakanchio[2] and his associate Tsitovich.* Price: 30 kopecks.

In The Clouds, a fourteen-part novel by Andrey Pechersky.* (Sequel to *On the Hills* and *In the Forests*).

Journalists and Nepotism, essays by a bankrupt editor.

Slavophile-Russian Dictionary: 40,000 words essential for reading the newspaper *Rus.**

!!! Ten Percent !!!

of a yearly income of 10,000 roubles to any doctors wishing to enter into a partnership with me.

Cherepov,[3] Master Coffin Maker

Ready-made *coffins* of all shapes and sizes available. Bulk discount for those dying en masse (epidemic). Those dying are kindly reminded to beware of fakes.

---

2   Comic invented name containing the Russian word for "cockroach."

3   Comic invented name containing the Russian word for "skull."

Cook Needed

must be sober, able to do laundry, and not employed exclusively by the *Moscow Sheet.** Apply to: Lieutenant Negodyaev,[4] own house, Zamoskvoretsky Lane, Bolshaya Ordynka Street.

Sausage-Free Worms

available from merchant Makhametov's shop on Okhotny Row.

Barrister I. N. Moshennikov[5]

conducts cases. Bail offered in the event of a guilty verdict.

Having lost all hope of getting married, I'm selling my dowry. Yegorushka! Come and get me! The Damsel Nevinnova.[6]

Clairvoyant From Tsvetnoy Boulevard

wishes to inform editors that she knows how many current and future subscribers any magazine has and will have in 1882. Payment per word: one rouble.

Merchant Vislyaev's[7] Legal Executors

wish to announce that the 10 roubles bequeathed by the deceased to anyone writing a ridiculously stupid comedy were paid on 15th November to the author of the comedy *The City is Being Abolished.**

---

4   Comic invented name containing the Russian word for "scoundrel."
5   Comic invented name containing the Russian word for "swindler."
6   Comic invented name containing the Russian word for "innocent."
7   Comic invented name containing the word for "loafer" or "rake."

It is with profound sorrow the one thousand one hundred and forty-four publishers of the *Russian Newspaper** inform their uncles, aunts, readers and colleagues of the irrevocable demise of their amiable offspring, *Russian Newspaper*, following a traumatic and prolonged period of decay. Due to lack of benefactors there will be no burial. The body of the deceased was taken to a theatre of anatomy. The postmortem revealed that the cause of death was atrophy of the brain and malnourishment. The mortal remains have been preserved and sent as a specimen to a secret department of the Winkler Museum* on Tsvetnoy Boulevard.

At The Winkler Museum,
on Tsvetnoy Boulevard,

in addition to all the rubbish from the countries of the Old and New World, the following curiosities are also on display:

1) **A stage carriage** constructed in 1343. It can carry 26 ballerinas,* 8 venerable fathers and 5 comic old women. It is not fit to go anywhere, but is truly majestic. The roof was perforated before a rehearsal last week by a sparrow that landed on the carriage in order to try and filch a piece of cotton wool which had fallen out of the coachman's cap.

2) **Two stage horses** of indeterminate colour harnessed to the aforementioned carriage, without manes or tails, and with legs shaped like corkscrews. One is 84 years old and the other is 67. A French general, the Marquis of Blancmange, was taken prisoner on one of them in 1812. They feed on straw and weeds. They are reputed to be the best stage horses in the business. They are certainly not fit for racing... They love the theatre and (oh, equina simplicitas!!)[8] consider themselves indispensable members of the Company.

3) **A portrait of the Jesuit Tsitovich** in a monk's cassock. His lips are parted and his right hand is impressively raised. Under him is the inscription: "Veni, vidi, non-vici,[9] I took and... naturally, left. Homo maximissimus."

---

8 *equina simplicitas*: "equine innocence" (Latin).

9 "I came; I saw; I did not conquer" (Latin).

4) **Apollo Belvedere.** A pearl of art. Acquired for 10,000 roubles. Taking into account that many mesdames, mesdemoiselles and young people under 25 visit our museum, out of a concern for morality, and on the advice of the inspector at the art school, we have dressed the statue up in top and tails. The clothes are by Ayé,* the top hat made by Posh and shoes made by Lvov.

5) **The nets** into which the beautiful Cleopatra enticed the depraved Anthony.

6) **A white rat** (stultum animal),[10] one-and-a-quarter foot tall. A rare specimen. It was found in a Filippov bread roll in 1880. Preserved in spirit. A novelty for young zoologists.

Dentist Lumpenmak

Displays teeth to the public. 35½ Akhakhaevsky Passage.

---

10   *Stultum animal:* "stupid animal" (Latin).

This and That

(Poetry and Prose)

'Tis a marvellous frosty afternoon. The sunlight plays on every snowflake. It is cloudless, windless. Two lovebirds are sitting on a boulevard bench.

"I love you!" he whispers.

Rosy cupids frolic on her cheeks.

"I love you!" he continues... "Ever since I first set eyes on you, I understood what I'm living for, I found my *raison d'être*! It is life with you or absolute non-existence! My darling! Maria Ivanovna! Yes or No? Manya! Maria Ivanovna... I love you... Manechka... Give me an answer, or I'll die! Yes or No?"

She looks up at him with her big eyes. She wants to say 'Yes'. She opens her cute little mouth.

"Ah!" she cries out.

On *his* snow-white collar, racing each other, are two enormous bedbugs... Oh, how awful!!..

* * *

"My dearest Mama," wrote a certain artist to his mother. "I am coming home. This Thursday morning, I shall know the joy of once again pressing you to my loving bosom. To render our rendezvous even sweeter, I am bringing... Guess who? No, you won't guess, Mama. You'll never guess. I am bringing a miracle of beauty, a pearl of human art. I am bringing (and I can just picture your smile)... Apollo Belvedere!"

"Kolechka, sweetheart!" his Mama replied. "I'm so happy you're coming home. God bless you! But please don't bring Mr. Belvedere with you, there isn't even enough for us to eat as it is!.."

* * *

The air is filled with fragrances conducive to languor: there is a scent of lilac and roses; a nightingale is singing, the sun is shining... and so on.

In the town park, on a bench under a wide acacia tree, sits a high-school student in his final year, wearing his new uniform, with a pince-nez on his nose and a scrawny moustache. Beside him is a pretty girl.

The schoolboy is holding her hand and trembling, going pale and red by turns, and whispering sweet nothings.

"Oh, how I love you! Oh, if only you knew how much I love you!"

"And I love you, too!" she whispers.

The schoolboy puts his arm around her waist.

"Oh, Life! You are beautiful! I am drowning, choking with happiness! Plato was right when he said that... Just one kiss! Olya! A kiss—and nothing more in the world."

She lowers her eyes languorously... Oh, she, too, thirsts for a kiss! He extends his lips toward her rosy little lips... The nightingale's song grows louder...

"Back to class!" resounds a rasping tenor above the schoolboy's head.

The schoolboy raises his head, and his cap falls off... Standing before him is the school inspector...

"Back to the classroom!"

"Um... but it's still the long recess, Alexander Fyodorovich..."

"Get moving! You have a Latin lesson now! I am giving you a two-hour detention today!"

The schoolboy stands up, puts his cap on, and walks off... as he walks, he feels her big eyes on his back... The inspector trips along behind him...

* * *

A performance of *Hamlet* is underway.

"Ophelia!" Hamlet cries. "Oh, nymph! Be all my sins remembered..."

"The right side of your moustache has come off!" Ophelia whispers.

"Be all my sins... Huh?"

"The right side of your moustache has come off!"

"Dammit!.. in thy saintly prayers..."

* * *

Napoleon I invites the Marquise de Chailly to the palace ball.

"I'll be coming with my husband, Your Excellency!" says Madame de Chailly.

"Come alone," says Napoleon. "I like good meat without mustard."

This and That

(Letters and Telegrams)

Telegram

Drinking all week to Sarah's health.* Ravishing! Dies as she stands. Those Parisians way ahead of us. Sitting in theatre as if in heaven. Greetings to Manka. Petrov.

* * *

Telegram

To Lieutenant Yegorov. Go take my ticket. Not going again. Rubbish. Nothing special. Waste of money.

* * *

From doctor of medicine Klopzon to doctor of medicine Verfluchterschwein[1]

Comrade! Yesterday I saw S.B. Chest—paralytic, flat. Bones and muscles—developed unsatisfactorily. The neck is so long and thin that not only the *venae jugulares*[2] but even the *arteriae carotides*[3] are visible. The *musculi sterno-clei-do-mastoidei*[4] are barely noticeable. From my second-row seat, I heard anaemic murmurs in her veins. No cough. She was all wrapped up on stage, which gave me reason to conclude that she has a fever. I diagnose anaemia and *atrophia musculorum*.[5] It's wonderful. Her lacrimal glands respond to volitional stimuli.

---

1 Both doctors have comic invented names, the first derived from the Russian word for "bedbug" (*klop*), the second from the German words "damned" (*verfluchter*) and "pig" (*Schwein*).

2 *venae jugulars*: "jugular veins" (Latin).

3 *arteriae carotides*: "carotid arteries" (Latin).

4 *musculi sterno-cleido-mastoidei*: "sternocleidomastoid muscles" (Latin).

5 *atrophia musculorum*: "muscular atrophy" (Latin).

Tears fell from her eyes and hyperaemia was observed on her nose whenever the rules of drama demanded that she cry.

* * *

From Nadya N. to Katya X.

Dearest Katya! Yesterday I was at the theatre and saw Sarah Beenheart there. Oh Katechka she has so many diemonds! I cried all night long at the thought that I will never have so many diemonds. I will describe her dress when we meet... How I wish I was Sarah Beenheart. They were drinking real shampain on stage! it's very odd Katya I speak excellent French but did not understand anything of what the actors said on stage they spoke differently somehow. I was sitting... in the gallery as my beast could not get another ticket. The beast! I regret that on Monday I was so cold with S. as he would have got me a seat in the stalls. S. will do anything for a kiss. To spite the beast, tomorrow S will be visiting he'll get a ticket for you and me.

Your, N.

* * *

From an editor to a columnist

Ivan Mikhailovich! This is outrageous! You go back and forth every day to the theatre with a press ticket and yet you haven't handed in a single line. What are you waiting for? Sarah Bernhardt is hot news today, so you've got to write about her today. For heaven's sake, get a move on!

Answer: I don't know what to write. Praise? Let's wait and see what our colleagues' come up with. There is time enough.

Yours K.

Will be at the editorial offices today. Have my money ready. If you can't spare the ticket, then send over for it.

* * *

Miss N.'s letter to same journalist

You are such a darling, Ivan Mikhailych! Thank you for the ticket. I have seen my fill of Sarah and order you to praise her. Could you ask at the editorial offices if my sister can also go to the theatre with press tickets?! I would be much obliged.

With cordial etc. etc.

Yours N.

Answer. She can... for a fee, of course. It's not a large fee: permission to visit you on Saturday.

* * *

To the Editor from his wife

If you don't send me tickets for Sarah Bernhardt today, don't bother coming home. Clearly your employees are better than your wife. Make sure I get to the theatre today!

* * *

From the Editor to his wife

Good Lord! Not you as well! My head is spinning with this Sarah without you pestering me too!

* * *

From the usher's notebook

Tonite, let in for. Forteen roub.
Tonite, let in five. Fifteen r.
Tonite, let in three and one madam. Fifteen roub.

* * *

...Just as well I didn't go to the theatre and sold my ticket. They say that Sarah Bernhardt acted in French. I wouldn't have understood a thing anyway...

Major Kovalyov.

* * *

Mitya! Do me a favour, drop a gentle hint to your wife that when she sits in a box with us, she raves about Sarah Bernhardt's dresses more quietly. At the last performance she was whispering so loudly that I couldn't hear what was being said on stage. Just a gentle hint, I would be much obliged.

Yours U.

* * *

From Slavist X. to his son

My son!.. I opened my eyes and saw the sign of depravity... Thousands of good Russian Orthodox folk, the type who talk about uniting with the people, were going in their droves to the theatre and laying their gold at the feet of a Jewess... Liberals, conservatives...

* * *

Darling! Even if you sprinkle the frog with sugar, I won't eat it...

*Sobakevich.**

The Sinner from Toledo

(Translated from the Spanish)*

"Whosoever reveals the present whereabouts of the witch who goes by the name of Maria Spalanço, or brings her before the judges' tribunal live or dead, will obtain the remission of sins."

The proclamation was signed by the Bishop of Barcelona and four judges on one of those days of yore that will forever remain an indelible stain on the history of Spain and, for that matter, of humanity.

All Barcelona read the proclamation. Searches got under way. Sixty women who resembled the witch in question were detained, and her relatives were tortured... There existed a ridiculous and at the same time deeply held belief that witches had the power to turn into cats, dogs or other animals, and definitely black ones. Tales were told of how, when attacked by an animal, a hunter would very often cut off its paw and carry it off as a trophy but, upon opening his bag, would find only a bloody hand, in which he would recognise the hand of his own wife. The inhabitants of Barcelona killed all the black cats and dogs, but did not recognise Maria Spalanço in these unnecessary victims.

Maria Spalanço was the daughter of an important Barcelona merchant. Her father was a Frenchman and her mother Spanish. From her father she inherited Gallic nonchalance and that boundless cheerfulness which is so attractive in French women, from her mother—a typical Spanish body. Beautiful, always good-humoured, intelligent, her life devoted to cheerful Spanish doingnothingness and the arts, she did not shed a tear until the age of twenty... She was as happy as a child... On the very day that she reached the age of twenty, she married the sailor Spalanço, famous in all Barcelona, a very handsome and, it was said, a most learned Spaniard. She married him for love. Her husband swore to her that he would kill himself if she did not find happiness with him. He was madly in love with her.

On the second day of the wedding festivities her fate was decided.

Towards evening, she set off from her husband's house to see her mother and got lost. Barcelona is a big city and not every Spanish woman can tell you the shortest way from one end of town to the other. She chanced to come upon a young monk.

"How do I get to St. Mark's Street?" she asked him.

The monk stopped and began looking at her while thinking about something... The sun had already gone down. The moon had risen and was casting its cold rays on Maria's lovely face. Not in vain do the poets speak of the moon when they sing women's praises! In the moonlight a woman is a hundred times more beautiful. Due to her quick pace, Maria's beautiful black hair had spread over her shoulders and heaving bosom as she drew deep breaths... As she tried to keep the headscarf in place on her neck, she exposed her arms, naked to the elbows...

"I swear by the blood of San Gennaro that you are a witch!" said the young monk suddenly and for no apparent reason.

"If you were not a monk, I would suppose that you were drunk!" she said.

"You are a witch!!"

The monk mumbled some kind of incantation through his teeth.

"Where is the dog that was running ahead of me just now? That dog turned into you! I saw it!.. I know... I have not yet lived even twenty-five years but I have already exposed fifty witches! You are the fifty-first! I am Augustine..."

With that, the monk crossed himself, turned on his heel, and disappeared.

Maria knew Augustine... She had heard a great deal about him from her parents... She knew him to be a most zealous destroyer of witches and the author of one learned book. In it he cursed women and hated man for being born of woman, and boasted of his love of Christ. And yet, Maria had often wondered, could someone who did not love man love Christ? When she had gone on a few hundred yards, Maria came across Augustine again. Through the gates of a large building with a long Latin inscription emerged four black figures. These four figures let her pass then followed her. One of them she recognised as that same Augustine. They followed her to her own door.

Three days after the encounter with Augustine, a man came to Spalanço's house dressed in black, with a puffy clean-shaven face, by all appearances a judge. The man ordered Spalanço to immediately go and see the bishop.

"Your wife is a witch!" the bishop declared to Spalanço.

Spalanço grew pale.

"Give thanks to God!" the bishop continued. "A man upon whom God has bestowed the precious gift of exposing the devil in people has opened your

eyes and ours. She has been seen to change into a black dog and the black dog
to change into your wife..."

"She is not a witch, she is... my wife!" Spalanço stammered, aghast.

"She cannot be the wife of a Catholic! She is the wife of Satan! Have you
really never noticed before, poor soul, that she has betrayed you many times
with the devil? Go home and bring her here immediately..."

The bishop was a very learned man. He derived the word "femina" from
the words "fe" and "minus," based on the ostensibly logical claim that a woman
has less faith...

Spalanço went whiter than a corpse. He left the bishop's chambers
and clutched his head in his hands. Where and to whom could he now
say that Maria was not a witch? Who would not believe what the monks
had believed? Now all of Barcelona would be convinced that his wife was
a witch! The whole city! There was nothing easier than convincing a stupid person that some dreamt-up fantasy was true, and Spaniards were all
stupid!

"There is no nation more stupid than the Spaniards!" Spalanço's dying
father, a doctor, once told him. "Disdain Spaniards and do not believe what
they believe!"

Spalanço did believe what the Spaniards believed but he did not believe
what the bishop had said. He knew his wife well and was convinced that wom-
en become witches only in old age...

"The monks want to burn you at the stake, Maria!" he told his wife once
he got home from visiting the bishop. "They say you're a witch, and they've
ordered me to take you to them... Listen to me, wife! If you really are a witch,
good luck to you! Turn into a black cat and run away somewhere; if you don't
have an evil spirit inside you, though, I won't give you up to the monks... They
will chain you by the neck and won't let you sleep until you tell a pack of lies
against yourself. If you're a witch, run away!"

Maria did not turn into a black cat, nor did she run away... She simply
began to cry and started praying to God.

"Listen!" Spalanço told his weeping wife. "My late father told me that
a time would soon come when people would laugh at those who believe in
the existence of witches. My father was a godless man, but he always spoke
the truth. So, what you need to do is hide somewhere and wait for that time
to come... It's very simple! My brother Christopher's ship is being repaired in
the harbour. I will hide you on the ship, and you will stay there until the time

comes that my father talked about. From what he said, that time is coming soon..."

By evening Maria was already sitting in the very bottom of the ship. Trembling from cold and fear, she listened to the noise of the waves and waited impatiently for that impossible moment of which Spalanço's father had spoken.

"Where is your wife?" the bishop asked Spalanço.

"She turned into a black cat and ran away from me," Spalanço lied.

"I expected this, foresaw it! But no matter. We will find her... Augustine has a great gift! Oh, wondrous gift! Go in peace and don't go marrying a witch again! There have been cases of evil spirits transmigrating from wives to their husbands... Last year, I burned one pious Catholic who gave his soul to Satan against his will after coming into contact with a possessed woman... Go!"

Maria sat in the ship for a long time. Spalanço visited her each night and brought her everything she needed. She sat there for a month, then another and a third, but the time they wished for did not come. Spalanço's father was right, but a few months is not much where superstitions are concerned. They are as long-lived as fish and it takes centuries for them to die... Maria got used to her new way of life and had already begun to laugh at the monks, whom she called crows. She would have gone on living there for a long time and would, most probably, have sailed with the ship once it was repaired, to faraway countries as Christopher Columbus said, far from stupid Spain, had it not been for one terrible and irremediable misfortune.

A proclamation by the bishop, passed from hand to hand among Barcelona's residents and glued to the walls in all its squares and markets, fell into Spalanço's hands as well. Spalanço read the proclamation and started to ponder. He was intrigued by the remission of sins that was promised at the end.

"It would be nice to obtain the remission of sins!" sighed Spalanço.

Spalanço considered himself a terrible sinner. On his conscience lay a multitude of sins for which many Catholics had been burned at the stake or tortured to death. In his youth Spalanço had lived in Toledo. Toledo at that time was a gathering place for magicians and sorcerers... In the twelfth and thirteenth centuries mathematics flourished more there than anywhere else in Europe. In Spanish towns it was one step from mathematics to magic... Spalanço, under his father's guidance, had also practised magic. He dissected animal entrails and collected rare herbs... One time he was pounding something in his iron mortar, and out of the mortar with a frightful splutter came an evil spirit in the form of a blue flame. Life in Toledo consisted almost entirely of sins of that kind. Having left Toledo after his father's death, Spalanço soon felt terrible pangs of conscience. An old and very learned physician monk told him that his sins would not be forgiven him unless he obtained the remission of sins for some kind of exceptional feat. Spalanço was ready to give everything he had for the remission of sins, if only to free his soul from the memory of his shameful life in Toledo and to avoid hell. He would have given half of his property, if only indulgences had been for sale in Spain at the time... He would have set off on pilgrimage on foot, if only his business had not detained him.

"If I were not her husband, I would give her up," he thought, having read the bishop's proclamation.

The thought that he had but to speak one word in order to obtain the remission of sins stuck in his head and gave him no peace day or night... He loved his wife, loved her very much... If it were not for that love, that weakness, so disdained by monks and even the doctors of Toledo, he could... He showed the proclamation to his brother Christopher...

"I would give her up," said his brother, "if she were a witch and if she were not so beautiful... Remission is a good thing... You know, we could do worse than to wait until Maria dies and then give her up, dead, to those crows... Let them burn her when she's dead... The dead feel no pain. She'll die when we're old, and it's when we are old that we will need remission"

With that, Christopher roared with laughter and slapped his brother on the shoulder.

"I may die before her," said Spalanço. "But, I swear to God, I would give her up, if I weren't her husband!"

A week after this conversation, Spalanço was walking about the deck of the ship and muttering:

"Oh, if only she were dead! I won't give her up alive, oh no! But I would if she were dead! I would cheat those cursed old crows and obtain remission from them!"

And stupid Spalanço poisoned his poor wife...

Maria's corpse was brought by Spalanço before the judges' tribunal and committed to the flames.

Spalanço obtained remission of his Toledo sins... He was forgiven for learning to cure people and for studying the science that was later to be called chemistry. The bishop praised him and gave him a book he had written himself... In the book, the learned bishop wrote that devils most often inhabit women with black hair because black hair is the colour of devils.

Supplementary Questions

*to the Personal Census Forms, suggested by Antosha Chekhonte**

16) Are you a *clever* man or a *fool*?

17) Are you an *honest man*? A *Swindler*? A *Robber*? A *scoundrel*? A *Lawyer* or?

18) Which columnist is most to your liking? *Suvorin*? *Bukva*? *Amicus*? *Lukin*? *Julius Schreier* or?*

19) Are you a *Joseph* or a *Caligula*? A *Susanna* or a *Nana*?*

20) Is your wife *blonde*? *Brunette*? *Chestnut*? A *redhead*?

21) Does your wife *beat* you or *not*? Do you *beat* her or *not*?

22) How many pounds did you weigh when you were ten years old?

23) Do you consume hot beverages? *Yes* or *no*?

24) What were you thinking about on the night of the census?

25) Have you seen Sarah Bernhardt? Or *not*?

At The Wolf-Baiting*

They say this is the nineteenth century. Do not take that for granted, dear reader.

It is Wednesday 6 January in that European and supposedly capital city of Moscow, and people have packed into the stands of the summer race-course to enjoy the entertainment, sitting so closely together they are treading on each other's toes. Not only the spectacle but its very description is an anachronism... Must it fall to us sensitive, lachrymose suit-wearers who have exchanged muscles for ideas, theatre-going liberals *et tutti quanti*,[1] to describe the baiting of wolves?! Us?!

Turns out it must... So be it, we will describe it.

The first thing to emphasise is that I am no hunter. I have never hit a living thing in my whole life. Unless you count fleas, but that was one on one, without hounds. The only firearms I am familiar with are the small tin pistols I bought my children for Christmas. Since I do not hunt, I apologise for any inaccuracies in my account. Non-specialists are habitually inaccurate. I shall endeavour to avoid talking about matters where I might display my ignorance of hunting terminology, and shall instead deliberate like the public does, i.e. superficially, and based on first impressions...

It is after midday. Behind the stands carriages, cabs and sleighs are jostling for space. There is noise and commotion everywhere... There are so many carriages that they are all squashed together...

Congregating in the horse racing stands, decked out in raccoon, beaver, fox and sheepskin, are experts on stallions, dogs, borzois, sparrow hawks and other miscellaneous beasts, and they are freezing and burning with impatience. Naturally, ladies have also come along... You cannot do anything without ladies, and for some reason, there are a great number of them who are prettier than usual... There are as many ladies as men. They too are burning with impatience. On the upper benches one can glimpse the odd school cap. Schoolboys have also come to gawp and they too are burning with

---

1   *et tutti quanti*: "and all of them" (Italian).

impatience and banging their galoshes together. Enthusiasts, connoisseurs and self-appointed critics who have made their way to Khodynka on foot without a rouble, crowding round the gates, knee-deep in snow, craning their necks for a view and also burning with impatience. In the arena there are a number of carts. On the carts are wooden crates. Inside the crates, the heroes of the day—wolves—are enjoying their lives. They, in all likelihood, are probably not burning with impatience...

Before the baiting begins, the audience admires the Russian beauties riding round the arena on fine horses... The nastiest and the most fanatical hunters criticise the dogs that have been prepared for the baiting. Each spectator clutches a flyer. The ladies are clutching flyers and binoculars.

"Most delightful way to pass the time, sir," remarks a scrawny-bearded old fellow in a cap and cockade to his neighbour, to all appearances a nobleman who has squandered his fortune a long time ago.

"Most delightful... One used to set off with companions... Set off at first light... And the ladies too."

"There is no point involving ladies," the neighbour interrupts the old man.

"Why's that?"

"Because you can't swear in front of ladies. And how can you not swear on a hunt?"

"True, it's impossible. But there have been ladies who themselves swear... There was the daughter of Baron Glanzer, if you please, Marya Karlovna— swore like a trooper! You devil, satan, damn you, so-and-so... Etcetera... Dot, dot, dot... She was the bane of all the low-ranks... She'd use her crop at the drop of a hat."

"Mama, are the wolves in the crates?" asks a high-school boy in an enormous hood, turning to a lady with plump red cheeks.

"Yes, they are."

"And they can't escape?"

"That's enough! You and your questions... Wipe your nose! Ask me something intelligent... Why ask such stupid questions?"

There is a stir of activity in the arena... Half a dozen men, all of them initiated into the mysteries of hunting, carry one of the crates and place it in the middle of the arena... A murmur runs round the audience.

"Sir, whose dogs are going in now?"

"Mozharov's! Hmm... No, not Mozharov's, Sheremetiev's!"

"They most certainly are not Sheremetiev's! It's Mozharov's borzois. There he is, Mozharov's black borzoi! Can you see it? Actually, maybe it is Sheremetiev's after all. Yes, yes, yes... Well well, well... Gentleman, they are indeed Sheremetiev's dogs! Sheremetiev's, and Mozharov's are over there."

They pound on the crate with a mallet... The crowd's excitement reaches fever pitch. They back away from the crate... One of them pulls a cord which makes the walls of the prison fall away, at which point the onlookers catch sight of that most revered of all Russian animals, a grey wolf. The wolf takes one look around him, gets to his feet, and runs... Sheremetiev's dogs race after him, racing behind them, against all the rules, is Mozharov's dog, and behind Mozharov's dog is the borzoi kennelman with a dagger...

The wolf barely manages to run a few dozen feet before it is already dead... The dogs and the kennelman have really distinguished themselves... "Bravoo!" cries the crowd, "Braaavo! Bravo! But why did Mozharov release his dog out of order? Mozharov, boo! Bra...vo!" Then the whole event is repeated with another wolf...

The third crate is opened. The wolf sits there and does not budge. The men crack a whip in front of his muzzle. Eventually he gets up, looking tired and beaten, barely able to pull his hind legs behind him. It looks around... There is no escape! But it yearns to live! He wants to live just as much as the people sitting in the stands, who listen to the gnashing of its teeth and look at the blood. He attempts to run but he has nowhere to go! Svechin's dogs grab it by his pelt, the kennelman plunges his dagger right into its heart and— *vae victis!*[2]—the wolf falls, taking to the grave a very dim view of humanity... Joking aside, mankind is shaming itself before wolves by contriving this pseudo-hunt!.. It is quite a different matter to hunting out in the steppe, in the woods, where human bloodlust can be slightly excused by the possibility of an equal fight, when a wolf can to defend itself or run away...

The spectators rage, so furiously as if all the dogs in the world have been unleashed on them...

"Might as well knife them right there in the crate! Some hunt this is! What a disgrace!"

"Why are you yelling if you have no idea what you are on about. You've obviously never been on a hunt, have you?"

"No, I haven't."

---

2   *vae victis:* "woe to the vanquished" (Latin).

"So why are you yelling? What do you know about this? You think the wolf should be set on the hounds, so it can tear them to pieces? Right? Is that what you think?"

"Listen! What pleasure is there in watching a wolf stabbed to death? The dogs aren't given a chance to run around!"

"Shush... Pipe down!"

"Whose are those dogs?" rages a gentleman in a raccoon fur coat. "Go and find out, lad, whose they are!"

"They're Lebushev's, Sheremetiev's, and Mozharov's!"

"Whose is the hound?"

"He's Mozharov's! Such a fine hound, too!.. Mozharov's!"

"Just stab it in its crate!.."

The crowd is rather unhappy about the wolf being stabbed so quickly... The wolf should have been chased around the arena for an hour or two bitten by dogs' teeth and trampled by horses' hooves, and only then stabbed... As if it were not enough that the animal had been already hunted down and captured, and had spent several weeks in captivity through no fault of its own.

The dogs and Stakhovich's kennelman capture the wolf alive... They return the lucky beast to its crate. One wolf jumps over the barrier. Dogs and kennelmen chase after it. Had the wolf managed to escape into town, Moscow would have been treated to a baiting on her streets and alleys unlike any other!..

During the intervals, full of wearisome expectation, the crowd guffaws and, would you believe, shouts 'bravo': it likes the ten-kopeck pony carrying the empty crates from the middle of the arena to their previous position. The pony does not so much walk as buck, and not with its legs but with a ripple of its whole body and its head. The crowd loves it and roars with delight.

Lucky pony! Could it or its forebears ever imagined it would be honoured with such applause?

Raucous barking heralds the arrival of a pack of hounds... A large wolf is given to them to rip to pieces. The hounds tear at it while the borzois, still tied up, yelp with envy.

"Bravo, bravo!" cries the audience. "Bravo, Nikolay Yakovlevich!"

Nikolay Yakovlevich bows to the crowd with the kind of flourish that any celebrated performer might envy.

"Bring out the fox!" he shouts in a frenzy.

In the middle of the arena a small crate is brought out and a pretty little vixen released. The fox runs and runs... the hounds give chase. No one can quite see at what point the dogs grab the fox.

"The fox has escaped!" cries the crowd. "They let it go! It's gone!"

Nikolay Yakovlevich appears with the fox in his hand and the crowd is taken aback. It takes a lot of time and men to gather the hounds back into a pack. The dogs are disobedient and ill-disciplined... The crowd does not like hounds.

In general, the crowd is completely frozen but very happy. The ladies are thrilled by the proceedings.

"It's good abroad," says one lady. "They have bull fights and cock fights there... Why don't they bring them to Russia?"

"Because, madam, they have bulls abroad but we do not!.." answers the old fellow sporting a cockade.

Finally, they release the last wolf. This wolf is slaughtered, and the crowd heads off home debating which dogs were good or bad.

By way of conclusion we have to ask: what is the point of this whole puppet-show? It cannot be about showing off dogs because it is such a small space and there is also nowhere to demonstrate prowess. What is the moral?

The moral is of the worst kind. It is just about giving the ladies a thrill and nothing else! The takings exceed a thousand roubles, it is true. But I would hate to think it was all about the takings. One can offset all the costs with the takings, but it is impossible to offset the small injuries which this baiting may have inflicted on the young soul of the aforementioned schoolboy.

Comic Advertisements and Notices

(Reported by Antosha Chekhonte)

An Announcement by the Dentist Gewalter*

It has come to my attention zat my patientz have been mizhtaking ze recently arrived dentist Gewalter for me; and so I have ze honour of informing zem zat I rezide in Mozhcow and I ask my patientz not to mix me with Gewalter. He is not Gewalter: it is I who am Gewalter. I fit false teeth, zell a ground chalk kompozed by me for brushing ze teeth and I have ze largest signboard. Home vizits I conduct in a white tie.

Ze dentist by ze Winkler menagerie—Gewalter.

~

The Following Terrible Titles Are
for Sale at Leukhin's Bookshop:*

Teach Yourself Passionate Love, or, **Oh, You Brute!** By Idiotov, price: 1 rouble, 80 kopecks.

Collected Letters. By doctor of profanity Merzavtsev.[1] Pr. 4 roubles.

The Mysterious Mysteries of Mysterious Love or **A Portfolio of Lovers' Delights**. Pr. 5 roubles.

Dictionary of all the indecent words used around the world. Pr. 7 roubles.

Notes of a female stocking, or **Oh, innocence!** Pr. 1 rouble, 50 kopecks.

How to seduce, flatter, corrupt, arouse, etc. A reference book for young people. Price: 6 roubles for 4 volumes.

---

1   Like Idiotov, self-explanatory also in Russian, this is an invented comic name derived from the Russian word "villain" (*merzavets*).

Nature's secrets, or **What is love?** A book for younger children with vignettes in text. Pr. 3 roubles, 50 kopecks.

25% discounts for subscribers. Customers spending more than 50 roubles will receive 50 free photographs and a winding key with a panorama.

⌣

Subscriptions for 1882 Now Open

for a major daily political, literary, commercial and astonishing newspaper

⌣

News and Stock Exchange Gazette.*

published by a joint-stock association with a base capital of 3,000,000 Finnish Marks, or approximately 1,200,000 roubles, divided into 3,000 shares at 1,000 F. Marks each.

The *News* has:

two paper mills of its own, its own very sharp-minded editor, its own printing house, its own bookshop

and, from 1882, will have:

its own building, its own stable for its own donkeys, its own lunatic asylum, its own debtors' prison and its own alehouse.

The newspaper's operations are financed by the shares of the aforementioned association.

⌣

Subscribers Have Absconded

Whoever finds them please deliver to the *Minute's* editorial office.* Reward— a handshake from the editor.

⌣

The Following Works by the Barrister Smirnov* are now
Available for Sale:

Fist-law. Translated from the Tatar. For trainee lawyers. Pr. 1 rouble.
To Bash or not to Bash? Pr. 3 roubles.
Anatomy of the Fist. Pr. 1 rouble.
　　Discount for booksellers and barristers.

—

Moscow—Arrivals:

French subject Nana Sukhorovskaya,* from St. Petersburg. Staying on Petrovskie Linii Street.
Moscow—Departures:
Journalist Molchanov,* for the South Pole.
One hundred and forty-five lawyers, for Taganrog.*

—

A MUSICAL-VOCAL-LITERARY-DANCE EVENING

Featuring

Mme Nana Sukhorovskaya

in aid of the victims of Vesuvius, the residents of Herculaneum and Pompeii,
at the Slavyansky Bazaar, on
29th February

Programme:
　　"How cold it is, pilgrims, how cold!" To be wept by Mr Ivanov-Kozelsky.*
"Where is the talent among us?!? Damn it!" To be declaimed with indignation by Mr Averkiev.*
　　"The Head hit a head in the head with a head." To be fizzed by the editor Mr Lanin.*
　　"Am I to blame..." To be sung by Mme Brenko.*
　　"Shortfall skips, deficit dances..." A gypsy dance to be performed by Pushkin Theatre artists.

"And here is Nikolay, the deceased, plus me..." Overture, to be performed by Mr. Shostakovsky*.

"Not every naked person's a beggar!" To be sung by Mme Nana Sukhorovskaya, while dancing.

"What's the use of modesty? Pushkin is first, Lermontov second and I—Velichkov[2]—am third..." To be read by friends on behalf of Mr. Velichkov, who is illiterate.

"Tomorrow, tomorrow, not today—this is what the lazy say!" To be sung by the editor of *the Blind Man*...

The programme commences at 7:30 p.m.

A doctor and free smelling salts will be on hand in case of fainting from stuffiness (45°C).

---

2   Velichkov is derived from the Russian word for "great" (*velikii*).

The Mad Mathematician's Maths Test

1. I was being chased by 30 dogs, of which 7 were white, 8 were grey, and the rest were black. Which of my legs did they bite—the right or the left?
2. Autolimedes* was born in the year 223, and he died after living for 84 years. He spent half of his life travelling and a third of it having a good time. How much does a pound of nails cost, and was Autolimedes married?
3. On New Year's Eve, 200 people were expelled from the masked ball at the Bolshoi Theatre for brawling. If there were two hundred brawlers, how many were quarrelling, drunk, slightly drunk and wanting, but not getting the chance to fight.
4. What is the total if you add up the above numbers?
5. 20 crates of tea were purchased. In each crate there were 5 bushels and each bushel contained 40 pecks. Of the horses carrying the tea, two dropped dead on the way, one of the drivers fell ill, and 18 pecks of tea were spilled. There are 96 pinches of tea in a peck. What is the difference between gherkin brine and bewilderment?
6. The English language has 137, 856, 738 words; French has 0.7 times as many. The English joined up with the French and combined both languages into one. What is the third parrot worth, and how long did it take to conquer these nations?
7. On Wednesday 17th June, 1881, a train was due to leave station 'A' at 3 o'clock in the morning in order to arrive at station 'B' at 11 o'clock that night, but, as it was about to leave, an order was received that the train should arrive at station 'B' at 7 o'clock in the evening. Who loves longest, men or women?
8. My mother-in-law is 75, but my wife is 42. What time is it?

As reported by Antosha Chekhonte

Forgotten!!

Ivan Prokhorych Hauptvakhtov,[1] a once nimble lieutenant, dancer, and ladies' man, but now a plump, short landowner twice struck down by paralysis, tired and worn out by doing the shopping for his wife, dropped into a big music store to buy some piano pieces.

"Good day," he said, on entering the shop. "If I may..."

The small German standing behind the counter extended his neck towards him, and composed a smiling question mark on his face.

"How can I help you, sir?"

"If I may... It's terribly hot! Nothing to be done with this climate, though! If I may... Mmmm... It's... Mm... If I may... I've forgotten!!"

"Try to remember, sir!"

Hauptvakhtov placed his upper lip over his lower one, wrinkled his small brow with great intensity, raised his eyes, and began to ponder.

"I've forgotten! Heavens, what a terrible memory! It's just... it's... If I may... Mm... I've forgotten!"

"Try to remember, sir..." "I told her: write it down! But no... Why didn't she write it down? I can't remember everything... But maybe you know it yourself? It's a foreign piece, you play it loudly... Eh?"

"We have so many, you know, that..."

"Of course... I understand! Hmm... Hmm... Let me recall... Well, what should I do? I can't go home without the piece—I'll get killed by Nadia, my daughter, that is; she does play it without the notes, you know, but awkwardly... it comes out wrong! She did have the music, but I must confess, I accidentally spilt kerosene on it and threw it behind the chest of drawers to avoid all the shouting... I don't like the sound of women shouting! She ordered me to buy... Well, yes... Humph... Oh, what a splendid cat!"

And Hauptvakhtov began to stroke the big grey cat sprawling on the counter... The cat began to purr and stretched contentedly.

---

1   Comic name derived from the German *Hauptwache* ("Main Police Station").

"Gorgeous... You're a Siberian rascal, I suppose! A pedigree troublemaker... Is it a tom or a female?"

"A tom."

"Hey, what are you looking at? Puss! Silly! Tiger! Do you catch mice? Meow, meow? That damned memory of mine!.. You fat rascal!.. I couldn't get one of his kittens from you, I suppose?"

"No... Hmm..."

"Otherwise I'd take one... My wife just loves cats to death! What am I to do now? I remembered all the way here, and now I've forgotten... I've lost my memory, and there's nothing to be done! I've become old, my time has passed... Time to die... You play it loudly, with flourishes, majestically... If I may... Hmm... Maybe I could sing it..."

"Do sing it... *oder*...[2] *oder*... or... whistle it!.."

"But it is bad luck to whistle indoors... Now, our friend Sedelnikov used to whistle indoors, and ended up whistling away all his money... Are you German or French?"

"German."

"That is what I thought from your appearance... It's good you're not French... I don't like the French... Oink, oink, oink... what piggery! During the war they ate mice! He whistled in his shop from dawn till dusk, and he whistled all his wealth up the chimney! He is in debt up to his eyebrows now... And he owes me two hundred roubles... I used to hum to myself sometimes under my breath... Hmm... If I may... I'll sing it... Hang on. Just a second... Hmm... Cough... Got an itchy throat..."

Hauptvakhtov clicked his fingers three times, closed his eyes and began to hum in a falsetto:

"To-to-ti-to-tom... Ho-ho-ho. I'm a tenor... At home I tend to sing descant... If I may... Tri-ra-ra... Ahem... I've got something stuck in my teeth... Pah! It's a seed... Ooh-to-to-ooh-ooh... Hmm... I must have caught a cold... I drank some cold beer at the bierkeller... Troo-roo-roo... it goes up high like that, you know... and then down, down... Sort of levels off, and then comes the top note, rather drawn out... to-to-tee... rooo. Do you get it? And then the basses start going: hoo, hoo, hoo, tootoo... Do you get it?"

"No, I don't..."

---

2   *Oder*: "or" (German).

The cat looked at Hauptvakhtov in amazement, burst out laughing it seemed, and jumped languidly off the counter.

"You don't recognise it? That's a shame... Though I am not singing it right... What a nuisance, I've completely forgotten it!"

"Play it on the piano... Do you play?"

"No, I don't... I used to play the violin once, on one string, but that was just, you know... fooling around... No one taught me... My brother Nazar plays... He was taught by... the Frenchman, Roquat, perhaps you know him—Benedikt Frantsych... Such a funny little Frenchman... We used to tease him by calling him Buonaparte... He would get angry... "I am not Buonaparte..." he would say, "I am the French Republic..." And his mug was Republican, to tell the truth... A dog's mug if ever there was one... My late father never taught me anything... "Your Grandfather," he would say, "was called Ivan, and you are Ivan, and therefore you must take after your grandfather in everything you do: into the military, you scoundrel! Smell some gunpowder!! Namby-pamby nonsense, my boy... boy... I, my boy... I, my boy, won't allow you any of that namby-pamby nonsense! Your grandfather basically ate horse meat, and so shall you! Put a saddle under your head instead of a pillow!.. I'm going to be in trouble at home! They will tear me to shreds! I'm not allowed to come home without the music... So in that case, goodbye, sir! I apologise for troubling you! How much does this grand piano cost?"

"Eight hundred roubles!"

"Woah... My goodness! That's called: buy yourself a piano and do without trousers! Ho-ho-ho! Eight-hundred-roubles! You know a good thing when you see it! Goodbye, sir! Sprechensie! Gebensie... ![3] I once had lunch with a German, you know... After lunch, I asked a certain gentleman, also a Teuton, how to say in German: "I humbly thank you for your hospitality?" And he says to me... and he says... If I may... And he says: "Ikh leebe dikh fon ganzen herzen!" What does that mean?"

"I... I love you," translated the German standing behind the counter, "with all my heart!"

"Well then! I went up to my host's daughter and said it straight out... She was embarrassed... It almost ended in hysterics... What a commission! Goodbye, sir! If your head isn't screwed on right you'll end up with sore feet...

---

3   *Sprechensie! Gebensie...* ! German for "Speak! Give!" (*sprechen Sie, geben Sie*).

That's how it is with me... It's a disaster having such a poor memory: I have to go back and forth twenty times... Your good health, sir! "

Hauptvakhtov cautiously opened the door, went outside, and took five steps before putting on his hat.

He cursed his memory and began thinking...

He began thinking about how his wife, daughter, and the little ones would come running up to him when he got home... His wife would examine what he had bought, berate him, call him some kind of animal, a donkey or a bull... The kids would pounce on the sweets and begin in a frenzy to spoil their already spoilt stomachs... Nadya would come and greet him in her blue dress with the pink scarf, and ask: "Did you buy the music?" On hearing "no," she would curse her old father, lock herself in her room, start howling, and not come and have lunch... Then she would emerge from her room and sit down at the piano in tears, heartbroken... At first she would play something mournful, and sing something, fighting back the tears... Towards evening Nadya would cheer up, and eventually, sighing deeply for the last time, she would play her favourite piece... "to-to-ti-to-to..."

Hauptvakhtov slapped himself on the forehead and ran straight back to the shop like a madman.

"To-to-ti-to-to, ohoho!" he cried out upon entering the shop. "I've remembered!! That's it! To-to-ti-to-to!"

"Ah... Now I understand. It's Liszt, Rhapsody Number Two*... *Hongroise* ..."⁴

"Yes, yes, yes... Liszt, Liszt! Well, I never did, Liszt! Number Two! Yes, yes, yes... My dear chap! That's the very one! My good friend!"

"Yes, Liszt is difficult to sing... Which do you want, the *original* or the *facilité*?"⁵

"Whichever! So long as it is Number Two, by Liszt! A troublemaker this Liszt is! To-to-ti-to... ha, ha, ha! I thought I'd never remember it! Just like that!"

The German pulled an edition down from the shelf, wrapped it up with lots of catalogues and advertisements, and gave the bundle to the beaming Haupvakhtov. Hauptvakhtov paid eighty-five kopecks and left, whistling.

---

4   *Hongroise*: "Hungarian"(French).
5   *facilité*: "easy version" (French).

Life in Questions and Exclamations

Childhood. Who has God blessed you with, a son or a daughter? How soon is the christening? What a big boy! Don't drop him, nurse! Oh, oh! He'll fall!! Has he cut his teeth? Is that eczema? Take the cat away from him, or it will scratch him! Have a tug at uncle's moustache! There! Don't cry! The bogeyman is coming! He is already walking! Take him out of here—he has no manners! What has he done to you?! Poor jacket! Well, never mind, we will dry it off! He's knocked over the inkwell! Go to sleep, poppet! He is already talking! Oh, what a joy! Come on then, say something! The coachmen nearly ran over him!! Sack the nanny! Don't stand in the draught! Shame on you, how can you smack such a small child? Don't cry! Give him some gingerbread!

Adolescence. You come here, I'm going to thrash you! How did you bash your nose? Don't disturb your Mama! You are not a baby! Don't come up to the table, your turn is later! Read! You don't know? Go and stand in the corner! Bottom marks for you! Don't put nails in your pocket! Why don't you obey your Mama? Eat properly! Don't pick your nose! Was it you who hit Mitya? You rascal! Read Krylov's fable *Demyan's Fish Soup** to me! What is the nominative plural of...? Add it up and subtract! Leave the class! No lunch for you! Time for bed! It's nine o'clock already! He is only naughty in front of guests! You're lying! Brush your hair! Leave the table! Come on then, show me your results! You've torn your boots already?! A big boy like you should be ashamed of bawling! How did you get your uniform dirty? You'll eat me out of house and home! Bottom marks again? When will I finally be able to stop thrashing you? If you are going to smoke, I will kick you out of the house! What is the superlative of *facilis?*[1] *Facilissimus?* You're lying! Who drank this wine? Children, they've brought a monkey into the yard! Why have you kept my son back a year? Grandma's arrived!

Youth. You are too young to drink vodka! Tell me about the sequence of tenses! It's much, much too early for you, young man! When I was your age, I had no idea about such things! Are you still scared of smoking in front of

---

1   *Facilis:* "easy" (Latin).

your father? Shame on you! Ninochka sends you her regards! Let's take Julius Caesar! Is it *ut consecutivum*[2] here? Oh, what a dear! Leave off, master, or I will... tell your Papa! Well well... you scoundrel! Bravo, I am already growing a moustache! Where? You drew it on, it's not growing there! Nadine has a charming chin! Which class are you in now? But, Papa, you have to agree that I cannot be without pocket money! Natasha? I know her! I've been to her place! So it's you? Oh, you kept that quiet! Give me a cigarette! Oh, if you knew how much I love her! She is a goddess! I will finish high school and I will marry her! It's none of your business, *maman*! I dedicate my verses to you! Leave me some smokes! I get drunk after just three shots! *Bis! Bis!* Braaavo! How come you haven't read George Born?* It's the sine, not the cosine! Where's the tangent? Sonka has bad legs! Can I kiss you? Shall we have a drink? Hooray, I've finished school! Add it to my bill! Lend me 25 roubles! I'm getting married, father! But I gave my word! Where did you spend the night?

Between 20 and 30 years of age. Lend me a hundred roubles! Which faculty? It's all the same to me! How much are you getting for the lecture? That's a bit cheap! All the way to Strelna* and back! *Bis, bis!* How much do I owe you? Come tomorrow! What's on at the theatre tonight? Oh, if you knew how much I love you! Yes or no? Yes? Oh my darling! Send him packing! Oi, barman! Do you drink sherry? Marya, bring us some gherkin brine! Is the editor in? I have no talent? That's strange! How will I make a living? Lend me five roubles! To the *Salon*! Gentlemen, dawn is breaking! I have dumped her! Lend me your tail coat! Yellow into the corner! I am already drunk, as it is! Doctor, I'm dying! Lend me some money for the medicine! I nearly died! Have I lost weight? Shall we go and eat at *Yar*?* It's worth it! Give me some work! Please! Aha... turns out you are just lazy! How can you be so late? It's not about the money! No sir, it is about the money! I'm going to kill myself!! This is the end! To hell with it and everything else! Farewell, foul existence! Actually... no! Is that you, Liza? I'm done for, *maman*! I've had a good run! Give me a job, Uncle! *Ma tante*, the carriage awaits you! *Merci, mon oncle*! I've changed, haven't I, *mon oncle*? Have I messed up? Ha-ha! Sign this document! Shall I get married? Never! Unfortunately, she is married! Your Excellency! Introduce me to your grandmother, Serge! You are enchanting, princess! You, old? Nonsense! You are fishing for compliments! Give me a seat in the second row!

---

2   *ut consecutivum*: "and consequently" (Latin).

Between 30—50 years of age. It fell through! Is there a vacancy? Nine without trumps! Seven of hearts! Your deal, *votre excellence.* You are terrible, doctor! I have a bloated liver? Rubbish! These doctors charge a fortune! How much is her dowry? You may not love her now, but you will grow to love her with time! Congratulations on your marriage! I can't live without gambling, my love! Gastric catarrh? Son or daughter? Spitting image of his father! He-he-he... I didn't know that! I've won, my love! I've lost again, damn it! Son or daughter? Spitting image... of his father! I swear to you, I don't know her! Stop being jealous! We're on our way, Fanny! A bracelet? Champagne! Congratulations on your promotion! *Merci!* What do you need to do to lose weight? Me, bald?! Stop nagging, mother-in-law! Son or daughter? I'm drunk, Karolinchen! Let me kiss you, my little German girl! That bounder is with my wife again! How many children do you have? Help a poor man out! What a charming daughter you have! They printed this in the newspapers, the devils! Come here, I'm going to thrash you, you nasty little boy! Was it you who crumpled my toupee?

Old age. Shall we go to the spa? Marry him, my daughter! He is stupid? Come, come! She may be a bad dancer, but she's got wonderful legs! A hundred roubles for... a kiss?! Oh, you little devil! He-he-he! Would you like some grouse, girl? You, son, have no... morals! You are out of line, young man! Shush! I ll... ove music! Bring shome sham... cham... pagne! Do you read the *Jester**? He-he-he! I've brought some sweets for the grandkids! My son is good, but I was better! Where have those days gone? I also haven't forgotten you in my will, dear Emmochka! That's me all over! Papashka, give me your watch! Dropsy? Really? May he enter the Kingdom of Heaven! Are his relatives crying? Mourning becomes her! He is giving off a smell! May you rest in peace, honest toiler!

Confession, or Olya, Zhenya, Zoya

(A Letter)

In your sweet letter, *ma chère*, my dear, unforgettable friend, you ask me among other things why I'm still not married, despite my 39 years.

My dear! I love family life with all my heart, and am not married only because wretched fate had no wish to see me married. I planned to get married about 15 times, but didn't, because everything in this world, and my life in particular, is subject to chance. Everything depends on it! Chance is a despot. Let me list a few of the chance incidents I have to thank for dragging out my life to this day as a miserable bachelor.

Incident Number One

It was a glorious morning in June. The sky was clear, like the clearest Prussian blue. The sun sparkled on the river, and its rays rippled along the dewy grass. The river and everything green seemed to be sprinkled with precious diamonds. The birds were singing as if from a score... We were walking along a little path sprinkled with yellow gravel, breathing in the fragrance of the June morning with happy chests. The trees were gazing down at us so affectionately, and whispering to us something which was no doubt extremely sweet and tender... The hand of Olya Gruzdovskaya[1] (who is now married to your district police chief's son) was resting in my hand, and her tiny little finger was trembling atop my thumb... Her little cheeks were flushed, and her eyes... Oh, *ma chère*, she had wonderful eyes! How much charm, truth, innocence, joy and child-like naiveté shone in those blue eyes! I was admiring her blond plaits and the small imprints left by her tiny little feet in the gravel...

"I have dedicated my life to science, Olga Maximovna," I whispered, fearing that her little finger might slide off my thumb. "A professorship awaits me in the future... There are questions on my conscience... scientific questions...

---

1   This surname is perhaps derived from the word for the milkcap mushroom (*gruzd'*).

A professional life, full of lofty concerns... how should I... Well, in a word, I will be a professor... I am being honest, Olga Maximovna... I am not rich, but... I need a partner who through her presence would (Olya lowered her eyes in embarrassment; her little finger began to tremble)... "who through her presence would... Olya! Look at the sky! It is clear... but my life is just as clear and limitless..."

My tongue had barely finished extricating itself from this nonsense when Olya raised her head, tore her hand away and began clapping. There were geese and goslings coming our way. Olya ran towards the geese and stretched out her hands to them with a loud chortle... Oh, what hands they were, *ma chère*!

"Honk... honk... honk...," said the geese, craning their necks and shooting Olya a sideways glance.

"Goosey, goosey, goosey," Olya cried, holding out her hand to a gosling.

The gosling was wise beyond its years. It fled from Olya's hand to its Papa, a very large and stupid gander, and clearly complained to him. The gander spread his wings. Mischievous Olya reached out towards another gosling. At that moment something terrible happened. The gander bent his neck towards the ground and started walking threateningly towards Olya, hissing like a snake. Olya squealed and ran back. The gander pursued her. Olya looked around, squealed some more and turned pale. Her beautiful, innocent little face was contorted in terror and despair. It seemed as if three hundred demons were after her.

I hastened to her aid and hit the gander on the head with my cane. The wretched gander had nevertheless managed to nip the hem of her dress. Wide eyed and face contorted, Olya fell on to my chest, trembling all over...

"What a cowardly girl you are!" I said.

"Give that goose a beating!" she said and burst into tears...

There was so much that was idiotic and not at all naïve or child-like in that frightened little face! *Ma chère*, I cannot stand pusillanimity! I cannot imagine myself married to a pusillanimous, cowardly woman!

The gander ruined the whole thing... Once I'd calmed Olya down, I went home, and I could not get her pusillanimous, almost idiotic little face out of my head... Olya lost all her charm in my eyes. I rejected her.

The Next Incident

You know of course, my friend, that I am a writer. The gods have ignited the sacred fire in my breast, and I do not believe I have the right not to take up the pen. I am Apollo's high priest... Everything, down to each beat of my heart, and every sigh, in short, my entire self, has been sacrificed on the altar of the muses. I write and write and write... Take away my pen and I am a dead man. You are laughing, you don't believe me... I swear, this is the truth!

But you know of course, *ma chère*, that this planet is a bad place for art. The earth is great and abundant, but it has no place for the writer. The writer is an eternal orphan, an outcast, a scapegoat, a defenceless child... I divide humanity into two categories: writers and those who envy them. The former write, while the latter die of envy and play dirty tricks on them. I've been ruined, am being ruined now, and will continue to be ruined by those who are envious. They have spoiled my life. They have taken the reins of power in literary matters into their hands, they call themselves editors and publishers, and they try with all their might to drown our brotherhood. A curse on them!

Now listen...

For a while I courted Zhenya Pshikova.[2] You will of course remember that sweet, raven-haired, dreamy child... She is now married to your neighbour Karl Ivanovich Wanze (à propos: in German, Wanze means... bedbug. Don't tell that to Zhenya, she'll be offended). Zhenya loved the writer in me. She believed in my life's purpose as devoutly as I did. She shared my hopes with me. But she was young! She did not yet understand the above-mentioned division of humanity into two categories! She didn't believe in this division! She didn't believe in it, and one fine day... disaster struck.

I was staying at the Pshikovs' dacha. They considered me a bridegroom, and Zhenya my bride. I wrote, and she read. What a critic she was, *ma chère*! She was just as fair-minded as Aristides, and as strict as Cato.* I dedicated all my works to her... One of these works Zhenya liked very much indeed. She wanted to see it in print. So I sent it to one of the comic journals. I sent it on the first of July and awaited the response two weeks later. The 15th of July arrived. Zhenya and I received the issue we'd been waiting for. We rushed to open it and read the response in the editorial mailbox. She blushed and I blanched. The following words addressed to me were printed in the editorial mailbox: "To Mr. M. D-ov, village of Shlendovo—You don't have an ounce of talent in

---

2   This surname contains the informal word for "nothing" (*pshik*).

you. The devil knows what this gibberish of yours is all about! Don't waste your stamps and leave us in peace. Find something else to do."

How stupid... It's clear now that dimwits wrote that.

"Mmm..." mumbled Zhenya.

"What wretched scoun-drels!" I muttered. "How do you like that? Perhaps now, Yevgenia Markovna, you will appreciate my division of humanity?"

Zhenya stopped to think and let out a yawn.

"Who knows?" she said. "Perhaps you really don't have talent! They should know. Last year Fyodor Fedoseyevich took me fishing the whole summer, while you do nothing but write and write... It's so boring!"

How do you like that? And this after sleepless nights spent writing and reading together! After our mutual sacrifice to the muses... Eh?

Zhenya lost interest in my writing and, consequently, in me. We separated. It couldn't have been otherwise...

Incident Number Three

You know of course, my unforgettable friend, of my great love for music. Music is my passion, my element... Mozart, Beethoven, Chopin, Mendelssohn, Gounod... these are names not of people, but of giants! I love classical music. Operetta I reject as a genre, as I reject vaudeville. I am one of the most faithful opera-goers. Khokhlov, Kochetova, Bartsal, Usatov, Korsov...* wondrous people! How I regret not being acquainted with singers! If I were acquainted with them, I would pour out my soul in gratitude to them. Last winter I went to the opera particularly often. I didn't go alone, but with the Pepsinov family. It's a shame you don't know this lovely family! The Pepsinovs reserve a box every winter. They are devoted to music, heart and soul... The crowning ornament of this lovely family is Colonel Pepsinov's[3] daughter Zoya. What a girl she is, my dear! Her little pink lips alone are enough to make a man like me lose his mind! She's slim, beautiful, clever... I loved her... I loved her madly, passionately, deeply! My blood raced whenever I sat next to her. You are smiling, *ma chère*... Go on, smile! You have no idea of a writer's love; it is alien to you... A writer's love is Etna plus Vesuvius. Zoya loved me. Her eyes were

---

3   Chekhov perhaps had in mind the enzyme pepsin when creating this surname (Theodor Schwann gave it a name derived from the Greek word for "digestion" when he discovered it in 1836).

always resting on my eyes, which were constantly fixed on her eyes... We were happy. The wedding was just one step away...

But then disaster struck.

It was at a performance of *Faust*. *Faust*, my dear, was written by Gounod, and Gounod is a truly great musician. On my way to the theatre, I decided to declare my love to Zoya during the first act, which I don't understand. The great Gounod wrote the first act for nothing!

The performance began. Zoya and I had retired to the foyer. She was sitting next to me and playing absent-mindedly with her fan, trembling with anticipation and joy. In the evening light, *ma chère*, she was beautiful, terribly beautiful!

"The overture has prompted me to make certain reflections, Zoya Yegorovna..." I said, declaring my love; "so much emotion, so much... You listen and you yearn... You yearn for a certain something and you listen..."

I hiccupped and continued:

"A certain something special... You yearn for something unearthly... Love? Passion? Yes, that must be it... love..." (I hiccupped.) "Yes, love..."

Zoya smiled, became flustered and started waving her fan frantically. I hiccupped. I can't stand hiccups!

"Zoya Yegorovna! Tell me, I beg you! Is that feeling familiar to you?" (I hiccupped.) "Zoya Yegorovna! Answer me!"

"I... I... don't understand you..."

"I've got an attack of hiccups... It'll pass... I'm talking about this all-encompassing feeling which is... what the devil!"

"Have a drink of water!"

"I'll finish declaring my love and then I'll go to the bar," I thought to myself and continued:

"I'll be brief, Zoya Yegorovna... You of course have noticed..."

I hiccupped and was so annoyed with hiccupping that I bit my tongue.

"Of course, you have noticed..." (I hiccupped.) "You've known me for about a year... Hm... I'm an honest man, Zoya Yegorovna! I work hard! It's true, I'm not rich, but..."

I hiccupped and jumped up.

"You should drink some water!" Zoya advised.

I took a few steps round the sofa, pressed my fingers against my throat and hiccupped again. *Ma chère*, I was in a most terrible predicament! Zoya got up and headed to the box. I followed. When I was letting her into the box,

I hiccupped and ran off to the bar. I drank about five glasses of water, and the hiccupping seemed to quieten down a bit. I smoked a cigarette and went to the box. Zoya's brother got up and gave me his seat—the seat next to my Zoya. I sat down and immediately... hiccupped. About five minutes passed and I hiccupped, hiccupped in a peculiar kind of way with a wheeze. I got up and went to stand by the door of the box. It is better, *ma chère*, to hiccup near the door than into the ear of the woman you love! I hiccupped. A schoolboy in the neighbouring box looked at me and started laughing loudly... How he enjoyed laughing, the little rotter! And how I would have enjoyed tearing off that young bastard's ear, root and all! He was laughing, while on stage they were singing the great *Faust*! What sacrilege! No, *ma chère*, when we were children, we were much better behaved. Cursing the insolent schoolboy, I hiccupped again... People started laughing in the neighbouring boxes.

"*Bis!*" the schoolboy hissed.

"What the devil... !" Colonel Pepsinov muttered into my ear. "You could have hiccupped at home, sirrah!"

Zoya blushed. I hiccupped again, and ran out of the box, clenching my fists furiously. I began walking up and down the corridor. I walked and walked and walked, but kept hiccupping. I ate all sorts of things, drank all sorts of things. At the start of the fourth act I called it quits and went home. When I arrived home, as if out of spite, I stopped hiccupping... I hit myself on the back of the head and exclaimed:

"Go on, hiccup! You can hiccup now, you hissed-out groom! No, you weren't hissed out! You didn't hiss yourself out... you hiccupped yourself out!"

The next day I visited the Pepsinovs as usual. Zoya did not appear for lunch and left word that she couldn't see me as she was indisposed, while Pepsinov droned on about how some young people were incapable of behaving themselves with decorum in public... Blockhead! He doesn't know that the organs that produce hiccups are not subject to volitional stimuli.

Stimulus, *ma chère*, means impulse.

"Would you give your daughter away, if you happened to have a daughter," Pepsinov turned to me after lunch, "to a man who allows himself to belch in public? Eh? What do you say, sir?"

"Yes, I would..." I mumbled.

"You'd be wrong!"

That was it for Zoya and me. She couldn't forgive my hiccups. I was done for.

Should I describe the remaining twelve incidents for you?

I would describe them but... enough! The veins on my temples are swollen, tears are gushing from my eyes, my liver is churning... Brother writers, something fatal lies in our destiny!* *Ma chère,* allow me to wish you all the best. I press your hand and send greetings to your Paul. I have heard that he is a good husband and father... More power to him! It's a shame that he's a hard drinker (that is not a reproach, *ma chère!*). Stay well and happy, *ma chère,* and don't forget your most faithful servant

Makar Baldastov.[4]

---

4   Comic surname derived from *balda,* an informal word meaning "blockhead."

The Greeting Of Spring

(A Treatise)

Zephyrus has taken over from Boreas.* There is a breeze blowing either from the west or the south (I am a recent arrival in Moscow and have not fathomed the cardinal direction here yet), it is blowing gently, barely brushing against my coat tails... It is not chilly, in fact it is so un-chilly that one can boldly go out in a coat and hat, with a cane. There is no frost, even at night. The snow has melted and turned into turbid water, tumbling down with a gurgle from mountains and hillocks into dirty ditches; the only places it has not melted are the lanes and side streets, where it rests serenely under an earthy brown layer five inches thick, and will continue to rest there right until May... Green grass is timidly springing up in the fields and the forests, and on the boulevards... The trees are still completely bare, yet they look more cheerful somehow. The sky is so lovely, clear and bright; only occasionally do rainclouds appear and release fine drops on to the ground... The sun shines so agreeably, so warmly and affectionately, as if it had drunk famously, eaten heartily and seen an old friend... There is a smell of young grass, manure, smoke, mould, every kind of rubbish imaginable, the steppe and something else quite distinctive... Wherever one looks, nature is abuzz with preparations, chores, endless cooking... The fact is that spring is fast approaching.

The public, who have become awfully tired of forking out for fire-wood, walking about in heavy fur-coats and galoshes that weigh ten pounds, and breathing bitingly cold air one moment, and indoor bathhouse fug the next, joyously, eagerly stand on tiptoes, stretching out their arms to greet the approaching spring. Spring is a welcome guest, but is she kind? How can I put it? In my opinion she is neither particularly kind nor particularly malevolent. In any case, she is eagerly anticipated.

Poets young and old, good and bad, have left book-keepers, bankers, railway workers and cuckolded husbands in peace for a while and are furiously scribbling madrigals, dithyrambs, salutatory odes, ballads and other rhyming things, rhapsodising over every single one of spring's delights... As usual, they are rhapsodising badly (present company excepted). The moon, the air, the haze, the horizon, desires, and "the beloved" are always centre stage for them.

Prose writers are also poetically tuned. Their features, diatribes and accolades begin and end with a description of their own feelings, imbued by the approaching spring.

Young ladies and suitors... They endure mortal suffering! Their pulse rate is 190 beats a minute, their temperature is ardent. Their hearts are full of the sweetest trepidation... Spring brings love in its wake, and love brings "So much happiness, so much torment!" Spring keeps Cupid on a leash in the picture we are painting. And rightly so. Love also requires discipline, otherwise what would happen if spring were to let Cupid loose, and set the scoundrel free? I am a thoroughly serious person, but thanks to the smells of Spring, even my head becomes filled with all sorts of devilry. I write, and lo, shady paths, little fountains, birds, "the beloved" and all that kind of things appear before my eyes. My mother-in-law has already started looking at me suspiciously, and my dear wife constantly lingers by the window...

Medical people are very serious people, yet even they cannot sleep peacefully... They're stifled by nightmares and have the most captivating dreams. The cheeks of doctors, medical assistants and pharmacists are flushed with a feverish glow. And no wonder! There are fetid mists floating above the cities, and these mists consist of microorganisms that cause illness... Chests, throats and teeth ache... Chronic cases of rheumatism, gout, and neuralgia flare up. There are countless multitudes of consumptives. The crush in pharmacies is terrible. The poor pharmacists have no time to either have lunch or drink tea. Berthollet salt, Dover's powder, herbal chest remedies, iodine and idiotic tooth treatments are sold literally by the pound. As I write I can hear the jingle of 5-kopeck coins at the pharmacy next door. My mother-in-law has gumboils on both sides of her jaw: a proper monster!

Small-time businessmen, pawnbrokers, bloodsuckers, Jews* and kulaks* are gleefully dancing a cachucha.* Spring is a benefactor for them too. A thousand fur coats are deposited with pawnbrokers, to be devoured by hungry moths. Anything warm that has still not lost its value is taken to Jewish benefactors. If you don't trade in your fur coat, you'll end up with no summer clothes and you'll have to parade about in your beaver or raccoon fur at the dacha. For my fur coat, which is worth at least 100 roubles, the pawnbroker gave me 32 roubles.

Berdichev, Zhitomir, Rostov, and Poltava* are knee-deep in mud. Sticky, brown, smelly mud... Passers-by sit at home and don't show their face outside; one look and you'll drown in the devil only knows what. You'll leave behind in the mud not only your galoshes, but your boots and socks too. If you have to, go outside either barefoot, or on stilts, but better still, just stay put. To be fair, you won't leave your boots in the mud in Mother Moscow, but you will definitely fill your galoshes with it. There are only a handful of places in Moscow where you will be parted for good from your galoshes (they are the corner of Kuznetsky and Petrovka Streets, Trubnaya Square and almost every other square). You won't get from one village to another, either by cart or on foot.

Everyone and everything is getting ready to go out and make merry save adolescents and youths. The young cannot see beyond exams as far as spring. All of May will be devoted to passing with flying colours or flunking. Spring is an unwelcome guest for flunkers.

Wait a while, about 5 or 6 days, a week at most, and the tomcats will start to howl louder below windows, the gooey mud will become thick, the buds on the trees will become fluffy, the grass will poke through everywhere, the sun will start to bake, and spring will come properly to life. Caravans of carts will stretch out from Moscow, loaded with furniture, flowers, straw mattresses and maids. Vegetable growers and gardeners will start to potter about... Hunters will begin to load their guns.

Wait a week or so, be patient, and in the meantime wrap your chests in sturdy bandages, so that your impassioned hearts which can brook no delay do not jump out...

By the way, how would you like me to depict spring on paper? In what form? In times gone by, she was portrayed as a beautiful maiden, scattering flowers over the ground. Flowers are a synonym for joy... Now times have changed, morals have changed, and spring has changed. She is also depicted as a young lady these days. She is not scattering flowers, though, for there are no flowers, and her hands are in a muff. She should be portrayed as gaunt, thin, and skeletal, with a consumptive flush, but let her be *comme il faut*! We'll grant her that concession, just because she's a lady.

Alarm Clock Almanac

For March–April 1882

Date and day of the week	Notable events, meteorology, predictions, world history, commerce, advice, recipes, and so on	Menu
8 Monday / Lundi / Montag	A great man will be born. Eclipse of the sun visible only in the town of Bakhmut, Yekaterinoslav province. Mental unrest on the island of Madagascar. The sun enters ● at 7.35 a.m. Frost and snow. Nothing in particular will occur regarding comets and planets. Yesterday there was a new moon. Sunrise is at 6.01 a.m. The same sun sets at 6.14 p.m. On this day Autolimedes II was defeated by the Persian Tsar Dodon IV* (in 342) and the Judgement of Paris took place.	1) Soup with oranges. 2) Canard *frit*. 3) Kasha* with burdock oil. 4) Chestnut jelly.
9 Tuesday / Mardi / Dienstag	The beginning of spring. Youths and young maidens, in agonising anticipation of happy days ahead, suffer heart palpitations (*affectio cordis;*[1] prescribed treatment: *kalium bromatum,*[2] *valeriana*[3] and ice). A fair in the village of Voznesensk. There will be no solar eclipse. Thaw and snow. A great writer will be born in Spain who will die on the 7th day after his birth. Sunrise at 5.58 a.m. The same sun sets at 6.16 p.m. Many years ago on this day there was a scientific revival (1441).	1) Pea soup with beans. 2) Fried goose à la Prince Meshchersky.* 3) Fried lemons in sauce. 4) Seedless grapes in vinegar.

---

1   *affectio cordis*: "heart attack" (Latin).

2   *kalium bromatum*: "potassium bromide" (Latin).

3   *valeriana*: "valerian drops" (Latin).

Date and day of the week	Notable events, meteorology, predictions, world history, commerce, advice, recipes, and so on	Menu
10 Wednesday / Mercredi / Mittwoch	Everyone will be happy. In the town of Lebedyan, Tambov province, a star with two tails and one wing will be visible: the sign of a failed potato crop. Frost. Hail in Algeria. A certain cashier will be captured. Fairs: in Alapayevsk, Perm province (chintz, wheels, needles, tar and raisins), in Samara, Samara province (mare's milk, felt and guitars), and in Rzhev, Tver province (plates, knives, forks, salt-cellars and snuff boxes). Sunrise at 5.55 a.m. The same sun sets at 6.19 p.m. On this day Pan Twardowski* died in the "Rome" inn (1811), and Caesar crossed the Rubicon (54).	1) "Little Russian"* cabbage soup. 2) Fried oysters. 3) Nightingale tongue sauce. 4) Maiden skin.
11 Thursday / Jeundi / Donnerstag	Along the Kursk-Kharkov-Azov railway line, a train near 'Collision!' station will be snowed under. Blizzard. In the city of Konotop, Chernigov province, an impostor will appear, claiming to be Hamlet,* the Danish prince. Astronomers are discovering something extraordinary on the moon. Diphtheria on the island of Borneo. Sunrise at 5.52 a.m. The same sun sets at 6.21 p.m. On this day Antony fell in love with Cleopatra (42), while Alexander Philipovich of Macedon* rode Bucephalus on pilgrimage (312).	1) Spineless chicken soup. 2) Stuffed cuttlefish. 3) Crayfish brains with mushrooms. 4) Belozersk smelt fish with vanilla.
12 Friday / Vendredi / Freitag	There will be a decline in morality in Shanghai. Thaw. Moscow barristers will dream of Themis with the long shears used in Professor Sklifosovsky's clinic for amputating swollen tongues. The barristers will grow pale and experience pangs of guilt.	1) Electric eel sour soup. 2) Suckling pig with horseradish.

continuation of the table ⟶

Date and day of the week	Notable events, meteorology, predictions, world history, commerce, advice, recipes, and so on	Menu
	No fair in Syzran. Universal Deluge in Na-khichevan. It will be drafty in Taganrog. In Shuya, Vladimir province there will be an earthquake which will soon be halted by the efforts of the local authorities. Sunrise at 5.48 a.m. The same sun sets at 6.24 p.m. On this day, in the year 148, Gaius Mucius 'Scaevola' lost his hand at cards.	3) Suckling pig without horseradish. 4) Horseradish without suck-ling pig. 5) Fried pine-apples with asparagus. 6) Rosin ice cream.
13 Saturday / Samedi / Son-nabend	A great man will be born. Gladstone will dine with the king of the Ashanti* and dis-cuss the state of affairs in China with him; the king of the Ashanti will give him an am-biguous reply. 25 ships will sink in Bukha-ra. Universal bewilderment in Carthage. The name day of all Africans. According to the actors of the Maly Theatre,* on this day the Northern Lights will be visible in Pol-tava, Poltava Province. Sunrise at 5.45 a.m. The same sun sets at 6.26 p.m. Vesuvius erupts at 8.32 a.m.	1) Consommé with saffron. 2) Boiled pork with Turkish delight. 3) Bay leaf in sauce. 4) Fig signs.
14 Sunday / Dimanche / Sontag	The management of the Kursk-Kharkov-Azov railway line will send a courier to "Collision!" station to find out whether the snow which buried the train on the 11th has melted. A great woman will be born. Solar eclipse and drought at the *Citizen* editorial office. A scholarly debate at a club in Tomsk about "which sea is the largest" and "which city is the smallest." The argu-ment will end in fisticuffs and police inter-vention. Sunrise at 5.42 a.m. The same sun	1) Ivory con-sommé. 2) Peas à la the *Jester* on lard. 3) Locusts with cloves. 4) Cherry lau-rel drops with poppy seed.

continuation of the table ➜

Date and day of the week	Notable events, meteorology, predictions, world history, commerce, advice, recipes, and so on	Menu
	sets at 6.29 p.m. On this day (1112), Othello strangled his wife Desdemona, while Authari, king of the Lombards, pressed the little finger of his bride, the demure Theodelinda* (738).	

Almanac Footnotes

1) All Almanacs lie, with the exception of ours.

2) The Almanac will continue to be published throughout 1882. We began it on 8th March because we foresaw that absolutely nothing would occur in January, February or the beginning of March, with the exception of those Tuesdays, Thursdays and so on that everyone is so fed up with. For reasons unknown to the Almanac editor, there was not even a 29th or 30th day this February.

3) It would be advisable to organise an Almanac Congress in some city or other as quickly as possible, so that:

a) Mr. Stalinsky* can attend as the Russian representative. The latter will explain to the Congress the motives behind which he, Stalinsky, dated one of the 1880 issues of the now defunct *Kharkov* newspaper as 30 February;

b) those born on 29th February can attend, in order to hear from Congress whether it is right that an honourable man should be prevented from celebrating his birthday each year. The Congress will either grant permission for the said dates to exist each year, or will indicate a date on which those born on 29th February could celebrate their birthday annually.

4) Those finding any sort of falsehood in the Almanac or wishing to share the fruits of their ability to prophesy and foretell are kindly requested to send their indications (in writing) to the *Alarm Clock* editorial office, marked for the attention of the Almanac editor.

5) Two professors of black magic and one professor of white magic have been hired to compile the Almanac. The Almanac editor is seeking a somnambulist or fortune-teller for the same task. The latter's salary is 1200 roubles per annum.

Editor, *Alarm Clock* Almanac

Antosha Chekhonte

Date and day of the week	Notable events, meteorology, predictions, world history, commerce, advice, recipes, and so on	Menu
15 Monday / Lundi / Montag	There will be no Northern Lights. In the town of Nezhyn, Poltava Province, two Ukrainians will drown in the mud while, Mondays apart, nothing will occur in the other cities of the Russian Empire. A great obstetrician will be born on the island of Madagascar. Out of boredom, the wives of two Zamoskvoretsky merchants will devour 16 kilograms of buckwheat and fall ill (course of treatment: Ol. Ricini[4] 300.0 grams per dose, Nux vomica[5] and diet). Fairs: in Stockholm, Stockholm province (Swedish matches, Swedish girls and cardboard) and in Pinega (smelt and tar). Fog. Sunrise at 5.39 a.m. Sunset at 6.31 p.m. On this day in the year 132 BC, Menelaus made the acquaintance of both Ajaxes* in an Athenian club, while the Germans invented the ape (1201 AD).	1) Spartan stew. 2) Fried drake spleen. 3) Boiled stork. 4) Its giblets. 5) Gingerbread ponies.
16 Tuesday / Mardi / Dienstag	On this day, conductors and signalmen on the A.B.C. Railway will for some reason be sober. Pyotr Boborykin's birthday.* Kursk nightingales are flying back to Kursk from abroad. Sowing begins in some parts of the Don region. The Astronomer Bredikhin will report to the mathematics society about two Jews he observed on the planet Saturn, who, in his opinion, ran off to that planet in order to dodge military service. Volcanic eruption in Tambov. A collision between a comet and Mr. Lentovsky.* Heavy snow. Fairs: in Makaryev, Kostroma	1) Cabbage soup with goldfinches. 2) Fried hawfinches. 3) Siskins in sauce. 4) Thoracic tea with honey. 5) Bullfinch ice-cream.

continuation of the table ⟶

---

4   *Ol. Ricini*: "castor oil" (Latin).

5   *Nux vomica*: "poison nut" (Latin).

Date and day of the week	Notable events, meteorology, predictions, world history, commerce, advice, recipes, and so on	Menu
	province (wooden spoons. Takings will be 7 roubles, 12 kopecks). Sunrise at 5.36 a.m. The same sun sets at 6.32 p.m. On this day Archimedes would have moved the earth if he had been given a fulcrum (312).	(this menu is called *The Choristers' dinner* in Madame Olga Molokhovets' *Classic Russian Cooking).**
17 Wednes- day / Mercredi / Mittwoch	The transit of Venus across the face of the sun will occur at the *Kaluga Provincial Ga- zette* editorial office. Name days: Messrs. Potekhin, Suvorin and the folk hero Al- yosha-Popovich.* Bloch will experience pangs of guilt,* but will not return what was stolen on this day or any other in the future. The Moscow Society of Acclima- tization will award the Baker Filippov* a medal for cultivating the best breeds of mice and cockroaches. On the Mos- cow-Brest Railway there will be a collisi- on... between the chief guard and a station master. Sunrise at 5.33 a.m. The same sun sets at 6.36 p.m. Abstraction. In Berdichev, there will be a refraction of light. On this day the Tsar of Persia Kardashian LX was defeated by Field-Marshal Kucheleba[6] (803).	1) Consommé with gravy. 2) Goat with currants. 3) Side of lamb with kasha. 4) Vermicelli with macaroni. 5) Johann Hoff Chocolate.

continuation of the table ➡

---

6   A parodic name derived from the Russian word for strychnine (*kuchelaba*), which was sold in the grocery shop run by Chekhov's father alongside buckwheat, soap, raisins, bay leaves and cigars.

Date and day of the week	Notable events, meteorology, predictions, world history, commerce, advice, recipes, and so on	Menu
18 Thursday / Jeudi / Donnerstag	Gladstone will lose his temper with the king of the Ashanti; the king of the Ashanti will make a vehement speech. There will be a vehement leading article in the *Don Bee* about the Israelites crossing the Red Sea. A battle of the elements in Tiraspol. It is our subscriber No. 18007's name day. The Pacific Ocean becomes ice-free; navigation resumes. A fair in Australia. Cold as hell. Sunrise at 5.30 a.m. The same sun set at 6.38 p.m. On this day in Saratov, Saratov province, Coverley was murdered (807; see the play *The Murder of Coverley*).*	1) Day-old cabbage soup with snipe. 2) Savoury pie made from Nestle flour. 3) Pea sausage with onion. 4) Sheep's head stuffed with sheep's brains. 5) Excellent blancmange.
19 Friday / Vendredi / Freitag	Three animals will die of 'not your aunt'* at the Zoo. Perturbation of minds at the Salamonsky circus.* In the town of Kineshma an honourable woman will give birth to sextuplets, all six of whom will in time grow up to be professors of black magic. Earthquake on the moon. There are, regrettably, no fairs anywhere. Sunrise at 5.27 a.m. The same sun sets at 6.41 p.m. Snowstorm, blizzard and winds. On this day Hannibal played checkers with his uncle Hamilcar (303).	1) Easy-cook cabbage soup Swabian style. 2) Stuffed sperm whale. 3) Fried vinegar. 4) Mushroom pudding.
20 Saturday / Samedi / Sonnabend	A 5% inc. in cap. gains from the circ. of dividends of the Anglo-Dutch loan bonds and the bonds of the Shuisko-Ivanovsk and Ryazan-Kozlovsky railways. The director of a certain bank will take a back seat. Warsaw munic. cred. bonds and shares Poti-Tiflis railway. Cutting of coupons at Bloch's office. Mr. Lokhvitsky's birthday.* Morning fog. There is a thaw at the *Kostroma*	1) Soup with stuffing. 2) Lamb cutlets with stuffing. 3) Brie with stuffing.

continuation of the table ➤

Date and day of the week	Notable events, meteorology, predictions, world history, commerce, advice, recipes, and so on	Menu
	Gazette editorial office. Sunrise at 5.24 a.m. She same sun sets at 6.43 p.m. On this day in 703 the Chinese defeated the Swedes on the island of Iceland.	4) Crayfish jelly with stuffing.
21 Sunday / Dimanche / Sonntag	Concert at the Theatre, concert at the Assembly Hall of the Nobility,* concert at the Manège and so on: 23 concerts in all. A clear day. A very clement day. Spring is in the air. Fairs: in Valdai (Valdai bells, jingle bells). The king of the Ashanti will lunch with Edison; Edison will give his opinion and resign. Skirmish between insurgents and émigrés on the island of Formosa. Bewilderment in Rybinsk. Sunrise at 5.21 a.m. The same sun sets at 6.45 p.m. On this day Savonarola predicted the birth of Dr. Lokhvitsky to Moscow barristers (1708). The end of the week. Issue No. 12 of the *Alarm Clock* goes on sale.	1) Lentils with beans. 2) Stuffing. 3) Gravy. 4) A side dish. 5) Stewed Adam's apples.

Almanac footnotes

1) Daily occurrences: morning, noon, evening: concerts, cases of fish poisoning, fire, scandal involving horse-drawn tram, leading articles, brilliant circus performances, the quartermaster's trial and Prince Meshchersky's feeble wit.

2) To Madame Olga Molokhovets: you have written to tell us that our menus are simply delicious, and have asked us to allow you to reprint these menus in your *Gift to Young Housewives*. By all means!

3) Those finding any sort of falsehood in the Almanac or wishing to share the fruits of their ability to prophesy and foretell are kindly requested to send their indications (in writing) to the *Alarm Clock* editorial office, marked for the attention of the Almanac editor.

4) To the Head Chef, editorial offices of *Kind Soul*,* Petersburg: Totally inedible and tasteless. Too bland, rancid and indigestible. More salt and less garlic.

5) To the *Rus** editorial offices: Merci. The kvass* is lovely. We'll recommend it. You write that kvass without cockroaches is a foreign contrivance. We do not agree with you. The answer is to strain it. Have the jugs washed: their putrescent smell is worse than the West!

Date and day of the week	Notable events, meteorology, predictions, world history, commerce, advice, recipes, and so on	Menu
22 Monday / Lundi / Montag	Singers, songstresses, pianists, choirmasters, theatre organ grinders and music agents are stuffing their suitcases with the gold they earned during Lent; a great joy fills their great hearts. *Au revoir* to the Strelna restaurant* until next winter. The weather is warm: +6 R., +7.5 C and 42° F. The secretary of the editorial offices of the *Kaluga Gazette* will lose his fur hat. Sunrise at 5.18 a.m; the same sun sets at 6.48 p.m.	1) *La-soupe-delicatesse.* 2) Strasbourg pie with cabbage. 3) Swans' necks in sauce. 4) Vanilla jelly with soya.
23 Tuesday / Mardi / Dienstag	There is a whiff of spring and the devil knows what else. Moscow is reminiscent of Venice with its quantities of excess water. We recommend that the city council go boating along Kuznetsky Bridge Street for charity. It is Misha Evstigneev's birthday.* Our lady-subscribers with name days today are: Nos 19012 and 13444. Fair in the town of Krasnoborsk, Vologda province (door latches and samovar pipes). Sunrise at 5.15 a.m. The same sun sets at 6.50 p.m. On this day Diogenes committed an indecent act in the presence of a Chinese envoy (303).	1) Radish Consommé. 2) Cayenne pepper with raisins. 3) Fried fluff. 4) Stewed trout.

continuation of the table ➝

Date and day of the week	Notable events, meteorology, predictions, world history, commerce, advice, recipes, and so on	Menu
24 Wednes-day / Mercredi / Mittwoch	The Donetsk Coal Mining Railway,* which carries fare-dodgers instead of coal, is to be renamed the Donetsk-Dodgers Railway. One-hundred and twenty-one great men will be born. Fair in Velizh, Vitebsk province (shafts, chisels and dolls). Zola, Shchedrin and Boborykin, who suffered defeat at the hands of the arch-oddball I. N. Pavlov,* will quit writing and take up the grocery trade. Sunrise 5.12 a.m. The same sun sets at 6.53 p.m. A decline in the arts and sciences in the town of Zvenigorod, Moscow province. On this day, the Russians, to the surprise of all foreigners, invented the samovar (1402).	1) Sauerkraut soup with pheasant. 2) Goldfish mayonnaise. 3) Fried ground squirrels. 4) Kvass *à la Russe* (strained about twenty times).
25 Thursday / Jeudi / Donner-stag	A good day. Everyone will be happy, apart from Prince Meshchersky and Prince Batalin,* who are always down in the dumps. On this day in the town of Syzran the age of pile dwellings will begin. From now on, *Rus* will be published with Church Slavonic Contractions. Messrs. Sadovsky, Musil and Pravdin* are to be transferred to Petersburg. The floors are being swept and locks are being cleaned in the theatres. In the town of Zhitomir, mud has brought to a halt the flow of... thoughts. Sunrise at 5.09 a.m. The same sun sets at 6.55 p.m. On this day in 132 in Portugal, nothing in particular happened.	1) Cabbage soup with parrots. 2) Tongue with peas. 3) Web-footed goose sauté. 4) Sugar water. 5) Spring water. (Olga Molokhovets calls this menu the "lawyers' dinner".)

continuation of the table ➤

Date and day of the week	Notable events, meteorology, predictions, world history, commerce, advice, recipes, and so on	Menu
26 Friday / Vendredi / Freitag	Mothers-in-law, wives, Mamas, aunties and grandmas will be baking *kulich* and *paskha** for Easter, shouting, arguing, and demanding money from the male sex, and driving everyone out of the house. Gentlemen, dandies and caballeros will be strolling along Kuznetsky Most Street, since it's spring cleaning at home. A touch of frost in the morning, but warm during the day. Name days: the poet Khrushchov-Sokolnikov,* our subscriber number 17037, and the late Derzhavin. Fair in the hamlet of Trofimov, London province. The secretary of the editorial offices of the *Kaluga Gazette* will find his hat, which he lost on the 22nd. Sunrise at 5.06 a.m. The same sun sets at 6.57 p.m. On this day Alexander Pushkin and Vissarion Belinsky were given bottom marks for their lack of ability in studying Russian literature.	1) Starfish soup. 2) Chinese style salanga. 3) Sautéed shark. 4) Boiled sweets.
27 Saturday / Samedi / Sonnabend	Eggs are painted in kitchens with inedible and edible dyes. Endless preparations for the following day. At laundries, tailors, and the establishments of *madames* all hell is let loose. Woe to all simpleton husbands and respectful sons-in-law: they will waste away running errands! Editors will look over the latest proofs and then rest on their laurels until Tuesday. In the town of Kineshma, Kostroma province, there will be no fair due to the absence of any goods. Strong sales of kopeck stamps. Mr. Gladstone's birthday. Sunrise at 5:03 a.m. The same sun sets at 7:00 p.m. A small snow storm in Arkhangelsk. On this day the	1) Shot of vodka. 2) Day-old cabbage soup with yesterday's kasha. 3) 2 shots of vodka. 4) Suckling pig with horseradish. 5) 3 shots of vodka. 6) Horseradish, cayenne

continuation of the table ⟶

Date and day of the week	Notable events, meteorology, predictions, world history, commerce, advice, recipes, and so on	Menu
	Sirens tried to lure King Odysseus with their song (812).	pepper, and soya. 7) 4 shots of vodka. 8) 8 bottles of beer. (In all cookery books this menu is called *The Journalists' Lunch*.)
28 Sunday / Lundi / Montag	An extremely bright, radiant, lengthy and most festive day... Bell-ringing, kisses, guests, snacks and shots. Everyone is celebrating, except for the postmen who... are run off their feet. The post office delivers one and a half tons of greeting cards. Many people are drunk, few are sober. The high and mighty take it easy, the underlings are panting with exhaustion from signing their names in the entrance halls of the high and mighty. The sky is pure, the sky is clear. While exchanging three Easter kisses with the merchant Baldastov's wife, lieutenant Akhakhaev[7] will scratch the latter's lips with his moustache, resulting in disfigurement. Sunrise at 5:00 a.m. The same sun sets at 7:02 p.m.	Instead of lunch it is customary to have an all-day, grandiose, colossal, chaotic chewing and swallowing of eggs, gammon, Easter cakes, snacks, wine, vodka *et cetera* ... Everyone will eat until they get heartburn, start hiccupping and belching. Some will fall ill with distended stomachs.

---

7   Comic invented name derived from the sounds for laughter ("ha ha" is spelled *kha kha* in Russian). Chekhov also recycles Baldastov ("blockhead") from his previous story "Confession, or Olya, Zhenya, Zoya" in this sentence and at the end of the Almanac.

Almanac footnotes

1) In an effort to avoid misunderstandings, the *Alarm Clock* staff have the honour to announce that they will exchange Easter kisses only with those who are attractive, while the Almanac editor will only do so with blondes.

2) During the current week, Spain and Austria will cease hostilities.

3) To Mr. NN—You write that the stuffed sperm-whale doesn't fit on your table. Well then! Buy yourself a bigger table!

4) Editorial offices, *News*, Petersburg: It will soon be the meat-eating season. Breed ducks.

5) There you have it, reader!

    The *Alarm Clock* Almanac editor—*Antosha Chekhonte*

29, Monday. Second day of the holiday. Heartburn, hiccups, burps. (Remedy: *magnesia alba*,[8] *ol. ricini*,[9] strict diet). People are resting after yesterday's visits and gluttony. There will be neither rain nor snow. A great deal of traffic on the boulevards. The zoo is shut for the holidays. Looking through the list of names signed yesterday in his entrance hall, Bayonet-Junker Frantoroznov[10] fails to find the name of Lieutenant Akhakhaev and swears that he will destroy the latter. Name day of the poet M. Yaron.* Sunrise at 4:47 a.m. The same sun sets at 7.05 p.m. On this day the author William Shakespeare exclaimed: "Oh women, women!" (1640)

30, Tuesday. A great fool will be born; the *Russian Satirical Sheet** will go under. Workers at printers and lithographers are as drunk as fiddlers, the typesetters are as drunk as cobblers. Kifa Mokievich* celebrates his name day. Krechinsky* and Khlestakov* will leave *The New Times** in order to publish their own newspaper *Loyal Goats*. Concerts on nearly every side street. *Sinichkin** is being performed at the Maly Theatre. Sunrise at 4:54 a.m. The same sun sets at 7:07 p.m. On this day the Great Migration of Peoples took place (707), and Kühner composed his *Latin Grammar.**

---

8   *Magnesia alba*: magnesium carbonate (Latin).

9   *ol. ricini*: "castor oil" (Latin).

10   Comic name derived from the word for "dandy" (*frant*).

31, Wednesday. Nothing will happen apart from Wednesday and the fair in Oryol, Oryol Province. Sunrise at 4:51 a.m., the same sun sets at 7:10. p.m. On this day Ephialtes betrayed his homeland to the Persians (803),* Prince Meshchersky invented the *Citizen* for the first time, Tsitovich* learned to write, and Mr. Batalin* was born.

April

A month possessing 30 days, 30 nights, 720 hours, 43 200 minutes, 2 592 000 seconds. A rainy, foggy, and muddy month. The grass will grow, the trees will turn green, the weather will get warmer. Commerce slows down. Getting married will not be forbidden. Fur hats are passed down to caretakers and footmen, and felt hats are put on instead. Fur coats are pawned. A trillion concerts, most of which, it goes without saying, are given by cats. Many great people are born this month. They will all be happy and live until the age of 90. Fleas are multiplying. It's time to think of the dacha!

Thursday 1st. April Fools' Day. Those who fool others are following tradition. Today we fool others and also deceive ourselves. "To live on this earth is extremely pleasant. Boborykin and Markevich are great writers.* Lokhvitsky has died.* The exchange rate goes up with each passing day. We do not live in order to eat, but eat in order to live..." And so on. Today is the day of lawyers, newspapers, and Ivan A. Khlestakov. It is warm. For those who are not fooling others there is *Sinichkin* at the Maly Theatre and *Arifa** at the Bolshoi. It is dead dull. The name-day of many Mashas. Sunrise at 4:48 a.m. The same sun sets at 7:00 p.m. On this day Lucullus ate and drank to the tune of 400 000 francs (43).

Friday 2nd. Everything is in fine shape. It is the name day of the Tituses, and they are living it up. The birthday of Madame Menter.* There is a scandal in the town of Yaroslavl: someone gave someone else a punch in the face. Woodcocks and snipe are returning. *The City Is Being Abolished* is on at the Maly Theatre, *The Maiden of Hell** at the Bolshoi. A solar and a lunar eclipse, visible simultaneously all over this world. Sunrise at 4:45 a.m., the same sun sets at 7:14 p.m. Etna is erupting onto Vesuvius. On this day Ivan Ivanovich quarrelled with Ivan Nikiforovich,* and Akaky Akakievich* sewed himself a new overcoat (1842).

Saturday 3rd. The Azov Sea will be drowned in Taganrog mud. The Black Sea will be covered in Odessa dust. Name days: the editor of *Current News* Mr. Gilyarov and the late N. I. Krylov.* Mr. Averkiev will start work on an 18-act drama in verse, *The Battle between the Russians and the Kabardians.** Sunrise at 4:42 a.m., the same sun sets at 7:17 p.m. The Medici Venus will pass across the surface of the sun. The moon will be visible only at four o'clock in the morning. Dark, star-studded, quiet nights. On this day Nebuchadnezzar, like the wild beast that he was, scoffed 35 pounds of hay (813).

Sunday 4th. First Sunday after Easter. First day of the sales. Great bargains. Terrible crowds in the shopping arcades. On this day one can purchase a shirt for 13 kopecks, chintz at 2 kopecks per yard, a dozen caps for 35 kopecks, a dress for a rouble and so on. Weddings are now permitted. *Alarm Clock* No. 13 goes on sale. Sunrise at 4:39 a.m., the same sun sets at 7:20 p.m. No need to wear galoshes. It was on this day that Agafya Fedoseyevna* bit off the assessor's ear (1854), Odysseus gave Penelope's suitors a thrashing (1030), and Sobakevich stepped on the governor's foot.

Monday 5th. A flood at the printing press. The garlands and evening dress of the late Nikolay Rubinstein* are to be pawned. It is the name day of our colleague Agafopod Yedinitsyn* (author of *Rockets of Five Feelings*). *Arifa* is on at the Bolshoi Theatre, *The Town is Being Abolished* at the Maly. Rain in the morning, clear at midday, rain in the evening. The weather will change by the hour. Sunrise at 4:36 a.m., the same sun sets at 7:22 p.m. On this day, Pythagoras invented the Pythagorean "Trousers."* (This was more than opportune because at that time he didn't have any trousers.)

Tuesday 6th. Remembrance of late grandfathers and grandmothers. There are picnics in the cemeteries. No fairs anywhere. The Turks are behaving like swine. Gladstone is perplexed. Troops are mobilised in Monaco. Storm clouds on the political horizon. Famine in London. Sunrise at 4:33 a.m., the same sun sets at 7:25 p.m. Two husbands, driven to ruin by the sales, hang themselves. May they rest in peace! Sarah Bernhardt is demanding a divorce. On this day King Alivemelekh of Nicomedia* had a fight with theatre touts.

Wednesday 7th. All Akulinas celebrate their name day. Sarah Bernhardt marries a black man. *Maiden of Hell* at the Bolshoi Theatre, *L. G. Sinichkin* at the Maly. Composers are up in arms in the town of Slavyanoserbsk. Sunrise at 4:30 a.m., the same sun sets at 7:37 p.m. Full moon. There will be no rain: no need for galoshes. On this day (in 1843) Pulkheriya Ivanovna* passed away.

Thursday 8th. The sun enters Capricorn at 7:30 a.m. It is the name day of all Pavselinas. Having gone hunting yesterday and the day before, hunters are buying wildfowl on Hunters Row. *Arifa* at the Bolshoi Theatre, *The City Is Abolished* at the Maly. Lentovsky is going to America in the morning and coming back in the evening. Sunrise at 4:27 a.m., the same sun sets at 7:30 p.m. In Krasnoyarsk the artist of arts Mr. Yukhantsev* is presented with a letter of gratitude. On this day, the first spot appeared on the sun (18) and Archimedes shouted: Eureka!!!

Friday 9th. A minimum number cross the Moscow River. The lead article in the *Current** scares its readers with fire and brimstone. *Maiden of Hell* at the Bolshoi Theatre, and *L. G. Sinichkin* at the Maly. The season opens in Slavyansk. Sunrise at 4:24 a.m., the same sun sets at 7:32 p.m. In the town of Volokolamsk the age of pile dwellings comes to an end. On this day Xanthippe emptied a chamber pot on to the learned head of Socrates, who said: "I know only that I know nothing!"

Saturday 10th. All Africans and Zenos* celebrate their name days. Sarah Bernhardt demands a divorce. There is a babel of languages in the town of Nakhichevan. *Arifa* at the Bolshoi Theatre, *The Town Is Abolished* at the Maly. Fair in Paris. (The works of Ponson du Terrail,* lace, and *those* ladies. 1,000,005 Francs will be handed out.) Sunrise at 4:21 a.m., the same sun sets at 7:35 p.m. Rainbow. Beelzebub will pop up out of Carl Heymann's sleeve* and frighten the public. The first tailor was born on this day (12).

Sunday 11th. Infants, adolescents and youths cram and go pale at the thought of exams. The Turks hire Mr. Lokhvitsky. Corporal punishment introduced at the *Citizen* editorial offices. *Maiden of Hell* at the Bolshoi Theatre, *L. G. Sinichkin* at the Maly. Sarah Bernhardt marries the deputy secretary of the Chinese Embassy. Sunrise at 4:19 a.m., the same sun sets at 7:37 p.m. Lilacs are in bloom in the south. The Marquise de Pompadour was born on this day.

Footnotes

1) The previous issue did not have an Almanac thanks to our professors of black magic, who were drunk.

2) The editor of the Almanac extends an invitation to a learned, sober and upright historian for joint scribbling. Any historian accepting this invitation should apply in writing, to the editor. For each event he contributes there will be a five-kopeck coin.

3) Mrs. N. N.: You ask what you should do to stop your husband hanging around the kitchen and getting in the way of the cooking? Here's what you should do: fire your kitchen maid... I expect she is pretty?

—on behalf of the *Alarm Clock* Almanac editor—G. Baldastov

Green Point

(A Small Novel)

Chapter I

On the shores of the Black Sea, in a place which appears as "Green Point" in my diary, and in the diaries of my heroes and heroines, stands a charming dacha. Perhaps this dacha would not appeal to an architect, or to lovers of all that is symmetrical, perfectly proportioned and stylish, but to a poet or artist it is an absolute delight. I appreciate its humble beauty—the fact that its own beauty does not impinge on the beauty of its surroundings, and that it exudes neither the coldness of marble nor the self-importance of columns. It looks welcoming, warm, romantic... Standing behind slender silver poplars, with its little towers, spires, crenellations and flag poles, it seems somewhat medieval. When I gaze at it I am reminded of sentimental German novels, with their knights, castles, doctors of philosophy, and mysterious countesses... The dacha stands on a hill; it is surrounded by a very dense, overgrown garden with paths, little fountains, conservatories, while below, beneath the hill, lies the stern blue sea... The air is constantly refreshed by a humid, playful breeze, there is every kind of birdsong, an eternally clear blue sky, limpid water—a wondrous little place!

The proprietress of the dacha, the wife of either a Georgian or perhaps a Circassian princeling, is Marya Yegorovna Mikshadze, a lady of about fifty, tall, plump, and, in her day, undoubtedly a beauty. She is a good woman, likeable, hospitable, but far too strict. Or rather, not strict, but capricious... She gave us excellent food, wonderful drink, lent us money very readily and at the same time tormented us horribly. Etiquette is her hobby horse. Being the wife of a prince is her other hobby horse. Riding these two hobby horses, she always overeggs the pudding. She never smiles, for instance, probably because she considers it to be improper, for herself and for grandes-dames in general. Those who are younger than she is, even if only by a year, are greenhorns. Gentility, in her opinion, is a virtue before which everything else is the most nonsensical rubbish. She is an enemy of flippancy and frivolity, loves silence, and so on and so forth. Sometimes we could hardly tolerate this lady. Were it not for her daughter, we would hardly be rejoicing now in our memories of Green Point. This good woman occupies the dullest patch in our memories. The adornment of Green Point is Marya Yegorovna's daughter, Olya. Olya is a petite, slender, pretty little blonde about nineteen years of age. She is full of life and no fool. She draws well, dabbles in botany, speaks excellent French, poor German, reads a lot, and dances like Terpsichore herself. She studied music at the conservatoire and plays really pretty well. We men loved this blue-eyed girl—we did not fall in love with her, we just loved her. We felt great affection for her, she was one of us... Green Point without her was unthinkable for us. Without her, its poetry would have been incomplete. She was like a pretty female figure in a charming landscape, and I don't like paintings without human figures. The splash of the sea and rustling of the trees are all very fine, but if you add to them Olya's soprano and the accompaniment of our basses, tenors, and grand piano, the sea and garden become an earthly paradise... We loved the little princess; it would have been impossible not to. We bestowed on her the title of daughter of our regiment. And Olya loved us. She gravitated toward our masculine company and it was only with us that she felt in her element. When we were absent, she would lose weight and stop singing. This company consisted of guests, the summer residents of Green Point, and neighbours. Belonging to the first category were Dr. Yakovkin, the Odessa journalist Mukhin, Fiveisky, holder of a master's in physics (now lecturing at university), three students, the artist Chekhov,* a Kharkov lawyer-baron, and yours truly, Olya's former tutor (who taught her to speak German poorly and to catch goldfinches). Every year we would descend on Green Point in May and occupy the spare rooms of the medieval castle and all its wings for the entire summer. Every March we would receive two written invitations to Green Point: one was self-important, stern, and full of lectures from the princess, and the other a very long, jolly note, full of all manner of plans, from her daughter, who missed us. We would arrive and stay until September. The neighbours who would come daily to visit us were: retired first lieutenant-artilleryman Yegorov,* a young man who had twice sat and twice failed the examination for the Academy, a very cultured, well-read fellow; the medical student Korobov* with his wife Yekaterina Ivanovna, the landowner Aleutov and a great multitude of landowners, retired, not-retired, merry and boring, idlers and good-for-nothings... This whole gang constantly ate, drank, played, sang, set off fireworks, cracked jokes day and night, all summer long... Olya loved the gang to death. She shouted, darted back and forth, and made more noise than the rest of us put together. She was the life and soul of the party.

Every evening the princess would assemble us in the drawing-room, her face crimson, and accuse us of "shameless" behaviour; she would scold us and swear it was due to us that she had a headache. She was fond of delivering homilies, which she delivered with sincerity, and was firmly convinced her homilies would do us good. Olya was on the receiving end more than anyone else. In her opinion, Olya was to blame for everything. Olya was afraid of her mother. She worshipped her and listened to her homilies standing up, silent, blushing. The princess treated Olya like a child. She would put her in the corner and leave her without breakfast and lunch. To stand up for Olya was to pour oil on the fire. If she could have, she would have put us in the corner too. She sent us to the all-night service, ordered us to read aloud from The Great Menaion Reader,* counted our linen, meddled in our affairs... Time and again we would walk off with her scissors, forget where she kept her smelling salts, and be unable to find her thimble.

"Scatterbrain!" she would shout constantly. "You walked past, dropped it and didn't pick it up! Pick it up! Pick it up right now! The Lord has sent you to punish me... Go away! Don't stand in the draught!"

Sometimes one of us would commit an offence for fun and be summoned to the old woman.

"Was it you who walked on the vegetable patch?" the trial would begin. "How dare you?"

"I accidentally..."

"Silence! I'm asking you, how dare you?"

The trial would end with a pardon, the kissing of her hand and, on exit from the court room, Homeric laughter. The princess never showed us any affection. Words of affection were reserved solely for old women and little children.

I never once saw her smile. She would whisper an assurance to the old general who visited her on Sundays to play piquet that we, doctors, holders of master's degrees, the odd baron, painters, and writers, would perish without her good sense... Nor did we try to dissuade her of this... Let her amuse herself, we thought... The princess would have been bearable had she not demanded that we get up no later than eight o'clock and go to bed no later than 12. Poor Olya went to bed at 11 p.m. To contradict her was forbidden. And, my, how we mocked the old woman for this unlawful encroachment on our freedom! We would all go together to ask for her forgiveness, compose panegyrics to her in the style of Lomonosov,* draw the family tree of the princes Mikshadze, etc. The princess would receive all this without irony in good faith, and we would guffaw. The princess was fond of us. She would sigh deeply and very sincerely when expressing her regret that we were not princes. She became used to us, as if we were children...

The only one of us she did not love was Lieutenant Yegorov. She loathed him with a vengeance, and harboured the most unimaginable antipathy towards him. She only received him because she had financial business with him and observed decorum. The lieutenant had previously been her favourite. He was handsome, witty, fairly taciturn and in the military (which the princess valued highly). But sometimes Yegorov was out of sorts... He would sit down, prop his head on his fists and begin to curse. He would curse everyone and everything, sparing neither the living nor the dead. When he began to curse, the princess would fly into a rage and chase all of us out of the house.

One lunchtime Yegorov propped his head on his fist and out of the blue started holding forth about Caucasian princes, then pulled a copy of *The Dragonfly* out of his pocket and had the audacity to read the following in front of Princess Mikshadze: "Tiflis* is a good city. Amongst the virtues of this fine city—in which 'princes' sweep the streets and polish boots in hotels, are..." etc. The princess got up from the table and silently left the room. Her hatred for Yegorov increased a hundredfold when he added our surnames next to our first names in her book of remembrance. In view of the fact that the lieutenant dreamed of marrying Olya, and Olya was in love with the lieutenant, this hatred could not have been more undesirable, or out of place. The lieutenant held fiercely on to his dreams, though he hardly believed that they would come true. Olya loved in secret, furtively, on her own, timidly, barely noticeably... For her love was contraband—a feeling on which a cruel veto had been placed. She was not permitted to love.

Chapter II

One of those silly medieval stories very nearly played out in the medieval castle.

About seven years ago, when Prince Mikshadze was still alive, Prince Chaikhidzev, an Yekaterinoslav* landowner and a friend of Mikshadze's, came to stay at Green Point. He was a very rich man. He had burnt the candle at both ends all his life and, despite this, remained rich until the end of his days. In the olden days, Mikshadze had been his drinking partner. With Mikshadze's help, Chaikhidzev had carried off a girl from her parents' home who subsequently became Princess Chaikhidzeva. This circumstance had bound both princes with the strongest ties of friendship. Chaikhidzev came to stay together with his son, a goggle-eyed, narrow-chested, dark-haired youth who was at high school. Chaikhidzev straight away started boozing with Mikshadze, for old time's sake, while his son set about wooing Olya, then a thirteen-year-old girl. His wooing did not go unnoticed. The parents winked at each other and remarked that Olya and the boy would make a pretty good match. The drunken princes ordered the children to kiss each other, shook hands and then they themselves kissed each other. Mikshadze was even moved to tears. "It is God's will!" said Chaikhidzev. "You have a daughter, I have a son... It is God's will!"

Both children were given a ring and were photographed together. This photograph hung in the hall and for a long time gave Yegorov no peace. It was the target of countless jokes. Princess Marya Yegorovna gave the happy couple her solemn blessing. She took to the fathers' idea out of boredom. A month after the Chaikhidzevs' departure, Olya received an extremely lavish gift in the post. Later on, she would receive such gifts annually. Contrary to expectations, the young Chaikhidzev was deadly serious about the matter. He was a rather simple-minded lad. Every year he would come to Green Point and stay a whole week, never saying anything and sending love letters to Olya from his room. Olya would read these letters and feel embarrassed. The bright girl was surprised that a grown-up person could write such stupid things! And he really did write stupid things... Two years ago Mikshadze died. On his deathbed, he said to Olya: "Look, don't get married to some idiot! Marry Chaikhidzev. He is an intelligent and worthy man." Olya knew how intelligent Chaikhidzev was but did not contradict her father. She gave him her word that she would marry Chaikhidzev.

"And it is Papa's will!" she would say to us, speaking with a certain amount of pride, as if she were accomplishing some heroic feat. She was proud that her father had taken her promise with him to his grave. It was such an out of the ordinary, romantic promise!

But nature and reason took their course: retired lieutenant Yegorov was constantly in view, while Chaikhidzev, in her view, became more and more stupid with every passing year...

When the lieutenant once dared to hint at his love for her, she asked him not to speak to her any more about love, reminded him of the promise she had given her father, and cried all night. Every week the princess wrote letters to Chaikhidzev in Moscow, where he was at university, and ordered him to graduate as soon as possible. "I've got men staying here who aren't nearly as bearded as you, and they graduated a long time ago," she wrote to him. Chaikhidzev answered her with the utmost deference, on pink notepaper, and took up two sheets to show that there was no way he could graduate before the allotted time. Olya also wrote to him. Olya's letters to me are far better than her letters to this fiancé of hers. The princess was convinced that Olya would be Chaikhidzev's wife, otherwise she would never have allowed her daughter to go out and "fritter away her time" in the company of troublemakers, numbskulls, godless youth, and "non-princes"... She could not allow any doubts... For her the will of her husband was sacred... Olya also believed that in time she would be signing her name as Chaikhidzeva...

But it was not to be. The two fathers' plan collapsed at the very moment of its fulfilment. Chaikhidzev's romance did not work out. The romance was destined to end in vaudeville.

Last year Chaikhidzev came to Green Point at the end of June. He came this time no longer as a student, having obtained an ordinary degree. The princess greeted him with solemn, ceremonial embraces and a very long lecture. Olya wore an expensive dress sewn specially for the meeting with her fiancé. Champagne was brought from town, fireworks were set off, and the next morning all of Green Point in one voice was talking about the wedding, supposedly set for the end of July. "Poor Olya!" we whispered as we lolled about, gazing malevolently at the windows which looked out on to the garden from the room of the eastern gentleman we found so odious. "Poor Olya!" Olya was walking around the garden, pale, thin, looking half-dead. "It's what Papa and Mama want!"—she would say when we began to pester her with friendly advice. "But this is absurd! Ridiculous!"—we would yell at her. She would shrug her shoulders and turn her face, which was full of anguish, away from us; the bridegroom sat in his room, sent tender letters to Olya via the footmen and, looking through the window, was amazed at the bold way we chatted and behaved with Olya. He left his room only to have lunch. He ate lunch in silence without looking at anyone, answering our questions stiffly. Only once did he venture to tell a joke, and even that turned out to be so old it was trite. After lunch the princess would sit him down beside her and teach him how to play piquet. Chaikhidzev played earnestly, thinking a lot, sticking out his lower lip and sweating... That sort of attitude to piquet went down well with the princess.

One day after lunch Chaikhidzev slipped away from the piquet and ran after Olya, who was making for the garden.

"Olga Andreyevna!" he began. "I know that you do not love me. Our betrothal is strange, stupid, it's true. But I—I hope that you will come to love me..."

After saying this he was profusely embarrassed and sidled his way back from the garden to his room.

Lieutenant Yegorov stayed at home on his estate and made no appearance anywhere. He could not stomach Chaikhidzev.

On Sunday (the second after Chaikhidzev's arrival), I believe it was the 5th of July, a student, the princess's nephew, turned up at our wing early in the morning and delivered a command. The princess' command was that by evening we should all be at the ready: we should be dressed in black with white ties and gloves; we should be serious, clever, witty, obedient, and sleek as poodles; we should be quiet; we should have tidy rooms. There was something like a betrothal afoot at Green Point. Wine, vodka and canapés were brought from town... Our servants were requisitioned and sent to the kitchen. Guests began to arrive after lunch and continued to arrive until late evening. At eight o'clock, after boat trips, the ball began.

Before the ball, we men had a pow-wow. At this pow-wow we unanimously agreed to rid Olya of Chaikhidzev, even if this cost us a major scandal. After the meeting I rushed off in search of Lieutenant Yegorov. He was living on his estate, about 13 miles from Green Point. I found him at home, but in what a state! The lieutenant was as drunk as a cobbler and sleeping like the dead. I shook him till he woke up, washed him, dressed him and, despite all his kicking and screaming, carted him off to Green Point.

At ten o'clock the ball was in full swing. There was dancing in four rooms, accompanied by two fine pianos. During the intervals, a third piano played on the mound in the garden. Even the princess herself admired our fireworks. We set them off in the garden, on the shore and on boats far out to sea. On the roof of the castle, multi-coloured Bengal lights went off, one after another, lighting up the whole of the Point. The boozing went on at two bars: one bar was in the summer house in the garden, and the other was in the house. The hero of the evening was supposedly Chaikhidzev. Squeezed into a tight tailcoat, with pink blotches on his cheeks and a sweaty nose, he was dancing with Olya, smiling wanly and feeling clumsy. He danced, watching every step he took. He desperately wanted to shine in something, but failed to shine at anything. Olya told me afterwards that she had felt extremely sorry for the poor princeling on this particular evening. He seemed pitiful to her. It was as though he sensed that his bride, whom he had thought about during every lecture, when he went to bed, and when he woke up, would be taken from him... When he looked at us, his eyes were full of supplication. He foresaw we would be strong and pitiless adversaries.

Judging from the champagne glasses being prepared and the way the princess kept looking at the clock, we concluded that the official ceremonial moment was approaching and that, in all likelihood, Chaikhidzev would be given permission to kiss Olya at midnight. It was time to act. At half past eleven I powdered my face so as to appear pale, twisted my tie to one side and, with an alarmed face and dishevelled hair, approached Olya.

"Olga Andreyevna," I began, grasping her arm, "I beg you!"

"What is it?"

"Please... Do not be afraid, Olga Andreyevna... It could not have been otherwise. We ought to have expected it..."

"What's the matter?"

"Don't be afraid... The thing is... Please, my dear! Evgraf..."

"What's the matter with him?"

Olya turned pale and turned her big, trusting, friendly eyes on to me...

"Evgraf is dying..."

Olya reeled and ran her fingers over her now pale forehead.

"It's just as I expected," I continued. "He's dying... Save him, Olga Andreyevna!"Olya grasped me by the arm.

"Where... where... is he?"

"Here in the garden, in the summer house. It's awful, my dear! But... we are being watched. Let's go on to the terrace... He doesn't blame you... He knows that you..."

"What... what is wrong with him?"

"It's bad, very bad!!"

"Let's go... I will go to him... I don't want him to... because of me... because of me..."

We went out onto the terrace. Olya's knees were buckling. I pretended to wipe away a tear... Running past us, back and forth on the terrace, were pale, alarmed members of our gang.

"The blood has stopped..." our friend with the master's degree in physics whispered to me in Olga's hearing.

"Let's go!" whispered Olya as she took me by the arm.

We went down the terrace steps... The night was quiet, clear... The sounds of the piano, the rustling of the dark trees, the chirping of crickets caressed the ear; the waves lapped gently below.

Olya could hardly walk... Her legs were buckling, and she was stumbling in her heavy dress. Trembling, she pressed herself against my shoulder in fear.

"But it's not my fault..." she whispered. "I swear to you, it's not my fault. It was Papa's will... He has to understand this... Is he in danger?"

"I don't know... Mikhail Pavlovich has done everything he could. He is a good doctor and loves Yegorov... We are almost there, Olga Andreyevna..."

"I... I won't see anything awful, will I? I'm afraid... I can't bear... What did he do this for?"

Olya burst into tears.

"It's not my fault... he should have understood. I will explain everything to him."

We had arrived at the summer house.

"Here we are," I said.

Olya closed her eyes and held on to me with both hands.

"I can't..."

"Don't be afraid... Yegorov, have you died yet?" I shouted, addressing the summer house.

"Not yet... Why?"

Lit up by the moon, the lieutenant appeared at the entrance to the summer house, dishevelled, pale from having drunk too much, and his waistcoat undone...

"Why?" he repeated.

Olya raised her head and caught sight of Yegorov... She looked at me, then at Yegorov, then at me again... I burst out laughing... Her face lit up. She shouted with joy, took a step forward... I thought she would be angry with us... But this girl did not know how to be angry... She took a step forward, thought for a moment, and rushed over to Yegorov. Yegorov quickly buttoned up his waistcoat and spread out his arms. Olya fell onto his chest. Laughing with delight and turning his head to one side so as not to breathe on Olya, Yegorov began to mumble some nonsense.

"You have no right... It's not my fault," Olya babbled. "It was what Mama and Papa wanted," and so on.

I turned back and quickly set off towards the illuminated castle.

Meanwhile, in the castle, the guests were preparing to congratulate the future bride and groom and were looking impatiently at the clock... Footmen with trays were crowding into the front hall; on the trays were bottles and champagne glasses. Chaikhidzev was impatiently kneading his right hand in his left, his eyes searching for Olya. The princess was walking through all the rooms and looking for Olya in order to edify her on how to behave, how to answer her mother and so on. We were all smiling.

"Do you know where Olga is?" the princess asked me.

"I don't."

"Go and look for her."

I went down to the garden and, clasping my hands behind my back, walked round the house twice. Our painter had struck up a few notes on the trumpet. This meant "Hold on, don't let her go!" From the summer house Yegorov answered with an owl's cry. This meant: "All right! I am holding her!"

Having walked round a bit, I went into the house. In the front hall, the footmen had put their trays down on the tables and were standing empty-handed, looking blankly at the guests. The guests, in their turn, were gazing with perplexity at the clock, whose minute hand showed it was already quarter past. The pianos went silent. In every room a profound, agonising, confused silence reigned.

"Where is Olya?" the princess asked me, crimson faced.

"I don't know... She's not in the garden."

The princess shrugged her shoulders.

"Surely, she knows she should have been here long ago?" she asked, tugging at my sleeve.

I shrugged my shoulders. The princess left me and whispered something to Chaikhidzev. Chaikhidzev also shrugged his shoulders. The princess tugged at his sleeve too.

"Nitwit!" she growled, and started running around the entire house. Maids and schoolboys, together with the princess's relations, ran noisily down the staircase and headed into the garden to search for the vanished bride-to-be. I also went into the garden. I was afraid that Yegorov would be unable to detain Olya and thus spoil the scandal we had thought up. I headed towards the summer house. I had no reason to be afraid! Olya was sitting beside

Yegorov, passing her fingers backwards and forwards over his eyes and whispering, whispering... When Olya stopped whispering, Yegorov would begin to murmur. He was instilling in her those notions that the princess called "ideas"... He sweetened each of his words with a kiss. He spoke, constantly raising his mouth to kiss her and at the same time turning it to one side so that she would not smell the vodka on his breath. They were both happy, and had evidently forgotten everything on earth and lost track of the time. I stood for a while by the entrance to the summer house, my spirit overjoyed, and, not wishing to intrude on their happiness, set off for the castle.

The princess was beside herself and sniffing at her smelling salts. Not knowing what to think, she was angry and ashamed before her guests and the bridegroom-to-be... She was never violent, but she slapped a maid when the latter reported that the young princess was nowhere to be found. The guests, tired of waiting for the champagne and congratulations, exchanged smiles and gossip and started dancing again.

The clock struck one, and Olya had not appeared. The princess was overcome by fury.

"This is all your doing!" she hissed every time she walked past one of us. "It will be curtains for her! Where is she?"

Finally, someone came to her rescue and told her where Olya was... This do-gooder turned out to be a paunchy little schoolboy, the princess's nephew. He came racing in from the garden like a madman, ran up to the princess, sat down on her lap, drew her head towards him and whispered in her ear... The princess turned pale and bit her lip until she drew blood.

"In the summer house?" she asked.

"Yes."

The princess rose to her feet and, with a grimace that resembled an official smile, announced to her guests that Olya had a headache and asked them to excuse her and so on and so forth. The guests expressed their sympathy, hastily ate their supper and began to disperse.

At two a.m. (Yegorov had done his best to detain Olya until then) I stood at the entrance to the terrace behind a wall of oleander bushes, waiting for Olya's return. I wanted to have a look at her face. I love happy female faces. I wanted to see how her love for Yegorov and her fear of her mother would co-exist on her face at the same time; and which would be the stronger: love or fear? I did not have to breathe in the oleanders' scent for long. Olya soon appeared. I fastened my eyes on her face. She walked slowly, lifting her dress a little and showing her dainty slippers. Her face was well lit by the moon and by the lanterns that were hanging on the trees, which spoilt the moonlight with their glimmer. Her face was serious and pale. Her lips alone smiled a bit. Her eyes looked thoughtfully at the ground; people usually solve difficult problems with eyes like that. When Olya put her foot on the first step, her eyes stirred and began to flicker: she had remembered her mother. Olya lightly touched her rumpled hair with her hand, stood indecisively on the step for some time and, shaking her head, boldly walked towards the door... But here I was destined to see the following picture... The door was flung open, and Olya's pale face was lit up by a bright light. Olya shuddered, took a step back and cowered. It was as though something had flattened her... On the threshold, her head raised, stood the princess, scarlet, trembling with anger and shame... The silence lasted for about two minutes.

"The daughter of a prince," the princess began, "and the bride-to-be of a prince goes to a rendezvous with a lieutenant!? With Evgrashka! Vile!"

Bent almost double and trembling, Olya slithered past the princess like a snake and fled to her room. She sat down on her bed and with eyes full of horror and alarm stared at the window all night long...

At three a.m. we held another pow-wow. At this meeting we laughed at Yegorov, who was drunk with happiness, and designated the lawyer-baron from Kharkov to deal with Chaikhidzev. The Prince was still awake. The Kharkov lawyer-baron was to point out to Chaikhidzev in a "friendly" manner the awkwardness of his, Chaikhidzev's, position, and ask that he, the prince, as a mature person, take upon himself the trouble of clearing up this awkwardness and also ask that he, among other things, forgive us for our meddling, forgive us "in a friendly manner" as a mature person... Chaikhidzev told the baron that he "understood all this very well," that he attached no importance to his father's behest, but that he loved Olya, and for this reason alone had been so persistent... He shook the baron's hand with feeling and promised to leave the very next day.

The next morning Olya appeared for tea looking pale, worn out, full of the most desperate thoughts, and both scared and ashamed... But her face shone when she saw and heard us in the dining room. We stood before the princess and shouted. We shouted in one voice. We threw off our little masks and loudly impressed upon the princess "ideas" very similar to the ones that Yegorov was impressing upon Olya the evening before. We spoke about a woman's individuality, about the legitimacy of free choice and so on. Not saying a word, the princess listened to us glumly and read a letter that Yegorov had sent her—this letter had been composed by us and was overflowing with words like: "due to youthfulness," "due to inexperience," "with your blessing," etc. The princess heard us out, read Yegorov's long letter from start to finish and said:

"It is not for you, greenhorns, to teach me, an old woman. I know what I am doing. Drink your tea and off you go to befuddle other heads. You should not live with me, an old woman... You are intelligent people, and I am a fool... Good luck to you, gentlemen!.. I will be ever grateful to you!"

The princess turned us out. We wrote her a letter of thanks, kissed her hand and, with heavy hearts, left for Yegorov's estate that very day. Chaikhidzev left with us. At Yegorov's all we did was booze, pine for Olya and comfort Yegorov. We spent about two weeks at his estate. During the third week our lawyer-baron received a letter from the princess. The princess asked the baron to come to Green Point and draw up some kind of documents for her. The baron set off. About three days after his departure we also went there, ostensibly to pick up the baron. We arrived at Green Point before lunch. We did not enter the house, but wandered round the garden, eying the windows. The princess saw us through the window.

"Is that you?" she shouted.

"It is."

"Do you have business here?"

"We've come for the baron."

"The baron has no time to consort with you hangmen! He is busy writing."

We took off our hats and approached the window.

"How are you, princess?" I asked.

"What are you hanging about for?" answered the princess. "Come inside!"

We went inside and meekly sat down. The princess, who had missed our company frightfully, liked this meekness. She gave us lunch. When one of us dropped a spoon during lunch, she scolded him for being a scatterbrain and reproached us for our poor table manners. We went for a walk with Olya, and stayed the night... We stayed the next day too and ended up staying at Green Point all the way through to September. The world had pieced itself back together again.

Yesterday I received a letter from Yegorov. The lieutenant writes that he has been "buttering up" the princess all winter, and has managed to turn the princess's anger to mercy. He assures me his wedding will take place this summer.

Soon I should be receiving two letters: a severe, official one from the princess, and the other—long, jolly, full of plans, from Olya. In May I am going to Green Point again.

"The Rendezvous
did Take Place, But..."

After passing his exam, Gvozdikov got into the horse-drawn tram and for six kopecks (he always sat "on the top deck") travelled as far as the edge of town. From the edge of town to the dacha it was about a two-mile slog on foot. The owner of the dacha, a young lady, met him at the gate. He tutored this young lady's boy in arithmetic, for which he received room and board at the dacha, and five roubles a month in cash.

"Well?" asked the lady of the house, stretching out her hand. "Did it go all right? Did you pass the exam?"

"I did."

"Bravo, Yegor Andreyevich! Did you do well?"

"As per usual... I got an A... Hmm..."

Gvozdikov was only awarded a C plus, not an A, but... but why not lie, if you can? Exam-takers are just as game when it comes to lying as hunters are. When he went into his room, Gvozdikov found a diminutive letter with a delicate pink wafer on his desk. The letter smelt of wild mignonette. Gvozdikov tore open the envelope, ate the wafer, and read the following:

"So be it. Meet me punctually at 8 o'clock next to the ditch your hat fell into yesterday. I will be sitting on the bench under the tree. And I love you, but don't be such a lump. You must be bold. Impatiently awaiting this evening. I love you madly. Your S.

P.S. *Maman* has left, so we can be out until midnight. Oh, how happy I am! Grandma will be asleep—she won't notice a thing."

When he finished reading the letter, Gvozdikov grinned broadly, leapt high into the air, and paced around the room in triumph.

"She loves me! She loves me!! She loves me!!! I'm so happy, damn it! O-o-oh! Tra-la-la!"

Gvozdikov read the note again, kissed it, then carefully folded and hid it in his dissecting table. Lunch was served. Dazed by the contents of the letter and forgetting all else, he ate everything they brought him: soup, meat, and bread. When he had finished, he lay down and began dreaming about all sorts of things: friendship, love, work... Sonya's image hovered before his eyes.

"What a shame I don't have a watch!" he thought. "If I had a watch, I could calculate how much time is left until evening. Time, just to spite me, is dragging its heels."

When he tired of lying around and dreaming, he got up, paced backwards and forwards, and sent the cook for some beer.

"In the meantime..." he thought, "we'll have a drink. Time will go by faster."

The beer arrived. Gvozdikov sat down, set all six bottles in a row before him, and, ogling them, got down to drinking. After three glasses, he felt as if lamps had been lit inside his chest and head: it felt so warm, bright, and pleasant.

"She will make me happy!" he thought, starting another bottle. "She... she is exactly the person I've been dreaming of... Oh yes!"

After the second bottle he felt that the lamp in his head had been extinguished, and things had become somewhat dim. But oh, how cheerful he was! Life is good after a second bottle! Starting his third bottle, Gvozdikov waved his hand in front of his face and swore that there was no happier person on this earth. He witnessed this oath himself and believed it categorically.

"I know why she fell in love with me," he muttered. "Oh, yes! She fell in love with the outstanding person in me! That's right! She knows whom to love and what to love about them... An outstanding person! I am not just some... I am Gvozd... I..."

Picking up the fourth bottle, he exclaimed:

"Yes, sir! I'm not just some... ! She fell in love with the... genius in me! Ge-ni-us! A world-class genius! Who am I? And what am I? Gvozdikov, you think? Yes, I am Gvozdikov, but what kind of Gvozdikov? What do you think?"

Half-way through the fourth bottle, he slammed his fist on the table, raffled his hair, and said:

"I'll show them who I am! Just let me graduate! Just let me study a bit! I'm a priest of science... She fell in love with the priest of science in me. And I'll prove she's right! You don't believe me? Get out of here! And she doesn't believe me? Who? Sonya? She can get out of here too in that case! I'll prove it! I'm going to start studying right away!.. Let me just finish this glass... You're all scoundrels!"

Gvozdikov became angry, emptied his glass, grabbed his lecture notes off the shelf, opened them, and began to read from the middle:

"'Dis… dislocation of the mandible can also result from a fall, a blow to the open mouth…'"

"Nonsense! Mandible… a blow… this and that… nonsense!"

Gvozdikov closed his lecture notes and grabbed the fifth bottle. When, at last, he finished the fifth and sixth bottle, he was overcome by sadness and began pondering the worthlessness of the universe overall and of humanity in particular… Still thinking, he mechanically positioned the cork on the neck of the bottle and took aim, trying to flick it at a green spot flashing before his eyes. Black, green, and blue spots flickered before his eyes when he hit the green spot with the cork. One of the spots, brownish-red with green needles, flew smiling toward his eyes, and gave off something like glue… Gvozdikov felt his eyelids getting heavy.

"Someone's… squeaking in my eyes!" he thought. "I have to get some air or I'll go blind. I must… go… go for a walk… It's stuffy in here. They are still heating the stoves… Oh, o-oh those asses! Squeaking and heating the stoves! Fools!" Gvozdikov put on his hat and left the room. Outside it was already dark. It was after nine. The stars were twinkling in the sky. There was no moon, and it promised to be a dark night. Gvozdikov could smell the forest's May freshness. He was presented with all the necessary attributes of a lovers' rendezvous: whispering leaves, a nightingale singing, and… even "the beloved" herself lost in thought and pale in the gloom. Without realising it, he had reached the spot mentioned in the letter.

She rose from the bench and walked toward him.

"Georges!" she said, scarcely breathing. "I'm here."

Gvozdikov stopped, listened carefully, and began to look up at the tree-tops. It seemed to him that someone was calling his name from above.

"Georges, it's me!" she repeated, coming closer to him.

"Huh?"

"It's me!"

"What? Who's me? Who is it?"

"It's me, Georges… Come… Let's sit down."

Georges rubbed his eyes and stared at her…

"What do you want?"

"You're funny! Don't you recognise me? Do you really not see anything?"

"A-a-a-ah... Allow me to... What r-r-r-iiight do you have to walk around someone else's garden at night? Good sir! Answer me, good sir, otherwise I'll s-s-sock you r-r-right in the kiss... kisss-er."

Georges reached out and grabbed her shoulder. She burst out laughing.

"You are so funny! Ha ha ha... You do put on a good show! But, come here... Let's chat."

"Who with? You? Why you? Why me? Are you joking?"

She laughed louder still, took him by the arm, and pulled herself forward. He backed away. He played the stubborn shaft-horse, and she the eager trace-horse.

"I... I want to sleep... Let me go..." he muttered. "I have no wish to occupy myself with trifles..."

"Come on, that's enough now... Why were you half an hour late? Were you studying?"

"I was studying... I am always studying... Dis... dis... dis-location of the mandible can result from a fall, a blow to the open mouth. Mandibles get knocked loose most often in pubs, taverns... I want some beer... a bottle of Tryokhgornoe."*

They dragged themselves to the bench and sat down. He propped his face up on his fists, resting his elbows on his knees, and snorted. His hat slipped from his head and fell into her hands. She leaned forward and looked him in the eye.

"What's the matter with you?" she asked quietly.

"It's none of your... none of your... business... No one has the right to meddle in my affairs... They're all fools and you're... fools."

After a short pause, Gvozdikov added:

"And I'm a fool..."

"Did you get my letter?" she asked.

"Yes, I... from Son... ka... From Sonya... Are you Sonya? Well, what of it? Silly... The word 'impatiently' is spelled with a 't' even though it sounds like a 'sh.' Grammarians! Devil take you all!.."

"Are you drunk or something?"

"N-n-no... But I am just! You have no... right... One can't get drunk on beer... What, which kind?"

"Why are you spouting this nonsense then, you shameless man, if you're not drunk?"

"N-no... Nominative: me, genitive: you, dative, nominative... *Processus condyloideus et musculus sterno-cleido-mastoideus.*"[1]

Gvozdikov guffawed and dropped his head to his knees...

"Are you asleep?" she asked.

There was no answer. She burst out crying and began wringing her hands.

"Are you asleep, Yegor Andreyevich?" she asked again.

As if in answer to this question, a loud, hoarse snore could be heard. Sonya stood up.

"You wretch!!" she muttered. "Good-for-nothing! So this is what you are like? Take that! And that! And that!"

And Sonya touched the back of Gvozdikov's head with her little hand about five times, and, oh, how she touched him! She stamped on his hat. Women like getting their own back!

The next day Gvozdikov sent Sonya a note which read as follows:

"I ask your forgiveness. I was not able to come last night because I was terribly sick. Pick another time, tonight, for example.

Lovingly, Yegor Gvozdikov."

The answer to the note went as follows:

"Your hat is lying somewhere near the summer house. You will find it there. You enjoy beer-drinking more than loving, so drink beer. I don't want to get in your way.

No longer yours, S...

P.S. Don't answer this. I hate you."

---

1   *Processus condyloideus et musculus sterno-cleido-mastoideus*: "condyloid process and sterno-cleidomastoid muscle" (Latin).

The Correspondent

There were eight musicians in the group. Their leader, Gury Maximov, was told that if they did not play continuously, the musicians would not see a single glass of vodka, and they would be lucky to be paid. The dancing began at exactly eight in the evening. At one a.m. the ladies took offence at the gentlemen, the tipsy gentlemen took offence at the ladies, and the dancing broke up. The guests split into groups. The old men occupied the drawing-room, where there was a table with forty-four bottles and as many plates of food; the ladies crammed into a corner, started whispering about the shocking behaviour of the gentlemen and began to discuss how a fiancée could straightway use the informal form of address with her intended. The gentlemen took over another corner and they all started talking at once, about their own affairs. Gury, the first and next-to-worst violinist and also conductor, struck up the Chernyaevsky March* with his seven musicians... He played continuously and only stopped for a shot of vodka or to hitch up his trousers. He was angry: the second and worst violinist was hopelessly drunk and improvising like hell, while the flautist kept dropping his flute, never looked at the music and laughed for no reason. The noise they made was terrible. Bottles began falling off the small table... Someone hit Karl Karlovich Fünf the German on the back... Several people with red physiognomies came rushing out of a bedroom; an alarmed footman chased after them. Deacon Manafuilov, wishing to dazzle the inebriated and highly respected company with his wit, stood on the cat's tail and kept his foot on it until a footman pulled the rasping cat out from under his foot, remarking to him that this was just ridiculous. The mayor thought that he had lost his watch. Taking fright, he broke into a sweat and began to curse, maintaining that his watch was worth one hundred roubles. The bride-to-be developed a headache... In the hall someone dropped something heavy, and a crack could be heard. In the drawing-room, by the bottles, the old men were not comporting themselves like old men. They were reminiscing about their youth and prattling on about the devil knows what. They told salacious anecdotes, had a dig at their host's romantic exploits, cracked jokes, and sniggered, while their host, evidently pleased, lounged in an armchair, and said: "You are just as bad, you sons of bitches; I know you well, and I've brought your lady-loves gifts on more than one occasion..." The clock struck two. Gury began to play a Spanish serenade for the seventh time. The old men got into the spirit of it.

"Take a look, Yegory!" one toothless old man mumbled, turning to his host and pointing to a corner of the room. "Who is that fidgety person sitting over there?"

In the corner by the bookcase, wearing a dark green, worn frock-coat with mismatched lightly coloured buttons, sat a little old man, his legs meekly tucked up under him, idly leafing through a book of some kind. The host looked over to the corner, thought for a second, and grinned.

"That is a newspaper man, my friends," Yegory said. "You mean you don't know him? He is a splendid person! Ivan Nikitich," he said, addressing the old man with the mismatched buttons, "why are you sitting over there? Come and join us!"

Ivan Nikitich gave a start, raised his blue eyes and became terribly embarrassed.

"Gentlemen, this is a writer, a journalist!" Yegory continued. "We are drinking, but he, you see, is sitting in the corner, thinking all sorts of clever things, and smirking at us. Shame on you, old fellow. Go and have a drink—it's a sin not to!"

Ivan Nikitich got to his feet, went meekly over to the table and poured himself a shot of vodka.

"May the..." he muttered, slowly downing the vodka, "may you... all the best..."

"Have a bite, old fellow! Eat!"

Ivan Nikitich blinked and ate a sardine. A fat man with a silver medal around his neck approached him from behind and sprinkled a handful of salt on his head.

"He will be saltier now, and he won't get worms!" he said.

The assembled company burst out laughing. Ivan Nikitich shook his head and blushed profusely.

"Now don't you take offence!" the fat man said. "What's the point of taking offence? It was a joke. You're such a queer fish! Look, I'll pour salt on myself!" The fat man picked up a saltcellar from the table and poured some on to his own head.

"I'll sprinkle salt on him, too, if you like. Why take offence?" he said and salted the host's head. The assembled company burst out laughing. Ivan Nikitich smiled too and ate another sardine.

"Why aren't you drinking, you conniver?" the host asked. "Drink! Come on, drink with me! No, we'll all drink together!"

The old men got to their feet and surrounded the table. The glasses were filled with brandy. Ivan Nikitich coughed and cautiously picked up a glass.

"That's enough for me," he said, turning to his host. "I'm already quite drunk as it is. Well... all the best to you, Yegor Nikiforych. But what are you all staring at me for? Is there something weird about me? Hee hee hee. Well, all the best! Listen, Yegor Nikiforych, old chap, would you be so kind and gracious as to instruct Gury to tell Grigory to stop drumming? He's torturing me, the lout. His drumming has set my stomach churning... Your good health!"

"Let him drum," said the host. "How can music exist without a drum? You don't even understand that, yet you keep composing your compositions. Well, have a drink with me now!"

Ivan Nikitich hiccupped and began to shuffle his feet. The host poured out two glasses.

"Drink up, my friend," he said, "and don't you dare go and hide. If you write that at L-ov's everyone was drunk, you'll be writing about yourself. Well? I wish you good health. That's it, well done! Goodness, you are a shy one! Drink up!"

Ivan Nikitich coughed, blew his nose and clinked glasses with the host.

"I hope that evil, ruin and misfortunes of all kinds... avoid you!" quipped a small-time merchant; the host's eldest son-in-law guffawed.

"Hurrah for the newspaper man!" the fat man shouted, grabbing Ivan Nikitich and hoisting him into the air. The other old men ran up, and Ivan Nikitich found himself lifted way above his head, on the hands, heads and shoulders of the most venerable and drunk intelligentsia of the town of T-.

"Toss him! Toss him, the rascal! Bring the old fidget! Drag him over here, the dark green scoundrel!" the old men shouted as they carried Ivan Nikitich into the hall.

In the hall the gentlemen joined forces with the old men and began to toss the poor newspaper man right up to the ceiling itself. The ladies clapped their hands, the musicians fell silent and put down their instruments, and the waiters, who had been hired from the club for show, were so surprised by the "outrageous antics" that they started sniggering stupidly into their aristocratic fists. Two buttons leapt off Ivan Nikitich's frock-coat and his belt came undone. He puffed, grunted, groaned, squeaked, and suffered, but... also smiled beatifically. He had not expected such an honour to be accorded to a "nonentity" like himself, who, as he put it, "was hardly visible and barely noticeable among men..."

"Haa-ha-ha-ha!" roared the fiancé, drunk as a cobbler, as he grabbed on to Ivan Nikitich's legs. Ivan Nikitich swayed, slithered from the grip of the T-intelligentsia and grasped the neck of the fat man with the silver medal.

"I'm going to get hurt," he muttered. "I'm going to get hurt! If you wouldn't mind! Just a little bit! Yes, like that... Oh, no, not like that!"

The fiancé let go of his legs, leaving him hanging from the fat man's neck. The fat man shook his head and Ivan Nikitich fell to the floor, groaned, then got to his feet giggling. Everyone laughed, and even the civilised waiters from the uncivilised club twitched their noses condescendingly and smiled. Due to his beatific smile, Ivan Nikitich's face was covered in wrinkles, little tears fell sparkling from his moist, blue eyes, and his mouth was twisted to one side, with his upper lip, moreover, twisted to the right, and his protruding lower lip twisted to the left.

"Honourable Sirs!" he said, addressing them in his feeble tenor voice, as he spread his hands and adjusted his belt, "honourable sirs! May God grant you all that you desire from God. Many thanks to him, my benefactor, that is to say, to Yegor Nikiforovich... He did not scorn an insignificant person. We met the day before yesterday in Gryazny Lane, and he said: "Come to the party, Ivan Nikitich. Look, you really must come. The whole town will be coming, and you, nationally renowned gossip, must come! He didn't spurn me, God bless him. I'm overjoyed by your sincere kindness, you did not forget the newspaper man, a ragged old gent. Thank you. And should not forget our fellow brethren, honourable sirs. It is true that our fellow brethren are insignificant, but they are harmless souls. Do not neglect them, do not scorn them, for they will feel it! Compared to other people, we are insignificant and impoverished, but meanwhile we are the salt of the earth, and we were created by God to be useful to the fatherland, we bring edification to the whole universe, we extol what is good, we revile human evil..."

"What are you babbling on about?" the host shouted out. "Ivan the Clown, you're speaking twaddle! Give us a speech!"

"Speech, speech!" the guests cried.

"A speech? Ahem. I am at your service. Allow me to think!"

Ivan Nikitich began to ponder. Someone shoved a glass of champagne into his hands. After a moment's pondering, he straightened up, raised his glass abruptly and began addressing Yegor Nikiforovich, in his thin tenor voice:

"My speech, dear ladies and gentlemen, will be brief and its length will not be in keeping with the present, extremely moving event. Ahem. The great poet said: "Blessed is he who in his youth was young!"* I have no doubt in the truth of this, and even surmise that I will not be mistaken if I add a few further thoughts to it, and make the following verbal appeal to the young perpetrators of this celebration and accompanying events: may our young people be young not only now, when they are naturally still physically young, but also in their old age, for blessed is he who was young in his youth, but a hundredfold more blessed is the man who preserves his youthfulness until the very grave. May they, the subjects of my present prolixity, be old in body in their old age, but young at heart, that is, in their life-giving spirit. May they preserve unto the grave their ideals, which constitute the sum of true human beatitude. May their joined lives merge into one, pure, good and most honourable life, and may the tenderly loving wife... hee-hee-hee... sound as an octave, as it were, for her husband, a husband strong of thought, and may they produce a sweet-sounding harmony! A long and happy life to them—hurra-a-ah!"

Ivan Nikitich drank the champagne, stamped the floor with his heel and surveyed those who surrounded him like a conqueror.

"Well said, well said, Ivan Nikitich!" yelled the guests.

Staggering and nearly falling over as he attempted to click his heels, the fiancé came up to Ivan Nikitich, clasped the orator by the hand and said: "Bookoo... bookoo merci. Your speech was ve-ve-ve-ry, ve-ry good and not without a certain bi-bias."

Ivan Nikitich leapt forward, embraced the fiancé and kissed him on the neck. The fiancé was taken aback and, in order to hide his embarrassment, began to embrace his father-in-law.

"You are pretty adept at explaining feelings!" the fat man with the medal said. "You cut such a figure, that... it was the last thing that I expected! It is true... forgive me!"

"Adept?" Ivan Nikitich began to squeak. "Adept? Hee-hee-hee. Ahaa! I know myself, I was adept! It is just ardour that is lacking, but where am I going to get it from, this ardour? The horse has bolted, honourable sirs! There used to be a time when one would say or write something that would bring you to tears yourself, and you'd be amazed at your own talent. Ah, those were the days! We should drink, Fra Diavolo, to those days! Come on, friends, let us drink! What marvellous days they were!"

The guests went over to the table and each took a shot glass. Ivan Nikitich was transformed. He poured himself not a glass, but a tumbler.

"Let us drink, honourable sirs," he continued. "You have shown kindness to an old man, so now honour the days when I was a great man! They were glorious days! *Mesdames*, my beauties, clink glasses with the asp and with the basilisk, who is astonished by your beauty! Clink! Hee-hee-hee. I had my little romances. Those were the days, *sacramento*! I loved and suffered, I conquered and was conquered repeatedly. Hurra-a-ah!"

"Those were the days," Ivan Nikitich continued, perspiring and agitated. "Those were the days, my good sirs! The days are good now, but for our colleagues at the newspaper, those days were better, for the simple reason that people had more ardour and truth. It used to be that every scribbler was a heroic warrior, a knight without fear and reproach, a martyr, a sufferer and an honest person. But now? Look, Russian land, upon your sons who write, and hang your head in shame! Where are you, true writers, journalists, and other justice-seekers and labourers in the field of... hic... hic... ahem... of free speech? They're nowh-where to be seen!!! Now everybody writes. Whoever wants to, writes. Even the man with a soul dirtier and blacker than my boot, whose heart was manufactured not in his mother's womb but in the smithy, who has as much truth about him as I have houses of my own, now dares to tread the path of glory—the path that belongs to prophets, to lovers of truth and haters of money. My dear sirs! Today this path has become wider, but there is no one to walk on it. Where are the true talents? Go look for them: by God, you will not find them! Everything has become threadbare and impoverished. Even the young daredevils and stalwarts from the old days who are still alive have become spiritually impoverished hacks now. They used to go after the truth, but today they've begun chasing after fine words and kopecks, damn it! A strange spirit is afoot! It's a tragedy, my friends! And I too, wretched soul that I am, unashamed by my grey hair, also began to chase after fine words! Once in a while I try to sneak in something of that kind into my articles. I thank you, Lord, creator of heaven and earth, that I am not mercenary, so do not venture to write from hunger. Nowadays, whoever wants to eat writes, and writes whatever he wants to, so long as it bears some resemblance to the truth. Do you want to earn a bit of money from newspaper editors? Yes? Well, then, if that is the case, go ahead, write that in our town of T. on such and such a date there was an earthquake, and that the other day a peasant woman called Akulina, excuse my shamelessness, *mesdames*, gave birth to six children at once... You are embarrassed, my beauties! Be so magnanimous as to forgive this ignoramus! I am a doctor of ribaldry, and in antiquity I repeatedly defended my dissertation on this theme in taverns and was victorious in various debates with knaves. Forgive me, my dear friends! Oh-ho-ho... write what you want, you can get away with anything. It didn't use to be like this! If we did write lies, it was due to our dull wits and stupidity, and did not have lies in our armoury because we considered our work to be sacred and worshipped it!"

"Why do you wear mismatched buttons?" said some dandy with four tufts of hair on his head, interrupting Ivan Nikitich.

"Mismatched buttons? It's true they don't match... I've just got used to them... In the olden days, about 20 years ago, I ordered a frock-coat from a tailor; and the tailor went and sewed lightly coloured buttons on instead of black ones by mistake. And so I got used to the mismatched buttons, because I wore that frock-coat for about seven years... Well, there we are, that's how it used to be, my dear sirs... What darlings they are—the young beauties are listening to me, an old codger, like dear friends... Hee hee hee. May God grant you health! My heavenly young beauties! You should have lived forty years ago, when I was young and was able to set hearts on fire. I would have been your slave, young ladies, and would have worn holes in my knees for you... The little petals are laughing! Oh, you are my... You have honoured an old man with your attention."

"Are you writing anything now?" asked an attractively snub-nosed young woman, interrupting Ivan Nikitich, who had got carried away.

"Am I writing anything? Of course, I am! I won't bury my talent, tsarina of my soul, until I am in the grave! Of course, I am writing! Haven't you read anything by me? And who, may I ask, in 1876 published an article in the *Voice**? Who? Didn't you read it? It was a splendid piece! In 1877 I wrote another piece for the *Voice*—however, the editor of that respected newspaper found my article not suitable for publication... Hee-hee-hee... Not suitable... Well! My article had a nasty smell to it, you see, a nasty smell. "There are people," I wrote, "who appear to be patriots, but the waters run deep as to where their patriotism lies—in their hearts or in their pockets?" Hee-hee-hee... a nasty smell. And I went on: "Yesterday," I wrote, "a memorial service was held at the cathedral for those who lost their lives at Plevna."* The dignitaries and ordinary

citizens were all present at the service, with the exception of the gentleman ful-
filling the post of police chief of T., who was conspicuous by his absence, because he found the end of a game of Preference* more interesting than participating in the feelings of national gratitude with his fellow citizens." That hit the
nail on the head! Ho-ho-ho! It wasn't published! But I really did my best then,
my friends! Last year, in 1879, I sent an article to the newspaper *Russian Courier*, which is published in Moscow. I wrote an article about our district schools
for Moscow, my friends, and it was published, and I now receive the *Russian
Courier* for free. How about that! Are you surprised? Be surprised at geniuses,
not at nonentities! I am a nonentity! He-he-he... I write rarely, honourable sirs,
very rarely! Our city T. is lacking in events that I could describe, and I do not
want to write nonsense, I am too proud and I fear my conscience. All of Russia
reads newspapers, and what is T. to Russia?? Why bore it with trifles? Why
would Russia want to know that they found a dead body in our tavern? But in
the old days, how I wrote, back in times gone by... I used to write then for the
Northern Bee, for *Son of the Fatherland,* for the *Moscow Gazette*... I was a contemporary of Belinsky,* once I even poked fun in parentheses at Bulgarin*...
Hee-hee-hee... You don't believe me? I swear to God! Once, I wrote a poem
about martial valour... But what I suffered at that time, my friends, God alone
knows... When I remember what I was like then, I am deeply moved. I was
a young stalwart and a daredevil! I suffered and was tormented for my ideas
and opinions; I went through torture for a feeble return from noble work. In
1846, as a result of an article that I submitted to the *Moscow Gazette,* I was
beaten up so badly by the local townsfolk that I was laid up in hospital for
three months. I have to presume that my enemy paid those Philistines a great
deal for their cruelty: they bludgeoned this servant of God so much that I still
bear the scars. And once, in 1853, I was summoned by the local mayor, Sysoi
Petrovich... You do not remember him, and be glad that you don't. My recollections of that man are the most bitter of all recollections. He summons me
one day and says: "What is this slander about me that you have written in the
Bee, eh?" Well, in what way did I smear him? I simply wrote, you know, that
a gang of swindlers had turned up in our city and that their den was at Guskov's
little tavern... Today that little tavern has vanished without trace, as in 1865 it
was shut down and gave way to Mr. Lubtsovatsky's grocery store. At the end of
my article I added a little piquancy. I went and wrote, you know: "It would not
be amiss, in view of the reasons mentioned above, for the police to focus their
attention on Mr. G...'s tavern." Sysoi Petrovich began to bawl at me and stamp

his feet: "Do you think I don't know? Are you trying to show me how to do my job, you mug? Are you my mentor, eh?" He went on shouting and shouting and put me, trembling, in jail. I spent three days and three nights in jail, recalling Jonah and the whale, suffering every kind of humiliation... I will remember it until my dying day! There is not one bedbug, nor a louse, if you please—not even the smallest insect, which was ever so humiliated as I was by Sysoi Petrovich, may God rest his soul! As for the archpriest, Father Pankraty, whom I had humorously dubbed in my mind as 'the parchpriest,' well, there was once a time when he read somewhere about some archpriest or other, and imagined that it referred to him, and that I was the thoughtless author; when it was not written about him at all and it wasn't written by me. I was once walking past the cathedral when someone whacked me on the back, and on the back of my head, with a walking stick, you know; hit me once, then another time, and a third... Confound it! What on earth's going on? I look round, and there is Father Pankraty, my confessor... He did this in public!! Why? What had I done? And I endured that with humility too... I have put up with a lot, my friends!"

Gryzhev, the prominent merchant who was standing nearby, grinned and slapped Ivan Nikitich on the shoulder.

"Write something!" he said. "Write! Why not write, if you can? Which newspaper will you send it to?"

"To the *Voice*, Ivan Petrovich!"

"Will you let me read it?"

"Hee-hee-hee... Without fail, sir."

"We will see where your talents lie. So, what are you going to write about?"

"Well, if Ivan Stepanovich were to make a donation to the secondary school, then I would write about him!"

Ivan Stepanovich, smooth-shaven, and the opposite of a traditional kaftan-wearing merchant, grinned and blushed.

"In that case, write something!" he said. "I will make a donation. Why not? Let's make it a thousand roubles..."

"Do you mean it?"

"Yes."

"Seriously?"

"Oh, come on... Of course I do."

"Are you sure you are not joking?.. Ivan Stepanovich!"

"Quite sure... Only that... Mmm... What if I make a donation, and you don't write anything?"

"Impossible! I give my word, Ivan Stepanych..."

"In that case... Hm... So, when are you going to write it?"

"Soon, very very soon, sir... Are you sure you are not joking, Ivan Stepanych?"

"Why would I joke? You wouldn't pay to joke, would you? Hmmm... Well, and what if you don't write anything?"

"I will write, Ivan Stepanych! Honest to God, I will!"

Wrinkles appeared on Ivan Stepanovich's large, glossy forehead as he began to think. Ivan Nikitich shuffled from one foot to the other, hiccupped, and fixed his shining eyes on Ivan Stepanovich.

"Look here, Nikita... Nikitich... it's Ivan, right? Look here... I'll give... I will give two thousand silver roubles, and later on perhaps a bit more... But only on the condition, my friend, that you do indeed write something..."

"I swear to god I will!" Ivan Nikitich squeaked.

"Go ahead and write something, but give it to me to read before sending it to the newspaper, and then I'll fork out the two thousand if it is well written..."

"Yes, sir... Ah... ahem... Heard and understood, you are a noble and magnanimous human being! Ivan Stepanovich! Be kind and gracious and don't leave your promise unfulfilled, so it won't just be hot air! Ivan Stepanovich! Benefactor! Honourable sirs! I might be drunk, but I am still compos mentis! Most humane philanthropist! I bow to you! Do your best! Do your utmost to support public education, give from the bounties of your... Oh, Lord!"

"All right, all right... You will see..."

Ivan Nikitich clung to Ivan Stepanovich's coat tail.

"Most magnanimous!" he cried in a shrill voice. "Let your hand join with the hands of the greats... Add oil to the lamp which lights up the universe! Permit me to drink to your health. I drink to you, gracious sir, I drink to you! May you live lo..."

Ivan Nikitich had a coughing fit and downed a shot of vodka. Ivan Stepanovich looked at those around him, winked at Ivan Nikitich and went out of the drawing-room into the hall. Ivan Nikitich stood for a moment thinking, stroked his bald pate and advanced sedately between the dancers to the hall.

"Your good health," he said, turning to his host and clicking his heels. "Thanks for your kindness, Yegor Nikiforovich! I will never forget it!"

"Goodbye my friend! Drop in again. Come to the store, if time permits, you can have a cup of tea with the lads. Come to the wife's name day, if you like... you can give a speech. Well, farewell, my friend!"

Ivan Nikitich shook the extended hand vigorously, bowed low to the guests and shuffled over to the entrance hall where his small, worn overcoat was buried among the mass of fur coats and overcoats.

"A tip would not go amiss, your Honour!" a footman suggested to him courteously while searching for his overcoat.

"My dear fellow! It would be fitting for me to be asking for tips myself, not giving them..."

"Here's your overcoat! Is this yours, your Honour? You can sieve flour through it! You'd be better off passing time in a pigsty than paying calls in this overcoat."

Having put on his overcoat in a state of embarrassment, Ivan Nikitich rolled up his trousers, left the house of the wealthy Yegor L-v, the bigwig of T-, and set off, sloshing through the mud, to his apartment.

He lived on the main street, in an annexe, for which he paid sixty roubles a year to the heirs of some merchant's wife. The annexe stood on the corner of a huge courtyard, overgrown with burdock, and through the trees it looked as humble, as... only Ivan Nikitich himself could look. He closed the latch on the gate and headed to his grey annexe carefully avoiding the burdock. A dog growled from somewhere and barked at him lazily.

"Chisel, Chisel, it's me... your old friend!" he muttered. The door into the annexe was not locked. After cleaning his boots with a small brush, Ivan Nikitich opened the door and entered his den. Grunting as he took off his overcoat, he prayed to the icon and walked through his rooms, which were lit up by the icon-lamp. In the second and last room he again prayed to the icon and tip-toed over to the bed. There was a pretty girl, about 25 years old, lying asleep on the bed.

"Manichka," Ivan Nikitich said, trying to wake her up. "Manichka!"

"Zzzzzz..."

"Wake up, daughter!"

"But I... I... I..."

"Manichka, hey, Manichka! Arise from your slumber!"

"Who's there? What is..., eh? Oh?"

"Wake up, my angel! You are my little musician; my breadwinner and you've got to get up... Beloved daughter! Manichka!"

Manichka turned over and opened her eyes.

"What do you want?" she asked.

"My dear, give me two sheets of paper, please!"

"Go to bed!"

"Daughter, don't refuse my request!"

"What do you want them for?"

"To write a piece for the *Voice*."

"Forget it... go to bed! I left some supper for you!"

"You're my only friend!"

"Are you drunk? That's wonderful... Let me sleep!"

"Give me the paper! What will it cost you to get up and humour your father? My dearest! Do I have to get down on my knees?"

"Aaaah... the devil! Just a minute! Get out of here!"

"All right."

Ivan Nikitich took two steps back and ducked behind the screen. Manichka jumped out of bed and wrapped herself tightly in a blanket.

"More time wasting!" she muttered. "You are a nightmare! Mother of God, when is this all going to end? I never get a moment's rest! You're totally shameless!"

"Daughter, don't insult your father!"

"No one is insulting you! Here you are!"

Manichka took two sheets of paper out of her briefcase and flung them on to the table.

"*Merci*, Manichka! Sorry to have troubled you!"

"All right!" Manichka fell onto the bed, covered herself with the blanket, curled up and immediately fell asleep.

Ivan Nikitich lit a candle and sat down at the table. Having thought for a moment, he dipped his pen in the ink, crossed himself and began to write.

The next day at eight o'clock in the morning, Ivan Nikitich stood at Ivan Stepanovich's front door and pulled the bell with a shaking hand. He pulled it for ten whole minutes and in those ten minutes he nearly died of fear at his own daring.

"You rang? What do you want?" Ivan Stepanovich's manservant asked, opening the door and wiping his sleepy, swollen eyes with the tails of a worn brown frock-coat.

"Is Ivan Stepanovich at home?"

"The master? Where else would he be? What do you want?"

"...I've come to see him."

"Are you from the post office? He's asleep!"

"No, I've come on my own behalf... Actually..."

"Are you an official?"

"No... but... can I wait?"

"Why not? You can! Go into the entrance hall!"

Ivan Nikitich sidled into the entrance hall and sat down on a couch, which was strewn with the servant's rags.

"Ahhh... Hrrrmmm... Who's there?" could be heard from Ivan Stepanovich's bedroom. "Seryozhka! Come here!"

Seryozhka leapt up and ran like a madman to his master's bedroom, while Ivan Nikitich took fright and began to do up all his buttons.

"Eh? Who?" reached his ears from the bedroom. "Who? Don't you have a tongue, you lout? What? Is it someone from the bank? Come on, out with it! An old man?"

Ivan Nikitich's heart thumped, his eyes blurred, and his feet went cold. The critical moment was approaching!

"Call him in!" was heard from the bedroom.

Seryozhka appeared, covered in perspiration, and, clutching his ear, took Ivan Nikitich to Ivan Stepanovich. Ivan Stepanovich had just woken up: he was lying in his double bed, peering out from under a calico blanket. Next to him, under the same blanket, snored the fat man with the silver medal. The fat man had not bothered to undress before getting into bed: the toes of his boots stuck out from under the blanket, and the silver medal had slipped off his neck onto the pillow. The bedroom was stuffy and hot, and smelt of tobacco. The floor was graced with the shards of a broken lamp, a puddle of kerosene and the tatters of a woman's skirt.

"What do you want?" Ivan Stepanovich asked, peering into Ivan Nikitich's face and frowning.

"I apologise for any disturbance I've caused," Ivan Nikitich carefully enunciated, taking a piece of paper out of his pocket. "Most honourable Ivan Stepanovich, allow me..."

"Listen, don't beat about the bush: come to the point. What do you want?"

"I've come, in order to ah... ahem respectfully present..."

"And who on earth are you?"

"Me? Ah... ah... hem... Me? Have you forgotten, sir? I am the newspaper correspondent."

"You? Ah yes. Now I remember. Why are you here?"

"I wanted to submit for your perusal the promised article..."

"You've already written it?"

"Yes, sir."

"Why so quickly?"

"Quickly? I've only just finished writing it."

"Hm... But you... not like this... You should have spent more time on it. What is the hurry? Go off and write some more, old fellow."

"Ivan Stepanovich! Neither place nor time can act as brakes on talent... Even if you had given me a whole year—by God—I would not have written it any better!"

"Ah well, give it here then!"

Ivan Nikitich unfolded the sheet of paper and with both hands took it over to Ivan Stepanovich's head.

Ivan Stepanovich took the sheet of paper, screwed up his eyes and began to read: "'Every year several buildings are erected here in T-, for which purpose architects are sent from the capital, building materials are obtained from abroad, huge amounts of capital are spent—and all this is done, one has to admit, with mercantile aims... It is such a shame! We have over 20 thousand inhabitants, T. has existed for several centuries, various buildings go up; but there is not even a single shack which could give shelter to the power that severs the deep-seated roots of ignorance... Ignorance...' What's that written there?"

"That? *Horribile dictu...*"[1]

"And what does that mean?"

"God only knows what it means, Ivan Stepanovich! But if you write anything bad or terrible, then you put this expression in brackets next to it."

"'Ignorance...' Hmmm... 'lies here in thick layers and enjoys full rights of citizenship in every layer of our society. But at long last the fresh breeze that is breathed by all of educated Russia has blown on us too. A month ago we obtained permission from a government minister to open a secondary school in our city. This decision was greeted by us with genuine enthusiasm. There were some people who did not confine themselves to expressions of enthusiasm, and who also wished to show their love though their actions. Our merchants, who never turn down invitations to provide financial support for

---

1   *Horribile dictu:* "horrible to say" (Latin).

worthwhile undertakings, did not say no in this instance either...' Dammmn it! How quickly he wrote it, and how eloquently! Good for you! Fancy! 'I consider it necessary here to name the main donors. They are: Gury Petrovich Gryzhev (2000), Pyotr Semyonovich Alebastrov (1500), Aviv Inokentievich Potroshilov (1000) and Ivan Stepanovich Trambonov[2] (2000). The latter has promised...' Who is this latter person?"

"The latter, sir? Why, it's you, sir!"

"So you think I am the last?"

"The latter... That is to say... ah... ah... ahem... in the sense of..."

"So I am the last?" Ivan Stepanovich got to his feet and went purple. "Who is the last? Me?"

"You, sir, but in what sense?!"

"In the sense that you are a fool! Do you understand? Fool! To hell with you and your article!"

"Your excellency... Ivan... Ivan..."

"So I am the last? Ah, you're a pimple! A goose!"

Elaborate expressions came flying from Ivan Stepanovich's lips, each one more unprintable than the one before... Ivan Nikitich was panic-struck, sank into a chair and began fidgeting.

"Oh, you ssswine! I'm the last?!? Ivan Stepanovich Trambonov never was and never will be the last! You are the last! Get out of here, and never set foot here again!"

Ivan Stepanovich crumpled the article into a ball in a complete frenzy, and flung it at the face of the correspondent of Moscow and St. Petersburg newspapers... Ivan Nikitich blushed, got to his feet and, waving his hands, scurried from the bedroom. He was met in the entrance hall by Seryozhka who opened the front door for him with the most stupid smile on his stupid face. After finding himself on the street, Ivan Nikitich plodded through the mud back to his apartment, white as a sheet. About two hours later, as he was leaving the house, Ivan Stepanovich caught sight of a peak cap forgotten by Ivan Nikitich on the window ledge in the entrance hall.

"Who does that cap belong to?" he asked Seryozhka.

---

2   Of the four donors' names, two are invented (Gryzhev, Trambonov); all have comic associations. Gryzhev is derived from the word for hernia (*gryzha*), Potroshilov from the verb to gut (*potroshit'*—the Russian word for giblets is *potrokha*). Trambonov and Alebastrov are self-evident.

"The nobody you ordered to be thrown out the other day."

"Chuck it out! What's the point of it lying here?"

Seryozhka took the peak cap, went outside and threw it into the stickiest mud.

Rural Aesculapiuses*

The zemstvo surgery.* It is morning.

In the absence of the doctor, who has gone shooting with the village policeman, the patients are being seen by the orderlies: Kuzma Yegorov, and Gleb Glebych. There are about thirty patients. While he waits for the patients to register, Kuzma Yegorov sits in the consultation room, drinking chicory coffee. Gleb Glebych, who has not washed his face or combed his hair since the day of his birth, is leaning over the table with his chest and belly, getting cross as he registers the patients. The registration is for statistical purposes. Noted down are: name, patronymic, surname, occupation, address, level of literacy, age, and then, after the patient has been examined, the nature of the ailment and the prescribed medicine.

"Damned quills!" Gleb Glebych mutters angrily, slowly writing huge "M"s and "A"s on tiny sheets of paper in a big book. "What kind of ink do they think this is? It's tar, not ink. I am amazed at that zemstvo! They tell you to register the patients, and then give you two kopecks a year for the ink! Next!" he shouts.

A peasant with a bandaged face and Mikhailo "the bass" approach.

"Who are you?"

"Ivan Mikulov."

"Huh? What? Speak Russian!"

"Ivan Mikulov."

"Ivan Mikulov! I'm not asking you! Move away! You! What's your name?"

Mikhailo grins.

"Don't you know?" he asks.

"What are you laughing at? Hell knows! We are up to our ears here, time is precious, and they go and make jokes! What's your name?"

"How can you not know? Are you wasted?"

"Of course, I know, but I have to ask, it's a formality... And there's nothing to get wasted on... I'm not such a drunkard as you are, Your Worship. I don't drink myself into the ground... Name and surname?"

"What's the point in me telling you when you already know? You have known for the last five years... Or have you forgotten, now we are into the sixth year?"

"I haven't forgotten, it's a formality! Do you understand? Or don't you understand the Russian language? A formality!"

"Well, sod it then, if it is a formality! Write it down! Mikhailo Fedotych Izmuchenko..."

"Not Izmuchenko, but—Izmuchenkov."[1]

"Let it be Izmuchenkov then... As you like, so long as you make me well again... You can even call me Ivan the Clown... 'Tis all the same..."

"Occupation?"

"Bass."

"Age?"

"Who knows? I wasn't at my christening, so I wouldn't know."

"Are you over forty?"

"Maybe—but then, maybe not. Write whatever you think."

Gleb Glebych gazes at Mikhailo for some time, thinks it over, and writes down—37. Then, after more thought, he crosses out 37, and writes 41.

"Can you read and write?"

"Do you think there can be a chorister who can't? What a question!"

"In public you should use the polite form of address, and you shouldn't yell at me like that. Next! Who is it? What's the name?"

"Mikifor Pugolova, from Khaplovo."[2]

"We don't treat people from Khaplovo! Next!"

"Have mercy, for Christ's sake... Your Honour... I have walked about thirteen miles to get here..."

"We don't treat people from Khaplovo! Next! Move aside! No smoking here!"

"I am not smoking, Gleb Glebych!"

"What's that in your hand, then?"

"It's my bandaged finger, Gleb Glebych!"

"Not a fag? We don't treat people from Khaplovo!!! Next!"

---

1 Mikhailo's surname has a Ukrainian ending, which the orderlies insist should be Russified.

2 The parodic invented surname Pugolovo is suggestive of "scarecrow" (*pugalo*). The name of the village is also invented, and contains the verb *khapat*, meaning "to grab."

Gleb Glebych finishes registering the patients. Kuzma Yegorov finishes his coffee, and the patients begin to be seen. The former deals with the medications, and goes to the pharmacy; the latter adopts the physician's role and puts on an oilcloth apron.

"Marya Zaplaksina!"[3] Kuzma Yegorov calls out, summoning the first person on the register.

"Here, sir."

A tiny withered old woman who looks as if she's been flattened by an evil fate enters the consultation room. She crosses herself and bows reverently to the orderly playing the part of Aesculapius.

"Hm... Close the door!.. What hurts?"

"My head, sir."

"Riiight... All of it, or just half of it?"

"All of it, sir... absolutely all of it..."

"Don't wrap up your head like that... Take this rag off! Your head should be kept cold, your feet warm, and your torso in an average climate... Does your stomach hurt?"

"It does, sir..."

"Riiight... Well then, pull down your lower eyelid! Good, that's enough. You have anaemia. I will give you some drops... 10 drops in the morning, at lunchtime, and in the evening."

Kuzma Yegorov sits down and writes out a prescription:

"Pr: for Marya Zaplaksina, Liquor ferri, *3 grams from the one on the window-sill, 10 drops three times a day, and the one on the shelf Ivan Yakovlich said not to open without him.*"

The old woman asks what to take the drops with, gives a low bow and leaves. Kuzma Yegorov tosses the prescription into the pharmacy through the small window cut into the wall and calls the next patient.

"Timofey Stukotey!"[4]

"Here!"

Stukotey comes into the consultation room—he is tall and thin, with a big head, and from a distance he looks very much like a walking-stick with a knob.

---

3   The name Zaplaksina suggests "tear-stained" (*zaplakannyi*).

4   Invented surname suggestive of the word for knocking (*stukotnya*) which seems appropriate for a tall, thin patient who looks like a walking-stick.

"What hurts?"

"My heart, Kuzma Yegorych."

"Whereabouts?"

Stukotey points at the pit of his stomach.

"Riiight... Has this been going on for a long time?"

"Since Holy Week... I was walking somewhere recently, and I had to sit down about ten times... I feel shivery, Kuzma Yegorych... Feverish, Kuzma Yegorych..."

"Hm... What else hurts?"

"To be honest, Kuzma Yegorych, everything hurts, but well, you just sort my heart out and don't worry about all the rest... That's a job for the women folk... Give me spirits of some sort to protect my heart from worry. It all gets to your heart, more and more and more, and then suddenly it grips it, I mean, this place here... it grips... then it... like this... My back hurts like hell... It feels as if there is a stone in my head... And I have a cough too."

"How is your appetite?"

"Not a whit..."

Kuzma Yegorov goes up to Stukotey, bends him over, and pushes down with his fist on the pit of his stomach.

"Does that hurt?"

"Ouch... ouch... ahhh... It really hurts!"

"And does this hurt?"

"Ahhh... Like death!!"

Kuzma Yegorov asks him several other questions, has a think, and summons Gleb Glebych for a medical consultation.

"Show your tongue!" Gleb Glebych says to the patient.

The patient opens his mouth wide and sticks out his tongue.

"Stick it out more!"

"It's impossible to stick it out more, Gleb Glebych."

"Everything is possible in this world."

Gleb Glebych gazes for a while at the patient, agonises over something, shrugs his shoulders, and without a word leaves the consultation room.

"Must be catarrh!" he shouts from the pharmacy.

"Give him olei ricini[5] and ammonii caustici!"[6] shouts Kuzma Yegorov. "Rub the abdomen morning and evening! Next!"

---

5 *olei ricini*: "castor oil" (Latin)

6 *ammonii caustici*: "ammonia" (Latin)

Stukotey leaves the consultation room and goes to the window which connects the corridor to the pharmacy. Gleb Glebych pours out a third of a teacup of castor oil and gives it to him. Stukotei drinks it slowly, licks his lips, closes his eyes and rubs his fingers together, thus indicating a request for something edible to go along with it.

"Here's your spirits!" Gleb Glebych shouts, handing him a glass jar with liquid ammonia. "Rub your abdomen, morning and evening, with a cloth rag... Jar to be returned! Don't lean on that!!! Move away!!"

Covering her mouth with a corner of her shawl and grinning, Father Grigory's cook, Pelageya, approaches the little window.

"What can I do for you?" Gleb Glebych inquires.

"Lizaveta Grigorievna sends her regards, Gleb Glebych, she would like some peppermint lozenges."

"With pleasure! For fair specimens of the female sex I am ready to do anything!"

Gleb Glebych takes a jar containing peppermint lozenges down off the shelf and pours half of its contents into Pelageya's shawl.

"Tell her," he says, "that Gleb Glebych was smiling with affection, when he gave you the lozenges. Did she get my letter?"

"She got it and tore it up. Lizaveta Grigorievna does not do love."

"What a grisette she is! Tell her that she is a grisette!"

"Mikhailo Izmuchenkov!" Kuzma Yegorov summons the next patient.

Mikhailo "the bass" comes into the consultation room.

"Mikhailo Fedotych! Our deepest... ! What hurts?"

"My throat, Kuzma Yegorych! I have come to you, actually, so that you, with your permission, regarding my health... It is not so much painful as unprofitable... I can't sing because of my illness, and our choirmaster deducts forty kopecks for each liturgy I have to miss. He deducted a quarter yesterday for Vespers... Today there was a requiem mass at the manor house, all the singers got three roubles each, and I ain't got a thing cause of my illness. And, with your permission, regarding my throat I could suggest to you that it really is sore and hoarse. It's like you have some cat sitting inside you and its paws are... Scratch... Scratch..."

"Is this due to strong drinks perhaps?"

"I don't know the exact cause of my illness, but with your permission, I can tell you that strong drinks do affect tenors, but don't affect basses at all.

The bass becomes deeper and more resonant with drinking, Kuzma Yego-rych... Basses get affected by cold more."

Gleb Glebych's head pokes through the little window.

"What shall I give the old woman?" he asks. "The iron that was on the window has run out. I'll open what's on the shelf."

"No, no! Not without Ivan Yakovlich's permission! He will be angry!"

"What can I give her, then?"

"Something!"

In Gleb Glebych's parlance "something" means "soda."

"You shouldn't consume strong drinks."

"I have not been consuming them for three days now anyway... I've got this because of a cold... It's true that vodka makes bass voices sound hoarse but, as you know, Kuzma Yegorych, hoarseness helps us with the deep notes... Our lot can't do without vodka... What sort of a chorister would you be, if you didn't drink vodka? Not a chorister, but, with your permission, just one big joke! If it weren't for my job, the damned stuff wouldn't have ever passed my lips! Vodka is Satan's blood..."

"Now listen... I will give you a powder... Dissolve it in a bottle, and gargle morning and evening."

"Can I swallow it?"

"Yes."

"Very good. It is a shame when you can't swallow. You gargle, and gargle, and then spit it out—what a waste! And then, this is what I actually wanted to ask you... Since I have stomach trouble, and because of this, with your permission, I let my blood and drink herbal remedies every month, is it all right for me to enter into lawful matrimony?"

Kuzma Yegorov ponders for some time, and says,

"No, I don't advise it!"

"My most heartfelt thanks... You are our wonderful healer, Kuzma Yego-rych! Better than any doctor! I swear to God! The number of people who pray for you! Ahh! Incre-edible!"

Kuzma Yegorov modestly lowers his eyes, and boldly prescribes *natri bi-carbonici*—that is, bicarbonate of soda.

A Lost Opportunity

(A vaudeville incident)

I desperately want to cry! If I were to have a good bawl, I think I would feel better.

It was a delightful evening. I dressed smartly, combed my hair, sprayed myself with scent, and headed off, Don Juan-style, to see her. She is staying at a dacha in Sokolniki.* She is young, beautiful, has a dowry of 30,000, a bit of education, and loves me, the present author, like a cat.

Upon arriving in Sokolniki, I found her sitting on our favourite bench under the tall, slender fir trees. When she saw me, she leapt to her feet and came up to me, beaming.

"How cruel you are!" she began. "How can you be so late? You know how much I miss you! You're terrible!"

I kissed her pretty hand and, trembling, walked with her to the bench. I was all a-quiver, aching, and felt as if my heart was on fire and ready to explode. My pulse was racing.

And no wonder! I had come here to settle my destiny once and for all. It was all or nothing... Everything depended on this evening.

The weather was wonderful, but that did not interest me. I did not even hear the nightingale singing above our heads, in spite of the fact that listening to a nightingale is an obligatory part of any more or less decent rendezvous.

"Why are you so silent?" she asked, looking straight at me.

"Well... What a lovely evening it is... Is your Maman in good health?"

"She is, yes."

"Hmm... Well... The thing is, Varvara Petrovna, I have something to say to you... And that is precisely why I have come... I have kept silent for so long, but now... I am your humble servant! I can no longer keep quiet."

Varya bent her head and began to tear a flower apart with trembling fingers. She knew what I wanted to say. I hesitated for a moment and then went on:

"What is the point in keeping silent? However quiet and timid a person may be, sooner or later he will have to give free rein to his... feelings and his tongue. Perhaps you will be offended... perhaps you will not understand, but... well?"

I paused. I needed to find the right words.

'Go on, speak!' her eyes protested. 'You mumbler! Why are you tormenting me?'

"Of course, you must have guessed a long time ago," I continued after a pause, "why I come here every day, plaguing you with my presence. How could you not have guessed? With your characteristic perceptiveness, you probably guessed ages ago how I feel about... (*Pause*). Varvara Petrovna!"

Varya hung her head even lower. Her fingers fidgeted.

"Varvara Petrovna!"

"Well?"

"I... What can I say?! It's already clear... I love you, that's all... What else is there to say? (*Pause*). I love you desperately! I love you so much that... In a word, if you were to gather together all the existing novels in this world and read all the declarations of love, vows and sacrifices they contain... you would end up with... that which is now in my heart... Varvara Petrovna! (*Pause*). Varvara Petrovna!! Why are you silent?!"

"What do you want?"

"Surely you won't say... no?"

Varya looked up and smiled.

'Oh, to hell with it!' I thought. She smiled, moved her little lips and said almost inaudibly: "Why should I say no?"

I grabbed her hand in desperation, kissed it in desperation, then frantically grabbed her other hand... She was brilliant! As I busied myself with her hands, she rested her head on my chest, which made me aware for the first time of the luxuriant wonder that was her hair.

I kissed her on the head, and my chest was filled with such warmth, it was as if a samovar had been lit inside it. Varya looked up, and there was nothing to be done but kiss her on her little lips.

And at this point, when Varya was at last in my arms, and the thirty thousand were about to be signed over to me, when, in a word, a good wife, good money and a good career were within my grasp, the devil took hold of my tongue...

I wanted to preen a little before my intended, dazzle her with my principles and show off. However, the truth is, I have no idea what came over me... It turned out so very badly!

"Varvara Petrovna!" I began, after our first kiss. "Before you make a promise to be my wife, I consider it my sacred duty to say a few words in order to avoid any possible future misunderstandings. I will be brief... Varvara Petrovna, do you know who and what I am? Yes, I am honest! I am hard-working! I... I am proud! But that is not all... I have prospects... But I am poor... I have nothing."

"I know that," said Varya. "Money does not bring happiness."

"Indeed... Who said anything about money? I... I am proud of my poverty. I earn a pittance for my literary work, but I wouldn't exchange it for the thousands that... which..."

"I understand. So..."

"I am accustomed to being poor. It does not matter to me. I can go without lunch for a week... But what about you? You! You, who are incapable of taking two steps without hiring a cab, who put on a new dress every day, who throw money about, who have never experienced need, and to whom an unfashionable flower is already a cause of great misery, could you really agree to part with all your earthly wealth for my sake? Hmm..."

"I have money. I have a dowry!"

"Forget it! Ten or so thousand will only keep you going for a few years... But what then? Hardship? Tears? Believe me, my dear, I speak from experience! I know! I know what I am talking about! In order to confront poverty, you need a strong will and a super-human character!"

'What nonsense I am spouting!' I thought, and continued:

"Just think about it, Varvara Petrovna! Think about this step you are proposing to take! There would be no turning back! If you have the strength, then marry me, but if you do not, reject me! Oh! I would rather be deprived of you than... have you deprived of your comfort! The hundred roubles that literature brings me every month are nothing. They are not enough! Think about it, before it is too late!"

I leapt up.

"Think about it! Where there is weakness, there are tears, reproaches and premature grey hair... I am warning you because I am an honest man. Do you really feel strong enough to share a life with me which would, to all appearances, be quite unlike your own, if not alien to you?" (*Pause*).

"But I have a dowry!"

"How much? Twenty or thirty thousand! Ha-ha! A million? Besides, how could I allow myself to appropriate what is... No! Never! I am proud!"

I paced up and down in front of the bench several times. Varya pondered. I had triumphed. If I had caused someone to think, then that meant I was respected.

"So, a life of deprivation *with* me, or a life of riches *without* me... Make your choice... Are you strong enough? Is my Varya strong enough?"

And I talked at length in that vein. I became carried away without realising it. While I was speaking, I felt as if I had been split in two. One half of me was carried away by what I was saying, while the other half dreamed: "Hang on a minute, my dear! We could live quite handsomely on your thirty thousand! It would keep us going for a long time!"

Varya listened and listened... Eventually she rose and held out her hand to me.

"I thank you!" she said, in a tone of voice which made me tremble and look into her eyes. Her eyes and cheeks were glistening with tears...

"I thank you! You have done well to be so open with me... I am too spoilt... I cannot... I am not the one for you..."

Then she began to cry. I had messed up... I am always at a loss when I see women crying, and even more so in this case. While I was wondering what I should do, she stifled her sobbing and wiped away her tears.

"You are right," she said. "To marry you would be to deceive you. I cannot be your wife. I am wealthy and spoilt, I take cabs, and I eat snipe and expensive pastries. I never have broth and cabbage soup for dinner. Even my mother constantly reproaches me... But I cannot live without such things! I cannot walk... I get tired... And as for dresses... They would have to be sewn at your expense... No! Farewell!"

Then, with a tragic gesture of her hand, she said without rhyme or reason: "I am not worthy of you! Farewell!"

Having said this, she turned round and went home. And what did I do? I stood there like a fool, my mind a blank, watching her go, and feeling as if the earth had crumbled beneath my feet. When I came to my senses and recalled where I was and what utter stupidity had overcome my tongue, I howled. I wanted to call out to her 'Come back!!', but she was long gone.

I set off for home, ashamed and empty-handed. There were no more trams by the city gate. Nor did I have money for a cab. I had to walk home.

About three days later, I went to Sokolniki. At the dacha, I was told that Varya was indisposed and about to go to St. Petersburg with her father to see her grandmother. I achieved nothing...

Now I am lying on my bed, biting my pillow and beating myself about the head. It feels like cats are clawing at my heart... Reader, how can I put things right? How can I take back my words? What can I say or write to her? It's impossible to fathom! The opportunity was lost—and how stupidly it was lost!

Flying Islands

Written by Jules Verne
Translated by A. Chekhonte

Chapter I
The Speech

"...And with that, gentlemen, I conclude," declared John Lund, a young member of the Royal Geographical Society, and he sank, exhausted, into an armchair. The lecture theatre shook as it rang to fervent applause and shouts of "bravo." One after another, gentlemen began approaching John Lund to shake his hand. Seventeen gentlemen signalled their astonishment by breaking seventeen chairs, and eight gentlemen, one of whom was the captain of the 100,009-ton yacht *Katavasia,** dislocated their long necks...

"Gentlemen!" said a touched John Lund. "I consider it my most sacred duty to thank you for your diabolical patience in listening to my speech, which lasted 40 hours, 32 minutes and 14 seconds! Tom Snipe,"[1] he addressed his elderly servant, "wake me in five minutes. I'll sleep for as long as the gentlemen will excuse me for daring to sleep in their presence!!"

"Yes, sir!" said old Tom Snipe.

John Lund threw back his head and immediately fell asleep.

John Lund was a Scot by birth. He had never received an education anywhere or studied anything, yet he knew everything. He was one of those fortunate beings who by dint of their own intellect arrive at an understanding of all that is beautiful and great. The excitement produced by his speech was wholly deserved. In the course of 40 hours he had outlined for the respected gentlemen's consideration a grandiose project, whose realisation was later to gain great glory for England and to demonstrate just how far the human intellect may occasionally reach! *"Drilling through the Moon with a Colossal Bit"*—such was the subject of John Lund's speech!

---

1   In the original, the servant's surname is Bekas, which means "snipe" in Russian.

Chapter II

The Mysterious Stranger

John Lund slept less than three minutes. Someone's heavy hand came down
on his shoulder and he woke up. Before him stood a seven-foot, one-inch tall
gentleman, as slender as a lance, and as lean as a desiccated snake. He was completely bald. Dressed all in black, he had four pairs of spectacles on his nose,
a thermometer on his chest, and another on his back.

"Follow me!" said the bald gentleman in a sepulchral voice.

"Where to?"

"Follow me, John Lund!"

"And if I don't?"

"Then I shall be forced to drill through the moon before you!"

"In that case, sir, I am at your service."

"Your servant will come with us!"

Mr. Lund, the bald gentleman and Tom Snipe left the lecture theatre and
set off walking through the illuminated streets of London. They walked for
a very long time.

"Sir," Tom Snipe addressed Mr. Lund, "if our route is as long as this man is
tall, then based on the laws of friction, we will wear out the soles of our shoes!"

The gentlemen considered the matter and, ten minutes later, having
found Snipe's words to be witty, they burst into loud laughter.

"With whom do I have the honour of laughing, sir?" Lund asked the bald
gentleman.

"You have the honour of walking, laughing, and talking with a member of
every geographical, archaeological, and ethnographic society, master of every
science, past and present, member of the Moscow Artistic Circle, honorary
trustee of the School for Bovine Obstetrics in Southampton, subscriber to the
Illustrated Demon, professor of yellow-green magic and introductory gastronomy at the future University of New Zealand, and director of the Nameless
Observatory, William Doltius.[2] I am taking you, sir, to..."

John Lund and Tom Snipe knelt before the great man, of whom they had
heard so much, and bowed their heads in respect...

"I am taking you, sir, to my observatory, located 20 miles from here.
Sir! I need an ally in my endeavour, the significance of which you will be

---

2   In the original, the surname is Bolvanius, which contains the word for dolt (*bolvan*).

able to grasp only if you apply both hemispheres of your brain. I have chosen you... After your forty-hour-long speech, you will hardly want to engage me in conversation, and I, sir, love nothing more than my telescope and prolonged silence. Your servant's tongue will, I hope, be bound, sir, by your command. May silence reign!!! I am leading you... You have nothing against this?"

"Nothing, sir! It remains for me only to regret that we are not fast walkers and that under our feet we have soles which cost money and..."

"I'll buy you new boots."

"Thank you, sir."

Those of my readers enflamed with a desire to become more closely acquainted with Mr. William Doltius should peruse his remarkable work *Did the Moon Exist before the Flood? If It Did, Why Was Not It Submerged Too?* To this work is appended the banned brochure written a year before his death: *A Method for Pulverising the Universe without Simultaneously Perishing.* The personality of this most exceptional individual could not be better characterised than in these writings.

Among other things, in the above works Doltius describes how he spent two years in the Australian bulrushes, where he fed on crayfish, slime, and crocodile eggs, and in these two years never once saw a fire. While living in the bulrushes, he invented a microscope absolutely identical to our standard microscope and discovered the spine in fish of the *Fisch* species. On returning from his long journey, he settled a few miles from London and dedicated himself entirely to astronomy. Since he was a proper misogynist (he had been married three times, and consequently had three pairs of magnificent branched horns), and did not want to be exposed until the time was ripe, he lived as an ascetic. Possessing a subtle, diplomatic mind, he contrived to make sure that his observatory and his works on astronomy would be known only to himself. To the chagrin and dismay of all right-thinking Englishmen, this great man has not survived to the present day. He died peacefully last year: while swimming in the Nile, he was devoured by three crocodiles.

Chapter III
Mysterious Spots

In the observatory to which Lund and old Tom Snipe were led (*a long, tedious description of the observatory follows which, in order to save space and time, the translator has decided to omit)...* stood the telescope perfected by Doltius. Mr. Lund went over to the telescope and began observing the moon.

"What do you see, sir?"

"The moon, sir."

"And what do you see next to the moon, Mr. Lund?"

"I have the honour of seeing only the moon."

"Do you not see pale spots moving about beside the moon?"

"I'll be damned, sir! Well, call me an ass if I don't see them now! What sort of spots are they?"

"They are spots which are visible only through my telescope. That's enough! Hands off the telescope! Mr. Lund and Tom Snipe! I simply have to find out what sort of spots they are! I will soon be there! I'm going to those spots! You are coming with me!"

"Hurrah! Three cheers for the spots!" cried John Lund and Tom Snipe.

Chapter IV

A Scandal in the Sky

In half an hour's time, Messrs William Doltius, John Lund and the Scot Tom Snipe were already flying toward the mysterious spots on 18 aerostats. They were sitting in a hermetically sealed cube containing compressed air and an apparatus to produce oxygen [A spirit invented by chemists. People say it is impossible to live without it. Nonsense. It is only impossible to live without money. Translator's note]. The first stage of this grandiose, hitherto unprecedented flight was completed on the night of 13 March 1870. A south-westerly wind was blowing. The magnetic needle indicated NWW (*an incredibly boring description of the cube and the 18 aerostats follows)*... A profound silence reigned in the cube. The gentlemen were wrapped in capes and smoking cigars. Stretched out on the floor, Tom Snipe was sleeping just as though he were at home. The thermometer registered below zero. For the first twenty hours not a single word was spoken and nothing in particular happened. The balloons reached the clouds. A few bolts of lightning chased the balloons, but could not catch them, since they belonged to an Englishman. On the third day, John Lund contracted diphtheria and Tom Snipe was overcome by spleen. The cube collided with an aerolite and received a terrible blow. The thermometer showed –76.

"How are you feeling, sir?" Doltius addressed John Lund on the fifth day, finally breaking the silence.

"Thank you, sir," replied Lund, genuinely touched. "I'm touched by your attention. I'm suffering horribly! Where is my faithful Tom?"

"He's now sitting in the corner, chewing tobacco and trying to look like a man who's married ten women at once."

"Ha, ha, ha, Sir Doltius!"

"Thank you, sir!"

Before William Doltius managed to shake young Lund's hand, something terrible occurred. There was a frightful cracking sound... Something burst; a thousand cannon shots rang out, resulting in a whooshing roar, and a furious whistling. Entering a less dense medium, the brass cube could not sustain the internal pressure; it burst, and its fragments hurtled into infinite space.

This was a most terrible moment, unlike any other in the history of the universe!!

Mr. Doltius grabbed onto Tom Snipe's legs; the latter, in turn, grabbed John Lund's legs, and all three hurtled at lightning speed into the unfathomable abyss. The balloons disengaged from them, and, once free of their weight, spun round and popped with a bang.

"Where are we, sir?"

"In the ether."

"Hmm... If we're in the ether, what shall we breathe?"

"Where's your willpower, Sir Lund?"

"Sirs!" cried Snipe. "I have the honour of informing you that, for some reason, we are flying up, not down!"

"Hmm... The devil take it! That means we're already beyond the Earth's gravity... Our goal is drawing us towards itself! Hurrah! Sir Lund, how are you feeling?"

"Thank you, sir. I see the Earth above us, sir!"

"That's not the Earth; it's one of our spots! We are just about to crash into it!" Crrrrash!!!!

Chapter V
Prince Meshchersky's* Island

Tom Snipe was the first to regain consciousness. He wiped his eyes and began to inspect the place where he, Doltius and Lund were lying. He took off a sock and proceeded to rub the gentlemen with it. The gentlemen were not slow in coming to.

"Where are we?" inquired Lund.

"You're on an island belonging to the group which flies! Hurrah!"

"Hurrah! Look up, sir! We've eclipsed Columbus!"

Several other islands were flying above them on the island (*a description of a scene comprehensible only to English people follows*)... They set off to explore the island. Its width was..., its length... (*numbers and more numbers... Forget it!*) Tom Snipe managed to find a tree whose sap reminded him of Russian vodka. It was strange that the trees were shorter than blades of grass. The island was uninhabited. Not one living being had ever trod its soil...

"Look, sir! What is this?" Lund asked Doltius, as he picked up some bundle.

"Strange... Surprising... Astounding..." muttered Doltius.

The bundle turned out to be the works of a certain Prince Meshchersky, written in one of the barbarian languages, Russian it seems.

How had these works found their way here?

"Curses!" shouted William Doltius. "Has someone been here before us?!!? Who could have been here?!.. Tell me—Who? Who? Curses! Oooooh! Oh, heavenly thunders, smash my great brains to smithereens! Bring him here! Give him to me! I'll devour him along with his works!"

And William Doltius, raising his arms skywards, began cackling in a terrifying manner. A suspicious gleam flickered in his eyes. He had gone mad.

Chapter VI
The Return

"Hurrah!!" shouted the residents of Le Havre who were crowded along the whole of the seafront. The air was filled with joyful shouts, the pealing of bells, and music. The dark mass that had been threatening everyone with death was coming down into the bay, and not on to the town... Ships rushed to get out into the open sea. After blocking out the sun for so many days, the dark mass plopped gravely (*pesamment*)[3] into the bay, splashing the entire seafront, to the accompaniment of triumphant shouts from the crowd and thunderous music. After dropping into the bay, it sank. A minute later the bay was already

---

3   *Pesamment*: "heavily" (French)

clear. Waves furrowed it in every direction... Three people were floundering in the middle of the bay. They were the mad Doltius, John Lund, and Tom Snipe. Boats hurried out to pick them up.

"We haven't eaten for fifty-seven days!" mumbled Mr. Lund, who was as thin as a starving artist, and he explained what had happened.

Prince Meshchersky's island no longer exists. When it took on the three intrepid men, it became heavier, slipped out of its neutral orbit and was pulled towards the Earth where it sank in the Bay of Le Harve...

Conclusion

John Lund is now occupied with the problem of drilling through the moon. The time is already approaching when the moon will be embellished by a hole. This hole will belong to the English. Tom Snipe now lives in Ireland and has taken up farming. He raises chickens and flogs his only daughter, whom he is bringing up according to Spartan methods. He even takes interest in scientific problems: he's furious with himself for forgetting to bring back from the Flying Island some seeds of the trees whose sap reminded him of Russian vodka.

A Rotten Story

(*Something Vaguely Novelistic*)

It all began back in the winter.

A ball was underway. The music was blaring, the chandeliers were blazing, the gentlemen were keeping their hopes up, and the young ladies were enjoying life to the hilt. There was dancing in the ballrooms, card-playing in the salons, drinking at the bar, and declarations of desperate love in the library.

Lyolya Aslovskaya, a plump, pink-cheeked blonde with large blue eyes, very long hair, and the number 26 in her passport, was sitting on her own and feeling angry, to spite everyone, the whole world and herself. She was sick at heart. The fact is, the men were behaving more than swinishly towards her. Their behaviour had been particularly deplorable for the last two years. She had noticed that they had stopped paying her attention. They were reluctant to dance with her. That was the least of it. Those scoundrels would walk past and not even look at her—as if she had stopped being beautiful. And if one of them did happen to cast a glance in her direction, sort of in passing, accidentally, it would not be a rapturous or platonic look, but rather the way one might eye a luscious pie or a roasted piglet before dinner.

Whereas in the old days...

"And it's the same story every evening, at every ball!!" Lyolya thought angrily, biting her lip. "I know why they ignore me, I know! It's their revenge! They're getting their own back because I despise them! But... but when will I finally get married? How can one get married like this? Time is flying by, after all! What a load of scoundrels you all are!"

On the evening in question, Fate took pity on Lyolya. When Lieutenant Nabrydlov[1] got sloshed to the gills instead of dancing the promised third quadrille with her, and then smacked his lips in a particularly idiotic way as he walked past, thus showing his utter contempt for her, she could not take it any

---

1   An invented surname derived from the Ukrainian *nabridlo*, meaning "fed up."

longer... Her anger reached its peak. Her blue eyes misted over, her lips began to quiver. Tears were about to spring forth... In order to hide her tears from people who did not respect her, she turned towards the dark, steamed-up windows, and—oh, glorious moment, you've arrived!—by one of the windows caught sight of a handsome young man who did not take his eyes off her. The young man presented a touching picture which pierced her very heart. His pose was graceful; his eyes were full of love, amazement, questions, answers, and so forth; his face was wistful. Lyolya instantly perked up. She adopted the requisite pose and began the requisite scrutiny. As a result of her observations it became apparent that the look the young man gave her was not accidental or casual, he was staring with exultation and delight.

"Dear Lord!" thought Lyolya. "If only someone would have the wit to introduce us! That's the value of a new man on the scene! He noticed me right away!"

The young man soon began to dash about, hurrying from one room to the next, and began pestering the other men.

"He wants to meet me! He's looking for someone to introduce him!" Lyolya thought, panting with excitement.

Indeed it was so. About ten minutes later, an amateur actor with a rakish clean-shaven face gave in to the young man's pleas and shuffled over to introduce him to Lyolya. The young man turned out to be "one of us"—the insanely talented artist Nogtev. Nogtev is about twenty-four years old, dark-haired, with passionate Georgian eyes, a dashing little moustache, and pale cheeks. He never paints anything, but he is an artist. He has long hair, a goatee, a charm in the shape of a golden palette hanging off his watch chain, golden palettes for cufflinks, elbow-length evening gloves, and shoes with exceedingly high heels. He is a good sort, but as dumb as they come. He has a noble Papa, a Mama to match, and a rich Grandmother. He is a bachelor. He shook Lyolya's hand timidly, sat down timidly, and, as soon as he was seated, began to devour Lyolya with his large eyes. He started talking reluctantly and timidly. Lyolya prattled on, but he said only 'Yes... no... well, you know...,' hardly breathing as he spoke, answering her questions at random, and rubbing his (and not Lyolya's) left eyelid in embarrassment. Lyolya applauded herself inwardly. She decided that the artist had fallen for her, and was triumphant.

The day after the ball, Lyolya was sitting by the window in her room and looking triumphantly at the street. Nogtev was outside, pacing up and down in front of her windows. He was pacing up and stealing glances at her windows.

He glanced sadly, yearningly, tenderly, passionately, as if he were about to die. On the third day it was the same story. On the fourth day, it rained, and he was not there. (Someone had convinced Nogtev that an umbrella did not suit him). On the fifth day, Nogtev paid a formal visit to Lyolya's parents. The acquaintance was tied with a Gordian knot—a knot impossible to unravel.

About four weeks later there was another ball. (See the opening paragraph).

Nogtev stood by the doors, leaning against the doorframes, devouring Lyolya with his eyes. Lyolya, wanting to make him jealous, was flirting with Lieutenant Nabrydlov, who was drunk, but not yet totally sloshed—just a wee bit tipsy, on his first round.

Lyolya's Papa sidled up to Nogtev.

"So you paint?" Lyolya's Papa asked. "You're an artist?"

"Yes."

"I see... That's a good occupation... Good luck to you... Hmm... So God gave you talent, eh... I see... To each his own talent..."

Papa fell silent for a moment, then continued: "You know, young man, here's what you should do, since you... do all that painting. Come and stay in the country with us this spring. There are some quite enchanting places there! Stunning views, I tell you! Rakhvael* never had the chance of painting anything similar. We'll be very happy to have you. Seeing as my daughter and you are... such good friends... Ahem... ahem... You young people, you young people! Heh-heh-heh..."

The artist bowed and on the first of May of this year he set off with his personal effects for the Aslovsky estate. These personal effects consisted of a superfluous box of paints, a piqué waistcoat, an empty cigarette case, and two shirts. He was welcomed with extremely open arms and given two rooms, two servants, a horse, and whatever else he desired, as long as things kept looking promising. The artist made excellent use of his situation: he ate huge amounts of food, drank a lot, slept long hours, admired nature, and could not keep his eyes off Lyolya. As for Lyolya, she was more than happy. He was right beside her: young, good-looking, so timid... and so in love! He was so timid that he did not dare approach her, just kept peeping at her from a distance, from behind a curtain or a bush.

"Timid love!" Lyolya thought, sighing...

One fine morning, her Papa and Nogtev were sitting on a garden bench and chatting. Papa kept praising the delights of family life, while Nogtev listened patiently, trying to catch a glimpse of Lyolya's body.

"Are you per chance an only son?" Papa asked him casually.

"No... I've got a brother, Ivan... He's a good fellow! Really marvellous person! You don't know him?"

"I haven't had the honour..."

"It's a shame you don't know him. He's a great wit, you know, a lot of fun, just terrific! He's a writer. Gets commissions from all the editors. He writes for the *Jester.** It's a shame you don't know him. He would be happy to meet you... Here's an idea! Do you want me to write to him and invite him to come and stay? What do you think? Honest to God! It would be even jollier!"

When Papa heard this proposal, his heart sank, but—there was nothing for it!—he had to say: "I'd be delighted!"

Nogtev leapt up as a sign of his happy disposition and immediately despatched an invitation to his brother.

Brother Ivan wasted no time in turning up. And he arrived with an entourage—his good friend Lieutenant Nabrydlov and an enormous toothless old dog named Turk. He brought them along so that, as he put it, he would not be ambushed by highwaymen along the way and would have a drinking buddy. Three rooms, two servants, and a horse between the two of them were put at their disposal.

"Don't you worry about us, now," Ivan said to his hosts. "We wouldn't want that! We don't need any of your feather eiderdowns, your sauces, your pianos—we don't need anything! But if, out of the kindness of your hearts, you'd get in some beer and vodka for us... that's another matter altogether!"

If you can picture a massive thirty-year-old man, with a big, fat face, scruffy little beard and puffy eyes, sporting a sailcloth shirt and a tie off to one side, you'll spare me from having to describe Ivan. He was the most obnoxious person in the world.

When he was sober, he was more or less tolerable: he just lay silently on his bed. When he was drunk, however, he was as unbearable as prickly burdock burrs on bare skin. When he was drunk, he talked non-stop, and cursed a blue streak too, regardless of whether or not women and children were present. His topics of conversation were lice, bedbugs, underpants, and the devil knows what else. He had no other more up-to-date themes. Papa, Mama, and Lyolya did not know what to think and blushed when Ivan started cracking jokes at the dinner table.

Unfortunately, during his entire stay at the Aslovsky estate, he was never once sober. Nabrydlov, the runty little lieutenant, meanwhile, tried his darnedest to be just like Ivan.

"He and I aren't artists!" he kept saying. "Much too grand for us! We're just peasants!"

The first thing that Ivan and Nabrydlov did was to move out of their fancy rooms in the main house, which they decided were too stuffy, and into the wing with the steward, who did not mind having a couple of drinks in good company. The second thing they did was to get rid of their frock coats and parade around the courtyard and the garden in their shirtsleeves. Lyolya kept running into Ivan or else the lieutenant sprawled out under a tree in a state of undress. Ivan and the lieutenant drank, ate, fed their dog liver, made fun of their hosts, chased the cooks round the yard, raised a riot every time they went swimming, slept like the dead, and blessed fate for chancing to bring them to a place where they could live it up *à la* pigs in clover.

"Hey, listen you!" Ivan said to Nogtev one day, winking drunkenly in Lyolya's direction. "If you're after her... so be it! We won't come near. You were there first, so it's in your hands. All due respect! We are decent people... We wish you every success!"

"We won't try to snatch her away! No way!" Nabrydlov confirmed. "That would be dastardliness on our part!"

Nogtev shrugged his shoulders and went back to feasting his eyes on Lyolya.

When you are bored with quiet, you long for a storm, and when you get bored of being all prim and proper, you want to raise a ruckus. When Lyolya got bored with timid love, she began to grow angry. Timid love will not butter any parsnips. To everyone's great annoyance, Nogtev was as timid in June as he was in May. In the main house they were sewing Lyolya's trousseau; Papa was dreaming day and night of getting a loan for the wedding, and meanwhile their relationship had still not taken any definite form. Lyolya made Nogtev go fishing with her for days on end. But that did not help. He stood beside her silently with his fishing rod, stammering something once in a while, and devouring her with his eyes. That was all. Not one deliciously terrifying word! Not a single declaration of love!

"You know..." Papa said to him one day, "we don't need to be so formal... You know, I'm fond of you... Call me... call me 'Papa' from now on... I'd like that..."

Like an idiot, Nogtev started to call Lyolya's father Papa, but even that did not help. Just as before, he remained silent at times when he should have been cursing gods for giving a man one tongue instead of ten. Ivan and Nabrydlov soon got wise to Nogtev's tactics.

"What the hell is wrong with you!" they grumbled. "You're like a dog in the manger: won't eat the hay yourself and won't let anyone else have it! You're a regular swine! When a piece of pie is about to pop into your mouth, be sure to gobble it up! Cause if you don't want it, we'll take it! Mark our words!"

But everything in this world comes to an end. And our story will too. And the lack of definition surrounding the Nogtev-Lyolya relationship also came to an end.

The denouement took place in the middle of June.

It was a quiet evening. The air was fragrant. The nightingale was singing its heart out. The trees were whispering. To resort to the fancy turn of phrase beloved by Russian novelists: languor was in the air... Obviously, the moon was also in evidence. The only thing missing from this sublimely poetic scene was Afanasy Fet,* who, if he had been standing behind some bush, would be reciting his enchanting verse for all to hear.

Lyolya, huddled in her shawl, was sitting on a bench, gazing pensively at the river through the trees.

"Am I really that unapproachable?" she wondered. She imagined herself standing there: majestic, proud, arrogant... Her musings were interrupted by the arrival of Papa.

"Well?" Papa asked. "Any news?"

"No."

"Hmm... Damn it!.. When will all this end? It costs me an arm and a leg to feed these loafers, you know! Five hundred roubles a month! That's no joke! The dog alone eats thirty kopecks worth of liver per day. If he wants to propose, he should jolly well propose, and if he doesn't, then to hell with him, and his brother and his dog! What does he say, anyway? Has he spoken to you? Has he told you he loves you?"

"No. He's so shy, Papa!"

"Shy... I know his kind of shyness! He's trying to pull the wool over our eyes! Stay right where you are, and I'm going to send him over here. Be done with him, young lady! No point in standing on ceremony... It's high time. Be so kind, my dear, as to... You're no spring chicken... You must know every trick in the book by now!"

Papa disappeared. After about ten minutes, Nogtev appeared, poking his way timidly through the lilac bushes.

"Did you want to see me?" he asked Lyolya.

"I did. Come over here! That's enough of you avoiding me! Take a seat!"

Nogtev approached Lyolya gently and gently sat down on the edge of the bench.

"How good looking he is in the dark!" Lyolya thought, and, turning to him, she said:

"Talk to me, Fyodor Panteleyevich... Why are you always so secretive? Why are you always so quiet? Why don't you open up your heart to me? What did I do to earn your distrust? I'm offended, really I am... You'd think we weren't friends... Start talking!"

The artist cleared his throat, heaved a sigh, and said:

"There's a lot that I need to tell you. A lot!"

"So what's stopping you?"

"I'm afraid that you might get upset, Elena Timofeyevna. You won't, will you?"

Lyolya giggled.

"The time has come!" she thought. "He's shaking! He's shaking all over! Have I hooked you, my dear?"

Lyolya was going weak in the knees herself. She was overcome with the trembling favoured by every novelist.

"In about ten minutes the embraces, kisses, and vows will all begin... Ah!"—she daydreamed, brushing the artist with her bare, hot elbow to fuel the flames.

"Well? What's the problem?" she asked. "I'm not as stand-offish as you think..." (There was a pause.) "Go on, say something!.." (Another pause.) "Out with it!!"

"Well, the thing is... There's nothing on earth I love so much, Elena Timofeyevna, as the fine arts... painting, in other words. My colleagues think that I've got talent and that I could be a decent artist..."

"Oh, I'm sure! *Sans doute!*"[2]

---

2   *Sans doute*: "without a doubt" (French).

"So yes... Anyway... I love my art. That is to say... I prefer genre painting, Elena Timofeyevna! Art... Art, you know... It's a magnificent night!"

"Yes, an exceptional night!" said Lyolya, wriggling like a snake as she snuggled in her shawl, her eyes half-closed. (Young women are brilliant when it comes to romantic touches—absolutely brilliant!)

"You know," continued Nogtev, wringing his pale hands, "I have been wanting to speak to you for a long time, but I was... afraid. I thought that you might get angry. But if you understand me in the right way... then you won't get angry. You too love art!"

"Oh... Well, yes... Of course! It's art, after all!"

"Elena Timofeyevna! Do you know why I'm here? Can't you guess?"

Lyolya grew terribly embarrassed, and put her hand on his elbow, as if by accident.

"It's true," continued Nogtev after a pause, "that there are some artists who act like pigs... That's true... They don't give a hoot about a woman's modesty... But I—I'm not like that! I've got tact. A woman's modesty is... the kind of thing that you can't just ignore."

"Why is he telling me all of this?" thought Lyolya, covering her elbows with her shawl.

"I'm not like them... For me, a woman is sacred! So you've nothing to fear... I'm not like them, I'm the kind of man who won't stupidly act out of line... Elena Timofeyevna! Will you permit me to—? Just hear me out; I'm being sincere, honest to God, because it's not for myself that I'm doing this, but for the sake of art! For me, art comes before the satisfaction of base instincts!"

Nogtev seized her by the hand. She leaned ever so slightly towards him.

"Elena Timofeyevna! My angel! My only joy!"

"Yes?..."

"May I ask you something?"

Lyolya giggled. She was already puckering her lips for that first kiss.

"Could I ask you a question? I beg you! Honest to God, it's for the sake of art! I have taken such a liking to you, I really have! You're the very one I need! To hell with everyone else! Elena Timofeyevna! My friend! Will you be—"

Lyolya drew herself up, getting ready to fall into an embrace. Her heart began to race.

"Will you—"

The artist grabbed her by the other hand. She put her head on his shoulder submissively. Tears of joy glistened on her eyelashes...

"My dear friend! Please be... my model!"

Lyolya lifted her head.

"What?!"

"Will you model for me?"

Lyolya stood up.

"What was that? What did you just say?"

"Model for me... Please!"

"Hm... Is that all?"

"I'll be forever in your debt! You'd give me the chance to paint a picture... and what a picture!"

Lyolya blanched. Her tears of love suddenly turned into tears of desperation, anger, and other bad feelings.

"So... that was it all along?!" she asked, trembling all over.

The poor artist! The echo of a loud slap reverberated through the dusky garden, and one of Nogtev's pale cheeks turned a blazing red. He scratched his cheek and fell into a stupor. He felt himself plummeting through space... He saw stars in front of his eyes...

Trembling, as white as death, and struck dumb, Lyolya took a step forward, then reeled. She felt as if she had been run over. Gathering all her strength, she set off towards the house, staggering as if she was ill. Her legs were giving way under her, she could not see where she was going, and her hands were reaching for her hair with the obvious intention of tearing it out...

She was almost at the house when she had cause to blanch once again. Blocking her way near the summer house, which was covered with wild grapevine, stood Ivan, drunk, dishevelled, with his waistcoat unbuttoned and his arms outspread. Bringing his fat face right up to Lyolya's, he sneered sardonically, and befouled the night air with a Mephistophelean "ha-ha." He grabbed Lyolya by the hand.

"Get out of my way!" hissed Lyolya and yanked her hand back...

A rotten story!

The Twenty-Ninth of June*

(The Tale of a Hunter Who Could Never Hit His Target)

It was four in the morning...

The steppe was bathed in the gold of the sun's first rays and, covered in dew, was sparkling as if strewn with diamond dust. The mist had been chased away by the morning breeze and had settled beyond the river in a leaden wall. Ears of rye and the tops of burdock and dog rose stood motionless, occasionally bowing to each other and whispering. Kites, merlins and owls were flying over the grass and over our heads, flapping their wings evenly. They were out hunting...

All six of us—Akim Petrovich Otletayev,[1] the magistrate, the zemstvo doctor, Otletayaev's son-in-law Predpolozhensky, the village elder Kozoyedov and I—were going hunting in Otletayev's low-slung carriage. Four dogs, their tongues hanging out, were running behind the carriage. The zemstvo doctor and I were skinny types, but the others were as fat as hundred-gallon barrels, and while the ancient carriage was both wide and deep, we felt horribly squashed. Indeed, my elbow and rifle butt kept prodding Kozoyedov in the belly. We were all jostling and huffing and puffing and hating each other's guts, and longing for the moment when we would be able to get out of the carriage. We were going some distance into the steppe to shoot partridges, little bustards, quails, marsh game and, should fortune smile on us, great bustards. We were being marshalled by Otletayev, the owner of the carriage and horses, thanks to whom we were going hunting. Our bodies were crushed, but our souls were overflowing with happiness of the highest quality!

A person who has never gone hunting, whether by carriage or on foot, will never understand these joys. We held on to our guns and gazed at them as lovingly, as mothers gaze at beloved sons who hold great promise.

---

1   Otletayev, Predpolozhensky and Kozoyedov are all humorous names concocted by Chekhov which derive from the words for "fly away," "supposition," and "goat eater."

"What route are we going to take?" I asked, when Otletayevka was about six miles behind us.

"We are making for Yelanchik now," Otletayev replied, "to shoot snipe... It is about five miles from here. And we will also shoot quail in the millet field too... When we've done with the quails, we'll bed down for the night, and tomorrow at crack of dawn, the real shooting will begin..."

"Gentlemen, what do you think?" I asked, pointing at a kite flying far above us in the azure heights, could we hit it from here? What do you think?"

"No, we couldn't!" Otletayev said. "It's too far away! Though, you could with my gun..."

"You wouldn't hit it even with your gun," Predpolozhensky remarked.

"Yes, you would. You couldn't hit it with a pellet, it's too far off, but with a bullet you might..."

"Even with a bullet you wouldn't hit it."

"It's for me to say if I'm going to hit it or not! You don't know my gun like I do... You've never seen a good gun in your life, and that's why it seems so unlikely to you... I've hit things even further away..."

Predpolozhensky threw back his head and laughed...

"What's so funny?" Otletayev continued. "You don't believe me, is that it?"

"Of course, I don't believe you."

"Hm... You obviously don't know my gun... It's a marvellous gun! It cost six hundred roubles for a reason."

"How... much??" Predpolozhensky asked, stretching his neck... "How much did you say, Papa?"

"Six hundred roubles... What's so funny? Have a look at the gun, and then you'll change your tune!"

"I can see it... What make is it?"

"Lepellier... Marseilles..."

"Lepellier? Never heard of it... It's a gun like any other... Costs about one hundred roubles... I don't like it, father-in-law, when you lie! Why lie? I can't understand, why you have to lie?"

"It is a good gun," the magistrate commented, "but it is not worth six hundred. You overpaid, Akim Petrovich!"

"He didn't overpay at all!" Predpolozhensky said, getting worked up. "He's lying! Lying like a schoolboy!"

Otletayev was getting flustered and turned red.

"I'm not the type to lie," he said. "So there! As for you... you're an out and out liar! Yes! And you're just trying to wind me up! I should never go anywhere with you. I don't know why I did this time!.."

"You shouldn't have done... Why lie, that's what I can't understand! He lies like a pig!"

"You're a pig yourself! A pig and a fool, added to which..."

We began appealing to Predpolozhensky's conscience.

"He shouldn't lie!" said the defiant son-in-law in justification. "I get really angry when someone lies... And he should leave pigs out of it. He is a pig himself, that's what! And if he doesn't like the fact I've come along... to hell with him! I can leave!"

"That's enough! Akim Petrovich never meant to offend you! Why make a mountain out of a molehill?"

Predpolozhensky puffed up like an over-fattened turkey and fell silent.

"It's not right!" Kozoyedov said, addressing Predpolozhensky after a moment's pause. "It's not right! He is your parental replacement now, one could say, he is your father-in-law, and you are being rude to him... It is a sin!"

The son-in-law glanced contemptuously at the village elder, and smirked...

"Did someone ask for your opinion?" he inquired. "Did they? Shut up when... Mind your own business!.. Parental replacement... You can't even talk properly yet, but you're also sticking your snout in... Hmm... Pleb... Lout!"

"There you are, see what you are like? You don't like it when people are sitting quietly. Although it might be I come from a lowly class, and although it might be I've had no education, I can tell you I have all kinds of feelings in my chest, in my heart and in my soul, and you don't, even though you've got all kinds of scientific degrees... So there!"

"That's enough, gentlemen!" I intervened. "Enough preaching morals to each other! Let's keep quiet..."

Breathing heavily, Otletayev pulled a large and extremely battered cigarette-case from his side pocket and slipped his fat fingers inside. The doctor and the magistrate extended their hands towards the case.

"I am sorry, no!" Otletayev said in an imperious tone. "Friendship is one thing, but tobacco is quite different. I don't have enough even for myself... We've a long journey and I've only brought four dozen along with me..."

The doctor and the magistrate were overcome with embarrassment and started whistling a tune from *La Fille de Madame Angot** in order to conceal their embarrassment from the world.

Otletayev was as foolish as forty thousand brothers,* and a terrible ignoramus...

We could not stand him. The embarrassed doctor lit up a cigarette of his own and began telling jokes. He told us about twenty jokes of which only one wasn't salacious; the rest made our ears go red.

"You're really good, you know!" I said, praising the doctor. "I didn't know you were such a comedian!"

"Yes... I do know the odd joke," said the doctor. "If I wanted to write for the magazines, I would have made millions. I would have earned more than you."

"I don't doubt it... Why don't you contribute anything?"

"I don't want to!"

"And why's that?"

"I just don't want to, that's all! I have a conscience! How could anyone with a conscience write for your magazines? Never! I don't even read the newspapers! I consider the people who subscribe to them to be blockheads wasting their money..."

"With me it is vice versa," remarked the magistrate. "I think that the blockheads are those who don't spend money on newspapers..."

"The doctor is in a bad mood today," I said. "Let's leave him alone..."

"Who told you I'm in a bad mood? I feel fine... You defend newspapers because you write for them, and in my opinion they are... lousy! They aren't worth one rotten egg! They lie endlessly. They are the biggest liars and gossips! Journalists are just like lawyers... They lie and have no conscience!"

"I used to be a lawyer," the magistrate said, "and I had a conscience."

Predpolozhensky and Kozoyedov exchanged glances and grinned maliciously.

"I am not talking about you... I meant in general... Generally speaking, they are all scoundrels... Journalists, lawyers, the lot of them..."

Instead of keeping my mouth shut, I went on sticking up for journalists. And the magistrate continued his defence of lawyers... An argument got underway in the carriage.

"And what about your medicine?" I chimed in. "Medicine? What is its value? Sure you're not lying? You just take money from us! What is a doctor?

A doctor is just the prelude to a grave-digger... that's what! But why am I arguing with you? Do you have any logic? You may have graduated from university, but you argue like a bath-house attendant..."

"Keep your hat on! There is no need for insults!"

"We are criticizing journalists and lawyers," Predpolozhensky boomed in his bass voice, "but cannot spot a true liar ourselves... Talk it over with my dear father-in-law, as when it comes to telling lies, he outdoes any lawyer..."

And so on and so forth... Words, grimaces and gossip provoked yet more words, grimaces and gossip, and things got awfully out of hand...

We began to say everything that had been building up in our hearts against each other all winter. We outdid old maids.

In the meantime, while we continued to attack each other, bleary-eyed and half-drunk, the sun rose higher and higher... The mist had lifted altogether, and the summer day had begun... All around was quiet, glorious...

It was just us breaking the silence...

Arriving at the first marsh we came across, we got out of the carriage and wandered off, angrily, in different directions. Kozoyedov tried to restore peace amongst us. He threw a three-kopeck coin high into the air, shot at it and hit it. Together, we picked up the coin, counted the traces of shot on it, and somehow fell back into conversation.

Predpolozhensky went after a corncrake and killed it. We congratulated him and shouted 'Hooray!' Peace would have been re-established once and for all had it not been for the doctor. While we were congratulating Predpolozhensky on his first success, the doctor went over to the carriage, unwrapped the provisions and helped himself to vodka and a snack.

"Doctor, what are you doing there?" Otletayev shouted.

"Eating and drinking."

"What gives you the right to be in charge?"

"What have I done wrong?"

"Was that stuff for you? I don't understand this, pardon me, swinish behaviour! Couldn't you wait? What that you have uncorked? Holy mother! That is my liqueur! How dare you, sir?"

"Please, don't shout! Calm down!"

"I brought this homemade liqueur along for myself! My health is weak, so I brought a bottle of liqueur and... damn it! It has been opened! Who asked him to open it! Wrap up that sturgeon!"

"No, I won't! You should know, you tactless boor, that when one goes hunting everything is shared... What a, pardon me, lout you are!

The doctor downed a glass of liqueur and, to spite Otletayev, cut himself a massive piece of sturgeon. Predpolozhensky hurried over to the carriage, and, in order to annoy his father-in-law, drank half of what remained of the liqueur from the neck of the bottle... Tears welled in Oteletayev's eyes.

"Did you do that on purpose?" he whispered. "Very well! Very well! So that's how you... *Merci beaucoup...*"[2]

The magistrate, not knowing what was going on, walked up to the carriage.

"Aha?.. Having a bite?" he asked. "Isn't it a bit early? Well, one shot wouldn't do any harm, I guess... Your good health!"

The magistrate poured himself a glass of homemade vodka and knocked it back.

"Oh, that's very good! That's fabulous!" Otletayev was shouting by now.

"What's fabulous?" asked the magistrate.

"Nothing..."

Otletayev got into his carriage, threw the bag with the provisions down on to the grass, bowed ironically to us, and hit Pyotr the coachman on the back.

"Drive on!" he shouted.

"Where are you going?" we exclaimed in surprise...

"Since you find me repulsive... uneducated... Kozoyedov! Get in, my dear fellow! How come us peasants thought of going hunting with the likes of them gentlemen academics? We will relieve them of our presence! Come on, my dear!"

"Where are you off to? Why are you fooling around?"

"If I am a fool, why bother you?... So be it! I am a fool... Goodbye... I'm going home..."

"But how are we going to get home?"

"That's your problem... It's my carriage."

"Are you out of your mind, dear father-in-law?" shouted Predpolozhensky.

Kozoyedov settled into the carriage beside Otletayev and meekly took off his hat.

"Have you gone mad?" Predpolozhensky continued. "Get out of the carriage!"

---

2   *Merci beaucoup:* "thank you very much" (French).

"No, I won't. Goodbye, son-in-law! You are an educated, humane, and civilised man... And I... What am I?"

"You are a fool! Gentlemen, what on earth is going on? Who set him off? Was it you, doctor? To hell with you! You are always sticking your academic nose in other people's business!"

"I'm not your father-in-law... And please don't yell," said the doctor a huff. "If you're going to yell, I'll leave too..."

"Go on, then! It will be no big loss! Really!"

The doctor shrugged his shoulders, sighed, and got into the carriage. Giving it up as a bad job, the magistrate also got into the carriage.

"It's always like this with us," he sighed. "Nothing works out..."

"Drive on!" shouted Otletayev.

Pyotr smacked his lips, tugged on the reins, and the carriage moved off.

Predpolozhensky and I exchanged glances.

"Stop!" I shouted and ran after the carriage. "Stop!"

"Stop!" Predpolozhensky yelled. "Stop, you swine!"

The carriage stopped, and we climbed in.

"You won't get away with this!" Predpolozhensky said, his eyes flashing as he shook his fist at his father-in-law. "You are going to remember this day until you die!"

We travelled back home all the way in silence. Joy of the highest quality had given way to the nastiest of feelings in our hearts. We were ready to gobble each other up and only did not because we were not sure which end to begin with... When we reached the Otletayev's house, Madame Otletayeva was sitting on the veranda, drinking coffee...

"You're back?" she asked in surprise. "Why so early?"

We got out of the carriage and silently headed towards the gates.

"Gentlemen, where are you going?" Madame Otletayeva cried. "What about a cup of coffee? Or lunch? Where are you going?"

We turned towards the porch and silently threatened it with our enormous fists. Predpolozhensky spat in the direction of the porch, swore and went off to the stables to sleep.

About two days later, Otletayev, Predpolozhensky, Kozoyedov, the magistrate, the zemstvo doctor* and I were sitting in Otletayev's house playing snap. We were playing snap and picking on each other as usual...

About three days later we had an almighty row, but five days after that, we were setting off fireworks together...

We quarrel, gossip, hate and despise each other, but cannot go our separate ways. Do not be surprised and do not laugh, dear reader! Go to Otletayevka, spend a winter and a summer there, and you will find out why...

The backwoods are not the capital... In Otletayevka a crab is a fish, doubting Thomas is a man of conviction, and a quarrel is the living word...

Which of the Three?

(An Old, Yet Eternally New Tale)

Standing on the veranda of the palatial old dacha belonging to the State Councillor's* wife Maria Ivanovna Langer were her daughter Nadya and Ivan Gavrilovich, the son of a prominent Moscow businessman.

It was a glorious evening. If I was skilled in describing nature, I would describe the moon peeping out affectionately from behind small clouds, and bathing the forest, the dacha, and Nadya's sweet face in its pleasant light... I would also describe the hushed whispering of the trees, the nightingale's song, and the faint gurgle of the little fountain... Nadya was standing with one knee pressed against the edge of an armchair, her hand clasping the balustrade. Her languorous, velvety, expressive eyes were fixed on the dark green copse... Little spots of dark shadow played on her pale, moonlit face: she was blushing... Ivan Gavrilovich stood behind her, nervously tugging at his wispy beard. When he grew tired of tugging at his beard, he began to stroke and fiddle with his unattractive high jabot. Ivan Gavrilovich was not handsome. He bore a strong resemblance to his Mama, who looked like a village cook. His forehead was small and narrow, as if it had been flattened; he had a snub, flat nose which was distinctly concave instead of being aquiline, and his hair was bristly. His narrow little eyes, like those of a young kitten, were gazing enquiringly at Nadya.

"Please forgive me," he said, stammering, breathing haltingly, and repeating himself, "forgive me for telling you... about my feelings... But I have fallen in love with you so deeply that I'm no longer certain whether I'm in my right mind... My chest is bursting with feelings for you that are impossible to put into words! Nadezhda Petrovna, as soon as I set eyes on you, I was nuts about you, I mean, I fell in love with you. You will forgive me, of course, but... after all, that... (Pause). Nature is looking nice today!"

"Yes... the weather is glorious..."

"And how nice it is in such nature, you know, to love such a nice person as you... But I'm unhappy!"

Ivan Gavrilovich sighed and pulled at his little beard.

"I'm very unhappy! I love you, I'm suffering, but... what about you? Is it possible you could really feel feelings for me? You are cultured, educated... all very noble... But me? I'm from the merchant class and... that's it! It really is! I do have plenty of money, but what is the point of that money without true happiness? Having all that money without happiness is just sinful... and meaningless. You eat well, and... you don't have to walk anywhere... but life is meaningless... Nadezhda Petrovna!"

"Well?"

"It's... nothing! Actually, I did want to bother you..."

"What is it?"

"Can you love me? (Pause). I offered your Mama... your mother, that is, my heart and hand in regard to you, and she said it is all up to you... She said you can... without your parents' approval... What is your answer to me?"

Nadya remained silent. She gazed at the dark green copse where the outlines of tree trunks and patterned leaves were only just visible... She was absorbed by the moving black shadows of the trees, the tops of which were swaying slightly in the wind. Ivan Gavrilovich was suffocated by her silence. His eyes filled with tears. He was suffering. 'What if she rejects me?' he wondered, and this unhappy thought pierced his broad back like an icicle...

"Have mercy on me, Nadezhda Petrovna," he pronounced. "Don't torment me... If I am pestering you, it is out of love after all... Because... (Pause). If... (Pause). If you do not answer me, I might as well die."

Nadya turned her face towards Ivan Gavrilovich and smiled... She offered him her hand and spoke in a voice that sounded to the Moscow businessman's ears like a siren's song:

"I'm most grateful to you, Ivan Gavrilovich... I've known for a long time that you love me, and I know how much you love me... But I... I... I also love you, Jean... It is impossible not to be fond of you because of your kind heart, and your devotion..."

Ivan Gavrilovich opened his mouth wide, began to laugh and stroked his face with his palm in happiness: was this a dream?

"I know that if I marry you," Nadya continued, "I will be the happiest woman in the world... But do you know what, Ivan Gavrilovich? Wait a little bit longer for my reply... I cannot give you a definite answer right away... I have to consider this step carefully... I need to think it over... Be patient for a little longer."

"Do I have to wait long?"

"No, not long... A day, two at the most..."

"I can manage that..."

"If you leave now, I'll send you my answer by letter... Go back home now, and I will start thinking it over... Farewell... Give a day..."

Nadya held out her hand. Ivan Gavrilovich seized and kissed it. Nadya nodded, blew a kiss, hurried from the porch and vanished... Ivan Gavrilovich stood there thinking for two or three minutes, then made his way through the small flowerbeds and the copse towards his horses which were standing in the clearing. He felt drained of energy and weak with joy, as if he had been soaking in a hot bath all day... He walked and laughed with happiness.

"Trofim!" he said, waking his dozing coachman. "Get up! We're off! There's a tip of five roubles in it for you! Have you cottoned on? Ha ha!"

Meanwhile Nadya had slipped through all the rooms on to the other veranda, run down the steps and hurried to another clearing, weaving her way through trees, bushes and shrubbery. Waiting for her here was Baron Vladimir Strahl, a young man of about twenty-six who was a childhood friend. Strahl was a sweet, chubby, roly-poly German, with an already noticeable bald patch on his head. He had graduated from university that year, was travelling to his Kharkov estate, and had come to say his final farewells... He was tipsy, lounging on the bench, and whistling "The Marksman."*

Nadya ran up to him and flung her arms round his neck, breathing heavily from the running. Chortling loudly and tugging at his neck, hair, and collar, she covered his fleshy, sweaty face with kisses...

"I've been waiting for you an entire hour," said the baron, putting his arms round her waist...

"So, are you well?"

"I am..."

"Are you leaving tomorrow?"

"I am..."

"You wretch... Are you coming back soon?"

"I don't know..."

The Baron kissed Nadya on the cheek, and shifted her from his lap on to the bench.

"Well, that's enough kissing," said Nadya. "Later on... there will be plenty of time for that. Let's talk things over now. (Pause). Volya, have you thought about it?"

"I have..."

"Well then, what do you think? When is the... wedding?"

The baron frowned.

"You are on about that again!" he said. "It was only yesterday I gave you... a definite answer... A wedding is out of the question! I told you that only yesterday... Why bring it up again when it's been discussed a thousand times?..."

"But Volya, there has to be some outcome to our relationship! How can you not understand that? There has to be!"

"Yes, but not a wedding... Nadine, I'll say it for the hundredth time, you are as naive as a three-year-old child... Naivety suits pretty women, but not in this case, my dear..."

"So you don't want to marry me! Is that it? Come on, you shameless creature, out with it: you don't want to?"

"No, I don't... Why in the world would I want to ruin my career? I love you, but if I married you, it would be the end of me... You have neither fortune nor status to give me... Marriage, old girl, has to count as half of one's career, but you... There's no point in crying... One must use common sense... Marriages based on love never bring happiness and usually go up in smoke..."

"Lying... You're lying! That's what!"

"We'll marry, and then die of starvation... We'd breed beggars... One must be sensible..."

"Well why weren't you sensible back then... do you remember? You swore to marry me... You did, didn't you?"

"I did... but now my plans have changed... You wouldn't marry a pauper, would you? So why are you trying to force me to marry one? I have no intention treating myself like a swine. I have a future, for which I have to answer before my conscience."

Nadya wiped away a tear with her handkerchief, then suddenly and unexpectedly, she threw her arms around the neck of the russified German again with reckless abandon. She clung to him and began to shower his face with kisses.

"Marry me!" she implored. "Marry me, dear friend! You know I love you! You know I cannot live without you, my sweetheart! If you leave me, you'll destroy me! Will you marry me? Will you?"

The German thought for a while, then said in a firm tone:

"I cannot! Love is a good thing, but in this world it doesn't come first..."

"So you don't want to?"

"No... I can't..."

"You don't want to? You really don't?"

"I can't, Nadine!"

"A scoundrel, a rascal... that's what you are! A swindler! A Kraut! I cannot bear you, I hate you, I despise you! You're repulsive! By the way, I have never loved you either! I only gave in to you that evening because I took you for an honourable man and thought that you would marry me... I couldn't stand you even then! It was your money and title I was after!"

Nadya waved her arms around, took a few steps away from Strahl, aimed a few more choice insults at him and set off home... 'I shouldn't have gone to see him just now,' she thought as she walked home. 'I knew that he wouldn't want to marry me, didn't I? Scoundrel! What a fool I was that evening! Had I not given in to him then, I wouldn't have had to humiliate myself just now before that... Kraut.'

When she arrived at the courtyard in front of the dacha, Nadya did not go indoors. She walked around the yard and came to a halt in front of a dimly lit window. This window belonged to a room which was occupied for the summer by the young first violin, Mitya Gusev, who had just graduated from the conservatoire. Nadya began to look through the window. Mitya, who had broad-shoulders, blond curly hair and was not bad-looking, was at home. He had taken off his jacket and waistcoat and was lying on his bed reading a novel. Nadya stood and deliberated for a moment, then knocked on the window. The first violin raised his head.

"Who's there?"

"It is me, Dmitry Ivanych... Open the window for a moment!.."

Mitya quickly put on his jacket and opened the window.

"Come here... Climb out... " said Nadya. Mitya appeared in the window and a second later was already at Nadya's side.

"What can I do for you?"

"Let's go!" said Nadya as she took Mitya by the arm.

"See here, Dmitry Ivanych," she said. "Don't write me love letters, my darling! Please, don't! Don't love me and don't tell me that you love me!"

Tears glistened in Nadya's eyes and streamed down her cheeks and over her hands...

The hot, large tears were absolutely real...

"Don't love me, Dmitry! Don't play your violin for me! I am despicable, loathsome, wicked... People like me should be hated, despised, beaten..."

Nadya began to sob and laid her head on Mitya's chest.

"I am completely loathsome, and my thoughts are loathsome, and my heart..."

At a loss, Mitya began to mutter some nonsense and kissed Nadya on the head...

"You are kind, good... I swear I love you... But you must not love me! What I love, more than anything else on earth, is money, fine clothes, carriages... I feel like dying when I remember that I have no money... I am a despicable, selfish person... Don't love me, my sweetheart, Dmitry Ivanych! Don't write to me! I am getting married... to Ivan Gavrilych... See the sort of person I am! And you still... love me! Farewell! I will love you even when I'm married... Farewell, Mitya!"

Nadya quickly put her arms round Gusev, quickly kissed him on the neck and ran to the gates.

Upon entering her room, Nadya sat down at her desk and wrote the following letter, weeping bitterly: 'Dear Ivan Gavrilych! I am yours. I love you and want to be your wife... Your N.'

The letter was sealed and handed to the maid to be sent.

'Tomorrow... he'll bring me something...' Nadya thought, sighing deeply.

That sigh marked the end of her tears. After sitting by the window for a while and calming down, Nadya quickly undressed and on the stroke of midnight a costly eiderdown, embroidered and monogrammed, was already warming the slumbering, occasionally shuddering body of the pretty and depraved immoral young viper.

At midnight, Ivan Gavrilovich was pacing up and down in his study, dreaming aloud.

His parents were sitting in the study, listening to his dreams... They were overjoyed at their son's good fortune...

"She's a fine girl, and noble," Ivan Gavrilovich's father said. "A State Councillor's daughter, and she is beautiful. Just one problem: she's got a German surname! People will think you married a German..."

He and She

They live like nomads. To Paris alone they give months, but are stingy with Berlin, Vienna, Naples, Madrid, Petersburg, and other capitals. In Paris, they feel almost at home; for them, Paris is the capital, their true residence, while the rest of Europe is a dull, meaningless province, best viewed only through the lowered blinds of a *grand-hôtel* or from the front of the stage. They are not old but have managed to visit all the European capitals at least twice, if not three times. They are already bored with Europe and have begun talking about a trip to America, and will continue to do so until they realise that her voice is not so remarkable that it is worth presenting to both hemispheres.

It is difficult to catch sight of them. You cannot see them on the streets because they travel by carriage, and they travel when it is dark, in the evening and at night. They sleep until lunchtime. They usually wake up in a bad mood, and do not receive anyone. They only receive visitors sometimes, at odd moments, backstage or when sitting down to supper.

You can see her in the photographs which are on sale. She is a beauty in these photographs, but she was never beautiful. Do not believe these photographs of her: she is ugly. Most people see her when she is onstage. But onstage, she is unrecognisable. Grease paint, rouge, mascara and borrowed tresses cover her face like a mask. At concerts, it is the same story.

An ungainly twenty-seven-year-old, with a lined face and nose covered in freckles, she is made up to look like a slender, pretty, seventeen-year-old when she plays Marguerite.* She is least like her real self onstage.

If you want to see them, you should acquire the right to attend the dinners given for her, and which she sometimes gives herself before leaving one capital for another. To acquire this right is not as easy as it looks, as only a select company can gain access to the table... The latter includes critics, weasels posing as critics, indigenous singers, conductors and choirmasters, as well as admirers and connoisseurs with smoothed-down bald patches, who have become theatre regulars and hangers-on thanks to wealth and connections. These dinners do not turn out to be boring, and are interesting to those who are observant... They are worth attending once or twice.

The famous attendees (of whom there are many amongst the diners) eat and talk. Their posture is relaxed: neck on one side, head on other, one elbow on the table. The old men even pick their teeth.

The journalists occupy the chairs nearest to hers. They are almost all drunk and behave in a very free and easy manner, as if they have known her for a hundred years. Were they to step up their efforts ever so slightly in this direction, it would amount to over-familiarity. They crack jokes loudly, drink, and interrupt each other (not forgetting moreover to say *"Pardon!"*), pronounce bombastic toasts and are clearly not afraid to look stupid; several of them lunge over the corner of the table to kiss her hand like true gentlemen.

Those posing as critics chat condescendingly to the admirers and connoisseurs. The admirers and connoisseurs are silent. They envy the journalists, smile beatifically and drink only red wine, which tends to be particularly good at these dinners.

She, the queen of the dinner, is dressed quite simply, but extremely expensively. A huge diamond peeps out from under a lace frill on her neck. There is a massive smooth bracelet on each arm. Her hairstyle is highly amorphous: the ladies like it, the men do not. Her face glows and bestows a dazzling smile on the entire company present at the dinner. She can smile at everyone at once, and talk to everyone at once, while sweetly nodding her head: one nod for each person dining. Look at her face, and you will think she is surrounded only by friends, and that she is on the best of terms with these friends. At the end of the dinner, she gives her photograph to some people; while still at the table she writes the first name and surname of the lucky recipient on the back of the photograph and signs it. She speaks in French, obviously, but at the end of the dinner also in other languages. She speaks English and German ridiculously badly, but even this badness is endearing coming from her. Indeed, she is generally so endearing that for a long time you forget she is ugly.

And he? He, *le mari d'elle*,[1] sits five chairs away from her, drinks a lot, eats a lot, is silent a lot, rolls bread into little balls and studies the labels on the bottles. Judging from his appearance, it feels like he has nothing to do, and that he is bored, lazy and fed up...

He is fair-haired, with a bald patch which follows little paths over his head. Women, wine, sleepless nights, and constant traipsing around the world have furrowed his face and left deep wrinkles. He is about thirty-five, no more,

---

1   *le mari d'elle*: "her husband" (French).

but seems older. His face looks as if it has been marinated in kvass.* He has good, though lazy eyes... There was a time when he was not ugly, but now he is. Bowed legs, hands the colour of mud, hairy neck. Thanks to his crooked legs and very peculiar walk, in Europe they have for some reason nicknamed him "The Carriage." In his frock coat he reminds one of a wet jackdaw with a dry tail. The dinner guests do not notice him. He pays them back in kind.

If you go to one of these dinners take a look at them, this married couple, and tell me what brought, and still keeps these two people together.

Looking at them, you will answer as follows (approximately of course):

"She is a famous singer, while he is just the husband of a famous singer or, to resort to backstage jargon, the husband of his wife. She earns the equivalent of eighty thousand a year in Russian money, while he does nothing, and therefore has time to be her servant. She needs a bookkeeper and someone to deal with entrepreneurs, contracts, agreements... She only deals with her applauding public, and has nothing to do with the box-office, the prosaic side of her life—all that is beneath her. Consequently, she has need of him as a hanger-on, as a servant... She would have got rid of him if she could manage things herself. As for him, while receiving a good salary from her (she does not know the value of money!), it is clear as day that he robs her like her maids do, squanders her money, recklessly lives it up, maybe even putting some aside against a rainy day—and is satisfied with his position, like a worm that has burrowed into a good apple. Had it not been for her money, he would have left her."

So, think and say all those who observe them during these dinners. They think and say this because they can only make superficial judgements, not having the opportunity to penetrate to the heart of the matter. They look at her as a diva, and shun him as if he were a pygmy covered in frog slime; and yet this European diva is tied to this little frog by a most enviable and noble bond.

Here is what he writes:

"They ask me why I love this gorgon? True, this woman is not worth loving. She is also not worth hating. She is only worth not paying attention to and her existence being ignored. To love her, you need to be either me, or crazy which is actually the same thing.

She is not pretty. She was ugly when I married her, and now she is even uglier. She has no forehead; instead of eyebrows over the eyes, she has two barely perceptible strips; instead of eyes she has two shallow slits. Nothing shines through these slits, neither intelligence, desire, nor passion. Her nose looks like a potato. Her mouth is small and beautiful, but her teeth are terrible. She has no breasts and no waist. She makes up for the latter shortcoming, however, by the devilish, almost supernatural skill with which she tightens her corset. She is short and plump. Her plumpness is flabby. *En masse,* her entire body suffers from what is, as far as I am concerned, an insurmountable flaw—a total lack of femininity. I do not regard pale skin and weak muscles as being feminine, and here I disagree with many. She is neither woman nor gentlewoman, but a shopkeeper with awkward manners: when she walks, she swings her arms; when she sits, she crosses one leg over the other, rocking her whole body backwards and forwards; when she lies down, she lifts her legs, and so on...

She is untidy. Especially characteristic in this respect are her suitcases: clean underwear together with dirty underwear, shirt cuffs with shoes and my boots, and new corsets together with worn-out ones. We never receive anyone because our rooms are always in a filthy mess... Ah, what is there to say? Look at her at midday when she wakes up and crawls out lazily from under her blanket, and you will not recognise her as the woman with the nightingale voice. Uncombed with tangled hair, and sleepy, puffy eyes, in a nightgown torn at the shoulders, barefoot, cross-eyed, enveloped in a cloud of yesterday's tobacco smoke—does she look like a nightingale?

She drinks. She drinks like a hussar, whatever and whenever. She has been drinking for a long time. If she did not drink, she would have been better than Patti,* or in any case not worse. She has drunk away half of her career, and very soon will drink away the other half. German scoundrels taught her to drink beer, and now she does not go to bed without downing two or three bottles of the staff. If she did not drink, she would not suffer from gastric catarrh.

She is not polite, as witnessed by the students who sometimes invite her to their concerts.

She loves advertising. Advertising costs us several thousand francs a year. I wholeheartedly despise advertising. No matter how expensive the stupid advertisement is, it will always be cheaper than her voice. My wife likes to be coddled, and does not like to be told the truth. She will not accept criticism from the critics, as their job is to praise her. For her, a bought Judas' kiss is sweeter than unbought criticism. She suffers from a total lack of self-respect!

She is intelligent, but her mind is uncultivated. Her brains lost their elasticity long ago, they have become covered in fat and are dormant.

She is capricious, fickle, and has no lasting convictions. Yesterday she said that money is meaningless, that it is not the point of life, but today she gives concerts in four different locations because she is convinced that there is nothing in this world more important than money. Tomorrow she will repeat what she said yesterday. She does not want to have anything to do with her own country, she has no political heroes, no favourite newspaper, and no favourite authors.

She is rich, but she does not help the poor. Moreover, she often underpays milliners and hairdressers. She has no heart.

She is a thoroughly flawed woman!

But look at this gorgon when she is made up with slicked-back hair and tightened corset as she approaches the footlights to begin competing with the nightingales and the lark to welcome the May dawn. How much dignity and charm there is in her swan-like glide! Look closely, and I urge you to pay careful attention. When she first raises her arm and opens her mouth, her slits are transformed into big eyes and are filled with sparkle and passion... Nowhere else will you find such wondrous eyes. When she, my wife, starts to sing, and when the first trills fill the air, and I begin to feel that under the influence of these heavenly sounds my troubled soul is on the mend, then look at my face, and you will discover the secret of my love.

"Isn't she lovely?" I then ask the people sitting next to me.

They say 'yes,' but that is not enough for me. I am ready to destroy anyone who thinks that this extraordinary woman is not my wife. I forget everything that happened before and live only in the present.

Look what an actress she is! How much profound meaning is concealed in her every movement! She understands everything: love, hatred, the human soul... The theatre shakes with applause for good reason!

At the end of the final act I lead her, pale and exhausted, having lived a lifetime in one evening, from the theatre. I too am pale and exhausted. We get into the carriage and go to the hotel. In the hotel she throws herself on the bed, silently, without undressing. I sit down on the edge of the bed and kiss her hand silently. This evening she does not drive me away. We drift off together, sleep until morning and wake, in order to send each other to hell...

Do you know when else I love her? When she attends balls or dinners. I love the wonderful actress in her on those occasions too. Indeed, what an actress she must be, to be able to outwit and overpower her own nature... I do not recognise her at these stupid dinners... She is transformed from a plucked duck into a peacock..."

This letter is written in a drunken, barely legible hand. It is written in German and encrusted with spelling mistakes.

Here is what she writes:

"You ask me if I love this boy? Yes, sometimes... Why? God knows...

It is true, he is neither handsome nor nice. People like him are not born with the right to mutual love. People like him can only buy love, it is not given to them for free. Judge for yourself.

Day and night, he is as drunk as a cobbler. His hands shake, which is very unattractive. When he is drunk, he grumbles and gets into fights. He hits me too. When he is sober, he lies on whatever is to hand and is silent.

He is eternally scruffy, even though he has enough money for clothes. Half of my takings slip through his hands, heaven knows where.

I can never get around to check up on him. We poor married artists have extremely expensive bookkeepers! Our husbands get half of the takings for their labours!

He does not spend it on women, that I know. He despises women.

He is lazy. I have never seen him do anything. He drinks, eats, sleeps—and that's it.

He has never completed a year at university. He was expelled for insolence as a first-year student.

He is not a nobleman and, what is worst of all, he is German.

I dislike Germans. In every one hundred Germans there are ninety-nine idiots and one genius. I learnt that from a prince, a German with French ancestry.

He smokes disgusting tobacco.

But he has his good sides. He loves my noble art more than me. When it is announced that I cannot sing due to illness before a performance, when in other words I am being capricious, he walks about looking devastated, clenching his fists.

He is not a coward, and is not afraid of people. This is what I like most of all in people. I'll tell you a little episode from my life. It was in Paris, a year after I graduated from the conservatoire. I was still very young then and learning to drink. I caroused every night as much as my youthful energy would allow. I caroused, of course, in company. During one of those carousals, as I was clinking glasses with my distinguished admirers, a very ugly boy whom I didn't know approached the table, looked me directly in the eye, asked:

"Why are you drinking?"

We laughed. My boy was not embarrassed.

The second question was more impudent and came straight from the heart.

"Why are you laughing? The scoundrels who are plying you with wine now won't give you half a kopeck when you ruin your voice with drink and become a beggar!"

Talk about cheek! My companions began to protest. I sat the boy down next to me and ordered some wine for him. It turned out that this advocate of sobriety drank wine beautifully. Á propos, I refer to him as a boy only because he has a very small moustache.

For his impudence, I repaid him with marriage.

He is mostly silent. More often than not he will utter just two words. These words he pronounces in a guttural voice, with a tremor in his throat, and a shudder on his face. He is in the habit of resorting to these words when he is sitting in company, at a dinner or a ball... When someone (regardless of who it is) tells a lie, he will raise his head and say, not looking at anything, and not a bit put out:

"Not true!"

These are his favourite words. What woman could resist the shining eyes which accompany the annunciation of these words? I love those words, and that brilliance, that shudder on his face. Not everyone can utter these good, bold words, but my husband repeats them everywhere and on all occasions. I love him sometimes, and this 'sometimes,' as far as I recall, coincides with the pronouncement of these good words. Anyway, God knows why I love him. I am a bad psychologist, and here, it seems, we have touched on a psychological issue..."

This letter was written in French, in beautiful, almost male handwriting. You will not find one grammatical mistake in it.

The Fair

A small, barely visible little town. It is called a town, but it resembles a town about as much as a third-rate village resembles a town. If you are lame and use crutches, it would take you ten, fifteen minutes at most to go round it, across it and back again. The houses are all dismal and ramshackle. Fifteen kopecks paid in three instalments will buy you any house. The residents can be counted on the fingers of your hands: the town head, the jailer, the priest, the teacher, the deacon, the fire lookout, the parish clerk, two or three other locals, two policemen, and, that it would seem, is it... There are many members of the female sex, but members of the female sex are after all not counted by the census-takers in the majority of cases. (The census-takers know that a chicken is not a bird, that a mare is not a horse and that an officer's wife is not a lady...) There are a great many visitors: neighbouring landowners, summer residents, lieutenants from an artillery unit temporarily quartered here, the shaggy, lilac-cassocked deacon with a mammoth basso profundo from the neighbouring village, et cetera. The weather is middling. It often rains, which causes a certain melancholy to descend on the buyers and sellers. The air is wonderful. There is no trace of Moscow's odours. It smells of the forest, lilies of the valley, tar, and perhaps faintly of the manger. The spirit of commerce wafts out of every nook and cranny, and every side alley. Wherever you turn there is a stall. There are two rows of stalls stretching from one end of the main street to the other, filling the entire town square, where the main street ends up. Along the church fence there are women selling seeds. It's jam-packed. There are carts, horses, cows, calves, and piglets everywhere! Men are thin on the ground, but as for womenfolk... goodness!! There are crowds of peasant women everywhere. They are all wearing red dresses and black velveteen jackets. There are so many of them, and they are standing so close together that one could safely sprint over their heads to a fire if it was "all hands to the pump."

For some reason there are—alas!—not many drunkards. The air is filled with a constant hubbub of chirping, yelping, squealing, bleating and lowing. From the racket you would think a second Tower of Babel was under construction.

The residents' windows are all wide-open. Through them you can see samovars, teapots with broken spouts, and the residents' red-nosed mugs. Acquaintances are milling about under the windows with their purchases and complaining about the weather. The deacon in the lilac cassock who has straw in his hair, clasps everyone by the hand and bellows, "Grreetings! May I wish you a happy holiday! A... hem!!?"

The menfolk have congregated by the horses and cows. Trade here is conducted in the tens or even hundreds of roubles. The main big shots in the horse business are, of course, gypsies. Invoking the Almighty, they swear oaths, inviting every misfortune to rain down on them should they break their word. By tradition, the reins of a sold horse are handed over with a help of a coat-flap, therefore a person without a coat can neither buy nor sell a horse. The horses on offer are mostly plebeian animals, bred for labour.

The womenfolk swarm round the booths selling drapery and gingerbread. The inexorable march of time has taken its toll on these gingerbreads: they are coated in sweet-tasting rust and mould. By all means purchase these gingerbreads, but be sure to keep them a safe distance from your mouth to avoid misfortune! The same holds for the dried pears and boiled sweets. The pitiful bagels are covered with pieces of bast—and also with dust. The womenfolk could not care less. No one is going to look inside their bellies.

Flies cannot cling to honey like the boys cling to the toy stall. They have not a kopeck to their name... They just stand and feast their eyes on the toy horses, soldiers and tin pistols. So near and yet so far. Once in a while, a bold lad will pick up a bird whistle, hold it, twirl it around, blow on it, then put it back—and wipe his nose contentedly. There is no stall without two or three dozen boys crowded around it. They stand and stare for an hour, two, three, with truly diabolical patience. Buy any little Fedyushka, Pyotr or Vasyutka a toy pistol, or a lion with a cow's face and black stripes on its back, and you will fill his heart with boundless joy.

Girls peek in between the boys' elbows. Their attention is fixed on the same toy horses, and on dolls in gauze skirts. You will also see children by the ice cream vendors, who sell very poor-quality "sugar" ice-cream. Those with a kopeck eat out of a small green goblet; they eat slowly and with great relish, afraid to miss any moment of bliss, chomping their jaws, licking their lips and licking their fingers. One eats, while two dozen without a kopeck stand to attention, peering enviously into the lucky child's mouth. Meanwhile, the latter eats, lording it over the others...

"Pyotr, come on... gimme a spoonful!" groans a girl, watching the lucky boy's right hand.

"Clear off!" the lucky boy answers, squeezing the little green goblet tighter in his fist.

"Pyotr!" groans a boy wearing his father's large peaked cap. "Trade me!"

"What?"

"The sugar ice cream. A bit of it." (Pause.) "Will you? I'll give you five knucklebones."

"Clear off!" the lucky boy answers.

The lucky boy finishes his portion, spends a long time licking his lips and lives with the memory of the sugar ice cream for a long, long time.

Oh, for some money!! Where are you, five and fifteen-kopeck pieces? There is nothing worse, nothing more wearisome and tortuous than having to go around in your father's peaked cap at the fair, seeing and hearing, touching and smelling and, at the same time, possessing not so much as a kopeck. What luck to be Fedyushka or Yegorka, who can eat an ice cream for a kopeck, shoot as loud as they like with a toy pistol and buy a toy horse for five kopecks! A small piece of happiness, hardly visible, but denied to most all the same!

Scoffers, drunks, and those sauntering aimlessly round the fair are drawn to the show booths. There are two theatres. They have been put up in the middle of the square, next to each other and they look shabby. They have been cobbled together from broken sticks, rotten, wet, slimy boards, and rags. The roofs are a mass of patch upon patch, and stitch upon stitch. Terrible poverty. There are two or three clowns standing on the planks and boards that make up an outside platform, entertaining the audience below. The audience is thoroughly undemanding. It laughs, not because it is amused, but because you are supposed to laugh when watching a clown. The clowns wink, pull faces, fool about, but... alas! The progenitors of all our Pushkinian and non-Pushkinian scenes have long since outlived their day and done their service. In days gone by their heads were the bearers of cutting satire and truths from distant parts, but now their wit leads to bewilderment, while their paltry talent is rivalled only by the poverty of their fairground surroundings. You listen to them and you begin to feel sick. Before you stand not itinerant performers, but hungry, two-legged wolves. Hunger, and nothing else, has driven them towards their muse... They are ravenous! Starving, tattered and worn out, with sickly, gaunt countenances, they contort themselves on the platform, trying to pull a stupid face so as to tempt another scoffer to their show and get another ten kopecks... The result is a vulgar, not stupid face: a combination of apathy with a forced, banal grimace that does not express anything. It is just a lot of winking, slapping, and hitting each other on the back, unceremonious interactions with the crowd, talking down to it... and nothing more. Do not listen to what they say. By necessity these artists do not speak from inspiration or follow a pre-planned routine that has an aim. Their words have no meaning. They are uttered with buffoonery, and that is doubtless why they are rewarded with laughter.

"You seem straight enough!"

"I'm not Straitanoff—I'm Ivan Fedoseyev."*

This is an example of their wit. 'Jesters and children sometimes speak the truth,' but presumably one needs to be a jester by vocation in order to occasionally speak the truth and not just nonsense all the time...

The distinguished public gawps and roars with laughter. This is pardonable, however: a better performance they have not seen, and they want to make merry. All that is lacking from the poor-quality gingerbreads, their time off, and light tipsiness, is laughter. Prod them and laughter will happen.

There are two theatres. Each puts on dazzling shows every quarter of an hour. In the evenings there are special, extraordinary performances. I will describe one such performance.

The most dazzling performance was given before the artists left town, on the first Sunday after the day of the fair. The day before the show, clowns distributed posters (handwritten) round the town. One such poster was delivered to me too. Here it is:

In the Town of X

With the permishun of the Othoritees a Grande Show will take place on X Square a Jimnastic and Acrobbatic Show by the Troop of Artistes

N. G. B Affliates comprizing of Jimnastic and Acrobbatic Feets Humorus Cuplets Quatrains and Pantamime in two parts.

1st. Various wonderful And entertaining White Magick or Agility and Slight of Hand Tricks will be Performed up to 20 Items by urobert the Clown.

2nd. Dobert the Clown and Youths Andriyas and ivanson will Perform Leeps Jumps and Summersalts in air.

3rd. The English man without Bones or Kauchuk Man who's Hole Body is Flexible like Rubber.

4th. Youth ivanson Terokha will Perform a Comic Cuplet. (And so on in the same way.)

9 p.m. the Price of Seats

1st place — 50 k.
2nd place — 40 k.
3rd place — 30 k.
4th place — 20 k.
Galary — 10 k.

I have shortened the poster, but have added nothing.

The above show was attended by all the local gentry (district police chief and family, justice of the peace and family, the doctor, the teacher—17 people in all). The intelligentsia haggled and only paid twenty-five kopecks each for the best seats. The owner himself, a rather unexceptional individual, sold the tickets. He was the kind of person you might find on Grachovka* or Dyukovka Street. We paid, went in and occupied the best seats. People poured in and the theatre was full to bursting. The interior was far from luxurious. Instead of a stage curtain serving simultaneously as the wings, there was a piece of calico cloth, two metres square. Instead of a chandelier there were four candles. The artists graciously executed the duties of artists, ushers, and police. They can turn their hands to anything. Best of all was the orchestra, which was seated on a bench to the right. There were four musicians. One was sawing away on the violin, another was playing the harmonica, the third was playing the cello (with three double-bass strings), and the fourth was on the tambourine. They played the ever-popular "Marksman" for the most part, mechanically and horribly out of tune. The tambourine player was delightful. He hit the tambourine with his hand, elbow, knee and practically with his heel as well. He looked as if he was hitting it with enjoyment, with emotion, immersed in his own world. His hand danced around the tambourine in some unnaturally nimble way, tapping out notes that even the violinist could not produce. Such was its movement that his hand seemed to be pitching and rolling.

Before the show started, a peasant wearing a long kaftan came in, crossed himself and sat down in the best seats. A clown went up to him.

"Please sit in the gallery," the clown said to him. "These are the best seats."

"Clear off!"

"Why have you plonked yourself down like some bear? Go away! This isn't your seat!"

The peasant in the long kaftan did not budge. He pulled his peaked cap down over his eyes and refused to give up his seat. The magic tricks began. The clown asked the audience for a hat. The audience refused.

"Well, in that case there won't be any tricks!" said the clown. "Ladies and gentlemen, does anyone have a five-kopeck piece?"

The peasant in the long kaftan handed him a five-kopeck piece. The clown performed the trick and, when returning the five-kopeck piece, concealed it in his sleeve. The peasant in a long kaftan took fright.

"What the... Hey! Don't play tricks, brother! Gimme back my five kopecks!"

"Would anyone like a shave, Gentlemen?" the clown inquired.

Two boys came out of the crowd. They covered them with a dirty blanket and smeared their faces, one with soot and the other with flour paste glue. No standing on ceremony!

"Call this an audience?" the owner's wife cried. "Delinquents, the lot of them!"

The tricks were followed by an acrobatic show with the mysterious "sartali mortali," and then by a strongwoman who lifted an incredible number of kettlebells on her plaits. One wall of the theatre collapsed in the middle of the performance, and by the end of it, the whole thing had collapsed.

All in all, it was not up to much. The buyers and sellers would not have missed an awful lot had there been no theatre at the fair. The travelling artist has ceased to be an artist—these days he is a charlatan.

There are swings next to the theatres. For five kopecks you are raised in the air five times higher than all the houses and then lowered again five times. It makes young ladies feel faint but it is pure bliss for village girls. *Suum cuique!*[1]

---

1   *Suum cuique:* "to each his own" (Latin) .

The Mistress

I

Rustling and swishing through the dry, dusty grass, a carriage drawn by a pair of handsome Vyatka horses drove up to Maxim Zhurkin's log house. Sitting in the carriage were the mistress, Elena Yegorovna Strelkova, and her estate manager, Felix Adamovich Rzhevetsky. The estate manager nimbly jumped out of the carriage, went up to the house and knocked on the windowpane with his index finger. A light flickered in the house.

"Who's there?" asked an old woman's voice, and the head of Maxim's wife appeared in the window.

"Come outside, granny!" the mistress called.

A minute later Maxim and his wife came out of the house. They stopped by the gates and silently bowed to the mistress, and then to the estate manager.

"Pray tell me," Elena Yegorovna asked the old man, "what is all this about?"

"What do you mean, ma'am?"

"How can you ask that? Do you really not know? Is Stepan at home?"

"No, ma'am. He went to the mill."

"Who does he think he is? I really don't understand that man! Why did he leave my service?"

"That we don't know, mistress. How could we know?"

"It is terribly inconsiderate on his part! He's left me without a coachman. Thanks to him, Felix Adamovich now has to harness the horses and drive them himself. It is quite idiotic! You must understand that it really is idiotic! Did he think he wasn't being paid enough, is that it?"

"Lord knows!" the old man replied, looking sideways at the estate manager who was peering through the window. "He doesn't tell us anything, and we can't get inside his head. He just says he is going off and that's that! He has a mind of his own! I suppose he did think he wasn't being paid enough!"

"And who is that, lying on the bench under the icons?" Felix Adamovich asked, looking through the window.

"That's Semyon, sir! Stepan isn't here."

"It's most impertinent of him!" the mistress continued, lighting up a ciga-rette. "Monsieur Rzhevetsky, how much did he get in wages?"

"Ten roubles a month."

"If he thought ten wasn't enough, I could have given him fifteen! But he walked out without saying a word! Is that honest? Is that decent?"

"I did say that one should never indulge these people!" Rzhevetsky said, enunciating each syllable, and trying not to emphasise the penultimate one.* "You have cosseted these parasites! One should never pay the whole wage in one go! What's the point? And why do you want to put up his wages? He will come back anyway! He accepted the job, and was hired! Tell him," the Pole said, addressing Maxim, "that he is nothing but a swine."

"*Finissez donc!*"[1]

"Do you hear me, peasant? Once you are hired, you do the job, you can't just leave when you feel like it, damn it! Just let him try not turning up tomor-row! I'll show him what you get for disobedience! And you will get it in the neck too! Do you hear me, old woman?"

"*Finissez,* Rzhevetsky!"

"Everyone will get it in the neck! In which case, you had better not show up at my office, you old dog! Indulge you people?! Are you even human? Do you even understand kind words? You only understand when you are boxed about the ears and given a hard time! He had better turn up tomorrow!"

"I'll tell him. Why wouldn't I tell him? That's easy..."

"Tell him I'll put up his wages," said Elena Yegorovna. "I can't do without a coachman. When I find someone else, he can leave if he wants to. But tomor-row morning, he must be back at work! Tell him that I am deeply offended by his discourteous behaviour! And you, granny, tell him too! I hope that he will turn up and not force me to send for him. Come over here, granny! That's for you, dear! I suppose it must be difficult to manage such grown up children? Take it, my dear!"

The mistress took a pretty cigarette case from her pocket, pulled out a yel-lowish note from underneath the cigarettes and handed it to the old woman.

"If he doesn't come," she added, "then we'll have to fall out, which would be highly undesirable. But I hope... you will make him see sense. Let's be off, Felix Adamych! Farewell!"

---

1   *Finissez donc:* "so, finish" (French).

Rzhevetsky jumped into the carriage, picked up the reins, and the carriage rolled away along the soft road.

"How much did she give you?" asked the old man.

"A rouble."

"Give it here!"

The old man took the rouble, stroked it with the palms of both hands, folded it carefully and hid it in his pocket.

"Stepan, she's gone!" he said, entering the house. "I told her a lie, that you'd gone to the mill. She is scared out of her wits!"

As soon as the carriage had driven off and vanished out of sight, Stepan appeared in the window. Pale as death and trembling, he crawled halfway out of the window and shook his big fist towards the garden that was darkening in the distance. The garden belonged to the estate. Having shaken his fist about six times, he muttered something, crawled back inside and let down the window with a bang.

Half an hour after the mistress had left, it was supper time in the Zhurkins' house. Zhurkin and his wife sat at the grimy table in the kitchen right by the stove. Opposite them sat Maxim's eldest son Semyon, a soldier on temporary leave, with the red, haggard face of a drunkard, a long, pock-marked nose and lubricious eyes. Semyon resembled his father, except that he was not grey-haired or bald, and did not have his father's cunning, gypsy eyes. Stepan, Maxim's second son, sat next to Semyon. Stepan was not eating but was staring at the sooty ceiling and thinking hard about something, his handsome blond head propped up on his fist. Supper was served by Stepan's wife, Marya. The cabbage soup was eaten in silence.

"Here, take this!" Maxim said, when the soup was finished. Marya picked up the empty bowl, but did not manage to carry it back safely to the stove, even though the stove was close at hand. She began to wobble on her feet and collapsed on to the bench. The bowl fell out of her hands and slid from her lap on to the floor. Sobbing could be heard.

"Crying, is she?" Maxim asked.

Marya's sobbing became louder. About two minutes passed. The old woman got up and served the kasha* herself. Stepan grunted and stood up.

"Quiet!" he muttered.

Marya continued to cry.

"Quiet, I told you!" Stepan shouted.

"I can't stand womenfolk's wailing!" Semyon muttered fiercely, scratching the bristles on the back of his head. "She is blubbering and doesn't even know why! That's womenfolk for you! She can cry her heart out in the yard, if she wants!"

"A woman's tear is a drop of water!" Maxim said. "Luckily there is no need to buy tears, they are given for nothing. Come on, why are you blubbering? Hey! Stop it! They won't take your Styopka away from you! You've been spoilt! You are too delicate! Go get some kasha in you!"

Stepan bent down towards Marya and struck her lightly on the elbow.

"So, now what? I am telling you, be quiet! Uh-uh... you stupid cow!"

Stepan took a swing and slammed his fist down on the bench that Marya was lying on. A large, shining tear rolled down his cheek. He wiped the tear from his face, sat down at the table and began to eat his kasha. Sobbing, Marya got up and went to sit by herself behind the stove. The kasha was eaten.

"Marya, bring us some kvass*! Know your place, wench! You should be ashamed of your wailing!" the old man shouted. "You are not a child!"

Marya came out from behind the stove with a pale, tear-stained face, and handed the ladle to the old man without looking at anyone. The ladle was passed from hand to hand. Semyon picked it up, crossed himself, took a gulp and choked.

"What are you laughing at?"

"Nothing... It's nothing. I just remembered something funny."

Semyon threw back his head, opened his big mouth and began to snigger.

"So the mistress came?" he asked, giving Stepan a sidelong glance. "Eh? What did she say? Eh? Haha!"

Stepan looked at Semyon and turned bright red.

"She is offering fifteen roubles," said the old man.

"Imagine! And she would give a hundred, if you were only willing! God smite me, she would!"

Semyon winked and stretched.

"Ah, if I had a woman like that!" he continued. "I would suck the living daylights out of the little devil! Squeeze the juices out of her! Ooh..."

Semyon tensed, slapped Stepan on the shoulder and guffawed.

"So that's how it is, my dear! You are too shy! It doesn't do for the likes of us to be shy! You're an idiot, Styopka! Such a big idiot!"

"Of course, he's an idiot!" said their father.

The sobbing started up again.

"Your woman is wailing again! She must be jealous! I can't stand women squealing. It is like being stabbed with a knife! Ah, women, women! And for what purpose did God make you? What was the point? *Merci* for supper, ladies and gentlemen! It would be nice to have some wine now so I could have beautiful dreams! Your mistress, I would imagine, has tons of wine! You could drink to your heart's content!"

"You are an insensitive brute, Senka!"

Having said this, Stepan sighed, grabbed a carriage rug and went out into the yard. He was followed by Semyon.

Outside, a quiet and serene Russian summer's night had begun. The moon was rising from behind the distant kurgans.* Ragged little clouds with silvery edges floated towards it. The horizon became paler, and pleasant pale greenery spilled right across its entire breadth. The stars grew fainter and, as if frightened by the moon, drew in their tiny rays. A nocturnal, cheek-caressing dampness began to spread in all directions from the river. When the clock in Father Grigory's log house struck nine, the chime reverberated throughout the whole village. The Jewish tavern keeper banged his windows shut and hung a greasy lantern over the tavern door. Not a soul, not a single sound could now be heard in the street and in the yards... Stepan spread his rug on the grass, crossed himself and lay down, tucking his elbow under his head. Semyon grunted and sat down at his feet.

"Ummm..." he said.

After a short silence, Semyon settled himself more comfortably, lit a small pipe and began to talk:

"I was at Trofim's today... Drinking beer. Drank three bottles. Do you want a smoke, Styopa?"

"No, I don't"

"It's good tobacco. Some tea would be nice now! Did you used to drink tea at the mistress's? Was it good? It must have been very good, right? It must have cost five roubles a pound. You know, there is tea that costs a hundred roubles a pound. Honest to God, there is. I know there is, even though I haven't drunk it. When I was working as a clerk in town, I saw it... One lady I knew used to drink it. The smell alone was good enough! I sniffed it. Shall we go to the mistress's tomorrow?"

"Leave me alone!"

"Why are you angry? I am not scolding you, I'm just talking. No need to get angry. But why won't you go, you nutter? I don't understand! It's good money, and the food is good, and you can drink to your heart's content... You'll smoke her cigarettes, and drink good tea..."

Semyon fell silent for a bit and continued:

"And she is beautiful. It's a misfortune to get involved with an old crone, but with her it's pure joy! (Semyon spat and fell silent.) That woman is a ball of fire! A fiery fire! She's got a magnificent neck, so lovely and plump..."

"And what if it's a sin on your soul?" Stepan asked suddenly, turning to Semyon.

"Sin? What sin? Nothing is a sin for a poor man."

"Even a poor man would go through hellfire to the devil himself if... But am I a poor man? I'm not poor."

"But where is the sin anyway? After all, she's the one after you, not the other way round! You are a dummy!"

"And you are a crook, and your reasoning is crooked."

"You're a foolish man!" Semyon said, sighing. "Foolish! You don't know how lucky you are! You don't get it! I suppose you have a lot of money... You don't need money, then."

"I do, but not other people's."

"You wouldn't be stealing, she will give it to you with her own little hand. But there is no point trying to reason with an idiot like you! It's like talking to a wall... It's just hot air."

Semyon stood up and stretched.

"You'll regret this, but then it will be too late! I don't even want to know you after this. You are no longer a brother to me. To hell with you... Hang around with your stupid cow..."

"Are you calling Marya a cow?"

"Yes, I am."

"Um... And you are not worth that cow's little finger. Go away!"

"It would have been good for you and... good for us. You're a real idiot!"

"Go away!"

"Don't worry, I'm off... What you need is a good thrashing!"

Semyon turned round and, whistling softly to himself, made his way back to the house. About five minutes later, the grass by Stepan rustled. Stepan raised his head. Marya was walking towards him. She came up to him, stood for a while and then lay down beside him.

"Don't go, Styopa!" she whispered. "Don't go, my dearest! She will ruin you! That Pole was not enough for that cursed woman, now she wants you as well. Don't go to her, Stepunka."

"It's none of your business!"

Marya's tears began to fall on to Stepan's face in a hot, fine shower.

"Don't ruin me Stepan! Don't allow sin to enter your soul. Love only me, don't go to other women! God wed you to me, so live with me. I am an orphan... You are all I have."

"Leave me alone! Aargh... damn it! I said I won't go!"

"That's good... And don't go, dearest! My heart is heavy, Stepushka... We'll have kids soon... Don't abandon us, or God will punish you! Father and Syomka can't wait for you to go to her, but don't go... Don't listen to them. They are beasts, not human beings."

"Go to sleep!"

"I am sleeping, Styopa... I am."

"Marya!" Maxim's voice called. "Where are you? Come here, mother needs you!"

Marya jumped up, tidied her hair and ran back to the house. Maxim slowly approached Stepan. He had already undressed and looked like a corpse in his underwear. The moon played on his bald patch and shone in his gypsy eyes.

"Are you going to the mistress tomorrow or the day after?" he asked Stepan.

Stepan didn't answer.

"If you are going, go tomorrow and go early. The horses, I bet, haven't been groomed. And don't forget, she promised fifteen. Don't go for ten."

"I'm not going at all," Stepan said.

"What do you mean?"

"I mean... I just don't want to..."

"Why not?"

"You know yourself."

"I see... Look, Styopa, I hope I don't have to thrash you in my old age!"

"Go ahead, thrash me."

"How can you speak like this to your parents? Who do you think you're talking to? Just look at you. Still wet behind the ears, and you are rude to your father."

"I'm not going, that's all there is to it! You go to church, but you aren't afraid of sin."

"I just want to set you up, you fool! Do we need to build a new house or not? What do you think? Who will you turn to for timber? To Madam Strelchikha? Who will you borrow from? From her or not from her? She will give you timber, and money. She'll reward you!"

"Let her reward others. Not me."

"I'll flay the skin off you!"

"Go ahead! Flay the skin off me!"

Maxim smiled and held out his hand. He was holding a whip.

"I'm going to flog you, Stepan."

Stepan turned over and pretended that he was being prevented from sleeping.

"So you won't go? Do you mean it?"

"I mean it. Let God punish my soul if I go."

Maxim raised his hand, and Stepan felt a sharp pain on his shoulder and cheek. He jumped up like a mad man.

"Don't flog me, Pa!" he cried. "Don't flog me! D'you hear? Don't flog me!"

"Why not?"

Maxim thought it over and struck Stepan once again. Then he hit him for a third time.

"Listen to your father when he gives you an order! You'll go to her, you scoundrel!"

"Don't flog me! D'you hear me?"

Stepan began to howl and quickly sank on to the rug.

"I'll go! All right! I'll go... But you mark my words! You will live to regret this! You'll be cursing!"

"All right. Go for your own sake, not for mine. It's you, not me, who needs a new house. I said I'd thrash you, and I did."

"I'll... go! Only... mark my words, you'll remember this flogging!"

"Go on. Scare me. Save your breath!"

"All right... I'll go..."

Stepan stopped howling, turned over on to his stomach and went on crying quietly.

"Look at him, twitching his shoulders! Whimpering! Weep some more! You'll head off early tomorrow. Ask for a month's wages in advance. And for the four days you've already worked. It will do for a scarf for that wench of yours. And don't be angry about the flogging. I am your father... If I want to, I'll hit you, and if I want to spare you, I will. That's how it is... Go to sleep!"

Maxim stroked his beard and headed back to the house. When he went into the house, Stepan thought he heard Maxim saying: "I flogged him!" And Semyon's laughter could be heard.

An out of tune piano began playing mournfully in Father Grigory's house: at nine o'clock the priest's daughter usually did her music practice. Quiet, strange sounds travelled round the village. Stepan got up, climbed through the fence and began walking along the street. He walked down to the river. The river was gleaming like mercury, and reflected the sky and the moon and the stars. It was deathly quiet. Nothing stirred. Only a cricket chirruped once in a while... Stepan sat on the riverbank, right above the water, and propped his head on his fist. Gloomy thoughts, one after another, began to swirl in his head.

On the other side of the river soared the tall slender poplars which surrounded the garden of the estate. A light from the mistress' window could be seen through the trees. The mistress was awake, clearly. Lost in thought, Stepan sat on the bank, until the swallows began flying over the river. When he got to his feet, it was no longer the moon that was reflected in the river, but the rising sun. He washed his face, prayed to the east and quickly strode along the riverbank to the ford. After crossing the shallow ford, he set off towards the estate.

II

"Has Stepan come?" Elena Yegorovna asked when she woke the next day.
"He has!" replied the maid.
Strelkova smiled.
"I see... Good. Where is he now?"
"In the stables."
The mistress got out of bed, dressed quickly and went into the dining room to have her coffee.

Elena Strelkova was still quite young-looking, younger than her years. Her eyes alone betrayed the fact that she had already lived through most of the time allotted to a woman, and that she was over thirty. Her eyes were brown, deep and mistrustful, more like a man's than a woman's. She was not beautiful, but she could charm. Her face was plump, attractive, and healthy, and her neck, mentioned by Semyon, was magnificent, as was her bust. Had Semyon appreciated beautiful legs and arms, he would probably not have kept silent about the mistress's lovely legs and arms. She was dressed in plain, light, summery clothes. Her hair was done very simply. Strelkova was lazy and did not like to spend a lot of time on her appearance. The estate on which she lived belonged to her brother, a bachelor who lived in St. Petersburg and rarely thought about his property. She had lived there ever since separating from her husband. Colonel Strelkov, her husband, a very respectable man, also lived in St. Petersburg, and thought about his wife less than her brother thought about his estate. She had separated from him after living with him for less than a year. She was unfaithful to him on the twentieth day after their wedding.

Having sat down to drink her coffee, Strelkova sent for Stepan. Stepan came and stood by the door. He was pale, his hair was not brushed, and he looked at her as a captured wolf might, malevolently and balefully. The mistress glanced at him and blushed slightly.

"Good morning Stepan!" she said, pouring herself some coffee. "Tell me, please, what are these tricks that you are playing? Why on earth did you leave? You spent four days here and then you left! Left without asking. You should have asked!"

"I did ask," Stepan grunted.

"Whom did you ask?"

"Felix Adamych."

Strelkova fell silent and then continued:

"Was it because you were angry, was that it? Stepan, answer me! I'm asking you! Was it because you were angry?"

"If you hadn't said those words, I wouldn't have left. I was assigned to the horses, not to..."

"Let's not talk about it... You misunderstood me, that's all. No need to be cross. I didn't say anything much. And even if I said something that you found offensive, then you... then you... After all, I am... I have the right to say more than I should... Hmm... I am raising your salary. I hope that from now on there won't be any more misunderstandings between us."

Stepan turned round and started walking off.

"Wait, wait!" Strelkova stopped him. "I haven't said everything yet. You know what, Stepan... I have some new coachman's clothes. Take them and put them on. What you are wearing won't do at all. The new clothes are nice. I'll send them to you with Fyodor."

"Yes, ma'am."

"Your face... Are you still sulking? Could it have been that offensive? Well, that's enough... I didn't mean anything... You'll have a good life here... You'll be pleased with everything. Don't be cross... You're not cross, are you?"

"As if we were allowed to be cross."

Stepan made a dismissive gesture with his hand, started blinking and looked away.

"What's wrong, Stepan?"

"Nothing... As if we were allowed to be cross! We are not allowed to be cross..."

The mistress got up, put on a concerned expression and approached Stepan.

"Stepan, are you... are you crying?"

She took Stepan by the sleeve.

"What's wrong, Stepan? What is it? Speak out? Who wronged you?"

Tears welled up in her eyes.

"Come on!"

Stepan gestured again with his hand, started blinking vigorously and burst into tears.

"Mistress!" he muttered. "I will love you... I'll do whatever you want! I agree to it! Only don't give anything to those devils! Not a kopeck, not a woodchip! I agree to everything! I will sell my soul to the Satan, so long as you don't give them anything!"

"Who do you mean?"

"My father and my brother. Not a woodchip! I hope they die of rage, damn them!"

The mistress smiled, wiped her eyes, and burst out laughing.

"Good," she said. "Well, go now! I will send the clothes to you straight away."

Stepan departed.

"What a good thing it is that he is stupid!" the mistress thought, watching him walk away and admiring his extremely broad shoulders. "He spared me from having to give him an explanation... He was the first to speak about 'love'..."

Towards evening, when the setting sun was flooding the sky with purple and the earth with gold, Strelkova's horses were galloping at a frantic pace from the village to the distant horizon along the endless steppe road... The carriage was bouncing up and down like a ball, mercilessly mowing down the heavy, bent heads of rye which lined the road. Stepan was sitting on the coachman's seat, furiously whipping the horses and it seemed that he was trying to tear the reins into a thousand pieces. He was dressed with great taste. It was obvious that a lot of time and money had been spent on his coachman's outfit. Expensive velvet and red calico tightly clad his sturdy figure.

A chain with charms hung on his chest. His boots, with pleats like a harmonica, had been polished with real beeswax. The coachman's hat with its peacock feather barely touched his curly blond hair. Dull resignation could be read on his face, together with raging fury, the brunt of which the horses bore... The mistress lolled back in the carriage, every part of her body feeling totally relaxed, her ample bosom breathing in the healthy air. A youthful blush was playing on her cheeks... She felt she was enjoying life...

"This is marvellous, Styopa! Marvellous!" she shouted. "Whip them! Faster! Godspeed!"

Had there been rocks under the wheels, they would have given off sparks... They were leaving the village further and further behind... The log houses and the estate barns disappeared from view... Soon even the bell tower was not visible... Eventually the village was reduced to a smoky strip and dissolved into the distance. Stepan continued to whip his horses. He wanted to get as far away from the sin that terrified him so much. But no, the sin was sitting right behind him in the carriage. He could not flee. That evening, the steppe and the sky bore witness to him selling his soul.

Around eleven o'clock, the horses came galloping back. The trace horse was limping and the shaft horse was covered in a lather of sweat. The mistress was sitting in a corner of the carriage, huddled inside her cloak with half-closed eyes. A contented smile was playing on her lips. She was breathing so lightly, so calmly! As Stepan drove the horses, he thought he was dying. His head was empty and foggy, and sorrow gnawed at his heart...

Every evening fresh horses were led out of the stables. Stepan harnessed them and drove to the garden gate. The radiant mistress walked through the gate, climbed into the carriage, and the frantic ride began. There was no day free from this ride. To Stepan's misfortune, there was not a single rainy evening on which he could have avoided going.

After one of these trips, Stepan left the yard when he returned from the steppe, and took a walk along the riverbank. As usual, his head was fuzzy, there was not a single thought in it, but there was a sickening sorrow in his heart.

It was a fine, quiet night. The air was full of subtle fragrances which caressed his face tenderly. Stepan remembered the village, which loomed in the dark across the river.

He remembered the house, the garden, his horse, the bench on which he slept with his Marya, and was so happy... He felt inexpressible pain...

"Styopa!" he heard a faint voice.

Stepan turned round. Marya was walking towards him. She had just crossed the ford and was holding her shoes in her hands.

"Styopa, why did you leave?"

Stepan gave her a blank look and turned away.

"Styopushka, I am an orphan, whom have you left me for?"

"Leave me alone!"

"You know God will punish you, Styopushka! He will punish you! He will send you a violent death without repentance. Mark my words! Uncle Trofim lived with that soldier's wife, remember? And how did he die? God forbid!"

"Why are you pestering me? Ah..."

Stepan took two steps forward. Marya clutched his kaftan with both hands.

"I am your wife, Stepan! You can't abandon me like this! Styopushka!"

Marya began to wail.

"My darling! I will wash your feet and drink the water! Let's go home!"

Stepan pulled away and hit Marya with his fist; he hit her out of grief, for no other reason. The blow landed right on her stomach. Marya gasped, grabbed her stomach and sank to the ground.

"Ah!" she groaned.

Stepan started blinking, hit his temple with his fist, and set off for the yard without looking back.

After returning to the stables, he collapsed on to the bench, put a pillow over his head and painfully bit his hand.

Meanwhile the mistress was sitting in her bedroom, trying to predict whether or not the weather would be fine the following evening. Her cards indicated that it would.

III

Early one morning Rzhevetsky was driving home after paying a visit to a neighbour. The sun had not yet risen. It was no later than four in the morning.

Rzhevetsky's head was buzzing. He was steering the horse and swaying slightly from side to side. About half of his route lay through the wood.

"What the hell?" he thought as he approached the estate that he managed. "It looks like somebody is cutting down trees!"

The sound of an axe and splintering branches reached Rzhevetsky's ears from the thicket. Rzhevetsky pricked up his ears, thought about it, cursed, climbed clumsily out of the carriage, and made for the thicket.

Semyon Zhurkin was sitting on the ground and chopping up green branches with an axe. Three felled alder trees lay beside him. A horse harnessed to a cart was standing a little way off and eating grass. Rzhevetsky caught sight of Semyon. His tipsiness and drowsiness vanished instantly. He turned pale and sped towards Semyon.

"What do you think are you doing? Eh?" he yelled.

"What do you think are you doing? Eh?" the echo repeated.

But Semyon did not answer. He lit his pipe and continued with his work.

"I'm asking you what you are doing, you scoundrel?"

"Can't you see? Have you lost your sight or something?"

"Whaat? What did you just say?! Repeat it!"

"I said that you should keep going!"

"What, what?"

"Keep going! No need to shout..."

Rzhevetsky turned red and shrugged his shoulders.

"What the blazes? How dare you?"

"Quite easily, as you can see. What's it to do with you? You can't scare me! There are a lot of your kind! If I were to please each one of you, I would need a lot of..."

"How dare you chop down the wood? Is it yours?"

"Not yours either."

Rzhevetsky raised his whip in the air and only did not strike Semyon because the latter drew his attention to the axe.

"Do you know whose wood this is, you scoundrel?"

"I do, Pan! It is Strelchikha's wood, and it is Strelchikha I will be speaking to. It's her wood and so it's her I will answer to. What's it got to do with you? You are a lackey! A servant! I don't know you. Be on your way, passer-by! Quick march!"

Semyon tapped out his pipe on the axe and smiled sarcastically.

Rzhevetsky ran back to the carriage, pulled on the reins and flew off like an arrow towards the village. In the village he collected together some witnesses and rushed back with them to the scene of the crime. The witnesses caught Semyon red-handed. An indictment was immediately drawn up. The village elder, his deputy, a clerk, and some constables appeared. They wrote out several documents. Rzhevetsky signed them, and Semyon was forced to sign them too. Semyon just laughed quietly to himself...

Before lunch, Semyon came to see the mistress. She already knew about the felling. Without greeting her, he began by saying that it was no way to live, that the Pole was flogging people, that it was only three trees, and so on.

"How dare you chop down someone else's trees?" the mistress fumed.

"He just causes trouble," muttered Semyon, admiring the mistress's outburst and wishing to do whatever it took to get his own back on the Pole. "With every word comes a blow! Is that a way to proceed? And it is the face he goes for! You can't do that... We are human too."

"And I'm asking you how you can dare chop down my trees? Scoundrel!"

"He lied to you, mistress! It's true I... chopped some trees down... I admit it. But why did he have to beat me?"

The mistress's aristocratic blood boiled. She forgot that Semyon was Stepan's brother, forgot her good breeding, and everything else in the world, and slapped Semyon on the cheek.

"Get your peasant mug out of here this very second!" she screamed. "Get out! Now!"

Semyon was flummoxed. He had in no way expected such a scandal.

"Farewell, ma'am!" he said, and sighed deeply. "Nothing to be done! Oh, well!"

Semyon muttered something and left. When he went outside, he even forgot to put on his hat.

About two hours later, Maxim came to see the mistress. He had a long face and his eyes were gloomy. It was clear from his expression that he had come to say or do something insolent.

"What do you want?" the mistress asked.

"Good day! I am here, mistress, to ask you for something. Some timber would be good, mistress. I want to build a house for Stepan, but I have no timber. A few little planks..."

"Well, all right."

Maxim's face beamed.

"We have got to build a house, but there's no timber. It's a lost cause! Like sitting down to eat soup, and there is no soup. He-he. Some little planks, bits of board... No doubt Semyon was rude... But don't be angry, mistress. He is a total idiot. His head is still full of foolishness. He lacks common sense. There are people like that. So would you give the order, mistress, so I can come and collect the timber?"

"Yes, you can come."

"Then please tell Felix Adamych. May God grant you good health! Now Styopka will have a house."

"But it will cost you, Zhurkin! As you know, I don't sell my timber, because I need it myself. And if I do sell it, it is at a high price."

Maxim's face fell.

"How do you mean?"

"I mean, first of all, money in advance, and second..."

"I don't want to pay money for it."

"Then how do you want to do this?"

"It's obvious how... You know yourself. What kind of money does a peasant have these days? A kopeck, and not even that."

"I'm not giving it away for nothing."

Maxim clenched his hat in his fist and began staring at the ceiling.

"Are you sure about that?" he asked after a pause.

"Yes, I am sure. Have you anything else to say?"

"What is there to say? You won't give me the timber, so why would I want to talk to you, ma'am? Farewell. But it's a shame you won't give me the timber... You'll regret it... I couldn't care less, but you will regret it... Is Stepan in the stables?"

"I don't know."

Maxim gave the mistress a significant look, coughed, hesitated, then left. He was shaking with rage.

"So this is what you are like, you witch!" he thought as he made for the stables. At that moment in the stables Stepan was sitting on a bench, lazily brushing the flank of the horse standing in front of him while remaining seated. Maxim stood at the door rather than entering the stables.

"Stepan!" he said.

Stepan did not answer or look at his father. The horse shook itself.

"Get your things together and come home!" Maxim said.

"I don't want to."

"How can you say such a thing to me?"

"Obviously I can if I am saying it."

"I'm ordering you!"

Stepan jumped up and slammed the stable door in Maxim's face.

In the evening, a boy from the village came running to Stepan and told him that Maxim had ordered Marya out of the house and that Marya did not know where to spend the night.

"She is sitting by the church, crying," the boy said, "and people have gathered round her and are blaming you."

Early in the morning the next day, when everybody at the manor house was still asleep, Stepan put on his old clothes and went to the village. The church bells were ringing for matins. It was a bright, cheerful Sunday morning with so much to be glad about! Stepan walked past the church, looked blankly at the bell tower and made for the tavern.

Unfortunately, the tavern opened before the church. When he entered the tavern, there were drinkers already hanging about the counter.

"Vodka!" Stepan ordered. They poured him a shot of vodka. He drank, sat for a bit, and had another shot. Stepan got drunk and began buying rounds. A rowdy drinking spree got underway.

"Do you earn a lot at Strelchikha's?" Sidor asked.

"As much as I should. Drink up, you ass!"

"It's very kind of you. Compliments of the season, Stepan Maximych! Happy Sunday to you! And why are you not…"

"I am… I am drinking too…"

"Jolly good… This is all most satisfactory and enticing, actually, Stepan Maximych! So… May I ask you, do you get about ten roubles then?"

"Haha! Do you think a gent can live off ten roubles? Are you kidding? He gets a hundred!"

Stepan looked at the person who said this and recognised his brother Semyon who was sitting on a bench in the corner, drinking. The drunken face of Manafuilov, the sacristan, peered out from behind Semyon and smiled spitefully.

"May I ask you sir," Semyon said, taking off his hat, "does the mistress have good horses or not? Do you ll… ike them?"

Stepan poured himself a shot of vodka in silence and drank it in silence.

"They must be very good," continued Semyon. "Only it's a pity there's no coachman. It's not the same without a coachman…"

Manafuilov approached Stepan and shook his head.

"You... you're a... pig!" he said. "A pig! Don't you feel sinful? Ye men of Orthodox faith! He doesn't feel sinful! And what does it say in the Scriptures, eh?"

"Leave me alone! Half-wit!"

"Half-wit... You're smart though. A coachman, but without horses. He-he... Does she give you coffee too?"

Stepan swung his arm and hit Manafuilov's big head with a bottle. Manafuilov staggered and went on:

"Love! What a feeling... Huh... Shame you can't get married. You'd be the master! He would have made a fine master, lads! Strict, and clever too!"

Laughter could be heard. Stepan swung his arm and hit the same head with a bottle again. Manafuilov staggered and this time fell to the ground.

"Why are you brawling?" Semyon shouted, advancing towards his brother. "Get married—then you can brawl! Why is he brawling, lads? I'm asking you, why are you brawling?"

Semyon narrowed his eyes, grabbed Stepan by the chest and hit him in the pit of the stomach. Manafuilov got to his feet and started waving his long fingers in front of Stepan's eyes.

"Guys! It's a fight! God is witness, it's a fight! Pile in!"

The tavern became very noisy. The chatter mixed with laughter.

People began crowding around the doors. Stepan grabbed Manafuilov by the collar and flung him through the door. The sacristan screamed and rolled down the steps like a ball. The laughter became even louder. The tavern was crammed with people. Sidor intervened in what was not his business and, without knowing why, hit Stepan on the back. Stepan grabbed Semyon by the shoulder and flung him through the door. Semyon hit his head on the doorpost, ran down the steps and fell wet-faced, into the dust. His brother ran over to him and started dancing on his stomach. He danced as if possessed, with gusto, jumping high into the air. He went on jumping for a long time...

The bells rang for the prayer "It is truly meet..." Stepan surveyed the scene. He was surrounded by laughing mugs, each one drunker and merrier than the other. A multitude of mugs! The dishevelled and bloodied Semyon was picking himself up from the ground, his fists clenched, and with a savage expression on his face. Manafuilov was lying in the dust, crying. The dust clung to his eyes. The devil knew what was happening all around!

Stepan roused himself, turned pale and took to his heels like a madman. His pursuers set off behind him.

"Catch him! Get him!" they shouted after him. "Stop him! He's killed someone!"

Stepan was overcome by terror. It seemed to him that if they caught up with him, he would surely be killed. He started running faster.

"Get him! Stop him!"

Without realising it, he had run to his father's house.

The gate was wide open, its two halves swaying in the wind... He ran into the yard.

His Marya was sitting on a pile of wood chips and shavings, three steps from the gate. With her legs tucked beneath her and her limp arms stretched out in front of her, her eyes were fixed on the ground. At the sight of Marya, a bright thought flashed through Stepan's wound up and drunken mind...

I must run away from here, run far away with this deathly pale, battered, dearly loved woman. Run as far as possible from these brutes, to Kuban* for example... Kuban is so wonderful! If Uncle Peter's letters can be believed, there is a wondrous freedom in the Kuban steppe! Life has more to offer there, the summer is longer, and the people are bolder... Stepan and Marya would start off as labourers, but afterwards they would acquire their own little piece of land. There would be no bald Maxim with his gypsy eyes, no Semyon with his drunken, sneering smile.

It was with this thought in his mind that Stepan went up to Marya and stood in front of her... Meanwhile his head was spinning from the drunkenness, coloured spots were flashing before his eyes, and he felt pain all over his body... He could barely stand on his feet...

"To Kuban... and..." he said, feeling that he was losing the ability to speak. "To Kuban... To Uncle Pyotr... You know? The one who wrote the letters..."

But no such luck! The idea of Kuban was blown to smithereens... Marya raised her pleading eyes to his white, distraught face, half-hidden by hair which had not seen a comb in a long time, and got to her feet... Her lips trembled...

"Is that you, you scoundrel?" she wailed. "You? Got your mug slit in the tavern? You damned wretch! You are my torturer! May you suffer in hell, the same way as you sucked all the life out of me! You've killed me, an orphan!"

"Shut up!"

"Cruel-hearted people! You have no pity for a Christian soul! You've tormented the life out of me, you scoundrels... You're a murderer, Styopka!

The Mother of God will punish you! You just wait! You won't get away with this! Do you think that I am the only one who is suffering? Oh no... You'll suffer too."

Stepan started blinking as he staggered.

"Shut up! For Christ's sake!"

"Drunkard! I know whose money you've got drunk on... I know, scoundrel! Are you drinking for joy? So you're happy?"

"Shut up! Mashka! Please..."

"Why have you come? What do you want? Did you come to gloat? We don't need your gloating to know... The whole world knows... They probably make an example out of you all day long, you wretched..."

Stepan stamped his foot, staggered, and pushed Marya with his elbow, his eyes flashing...

"Shut up, I'm telling you! Don't wring my heart!"

"I'll keep talking! Are you going to hit me? Go ahead then... hit me... Hit an orphan. There is only one end to this... What kind of affection could I expect? Beat me... Finish me off, scoundrel! What do you need me for? You have got the mistress... She is rich... She is beautiful... I'm scum, and she is a noblewoman... Why don't you hit me, you scoundrel?"

Stepan swung his arm and with the full force of his fist hit Marya's face, which was distorted with rage. The drunken blow landed on her temple. Marya shuddered and fell to the ground without making a single sound. As she was falling, Stepan hit her once more on the chest.

The husband bent over his wife's warm, but already dead body, stared blankly at her emaciated face, worn out with suffering, and, without understanding anything, sat down beside the corpse.

The sun had already risen over the log houses and was now scorching. The wind turned hot. An oppressive sorrow hung in the sultry air as a dense crowd of trembling people surrounded Stepan and Marya... They could see and understand that a murder had taken place here, but they could not believe their eyes. Stepan surveyed the crowd with dull eyes, gnashing his teeth and muttering incoherently. No one tried to tie Stepan up. Maxim, Semyon and Manafuilov stood in the crowd, huddled together.

"Why did he do it?" they were asking, pale as death.

Stepan's mother was running about, wailing...

The incident was reported to the mistress. The mistress gasped, and took hold of a vial of smelling salts, but did not faint.

"What terrible people!" she whispered. "Terrible people! Scoundrels! Very well then, I'll show them! They'll find out now what sort of a woman I am!"

Rzhevetsky turned up to console her. He consoled the mistress and once again took up the position which had been taken from him by his capricious mistress and given to Stepan. It was lucrative, snug and suited him perfectly. Ten times a year he was dismissed from this position and each time he was paid compensation. He was paid quite a lot.

A Hollow Victory

(A Story)

Chapter I

The sun was setting in the west when Zwiebusch and Ilka Dog Teeth* turned off the highway and headed towards the orchard of the Counts Goldaugen. It was hot and humid.

In June, the Hungarian steppe* makes its presence felt: the earth cracks, and the road turns into a river in which grey dust ripples instead of water. The wind, if there is any, is hot and dries the skin. There is a stillness in the air from morning to evening. This stillness brings on melancholy in the traveller. Only the splendid, world-famous Hungarian orchards and vineyards do not wither and dry up under the burning rays of the steppe sun. Scattered by the hand of civilised humans along the banks of numerous rivers and streams, they show off their greenery from early spring until late autumn, luring passers-by and serving as a shelter for all living things fleeing the scorching sun. They are a haven of shade, coolness, and wonderful air.

Zwiebusch and Ilka set off down a long path. This path covered the shortest distance between the gate leading to the steppe and the gate in front of the count's orchard. It divided the orchard into two equal parts.

"This path reminds me of the ruler they used to hit your father's hands with at school in days of yore," said Zwiebusch, trying to make out the end of the drive. The end of it disappeared and merged with the green horizon. The sun did not reach it. The drive was no more than two yards across, and the branches of the trees lining it stretched towards each other. It was a tunnel built by nature out of olive, oak, linden, and alder tree branches.

Zwiebusch and Ilka entered it and almost had a roof over their heads. The fat and short-legged Zwiebusch was dripping with sweat. His face was as crimson as a boiled beetroot. He kept on wiping his moist chin with the edge of his short jacket. He was huffing and puffing like a badly lubricated steam-powered thresher.

"This cool air is divine, my little chaffinch!" he muttered, unbuttoning his waistcoat and shirt with his fat fingers. "I swear by my fiddle! We've left hell and arrived in heaven, don't you think?"

Ilka's face was no paler than her little pink lips. Beads of sweat gleamed on her large forehead and on the arch of her nose. The poor girl was exhausted, and could barely stand upright. The strap from her harp was pressing on her shoulder, while its sharp edge chafed her side. The shade made her smile a few times and breathe more deeply. She took her shoes off and went barefoot. Her pretty little bare feet revelled in the sensation of the cold sand underfoot.

"Why don't we sit down for a bit?" suggested Zwiebusch. "The drive is as long as an old maid's tongue. It must stretch for the best part of two miles!"

"No, Papa! If we sit down, it will be difficult to get up again! Better to get to the end and rest there."

"All Right... Today is your birthday, my little chaffinch. Fate will give you a present, but what will it be?"

"I'd like to wish that fate gives me the present of some lunch today..."

"That's a tall order! Ha-ha! You are asking too much! Isn't that overdoing it, my girl? Perhaps you would like some supper too?"

"It's been a long time since I have eaten hot food... You can't imagine, Papa, how dry my throat is from all that dry bread and smoked sausage! If fate were to offer me today a choice between ten extra years of life or a cup of broth, I would choose the broth without a second thought."

"And you would be quite right. The worst broth is many times better than our idiotic life."

"I would choose the broth and would gulp it down with an enormous great appetite! I am terribly hungry."

Zwiebusch gave Ilka a sympathetic look, sighed, and whistled with his thick lips. He always made short whistling sounds when something worried him or forced him to think. After a brief pause, he focused on Ilka his thick overhanging eyebrows, from under which peered his smiling eyes, and said:

"Well, you have to wait a bit and be patient... I foresee that the gift fate will bring you today will be worthy of our attention... He-he... I foresee that we are not trudging in vain towards the courtyard of the noble Counts Goldaugen! He-he... When we enter the courtyard and begin to play, we'll be pelted with filthy lucre. We'll stuff our pockets with coins. Ilka will be treated to lunch... He-he... Dream on, Ilka! Anything can happen on this earth! Perhaps, everything I've been saying will come true!"

Ilka adjusted the harp strap on her shoulder and laughed.

"The Count himself will listen to us!" continued Zwiebusch. "And, my dear, just suppose that the thought occurs to him, the count, that we should not be turned out of the courtyard! And suppose Goldaugen listens to you and smiles... If he is drunk, he will throw a gold coin at your feet, I swear by my fiddle! A gold one! He-he-he. And suppose, by some good fortune, he is now sitting at the window and as drunk as forty thousand brothers! The gold coin is yours, Ilka! Ho-ho-ho..."

"But why does he have to be drunk?" asked Ilka.

"Because a drunk man is kinder and cleverer than a sober man. A drunk man loves music more than a man who is sober. Oh, my golden-voiced quint! Had there been no drunks in this world, art wouldn't have progressed very far! So, pray that those who are going to listen to us are drunk!"

Ilka thought it over. Yes, Zwiebusch was right to some extent! Up to now, it had mainly been drunks who would throw her coins. Were it not for them, she and her father would have gone hungry much more often. They would play most often outside inns and taverns, rather than in front of the clean porches of sober burghers. It was mostly men whose distinguishing traits were a sagging face, big red nose and incoherent, vulgar talk who listened to them. Ilka began to ponder this joyless subject, and felt bitter and frustrated. She understood now why more attention had been paid to her father's bleating vocals and vulgar jokes than to her songs, and why so often they would ask for a dance tune instead of her songs. Often, her song would be interrupted halfway through and replaced with a pointless dance tune accompanied by the squeaking of her father's fiddle. Up to now, not a single listener had bothered to enquire who had written the songs she sang with such feeling. *The Song of the Three Knights* and a trite dance tune were listened to with equal interest.

"The sober despise us because they see us as beggars, but the drunks welcome us because our music drowns out their headache a bit."

With these words Zwiebusch drove the frustrated Ilka to despair. She felt like bursting into tears and breaking something in her body... her fingers, for instance. But her fingers would not break whatever she did with them, so she had to be content with tears.

"Greeting to the abode of the esteemed counts Goldaugen!" muttered Zwiebusch. He had caught sight of a small gate made out of thin wire overgrown with blooming sweet peas.

"Greetings! A man without forefathers enters the lair of people with fore-fathers, scoundrel forefathers! Better to be nothing rather than dishonourable! In the seventeenth century, Count Karl Goldaugen died of remorse after mar-rying a commoner, while his brother, Moritz, spent a whole month dancing for joy after the priest gave him permission to divorce a woman whom he, Moritz, had robbed and driven to consumption."

"Do you see this house, my chaffinch? If it was possible to reveal to you the history of this house and you could glance into it, you would exclaim: "Man is a beast!"—and you, who do not know a single swear word, would curse like... maybe only the Russians curse! Do you remember the Russians, my darling? Their language is as tough as their winter. Let our instruments be tuned!

Zwiebusch tuned his fiddle. Ilka wiped the dust off her harp with her pinafore.

"Fate, we challenge you! Pick up the non-existing gauntlet!"

Zwiebusch and Ilka straightened up, assumed happy faces and entered the count's courtyard. Despite the heat, the courtyard was not empty. Work was abuzz there. About twenty workers in blue shirts, covered with dust, soot and sweat, were laying asphalt in the yard. Grey smoke was pouring out of three vats.

Zwiebusch and Ilka walked boldly up to the house itself. When they glanced at the windows, they caught sight of a big face in the biggest window... The face was red.

"The Count!" muttered Zwiebusch. "I think that's him! My prophecy is coming true! And, he's drunk, too... Off you go!"

Ilka plucked the strings of her harp. Zwiebusch stamped his foot and lift-ed the fiddle to his chin. When the workers heard music, they turned round. The red face in the window opened its eyes, frowned and sat up. There was a glimpse of a woman's face and a pair of arms behind the red mug... The win-dow was flung open...

"Go away!" came from the window. "Get out of the courtyard, you musi-cians! To hell with you and your music!"

The red face leaned out of the window and gesticulated with his hand.

"Play, play!" cried a female voice.

The workmen stopped working and approached the musicians, scratching themselves. They stood right in front of them, so they could see Ilka's face.

"There are many countries in the world," Ilka started to sing, plucking the strings with her fingers, "beautiful countries, as radiant as the sun, and rich; but the best of them all is Hungary with her orchards, paddocks, climate, wine, and bulls who have horns a yard long. Ilka loves this country. And she loves the people who inhabit it."

The red face smiled and stared at Ilka with moist little eyes.

"Her people are good," Ilka went on singing. "They are beautiful and brave, and they have beautiful wives. They are unbeatable in war or in battles of words. Nations envy them. They have but one shortcoming: they don't know any songs. Their singing is pitiful. It lacks passion. It makes one feel sorry for Hungary..."

"Mister Pichterstei, His Grace's chief estate manager, commands you to sing something more cheerful!" boomed a lackey in a red jacket, who had come up to Ilka.

Ilka fell silent. The girl did not get the chance to express herself fully.

"More cheerful? Hmm... Tell his excellency Mister Pichterstei that his wish will be faithfully carried out! However, I would like to have the honour of talking to him myself!"

After saying this, Zwiebusch took off his hat, walked up to the big window and clicked his heels.

"You command that we sing something more cheerful?" he asked, smiling respectfully.

"Yes."

"What about a diplomatic song? My own composition! This song resolves one of the most vital of European problems. Your Serene Highness, do you have the honour of being a Magyar?"

The red face exhaled a column of tobacco smoke and graciously nodded.

"I invite gentlemen patriots to pay attention! May I hope, gentlemen, for discretion? Are there in your midst..."

Zwiebusch looked at the workers who nodded their heads and, intrigued, came closer.

"What is Austria?" sang Zwiebusch in a shrill voice. "Politicians, princes of the realm, tell me, what is Austria? Is it not a mixed salad, which greedy neighbours are ready to devour? And devour it they would if, in that mixed salad, there was not a golden ruff that one might choke on. This ruff is Hungary."

"Bravo, bravo!" muttered a fat man.

"Austria is a bird painted in a hundred colours!" Zwiebusch continued to sing. "It consists of a hundred parts. It has many legs, many wings, many stomachs, but only one head. This head is Hungary. A wild beast could attack the bird, swallow all its parts, but it won't crack its skull! The skull is as hard as ivory."

"Bravo, bravo!"

"There is the French language, there is German, Russian, and there is Magyar. All the wise men marvel at the richness of the Magyar language. So, please, go to Vienna and ask: where does the sphinx live which speaks Austrian?"

"Bravo, bravo! This is for you!"

A large shiny, silver coin, was thrown through the window and rolled to Zwiebusch's feet with a tinkling sound. A similar coin hit Ilka's shoe. Zwiebusch picked up the coin and shouted:

"A thousand thanks! I shall go and drink to your Honour's health! I shall drink and, I swear on my fat face, I won't breathe! I will drink to your health with two throats: the common throat and the respiratory one! I won't have time to breathe!"

Zwiebusch doffed his hat. At that moment something unexpected happened at the window. The red face turned crimson, the girl screamed, and the window suddenly slammed shut. The workers backed away and lined up. Zwiebusch flung his hat back and sensed a certain obstacle behind his hat. He looked round and his knees went wobbly. A beautiful black horse, scared by the tactless waving of his hat, was rearing on its hind legs right by him. Sitting on the horse was a tall, slender beauty known to the whole of Hungary—the wife of count Goldaugen, née Baroness von Heilenstrahl. Zwiebusch saw before him a most beautiful woman, full of grace, youth, dignity and... anger. She steadied the horse and, very pale, trembling with anger and shooting daggers with her eyes, raised her whip.

"You swine!" she whispered, almost falling off her saddle, while Zwiebusch, stunned by the blow, swayed and fell to the ground, his corpulent body hitting the black horse's front legs. He could not help but fall.

Zwiebusch's temple, cheek and upper lip took the full force of the blow. The countess had struck him really hard.

The other female face, beautiful and young and framed by a billion strands of blonde hair, the face of Goethe's Gretchen and of Ilka, was distorted with anger and inexpressible despair. It was drained of colour and contorted...

Her face twitched. Ilka bared her white teeth like a dog, took a step forward and, failing to find a rock on the ground, threw the silver coin at Countess Goldaugen. The coin barely touched the veil billowing in the wind and flew towards the house. A strange, heavy silence ensued. The countess and the little blonde head stared each other down. The silence lasted a minute. The countess raised her whip but, seeing the pale, wretched, distorted face, slowly lowered her arm, and rode off towards the house. When she reached the front porch, she turned her head back twice.

"Turn them out!" she shouted.

Zwiebusch got to his feet, shook the dust off himself and, smiling through the blood streaming down his face, approached the petrified Ilka.

"Are you surprised, my dear, that your father has been whipped? If so, don't be! This isn't the first time that he has been beaten up, it's the forty first! It's time you got used to it!"

Ilka grabbed her father's hand and clung to him, shaking all over.

"Oh, how happy I am!" said Zwiebusch, trying to prevent the blood from dripping off his face onto Ilka's head. "How happy I am! How can I thank her Grace! My fiddle is intact! I didn't crush my fiddle!"

Zwiebusch took hold of the harp in one arm, put his other round Ilka's shoulders, and started walking quickly towards the drive.

Chapter II

At the very moment when the end of the drive, which leads out on to the steppe, appears in sight, one must start counting the beech trees on the left. Between the eighth and ninth beech tree, an experienced eye will be able to make out the traces of a previously existing but now abandoned path. This path winds like a snake towards a chapel near to which one can find water. Zwiebusch knew of this path's existence. He counted up to eight and turned left. Ilka followed him. They had to fight their way through a dense thicket of burdock, wild hemp, hemlock and nettle. Nettles stung their hands, neck and face pitilessly, and the heavy smell of wild hemp and hemlock made it difficult for them to breathe. Zwiebusch and Ilka's shoulders became covered with cobwebs in which little spiders, big flies and grasshoppers were scrabbling about and becoming entangled. Large spiders performed unusual *salti mortali* from Zwiebusch' and Ilka's shoulders on to the grass. Our travellers were disrupting the peace of a thousand lives.

The chapel stood in a clearing overgrown with tall grass, a quarter of an hour's walk from the drive. It was a decrepit little church covered with moss, goosefoot and ivy, which timidly overhung the grass. On top of its smooth, cone-shaped roof, discoloured by the sun, stood a tall, bronze cross. This cross served as a lode star for Zwiebusch.

"If the brook has dried up," said Zwiebusch, "then fate's gift will be much nastier than the one her Grace brought us. My innards are as dry as parchment."

But the brook had not dried up. When Zwiebusch and Ilka reached the chapel and removed the cobwebs from their shoulders, they felt a waft of fresh air and heard a murmuring sound. Zwiebusch smiled broadly, put the harp and fiddle down on the chapel steps, and quickly started walking round the chapel, tracing a circle with his short legs.

"It's gurgling... but in which direction, dammit?" he laughed. "Brook, where art thou? How can I find you? Darn my stupid memory! I drank from you a couple of times, brook, and, ungrateful that I am, have forgotten where you are! I recognise the human being in myself! We don't forget anything, except, that is, our benefactors! Oh, humans! Ha-ha..."

Ilka, whose hearing was more acute, could have pointed out from which direction the noise of running water came, had there not been that terrible insult to which her old, and in her opinion, sick father, had so recently been subjected. She followed her father instinctively, unable to see, hear or understand anything. She was oblivious to fatigue and thirst. Everything paled before a powerful, young, righteous anger. She walked, staring at the ground and biting her upper lip.

Deaf in one ear, Zwiebusch walked round in circles until he came upon a place where the gurgling of running water could clearly be heard, and where soft, moist soil could be felt underfoot.

"The brook must be under the linden trees!" said Zwiebusch. "Here is one linden. But where are the other two? There were exactly three of them when I was here drinking water ten years ago... They must have cut them down! Poor little lindens! Someone must have needed them too. But here is what we are looking for... My respects! Let us drink, Ilka, to your health!"

Zwiebusch knelt down, tossed his hat aside and lowered his burning face to the cold, sparkling surface... Ilka instinctively went down on one knee and followed her father's example. Zwiebusch drank with his mouth and eyes. In the water he could see his reflection, covered with blood, he began to think of a suitable witticism as he looked at the bruises and grazes. But the witticism went right out of his head and the water ran out of his mouth when he caught sight of Ilka's face on the mirror-like surface next to his face. He stopped drinking and raised his head.

"Ilka!" he said, frowning. "Do you hear me, girl? Stop snarling! You're not a dog! I don't like this sort of thing. Don't be a fool!"

Ilka raised her head and passed the wet palm of her hand over her forehead.

"I don't like it!" Zwiebusch went on. "Give up your silly habit of baring your teeth at every trifle! Be a good girl! Why get worked up? You are as pale as a corpse and you're trembling! Watch out you fool, or you will die of anger, and that'll teach you! Stop it! Come on!.."

"I can't... No-one has the right, papa Zwiebusch, to hit you in the face. No-one!"

"Is that so? And do you think I didn't know that? I know that full well without you telling me! Not on the face, or on the back, or on the belly... But what can one do?"

Ilka passed the palm of her hand across her forehead once more and whispered:

"I don't want anyone to hit you. I want... I want revenge on her."

Zwiebusch made a whistling sound, bent over the water and started washing his face. When he had washed his face, he wiped it with his sleeves and said:

"That's nonsense, Ilka! Drink some more, if you haven't had enough already, and let's get back to our instruments. Enough talking rubbish!"

Zwiebusch lifted Ilka up by her hand and, stroking his belly, made for the chapel.

"Instead of being angry, let's look at the chapel!" Zwiebusch suggested.

A great number of green and grey lizards scuttled off into the cracks in the ground and the grass as Zwiebusch and Ilka approached the chapel. The chapel door and its rusty hinges had been securely boarded up. Some copper letters were nailed onto a smooth wooden plaque above the door. The letters were, of course, in Latin. Zwiebusch read out and translated to Ilka the following: "Francis Goldaugen—1806. Passer-by, please pray that the holy angels bore his soul to Paradise!" The glass panes in two windows were broken. Shards of glass protruding from semi-rotten frames reflected all the colours of the rainbow. The third window was plugged with a sheaf of barley. The windows were a kingdom of cobwebs and dust.

"Francis Goldaugen!" Zwiebusch shouted into the window.

"Goldaugen!" the echo responded.

"Francis Goldaugen was the current count's grandfather's brother," Zwiebusch said, turning to Ilka. "In 1806, on his way home from a tryst, he was killed on this very spot by his old valet who was avenging his daughter. That is what some say, others say that he got into a fight with his nephew over some girl and was killed. Whatever the truth of the matter, the valet was hanged right here. "Thou shall not kill," says the holy commandment; but, in the Goldaugens' houses, forests and orchards, they did not know the holy commandments. Look through the window, Ilka... Can you see St. Francis? His face is yellowish-green and rather scary... This image has faded now, but in days gone by it was perfectly visible and instilled terror in stupid people and women. This face was particularly frightening, I remember, when a blue lamp burned before it... I used to get shivers down my spine when I looked at this face. The point is, my girl, that the artist who painted this image ran off without completing the job. He did not finish painting the left eye, which is why the right eye stood out so much and bothered our superstitious eyes. The face was also left unfinished. There was just the underpainting, as artists call it. The artist ran off because he had fallen in love with the countess. The eccentric fellow saw her as an impregnable fortress. Idiot! All he needed to do was to let her know, and she would have thrown herself at him. Women have always been weak in this respect. They are not different to men when it comes to the subject you shouldn't know about, my innocence."

Zwiebusch fell silent and looked at Ilka. Ilka was not listening to him. She was staring at the ground, whispering something and waving her fingers as if talking to herself. Zwiebusch made a whistling sound and began to ponder.

"Listen, redhead!" he said, frowning. "I don't like this! You're starting to bare your teeth again! Let's go and sit down!"

Zwiebusch and Ilka sat down on the chapel's sunbaked steps.

"Where are your brains, girl?" Zwiebusch continued, gazing at his daughter's pale face. "Why don't you think logically? One cannot make steel out of wood; one cannot make a bell out of rags. A rat cannot give birth to a swan. One cannot expect angelic behaviour from that woman, as she was born from a certain breed of people. Her father and grandfather were wolves, so, how could she, contrary to the laws of nature, be born a lamb? She is a wolf too! A wolf from head to toe! And since she is a wolf, she could not have acted otherwise... What did you expect? Teaching wolves to eat hay is not our business... Think logically! She was born the baroness Heilenstrahl; and who are the Heilenstrahls? They are the same as the Goldaugens. The first Heilenstrahl was the illegitimate son of Arthur Goldaugen. He only obtained the title of baron during the Thirty Years War because he was related to the Goldaugens. Later on, the Goldaugens took the Heilenstrahls as wives, the latter would take the former as husbands, and so on. The result was two identical families. What do you expect? Would you like a Heilenstrahl to smother you with kisses while a Goldaugen was beating you? Hmm... No, my dear! Only greenhorns like you can be angry with the wolves for the sharp teeth given them by nature."

Zwiebusch paused for a moment and then went on:

"And the importance of nature's role here can be clearly seen from the history of the Goldaugens. The first Goldaugen appeared at the end of the Crusades. They called him the Golden-eyed vampire. His hair and his beard were as black as coal, while his eyebrows and eyelashes were blond. Thanks to this freak of nature he was nicknamed Goldaugen. History tells us that, along with a remarkable mind, and a mixture of the cunning and prowess of a lynx, the bloodthirstiness of a hungry leopard gleamed in his golden eyes. He was a rabid dog in the worst sense of the word. He drank human blood as easily as we do water; he bought and sold people with the brazenness of a Judas. To burn a village to the ground was much easier for him than it would be to smoke a cigar for us. He would set it alight and watch the flames with glee. While the victors, led by Godefroy de Bouillon,* were praying for the first time at the Holy Sepulchre, Goldaugen was scouring the suburbs of Jerusalem and threading the heads of Saracens on pikes. Even at this great moment he remained true to himself! As the annals tell us, he passionately wanted to pray, but the instinct of a rabid dog pulled him in a different direction: to destruction, blood. This is a terrible deformity, my dear! One cannot believe that the golden-eyed man was guilty of his deformity. A man cannot sink to such horrifying atrocities on his own, just as he cannot think up a sixth finger on his hand. It is nature which is to blame. It gave him the brain of a wolf. A son was born to the Golden-eye, who differed from his father only in that he did not have golden eyes... the deformity passed on to him; the grandson had golden eyes and the same deformity. And so on. The present count does not have golden eyes. Last year his son died; a boy who did have golden eyes. The golden eyes thus skip a generation, but the deformity has become everyone's lot. As you see, my dear, it is as difficult for the Goldaugens to get rid of their wolf's brains, as it is for them to get rid of their golden eyes. So, judge for yourself, how could that beauty not strike me on the lips? Nature took precedence over reason, and it couldn't do otherwise!"

"You are lying, father!" screamed Ilka, stamping her foot. "You're lying! Your lips don't care about her deformity or her nature! It is not our business! You're only saying this, because being angry is not good for me. But I'll show her! I won't... won't forgive her! May God punish me if I forgive her this insult!"

"Let someone else, not you, my lamb, make a show of bravery! A lamb standing up to a wolf just means a waste of breath... We'd do better to stop talking!"

Ilka rose to her feet, threw the harp's strap over her shoulder and indicated the path with her chin.

"Don't you want to rest a bit?" asked her father.

Ilka remained silent. Zwiebusch stood up, took the fiddle under his arm, wheezed, and started walking towards the drive. He was used to obeying Ilka.

An hour later they were back walking on the dusty, hot road, barely able to drag their tired feet along. Ahead of them, beyond the strip of blueish thickets and orchards, stood white bell towers and the town hall of a small Hungarian town. To the left was the attractive and colourful village of Goldaugen.

"Where is the courthouse? Here or there?" asked Ilka, pointing to town and village.

"Courthouse? Hmm... There is a courthouse in both the town and the village. In the town, my precious, they judge the townsfolk, and in the village, the Goldaugen folk."

Ilka stopped and, after some thought, started walking along the road which led to the village.

"Where are you going? Why?" asked Zwiebusch. "What is the point? May God keep you from those peasants!"

"I am going, papa Zwiebusch, to the place where they judge the Goldaugens."

"Whatever for? For God's sake! You're a madcap, my dear! We can have lunch and drink some beer in the town, but what are we going to do here?"

"What are we going to do? It's quite simple: we are going to sue that shameless scoundrel of a woman."

"You are a fool, daughter! You've gone out of your mind! You've lost all ability to reason, my dove! Or maybe you are joking?"

"I'm not joking, father! I even wonder how you, with all your self-esteem, can act so coolly in regard to this insult! Go to the town If you want! I will go to court on my own and will demand that they punish her!"

Zwiebusch glanced at Ilka's face, shrugged his shoulders, and started walking after his disobedient daughter, muttering, gesticulating with his hands and making whistling sounds.

"You are a fool, Ilka," he said with a sigh as they crossed the bridge over the river. "A fool! I swear on my fiddle, it will come to nothing! Forgive me, daughter, but, honestly, today you are as stupid as a gudgeon!"

They had crossed the bridge and entered the village. There was not a soul on the streets. Everyone was busy working in the fields and orchards. They spent a long time walking in circles round the village until eventually they came across a little old woman, who was as wrinkled as a desiccated melon rind.

"May I ask," Ilka said, addressing the old woman, "where does the judge live here?"

"The judge? We have three judges, young lady," the old woman answered. "One of them hasn't judged anyone for a long time. He's been lying paralyzed for ten years now. The second one gave up working, and is a landowner now. He married a rich woman and took her land as a dowry—what does he care about the court now? But he is already an old man too... He got married about fifteen years ago, when my eldest son died, may God have mercy on his soul..."

"And the third one? Where does the third one live?"

"The third one? The third one still judges... But, he too, is pretty hopeless... He's an old codger! He should be sleeping in the grave, not sorting out disputes... He lives... See that green porch? See it? Well, that's where he lives..."

Zwiebusch and Ilka thanked the old woman and set off towards the green porch. They found the judge at home. He was standing in his courtyard under a sprawling old mulberry tree, knocking down black, overripe berries with a stick. His lips and chin were stained purple, blue and bright red. His mouth was full. The judge was chewing more lazily than bulls who are tired of chewing their cud.

Zwiebusch took his hat off and bowed to the judge.

"I wonder if I might bother your honour with a single question," he said. "Are you the judge, sir?"

The judge eyed his uninvited guests and, having swallowed the cud, said:

"I am the judge, but only before lunch."

"And have you already eaten, sir?"

"Well, yes... I lunch at half past two... You should know that. On days off, I lunch at half past one."

"*Plenus venter non studet libenter,*[1] your honour! Heheheh... You speak the truth. But there are no rules without exceptions, your honour!"

"There are with me... I admit no exceptions in this particular case. I only judge people on an empty stomach, old fellow, when I am least likely to be sentimental. Ten years ago, I tried to judge after lunch... And what happened? Do you know what happened, old fellow? I handed out sentences one grade more lenient... And this is not always fair! But you are as fat as a hundred-bucket barrel! You probably eat a lot, do you? Doesn't it make you hot to carry all that extra flesh? And who is this girl?"

"This, your honour, is my daughter... She is the one who is your plaintiff."

"Hmm... So... Come closer, my beauty! What do you want?"

Ilka approached the judge and told him about everything that had occurred in the Goldaugen courtyard, in a trembling voice. The judge listened to her, looked at Zwiebusch's lips, smiled and asked:

"So, what is it you want, my beauty?"

"I want you to punish that woman!"

"I see... All right... With great pleasure! We will chuck her into prison, right now... Listen, old fellow," the judge addressed Zwiebusch. "Where did you sire this beauty, on the moon or on earth?"

"On earth, your honour! There are no women on the moon, your honour, so it's hardly possible to drink a glass of wine to the health of the new mother!"

"If on earth, then, why doesn't she know that... What fools you are! Ah, what fools! You are both fools and eccentrics!"

"Why is that?" asked Ilka.

"Probably because you have no brains... The Goldaugens wine and dine me, so why would I want to judge them?! Hahaha! The Goldaugens are the counts, and she is the daughter of a gypsy, a lousy fiddler who should be flogged for playing the fiddle so poorly! You are a strange lot! No, you were not born on this earth! Do you think she would want to litigate with you? On the

---

1   *"Plenus venter non studet libenter"*: a Latin proverb "a full belly does not like studying."

writ I'd send her, she would draw a face with a big nose and throw it under her desk! And where are your witnesses? The workers? Fat chance of that! They are not such millionaires to give up a piece of bread! Hahaha! You found just the right person to sue! You odd girl! No, my beauty, don't be silly! It's upsetting, I agree... But, what's to be done? You can't change the world!"

"But what should I do?"

"Give your dad a rag so that he can bandage up his lip. The flies might make the wound go septic... Buy some zinc ointment... That's the only advice I can give... Want another piece of advice, my beauty? Be my guest! Take your fat papa by the hand and go away... I can't stand fools! Deliver yourselves from the presence of an unjust judge and give me the option of not conversing with you."

"But what should I do?" asked Ilka again, wringing her hands.

"Hmmm... Want a third piece of advice? Here you are! Make yourself a countess, just like she is. Then, you will have every right to sue her! Every right! Hahaha! Become a countess! Upon my honour! Then you can sue her to your heart's content! Anyway... farewell! I'm busy! Leave me alone. As you are not a countess yet, I am fully justified in driving you, so indelicately, away from my full stomach and lazy tongue! Quick march, old fellow! Don't forget to buy the zinc ointment."

The judge turned round and began tucking into the berries. Zwiebusch and Ilka left the yard and headed towards the bridge. Zwiebusch wanted to stay in the village and have a rest but he did not want to go against Ilka's wishes... He trudged after her, cursing the hunger pinching his stomach. The hunger was preventing him from thinking...

"Are we going to the town, daughter?" he asked.

Ilka didn't answer. When they entered a grove belonging to the Goldaugen peasants, Zwiebusch asked:

"Are you angry, Ilka? Why don't you answer my question?"

Instead of answering, Ilka swayed and grasped her head.

"What's the matter with you, daughter?"

The daughter stopped and turned her face to her father. Her face was distorted by a wicked and malicious smile. Her teeth were bared as if she were a dog...

"Please tell me, what is the matter?"

Ilka raised her arms, threw her head back and opened her mouth wide... A harsh deep cry resounded through the grove. Large tears started streaming from the blue eyes of a daughter whose father was insulted... Ilka began to sob and laugh.

"What's the matter? How can you be so angry?"

Zwiebusch burst into tears himself and began kissing his daughter.

"How can you get yourself into such a state? Sit down, Ilka! I beg you, sit down! Come on, sit down!"

Zwiebusch placed his large sweaty hands on her heaving shoulders and pressed.

"Sit down! We will sit for a while in the shade, and you will feel better! Let's go sit under that willow! And here's the brook! Want some water? Willows always grow near water. Where there are willows, one should look for water! Let's sit down!"

Zwiebusch carried Ilka to the willow tree, bent her knees and sat her down on the grass. The sobbing was becoming louder and louder...

"That's enough, daughter! Do we have the right to be so insulted? Do we never insult anyone? Can you vouch that your father never insulted anyone with impunity? I have insulted people! And I have only paid for it today."

A shot was heard. Catching on the branches, rustling and flapping its wings, a bird fell out of the willow on to Ilka's pinafore. It was a young female eagle. One pellet had lodged in her eye, and another had crushed her beak...

"Look, my dear! If we take nature to be represented by this bird, it has been greatly insulted... This insult is much greater than ours... Nature puts up with it... It does not punish or take revenge..."

The sound of snapping twigs came from the bushes, and Zwiebusch saw in front of him a tall, statuesque, supremely handsome man with a large, full beard and a swarthy complexion. He was holding a gun in one hand, and a wide-brimmed straw hat in the other. Seeing his prey in the lap of a pretty girl who was crying, he stopped dead in his tracks.

"This man, though, has already been punished!" said Zwiebusch. "And punished severely! His sins pale in comparison to his penitence! May I commend to you, Ilka: Count Vunic, Baron Seinitz. Hello, Count and Baron! Are you more of a count or a baron? There's a lot of both in your devilishly handsome figure... Here is your prey! My daughter is presiding over its funeral."

Baron Arthur von Seinitz was about twenty-eight years of age—not more than that, but he looked over thirty. His face was still handsome and fresh, but there were little wrinkles on it, near the eyes and in the corners of his mouth, such as can be seen in people who have already lived and suffered a great deal. Youth, with its failures, joys, woes, drunken parties and debauchery, had furrowed his handsome, swarthy face. There was satiety and boredom in his eyes... His lips had formed into a submissive and, at the same time, derisive smile that had become habitual... The baron's black hair was long and curly. It reminded one of the hair of a young boarding school girl who has not started braiding her hair into plaits yet. Arthur rarely bathed, and, for this reason, both his hair and his neck were dirty and glistened in the sun. He was dressed modestly and simply... His clothing was unfussy and extremely unspecific... The collar of his dirty shirt betrayed the fact that he was not fashion-conscious. People wore collars of that sort four years ago. His worn black necktie was like a ribbon; its knot, tied hastily and clumsily, had shifted to one side and was in danger of becoming undone... His jacket and waistcoat were fabulous; they were covered with stains, but they were new. They were made of expensive grey material, woven from the best goat wool. His worn silk breeches, which had seen better days, clung snugly to his muscular thighs and disappeared handsomely above the knees into the folds of high shiny boots. The heels of his boots were crooked and half worn-down. A new metal chain rested on the goat-wool waistcoat. Six gold lockets were attached to the chain, as well as a gold stork with diamond eyes, and a small, meticulously crafted gun with a gold barrel and a platinum butt. On the butt of this tiny gun, one could read the following inscription: "To Baron Arthur von Seinitz. The Society of Weistaff and Solenogorsky Hunters." Do not ask the baron what time it is; instead of a watch, a key and a tin whistle were attached to the pocket end of the chain.

The family of the barons Seinitz cannot boast a long history. It goes back to the first decade of the present century, no further. Arthur has a small brochure, *The History of the Barons von Seinitz*, which was commissioned long ago by Arthur's father Karl from some visiting scholarly Swedish pastor. The obliging pastor charged a large sum and spared neither paper nor the truth when composing the genealogical tree of the gracious barons. He traced the von Seinitz family back to the eleventh century. Naturally, many believed the brochure; especially those who had no reason to check the pastor's accuracy. But the brochure gave the Seinitzes a reason to blush when one very helpful illustrated newspaper, wishing to be of service, printed their coat of arms and a family history which was closer to the truth than the one for which the pastor had been paid. The first baron Seinitz was just an ordinary member of the gentry who had married the daughter of a banker, a baptised Jew. This was an individual who was contemptible in every respect—sycophantic, perpetually hungry, and loving money above all else in the world. He would have lived his life invisibly and disappeared from human memory forever had it not been for fortune, which smiled at him both graciously and constantly... The first Seinitz had two brothers. One of them was a Jesuit, who lectured in physics at some university and made his own way to a cardinalship. The other brother was a court poet and the son-in-law of the king's personal physician. Thanks to both the powerful protection of these two brothers and money from his banker father-in-law, who had major financial connections, it was much easier for him to obtain the title of Baron von Seinitz than that first Seinitz, about whom the Swedish pastor had written all those fibs. The second Seinitz, Arthur's grandfather, fought at Austerlitz and died as a professor of the military academy. This Seinitz was the spitting image of his uncle the cardinal and, like him, was a more bookish man than a soldier or a country squire. Arthur's father resembled the first Seinitz. He too was a petty, nondescript, worthless person. Poorly educated, dim-witted, physically and morally weak, he made it his goal to squander, once and for all, everything that smiling Fortune had bestowed on his grandfather and father. This task, however, did not prove to be an easy one. The barony of Seinitz occupies no small amount of land. A railway crosses it in two places. It is considered, thanks to its orchards, vineyards and soil, to be one of the richest and most sumptuous estates. A stud farm and a textile mill on its territory earned the barons two thousand four hundred francs a day between them; not to mention all the rest. To squander such a fortune is not easy, but Karl von Seinitz had excellent helpers. He was helped by his philandering, his lack of reason, his kindness, and his... son. To the end of his days, he never gave up loving women. He loved desperately, madly, without reason and without letting any obstacles get in his way. Women constituted his main item of expenditure, and without them he would have been hard-pushed to squander *everything*. He had a mistress for a while in Vienna. He would travel to go and see this mistress on a special express train with a multitude of libertine hangers-on who would drink only champagne. Every train would deliver stunningly luxurious presents to his mistress that would speak too eloquently of the baron's madness. The presents consisted of family jewels, expensive horses, promissory notes... The chambermaid of his Viennese love received a thousand francs a month and had her own carriage just in case. Lucullan feasts* were held upon the arrival and before the departure of the special trains. In Prague, there was a second mistress, in Budapest, a third, etc. Women adored him, naturally, for his generosity more than anything else.

The mass of anecdotes still told about Karl von Seinitz are the best illustration of this adoration. From that mass of anecdotes we will cite just one.

A young actress, who had just graduated from drama school, made her debut at one of the leading German theatres. (Today she is a very famous actress, particularly noted for her portrayal of dramatic characters and tragic old mothers.) She was young, good-looking and gave a first-class performance. The theatre rang with applause. After the first act, she was presented with a bouquet of flowers decorated with a most precious necklace belonging to the late Baroness von Seinitz, Karl's mother. The baron gave away this necklace because it had been sitting in his side pocket and jabbing his side with the sharp end of the locket fastener. After the second act, several high-ranking persons who happened to be in the theatre went backstage to express their admiration to the debutante. Von Seinitz, too, was present among these high-ranking figures. He felt at home backstage. After a glass of champagne in the dressing-room of the male lead, he headed to the dressing room of the up-and-coming star. The door of the dressing room was locked. He knocked.

"What are you doing!?" the high-ranking fans exclaimed in amazement... "You forget yourself! You forget that this is not a circus, or an operetta... Not the *Salon de Madame Deleaux*! You are devilishly impertinent, baron!"

"You think? I'm just impatient..." replied the baron.

"She will appear any minute! Won't your patience last two or three minutes?"

"No, it won't."

"But this is indecent! Maybe, she is getting dressed right now!"

"Maybe," answered the impatient baron, and he knocked on the door once more.

"Who is there?" a young female voice was heard from the dressing room.

"Me!" replied the baron.

"Who are you?"

"One of the admirers of your talent. I don't actually understand a thing about your talent, but I'm told that you are a wonderful actress, and I'm in the habit of believing what people say. Open up!"

"That's odd... I'm in my dressing room! You can't come into a dressing room. Who are you anyway?"

"I am Baron von Seinitz. I have something to discuss with you."

The voice from the dressing room started talking more quietly and not so boldly:

"I'm delighted, Baron... But, I'm not dressed... Please, wait five minutes."

"I have no time to wait. I'm leaving in two minutes. It's now or never!"

"You can't come in!"

"Up to you... Farewell! Who is yanking at my sleeve, dammit?"

A crowd of the debutante's admirers had gathered round the baron. The crowd was thoroughly scandalised by the baron's brazen behaviour. They demanded that he step away from the door. The debutante's fiancé, who was in the crowd, yanked at his sleeve.

"Would you please step away from the door!" shouted the admirers.

"And what will happen if I don't?" asked the baron, and he knocked on the door, this time with his fist rather than his finger.

"*Mademoiselle*, I suppose you want these gentlemen to have a row with me!" he said through the door to the debutante. "Open up! I'm leaving in a minute and a half... Now or never! I, Baron von Seinitz, like to do everything now or never! Won't you please talk to Baron Seinitz, who has business to discuss with you? "

The debutante was evidently hesitating.

"What do you want?" she asked.

"Oh, dammit! Isn't it obvious what I want!? I have no time to talk! Well, I'll count to three. If you don't open up when I say "three", I'll leave, and you will never see me again... But what a lot of admirers you have! I can tell from the number of pinches I am getting on my back and on my sides... Well, I'm starting to count... one...two... Well... well..."

Light steps could be heard near the door of the dressing room.

"Three!" said the baron.

The lock clicked. The door opened quietly. A pretty maid with a smile darted out of the dressing room right in front of the baron's nose. The baron took a step forward, and his sense of smell was pervaded by the fine fragrances of the dressing room. She was standing at the darkened window, wrapped in a shawl. A dress that she was going to put on lay next to her... Her cheeks were red. She was dying of shame...

"My God, she is still so innocent!" thought the baron. He bowed and said:

"My apologies! I'm leaving in a minute, therefore..."

The debutante lifted her eyes. Her eyes were full of curiosity. She was seeing him for the first time, but she had heard so much about him back at drama school! She had long adored him from hearsay.

"What do you want, Baron?" she asked after a tense, minute-long silence.

"I beg your pardon, *mademoiselle*, for my persistence, but... the honest truth is that I like you!"

The debutante stared at the floor. Her cheeks became even redder.

"I don't like compliments," she said.

"Dear God, how innocent she is!" the baron thought, and asked:

"What sort of fee is the theatre paying you?"

"That is still to be decided... How much—I'm not sure... For a start, probably, not more than two thousand thalers..."

"Hmm... That is good... Enough to start off with."

The baron fell silent and stared hard at the debutante. The debutante was ready to sink into the ground from shame and expectation.

"If you come to me," said von Seinitz after a pause, "you will get a hundred and fifty times more."

The debutante's rosy cheeks became as white as the baron's shirt. The debutante shrieked, clasped her hands together and, as if stunned by the shot of a hundred cannons, promptly fell onto a velvet-upholstered armchair. She had a fit of hysteria. Von Seinitz bowed and left. When the maid entered the dressing room, the debutante was sobbing. The sobs were spasmodic and mingled with laughter... The maid took fright and ran out of the dressing room, and within a minute the crowd outside had divided into little groups. These groups were whispering, looking askance at the dressing-room door and not knowing what to do: to fume over the baron's daring deed, or... to envy the sobbing debutante's luck? The fiancé stormed into the dressing room like a madman, threw himself at her feet and yelled:

"Don't cry, my darling! He will pay for this insult! But... why, god damn it, did you open the door to that demon?"

The debutante rested her tear-streaked face on her fiancé's white shirt-front, put her hands on his shoulders and whispered:

"Oh, Georges! How lucky I am! How lucky you and I are! He promised me one hundred and fifty times more, and we were taught at drama school that Baron von Seinitz keeps his word! What a pity, though, that he is not handsome! But... a hundred and fifty times more!! Go, my friend, and ask them to announce to the public that I am indisposed and cannot go on with the play!"

The next day, the debutante received from the "adored" von Seinitz three months' worth of salary in advance...

This anecdote is plausible, but I do not know how truthful it is.

The baron's second main item of expenditure was cards. Von Seinitz gambled very rarely. He was bored by card games; but, once he sat down to play cards, he used to lose enormous sums of money out of boredom. Boredom also led him to invent his own card game. His game was too simple. It was called *Blacks and Reds*.

"Red or black?" Seinitz would ask his partner, showing him the back of a card. "If you guess, you win, and if you don't, I win."

Von Seinitz would have been hard-pushed to invent anything cleverer than this game. However, he managed over two evenings to lose the county of Vunic that had been bought by Arthur's grandfather in Galicia. The county of Vunic was his first significant loss.

The second loss was his wife, Baroness von Seinitz, whom he drove to her death with his behaviour. The third loss was his daughter, a hypocritical prude and an idiot, who, in order to boost a faltering business, had to be married off to a Jewish banker who was climbing the social ladder towards nobility. The barony of Seinitz met a most pitiful fate. It was mortgaged for a pittance to the banker son-in-law who left it for himself at the auction. Karl ended up unsuccessfully committing suicide (the bullet lodged in his shoulder), and he died in the arms of his daughter and some Catholic priests, having left the banker several promissory notes for a hefty sum, "just in case."

His son Arthur, following his mother's death, was sent when he was twelve to Vienna, where he was put in a boarding school. After leaving boarding school, where he learnt to speak three languages, he went to university, entering the faculty of philology. It was not long before Arthur abandoned philology and began to study mathematics. In this faculty he was lucky. He received a prize for the best student essay on differential calculus. After completing his studies in mathematics, he resumed his studies in philology. This wandering from one harbour to the next, could possibly have led to something good, had it not been for those thousands he received every month at the post office and from his father's agents. These thousands went to his head. When he got tired of collecting a library, on which he had been spending large sums ever since he entered university, he lost his bearings and followed in his father's footsteps... He went to Paris. Thousands of letters flew from Paris to the barony of Seinitz with demands for money. Karl was kind, and so not a single letter was left unanswered; every answer was made in the form of cheques. To Arthur's good fortune the packages of money he received from home became smaller every month, and began to arrive in

Paris less and less frequently... Hundreds gradually replaced the thousands. Along with the news of his father's death, Arthur received a thousand francs, and a letter from his banker brother-in-law. The banker wrote that the enclosed thousand was *all* that was left of the von Seinitz fortune and that he, Arthur, had nothing left to fall back on... Arthur read the letter and turned bright red.

He began to feel terribly ashamed of himself and of his father. He did some serious thinking, and started to fear for his future, which he had so cherished and pitied when he was a university student. He tore his brother-in-law's letter into pieces and punched himself in the face with all his might... He wanted to throw the thousand francs out the window, but... did not in the end. And just as well. That thousand came in handy. It was spent on running away from his debts in Paris. His creditors were hotel keepers, money lenders and, most shamefully, courtesans... During his last days in Paris he had to live at the expense of courtesans... He fled back to his homeland, worn out by drinking, dissipation, and dishonesty, though, luckily, not entirely. His health had not yet broken down, and not once had he been deliberately mean. Luckily, Arthur had a resilient nature. In Vienna he took up his studies again, and with greater zeal than before. In order to put bread on the table and not pester his relatives for money, he became an algebra teacher in a military college and a journalist for two big newspapers in Paris. He also earned a little by writing poems, which he placed in French magazines. (Like Frederick the Great, he could not stand the German language.) His life became quiet, simple, and tolerable, the direct opposite of his Parisian lifestyle, but it did not stay like this for long... His life was ruined at the most interesting point, namely in the golden year when he became a Doctor of Philosophy and a Master of Mathematical Sciences. Fate tripped him up on the road of opportunity without him noticing it. He got into debt. Anyone who used to be rich and is now poor, will understand the meaning of "without noticing it." In addition, Arthur married a pretty girl, of impoverished noble stock, who had fallen in love with him. He married out of both love and compassion. The marriage increased his expenditure. He was obliged to turn to his sister. Arthur wrote his sister a letter, in which he asked her to let him know the fate of their mother's estate, and, if it had not been sold to cover the debts, to assign him a share of the income received from it. In the same letter he also asked his sister to send to him in Vienna his library, which she had once taken care of. In response to this letter, Arthur received a telegram from his brother-in-law asking him to come to Seinitz immediately. Arthur went. When he arrived at Seinitz, they asked him to enter on foot.

"Madame Peltzer," they told him, "doesn't like the sound of wheels. Be so kind as to come to the house on foot."

Arthur was received in the drawing-room by his brother-in-law and sister. His sister was sitting in an armchair, crying. When he came in, his brother-in-law buried his nose in a newspaper...

"Here I am!" Arthur said to them. "Don't you recognise me?..."

"We can see you," answered the banker. "You did well to obey us and come... We are very glad, Baron, that you still possess the ability to obey... The word "obedient" reeks of something slavish, but you will forgive us... For people like you, obedience is necessary..."

"I don't understand you," said the bewildered baron. "Sister, what are you crying about? Your brother Arthur has come, and you are crying... Answer my "hello" with something! That's enough crying!"

"She started crying, Sir," said the banker, "as soon as we were told you were on your way... Please, sit down... Your sister, thank God, still has some chairs. Not everything was squandered by you and your father. My wife is crying because she still loves you..."

Arthur's eyes widened, and he drew the palm of his hand across his forehead. He did not understand.

"Yes," continued the banker, not taking his eyes off his newspaper, "she cannot easily give up that feeling which, one must acknowledge, is unnatural, because she has basically already ceased to be your sister... Hmm... You are no brother to her. She is immeasurably better than you are. You are too ignoble to be a brother to this woman... Sir! Thank this woman! If it were not for her, you wouldn't dare put a foot inside this house."

"Explain to me, sister," Arthur said, turning pale, "what I should understand from your husband's words? I absolutely don't understand anything! And then, your tears... I don't understand!"

The banker's wife took the handkerchief away from her face, jumped to her feet and started walking round the drawing-room, her heavy dress rustling. Genuine, large, real tears were dropping from her eyes on to the floor.

"You don't understand?" she shouted in a shrill voice. "It is time you understood once and for all that you are killing us with your behaviour! Your immorality shocks us! I'm incensed as a sister and as a Christian!"

"Explain yourself, sister!" said Arthur. "I just don't understand what you are trying to tell me?"

"Be quiet! I don't want to hear your voice! What was that piece of trash you married there?"

"Yes, Baron!" the banker said, joining in the conversation, in a high, quivering tenor voice. "By marrying that worthless woman, you have disgraced the name of the barons von Seinitz and those who consider themselves their relatives!"

The arm of the chair that the baron was clutching made a cracking sound. Arthur began to shake with anger.

"Sylvia!" he said, turning to his sister. "I didn't say a word to you when you were marrying the scoundrel Peltzer. I respected your will. But you? You allow yourself to be dictated to by Peltzer and insult me deeply! Don't forget yourself!"

"Me, a scoundrel?" shouted Peltzer. "I forgive you this word, Baron! I forgive you!"

Sylvia stamped her foot and took a step towards her brother.

"I know everything about you!" she hissed, swallowing her tears. "Everything! As if marrying that street scum, that beggar, was not enough! You are also an atheist! You never go to church! You've forgotten God! You have forgotten that at any minute your soul could separate from your body and be delivered into the hands of the devil!"

"If only scoundrels were like me!" Peltzer was shouting in the meantime. "Ha! Things would be different on earth then! There would be no people on earth who didn't care about anything, either their name, or their honour... There wouldn't be those women, street walkers who..."

Peltzer suddenly fell silent. He looked at Arthur's face, and he began to feel scared.

"Even Lutherans don't behave like you do!" Sylvia was shouting. "We summoned you to let you know how ignoble you are! You must repent! Divorce her and... change your way of life! Straight away! Do you hear me? Do you understand?"

"Since you adhere to class traditions," said Arthur in a muffled voice, "then you should know that it's not becoming for Baron Arthur von Seinitz to bicker with a Jewish emigrant from Russian Poland and his wife! However... I will condescend to ask you one question. I will ask it and leave. What can you tell me regarding the estate of my late mother?"

"It belongs to Sylvia," said Peltzer, "to her alone."

"By what right?"

"Don't you know about your mother's will?"

"Why are you lying? There was no will. I know that!"

"There is a will!"

"If there is one, it is a forgery! And where is my library?"

"It was sold for the thousand francs that were sent to you in Paris..."

"It was worth not a thousand, but two hundred thousand francs!"

Peltzer shrugged his shoulders and snorted.

"Despite all my efforts, I couldn't sell it for more."

"Who bought it?"

"I, Boris Peltzer, did..."

Arthur felt he was choking. He grasped his head with his hands and ran out of the drawing-room.

"Come back, brother! Come back!" Sylvia shouted after him.

Arthur wanted not to come back but it was impossible. He still loved his sister.

"Repent, Arthur!" said Sylvia to her brother when he came back into the drawing-room. "Repent while there's still time!"

Arthur ran out of the drawing-room and, within a minute, choking and trembling with anger, he was racing towards the railway station.

Locking himself in a second-class compartment, he lay on the seat, face down, and travelled in this position all the way to Vienna. In Vienna, fate tripped him up again. When he arrived home, his wife was not there. During his absence, his dearly beloved wife had run off with her lover... She left a letter, asking for forgiveness. Arthur was thunderstruck by this infidelity...

A week later, his wife was thrown out by her lover and returned to him, only to poison herself and die on the threshold of his apartment... When Arthur returned home from the cemetery after burying his wife, he was met by his servant with a letter. The letter was from his sister Sylvia and it read as follows:

"My dear brother! We know everything... The secret murder you committed in order to erase from the face of the earth the traces of the crime that disgraced our name is repugnant to God... We only demanded your repentance, but your wife could have lived... Her death was not necessary. All that was required was her removal. But do not despair. We are praying for you, and believe me, our prayers are not in vain. You should pray too.

Your Sylvia."

Arthur tore the letter into tiny pieces. Then he began to stamp on the pieces, on which God's name had been written by a sacrilegious hand... Arthur began to howl and fell unconscious to the ground...

The teaching, philosophy, mathematics, French poetry—Arthur abandoned and forgot it all. When he finally came back to his senses, he got terribly drunk, and since then, after slinging a double-barrelled gun over his shoulder, he has led a life of wandering as "the wild Seinitz" in the environs of Seinitz, Goldaugen and other villages, drinking copious amounts of wine and exterminating game. He started to lead a strange life... People only saw him at the inns and taverns which adorn the crossroads with their intricate bright colours. All the foresters and most of the shepherds who saw him knew who he was.

No one knew where he lived and what he ate. He would have been considered a madman if he did not strike up such clever conversations with people he chanced to meet. No-one knew what to make of him. They called him "the wild Seinitz," the wandering hermit and "unlucky Baron Arthur." The gutter press started writing about him: about some huge lawsuit that Seinitz was going to bring against the Peltzers; about his sister who had legally robbed her brother; anecdotes and little novels from the lives of Arthur von Seinitz and his father began to appear out of the blue. There was even a newspaper which lamented that the Seinitz family had vanished off the face of the earth...

Arthur mostly wandered through the orchards and groves. There was more game there than in the fields or near the rivers. Orchard owners did not forbid him from hunting on their property. They hated his sister, and they saw in him Peltzer's worst enemy. The female owners even rejoiced at the fact that von Seinitz visited their orchards and groves.

"One can't say," they would chatter, "that he is an *Erlking*,* no! He is too young for that... He is more like the *Erl-Crown-Prince*!"

When he met people, the Erl-Crown-Prince would usually bow very politely. When he bumped into Zwiebusch and Ilka, however, he stopped in his tracks. As an artist, he was struck by the beauty and the true-to-life quality of the group which was made up of Zwiebusch, Ilka, the harp, the fiddle, and the bird.

Hearing sobbing, Arthur frowned and coughed angrily.

"Why is she crying?" he asked.

Zwiebusch chuckled and shrugged his shoulders.

"She is crying," he said, "probably because she is a woman. If she was a man, she would not be crying."

"Was it you who upset her?"

"It was, Baron! I repent..."

The baron looked indignantly at Zwiebusch's fat, glistening physiognomy and clenched his right fist.

"What did you do to upset her, you old swine?"

"I upset her, your Grace, because I possess a mug that can be whipped with impunity... She is my daughter, Baron, and well-mannered people refrain from scolding fathers in the presence of their daughters..."

"Why did you upset her, you rascal? Don't cry, girl! I will interrogate him right now, the scoundrel! Did you beat her up?"

"You guessed correctly, Baron, though only partially... Yes, there was some beating, only it wasn't her who was beaten, and it wasn't me who was doing the beating... Your concern for my daughter touches me, Count! Thank you!"

"Buffoon!" said the baron, waving his hand dismissively before bending over Ilka.

"What's the matter, my dear?" he asked. "What are you crying about? Who hurt you? Tell me who hurt you, and I... will hurt him, and hurt him hard!"

The baron stroked Ilka's hair with his large, sunburnt hand. His eyes lit up with a warm glow.

"We men must stand up for women, because the strong must protect the weak. So why are you crying?"

And, peering into a face covered by her moist little fingers and her loose hair, von Seinitz sank to his knees and carefully sat down next to Ilka. He started talking in a voice he had not used for a long time. Ilka heard a voice full of tenderness and feeling which came straight from the soul—a voice one could trust...

"Why are you crying? Tell me about your troubles! It is not a decrepit old buffoon that is now sitting beside you, but a strong man. You can trust me... I'm powerful and can do anything... What is it you are crying about? Well?"

When children are asked why they are crying, they start crying harder. The same happens with women. Ilka started crying harder...

"Judging by how hard you are crying, your troubles must be very great... You will tell me... You will, won't you? You can be frank with me. I am not asking you out of mere curiosity. I want to help you... Word of honour, my girl!"

Arthur leant over and kissed Ilka on the crown of her head.

"You won't cry anymore? Agreed? Now come on, my dear! You just need to talk it over, to lessen troubles a bit..."

"It's unlikely she will stop crying soon," said Zwiebusch. "Her nerves are as weak as the threads of a shirt that has been worn for five years. Let's give her time to cry her heart out, Baron... It's not good, Ilka! Shedding so many tears will make you thirsty."

"Ah, yes! She needs water!" said the baron. "There is water nearby..."

The baron got up and disappeared through the thick bushes; dry twigs and branches started snapping under the weight of his heavy body.

"What a great baron!" giggled Zwiebusch. "Gentle, polite, considerate! Hahaha! Anyone might think that he really is good-natured. Trust him, Ilka, but only a little. He is a good fellow, but give him an inch and he will take a mile. Don't tell him about what happened at the Goldaugens'. He is related to those Goldaugen cut-throats and will laugh at you as if you were a complete fool. Will you stop crying soon?"

The twigs snapped again, and Arthur appeared through the foliage with a huntsman's silver cup in his hand. The cup was full of water.

"Drink... What's your name? Ilka? Drink, Ilka!"

The baron knelt down and lifted the cold cup to Ilka's lips. Ilka took her hands off her face and drank half a cup...

"How miserable I am! Ah, how miserable!" she muttered.

"I believe you, I really do!" said the baron as he wetted her temples with cold water. "I would call you a liar, my dear, if you said that you were happy. Drink some more!"

"I beg you, please, don't scold my father!" whispered Ilka. "He is also very miserable!"

"I won't... I scolded him, because I got heated. At first I thought that he had upset you. I take my unkind words back. But he is treating your troubles in a cold-blooded manner that is unbecoming for any respectable father."

"All we need now is for you to be wetting my temples with water too!" laughed Zwiebusch. "I learnt not to howl back in the days when I grew accustomed to my father caning me. But how soft-hearted you are today, Baron! I don't recognise in you the Baron Arthur von Seinitz who six years ago punched two teeth out of a billiard marker's mouth in the *Black Stallion* restaurant in Prague... Remember, your Grace? One tooth you were good enough to knock out with a cue, and the other with your fist..."

"There were a lot of things that happened six years ago!" muttered von Seinitz. "Many things happened, including some things it wouldn't be proper to mention now. Well, Ilka! Tell me all about it! You've calmed down a bit now, and all you need to do to recover completely is to tell me everything... Well? Who insulted you?"

"It was not me they insulted, but my father!"

"Ah! So, you are crying because of your father?"

"He was insulted in a terrible way! You would be horrified if you saw how he, poor soul, was insulted!"

"So, that's what it is! Hmm... What a good girl you are, though! You have a good daughter, old fellow! A rare thing! Well, it's all the same, tell me... I will also stand up for him as eagerly as I would for you."

"You won't, Baron!" said Zwiebusch.

"Why wouldn't I?"

"Because it is impossible... I had the honour of getting slapped in the face by a very important person, not someone insignificant. No cannonball is capable of striking this person! And you shouldn't stand up for me anyway! My daughter is acting up."

"What rubbish! It's all the same to me, whoever the offender was! My cannonball, if need be, will strike anyone... Do tell me, Ilka. I will help you."

Stuttering, sighing deeply, and continually repeating herself, Ilka told Arthur von Seinitz about what was troubling her. When her story got to the point when the countess Goldaugen had raised her whip, Arthur frowned.

"So, it... was a woman?" he asked.

"Yes, the countess Goldaugen..."

"Hmm... Go on..."

The baron went terribly pale and scratched his forehead.

"Go on... I'm listening... So, a woman hit him? Not a man?"

"A woman, Baron!"

"Hmm... So... Why aren't you continuing with your story?"

When Ilka told him how her father had fallen under the horse's hooves, and how he was then covered in blood, the baron glanced at Zwiebusch...

"Was it she who cut your lip?" he asked.

"Is this worth discussing? We'd do better to talk about politics!"

"I am asking you, you old fool, was it she who cut your lip, or not?" shouted the baron, hitting the grass with his fist. "His daughter is suffering because of him, and he is joking! I don't like jokers!"

"It was her, yes!" said Ilka.

"I am putting the old fool into a young hide and returning him as appropriate!" grumbled Zwiebusch. "I'm not joking, I'm telling the truth! Politics is much better than conversations that definitely won't lead to anything good..."

Ilka showed with her hands approximately how much blood her father had shed, and how he limped when he was trudging towards the chapel. When she told him about the judge and repeated verbatim what he had said, the baron smiled contemptuously and spat to one side. The spit travelled two yards.

"Swine!" he grumbled. "Yes, he is right! That rascal is right! He couldn't have done anything! This Goldaugen Aristides is as much the Goldaugen slave as the horse that almost crushed this Shakespearean fool, your father."

"I don't get so upset when my father is beaten by drunken peasants or the police," concluded Ilka. "The police don't allow us to play in the big cities, Baron. But I am vexed, offended, insulted... offended, when it is a woman who is educated, noble, with a tender face... And what right does she have to look at us with such arrogance, such disdain? Nobody has the right to look at us like that!"

Ilka raised her fingers to her face and started crying...

"Surely she can't get away with it?... Oh my God, oh my God!! If this insult remains unpunished, I'll die... I'll die! Then father will have to play on his own! And he will have to sell my harp!"

Ilka buried her face in her pinafore and continued to weep softly. Zwiebusch looked at the ground and made whistling sounds. The baron began to ponder...

"It's a dreadful insult," he said after a prolonged thought. "But... first one should hear what's the matter and only then make promises. I lied, my darling. I am not as powerful as I bragged an hour ago. I can do nothing for you..."

"Why?"

"Because she's a woman... I can hardly fight her in a duel now, can I? It's a bad business, my darling. You must simply resign yourself..."

"I can't resign myself! Whatever makes you think I can?"

"Your powerlessness will force you to. You are powerless because you're the daughter of a beggar musician and I am powerless because, damn her, she's a woman..."

"What am I to do?" asked Ilka. "Don't believe my father, I implore you! He himself won't survive this insult! He is just pretending to be cold-blooded whereas in reality... I will go to Budapest or to Vienna! I will find justice!"

"You won't find it…"

Ilka jumped up and started walking round the baron and Zwiebusch.

"I will!" shouted Ilka. "You're a baron, after all; a noble, intelligent man, you know everyone, and all the noble people know you… You're not some commoner! Why don't you write a letter to some judge or other so that he convicts her according to the law? You only have to speak or write, and everything will be done!"

"Stop it, Ilka!" said Zwiebusch with authority. "The baron is bored of listening to your hopeless nonsense! You are wasting his time."

"You only think that way, Ilka," said the baron, "because you don't know life. Just now you were telling me that you were miserable and yet your outlook on life is just like that of a sybarite who can't tell copper from iron. How old are you? Seventeen? It's time to get to know life, my beauty! Life is such disgusting, vile and vicious nonsense, and it is such vulgar, aimless and inexplicable rot that it doesn't even bear comparison with a cesspit that has been dug in order to be filled with all sorts of filth. It's time to know it! What do you want from life? Do you want it to smile, to shower you with flowers and gold coins? Yes? Is that what you want?"

Von Seinitz blushed and put his hand into his large hunting bag.

"If so, then you want the impossible! The only life possible on Earth is unbearable… If that's what you want—then, live; if not,—then off with you to kingdom come. Poison is always at your service… You're just a child, that's what! You are a fool!"

Out of the bag appeared a wicker-encased bottle. The baron lifted it swiftly to his lips and took several greedy swigs.

"Life is loathsome!" he continued. "Its vileness is its unshakeable, everlasting law!.. It is given to man as a punishment for his crassness… My lovely pretty girl! If I were not so deeply aware of my own crassness, I would have long ago gone the way of all flesh. I would have had enough bullets… Suffer Arthur, I told myself! You deserve this suffering! Arthur, receive your due! You too, little girl, learn to engage in philosophical speculation of this kind yourself… It's a skill that makes living easier…"

Arthur took two more swigs.

"There is one element in the universe that somewhat reconciles a man to his life. This element, they say, was created by the devil, but… so be it! It takes the thorns out of my soul… for a while, of course. This element is in my bottle… Have a drink, Ilka! Just one swig! It's good vodka…"

Ilka shook her head. Zwiebusch glanced at the bottle, licked his lips and shyly lowered his gaze.

"Go on, take a swig, you weird girl!" von Seinitz went on. "You'll feel better. Go on, just try!"

"Have a drink, Ilka!" Zwiebusch advised.

Ilka took the bottle, sipped a little from it, and frowned.

"Now, you have a drink," Arthur addressed Zwiebusch. "You, too, old piece of lard, drink up!"

Smiling and pulling a face, Zwiebusch beamed as if he had seen a long-lost friend... He took the bottle in both hands and solemnly lifted it to his fleshy lips. After carefully taking two or three swigs, he set the bottle down on the grass.

"Bottoms up!" said the baron. "Don't hold back. I've got another bottle."

It took Zwiebusch a split second to carry out the order.

"Sometime somewhere I've seen you before, old man!" said von Seinitz. "Your physiognomy seems somehow familiar... Where have I seen you?..."

"I am, Baron, that same unfortunate billiard marker, whom you, Your Excellency, deigned to deprive of two teeth in Prague."

"Perhaps, perhaps... I see... I was very good at that sort of thing... I'm sorry I can't put them back in again..."

The baron took another bottle and a package wrapped in paper out of his bag. In the package were pies, cheese and sausage. Von Seinitz cut the sausage in half: he offered one half to Zwiebusch, and cut the other half in two, giving one piece to Ilka and keeping the other for himself.

"Please!" he said. "Tuck in, don't be shy. Eat, girl! The cheese is for your stomach alone. We won't touch it."

The hungry Zwiebusch and Ilka did not wait to be asked twice. They attacked the food with the eagerness of hungry ill-bred children... and in five minutes had devoured everything except a little piece of sausage. This piece was saved by Zwiebusch to be eaten after another shot of vodka.

The vodka Arthur drank had an immediate effect on him. His face reddened and lightened up. His eyes darted about like trapped mice and began to gleam. He stretched his legs out on the ground, propped his head up on his fists, and broke into a smile. The vodka had no effect on Zwiebusch. His head remained in the same state as before. The vodka had an oppressive effect on Ilka. She sat down on her own away from them, rested her head on the palms of her hands and became pensive.

"Drink up, old man!" said Arthur, offering his bottle to Zwiebusch. "Better to be drunk and merry than sober and dull. Good vodka is our salvation... Without it, man would perish! Let's drink to its existence! Why did I knock your teeth out? Do you remember?"

"How could I not? Of course, I do... You were slightly tipsy and demanded that I catch a billiard ball that had been thrown up in the air with my mouth. When I showed no desire to do your bidding, you took a stern course of action..."

"What a swine!" muttered Arthur.

"Who?"

"Listen, my beauty!" said von Seinitz, suddenly turning to Ilka. "You remind me awfully of a girl I was in love with when I was a child. There was no such girl, she didn't exist, but every night my nanny would tell me about her. I imagined her to be just like you. This girl, according to my nanny, lived far, far away, over hill and down dale, in an enormous tulip. She sat on the pistil and peeped out at God's world from behind the tulip petals. She had the most varied occupations. She looked after the flowers, poured the dew into bottles to be used for her baths and as drinking water; she sang songs. This girl, I forgot to tell you, was no taller than your little finger. She ate only honey brought to her by the bees. She wore the crimson petals of poppies. Her area of expertise was medicine. She would charm away toothache, bandage wounds, prepare drops and so on. She performed surgery on a grasshopper whose leg had been broken in a fight with a spider with such dexterity and expertise as might be envied even by Billroth.* In practising medicine, she did not shy away from other crafts. She made clothes for impoverished insects; mended the gold-beetles' chamberlain livery and the ladybirds' fur-lined sleeveless jackets... The insects respected her like their own mother and loved her more than anything in the world. And quite right too! She spent all she had on the penniless worms, who came crawling to her from every direction seeking alms; she lost her voice delivering sermons to the insects. Her sermons were the pinnacle of the art of oratory. Reliable sources reported that after listening to her sermon "On Idleness," ten drones wept with remorse and immediately began collecting honey. She found husbands for butterflies and moreover gave them the finest muslin dresses for a dowry. She found wives for crickets, giving them the sternest of orders not to disturb their wives with their chirping at night... She was a real mother! One day a tarantula presented himself to this girl and asked her to charm away his toothache. The girl did as she was asked, and the spider's gumboil vanished in an instant. "Good. Thank you," said the spider. "In return for your work, I will send you a sauce made of flies someday... Listen, I've just had a brilliant idea! Marry me! Well? Will you?" The girl laughed and said that under no circumstances could she be the spider's wife. "I don't love you," said the spider. "I don't even like you, but I want to collect a tax from the insects you cure, clothe and teach to read... I need money. You don't want to? Very well, then! If in three days you don't give me your consent, I will kill you with these teeth here!" The spider showed the girl his terrible teeth and went home. The girl told all her protégés about the spider's threat. And along they came, flying and crawling from all sides to take up a defensive position around her. "We'll die before we give you up!" they exclaimed. Along came the spider. "Do you give your consent?" he asked the girl. "No, I don't. Do not sow discontent, spider! Look how many defenders I have!" The spider looked and saw not defenders but cowards who were pale and trembling all over. He roared with laughter and then, as the whole insect community looked on, he killed the poor girl with his awful teeth. After he had killed her, he calmly headed home. The bees made a coffin out of wax and laid the girl in it... The ants set about digging the grave. The mosquitoes followed the hearse, singing beautifully and playing the trumpets. The gold beetle read the eulogy... In a word, it was a fine funeral. The feast at the wake was even better. The insects all ate and drank until they had stomach ache. After the wake, the insects slept in, gave the centipede the task of collecting money for a tombstone and flew off home...

"And the end?" asked Zwiebusch.

"What more do you need?" asked the baron. "Do you want the spider to be put in prison? Fat chance! My nanny was an excellent teacher. She didn't lie to me even in fairy tales. Goodness did not prevail in her tales. The spider is still sitting in his lair and scoffing his sauce made of flies, and those despicable insects, sick and unkempt, most probably remember the tasty funeral banquet more often than they do the girl. The Kingdom of Heaven to you, Nanny! You understood the nature of things very well! Let's drink, old man! Well, Ilka? Do you like my tale? For some reason, you remind me an awful lot of that girl... Surely a tarantula isn't going to eat you, too? Hahaha... It's quite possible... Why not eat, if one can? You have teeth, so go ahead, stuff yourself... But, you're not listening to me, Ilka! You look as if we are not here!"

Ilka gave a start and looked at Arthur with pleading, questioning eyes.

"I can't forget about her!" she whispered.

"Are you still on about that? One needs to resign oneself, my child! The advice of that wretched judge is still valid. You won't think up anything better... Buy your father some eau de plomb and make yourself a countess..."

"You're still joking! Dear God! A countess... Is that really possible?"

"It is if you manage to marry some count or other, but not if you don't. But I doubt you could do it... If one were to add a good deal of filthy lucre to your sweet face—well, then there'd be no need for doubt. I would marry you, dammit. Would you marry me, Ilka?"

"Are you a baron? I would... I would marry a baron..."

"I'm a count as well... Hahaha... Should I play a prank? Wait, wait... It would be an amazing prank..."

The baron thought for a minute.

"No..." he said. "It would be too much... It's not worth it. I love the girl in the tulip, but alas, marriage must bring me no less than a million francs!"

"It's not nice to marry for money, Doctor!" said Zwiebusch, who was now beginning to feel the effects of the vodka. "Marrying for money, Doctor, is regarded as a low act."

"What is to be done?! I will settle for a low act. I need a million no matter what. With a million in my hands... Actually, you don't need to know that. I would show them!"

"And would you marry an old woman?"

"I would marry the devil... Anything for a million! A million is the lever with which I will turn hell itself upside down, with its demons and its fire. I'm not talking about a future hell but the one I'm in right now. Unless I commit a low act, I will give others the chance to commit a thousand. Tulip Girl," said Arthur, addressing Ilka, "why don't you have a million? If you had a million, I would have a pretty little wife, and you would be a countess. You would have carried out one of the judge's pieces of advice..."

"All you do is joke!" sighed Ilka.

"I'm not joking at all... Try to come by a million, go on! Then I will definitely make you a baroness! Go on, try!"

"Should we have a drink, Doctor?" suggested Zwiebusch. "An element of fantasy is beginning to creep into our conversation... Let's leave the fantasy behind! Are we the kind of people to be talking about millions? It would be easier for me to swallow my own head than ever to set eyes on a million... Please let's not talk about money! Talking begets envy..."

"Be quiet, please! Why not dream a little, if there's nothing to be done? I tell you again, you old piece of lard, that if you had a million, I'd take the girl from you and sit her in a tulip... You think I'm drunk? Fine! I swear, I do like her! Just look at that little nose! Ah, damn it! Get hold of a million, Ilka!"

"And how can I get hold of a million?" asked Ilka.

"Oh, naivety! *Sancta simplicitas!*[2] How do you get hold of a million? There are various methods one can employ. There are difficult and easy methods... The difficult method consists of endless hard work—rational work of your own free will involving sleepless nights, malnourishment and sickness. If you use this method, the million only comes along in old age, when it's not worth getting married. You're a woman, you're not rational enough and you want to get married, so this method won't work for you. The second method, which is easy enough in itself but sometimes has difficult consequences, consists in forgetting the one thing which holds everyone back—conscience. Rob and steal. The cleverer and more shameless you are, the sooner you'll be Baroness von Seinitz. It is not just on the highways that one can rob and steal. One can rob and extort while sitting in your own study. I don't recommend you go for this method. If you are not clever enough, it will be fraught with consequences: you could easily end up in hell. The third method is to come into an inheritance... And the fourth? The fourth method, the one most often employed by women and not always disdained by men, lies in the ability to use one's body. The better the body a person has, the closer he is to the million. That's the method most suited to you, Ilka!"

"It's the least suited!" said Zwiebusch. "It's not suited at all! Let's forget it, Baron! This piquant method seems a bit too salacious for my liking, and Ilka..."

"Is too young? Never mind—let her know! Why conceal from her what she needs to guard against? And so, let me continue... You must learn, Ilka, to dress with taste, show your pretty little foot under your dress at just the right time, be crafty and flirt... For each kiss you can earn a thousand francs... In your present circumstances, they will hardly give you much, but if you were seated in a box at the theatre or in a carriage, then..."

"Now, now... that's enough!" muttered Zwiebusch. "God knows what you're stuffing the girl's head with! Let's drop this conversation! Please, Doctor! I am changing the subject... So... Is it true what they say? That you adopted the Lutheran faith last week?"

---

2   *Sancta simplicitas*: "holy innocence" (Latin).

"It is... The last method is the easiest and not the most disgraceful. Acquire high society manners, Ilka, learn small talk and, trust my experience, you will have a million. This method is used too often. Seven eighths of women would employ it, if seven eighths were beautiful and had market value. Had you crossed my path seven or eight years ago, I would certainly have bought you... You pretty little creature!"

"Hush, Baron, for God's sake, hush," said Zwiebusch. "Let's not let our tongue loose!"

Zwiebusch looked at his daughter with apprehension. Ilka was sitting and listening to the baron attentively, seemingly not embarrassed by either the contents or the form of his speech.

"I understand," she said. "But are you really capable of marrying a woman who has sold herself?"

"Yes, I am. After all, by marrying for money, I am selling myself, too! And so on, and so forth... I have a favour to ask you, Ilka..."

The baron sat up and took a gold coin from his vest pocket.

"Take this money, my dear, and have your photograph taken in the first town you come across. Do you understand? Then send me the photo... to this address..."

The baron gave Ilka a gold coin and a card with an address written on it.

"I want to see the girl in the tulip more often... I want to carry her in my side pocket all the time... Will you send me the photo?"

"Yes."

"Excellent. And now, my friends, *adieu*! I want a nap."

The baron stretched out on the grass and put his hunting bag under his head.

"Farewell. Delighted to make your acquaintance. I'll be waiting for the portrait and will marry you if you get hold of a million..."

Zwiebusch stood up and bowed.

"Thank you, Baron," he said. "You've fed us, so would you allow us to play for you in return? Our dull music is an excellent aid to sleep!"

"By all means!"

Zwiebusch tuned his fiddle and started playing a scene from *Boccaccio*,* accompanied by Ilka on the harp. The baron nodded to show his pleasure and closed his eyes... When the musicians had finished playing and were about to leave, he opened his eyes and rested his bleary gaze on Ilka.

"Ah... I see," he muttered. "Is that you, Ilka? Take this as a souvenir!"

The baron detached one of the lockets from his chain, gave it to Ilka, lowered his head onto the bag and fell fast asleep.

Chapter III

When von Seinitz awoke, it was already evening. The tree tops and the stone buildings of the little town that stood on the hill were bathed in the golden light of the setting sun. This gold, tinged with crimson, spread like brocade across the sky eastwards from the sun and obscured a good third of the sky... Near the sun and above it there was not a single cloud; this latter circumstance augured a fine night. The pipe of a shepherd on his way home was playing far beyond the forest. It was playing a simple little tune with no name; the music was mundane and jumbled, but it is to this uncomplicated music that the forests of the Goldaugen counts fall fast asleep every evening, as do the rye fields, the feather-grass and the river...

Arthur saw two bottles and some newspaper lying on the grass beside him. The fat old man and the pretty fair-haired girl were gone. He remembered them, and his conversation with them, and he smiled—laughed even when he looked at his chest and saw a piece of paper attached to one of his buttons. Written on that piece of paper in pencil was the following:

"Dear Baron! You are the first human being to have treated us in a humane fashion. Before you, we knew about humane treatment only from hearsay... So you are the first person I will remember with pleasure, rather than bitterness. Your concern has deeply touched us. Farewell! May God grant you happiness! I will send the photo.

Your servant Ilka."

"Not a single grammatical mistake!" von Seinitz said aloud, after twice reading this letter, which was written in an attractive female hand. "That's remarkable! Well done, Ilka!"

The baron took a small metallic pencil from his notebook and wrote: "Received from the Tulip Girl on 13th June." After folding the letter in half, he hid it in the pocket of his notebook.

"I must be off! It's time for dinner!" Slinging the gun across his shoulder, the baron set off through the forest, heading for the town which had already started losing the golden light placed there briefly by the sun.

He had to walk down a long, narrow cutting strewn with gravel. The cutting stretched almost to the town itself. It was crossed in the middle by a railway. Not far from the crossroads formed by the cutting and the railway tracks stands the house of Blaucher the forester.

When he reached the crossing, Arthur turned, raised his hat and bowed: old Mrs. Blaucher was sitting on the veranda of the little house, embroidering a tablecloth... On her tiny head sat a large bonnet with the biggest of bows and from under the bonnet peeped a pair of ancient, grandfatherly spectacles; they sat upon a long snub nose, resembling a big toe... She responded to Arthur's bow with a cloying smile.

"Good evening, Frau Marta!" said the baron. "Are there any letters for me?"

"There is only one. With a coat of arms, Baron..."

"Is the address in Peltzer's hand?"

"It is..."

"Then throw it into the stove, Marta. I know its contents. The Jew has been dictated to by my sister and is cursing me for converting to Lutheranism... I know its contents without reading it. Is your husband well? And Fräulein Amalia too, I hope?"

"Yes, thank you... That will be the sixth letter I've had to burn... It's not a particularly pleasant thing to do if you know that people have laboured over a letter, put their feelings into it... How cruel you are! Where are you going now?"

"To have dinner... somewhere..."

"And to see someone?"

"Yes..."

The old woman sighed and shook her head.

"If my Blaucher weren't so cautious," she said, "I would give you dinner, too. My husband tears his hair out when noble gentlemen come to visit. General Frechtelsack comes to visit, but he is an old man—he's nothing to fear... And he gives my Blaucher no cause for concern... Whereas *you* terrify him. If you were to dine with us, the neighbours would say you were courting our daughter, and God knows what else. A nobleman visits not in order to marry, but well, you know why... And so Blaucher is afraid... But General Frechtelsack is a completely different matter!"

"Don't worry, Marta! I will dine elsewhere."

"And, truth be told, today's dinner isn't really up to much. Servants are a real problem, nowadays—one can't do anything with them."

"Good-bye, Marta! Regards to the family!"

"Good-bye, Baron!"

The baron bowed and headed for the cutting. Dark evening shadows were already falling on the ground. There was a freshness in the forest air. Behind Arthur, a local evening train, conveying city dwellers to the fields and forests, sped past noisily... The evening begins earlier in the forest than in the fields. In the fields, it was still bright enough to thread a needle... When the noise from the train died away, Seinitz heard the sound of horse's hooves behind him. He turned round and stopped; an Amazon was bearing down on him on a magnificent black steed. She raced past, glanced at Arthur, and then reined in her horse after riding on a few yards.

"Von Seinitz?" the rider asked loudly.

"The very same..."

Arthur approached the Amazon and bowed. It was dark in the forest but not so dark as to make it impossible to see how beautiful the rider was. Her whole form radiated an air of truly baronial magnificence.

Had Zwiebusch and Ilka been there, they would have recognised her as the same rider whom in the first chapter of our story, along with Zwiebusch, we named as Countess Goldaugen, née Heilenstrahl. She was holding the same whip that at midday had split Zwiebusch's lip.

"I recognised you at first sight," she said, offering Arthur her hand. "You have changed a bit... However... am I going to be able talk to you or not? Your last letter to me was full of hatred, outrage, and the most desperate contempt... Do you still hate me as much as you did?"

The baron shook her beautiful hand and smiled.

"My letter," he said, "is a crime for which the statute of limitations has run out. It was written four years ago. In that letter, I hated you for your mercenary nature, which would not allow you to marry the man you loved, the man who loved you but was ruined. Nowadays, I am not the slightest bit angry with you about your mercenary nature. Three hours ago, I was talking about marrying for money in the future myself... I am still in this world and am not dispatching myself to the next solely because I have a goal in life... That goal is—to marry for a million..."

"I see! In that case, your convictions have changed a great deal over the last four years. However, I'm glad... This is such an unexpected encounter! I'm very pleased, Baron, I am indeed! I'm grateful just to have met you again!"

"Under no circumstances could I have ever expected to have met you in these parts. How did you end up here?"

"I... Don't you know? I am a local resident... And have been for a long time now..."

"You, Baroness? How come?"

"I am no longer Baroness Heilenstrahl, but Countess von Goldaugen. Two years ago, I married your neighbour, Count Goldaugen..."

"I hadn't heard... What news, indeed! The count... I don't know him... Is he handsome?"

"No..."

"That's strange... You are an admirer of handsome men, from what I know of you. You loved me because I was, as they say, devilishly handsome. But is he young, rich?"

"He's nearly forty... He's very rich..."

"You are happy, of course?"

"Not at all. I too married for a million. Two years' experience has proved that I've made a terrible mistake. Happiness does not lie in having a million, as it turns out... All I'm concerned with now is trying to devise a way to run away from the million!"

The countess laughed, and her gaze rested for a moment on the darkening sky. After a brief silence, she continued to laugh:

"So we have switched roles, Baron. I now hate what I used to love, and you're the other way around... But how strangely circumstances change in this dull world!"

"You want to flee the million in order to be happy, but I am looking for a million but not in order to be classed as a happy man... Our objectives are different, as you can see..."

"Do you really know nothing about my new life?"

"Nothing..."

"So, the rumours have not spread very far yet... I have initiated divorce proceedings against my husband..."

"A jolly endeavour... But you're living with him at the moment?"

"Well, yes... It's a little strange, it's true... But, to avoid unnecessary gossip, we will separate only when our divorce is embellished by an official seal... I shall fly the nest once I am officially free... However, all this is of no interest to you... I was so thrilled to encounter an old acquaintance and... a friend that I'm prepared to shamelessly blurt out all my secrets and non-secrets... Let's talk about you instead... How are you?"

"As you can see. I live where I end up..."

"You've abandoned your studies? For good?"

"I have, and in all probability, for good."

"And is your conscience as a man of science clear?"

"Well... Science has lost not much more than zero in me... No great loss..."

The countess shrugged her shoulders and shook her head.

"Seinitz, you are making the excuses of a schoolboy..." she said. "Not much more than zero... Young scientists don't have a present, they have a future. Who knows: maybe, if you continued your studies, you would be worth a thousand times more than zero to science!"

"You are expressing yourself incorrectly," laughed von Seinitz. "Zero times a thousand equals zero."

"Are you completely ruined?" asked the countess, as if not listening to von Seinitz.

"Yes. Do you have any money on you?"

"Yes, a little. Why?"

"Give it to me."

The countess quickly took a little purse from her pocket and handed it to Arthur. Arthur tipped the money into his hand and handed the purse back to the countess.

"*Merci*," he said. "I'm just borrowing it. I will pay you back the day after the wedding. Are you surprised? Your eyes look so surprised! Not only am I asking and borrowing, I even regret that there was so little in your purse."

The countess looked into his eyes and thought: "He is lying."

"I am not in the least surprised," she said. "What is so strange and surprising in Arthur von Seinitz borrowing a little money from his friend? It's an ordinary everyday matter..."

"And who told you that you are my friend?"

"You are being strange... Farewell! It's an irksome business talking to you."

The countess nodded, raised her whip and trotted off along the cutting.

Chapter IV

When she reached the end of the cutting and rode into the open field, it was already dark... The town and the mountains were still visible but had lost their outlines. The people and horses wandering about looked like formless silhouettes. Lamps had been lit here and there. The countess stopped near a shack built out of reeds and straw in one of the Goldaugens' vegetable gardens. The Goldaugens had been leasing part of the municipal land for their vegetable gardens from time immemorial. They did so out of vanity. "The less my land is encircled by other people's property," one of the Goldaugens once said, "the more reasons I have to hold my head high."

Near the shack stood the gardener and his son. When they saw the countess racing towards them, they doffed their hats.

"Hello Old Fritz and Young Fritz!" said the countess to the gardener and his son. "I'm very glad to find you here. If I'm ever told that you are shirking your duties, I will have good reason not to believe it."

"We are always attentive to our duties," said old Fritz standing to attention. "We don't step an inch away from the garden. And yet, your Grace, should my face not please Herr Estate Manager or his minions for some reason, I will be sacked without your Grace's knowledge. We are little people and hardly anyone would bother your Grace on our account..."

"You think so, Fritz? No, you are very much mistaken... I know all our servants and, believe me, I can tell who is good, who's bad, and who's been dismissed. I know, for example, that Old Fritz is a decent servant, and I know that Young Fritz is an idle fellow and stole the pastor's gloves and walking stick last winter... I know everything."

"You know the poor pastor's gloves and walking stick were stolen but you don't know..."

Old Fritz stopped and smirked.

"What don't I know?" asked the countess.

"Your Grace doesn't know that three weeks ago the dogs of His Grace the Count's valet badly bit my wife and daughter? Your Grace hasn't heard anything of this, despite the whole village going out of their way to make it known. The valet's dogs cannot stand plain clothing and will attack anyone dressed like a peasant. Herr Valet enjoys it. I'll say! The dogs knock a woman to the ground, rip her clothes and... the naked body, your Grace... Herr Valet is a great lover of female flesh!"

"All right, all right... But what is it you want? That I don't know..."

"My wife is ill, and my daughter is ashamed to go outside because the men have seen her in her birthday suit, thanks to the dogs."

"All right, all right... I'll look into it. I want to ask you something. You didn't happen to see some musicians, a fat old man and a young girl with a harp, heading towards town today? Did they go past?"

"No, your Grace!" said Old Fritz. "Maybe they did, and maybe they didn't. So many different folks go by. One can't see and remember all of them."

The countess thought for a while, staring into the dark distance.

"That isn't them, is it?" she asked, pointing her whip at two black human silhouettes in the distance.

"Those are both men," said Young Fritz.

"It's quite possible that they've stopped to spend the night in the village," said the countess. "In which case they will pass by tomorrow... If you see them, be sure to send them to me."

"Certainly," said Old Fritz. "A fat old man and a young girl. Understood. And what do you need them for, your Grace? I suppose they've stolen something."

"Why should they have to have stolen something?"

"I don't know, your Grace. Hunting for thieves seems to be about the only business in Goldaugen County. It's the fashion. In Goldaugen County only the bigwigs steal, but everyone is considered a thief."

"Oh, really! I see... Tomorrow you can start looking for another job. Woe betide if there is a single Fritz left in this county tomorrow!"

With that, the countess turned her horse around and galloped back to the cutting.

"How beautiful she is!" said Young Fritz. "She cut such a handsome figure!"

"Yes, very beautiful," said Old Fritz. "But, what's that to us?"

"An extremely fine figure! I swear to you by almighty God, Father, that it wasn't me who stole the pastor's gloves and stick! I've never been a thief! May I go blind this very second if I'm telling you a lie. I've been slandered for no reason at all... And she believed the slander! Despicable people!"

Young Fritz fell silent for a while, then continued:

"But let these despicable people not slander in vain! Let them not laugh at us in vain... I will steal. When she was talking to you and I looked at her beautiful face, I solemnly swore to myself that I would steal... And I will! I will steal from Count Goldaugen something none of his estate managers can steal. And I shall keep my word."

Young Fritz sat down and began to ponder. His mind and heart were filled with new, supremely sweet dreams—Balzac dreams, not peasant dreams. In a matter of minutes his enflamed youthful imagination had constructed a magnificent castle in the air... Something that an hour before he would have thought insane, unfeasible, and immediately driven from his mind as the stuff of children's fairy tales, now suddenly took the form of a task which he had a genuine desire to perform at any cost. There was suddenly a need to make the castle in the air more solid...

With his head beginning to spin with wild dreams, Young Fritz jumped up, rubbed his eyes with his fingers and shouted to his father, laughing:

"I will definitely steal! Let them search me then!"

The countess rode home. On the way, she came across Baron von Seinitz who was still on his way to dine.

"We shall meet again, I assume?" the countess shouted to him.

"If you wish, then yes."

"We'll find things to talk about. Given the boredom I am experiencing right now, you come as a real boon. A little idea has occurred to me. You wouldn't like to celebrate your birthday on Thursday next week with me, would you? See how well I remember still? I even haven't forgotten your birthday... Do you want to?"

"If you like..."

"We'll need to meet somewhere... Here's what we'll do... Do you know the place where *The Bronze Deer* is?"

"Yes."

"We could reminisce about old times there without being interrupted. Be there at seven in the evening."

"I'll bring the wine."

"Excellent. *Adieu*! Incidentally, Baron: in future, we'll converse in French. I haven't forgotten that you don't like German. As for the "charlatan" and the clever folk—give it a thought. *Adieu*!"

The countess cracked her whip and the next minute vanished in the ever-darkening forest air.

Baroness Theresa von Heilenstrahl was that "pure, unearthly creature" on whom Arthur's eyes and feelings had first come to rest after his odious life in Paris. It was thanks not only to his respect for learning that Arthur had made a too sudden change of direction from debauchery to industry; the baroness, too, had greatly enabled that change of direction. Without her, his regeneration would have been incomplete.

Upon his arrival in Vienna from Paris, Arthur began to lead the life of a hermit. He would dream in solitude of restful work, curse this world and its inhabitants, and could not stop himself from sighing... for Parisian courtesans. It is not known how this solitude would have ended had Arthur not become a regular visitor to the house of the barons Heilenstrahl soon after his arrival. During Arthur's time in Vienna, anyone who wished could visit the Heilenstrahls. They actually never invited anyone, but were visited by all those who liked to go to the houses of the high and mighty without invitation, so long as the doors were open.

During those last years, this house resembled a righteous man who, upon learning of his approaching death, lets himself go and plunges into dissipation so he can enjoy life like a normal human being for at least one day.

Worn out and broke, searching for salvation and not finding it, anticipating the throes of death, the barons Heilenstrahl let everything go, and lost all ability to pay attention to anything. Everything was forgotten except the imminent terrible end. The horror of the imminent catastrophe was successfully alleviated by wine, love and dreams.

The Heilenstrahls still dreamt of the possibility of salvation. Their salvation, they thought, was in the hands of Theresa, who could marry a very rich man and improve the poor state of affairs of her family through marriage. But this hope, too, was only a dream.

Theresa was not on speaking terms with her father and swore that she would not give her relatives a single penny if she married a rich man.

The Heilenstrahls gave it up as a hopeless case and began consuming whatever had not yet been consumed. They did not consume in a simple way, but desperately, solemnly, with a hell of a racket, as if they had never eaten before. The doors of their house opened of their own accord, and through them rushed a semi-hungry throng of devourers of leftovers. The latter appeared in the form of impoverished aristocrats, writers, artists, actresses, musicians, with their splendid costumes, striking faces, sophisticated fragrances, remarkable instruments and empty stomachs. The devourers immediately occupied the barons' house, and the Heilenstrahls, impoverished and craving salvation, all of a sudden saw themselves as leading art patrons. They decorated their house with theatrical scenery, paintings, and rare watercolours. In the evenings, their neighbourhood would echo to the sounds of symphonies, nocturnes, waltzes and polkas. Their musical-literary evenings, at which people would play and recite, were very popular and attracted throngs of visitors from different levels of society. All these soirees and performances were attended by Theresa. Beautiful, as if chiselled from marble, and all in black, she would wander through the motley crowd of devourers, from one artist to another, trying with all her might to get rid of her deadly boredom. The people who made up the crowd were new to her. They stimulated her interest. Out of boredom, she began to study them. She would fix her eyes on the striking faces, listen, speak, read the works in the manuscripts brought to her and by way of long study she came to the conclusion that there were some decent fellows among them, but also some charlatans. This conclusion was the only result of her study. Not possessing more refined analytical skills, she was unable to separate decent people from charlatans. She admitted a few of them to her inner circle, but even among these few there were charlatans as well as enlightened persons. Von Seinitz was one of the chosen few.

He ended up at the Heilenstrahls' house by chance. He had been taken there by a friend and writer who wished to show him his comedy, which was being performed on the barons' stage. Not satisfied by performances and literary soirees, he soon began to visit the Heilenstrahl house during the day time as well. And Theresa, who used to go out riding in the evening, usually accompanied by a groom, soon began to go on these rides in Arthur's company. Every evening, Arthur would enthusiastically tell her what he had accomplished during the day; what he had read; what he had written. The report was followed by inevitable dreams, hopes, and proposals. Theresa would listen to him and talk herself. She would sprinkle into her conversation the names of famous scientists she knew... by hearsay, from Arthur. They became friends. They say there is only one step from friendship to love. Arthur was not thinking of love. He was more than happy in the company of an intelligent, new woman. He only began talking of love when Theresa confessed that she loved him, during one of their evening outings... She was the first to start talking about love. After this confession came the days which they say happen only once in a lifetime. Never at any other time had Arthur been so happy and contented with life as during these days, spent with the woman he loved. This happiness, however, did not last long. It was destroyed by Theresa. When he demanded from his beloved and undoubtedly loving girl that she become his wife, a baroness and the spouse of "Doctor" von Seinitz, she refused him point blank.

"I cannot marry you," she wrote to him. "You are poor, and I am poor. Poverty has already poisoned the first half of my life. Should I poison the other half? You are a man, and men don't comprehend all the horrors of poverty like women do. A poor woman is the most miserable creature... Arthur, you started this marriage conversation in vain... In doing so, you provoke discussions which cannot but leave a mark on our current relationship. Let's stop these difficult discussions and carry on as before."

Arthur tore this letter to pieces and wrote a reply in which he invoked heavenly thunder on Theresa's head... In the heat of the moment, he wrote to "the unearthly creature" an enormously long letter in which he cursed "the spirit of the times" and upbringing... Touching letters, which were later sent as justification of the refusal, would not be read and would be thrown into the fireplace. Arthur came to hate Theresa so much that everything that reminded him of her lost all value in his eyes. He came to hate everything grand, austere, and proud, and became attached with all his soul to everything miserable, downtrodden, and poor...

Arthur remembered all that on his way to dinner... His treatise *On the Spirit of the Times* seemed ridiculous to him now, but the old hatred stirred in him. He had not managed to get rid of it yet.

On Thursday, his birthday, Arthur remembered the promise he had given to Theresa that they dine together, so he set off for *The Bronze Deer*. That was the name given to a little clearing in the woods where a deer with a bronze-coloured coat had once been killed by the king. Others say that in days long past a statue called *The Hunt* had stood there—a deer cast in bronze, replacing Diana. They say that the king, by whose orders this statue was erected, was puritan in his tastes and regarded classical statues of women with disgust.

When Arthur arrived at the clearing, Theresa was already there. She was impatiently walking up and down on the grass and knocking off the heads of flowers with her whip. Her horse was tied to a nearby tree and lazily munching grass.

"What a fine reception for your guests!" said the countess, walking towards Arthur. "A fine host you are! You've been gallivanting, while your guest has been waiting for you for more than an hour already..."

"I went to buy some wine," Arthur excused himself. "Please, sit down! It's not the first time we've sat on the grass. Remember the old days?"

The countess and Arthur sat down on the grass and started recalling days gone by... They remembered, but did not touch upon either their love, or their break-up... The conversation circled around their Viennese lifestyle, the Heilenstrahl house, the artists, evening strolls... The baron talked and drank. The countess refused the wine. Having drunk a whole bottle, Arthur got slightly tipsy: he started laughing, cracking jokes and making caustic remarks.

"How do you support yourself these days?" he asked casually.

"How? Hmm... You know how... The Goldaugens are not poor..."

"So you eat and drink from the count's table?"

"I don't understand, what are you getting at?!"

"But answer me, Theresa, I beg you. You eat and drink from the count's table?"

"Well, yes!.."

"That's strange. You cannot stand the count, yet at the same time, you live at his expense... Hahaha... How's that? What rules are you following, damn it? Your wise men consider me a charlatan; what's their opinion of you, then? Hahaha!"

The countess's face momentarily clouded over.

"Don't drink any more, Baron," she said sternly. "You are getting drunk and starting to be insolent. You know that circumstances force me to go on living with Goldaugen for the time being."

"What circumstances? Fear of malicious talk? The same old tune! But, tell me, please, countess, how much will the count have to give you annually after the divorce?"

"Nothing..."

"But why are you lying to me? Now don't get angry... I'm talking like a friend. Don't fiddle with your whip. It's got nothing to do with it. Bah!"

The baron slapped himself on the forehead and sat up.

"Just a moment... How come I didn't notice this before?"

"What do you mean?"

The baron's eyes began to dart. They kept moving from the countess' face to the whip, from the whip to her face. He moved about nervously.

"How come I didn't remember earlier!" he muttered. "So, it was you who gave a treat to that old fatty and my Tulip Girl?"

The countess' eyes widened, and she shrugged her shoulders.

"Tulip... Fatty... What are you muttering about, von Seinitz? You're beginning to talk rubbish. You shouldn't be drinking!"

"And you shouldn't flog people, my lady!"

The baron went pale and hit his chest with his fist.

"You shouldn't flog people. To hell with you and your aristocratic habits! Do you hear me?"

The countess jumped to her feet. Her eyes widened and sparkled with anger.

"Don't forget yourself, Baron!" she said. "Would you care to retract your insult? I don't understand you!"

"No, I won't! To hell with you! Are you now going to deny your low deed?"

The countess' eyes grew even bigger. She did not understand.

"What deed? What do I need to deny? I don't understand you, Baron!"

"Who was it who hit an old fiddler in the face in Count Goldaugen's yard with this very same whip? Who pushed him under the feet of this very horse? I was told it was Countess Goldaugen, and there is only one Countess Goldaugen!"

A red flush, as bright as the glow of a fire, appeared on the countess' face. Starting at the temples, it spread all the way down to her lace collar. The countess was terribly embarrassed.

She began to cough.

"I don't understand you," she muttered. "What fiddler? What are you... blabbering about? Come to your senses, Baron!"

"Enough! Why lie? In years gone by you were good at lying, but not for the sake of trifles like this one! Why did you hit him?"

"Hit who? Who are you talking about?"

The countess' voice was soft and trembling. Her eyes were darting to and fro like trapped mice. She was terribly ashamed. And the baron, again half-lying on the grass, his gaze fixed on her beautiful eyes, was grinning malevolently and drunkenly. His lips were twitching in a malicious smile.

"Why did you hit him? Did you see how his daughter was crying?"

"Whose daughter? Explain yourself, Baron!"

"You can say that again! You can give free reign to your white hands and your long tongue, but you cannot see tears! She is still crying... A pretty blonde girl is still crying... She is weak and poor, and cannot exact revenge on the countess for her father. I sat with them for three hours, and for three hours she wouldn't take her hands from her eyes... Poor girl! I can't get her sobbing, noble, little face out of my mind. Oh, those cruel devils, well fed, never beaten and never insulted!"

"Explain yourself, Baron! Whom did I beat?"

"I see! You think I don't know where to find the cat that ate the mouse? Shame on you!"

The baron sat up and held his hand out.

"Show it to me!"

The countess obediently gave him the whip.

"Shame on you!" he repeated, and, twisting the whip into a spiral, he broke it into three parts and threw it away.

The countess was totally confused. Ashamed, and listening to a dressing-down for the first time in her life, blushing and not knowing where to hide her face and hands from the baron's accusatory gaze, she was lost for words. She was partly released from this awkward position by one small circumstance. While Arthur was breaking the whip into pieces, steps could be heard from behind the nearby trees. A minute later, the countess saw both Fritzes. They emerged from the trees and started walking across the clearing, looking at the countess and Arthur with curiosity. Walking in front was Young Fritz with a long fishing rod across his shoulder. Behind him, hardly moving his feet, came Old Fritz. A young pike was dangling off a string in Old Fritz's right hand.

"Herr Fritz, why aren't you wearing gloves?" the countess said addressing Young Fritz.

Fritz lowered his gaze and, giving the countess a sidelong glance, started mumbling.

"Where is your walking stick? Why don't you have your walking stick with you?"

Young Fritz went pale in the face and started walking quickly towards the trees. Near the trees he turned round once then disappeared. Old Fritz hobbled along after him silently, without looking at anyone.

"Forgive me," began the baron after the Fritzes had disappeared behind the trees. "I don't wish to insult you... But, I swear by my honour, I could avenge the fiddler, if you were not a woman... Shame on you, Theresa! I felt embarrassed for you before the girl!"

The baron got up and put his hat on.

"You cannot find words to justify yourself... That's great! Why lie? Your excuse is a lie."

"I still do not understand you, Baron!" said the countess.

"Honestly?"

"Yes... honestly..."

"Hmm... Good-bye! Your beautiful eyes are full of lies! Thank God you are still able to blush when you are lying."

Arthur stretched, nodded his head and started walking across the clearing towards the forest path.

Countess Goldaugen's forehead was furrowed with wrinkles. She was agonising, searching for words in her mind, and not able to find them... She passionately wanted to justify her deed to Arthur, a deed which was shameful to confess. While she was thinking, biting her pink lips and wringing her hands, Arthur disappeared behind the trees.

"Baron!" shouted Theresa. "Wait!"

Instead of an answer, the countess heard only the sound of Arthur's receding steps.

"Baron!" shouted the countess once more, and her voice started trembling with fear that the baron would leave. The noise of the steps was no more.

The countess stood there for a while, then lowered herself onto the ground, deep in thought. Two empty bottles lay near her. The third one, still containing a little wine, was standing on the grass at an angle, and ready to fall. Theresa drank the rest of the wine from the bottle, then got up and went towards her horse.

When she left the clearing, she saw a rider who was mounting a horse two or three steps from the trees surrounding the clearing. Noticing the countess, the rider's horse neighed merrily. The rider was a man of about forty-five; tall, thin, pale, with a puny little beard. Having mounted the horse, he took off after the countess.

"Wait!" he said in a quiet voice. By the timbre of that weak, non-masculine voice one could tell that it came from a sick chest. "Wait! I've a couple of things I want to say to you!"

The countess did not turn round...

"You've been spying?" she asked. "Snooping?"

"But I love you! I cannot live a single minute without seeing you. Just two words!!"

Chapter V

The countess glanced at her husband Count Goldaugen (for it was he) and began riding more slowly.

"The doctor forbade you to ride fast," she said. "Slow down... What do you want?"

"Just two words."

"Well?"

"Who is he?"

"Baron von Seinitz."

"Von Seinitz? Him? So, that's von Seinitz? The man you once... loved?"

"Perhaps... Well, yes, it is him. So what?"

"Hmm... He is still handsome... Why did you allow him to yell at you? What right does he have?"

The count fell silent, coughed, and asked:

"Perhaps, you might... fall in love with him again? Old love can be rekindled after all?"

"Give me your whip!" said the countess, and, taking her husband's whip, she pulled hard on the reins and took off down the cutting. The count also yanked on the reins with all his might. His horse began to canter, and he shook helplessly in the saddle. He lost strength in his thighs, winced from pain and reined in his horse. It slowed down. The count followed his wife with his gaze, lowered his head on to his chest, and sank into thought.

About three days later, Arthur bumped into Theresa near the house of Blaucher the forester. She was not wearing her riding outfit this time. She was strolling about in a peasant's dress. It looked like an ordinary peasant dress that had just been run up, but it was much more expensive than her riding habit of black silk. Turquoise, emeralds, corals, and pearls hung round her neck instead of different coloured pear-shaped garnets. There was a heavy bracelet on each wrist. The dress and her Hungarian-style jacket were made of expensive fabrics.

"Baron!" she shouted catching sight of Arthur. "One minute, please!"

When he came up to her, she said to him:

"You set me a puzzle with your words and sudden departure—remember? I only understood what you meant after much thought. Now I understand... You were referring to that old man... whom I hit with my whip! Right?"

"Well, yes... So what's the puzzle?"

"Well, this! I understand now who you were talking about... I have no need to excuse myself before you, Baron, but for the sake... for the sake of satisfying our mutual sense of justice... I hit him with good reason. Thanks to him, my horse threw me off... I almost broke my leg. And then... he dared to laugh..."

Arthur looked at the countess' face and laughed.

"Enough lies, your Grace!" he said. "Why feed each other lies? I don't need your justifications... What's the point of them? I'm looking at your pretty legs for the first time in my life, and that's quite enough for me... Your lovely legs are above all criticism! Let's go for a walk. I apologise for the insolent words I treated you to at *The Bronze Deer*. I was drunk..."

Arthur and Theresa walked for a long time. They talked about the most ordinary things, joked a lot, and laughed a lot... Not a word was said about the old musician, his daughter, wise men and *the charlatan*. The baron did not utter a single jibe... He was as gallant as in bygone years in Vienna at the Heilenstrahls' house. When he walked Theresa to her cabriolet, which was parked not far from Blaucher's house, it was totally dark.

"Will you give me lessons in shooting?" asked Theresa, as she seated herself in the cabriolet.

"As many as you like..."

"Please do, baron. I'm terribly bored. If you relieve my boredom just a little, you will be doing me a great service... Honest to God. Let's help each other."

Theresa shook Arthur's hand and drove off.

Four days later they met again, while half a month later there was not a single day when they had not met. The baron taught Theresa to shoot, and Theresa came to hunt every evening, and sometimes also early in the morning. Their relationship was totally undefined. When sober, von Seinitz would stun Theresa with his gallantry. When sober, he spoke softly, tenderly, apparently avoiding harsh words; he would smile sweetly, courteously offering his large hand, and speak not like an uncivilised 'lout,' but as a true ladies' man. The drunk von Seinitz, however, would shock her with his rudeness, cynicism and malicious laugh... When he was drunk, Theresa was forced to listen to the most unimaginable things. He would mock her, tell her to go to hell, say that he despised and hated her.

"I only forgive you, von Seinitz," Theresa once told him, "because you are drunk. One does not beat madmen, drunkards, and those who are already down..."

"Aaah... I see! Is that so? Then you should know," von Seinitz replied with a laugh, "that I only tell you the truth when I'm drunk. When I'm sober, I behave like a complete hypocrite with you. Don't believe me when I'm sober!"

"We shouldn't keep seeing each other..."

"Why not? You are bored, and I am bored... time passes faster in quarrels and in wars than in times of peace. Ha-ha! Fate did well to insert some coolness between us and instil in us disrespect for each other's virtues. You don't respect me because you regard me as a charlatan, and I don't respect you, because I see in you only a piece of good female flesh! Ha-ha!"

Theresa looked daggers at him, did not say a single word, and left. After that conversation, Arthur did not see her for a whole week. On the eighth day he met up with her and apologised.

Arthur was often drunk. Time and again, Theresa would leave him feeling insulted. She would leave and promise herself that she would stop seeing him, but...

The summer ended, and autumn set in. Yellowing leaves began to fall on to the moist, cold ground having come to the end of their short lives... The rains started. Autumn mud is not like summer mud: it does not dry out, and if it does, then it takes days and weeks, rather than hours... A wind reminiscent of winter started blowing. Blackened by the bad weather the forest scowled, having already stopped luring people under its foliage.

Von Seinitz swapped his jacket of fine goat's wool for a short, padded woollen coat. His boots lost their shine and became covered with mud... A ruddy glow from the cool, damp wind appeared on his pale face. His relationship with Theresa still had not acquired a definite shape. They still had things to talk about... Theresa felt that she still "had a lot to say" and kept riding to the forest as before.

It was necessary to find cover from the forest's dampness, mud and cold... Fate provided them with a refuge. They began to meet in the Goldaugen gardens, at the abandoned chapel, which was overgrown with moss and nettles. The forbidding eyes of the unfinished St. Francis saw Arthur and Theresa every autumn evening. They sat on the half-rotten bench in the flickering light of the lantern, and talked... As he was usually drunk, he would sit, yawn and say spiteful things... Pale as marble, with her head held high, having grown accustomed to his language, she would listen to him patiently, and then say spiteful things herself.

When he was sober, the spiders which had taken shelter in the corners of the chapel listened to tales of past happiness and saw a happy woman. Like an old man, he loved talking about the past. One could hear a note of old age in his voice: he did not regret anything and was content with just memories. She, on the other hand, being full of energy, youth and desires, regretted the past, and her voice was full of hope. She still passionately loved Baron von Seinitz...

On one of the most miserable of autumn days, Arthur dropped in on Madame Blaucher to take shelter from the rain. Madam Blaucher, with a little smile, gave him a package.

When he opened the package, he laughed like a child who had been shown a new toy. In it there was a photograph and a letter.

Both were from Ilka. The baron looked at the photograph and his eyes widened. The photograph was of Ilka, but not the Ilka he had seen several months ago; no, there was not a hint of that poor dress that was once drenched by the insulted Ilka's bitter tears in the photograph. Nor was there sight of the cheap velvet ribbon that held Ilka's fair hair in place. In the photograph Arthur saw a young aristocrat wearing a luxurious, fashionable dress. The hair, styled by a skilful hand, was crowned by a straw hat. There were flowers on the hat and, insofar as one could make out from the photograph, they were not cheap flowers; the smile on the pretty, little face was proud and arrogant, but it was a forced smile.

"Silly girl!" said Arthur with a laugh, and kissed Ilka's portrait. "You are a silly girl! A jackdaw in peacock's feathers! You put on a sumptuous dress and look triumphant! Go on wearing this dress for a little longer! We'll see what tune you'll be singing!"

The letter was written in an already familiar handwriting.

"Dear Baron!" Ilka wrote. "I'm sending you the photograph, and assure you that I and my father Zwiebusch are alive and well. I would also like to let you know that I am definitely going to have a million. I will have it very soon. We now live very well. When we meet, I will tell you what happened to us. You have probably already forgotten me. With this letter, I am reminding you of my existence and ask you not to forget what you promised me. I love you very much. I see many barons and counts here, but you are better than all of them. My papa sends his greetings. Write to me at the following address (there followed a long address). Write and let me know whether there is any hope for me or not.

Your I."

Laughing and not taking his eyes off the photograph, the baron asked Madame Blaucher for some paper and wrote as follows:

"Hello Ilka. Thank you. I'm waiting for you with your million. Do not do anything silly. Be smart and stay healthy. My best regards to that old, fat father of yours who has been beaten a hundred times and to whom you should give two or three gold coins out of your big million to spend on booze.

Your fiancé, Baron von Seinitz."

After giving this letter to Madame Blaucher to post, Arthur sat down at the table and started drawing a big tulip on the photograph. The pencil had been sharpened at both ends; one end was red, the other blue. Neither colour would stick to the film covering the photograph. And though Arthur sat at his drawing until it grew dark, he did not manage to place Ilka in the tulip.

Chapter VI

Something quite out of the ordinary had happened to Ilka and her father...

A week after their encounter with Baron von Seinitz, on a most scorching afternoon, they were sitting under the awning of a railway station. Despite the excruciating heat and humidity, there were a lot of people on the station platform: holidaymakers, landowners and the passengers of a train standing in the sidings were darting about the platform and crowding all the station buildings. The train standing in the sidings was a military one, and military trains stop at stations for two to three hours... The first class waiting-room was full of officers drinking. In the third class waiting-room, a military band was booming; it was the music played by the band that was attracting crowds of people to the station.

Zwiebusch and Ilka were sitting on a platform with large decimal scales, resting and gazing at the crowd: Zwiebusch was looking at the soldiers drinking beer, Ilka was looking at the ladies' dresses. Drunken officers were strolling past them and gazing at Ilka. They took a liking to the pretty girl... First, the junior officers hovered round her; and then, after their drinking session, Ilka saw some senior officers near her too. Half an hour before the train's departure, the senior and junior officers gathered together and started whispering while shooting drunken glances at Ilka.

"They are talking about you, Ilka!" said Zwiebusch. "Let's play something for them. They'll give us money. Just as well that lousy band has stopped playing."

Zwiebusch and Ilka got to their feet, tuned their instruments and started playing. Ilka started singing. The officers began to smile... Ilka sang that there was no one in the world more handsome and brave than Austrian soldiers who could conquer the whole world in a minute.

"Beautiful! Incomparable!" muttered the officers. "Old man, don't sing! You only spoil things with your bleating voice! Incomparable!"

"I have an idea!" shouted an officer with a large grey moustache, and he struck his cap. "On my honour, I swear it is a great idea!"

Turning to his comrades, he started whispering something to them... His fellow officers nodded affirmatively. Having secured their consent, the officer with the grey moustache walked on unsteady feet to Ilka, took her by her tanned hand and said:

"Listen, little bird! We want to take you with us on the train... You will sing and play for us all the way. We will give you lots of money for it. Agreed?" Without waiting for an answer, the officer pulled her by the hand and led her to his comrades.

"Yes, yes..." the drunken officers spoke up. "We will give you lots of money... Definitely..."

"And where are you going?" asked Ilka.

"To Bosnia, we think... We are not sure ourselves."

"We can't go!" said Zwiebusch, smiling.

But the officers did not hear Zwiebusch. They took the smiling Ilka to one side, and began persuading and convincing her... One took her by the chin.

Confident that Ilka would not agree, Zwiebusch stood a little way off, smiling. Ilka would not agree! She had always refused those kinds of propositions. She was a girl of proper morals. Imagine his fright and amazement when Ilka entered a first-class carriage with peals of laughter. She entered it and nodded to her father out of the window... Her father ran after her.

"I'm going, father!" she said. "Get in..."

"You are mad!" said the pale Zwiebusch, not brave enough to enter such a smart carriage.

"Get in!" the officers told him.

Bowing and feeling embarrassed, he climbed on to the train and started reasoning with Ilka. But the stubborn girl was unrelenting.

"I want to have a million!" she whispered to him. "If I don't have a million, I'll die."

"You won't get a million, you mad girl, but you will lose your honour! You will lose your honour! It is immoral!"

"Don't be afraid, Papa Zwiebusch. The men will see and hear nothing from me except the music... I've decided."

The train took off, but the old man was still trying to persuade her, begging and imploring. At one point he even started crying.

"This is boring, father!" she said and went off to join the officers.

Pale and sweating, with trembling fingers and lips, her father took refuge in a distant corner of the carriage, closed his eyes and started praying. He did not recognise his meek Ilka who often cried in this merry Ilka who was listening to the officers' platitudes. He could not believe his eyes and ears... These silly girls are a mystery and impossible to understand!

Ilka was given a separate compartment. She and her father were offered a luxurious breakfast, but they did not touch it. In the next town, where the train stopped for two hours, one of the officers drove to the shops and bought Ilka a new dress, a bracelet and some shoes...

"To the health of the daughter of the regiment!" shouted the officers when she came out of her compartment in her new attire. "Hurra-ah!"

The officers began drinking and made Ilka sing. She started singing and sang until the regiment reached the border...

Such was the first step in the new enterprise, from which the silly Ilka was expecting a million. This first step was successful. When Ilka ran away from the regiment a month later with Zwiebusch, she wore a dress that had cost the officers a thousand and a half francs. She ran away in a first-class carriage, in the company of five young girls, an old woman with a big, aquiline nose, and a fat German with a large bald patch on his head. Once they were on their way, the German began handing round his visiting cards which read: "Joseph Kelter, manager of an orchestra and Hungarian choir in Trieste." The old woman with the aquiline nose was his companion.

Chapter VII

The stubborn girl ran away once again, but for the last time.

It was a warm night in April... It had long struck midnight and, in Madame Blanchard's summer theatre, the performance was still underway. On stage, Mademoiselle Turie, a professor of black magic, was performing magic tricks. Having released a flock of doves from a woman's shoe, she pulled out a large lady's dress, to thunderous applause... A little boy in a Mephistopheles costume came out from under the dress after it had been lowered to the ground and lifted. The magic tricks were all as old as the hills, but one still could watch them with half an eye. The whole point of the performances at

Madame Blanchard's theatre was for a restaurant to be still called a theatre. The audience spends more time eating and drinking than looking at the stage. There were little tables behind the columns and in the boxes. The first-row audience sit with their backs to the stage, because their lorgnettes are fixed on the courtesans occupying the whole of the second row. The entire audience tends to dart about rather than sit still... It is too lively by half, and no amount of hissing will make it slow down even for a second... The audience moves from the stalls into the restaurant, and from the restaurant into the garden... Another reason Madame Blanchard keeps the theatre is to present "newcomers" to the public. After M-lle Turie's tricks, these "newcomers" were supposed to sing. While they waited for the magic tricks to finish, the excited audience were taking their seats and applauding the lady-magician for want of anything better to do. The fat Madame Blanchard herself was sitting in one of the boxes, smiling and toying with a bouquet. She was assuring "certain members of the public" hovering round her that the "newcomers" were superb... Her fat husband, sitting *vis-à-vis* and reading a newspaper, smiled and nodded his head affirmatively.

"Oh yes!" he muttered. "There is a reason why we had to pay so much for this choir! There's plenty to listen to and plenty to look at..."

"Listen," said a corpulent gentleman with grey hair, addressing the fat Madame Blanchard, "why aren't there any Hungarian songs in your programme today?"

The fat Madame Blanchard wagged her finger at the person asking in a coquettish way.

"I know why you want Hungarian songs, Viscount," she said. "The person you want to see is off sick today and cannot sing..."

"Poor thing!" sighed the viscount. "What is wrong with M-lle Ilka?"

Blanchard shrugged her shoulders.

"I don't know... She is certainly fabulous, my Ilka! You are the hundredth person this evening who has asked me about her. She is ill, Viscount! Even beauties succumb to illnesses..."

"Our Hungarian beauty suffers from a very noble malady!" said a young man in a dragoon's uniform, standing right there in the box. Yesterday she told that buffoon d'Omaren that she was homesick! Hey! Look, Viscount Saisies! What a... what a... what a... wonderful spectacle!"

The dragoon indicated that Viscount Saisies should look at the stage where the chorus of "newcomers" was taking up its position. Casting a quick look at the stage, Saisies resumed his conversation about Ilka with Blanchard...

"She is laughing at us!" he whispered to her a quarter of an hour later... "But she is stupid! Do you know what she demands from each of us for a moment of love? Do you know? One hundred thousand francs! Hahaha! We'll see what madman gives her that sort of money! For a hundred thousand I could get a dozen such girls! Hmm... Your cousin's daughter, Madame, was a thousand times more beautiful than she is, and cost me a hundred thousand, but that was over three years! And this one? Capricious little madam! One hundred thousand... You should explain to her, Madame, that it's terribly stupid of her... She is joking, but... one cannot always joke after all."

"And what does the handsome Alfred Désiré have to say on the matter?" said the laughing Madame Blanchard, addressing the dragoon.

"The girl is a tease," said Désirée. "She wants to sell herself at a higher rate... She will work you up and, instead of a thousand, will take two thousand francs from you. The girl knows that nothing strains and upsets bad nerves like the expectation... One hundred thousand is a cute little joke."

A fourth person joined in the conversation, then a fifth, and soon the whole box was talking about Ilka. There were about ten people in it....

During this conversation, Ilka was sitting in one of the multitudes of little rooms into which the backstage space was divided. The room, permeated with the smells of perfumes, powder and gas lighting, bore three names at once: dressing-room, reception room and the room of M-lle such-and-such... Ilka had the best room. She was sitting on a sofa, freshly upholstered in bright magenta-coloured velvet. Under her feet, a beautiful multi-coloured rug was spread. The whole room was flooded with pink light emanating from a lamp with a pink shade.

Before Ilka stood a young man of about twenty-five years old, a handsome brunette, dressed in a clean black suit. This was André d'Omaren, a reporter from *Le Figaro* newspaper. Due to his job, he was a regular visitor to places like the Blanchard theatre. His visiting card guaranteed him a free pass to all similar establishments which wanted their scandals reported in the press... A scandal described in *Le Figaro* is the best possible advertisement.

André d'Omaren was standing before Ilka, chewing his little moustache and beard, and unable to take his eyes off her.

"No, André," Ilka was saying in broken French, "I cannot be yours... There is no way! Don't swear to me you'll be faithful, don't follow me, don't demean yourself... It's all in vain!"

"Why?"

"Why? Ha-ha-ha! You are naïve, André... If you are rejected there must be a reason, is that it? First, you are poor, and I have told you a thousand times already that I cost a hundred thousand... Have you got a hundred thousand?"

"At the present moment, I don't even have a hundred francs... Listen, Ilka... What you're telling me is a pack of lies... Why are you slandering yourself so ruthlessly?"

"But what if I love someone else?"

"And does this 'someone else' know that you love him, and does he love you?"

"He knows, and he loves me..."

"Hmm... What a bastard he must be to allow you to work for the fat Blanchard!"

"He doesn't know that I'm in Paris. Don't berate him, André..."

Ilka got up and started pacing round the room.

"You, André," she said, "have said, on more than one occasion that you would do anything for me... You did, didn't you? Well, then do this for me... Stop my admirers from pestering me... They won't give me any peace... There are hundreds of them, and only one of me. Judge for yourself... And I must reject each and every one of them... Do you think it pleases me to see people upset by my rejection? Do this for me, please... I'm fed up to the back teeth with all this wooing and soliciting."

"I'll make sure that nobody annoys you, except for me... right?" said d'Omaren.

Ilka shook her head.

André went pale. Watching Ilka pacing round the room, he went down on his knees.

"But I love you," he said with a pleading voice. "I love you, Ilka!"

Ilka gave a sudden scream. The locket she'd been toying with clicked open. Up to now, despite all her efforts, it had remained firmly shut. When presenting her with this locket, von Seinitz had forgotten to tell her that it had a secret lock.

"At last!" Ilka shouted, and her face lit up with joy.

Now she would find out what was in it! His portrait, perhaps? And, in the hope of seeing a noble face with a big black beard, she hurried over to the lamp, took a look at the locket and went pale: instead of a bearded face, she saw a haughty female face, with a majestic smile. And Ilka recognised this face! On the little golden frame, into which the portrait was fitted, the following words were engraved: "Theresa Heilenstrahl loves you."

"So, that is how it is?!"

Ilka went scarlet and threw the locket to one side.

"So, that is how it is?! She loves him? Hmm... All right then..."

Ilka fell on to the sofa where she fidgeted about restlessly.

"She dares to love him?" she muttered. "No way! André! For God's sake!"

The reporter rose to his feet, hitting his knees with his hand, and went up to her.

"André... All right, I will love you, only you must do something for me, just one thing..."

"Anything you want! A thousand things, my dear!"

"I didn't want to do this until now, but... now I'm forced to... I am choosing you as my avenger... Have you ever been to my country?"

And Ilka, leaning on the reporter's shoulder, started whispering in his ear. She whispered for a very long time, energetically gesticulating with her hands. He jotted something down in his reporter's notebook.

"Will you do it?" she asked.

"Yes... I hate her after what you've told me..."

"Off you go then..."

"How will you know whether I've carried out your instructions?"

"I will take your word for it," said Ilka.

"And you, Ilka, give me your word that you... won't deceive me."

For a second, Ilka hesitated. Who would not? She was about to lie disgracefully, lie to a devoted, honest man and... for the first time in her life.

"I give you my word," she said.

The reporter kissed her hand and left. An hour later, he was already sitting in a train and, by the next day, he had left France.

Having bidden the reporter farewell, Ilka emerged from her dressing-room into the foyer full of little tables. Pale, agitated, and forgetting that patrons had been told she was indisposed that evening, she started pacing through the rooms. She did not want to think, but the most frightful, worrying thoughts floated, one after another, into her heated little mind. The thought that her baron was in love with or had loved *that* woman, was tearing her apart. When she entered the stalls, the audience's eyes turned to her and to Madame Blanchard in her box, who, only a few minutes ago had been insisting that Ilka was ill and lying in bed. Hearing hissing, whistling and applause, the "newcomers" who were treading the boards, began to bow... but it was not them whom the audience was hissing at and applauding...

"Onto the stage with you! Hungarian songs!" shouted the furious audience. "Quick march on stage! Ilka! Brava!"

Ilka smiled, pointing to her throat, and left, leaving fat Madame Blanchard to deal with the irate audience. She made her way to one of the restaurant's private rooms where she usually dined with "friends." Her fans followed her.

On this occasion, the supper was not a happy one. Ilka was silent and did not eat anything. Instead of merry laughter and broken French, her "friends" had to listen to deep sighs. And Saisies, usually the main toastmaster at these suppers, was also down in the dumps.

"The devil take these innocents with their innocent little faces!" he was muttering, devouring Ilka with his eyes. Désiré drank and was silent. Of late, the hapless dragoon had begun turning things over in his mind... He could not offer even two thousand to Ilka, who was demanding one hundred thousand. His father had recently died, and the estate was in the hands of creditors. He could not bank on altruistic love; he knew that he was not handsome and that these girls were mercantile...

Adolph, the son of the banker Bach, whose responsibility it was to ply everyone with champagne, was sitting next to Ilka and being over-familiar. As the richest of them all, he had the right to do so... He was drinking from Ilka's glass, whispering into her ear, etc. His behaviour was throwing the diners, who could not stand Adolph Bach for being rich, into the depths of gloom.

A few steps away from the table where the drinking was going on, two old men were sitting at the window. One of them was a manufacturer from Lyon, Marc Louvrer; the other...you would not recognise as our old acquaintance, Zwiebusch the fiddler, yet Zwiebusch it was. He had changed enormously. He had grown thinner, paler and his forehead no longer shone with sweat. In his eyes, there was apathy and acquiescence... Old Zwiebusch had given up on everything... For him and his Ilka, it was the end. He no longer wore tattered old rags. His increasingly skinny body was clothed in a white shirt with golden cufflinks and a black tailcoat... With Louvrer, one of Ilka's most ardent admirers, he was discussing... literature.

By three a.m., everyone except Zwiebusch, his daughter, and Louvrer was already drunk. The alcohol had shaken up the gloomy revellers to some degree. Hopeless love had ignited their drunken heads. They found their tongues...

By four a.m., Ilka was ready to go home with her father. Before she left, each man tried to have a few words with her on the quiet.

"I love you!" each man said to her, and each of them promised her paradise.

"One hundred thousand!" she would answer curtly.

On a quiet evening in May, there finally turned up a man who gave her a hundred thousand and put an end to all this comedy. This man was dragoon Désiré.

At three in the morning, when everyone was already drunk, the dragoon entered the room. Without greeting anyone, he went up to Ilka and took her aside.

"I've brought it..." he said in a hollow voice. "Take it... Do you know what I've done? I've robbed my uncle... I'll be taken to court tomorrow... Take it! I'm in!"

A cry of joy escaped from Ilka's chest. She now had a hundred thousand! At the same time, her face drained of colour: the time had come to pay for the hundred thousand...

Adolph Bach, who had been watching Désirée's movements, came up to Ilka and, having heard the words, "I'm in," grew pale.

"I'm in, too!" he said quickly and grabbed at his pocket... "I will give a hundred thousand, too!"

Désiré smiled derisively. In Bach, a mere boy, he no longer saw a worthy competitor.

"I was the first to agree... It wouldn't hurt you, Bach, if you went to bed now. Your nanny is waiting for you."

"I don't sleep with nannies, and I don't like your face that much, Désiré. It is begging for a slap! I will give one hundred and ten thousand!"

"And I—one hundred and twenty!"

Désiré had stolen exactly one hundred and twenty thousand from his uncle.

Drunken Saisies, devouring Ilka with his eyes like a snake devouring a rabbit, suddenly got to his feet and went up to Bach and Désirée.

"You... you... agree?" he muttered. "You've gone mad! You... you... have gone mad, boys! One hundred thousand! Ha-ha-ha! Pardon, mademoiselle, but, you must agree that..."

"I give one hundred and twenty!" Désiré repeated.

"And I give one hundred and twenty!" said milksop Bach and burst into laughter. "I'll give it this very minute, in cash!"

Saisies flinched. He did not want to believe his own ears. Do such fools really exist who would pay a hundred thousand for a woman whom he would be able to buy for five thousand at any time? And was it possible she would be bought by someone else... not him?

"It's out of the question!" he shouted.

"I, too, give one hundred and twenty!" said a fourth man joining the party. He was a strapping country squire from the outskirts of Marseille, named Arcôt; a very rich man. For him to throw a hundred thousand at this girl's feet meant nothing. He had recently lost his wife and only son and was now drowning his sorrow in wine and bought love.

"I agree, too!" said Botič, a Serb who passed himself off as the secretary of some embassy or other and squandered heaps of money every day.

Saisies started turning the pages of his notebook, jotting something down, calculating. His pencil was running to and fro over the paper.

"How come, gentlemen?" he was muttering. "Is money that cheap for you? Why does it have to be a hundred and twenty, and not an even hundred? Thirty... six hundred... Why not an even hundred?"

"One hundred and twenty-five!" shouted Bach, gazing triumphantly at his competitors.

"Agreed!" shouted Saisies. "Agreed! I agree, too, I'm telling you!"

"I don't want your extra five thousand," Ilka told Bach. "Take it back. I'm quite happy with a hundred and twenty... Only, gentlemen, not all of you... Just one... And who is it to be?"

"Me," said the dragoon. "I was the first to agree."

"That's splitting hairs," the others began. "Splitting hairs! What's the difference between first or second?"

"Yes, it's splitting hairs," said Ilka. "What shall we do, gentlemen? I like you all... You are all pleasant, polite... You all love me to an equal extent... What shall we do?"

"Draw lots!" suggested a young man who was not partaking in the auction and who had been gazing at the buyers with envy...

"Alright, we'll draw lots," Ilka agreed. "Agreed, gentlemen?"

"Agreed!" said everyone, except for the dragoon who was sitting on the windowsill, relentlessly chewing his big lower lip.

"And so, gentlemen, let's write out the lots... The person who draws the lot with my name on it will get me. Papa Zwiebusch, write out the lots!"

Obedient, as always, Papa Zwiebusch reached into the pocket of his new tailcoat and retrieved a piece of paper from it. The paper was then cut into little squares, and on one of the squares "Ilka" was written.

"Gentlemen, put your money on the table!" Ilka prompted. "The tickets are ready."

"How much should each of us put?" asked Bach. "How many of us are there? Eight? One hundred and twenty divided by eight equals... equals..."

"Put one hundred and twenty thousand each!" said Ilka.

"How much each?"

"One hundred and twenty thousand!"

"You are not good at arithmetic, my dear!" said the Serb. "Or, are you joking?"

"One hundred and twenty thousand each... otherwise, I quit," said Ilka.

Walking in silence away from Ilka, the men sat down at the table. They were indignant. Saisies started cursing and looking for his hat.

"That's a swindle!" he said. "It is what is known as cheating! To take advantage of the fact that we, idiots, drunken asses, have our blood on fire!?"

"I'm not giving a single centime," said Bach.

"I don't insist," said Ilka. "However, it's time to go home... Are you ready, Papa Zwiebusch? Let's go! Keep the tickets as a memento."

"Good-bye!" said the men. "Go back to your Hungary and look there for fools who'd give you a million! It is a million you're after, isn't it? If only you could understand, you weird one! One could buy the whole of Paris with a million! Good-bye!"

But almighty passion prevailed... After Ilka had offered to each man her warm hand, managed to say a few warm words by way of parting to each of them, and had sung "the last" song, the passion reached its apogee...

At five a.m., the first waiter they came across was taking little paper squares out of Bach's hat... When all these squares were gathered together and unfolded, laughter burst out of every man's chest. This laughter was the laughter of despair, laughter at the insanity and madness of fate.

The lot with the name "Ilka" on it was drawn by the Lyon manufacturer, old Marc Louvrer. Marc Louvrer had offered his one hundred and twenty thousand "in jest" and might well have been satisfied with just one kiss!

Chapter VIII

It was a frosty December evening. The first stars were flickering, and the cold moon was gliding through the sky. It was deathly quiet: there was not a single movement, not a single sound.

Arthur von Seinitz was walking along the big cutting to "lunch." He was walking from the chapel of St. Francis, where half an hour before he had bid goodbye to Theresa Goldaugen until the following day. Having dropped by the forester's house, as usual, he asked whether there was any post. Mrs. Blaucher gave him two envelopes: one very big, the other very small. The small one was from Paris, from Ilka. Seinitz did not want to read this letter and shoved it in his pocket. He knew its contents: "I love you!" Ilka would not have thought of anything more original or clever than that. The address on the big one was written in Peltzer's hand. Seinitz would have shoved this letter too into his pocket, had he not noticed the inscription "Securities." Arthur thought a little and opened the envelope. In it, he found his mother's will. He began to read the will. The more he got engrossed in reading the document, once signed by the dear hand which had nurtured the baron, the more surprised his face became. His mother had left *everything* to him and nothing to his sister... But why had the Peltzers sent him this will?

"Aha!" he thought. "They have repented! Long overdue..."

His mother's estate was not a big one. It would give no more than ten thousand thalers of income a year. But Arthur would have been glad of even that amount. And it would have pleased him to snatch even that amount from that miser Peltzer who would be prepared to commit the worst villainy in the world for a thaler.

Arthur asked Frau Blaucher for some paper, sat down at the table, and wrote Peltzer a letter. He wrote that he had received the will and that it would be desirable to know what had happened to the money that had been received to date from the estate that his mother had left him in her will. The letter was given to Frau Blaucher who duly sent it off to the posting station the next day. A week later, a reply from Peltzer was received. The reply was rather strange and unexpected. "I know nothing," Peltzer wrote. "I know neither about the will, nor about the money. Leave us alone..."

"What does it mean?" Arthur asked himself, having read the reply. "Rather strange! Or does he regret sending me the will? Hmm... Well, if that's the case, watch out!"

And the day after receiving Peltzer's reply, Arthur headed off to town where he contested the will. A court case got underway.

Arthur started travelling to town often. He would go first to the law court, and then to his solicitor. Theresa would often have to sit alone in the St. Francis chapel, pining from the wait and from boredom. She would sit in the chapel, look into St. Francis's forbidding eyes and listen intently to the sound of the wind. What happiness began to glisten in her eyes when she recognised the baron's footsteps among the noise outside the chapel; and how pallid she was when she would leave the chapel late in the evening, without having seen him! He would come to the chapel only to tease her, to speak obscenities, to laugh... Theresa was waiting impatiently for spring when it would be possible once again to walk together under the open sky.

But the spring brought her unhappiness...

Theresa was sitting by *The Bronze Deer* and waiting for Arthur. She was sitting on young blades of grass which had only just appeared through the soil, listening to the murmur of the stream which was gurgling somewhere near her... The sun was warming her beautiful shoulders pleasantly.

"Will he come or not?" she was thinking. Arthur had thrown himself into the litigation and came to *The Bronze Deer* reluctantly. But on this "after-dinner" occasion, he came. As usual, he arrived slightly tipsy, frowning and unhappy.

"You're here?" he asked Theresa, who was rejoicing at the sight of him. "My respects! It's nice not to have anything to do! I mean it, it's nice! Idle people always stroll about and sit on the green grass..."

After sitting down next to Theresa, he began to spit frenziedly to one side.

"What are you angry about?" asked the countess.

"Those scoundrels, the Peltzers. Do you know what they have done to me? The will they sent me is as false as a woman. It is a forgery. I contested it, and now I'll be tried for fraud... The Peltzers have mastered an insidious thing! They shrug their shoulders at the sight of this will and don't want to know about it. They have committed a forgery, and I will be put on trial! Dammit! They took a written undertaking from me to stay put, and soon I will be hassled by a court investigator. What do you think of that? Ha-ha! Baron von Seinitz made a fraudulent will! It takes the swindler Peltzer to invent such a trap! Well, your Grace, what about you? I heard yesterday that you and the count are divorced. All is finished between you. What, then, are you sitting here for? Why aren't you leaving your husband and all the places that remind you of this hateful man?"

"I don't want to leave," said Theresa.

"Hmm... Will you tell me why?"

"You don't know?"

"How would I know?"

A momentary silence ensued. Both knew why she was still there, and why she would not leave these parts, but Arthur had to tease a little...

"I... You don't know? I love you," said the countess, and a blush spread over her proud, stern face. "I love you, Arthur... If it were not for this love, I would be far away from *The Bronze Deer* now."

The countess lifted her eyes to Arthur's face. This drunken, derisive face told her the truth. The silence confirmed the same truth. He did not love her.

"Why, then, have you been coming here?" she asked softly, twisting her fingers. "Why didn't you leave me back then when our *rendezvous* were just beginning?"

"You were bored," said Arthur. "I haven't yet ceased being a ladies' man, and I do everything to please dear ladies. Ha-ha!"

"How silly that is!"

"What a pity I cannot reciprocate your love. I love someone else..."

Arthur reached into his side pocket with a laugh, pulled Ilka's photograph out of it, and raised it to Theresa's eyes.

"Here's my true love. Do you recognise her?"

"Is this that old man's daughter? But why is she dressed like that?"

"She is dressed very decently... A charming little face!"

"Where is she now?"

Arthur fell silent. The effect he had been counting on had not come off. The countess did not go pale or red in the face at the sight of the photograph... She just sighed and, strangely enough, kindness started glowing in her eyes at the sight of the pretty, almost child-like, face.

"Goodbye!" said Arthur. "Adieu! I'm going to read up about the law. Oh Peltzer, Peltzer! If I were to say in court that it was he who sent me the will, they would laugh at me!"

Arthur turned his back on Theresa and started walking into the heart of the forest, gesticulating with his hands.

Theresa walked over to her horse, which was standing nearby and grazing on young grass.

"Let's go away and never come here again," said Theresa, stroking the horse's forelock. "We are not loved. Let's not beg for alms."

Leaping on to the horse's back, Theresa took off into the forest. Her eyes were glowing with resolution. When she rode through the gate leading into the long path we told you about in the first chapter of our story, she heard steps behind her. She turned her head. Running after her horse was a young man she did not know who had a whip in his hand.

"One minute!" he shouted to her in French.

The countess reigned in her horse and nodded to the young man.

"Must be a petitioner," she thought.

Smiling and beaming, the reporter d'Omaren ran up to her and raised the whip in admiration of her beauty.

"You are as cruel as you are beautiful!" he said. "Nothing must go unpunished. Remember the old musician and his daughter!"

And the countess felt a burning pain on her face...

"So be it!" she said and gave a sharp tug at the reins.

D'Omaren stared after the beautiful countess for a long time. The Frenchman longed to speak to the woman he had struck and who had responded to his striking her with the words "So be it!" but when she disappeared from his sight he quickly turned back and started walking swiftly towards the railway station. He had fulfilled the assignment given him and now was going after his reward...

Chapter IX

"Some lady is seeking you!" Frau Blaucher said to Arthur one evening when he dropped by to get his mail. "She left a little note!"

"I am staying at *The Big Anchor* hotel," Arthur read in the note. "Come soon. Ilka."

Arthur headed off to town and met with Ilka on the dot of midnight. He burst into laughter when he saw her. How elegantly she was dressed, and how unlike that little singer girl he had once met in the forest, sobbing her heart out!

"Do you have a million?" he asked, laughing.

"Yes. Here it is!"

Arthur suddenly stopped laughing. Before him on the table, a million, a real million, was laid out.

"Dammit!" he said, refusing to believe his eyes. "You are counting, my child, in francs? I forgot to tell you to count in thalers... But no matter... This money is good, too! Where did you get it?"

Ilka sat down next to him and told him everything that had happened to her after they had parted.

"Well? And what did you do to the old man?" asked Arthur.

"Plied him with morphine and fled without looking back the same night."

"Honestly!" said Arthur. "Ha-ha-ha! Another time I would have whipped you, but now you must be the baroness von Seinitz! Here is my hand! Tomorrow we'll go to the mayor!"

The next day, von Seinitz and Ilka were at the mayor's office. Ilka became baroness von Seinitz on 2nd of June , at half past nine in the morning.

At two o'clock on the same day, Baron Arthur von Seinitz was stripped of his barony; the jurors found him guilty of forging a will... The Peltzers had achieved their goal.

Ilka saw the countess Goldaugen in court.

The countess was sitting in one of the back rows, far away from the public, with her eyes fixed on the accused. A dark veil hung down from her black hat. She evidently wanted to remain incognito. And it was only when she uttered aloud: "How silly it is!" after listening to the prosecutor's speech that Ilka recognised her by her melodious voice.

"What right does she have to stare at my husband?" Ilka thought, going pale with hatred and, at the same time, feeling victorious. She now believed in this victory: the man the countess loved had been taken from her.

The accused behaved very strangely in court. He was tipsy, and unkind witticisms poured from his tongue. Ignoring the judges and the jurors, he was silent when he should have been speaking, and he spoke when he should have remained silent. The prosecutor was his friend from university days, but did not spare him in his speech. He dug shamelessly into his past, which, as a friend, he knew about; he described his Parisian life, the bankruptcy, the lack of money, the hardship that Baron von Seinitz experienced thanks to this lack of money, and finished with a paean to Frau Peltzer who had sacrificed her feelings of brotherly love in the name of justice, and revenge for misdemeanours...

"Her actions have been those of an exemplary citizen!" he said.

"Shame on you," said Arthur. "Before, when you used to smoke my cigars in our university days, you were less skilful at lying!"

This was Arthur's only serious and sincere remark; the rest of what he said provoked laughter, and the bell of the Presiding Court Officer to sound.

The public, which consisted almost entirely of Peltzer's minions, met the verdict with applause. People who sympathised with Arthur had not been able to find a seat in the court; all the seats had been occupied by the banker's supporters early in the morning. Arthur listened to the verdict coolly.

"I can pull strings with the Emperor," he said, "and when I need a barony again, I'll pay him a visit. Vienna, which knows me, will laugh at this verdict!"

A bitter feeling of shame for people and disgust filled the countess' heart after she left the courtroom and took a seat in her carriage. An innocent man had been accused of fraud and convicted in her presence.

"I will restore his good name!" she decided indignantly. "He told them he can pull strings in Vienna, but he won't bother to do that for what he regards as the trifling matter of his good name. He is also lazy, and so full of inertia... I will do it for him..."

"I will give him alms," she added mentally, "and he will have to accept them against his will!"

The very next day she was at a charity ball given at the municipal club, selling tickets. In the garden, under an awning made out of flags, ornamental vines and fresh flowers, there stood several little tables. On the tables, there were wheels of fortune with lottery tickets.

Eight very beautiful and very prettily dressed aristocratic ladies were sitting at these tables selling tickets. The countess Goldaugen was doing the best. She was spinning the wheel continuously and giving out change. Peltzer, who was present at the ball, bought two thousand tickets from her.

"How is your wife's brother doing?" the countess asked Peltzer, as she took the money from him.

Peltzer sighed.

"He was dealt two blows, poor thing," he said. "He got married and... today he is no longer a baron..."

"I heard about that... Where is his wife now?"

"She is here. Haven't you seen her? How funny! Ha-ha... She is a baroness... If they had got married a few hours later, she would now be only burgher Seinitz..."

Ilka was at the ball. She had already walked past the countess once with her head held high and a proud, haughty smile. The countess was busy with her sales and did not notice her. She walked past the second time, surrounded by a crowd of onlookers who were lost in contemplation of her pretty face. The countess glanced at her and did not appear to recognise her. When she was walking past for the third time, their eyes met.

The countess became confused and, to Ilka's great pleasure, dropped some money. Several coins slipped out of her trembling hands and scattered noisily, rolling over the floor.

Ilka went up to the countess' table and, looking her straight in the face, bought several tickets.

"I want to present one little thing to the school charity fund," she said, and thrust a gold locket into the countess' hand without waiting for a response. The countess took the familiar locket into her hands, opened it and smiled. Her face had been scratched with a pin.

"You should take this thing to the club administration," she said, giving the locket back to Ilka. "We only sell tickets..."

Smiling sweetly, the countess added:

"Pardon me, I have no time for this!"

The countess' smile and composure confused Ilka. Not being used to confrontations of this sort, she became embarrassed and walked away from the table. She felt angry and awkward; those standing near the countess' table noticed her embarrassment, exchanged looks and smiled. Those perplexed smiles pierced Ilka's heart like darts.

"Allow me to pass, please," she said to some young people who stood before her like a wall and were watching her with curiosity.

The young people suddenly burst out laughing for some reason. Ilka heard the same laughter from behind her, too. She turned her head and saw a similar crowd of youths.

"Allow me to pass!" repeated Ilka.

Again, the laughter was heard, and a big beer cork hit Ilka's pink forehead. Another cork hit her right shoulder...

"Ha-ha... Hurrah! Baroness von Seinitz, the spouse of a demoted crook!" shouted someone, and hissing was heard...

The third and fourth corks hit her in the face together. Insulted, humiliated, and ready to faint, she looked at the countess, and it seemed to her that the countess was laughing... Ilka's eyes went blurry. Her spinning head felt as if it was being dragged to the ground.

"Arthur!" she shouted.

No-one responded to this call. The baron, stripped of his title, was far away. Drunk, he was lying fast asleep under a bush, not far from the Blaucher's little house, and dreaming about his million.

The countess, whom the insulted girl did not recognise due to her blurred vision, approached Ilka, seized her by the shoulders, and led her out of the crowd.

"Let me go! I want to kill her!" shouted Ilka, but she then passed out.

When she came to, she found herself in a little room whose furniture was upholstered in raspberry-coloured velvet. She was lying on a couch. A girl with a vial in her hand was sitting next to her.

"Where are we?" Ilka asked.

"At the club, Fräulein," answered the girl.

The sounds of a mazurka which reached Ilka's ears confirmed the girl's words. Ilka lifted her heavy head, thought a little, and remembered everything that had happened.

"Bring me a small glass of Rhine wine," she asked the girl.

The girl went out of the room. Ilka quickly pulled a purse out of her pocket. From the purse Ilka took a little vial of morphine. This was the morphine to which she had recently treated the old Louvrer! And now she was going to treat herself to it, because she took the insults people dealt her so close to heart... All the morphine in the vial was consumed. In anticipation of eternal sleep Ilka reclined on a velvet cushion and started thinking... She did not regret her colourless life. She felt sorry to leave Papa Zwiebusch—only him! She was not sorry for Arthur, who loved wine more than his young wife.

"How are you feeling?" she heard a melodious voice saying.

The countess, her worst enemy, had entered the room and was bending over her... Ilka saw a pair of shining eyes and cheeks with two pink spots on them in front of her face.

"D'Omaren!" she whispered, seeing a barely noticeable red line on the left cheek.

"Those who offended you will be punished," said the countess. "They were hired by Peltzer who hates Arthur... I will punish that scoundrel Peltzer... I am powerful... Are you still angry with me?"

Ilka turned her face away.

"Are you still angry, Ilka? Well... forgive me... I am guilty... I insulted both your father and you... I repent and ask for forgiveness."

And Ilka felt a kiss on her head.

"I have been searching for you for a long time... I had no rest day or night after meeting your gaze on that ill-fated day... Your burning gaze consumed me in my sleep..."

Ilka suddenly burst into tears.

"I'm dying," she whispered, falling asleep to the sounds of her repentant rival's tender voice.

"Please forgive me, Ilka, like I have forgiven you..."

Ilka extended her arm and touched the countess' neck... The countess leaned towards her and kissed her on the lips.

"I'm dying," Ilka whispered. "I took... mor... on the rug..."

The countess bent down and saw the vial on the rug. She understood everything. Within a minute, a doctor was found in the club and brought to Ilka. All the doctor managed to do, thanks to the presence of the vial, was to certify death by poisoning; he failed to resuscitate Ilka, who had fallen asleep.

The reporter d'Omaren arrived in Paris from Hungary on the night Ilka was raffled off. Having found nobody in the hotel room where the songstress lived except Louvrer, who was fast asleep in the armchair, he ran to Bach. Bach told him everything that had occurred during his absence.

"She's run away," decided the reporter and the next day he returned to Hungary, where he hoped to receive payment for his services.

In Hungary, he learnt about the death of the woman he loved. The news of this death was a cruel blow that forced him to take to his bed. After spending some time bedridden with a fever, he settled in the Goldaugen forest, collected facts from every source and wrote a story about the beautiful Ilka. Last year, while passing through the Goldaugen forest, I made d'Omaren's acquaintance and read his story.

It has now been translated into Russian, and is offered here to our readers.

Live Goods

*To F. F. Popudoglo**

I

Grokholsky embraced Liza, kissed every one of her little pink, nail-bitten fingers, then sat her down on the chaise longue, which was upholstered in cheap velvet. Liza crossed one leg over the other, placed her hands behind her head and lay down.

Grokholsky sat down on the adjacent chair and leaned towards her. His whole being was captivated by this vision.

How pretty she seemed, illuminated by the rays of the setting sun!

The setting sun, which was gold, flecked with dark crimson, was entirely visible through the window.

It lit up the whole drawing room, Liza included, with a bright, soft light and for a short moment turned everything to gold...

Grokholsky was lost in wonder. Liza was not, strictly speaking, a beauty. True, her little feline face with its brown eyes and snub nose was fresh and even alluring, her thin, curly hair was as black as coal, and her small, well-proportioned body was as lithe and graceful as that of an electric eel, but overall... Well, let's leave my taste out of it. Grokholsky, who had been in and out of love a hundred times in his life, and was spoiled by women, regarded her as a beauty. He loved her; but then blind love finds ideal beauty everywhere.

"Listen," he began, gazing straight into her eyes. "I've come to talk to you, my darling. Love cannot tolerate anything undefined or formless... Undefined relations, you know... I went over this with you yesterday, Liza... So today let's try and find a solution. Let's decide together... What shall we do?"

Liza yawned and withdrew her right hand from under her head, grimacing severely.

"What shall we do?" she repeated, barely audibly, after Grokholsky.

"Well, yes, what shall we do? Go on, decide, my clever girl... I love you, and a man in love is not a sharer. He's more than selfish. I'm incapable of sharing you with your husband. I mentally tear him to pieces when I think that he loves you too. And, secondly, you love me... For love to survive, it needs absolute freedom... And are you free? Are you not tormented by the thought that this man constantly hovers over you? A man you do not love, whom you perhaps, quite naturally, hate... That's the second thing... And the third... What was the third thing? Ah yes, we're deceiving him, and that's... dishonest... The truth before all else, Liza. Let us be rid of these lies!"

"Well, what shall we do?"

"That you can surely guess... I think it is essential we inform him of our relations and leave him, so we can live in freedom. Both things must be done as soon as possible... For example, perhaps even this evening you... you could come clean with him... It's time to make the break once and for all... Are you not tired of loving so furtively?"

"Come clean? With Vanya?"

"Yes!"

"That's impossible! I told you yesterday, Michel[1]—that's impossible!"

"But why?"

"He'll take it badly, make a scene, cause all kinds of unpleasantness... Do you really not know what he's like? Heaven help us! There's no need for him to know! What an idea!"

Grokholsky ran his hand over his forehead and sighed.

"Yes," he said. "He'll take it worse than badly... After all, I'll be depriving him of his happiness. Does he love you?"

"Yes. Very much."

"Oh, what a headache! Impossible to know where to begin. Hiding the truth from him is dishonest, but to come clean with him would mean killing him... Dammit! Well, what are we to do?"

Grokholsky was deep in thought. A scowl appeared on his pale face.

"Things between us will always be just as they are now," said Liza. "Let him find out for himself, if he so wishes."

"But it's... it's sinful and... Finally, you're mine, and no one has the right to think that you belong to someone else and not me! You're mine! I won't give you up for anyone! I pity him, Liza, God knows I pity him! When I see him it causes me pain! But... but what can be done about it? After all you don't love him, do you? So why continue to suffer with him? We must tell him! We'll tell

---

1   Author's mistake: Grokholsky is called Grigory or Grisha elsewhere.

him and you come home with me. You're my wife, not his. Let him do as he sees fit. He will get over his grief somehow or other... He is not the first, and he won't be the last... Do you want to run away? Well? Tell me! Do you want to run away?"

Liza sat up and looked at Grokholsky questioningly.

"Run away?"

"Well yes... To my estate... Then to the Crimea... We'll tell him everything by letter. We can leave tonight. There's a train at half past one. Well? Do you agree?"

Liza scratched the bridge of her nose idly and began to ponder.

"I agree," she said and... burst into tears.

Red patches flared up on her cheeks, her eyes became puffy, and tears flowed down her little feline face...

"What's the matter?" asked Grokholsky anxiously. "Liza! What's wrong? Eh? What are you crying about? What's this all about? Sweetheart! My dearest!"

Liza reached out towards Grokholsky and wrapped her arms round his neck. Sobbing could be heard.

"I'm sorry for him..." muttered Liza. "Oh, I feel so sorry for him!"

"For whom?"

"For Va...Vanya."

"And you think I don't? But what can we do? We will be the cause of his suffering... He'll suffer, and he'll curse us... But is it our fault that we love each other?"

After saying this, Grokholsky leapt away from Liza as if he had been stung and sat down in the armchair. Liza detached herself from his neck, and in the blink of an eye quickly sank onto the chaise lounge.

Both of them went bright red, lowered their eyes and started coughing.

A tall, broad-shouldered man in a civil servant's uniform, about thirty years old, had walked into the room. He had come in unnoticed. It was only the sound of him accidentally knocking a chair against the door frame that had given the lovers any indication of his presence and made them look round. It was Liza's husband.

But they had looked round too late. He had seen Grokholsky holding Liza by the waist, and Liza clinging to Grokholsky's white, aristocratic neck.

"He saw us!" thought Liza and Grokholsky simultaneously, trying to hide their heavy hands and embarrassed eyes...

The pink face of the stunned husband turned white.

The agonising, strange, gut-wrenching silence lasted three minutes. Oh, those three minutes! Grokholsky remembers them to this day.

The first to move and break the silence was the husband. He took a step towards Grokholsky, and offered him his hand, contorting his face into a nonsensical grimace resembling a smile. Grokholsky limply shook his soft, clammy hand and shuddered, as if he had just squashed a cold frog in his fist.

"Good evening," he muttered.

"How are you, Sir?" the husband croaked, barely audibly, and sat down opposite Grokholsky, adjusting the back of his collar...

The room was again filled with an agonising silence... But this silence was less inane than before... The first move, the most difficult and the most spineless, had been taken.

All that was left now was for one of the two men to withdraw in order to fetch matches or some other trivial item. They both were desperate to leave. They sat there, pulling on their beards, each avoiding the other's gaze, and searching in their agitated minds for a way out of this insufferably awkward situation. They were both sweating. They were both suffering horribly, and they were both consumed by hatred. They wanted to grab hold of each other, but... How to begin? And who would begin? If only she would leave the room!

"I saw you yesterday at the Assembly,"* muttered Bugrov (the husband).

"I was there... Yes... Did you dance?"

"Hm, yes. With... the young Lyukotskaya... She doesn't dance very well... She dances atrociously. She likes to talk. (Pause.) Talks non-stop."

"Yes... it was dull. I saw you there too..."

Grokholsky inadvertently glanced at Bugrov... His eyes met the wandering gaze of the deceived husband, and he could not bear it. He quickly got up, and quickly took Bugrov's hand, then pressed it, grabbed his hat and made for the door, acutely conscious of his back. He felt as if a thousand eyes were fixed on his back. An actor booed off the stage, or a fop who has been given a clip round the ear and is being dragged off by the police, feels the same way.

As soon as the sound of Grokholsky's steps had died away, and the door into the hall had clicked shut, Bugrov leapt to his feet, circled the drawing room several times, and walked over to his wife. Her little feline face cringed in fear and her eyes blinked, as if expecting a slap. Her husband came up to her and shook his arms, head and shoulders, his face pale and distorted as he stepped on her dress, his knees knocking against hers.

"If you let him in here once more, you piece of filth," he began in a muted, tearful voice, "I'll... Not one foot inside the door! I'll kill you! Do you understand? A-a-agh... You shameless hussy! You're trembling! What ffff-ilth!"

Bugrov seized her by the elbow, shook her, and hurled her towards the window like a rubber ball.

"Filth! Slut! You have no shame!"

She flew towards the window, her feet barely touching the floor, and caught hold of the curtains.

"Silence!" her husband shouted, as he came towards her and stamped his foot, his eyes flashing.

She said nothing. She looked at the ceiling and sobbed, the expression on her face like that of a penitent little girl about to be punished.

"So that's what you're like, eh? Running around with a rake, are we? Very well! And your vows before the altar? A good wife and mother you make! Silence!"

And he hit her on her beautiful, delicate shoulder.

"Silence! Filth! I'll do more than that! If that crook dares set foot in here one more time, if there is one more time... (mark my words!!) that I see you with that scum, then... don't ask for mercy! I'll kill you, even if they send me to Siberia! And him! It won't cost me anything! Get out! I don't want to see you!"

Wiping his forehead and eyes with his sleeve, Bugrov began pacing round the drawing-room. Sobbing louder and louder, her shoulders heaving and her little snub nose twitching, Liza started examining the lacework on the curtains.

"You're fickle!" her husband cried. Women's heads are stuffed with idiotic ideas. Endless flighty nonsense! I won't stand for any of that, Lizaveta! There is not to be a peep out of you, do you understand? I don't like that sort of thing! If you want to behave badly then... off you go! There's no place for you in my house! Quick march, if... You are married, so forget about it, drive these posers out of your stupid head! It's all foolishness! It'd better not happen again! Don't even think about it! Love your husband! You've been given to your husband, so love him! That's how it is! Is one not enough? Now go, before... Tormentors!"

Bugrov went quiet for a moment, then shouted:

"Go, I said! Go to the nursery! Why are you howling? You're the guilty one and yet here you are blubbering! Just look at you! Last year you were hanging onto Petka Tochkov's neck, and now you've attached yourself to this, Lord forgive me, devil... Ugh! It's high time you understood who you are! You are a wife! A mother! Last year we had unpleasantness, and now there'll be more unpleasantness... ugh!"

Bugrov sighed loudly and the air was filled with the smell of sherry. He had been out to lunch and was slightly drunk.

"Don't you know your duties? No?... You need to be taught then! You still haven't learnt! Your mamas are all hussies and so are you... Go on, cry your eyes out!"

Bugrov went over to his wife and pulled the curtain out of her hand.

"Don't stand by the window... People will see you crying... Don't you dare do that again. Or you'll go from embraces to ruin... You'll end up in a mess. You think I enjoy being cuckolded? If you insist on trailing around with these, with these louts, you'll... That's enough... If you do it again... I'll have to... Liza... Stop it..."

Bugrov sighed, enveloping Liza in sherry fumes.

"You're a young, foolish little thing, you don't understand anything... I'm never at home... And they take advantage of it! You have to be clever, sensible! They'll pull the wool over your eyes! But I won't put up with it then... That will be it... Finished! Then you might as well lie down and die. If you cheat on me, my dear, I'll... I'll be prepared to do anything! I can beat you to death... I'll chase you out of the house. Then you can run after your scoundrels."

And Bugrov wiped the wet, tear-stained face of his unfaithful Liza with his large soft palm (*horribile dictu!*).[2] He treated his twenty-year-old wife like a child!

"Well, that's enough. I forgive you now, but next time... God forbid! I forgive you for the fifth time, but I won't forgive you a sixth. As God is my witness... Not even God forgives your kind such things."

Bugrov bent down and extended his glistening lips towards Liza's head.

But he did not succeed in kissing her...

There was a slamming of doors in the hall, the dining room, the parlour and the drawing room, and Grokholsky flew into the drawing room like a whirlwind. He was pale and trembling. He was waving and crumpling his expensive hat with his hands. His frock coat hung loosely on him, as if on a hanger. He was fever incarnate. At the sight of him, Bugrov left his wife's side and began to look out of the other window. Grokholsky raced over to him and

2   *"horribile dictu!"*: "horrible to say!" (Latin).

said in a trembling voice, waving his arms about, breathing heavily, and not making eye contact with anyone:

"Ivan Petrovich! Let's put an end to this farce! We've deceived each other long enough! Enough! I don't have the strength. You do what you wish, but I cannot! It's vile and squalid after all! It's disgraceful! You've got to understand, it's disgraceful!"

Grokholsky was choking and gasping for breath.

"It's against my principles. And you're an honest man. I love her! More than anything in this world! You saw as much and... I'm obliged to say it!"

"What do I say to him?" Ivan Petrovich wondered.

"This must come to an end! This farce cannot continue! We need to come to some sort of agreement."

Grokholsky took a deep breath and continued:

"I cannot live without her. And she feels the same. You're an educated man, you will understand that under such conditions your family life is impossible. This woman isn't yours. Yes... In a word, I ask you to look at this affair from a compassionate... humane point of view. Ivan Petrovich! You have to understand that I love her, love her more than myself, more than anything in the world, and to resist this love is beyond me!"

"And what about her?" asked Bugrov, in a sullen, somewhat mocking tone.

"Ask her! Go on, ask her! For her to live with someone she does not love, to live with you, whilst loving another... it's clearly... it... it means suffering!"

"And what about her?" Bugrov repeated, his tone no longer mocking.

"She... she loves me! We have fallen in love... Ivan Petrovich! Kill us, despise us, persecute us, do what you wish... but we are no longer able to hide it from you! We are both here before you! Judge us with all the severity of a man from whom we... from whom fate has snatched away all happiness!"

Bugrov went as red as a lobster and took a quick look at Liza. He blinked. His fingers, lips and eyelids trembled. Poor man! Liza's tearful eyes told him that Grokholsky was right, that the affair was serious...

"Well?" he muttered. "If you... Nowadays... You are all so..."

"Honest to God," Grokholsky squeaked in a high tenor voice, "we understand you. Do you think we don't understand? That we have no feelings? I know what suffering I'm causing you. Honest to God! But have some compassion! I beseech you! We are not guilty! In love there is no guilt. Even with all the will in the world, it cannot be resisted! Give her to me, Ivan Petrovich!

Let her come with me! Take what you want from me for your suffering, take my life, but give me Liza! I'm prepared to do anything... Tell me what I can do to at least partly replace her for you! In exchange for your lost happiness, I can give you another happiness! Believe me, Ivan Petrovich, I can! I'll agree to anything! It would be dishonourable on my part to leave you dissatisfied... I understand what you are going through at this very minute."

Bugrov made a gesture with his hand as if to say, "Just leave, for God's sake!" His eyes started to cloud over with treacherous moistness... Now they would see what a cry-baby he was.

"I assure you, I do understand you, Ivan Petrovich! I'll give you another kind of happiness, such as you have never experienced! What do you want? I'm a rich man, and I'm the son of an influential man... Do you want that? How much do you want?"

Bugrov's heart began to thump. He seized the curtains with both hands.

"Would you like... fifty thousand? Ivan Petrovich, I beseech you... It's not a bribe, it's not a deal... I only want to make an offering to at least partly compensate you for your immeasurable loss... Do you want one hundred thousand? I can do that! A hundred thousand?"

Goodness! Two giant hammers began to strike the unhappy Ivan Petrovich's sweaty temples... Russian troikas* with bells and jingle bells started running in his ears...

"Take this offering from me!" Grokholsky continued. "I implore you! You will be taking a great weight off my conscience. I beg you!"

Goodness! A fashionable four-seated carriage went past the window through which Bugrov's moist eyes were staring; the road was slightly damp from the light May showers. The horses were fierce and swift, and well-trained. Seated in the carriage were people in straw hats, with happy faces, long fishing rods, and nets... A schoolboy in a white peaked cap held a gun in his hands. They were on their way to the dacha to catch fish, hunt, and drink tea in the fresh air. They were going to those blissful places where, as a boy in days of yore, the young Bugrov, son of the village deacon, had run through fields, woods and along riverbanks, barefoot and sunburnt, but infinitely happy. Oh, how devilishly seductive was this month of May! Happy are those who can shed their heavy civil service uniforms, sit in a carriage and fly to the wide, open spaces, where the trill of quails and the scent of fresh hay fill the air. Bugrov's heart contracted with a pleasant feeling that gave him the shivers... One hundred thousand! Flying past him together with the carriage were all of his most sacred dreams, in which he had loved to indulge throughout his life as a civil servant, while sitting in his provincial government office or in his pathetically small study... A deep river full of fish, a large garden with narrow paths, fountains, shadows, flowers, summer houses, a luxurious dacha with terraces and towers, an Aeolian harp and little silver bells... (He had learnt of the existence of Aeolian harps from German novels.) A clear blue sky; limpid, fresh air, filled with scents reminding him of his barefoot, hungry and downtrodden childhood... To rise at five o'clock, go to bed at nine; and, during the day catch fish, hunt, chat with the peasants... Bliss!

"Ivan Petrovich! Don't torment me! Do you want one hundred thousand?"

"Hmm... A hundred and fifty thousand!" Bugrov bellowed in a low voice, like that of a bull which has gone hoarse... He bellowed and lowered his head, ashamed of what he had said and waiting for an answer...

"All right," said Grokholsky. "I agree! Thank you, Ivan Petrovich... I shall now... I shall not keep you waiting."

Grokholsky jumped up, put on his hat and walked backwards before running out of the drawing room.

Bugrov gripped the curtains even more tightly... He was ashamed... In his heart he felt he had done something despicable, stupid, but what beautiful, brilliant hopes also began to stir between his throbbing temples! He was rich!

Fearing that Bugrov would come over to her window and cast her aside, Liza darted through the half-open door, trembling from head to toe, and not understanding anything. She went to the nursery, lay down on the nanny's bed and curled up into a ball. She was in the grip of a fever.

Bugrov was left alone. He began to feel suffocated, so he opened the window. How wonderful the air felt on his face and neck! How good it would be to breathe in such air while reclining on the cushions of a carriage... There, far beyond the town, near the villages and dachas, the air was better still... Bugrov even smiled as he dreamed of the air that would envelop him as he stepped out onto the veranda of his dacha to admire the view... He stood by the window dreaming for a long time... The sun had already gone down, but still he stood there plunged in daydreams, trying with all his might to cast out of his mind the image of Liza, which had been following him relentlessly through all his fantasies.

"I've brought it, Ivan Petrovich!" Grokholsky, who had returned, whispered in his ear. "I've brought it... Take it... There is forty thousand in this bundle. If you care to present this form to Valentinov the day after tomorrow, he will give you another twenty. Here's a promissory note... A cheque... The remaining thirty thousand will be with you in a few days. My administrator will deliver it to you."

Pink, excited, and all movement, Grokholsky laid out a pile of banknotes, papers and packets before Bugrov. It was a large, brightly coloured heap. Bugrov had seen nothing to equal it in his entire life! He spread out his fat fingers and began to go through the bundles of credit notes and forms without looking at Grokholsky...

Grokholsky laid out all the money and began mincing about the room, searching for his Dulcinea who had been bought and sold.

After stuffing his pockets and wallet, Bugrov hid the forms in his desk, drank half a jug of water, and rushed out into the street.

"Cabbie!" he called out in a wild voice.

At half past eleven that night he drove up to the entrance of the Paris Hotel. He walked noisily up the stairs and knocked on the door of Grokholsky's room. He was let in. Grokholsky was packing his things into a suitcase. Liza was sitting at a table trying on bracelets. Both of them took fright when Bugrov entered. They thought he had come for Liza, and to return the money, which he had taken in the heat of the moment rather than from conviction. But Bugrov had not come for Liza. Ashamed of his new outfit and feeling terribly uncomfortable in it, he bowed and stood like a footman in the doorway... His new attire was superb. Bugrov was unrecognisable. A brand new suit of the most fashionable French wool enveloped his large body, which up to then had worn nothing except the usual civil servant uniform. On his feet were shiny ankle boots with sparkling buckles. He stood there, ashamed of his new clothes, his right hand concealing a watch chain for which he had paid three hundred roubles just an hour before.

"I have come here because..." he began. "A man's word is worth more than money. I shall not give up Mishutka..."

"Who's Mishutka?" Grokholsky asked.

"My son."

Grokholsky and Liza exchanged looks. Liza's eyes swelled with tears, her cheeks reddened and her lips quivered.

"Very well," she said.

She remembered Mishutka's warm little cot. The cold hotel couch would be a poor substitute for it, and so she agreed.

"I will go on seeing him," she said.

Bugrov bowed, left the room and flew down the stairs in all his glory, cutting through the air with his expensive cane.

"Home!" he said to the cab driver. "I am leaving tomorrow morning at five o'clock... Come for me. If I am asleep, wake me up. We will be going out of town..."

II

It was a beautiful August evening. The sun, framed by a gold background and tinged with purple, hung over the western horizon, ready to sink behind the ancient kurgans* in the distance. The shadows and half-shadows had already disappeared in the gardens, and it had become dark, but a golden light continued to play amongst the treetops... It was warm. It had recently rained, and this made the already fresh, limpid, fragrant air even fresher.

I am not describing an August evening in the capital—all misty, drizzling, dark, with its chilly, horribly damp sunsets. God forbid! I am not describing our harsh northern Augusts. I am asking the reader to transport himself to the Crimea, to one of its shores near Feodosia, to the very spot where the dacha of one of my heroes stands. It is an attractive little house: spick and span, and surrounded by flower-beds and pruned hedges. About a hundred feet away behind it can be seen the blue shadow of an orchard in which holidaymakers are walking... Grokholsky pays a large sum for this dacha—one thousand roubles a year, I believe... It is not worth this sum, but it is a nice little place... Tall, slender, with slender walls and very delicate balustrades, it is painted light blue, and hung everywhere with curtains, door curtains and drapes—it reminds one of a sweet-looking, delicate, prim young lady.

On the evening we have described, Grokholsky and Liza were sitting on the veranda of this dacha. Grokholsky was reading *New Times** and drinking milk from a green mug. A syphon of soda water stood on the table before him. Imagining that he suffered from catarrh of the lungs and, on the advice of Dr. Dmitriev, Grokholsky was consuming huge quantities of grapes, milk and soda water. Liza was seated at some distance from the table in a soft armchair. With her elbows resting on the balustrade of the veranda, and her little face propped up on her fists, she was staring at the dacha opposite them... The sun was reflected in the windows of this dacha and the hot panes of glass cast blinding rays of light into her eyes... Beyond the front garden and the sparse trees surrounding the house, the sea was visible, with its waves, blueness, infinity and white masts... It was so lovely! Grokholsky was reading one of the feuilletons by Anon and casting his blue eyes on Liza's back after every ten lines... Shining in these eyes was the same, passionate, burning love... He was infinitely happy, regardless of his imagined catarrh of the lungs... Aware of his eyes on her back, Liza thought of Mishutka's brilliant future, and she felt totally relaxed and at peace...

It was not so much the sea, or the blinding glint of the window panes of the neighbouring dacha which occupied her attention, as the string of carts which were moving towards it, one after another.

The carts were full of furniture and various household items. Liza saw the lattice gates and large glass doors of the dacha open, and the delivery men busy themselves with furniture, bickering endlessly. Through the glass doors they carried large armchairs and a couch, all upholstered in a dark raspberry-coloured velvet, tables for the Parlor, drawing room and dining room, a large double bed, and a child's bed... They also carried in a large, heavy object wrapped in matting...

"A grand piano," thought Liza, and her heart started to beat faster.

She had not heard anyone play the piano for a long time, and she loved piano playing so much. In their dacha they did not have a single musical instrument. She and Grokholsky were only musicians in their hearts—no more.

After the grand piano came a lot of crates and bundles on which the word "Fragile" was written.

These crates contained mirrors and crockery. An expensive, shining carriage was brought through the gates plus two white horses which looked like swans.

"My God! What wealth!" Liza thought, remembering the little old pony bought for one hundred roubles by Grokholsky, who liked neither riding nor horses. Compared to these swan-like horses, her pony reminded her of a bedbug. Grokholsky, who was scared of going too fast, had on purpose bought Liza an inferior horse.

"What wealth!" Liza thought and whispered, as she watched the noisy delivery men.

The sun had disappeared behind the kurgans, the air had begun to lose its limpidity and dryness, but furniture was still being brought in. Finally it became so dark that Grokholsky stopped reading the newspapers, but Liza kept on watching.

"Shall we light the lamp?" Grokholsky asked, worried that a fly would fall into his milk and he would swallow it in the darkness. "Liza! Shall we light the lamp? Or are we going to sit in the dark, my angel?"

Liza did not reply. She had noticed a charabanc approaching the gates of the dacha opposite... What a sweet little horse was pulling it! Medium height, small, graceful... A gentleman in a top hat was sitting in the charabanc. Ensconced on his lap, waving his arms about, was a child of about three, evidently a little boy... He was shouting with delight.

Liza suddenly cried out, got to her feet and lunged forward.

"What's the matter?" asked Grokholsky.

"Nothing... It's just... I thought..."

The tall, broad-shouldered gentleman in the top hat jumped down from the charabanc, took the little boy into his arms and ran merrily towards the glass front door, jumping up and down.

The door opened noisily, and he disappeared into the darkness of the dacha apartments.

Two lackeys ran up to the horse harnessed to the charabanc and led it deferentially through the gates. Soon lamps shone from the dacha opposite, and the clink of plates and cutlery could be heard. The gentleman in the top hat had sat down to dine and, judging by the prolonged clinking of dishes, he ate for a long time. It seemed to Liza that she could smell cabbage soup with chicken and roast duck. After supper, a cacophony of sounds from the grand piano wafted over from the dacha. The gentleman in the top hat had probably wanted to amuse the child with something and had allowed him to have a tinkle.

Grokholsky walked over to Liza and put an arm round her waist.

"What wonderful weather!" he said. "What air! Can you feel it? I'm very happy Liza... very happy. My happiness is so great that I fear it will collapse. Great things often collapse... You know, Liza? In spite of my happiness, I am still not completely... at peace. I am still tormented by one haunting thought. It torments me terribly. It gives me no peace, day or night..."

"What thought?"

"What thought? A terrible one, my darling. I am tormented by the thought of... your husband. I have kept quiet about it till now, for fear of disturbing your peace of mind. But I can no longer remain silent... Where is he? How is he? Where has he gone with his money? It's terrible! Every night I see his face; haggard, suffering, beseeching... Well, judge for yourself, my angel! We stole his happiness! We destroyed it, crushed it! We built our happiness on the ruins of his... Can the money which he accepted so good-naturedly really replace you? He was very much in love with you, wasn't he?"

"Very much so!"

"So, you see! He's either become a drunkard by now, or... I fear for him! Oh, how I fear for him! Shall we write to him? We must comfort him... A kind word, you know..."

Grokholsky signed deeply, shook his head, and sank into his armchair, worn out by his heavy thoughts. Resting his head on his fists, he began to think. Judging from the look on his face, his thoughts were painful...

"I'm going to bed," said Liza. "It's time..."

Liza went to her room, undressed and dived under the covers. She went to bed at ten and got up at ten. She loved being a sybarite...

Morpheus soon took her into his embrace. All night long she had the most captivating dreams... She dreamed whole novels, stories, Arabian fairy tales... And the hero of all these dreams was... the gentleman in the top hat who had made her cry out that evening.

The gentleman in the top hat was taking her away from Grokholsky, singing, beating her and Grokholsky, flogging the little boy under the window, declaring his love for her and taking her for drives in his charabanc. Oh, dreams! One can sometimes live ten happy years, if not more, in the space of one night, lying down with one's eyes closed... That night Liza lived very intensely and very happily, even despite the beating...

Waking at some point after seven o'clock, she threw on a dress, quickly arranged her hair and ran out onto the veranda without even putting on her pointed Tatar slippers. Shielding her eyes from the sun with one hand while with the other holding up her dress, which was slipping down, she looked over to the dacha opposite... Her face lit up.

There was no doubt about it. It was him.

A table stood beneath the veranda of the dacha opposite, in front of the glass door. A tea service with a small silver samovar at its head shone, sparkled and gleamed on the table. Sitting at the table was Ivan Petrovich. He had a silver glass holder in his hand and was drinking tea. He was drinking with great relish, as was clear from the slurping sound that reached Liza's ears. He was wearing a brown dressing gown, embroidered with black flowers. Its huge tassels reached all the way to the ground. It was the first time Liza had seen her husband in a dressing gown, let alone such an expensive one... Mishutka was sitting on one of his knees, making it difficult for him to drink his tea. He was bouncing up and down, trying to grab his papa by his glossy lip. After every three or four gulps, Papa would lean over to his son and kiss the crown of his head. A grey cat wound itself around one of the table legs with its tail raised high and expressed its desire to eat in plaintive mews.

Liza hid behind the door curtain and drank in the sight of her former family. Her face shone with joy...

"Michel!" she whispered. "Misha! You're here, Misha! My little one! And look how much he loves Vanya! Good gracious!"

And Liza burst out laughing when little Misha stirred his father's tea for him.

"And how Vanya loves Misha! My darlings!"

Liza's heart was throbbing, and she felt dizzy with joy and happiness. She sank into an armchair and continued to watch them.

"How did they come to be here?" she wondered, blowing kisses to Misha. "Who suggested they come here? Good gracious! And does all that wealth really belong to them? Do those swan-like horses which were led through the gate yesterday really belong to Ivan Petrovich? Ah!"

After drinking his tea, Ivan Petrovich went back into the house. Ten minutes later he appeared on the porch and... flabbergasted Liza. The youth who had only stopped answering to Vanka or Vanyushka seven years ago, and was ready to bust someone's jaw and turn the whole house upside down over twenty kopecks, was now devilishly well-dressed. He was wearing a wide-brimmed straw hat, marvellous shiny high boots, and a piqué waistcoat... A thousand suns, big and small, sparkled on charms attached to his watch chain. In his right hand he held gloves and a cane, with great panache...

But how much haughtiness and ambition there was in his heavily built figure when he ordered the lackey to have the horse brought to the door with a graceful wave of his arm!

He seated himself in the charabanc with an air of importance, and ordered the servants standing there to hand him Mishutka and the fishing rods they were holding. After sitting Mishutka down beside him and putting his left arm round him, he tugged on the reins and set off.

"Giddyup!" Mishutka shouted.

Without noticing what she was doing, Liza waved her handkerchief after them. Had she looked in a mirror, she would have seen her little red face both laughing and crying at the same time. It pained her that she was not beside her jubilant Mishutka, and that for some reason she could not immediately smother him in kisses.

For some reason!.. To hell with all these delicate sentiments!

"Grisha! Grisha!" Liza cried, after running into the bedroom to wake Grokholsky. "Wake up! They're here! Darling!"

"Who's here?" Grokholsky asked as he woke up.

"Our... Vanya and Misha... They're here! In the dacha opposite. I was looking, and there they were... They were drinking tea... And Misha too... What a little angel our Misha has become, if only you had seen him! Heavens above!"

"Who? What are you... Who's here? Where?"

"Vanya and Misha... I was looking at the dacha opposite, and there they were, drinking tea. Misha already knows how to drink tea by himself... Did you notice that someone was moving in yesterday? It was them!"

Grokholsky frowned, rubbed his forehead and turned pale.

"He's here? Your husband?" he asked.

"Well, yes..."

"Why?"

"To stay here, probably... They don't know that we're here. Had they known, they would have been looking at our dacha, but they were drinking tea and... weren't paying any attention to this place..."

"Where is he now? Speak clearly, for God's sake! Agh! Well, where is he?"

"He has gone fishing with Misha... In a charabanc. Did you see the horses yesterday? Those are their horses... Vanya's... Vanya uses them. You know what, Grisha? Let's invite Misha over... Shall we? He's such a good-looking little boy! So adorable!"

Grokholsky became pensive, but Liza went on talking and talking...

"What an unexpected encounter," said Grokholsky after a long and, as usual, painful reflection. "Well, who would have thought that we would meet here? Well... fine... so be it... Fate has ordained it. I can imagine how awkward he'll feel when he meets us!"

"Can we invite Misha over?"

"Misha, yes... It would just be awkward to meet him... What am I going talk to him about? What? It would be awkward for him, and awkward for me... We shouldn't meet. We'll communicate, if need be, via the servants... Lizochka, I have an awful headache... My arms and legs... Everything aches. Is my head hot?"

Liza felt his forehead; it was hot.

"All night I had terrible dreams... I'm not going to get up today, I'm going to lie in... I must take some quinine. Send me up some tea, my dear..."

Grokholsky took some quinine and lay in bed all day. He drank warm water, groaned, had his sheets changed, whimpered, and made life a misery for all those who surrounded him. He was unbearable when he fancied that he had caught a cold. Time and again Liza had to break off her engrossing observations and run from the veranda to his room. At dinner time she had to put mustard plasters on his back. How boring all this would have been, my reader, had there been no dacha opposite at my heroine's service. Liza gazed at this dacha all day long, and was over the moon with happiness.

Ivan Petrovich and Mishutka had breakfast at ten o'clock after returning from fishing. At two o'clock they had lunch, and at four they went somewhere in their carriage. The white horses carried them off at the speed of light. Guests came to visit them at seven o'clock, all of them men. They played cards at two tables on the veranda right up to midnight. One of the men played the piano beautifully. The guests played cards, drank, ate and laughed. Ivan Petrovich, roaring with laughter, told them an Armenian anecdote, and spoke so loudly so that all the dachas heard it too. It was great fun! And Mishutka stayed up with them until midnight.

"Misha's happy, he is not crying," Liza thought to herself, "that means he doesn't remember his mama. He must have forgotten me!"

And Liza's heart sank. She cried all night. She was tortured by small pangs of conscience, annoyance, sorrow, and a passionate desire to talk to Mishutka, and kiss him... In the morning she woke with a headache and swollen eyes. Grokholsky thought her tears were on his account.

"Don't cry, my dear!" he said to her. "I am already better today... My chest aches a little, but it's nothing."

Breakfast was in progress at the dacha opposite while they were drinking tea. Ivan Petrovich had his eyes fixed on his plate, and saw nothing but his piece of goose, which was dripping fat.

"I am very pleased," Grokholsky whispered with a sideways glance at Bugrov. "Very pleased he finds life so tolerable! May this pleasant environment at least allay his grief. Cover yourself up, Liza! They'll see us... I don't want to talk to him now... God be with him! Why disturb his peace of mind?"

Lunch, however, was not so peaceful... At lunchtime occurred that very same "awkward situation" which Grokholsky had been so afraid of. When partridges were served, Grokholsky's favourite dish, Liza was suddenly overcome by embarrassment, and Grokholsky began to wipe his face with his napkin. They caught sight of Bugrov on the veranda of the dacha opposite. He was standing with his arms resting on the balustrade, staring straight at them, his eyes popping out of his head.

"Go indoors, Liza... Go indoors..." whispered Grokholsky. "I told you we should have lunch indoors! Really, you are..."

Bugrov stared and stared, and suddenly let out a shout. Grokholsky looked at him and saw a very surprised face...

"Is that you?!" Ivan Petrovich shouted. "You?! You're here too? Hello!"

Grokholsky ran his fingers from one shoulder to the other. He wished to indicate that his chest was weak, so yelling at such a distance was impossible. Liza's heart was beating loudly and her eyes went blurry... Bugrov disappeared from his veranda, ran across the road and within a few seconds, was already standing below the veranda where Grokholsky and Liza were having lunch. So much for the partridges!

"Hello," he said, blushing, and thrusting his big hands into his pockets. "So you're here too?"

"Yes, we're here too."

"How come you're here?"

"And what about you?"

"Me? That's a long story! A whole saga, old chap! But don't worry, do go on eating! I have been living, you know, ever since we... in Oryol province... I rented a little estate. An excellent estate! Do go ahead and eat! I lived there from the very end of May, but now I have given it up... It was cold there, you see, and the doctor advised me to go to the Crimea..."

"Are you suffering from some sort of illness?" asked Grokholsky.

"Yes... it's as if... something is rumbling in here..."

And at the word "here," Ivan Petrovich ran his hand from his neck down to the middle of his abdomen.

"So you're here too... So... What a pleasant surprise. Have you been here long?"

"Since June."

"And what about you, Liza? Are you well?"

"I'm fine," said Liza, and she felt embarrassed.

"I suppose you're missing Mishutka? Yes? He's here with me... I'll send him over to see you with Nikifor right away... What a pleasant surprise! Well, goodbye! I have to go now... Yesterday I met Prince Ter–Gaymazov... a delightful man, even though he's an Armenian! And today he's having a croquet match... We're going to play croquet... Goodbye! The horse is already at the door..."

Ivan Petrovich turned on the spot, shook his head, waved "adieu," and ran back to his dacha.

"Poor chap!" Grokholsky said, following him with his eyes and sighing deeply.

"Why 'poor'?" Liza asked.

"Seeing you and not having the right to call you his!"

"You fool!" Liza dared to think to herself. "Spineless creature!"

Before evening fell, Liza was hugging and kissing Mishutka, who had been brought over by Nikifor. At first, Mishutka burst into tears, but when he was offered some cornelian cherry jam, he smiled amiably.

Grokholsky and Liza did not see Bugrov for three days. He was busy somewhere during the day, and only came home at night. On the fourth day he came to call again at lunch time... He walked in, shook hands with both of them and sat down. His face was serious...

"There is something I want to discuss with you," he said. "Read this!"

And he handed Grokholsky a letter.

"Read it! Read it aloud!"

Grokholsky read aloud the following:

"My dear, beloved, unforgettable son Ivan! I have received your respectful and loving letter in which you invite your aged father to the luxuriant and serene Crimea to breathe in its beneficial air and behold *terra incognita*. To this letter of yours I would like to reply that I will come to see you when I take my vacation, but just for a short visit. My fellow priest, Father Gerasim, is a frail and feeble man, and cannot manage alone for long. I am very touched that you have not forgotten your parents, your father and your mother... And that you bestow affection on your father, and remember your mother in your prayers; as the Lord had ordained. Meet me in Feodosia. What sort of a town is Feodosia? What kind of place is it? It will be very nice to see it. Your godmother, who held you in her arms at the baptismal font, is called Feodosia. You write that God helped you win two hundred thousand roubles. I find that most impressive. But I do not approve of you leaving the service, having risen to a prominent rank. Even a rich man should be in service. I bless you always, now and forever. Ilya and Seryozhka Andronov send their greetings to you. Perhaps you could send them ten roubles each? They live in poverty!

Your loving father, Father Pyotr Bugrov."

Grokholsky read this letter aloud, then looked questioningly at Bugrov—as did Liza.

"You see, the thing is..." Ivan Petrovich began with a stammer. "While he is here, I would ask you, Liza, to stay out of his sight and hide. I have written to him and told him that you are sick and have gone to the Caucasus for treatment. If you were to bump into him... you know yourself... It would be awkward... Um..."

"All right," said Liza.

"We can do that," thought Grokholsky. "If he has made sacrifices, why shouldn't we?"

"Please... Otherwise, if he were to catch sight of you, there would be trouble... He is very straitlaced. He would put an anathema on me. Liza, just make sure you don't leave your room... He won't stay here long. Don't worry..."

It was not long before Father Pyotr arrived. One fine morning Ivan Petrovich ran in and hissed in a conspiratorial tone:

"He's arrived! He's asleep now! So please!"

And Liza was stuck within four walls. She did not dare to go into the courtyard, or on to the veranda. She could see the sky only from behind the curtains... Unfortunately for her, Ivan Petrovich's papa spent all his time in the open air, and even slept on the veranda. A diminutive little priest in a brown cassock and tall hat with a raised brim, Father Pyotr would usually stroll slowly round the dachas and peer with curiosity at this "terra incognita" through his grandfathers' spectacles. He would be accompanied by Ivan Petrovich with his Order of St. Stanislav* in his buttonhole. Usually he did not wear his medals, but Ivan Petrovich liked to put on airs in front of his family. When in the company of his family, he always wore his Stanislav.

Liza was dying of boredom. Grokholsky was suffering too. He had to go for walks alone, without his companion. He was close to tears but... he had to submit to fate. To cap it all, every morning Bugrov would come round and provide an unnecessary bulletin in hissed tones about the diminutive Father Pyotr's health. They became fed up with these bulletins.

"He slept well last night!" Bugrov would inform them. "Yesterday he was annoyed that I had no pickled cucumbers... He has become very fond of Mishutka. He keeps patting him on the head..."

Finally, two weeks later, the diminutive Father Pyotr walked round the dachas for the last time and, to Grokholsky's delight, departed. He had enjoyed his strolls and left extremely contented... Grokholsky and Liza once again picked up their old lifestyle. Grokholsky again thanked his lucky stars... But his happiness did not last long... A new misfortune presented itself which was even worse than Father Pyotr.

Ivan Petrovich got into the habit of coming to see them every day. Ivan Petrovich was a nice fellow, but to be honest, he was very heavy-going. He would arrive in the middle of dinner, eat with them, and stay for a very long time. This they could have put up with. But to accompany his dinner they had to buy him vodka, which Grokholsky could not stand. Ivan Petrovich would drink about five shots of the stuff and talk non-stop throughout the meal. This too they could have put up with... But he would sit around until two in the morning and would not let them go to bed... And worst of all, he took the liberty of saying things that he should have kept quiet about... At two o'clock, when he had drunk his fill of vodka and champagne, he would take Mishutka in his arms and, sobbing, say to him in front of Grokholsky and Liza:

"My son! Mikhail! What am I? Who am I? I'm... a scoundrel! I sold your mother! I sold her for thirty pieces of silver... May the Lord punish me! Mikhail Ivanovich! My little piglet! Where is your mother? Whoosh! She's gone! Sold into slavery! Well... that means I'm a scoundrel..."

These tears and words wrenched at Grokholsky's heart. He would look sheepishly at Liza's pale face and wring his hands.

"Go home and sleep, Ivan Petrovich!" he would say timidly.

"I will... Let's go, Mishutka! May the Lord judge us! I cannot think of sleep when I know that my wife is a slave... But Grokholsky is not guilty... It was my asset, his money... To each, his own..."

During the day, Grokholsky found Ivan Petrovich's company no less unbearable. To Grokholsky's great dismay, Ivan Petrovich would not leave Liza's side. He would go fishing with her, tell her jokes, and go for walks with her. And once, he even took advantage of Grokholsky having a cold and carried her off in his carriage, God knows where, until late into the night.

"This is outrageous! Inhumane!" thought Grokholsky, biting his lip.

Grokholsky liked to kiss Liza all the time. He could not live without these sugary kisses but kissing in Ivan Petrovich's presence was somewhat awkward... Talk about torment! The poor fellow felt quite lonely... But fate soon took pity on him... Ivan Petrovich suddenly disappeared somewhere for a whole week. Some guests arrived and dragged him off with them. And they took Mishutka too.

One fine morning a beaming Grokholsky returned to the dacha from his walk in a most cheerful frame of mind.

"He has come back," he said to Liza, rubbing his hands. "I'm very happy he's back... Ha ha ha!"

"Why are you laughing?"

"There are women with him..."

"What women?"

"I don't know... It's good he's got himself some women... Excellent, even... He's still so young, so spritely... Come over here! Take a look..."

Grokholsky took Liza out on to the veranda and pointed at the dacha opposite. They both almost split their sides laughing. It was hilarious. Ivan Petrovich was standing on the veranda and smiling. Two dark-haired ladies and Mishutka were standing below the veranda. The ladies were discussing something in French in loud voices and laughing.

"They're French," said Grokholsky. "The one closest to us is reasonably pretty. They're ladies of easy virtue, but that doesn't matter... There are good women even among those kinds... But, my goodness... how brazen they are!"

What was funny that Ivan Petrovich had lent over the balustrade, lowered his long arms, seized the shoulders of one of the French women, lifted her into the air, and deposited her, giggling, on the veranda.

Having lifted both ladies on to the veranda, he lifted up Mishutka too. The ladies ran back to where they had started from and the lifting began all over again...

"He's certainly got strong muscles!" muttered Grokholsky as he watched the scene.

The lifting was repeated half a dozen times. The ladies were so good-natured that they were not in the least embarrassed when, during the lifting, a gusty breeze did what it liked with their billowing skirts. Grokholsky bashfully lowered his eyes when the ladies flipped their legs over the balustrade as they reached the veranda. But Liza watched and laughed! It was all the same to her! The miscreants were not the men, whom, as a woman, she might have found embarrassing, but the ladies!

That evening, Ivan Petrovich came flying into their dacha and declared in embarrassment that he was now a family man...

"Don't think that they are just anybody," he said. "It's true, they are French, they shout all the time, drink wine... But we all know that! The French are brought up to be like that! It cannot be helped... The prince let me have them..." Ivan Petrovich added, "for next to nothing... Take them, take them... I must introduce you to the prince some time. A man of education! He is forever writing and writing... And do you know what their names are? One is called Fanny; the other Isabella... That's Europe for you! Ha ha ha... The West! Goodbye!"

Ivan Petrovich left Grokholsky and Liza in peace and attached himself to his ladies. All day long the sounds of talking and laughter and the clatter of cutlery could be heard from his dacha... The lights were on until late at night... Grokholsky began to unwind... Finally, after a long and painful interval, he felt happy and at peace once more. Ivan Petrovich, even with his two ladies, did not experience such happiness as he had with one... But—alas! Fate has no heart. It plays with the Grokholskys, Lizas, Ivans, and Mishutkas of this world as if they are pawns... Grokholsky was about to lose his peace of mind again...

After waking up late one day (a week and a half later), he went out on to the veranda and saw a scene that shocked and outraged him and made him feel highly indignant. Under the veranda of the dacha opposite stood the French ladies, and between them was... Liza. She was chatting, casting sidelong glances at her own dacha as though to check whether that tyrant—that despot— had woken up. (Or at least this was how Grokholsky interpreted these glances). Standing on the veranda with his sleeves rolled up, Ivan Petrovich lifted Isabella, then Fanny and then... Liza. While he was lifting Liza, it seemed to Grokholsky that he was pressing her to his chest... Liza also flipped one leg over the balustrade... Oh, these women! They are all enigmas, each and every one of them!

When Liza came back home after visiting her husband and tiptoed into the bedroom as though nothing had happened, Grokholsky was lying there, pale, and with pink blotches on his cheeks, in the pose of an utterly exhausted man, groaning.

On seeing Liza, he jumped up from the bed and began pacing round the room.

"So that's what you're like?" he shrieked in a high tenor voice. "So that's what you're like? Thank you very much! This is outrageous, madam! Above all else, it is immoral! You must understand that!"

Liza turned pale and of course burst into tears. Women usually make a scene and cry when they feel they are in the right, but when they know they are guilty, they only cry.

"Putting yourself on the same level as those loose women?! It's... it's... it's... it's beneath all contempt! Do you know who they are? They are harlots! Courtesans! And you, an honourable woman, descended to their level?! And as for him... him! What does he want? What else does he want from me? I don't understand! I have given him half my fortune, even more! You know that! I have given him what I don't have... Almost everything... But he! I have tolerated your familiarity with him, to which he has no right. I have put up with your walks, your kisses after lunch... I have put up with everything, but this I will not... It's either me or him! He's got to leave, or else I will! I can't live like this anymore... no! You know that very well... It's either me or him... Enough! My patience is exhausted... I've suffered so much already, as it is... I'll go and talk to him right away... This very minute! What does he think he is doing? Just who does he think he is? No, sir... He has no reason to think so highly of himself."

Grokholsky uttered many more brave and stinging things, but he did not go "right away": he lacked the courage and felt ashamed. He went over to Ivan Petrovich three days later...

His mouth fell open when he entered his apartments. The luxury and wealth with which Bugrov had surrounded himself astonished him. The velvet wallpaper, the exorbitantly expensive chairs... He felt nervous even about taking a step forward. Grokholsky had come across a lot of rich people in his life, but he had never witnessed such wanton luxury. And what an unholy mess it was that he encountered when with inexplicable trepidation he entered the drawing room! Plates with pieces of bread on them littered the grand piano; there was a glass standing on a chair; and under the table was a basket with some sordid rags. Nutshells were scattered on the windowsills... Bugrov himself was not particularly presentable when Grokholsky entered... Pink-faced, his hair uncombed and in a state of undress, he was pacing about the room and talking to himself... He was clearly very worried about something. Mishutka was sitting on a sofa right there in the drawing room, shrieking his head off.

"It's awful, Grigory Vasilich!" Bugrov said when he saw Grokholsky. "Such a mess... such a mess... Please sit down! You'll have to excuse me, I'm in my birthday suit... Don't take any notice... Such a terrible mess! I don't understand how people can live here? I really don't! The servants don't obey orders, the climate is awful, everything is so expensive... Be quiet!" he suddenly shouted as he stopped in front of Mishutka. "Be quiet, I told you! You little brute, why won't you stop crying?"

And Bugrov pulled Mishutka hard by the ear.

"Ivan Petrovich, this is appalling!" said Grokholsky in an emotional voice. "How can you hit such a young boy? Really, what kind of a person..."

"He had better stop blubbering... Be quiet! Or I'll flog you!"

"Misha, don't cry poppet... Daddy won't hurt you anymore. Don't beat him, Ivan Petrovich! After all, he's still a child... Now, now... Would you like a little horse? I'll send you one... Really... how cruel you are..."

Grokholsky paused for a moment, then asked:

"And how are your ladies doing, Ivan Petrovich?"

"They aren't. I sent them packing... I might have kept them on a bit longer, but it's awkward: the boy is growing up... I don't want to set him a bad example... Had I been alone, well, that would have been a different matter. But what was the point in me keeping them? Pfff... It was a farce! I spoke to them in Russian; they answered me in French... They didn't understand a word I said, it was like talking to a brick wall."

"I have come to you for a reason, Ivan Petrovich, to have a chat... Hm... It's nothing very important... just a quick word... Actually, I have a request to make of you."

"What's that?"

"Ivan Petrovich, might you consider... going away? We are very glad that you are here, it is very pleasant for us—but, you know, it's uncomfortable... I'm sure you understand. It's sort of awkward... Undefined relationships, a certain ongoing unease in regard to each other... We must part ways... It's essential, actually... Please excuse me, but... you, yourself, of course, understand... you know that in such cases living at close quarters leads to... certain thoughts... Or rather, not so much thoughts, as to a certain awkward feeling."

"Yes... that is true. I have thought as much myself. All right, I'll go."

"We would be very grateful. Believe me, Ivan Petrovich, we'll retain the most flattering memory of you! The sacrifice that you..."

"Fine... But what will I do with all these things? Listen, why don't you buy this furniture from me! Would you like to? It's not expensive... About eight thousand... or ten... for the furniture, the carriage, and the grand piano..."

"All right... I'll give you ten..."

"Well, that's great! I'll leave tomorrow... I'll go to Moscow. It's impossible to live here! Everything is expensive! Terribly expensive! Money just melts away... you can't take a step without spending a thousand... I can't live like that... I have a family... Well, thank God you're buying my furniture. And that there's more money on the way, otherwise I'd be totally bankrupt..."

Grokholsky stood up, bid farewell to Bugrov and went home jubilant. That evening, he sent him ten thousand.

By early morning of the next day, Bugrov and Mishutka were already in Feodosia.

III

Several months passed. Spring arrived.

With spring came those clear, bright days, when life seems less hateful and dull, and the earth is at its most noble... There was a warmth that came in from the sea and the land... The earth was covered in new grass, and the new leaves on the trees turned green. Nature was reborn and appeared in new attire...

One would have thought that new hopes and desires would begin to stir in a person when everything in nature is renewed, young and fresh... But it is difficult for people to be reborn.

Grokholsky was still living in the same dacha... His hopes and desires, small and undemanding, were still focused on the same Liza, on her alone and nothing else! As before, he could not take his eyes off her, and indulged himself with the thought: "How happy I am!" The poor fellow actually did feel awfully happy. As before, Liza sat on the veranda, gazing dumbly and drearily at the dacha opposite and the trees round it, through which the blue sea could be seen... As before, she was mostly silent, but also cried often, and from time to time put mustard plasters on Grokholsky. However, she may be congratulated on a new acquisition. There was a worm growing within her. This worm was longing... She was struck with a deep longing for her son, for her past life and for merriment. Her past life had not been particularly merry, but it was still merrier than her present one... While living with her husband, she had occasionally gone to the theatre, to the Assembly, to visit acquaintances. But here, with Grokholsky? It was empty and quiet... There was one person there, but he was like a docile old grandfather with his ailments and incessant saccharine kisses, his eyes constantly misting up with happiness. It was boring! There was no Mikhey Sergeyich, who liked to dance the mazurka with her here, no Spiridon Nikolayich, the son of the editor of the regional newspaper. Spiridon Nikolayich sang well and would recite poetry. There was no table with appetisers, no guests, no Gerasimovna, the old nanny, who would constantly grumble that she was eating a lot of jam. There was no one here at all! She might as well lie down and die of melancholy. Grokholsky rejoiced in his solitude, but... he rejoiced in vain. All too soon he would pay for his selfishness. In early May, when it seemed that the air itself had fallen in love and was drunk with happiness, Grokholsky lost everything: both the woman he loved and...

Bugrov came to the Crimea this year too. He did not rent the dacha opposite but kept moving with Mishutka from one Crimean town to another. He drank, ate, slept and played cards in these towns. He had lost all desire for fishing, hunting, and those French women who, just between you and me, had stolen a few things from him. He had lost weight, had stopped beaming and smiling broadly, and now dressed in sailcloth. Every now and again Ivan Petrovich would visit Grokholsky's dacha. He would bring Liza jam, confectionery and fruit, and seemed to be trying to dispel her boredom. Grokholsky was not worried by these visits, especially as they were infrequent, short, and were evidently for the sake of Mishutka, who could not be deprived of the right to see his mother without good reason. Bugrov would arrive, lay out his presents, say a few words, and depart... And he would address those few words not to Liza, but to Grokholsky... With Liza he was totally silent. And Grokholsky was at peace... But there is a Russian proverb that Grokholsky would have done well to remember: "Fear not the dog that barks; fear the dog that is silent..." It is a mean proverb, but in real life it is sometimes highly relevant.

One day, walking in the local park, Grokholsky heard two voices talking. One was a man's voice and the other—a woman's. The first belonged to Bugrov, the second to Liza. Grokholsky listened to the voices and, pale as death, walked quietly towards them. He stopped behind a lilac bush and began to watch and listen. His legs and arms turned cold. His forehead broke out into a cold sweat. He had to grab hold of several lilac branches to avoid staggering and falling. It was all over!

Bugrov was holding Liza by the waist and saying to her:

"My dearest! Well, what shall we do? It must mean this was God's will... I am a scoundrel... I sold you. I was lured by Herod's wealth, a plague be upon him... And what good did this wealth bring? Nothing but anxiety and bragging! Neither peace, nor happiness, nor status... You're stuck like a lump in the same place, and have not taken one step forward... Have you heard? Andryushka Markuzin has been appointed Head Clerk... Andryushka, that fool!

And I'm stuck here... Good Lord! I have lost you; I have lost my happiness. I am a scoundrel! A rogue! You think I'll have a good time on Judgement Day?"

"Let's leave this place, Vanya!" cried Liza. "I'm bored... I'm dying of misery."

"We can't... I took his money."

"Well, give it back!"

"I would gladly pay it back, but alas... as they say: that horse has bolted! I have spent it all! We will have to resign ourselves, my dear... God is punishing us; me for my greed and you for your frivolity... So what? We will suffer torment... It will be easier in the next world."

And in a rush of religious feeling, Bugrov raised his eyes to heaven.

"But I can't live here! I'm bored!"

"What can we do? Do you think I am not bored? I'm bored too, don't forget that. Do you think that I have fun without you? I'm pining away, withering to nothing! And I've got a pain in my chest! You're my lawful wife, my flesh and blood... we are one flesh... Live and endure! Well, and I... will come and visit you..."

Leaning over towards Liza, Bugrov whispered, but so loudly that it could be heard several yards away:

"I'll come to you at night too, Lizanka... Don't worry... I'm in Feodosia, not far away... I'll live here, near you, until I have spent everything... And it won't be long before I have spent it all, down to the very last kopeck! Ahh! What kind of life is this? Boredom, illness... my whole chest aches, and my stomach aches..."

Bugrov fell silent. It was Liza's turn... My God, how cruel that woman is! She began to weep and complain, enumerating all her lover's shortcomings, and her torments... Listening to her, Grokholsky felt like a robber, a villain, a destroyer...

"He has driven me insane!" Liza concluded...

After kissing Liza goodbye and going through the gates of the park, Bugrov bumped into Grokholsky, who was standing at the gates waiting for him.

"Ivan Petrovich!" Grokholsky said in the tone of a dying man. "I heard and saw everything... It's dishonourable on your part, but I don't blame you... you love her too... But you must understand that she is mine! Mine! I can't live without her! How can you not understand? Well, let's suppose let's assume you do love her, and are suffering, but didn't I pay you for at least a part of your suffering? Go away, for God's sake! Leave this place forever. I beg you! Otherwise, you will kill me..."

"I have nowhere to go," Bugrov said indistinctly...

"Hmm... you've already spent everything... You get carried away... Well, all right... Go off to my estate in Chernigov province... Would you like to? I'll give it to you... It's a small estate, but a good one... I promise, it's a good one!"

Bugrov smiled broadly. He suddenly felt as if he were in seventh heaven.

"I am giving it to you... I will write to my steward this very day and send him my power of attorney for the deed of purchase. You can tell everyone that you bought it... Now leave! I beg you!"

"All right... I will go. I understand."

"Let's go to a notary... at once," said the now more cheerful Grokholsky, and he went to order the horses to be harnessed.

The next day, in the evening, when Liza was sitting on the bench where her rendezvous with Ivan Petrovich usually took place, Grokholsky quietly approached her. He sat down beside her and took her hand.

"Are you bored, Lizochka?" he said after a short silence. "Are you bored? Then why don't we go out somewhere? Why do we always sit at home? We should go out and enjoy ourselves, make new acquaintances... We should, shouldn't we?"

"I don't want anything," said the pale and thin Liza as she looked at the path Bugrov would walk up on his way to meet her.

Grokholsky pondered. He knew who she was waiting for, and who she wanted.

"Let's go, Liza, let's go home," he said. "It's damp here..."

"You go... I'll come in a minute."

Grokholsky thought once again.

"Are you waiting for *him*?" he asked and made a face as if a pair of red-hot pincers had gripped his heart.

"Yes... I want to give him the socks for Misha..."

"He's not coming."

"How do you know?"

"He's left..."

Liza's eyes widened...

"He's left... Gone to Chernigov province. I have given him my estate..."

Liza turned terribly pale and gripped Grokholsky by the shoulder so as not to fall.

"I saw him on to the boat... At three o'clock..."

Liza suddenly clutched her head, shuddered, and fell on to the bench, shaking all over.

"Vanya!" she wailed. "Vanya! I am coming too, Vanya!.. My darling!"

She had a fit of hysterics...

And from that evening right up until July, two shadows were to be seen in the park in which holidaymakers strolled. The shadows wandered about the park from morning till night and depressed the other holidaymakers. Grokholsky's shadow tenaciously followed in the footsteps of Liza's shadow. I call them shadows, because both of them had lost their previous appearance.

They had become thin, pale and shrivelled, and resembled shadows more than living people... Both languished like the flea in that classic joke about the Jew selling flea powder.

In early July, Liza ran away from Grokholsky, leaving him a note in which she wrote that she was going to see "her son" for a while... For a while! She ran away at night, when Grokholsky was asleep...

After reading her note, Grokholsky wandered around the dacha like a madman for a whole week; he neither ate nor slept. In August, he suffered from another bout of tick fever, and in September he went abroad. While he was abroad he began to drink, hoping to find solace in wine and debauchery. He squandered his whole fortune, but he did not succeed, poor fellow, in expelling the image of the beloved woman with the cat-like face out of his mind... People do not die of happiness, nor do they die of unhappiness. Grokholsky's hair went grey, but he did not die. And he is alive to this day... Having returned from abroad, he went to take a "quick peek" at Liza. Bugrov met him with open arms and allowed him to be his guest for an indefinite time. And he is still living as Bugrov's guest...

This year, I had to travel through Grokholevka, Bugrov's estate. I found the proprietors at dinner... Ivan Petrovich was terribly glad to see me and invited me to join them. He had put on weight and become a little flabby. His face glowed with wellbeing, as it had before, and was shiny and pink. He was not yet bald. Liza had also gained weight. Plumpness did not suit her. Her face had begun to lose its cat-like look and—alas!—was becoming more seal-like. Her cheeks had puffed out upwards, outwards, and at the sides. The Bugrovs lived in fine style. They had plenty of everything. The house was stuffed with servants and food...

When we finished dinner, a conversation ensued. Forgetting that Liza was not a musician, I asked her to play something on the piano.

"She doesn't play!" Bugrov said. "My Liza is not the musician... Hey! Who's there? Ivan! Tell Grigory Vasilich to come here! What's he up to there?" and turning to me, Bugrov added, "here comes our musician... He plays the guitar. We're keeping the grand piano for Mishutka, he's having lessons..."

About five minutes later, Grokholsky came in, looking sleepy, unkempt and unshaven. He came in, bowed to me and sat down a little way away.

"No one goes to bed this early!" Bugrov said to him. "What's it all about, old fellow? You're always asleep, always asleep... Sluggard! Now, play us something cheerful..."

Grokholsky tuned the guitar, plucked the strings, and began to sing:

"Yesterday I waited for my dear friend..."

I listened to his singing, looked at Bugrov's well-fed face and thought: "What a foul mug!" I felt like crying... After finishing his song, Grokholsky bowed to us and left...

"What am I to do with him?" Bugrov turned to me after Grokholsky had left the room. "He's such a nuisance! During the day, he's always thinking... and at night he moans. He moans and groans in his sleep... It's some kind of illness... What I am to do with him, I haven't the faintest idea! We can't sleep... I'm afraid he'll lose his mind. People will think that we are treating him badly here... but what's bad about it? He eats with us, drinks with us... The only thing we don't give him is money... For if we did, he would spend it all on drink or fritter it away... Another load on my mind! Lord, forgive me, a sinner!"

They invited me to spend the night. When I woke up the next morning, Bugrov was scolding somebody in the adjoining room:

"Give a fool rope enough and he will hang himself! Who paints oars green? Think, you knucklehead! Use your brain! Why are you silent?"

"I... I... made a mistake..." a hoarse tenor voice apologised...

The voice was Grokholsky's...

Grokholsky accompanied me to the station...

"He is a despot, a tyrant," he whispered to me the whole way. "He is an honourable man, but a tyrant! He is immature in both heart and mind... He torments me! If it were not for this noble woman, I would have left him a long time ago... I feel sorry for her. It's easier to suffer together."

Grokholsky sighed and continued:

"She's pregnant... Did you notice? It is actually my child... Mine... She soon acknowledged her mistake and gave herself to me again. She cannot stand him..."

"You are a doormat!" I could not refrain from saying to Grokholsky.

"Yes, I am weak-willed... All this is true. It is the way I was born. Do you know how I came into the world? My late father bullied an insignificant little clerk. He bullied him mercilessly! Poisoned his life! Well... And my mother, who is no longer with us, was tender–hearted, she was from the common folk, lower class... She pitied this little clerk and allowed him to get close to her... Well... And that's how I came into the world... From the oppressed clerk... In such circumstances, where would I get strength of character from? From where? But that's the last bell... Goodbye! Come back to visit us, but don't tell Ivan Petrovich what I said about him!"

I shook hands with Grokholsky and jumped on to the train. He bowed in the direction of my carriage then went over to the water butt. I suppose he was thirsty.

Late-Blooming Flowers

Dedicated to N. I. Korobov*

I

It was a dark autumn afternoon at the house of the princes Priklonsky.

The old princess and young Princess Marusya stood in the young prince's room, wringing their hands and pleading with him. They pleaded as only unhappy, weeping women can: invoking Christ the Lord, the family honour, and the ashes of the prince's late father.

The old princess stood motionless before her son, sobbing.

Giving free rein to her tears and entreaties, and interrupting Marusya's every word, she bombarded the prince with reproaches, and cruel, even blasphemous words, endearments and requests... A thousand times she mentioned the merchant Furov, who had initiated a claim against their promissory note, and her late husband, whose bones now were turning over in his grave, and so forth. She even mentioned Doctor Toporkov.[1]

Doctor Toporkov was a thorn in the Priklonskys' side. His father had been a serf, the late prince's valet Senka. Nikifor, his maternal uncle, still served as Prince Yegorushka's valet. And Doctor Toporkov had himself in early childhood endured many a cuff on the back of the neck for cleaning the prince's knives, forks, boots, and samovars badly. But now—was it not bizarre?—he was a brilliant young doctor, lived like a lord in an absolutely enormous house, and had his own coach and pair, as if to pique the Priklonskys, who went about on foot and spent a long time haggling whenever they hired a carriage.

"Everyone respects him," said the old princess, letting the tears flow down her cheeks; "everyone loves him; he's wealthy, handsome, received everywhere... Your former servant, Nikifor's nephew! It's shameful even to

---

1   Toporkov: an apparently carefully chosen surname suggestive of the words for "axe" (*topor*), and "crude" or "uncouth" (*topornyi*). Priklonsky, meanwhile, is a recognised noble surname whose associations are with the verb *priklonit*, meaning to "bend," "incline," or "lay" (one's head).

mention! And why? It's because he behaves well, doesn't go out carousing, and doesn't keep bad company... He works from morning to night... Whereas you? Dear Lord!"

Princess Marusya, a girl of twenty, as pretty as the heroine of an English novel, with marvellous flaxen curls and large intelligent eyes the colour of the southern sky, pleaded with her brother Yegorushka as fervently as her mother.

She talked at the same time as her mother, kissing her brother on his prickly moustache, which smelled of rancid wine, stroking him on his bald spot and on his cheeks, and clinging to him like a frightened little dog. She spoke only tender words. The young princess was incapable of saying anything remotely acrimonious. She loved her brother so much! As far as she saw it, her dissolute brother, the retired hussar, prince Yegorushka, exemplified the loftiest truth and was a paragon of virtue! She was sure, to the point of fanaticism, that this drunken ignoramus's heart would be the envy of all fairies. She saw him as a man down on his luck, whose true qualities were misunderstood and unrecognised. She forgave his drunken debauchery with near rapture. Of course she did! Yegorushka had long ago convinced her that he drank to drown his sorrows: wine and vodka were a refuge from the hopeless love that consumed his soul, and it was in the arms of loose women that he tried to banish *her* wondrous image from his hussar's mind. And what Marusya or any other woman does not consider love by far the most valid and all-forgiving excuse? What woman?

"*Georges!*" said Marusya, clinging to him and kissing his haggard, red-nosed face. "You drink from sorrow, it's true... But if so, forget your sorrow! Do all unhappy men really have to drink? Endure, take courage, and fight! Be a warrior! With a mind like yours, and such an honest, loving soul, the blows of fate can be endured! Oh! You victims of fortune are all so faint-hearted!.."

And Marusya (forgive her, reader!) recalled Rudin from Turgenev's novel and began explaining him to Yegorushka.

Prince Yegorushka lay on his bed staring at the ceiling with his red, rabbit-like eyes. There was a slight buzzing in his head and a pleasant feeling of satiety in the region of his stomach. He had just eaten dinner, and drunk a bottle of red wine, and now he was in a state of bliss puffing on a three-kopeck cigar. The most varied feelings and thoughts were swarming around his foggy brain and pathetic little soul. He pitied his weeping mother and sister, but at the same time he desperately wanted to get rid of them: they were getting in the

way of him taking a nap and having a snooze... He was angry that they dared
to lecture him, though at the same time he was tormented by small twinges
of his (probably also very small) conscience. He was dim-witted, but not to
the extent that he was unaware the Priklonskys' home really was in peril, and
partly thanks to him...

The old princess and Marusya went on pleading for a very long time. The
lamps in the drawing-room were lit, and some lady came to visit, but still they
kept on pleading. Eventually Yegorushka got bored of lying in bed unable to
sleep. He stretched, cracking his joints, and said:

"All right, I'll mend my ways!"

"Word of honour?"

"May God strike me down!"

His mother and sister took hold of him and made him swear again to God
and on his honour. Yegorushka swore to God again, and on his honour, and
appealed for lightning to strike him down on the spot if he did not give up
leading a disreputable life. The old princess made him kiss the icon. He duly
kissed the icon, and moreover crossed himself three times. In short, the most
genuine of oaths was sworn.

"We believe you!" said the old princess and Marusya, and they rushed to
embrace Yegorushka.

They believed him. How could they not believe his word of honour, desperate swearing to God, and kissing of the icon, all taken together? Besides,
where there is love, there is reckless faith. They cheered up, and both went
off to celebrate Yegorushka's restoration, beaming like the Judeans celebrating the restoration of Jerusalem. After sending their guest on her way, they
settled in a corner and began whispering about how their Yegorushka would
reform, about the new life he would begin to lead... They decided that Yegorushka would go far, that he would soon put their circumstances in order
and halt their descent into destitution—this ignominious Rubicon which all
profligates must cross. They even decided that Yegorushka was destined to
marry a beautiful heiress. He was so handsome and clever, so distinguished
that there could hardly be any woman who would dare not to fall in love with
him! The old princess concluded by recounting the biographies of ancestors
whom Yegorushka would soon emulate. Grandfather Priklonsky had been
a diplomat who knew all the European languages; their father had commanded a famous regiment, and the son would become... would become... what
would he become?

"Just wait! You'll see what he will become!" decided Marusya. "You'll see!"

After helping each other to bed, they went on talking about the wonderful future for a long time. When they fell asleep, they had the most marvellous dreams. They smiled with happiness as they slept, so wonderful were their dreams! In all likelihood, fate sent them those dreams to compensate them for all the horrors they experienced the following day. Fate is not always miserly: sometimes it also pays in advance.

Around three in the morning, just as the old princess lay dreaming about her *bébé* in the brilliant uniform of a general, and Marusya in her dream was applauding a brilliant speech her brother had given, an ordinary hired carriage drove up to the Priklonsky house. In it sat a waiter from the *Château de Fleurs*, propping up in his arms the noble body of Prince Yegorushka, stone drunk. Yegorushka was in a completely unconscious state, and was flopping about in the arms of the 'wai… ddderrrr' like a freshly slaughtered goose being taken to the kitchen. The driver jumped down from the box and rang at the front door. Nikifor and the cook came out, paid the driver and carried the drunken body up the stairs. Expressing neither surprise nor horror, old Nikifor undressed the inert body with an accustomed hand, tucked it deeply into the feather bed and covered it with a blanket. The servants did not say a single word. They were long accustomed to seeing their master as something that needed to be carried, undressed, and tucked into bed, so they experienced neither surprise nor horror. The drunken Yegorushka was the norm for them.

The time to be horrified was the following morning.

At eleven, when the old princess and Marusya were drinking coffee, Nikifor came into the dining room and reported to their highnesses that something was not quite right with Prince Yegorushka.

"Looks as if he must be dying, ma'am!" said Nikifor. "Would you take a look, ma'am?"

The faces of the old princess and Marusya turned as white a sheet. A piece of sponge cake fell out of the old princess's mouth. Marusya knocked over her cup and with both hands clutched her chest, in which her anxious heart, caught unawares, had begun to pound.

"He came back at three in the morning, and must have been a bit merry," reported Nikifor in a trembling voice. "Like as usual… But now, Lord knows why, he's tossing about and groaning…"

The old princess and Marusya clasped hold of each other and rushed to Yegorushka's bedroom.

Dishevelled, severely emaciated and his face pale green, Yegorushka was lying under a thick flannel blanket, breathing heavily, shivering and tossing about. His head and hands could not stay still for a minute and were twitching and shuddering. Groans burst out of his chest. Something small and red, evidently a drop of blood, hung from his moustache. If Marusya had leaned over his face, she would have seen a small wound on his upper lip and the absence of two teeth from his upper jaw. His entire body was hot with fever and reeked of spirits.

The old princess and Marusya fell to their knees and burst into tears.

"It's our fault he's dying!" said Marusya, clutching at her head. "We upset him with our reproaches yesterday and... he couldn't bear it! He has such a tender soul! It's our fault, *Maman*!"

Both opening their eyes wide in acknowledgement of their guilt, they clung to each other, trembling all over. This is the way people tremble and cling to each other when they see that the ceiling above them is about to collapse with a great clatter, and crush them under its weight.

The cook had the presence of mind to run for the doctor. Ivan Adolfovich, the doctor who turned up, was a small man consisting entirely of a very large bald patch, dull, piggish eyes and a pot belly. They greeted him with joy, like a long-lost father. He sniffed the air in Yegorushka's bedroom, took his pulse, heaved a deep sigh and frowned.

"Don't you worry, your highness!" he implored the old princess. "I not know, but in mine opinions, your highness, I don't find that your son is in grave, so to speak, danger... Es ist nothing!"'

To Marusya, though, he said something completely different: "I not know, princess, but in mine opinions... Everyone has his own opinions, princess. In mine opinions, his highness... *pff!.. schwach,*[2] like the Germans say... But it all depends... it depends, so to speak, on the crisis."

"Is he in danger?" asked Marusya quietly.

Ivan Adolfovich wrinkled his brow and began to prove that each person has his own opinion... He was given a three-rouble note. He expressed thanks, became embarrassed, gave a little cough, and vanished.

When they had collected themselves, the old princess and Marusya decided to send for someone famous. Famous doctors are expensive, but... what could they do? The life of someone close to you is worth more than money.

---

2   *schwach*: "weak" (German).

The cook dashed off to fetch Toporkov. He did not find the doctor at home, of course, and had to leave a note.

Toporkov took his time to respond to the invitation. They waited anxiously all day with their hearts in their mouths, then waited all night, and the next morning... They were even about to send for another doctor, and had decided that when Toporkov came, they would call him a lout, straight to his face, so that he would never again dare to force anyone to wait as long. Despite their woe, the residents of the Priklonsky home were absolutely incensed. Finally, at two o'clock on the following day a carriage drove up to the front entrance. Nikifor shuffled as fast as he could to the door and in the space of a few seconds had removed his nephew's overcoat in a most ingratiating manner. Toporkov alerted the household to his presence with a cough, and went to the patient's room without greeting anyone. He strode through the reception room, the drawing room, and the dining room like a general, not looking at anyone, his gleaming boots squeaking throughout the house. His enormous figure commanded respect. He was awe-inspiring, imposing, full of dignity and thoroughly proper—as if he had been chiselled from ivory. Gold-rimmed spectacles and an extremely serious, immobile face completed his haughty bearing. He was plebeian by birth, but there was nothing plebeian about him except his strongly developed muscles. Everything else about him was noble, even gentlemanly. His face was pink, handsome, and even—if his female patients were to be believed—very handsome. His neck was white like a woman's. His hair was as soft as silk, and attractive, but unfortunately cut short. If Toporkov were to pay attention to his appearance, he would not cut his hair, but allow it to curl all the way down to his collar. His face was handsome, but too stiff and serious to seem pleasant. Stiff, serious, rigid, it expressed nothing but exhaustion from working hard all day, every day.

Marusya stepped forward to greet Toporkov, and began to plead with him, wringing her hands. She had never pleaded with anyone before.

"Save him, doctor!" she said, raising her big eyes to his face. "I implore you! You are our only hope!"

Toporkov walked round Marusya and headed off to see Yegorushka.

"Open the vents!" he commanded, entering the patient's room. "Why are the vents closed? How can one breathe in here?"

The old princess, Marusya and Nikifor rushed to the windows and the stove. There was no way to let air in through the windows, which had already had their double frames installed. The stove had not been lit.

"There's no ventilation," said the old princess timidly.

"That's strange... Hmm... You try and treat someone in such conditions! I am not going to treat him!"

Raising his voice slightly, Toporkov added:

"Take him into the reception room. It's not so stuffy in there. Call the servants!"

Nikifor rushed over and stood at the head of the bed. The old princess took hold of the bed, blushing because she had no other servants besides Nikifor, the cook, and a half-blind maid. Marusya also took hold of the bed and pulled with all her might. The decrepit old man and the two weak women lifted the bed with a groan, and began to carry it, stumbling, afraid they might drop it and not believing in their own strength. The old princess's dress ripped at the shoulder and she felt something tear in her stomach. Everything went green before Marusya's eyes, and her hands ached—Yegorushka was so heavy! But Dr. Toporkov walked pompously behind the bed, frowning irritably at the time he was wasting on such trifles. And he did not so much as lift a finger to help the ladies! What a swine!..

They set the bed down next to the grand piano. Toporkov pulled back the blanket and asked the old princess various questions as he began to undress Yegorushka, who was tossing about. The patient's shirt was off in a matter of seconds.

"Be more concise, please! That has no bearing on the matter!" he said curtly, after listening to the old princess. "Anyone not needed may leave!"

He tapped Yegorushka's chest with a little hammer, turned the patient on to his stomach and tapped again. Breathing heavily through the nose (as doctors always do when they are sounding a patient), he arrived at his diagnosis: a straightforward case of *delirium tremens*.

"It wouldn't hurt to put him in a straitjacket," he said in his even voice, clipping each word.

After giving some more advice, he wrote out a prescription and headed briskly for the door. While he was writing the prescription, he asked, among other things, for Yegorushka's surname.

"Prince Priklonsky," said the old princess.

"Priklonsky?" repeated Toporkov.

"How quickly you have forgotten the name of your former... squires!" thought the princess.

The princess was incapable of summoning up the word "masters": the figure of their former serf was too imposing!

She went up to him in the hall and asked anxiously:

"Is he in danger, doctor?"

"I don't think so."

"Will he get better, in your opinion?"

"I presume he will," the doctor answered coldly, and, with a slight nod, he went down the stairs to his horses, which were as awe-inspiring and imposing as he was himself.

After the doctor left, the old princess and Marusya breathed freely again for the first time after their exhausting vigil. The famous Doctor Toporkov had given them hope.

"How solicitous he is, how kind!" said the old princess, mentally blessing all the doctors of the world. Mothers love medicine and believe in it when their children are ill!

"That's one important gentleman!" remarked Nikifor, who had not seen anyone in the master's house besides Yegorushka's drinking companions for quite some time. It was beyond the old man's wildest dreams that this important gentleman could be none other than little Kolka, the filthy boy whom he used to drag by the feet from under the water cart and flog.

The princess had concealed the fact that his nephew was a doctor from him.

That evening, after the sun had set, the exhausted and grief-stricken Marusya was suddenly overcome by a severe chill; the chill forced her to take to her bed. The chills gave way to a high fever and a pain in her side. She spent the whole night delirious and groaning, "I'm dying, *Maman*!"

So when he arrived at ten in the morning, Toporkov had not just one patient to treat, but two: Yegorushka and Marusya. He diagnosed Marusya with pneumonia in one lung.

The spirit of death began to haunt the Priklonsky household. Invisible, frightening, it flitted over both beds, threatening any minute to carry away both of the old princess's children. She was out of her mind with despair.

"I don't know, ma'am!" said Toporkov. "I cannot know, I'm not a prophet. All will be clear in a few days."

He uttered these words drily and coldly, and his words cut deep into the heart of the distraught old woman. If only there could be one word of hope!

To complete her misery, Toporkov prescribed his patients practically nothing, but just tapped, listened, and made criticisms that the air was not pure, and that the compress had been applied to the wrong place, and at the wrong time. The old princess considered all these newfangled remedies to be a waste of time. Day and night she paced ceaselessly from one bed to the other, forgetting everything else in the world, making vows and praying.

She regarded fever and pneumonia as the most dangerous, lethal illnesses, and when blood was detected in Marusya's phlegm, she assumed that her daughter was in the "final stage of consumption" and fainted.

You can imagine her joy when on the seventh day of her illness Marusya smiled and said:

"I feel well."

Yegorushka came to on the seventh day as well. Praying to Toporkov as if to a demi-god, laughing with happiness and crying, the old princess went up to him when he arrived and said:

"I am indebted to you for saving my children, doctor! Thank you!"

"What, ma'am?"

"I owe you so much! You've saved my children!"

"Ah... The seventh day. I had assumed it would be on the fifth. Anyway, no matter. Give them this powder once in the morning and once at night. Continue with the compress. You may replace this heavy blanket with something lighter. Give your son something fermented to drink. I'll come by tomorrow evening."

And the famous doctor nodded his head and walked towards the stairs in his measured general's gait.

II

A clear, bright day with a light frost—one of those autumn days when you gladly reconcile yourself to cold, dampness, and heavy galoshes. The air is so transparent that you can see the beak of a jackdaw sitting atop the highest belfry; it is saturated with the smell of autumn. If you go outside, a healthy blush will spread over your cheeks, reminiscent of a crisp Crimean apple. The long-fallen yellow leaves, patiently awaiting the first snow and trodden underfoot, gleam in the sun like gold ten-rouble coins. Nature is sinking quietly and submissively into slumber. There is no wind, nor any sound. Motionless and mute, as if exhausted by spring and summer, nature basks in the sun's gentle, warming rays, and as you gaze at this incipient repose, you want to become still yourself...

On just such a day Marusya and Yegorushka sat by the window, awaiting Toporkov's arrival for the last time. A gentle warming light shone through the Priklonsky's windows; it danced on the carpets, the chairs, and the piano. Everything was bathed in this light. Marusya and Yegorushka looked out through the window, celebrating their recovery. People recovering from an illness always brim with happiness, especially if they are young. They feel and understand good health in a way that an ordinary healthy person does not. Good health is freedom, and who savours the feeling of freedom more than a liberated slave? Marusya and Yegorushka felt like liberated slaves each waking moment. How good they felt! They wanted to breathe, look out of the windows, move around—in short, to live, and every second all these desires were fulfilled. Furov and his claim about the promissory note, gossip, Yegorushka's behaviour, poverty—all was forgotten. Only pleasant, unstressful things remained: good weather, upcoming balls, kind *Maman*, and... the doctor. Marusya laughed and chattered ceaselessly. The main topic of conversation was the doctor, who was expected at any moment.

"He's an amazing person, he's almighty!" she said. "What almighty skill! Think about it, *Georges*, what a great, lofty feat: to battle with nature and prevail!"

As she spoke, she used her hands and eyes to place a great exclamation mark after each grandiose but sincerely meant phrase.

Yegorushka listened to his sister's rapturous speech, blinking and nodding approval. He too respected Toporkov's stern face and was sure that he owed his recovery solely to him. Beaming and jubilant, *Maman* sat next to them, sharing in her children's rapture.

She liked Toporkov not only for his skills as a doctor, but also for the "good character" which she had managed to read in his face.

For whatever reason, this "good character" has a strong appeal for old people.

"It's just a shame he's... of such low origin," said the old princess, glancing timidly at her daughter. "And his trade... is not the cleanest. Always handling all kinds of things... Ugh!"

The young princess flushed and moved to another armchair to get away from her mother. Yegorushka was also riled.

He could not stand pretension and upper-class snobbery.

Poverty can educate anyone! He himself had on more than one occasion personally experienced the pretensions of people wealthier than he was.

"Nowadays, *Mutter*,"[3] said he, twitching his shoulders contemptuously, "anyone with a head on his shoulders and a big pocket in his trousers is of good background; whereas the kind of person who has buttocks instead of a head, and a soap bubble instead of a pocket, that person is... a nonentity, so there you are!"

In saying this, Yegorushka was parroting someone. He had heard these very words a couple of months ago from a seminary student with whom he had got into a fight in a billiards room.

"I would gladly exchange my princely title for his head and his pocket," added Yegorushka.

Marusya raised her eyes, brimming with gratitude, to her brother.

"There is a lot I could say, *Maman*, but you wouldn't understand," she sighed. "Nothing will dissuade you... And it's a great shame!"

The old princess, exposed as a stick-in-the-mud, was embarrassed and tried to justify herself.

"Actually, in Petersburg I used to know a doctor who was a baron," she said, "I did... And abroad as well... It's true... Education means a lot. It does..."

Toporkov arrived after midday. He entered in the same manner as the first time: pompously, not looking at anyone.

"Refrain from alcohol, and avoid excess if possible," he said to Yegorushka, after putting down his hat. "Take care of your liver. It's already significantly enlarged. And that is completely due to your consumption of alcoholic beverages. Drink the waters I've prescribed you."

Then, turning to Marusya, he imparted to her some final instructions.

Marusya listened attentively, as though it was an interesting tale, looking straight into the learned man's eyes.

"Well? May I presume you have understood?" asked Toporkov.

"Oh yes! *Merci*!"

The visit had lasted exactly four minutes.

Toporkov cleared his throat, reached for his hat and gave a nod. Marusya and Yegorushka glared at their mother. Marusya even blushed.

---

3 *Mutter*: "Mother" (German).

The old princess, waddling like a duck and blushing, went up to the doctor and slipped her hand awkwardly into his white fist.

"Most obliged to you!" she said.

Yegorushka and Marusya lowered their eyes. Toporkov lifted his fist to his glasses and beheld a bundle of banknotes. Without the slightest embarrassment or lowering his eyes, he licked his finger and softly counted out the banknotes. There were twelve twenty-five rouble notes. It was not for nothing that Nikifor had run over to a certain place with her bracelets and earrings the previous day! A bright little cloud, something like the aura that saints are depicted with, flitted across Toporkov's face; his mouth twitched into a slight smile. He was clearly quite satisfied with the recompense. Having counted the money and tucked it into his pocket, he gave another nod and turned toward the door.

The old princess, Marusya and Yegorushka stared at the doctor's back, and all three of them felt a twinge in their hearts. Their eyes lit up with good feelings: this man was leaving and would not come back, but they had already become accustomed to his measured step, his clipped tones, and his serious face. A little idea flashed through the mother's mind. She had a sudden desire to bestow some tenderness on this wooden man.

"He's an orphan, poor thing," she thought. "All alone."

"Doctor," she said in a soft, old-woman's voice.

The doctor looked round.

"What is it?"

"Would you have a cup of coffee with us? Please do!"

Toporkov frowned and slowly drew his watch out of his pocket. He glanced at the time, thought for a moment, then said:

"I'll have some tea."

"Please have a seat! Over here!"

Toporkov put down his hat and sat down; he sat rigidly, like a mannequin whose knees have been bent and whose neck and shoulders have been straightened. The old princess and Marusya bustled about. Marusya's eyes widened and took on an anxious look, as though she had been assigned an impossible task. Nikifor darted from room to room in his worn black frock coat and greying gloves. The clatter of crockery and the clinking of teaspoons could be heard throughout the house. Yegorushka was briefly summoned from the room, discreetly and mysteriously.

Toporkov sat for about ten minutes, waiting for the tea. He stared at the piano pedal, without moving a limb or uttering a sound. At last, the drawing room door opened. Nikifor appeared, beaming, bearing a large tray. On the tray, in silver holders, were two glasses: one for the doctor, the other for Yegorushka. Around the glasses, in strictest symmetry, stood jugs with fresh and clotted cream, sugar lumps with tongs, lemon slices with a little fork, and sponge cakes.

Walking behind Nikifor was Yegorushka, his expression blank from the solemnity of the occasion.

Bringing up the rear were the old princess with beads of sweat on her brow, and a saucer-eyed Marusya.

"Please help yourself!" the old princess said to Toporkov.

Yegorushka took a glass, stepped to one side and sipped cautiously. Toporkov took a glass and also sipped. The old princess and Marusya sat to one side, observing the doctor's face.

"Maybe it's not sweet enough for you?" asked the old princess.

"No, it's fine."

And as might have been expected, silence set in—the kind of awful, unpleasant silence during which one for some reason feels the terrible awkwardness of the situation and the impulse to be embarrassed. The doctor sat and drank without speaking. He was clearly ignoring those around him and had eyes for nothing but his tea.

The old princess and Marusya were eager to engage this intelligent man in conversation, but had no idea how to begin; they were both afraid of appearing stupid. Yegorushka looked at the doctor, and it was obvious from his eyes that he was on the verge of asking something, and just could not get it out. A grave silence reigned, disturbed from time to time by the sound of swallowing. Toporkov swallowed very loudly. He evidently felt no constraint and drank the way he wanted to. As he swallowed, he produced sounds which were very like the sound "glug." It was as though each gulp plunged from his mouth into some kind of abyss, where it plopped against something big and smooth. The silence was also occasionally disturbed by Nikifor, who from time to time smacked his lips and made chewing motions, as though trying out the doctor for taste.

"Is it true what they say that smoking is bad for you?" Yegorushka finally managed to ask.

"Nicotine, an alkaloid of tobacco, has a strong toxic effect on the body. The toxin that each cigarette introduces into the body is insignificant in quantity, but it is ingested over a prolonged period. The amount of poison, like its energy, is in inverse proportion relationship to the duration of ingestion."

The old princess and Marusya exchanged glances: what an intelligent man! Yegorushka blinked and lengthened his fish-like physiognomy. The poor fellow had not understood the doctor.

"In our regiment," he began, hoping to lower the scholarly tone of conversation to an ordinary level, "there was this one officer. His name was Koshechkin, a very decent fellow. He looked awfully like you! Awfully like you! Like two peas in a pod. Impossible to tell you apart! He is not a relative of yours, is he?"

Instead of answering, the doctor produced a loud swallowing sound, and the corners of his lips rose slightly and wrinkled into a contemptuous smile. It was obvious he despised Yegorushka.

"Tell me, doctor, am I completely cured now?" asked Marusya. "Can I count on a full recovery?"

"I suppose so. I predict a full recovery, based on..."

Holding his head high and looking straight at Marusya, the doctor began to discuss the outcomes for lung infections. He spoke in measured tones, clipping each word, without raising or lowering his voice. They listened to him more than eagerly, with pleasure, but unfortunately this dry man was unable to speak in a way that ordinary people could understand, and did not consider it necessary to adjust to other people's mental level. He mentioned the word "abscess" and "caseous necrosis" a few times, and generally had a fine and eloquent manner of speaking, but what he said was very hard to understand. He gave an entire lecture, sprinkled with medical terminology, and did not utter a single phrase that his listeners might have understood. But that did not prevent them from sitting with their mouths hanging open, gazing at the learned man with a feeling close to reverence. Marusya could not tear her eyes away from his mouth and strained to catch every word. She looked at him and compared his face with those of the people she came across every day.

How different was that learned, weary face from those dull, drunken faces of her suitors, Yegorushka's friends, who bored her every day with their visits! Faces of carousers and debauchees, from whom she, Marusya, had never heard a single kind, decent word, could not even hold a candle to this cold, aloof, but intelligent, haughty face.

"What a marvellous face!" thought Marusya, admiring his face, his voice, and his speech. "What a mind! And so knowledgeable! Why is Georges in the army? He should be a man of science too."

Yegorushka looked affectionately at the doctor, thinking:

"If he's talking about such clever things, he must think we're clever too. It's a good thing that we have that reputation in society. It was very stupid of me, though, to tell that lie about Koshechkin."

When the doctor finished his lecture, the listeners sighed deeply, as though they had performed some heroic feat.

"How wonderful it is to know everything!" sighed the old princess.

As if to thank the doctor for his lecture, Marusya stood up, sat down at the piano and struck the keys. She yearned to lure the doctor into conversation, to draw him in deeper, to touch him emotionally, and music always leads to conversation. And she also wanted to show off her abilities in front of an intelligent, perceptive man...

"It's Chopin," said the old princess, smiling languidly and holding her hands primly like a boarding-school pupil. "A delightful piece! If I may boast, doctor, she is also a delightful singer. And my student... I possessed a marvellous voice in my day. But that student of mine... Do you know her?"

And the old princess mentioned the name of a famous Russian singer.

"She's indebted to me... Yes, indeed... I gave her lessons. She was a nice girl! She was related to my late prince... Do you like singing? But why am I even asking? Who doesn't like singing?"

Marusya began to play the best part in the waltz and turned to the doctor with a smile. She wanted to see his face, to gauge the impression her playing made on him.

But she could not gauge anything. The doctor's face was just as serene and stiff as before. He was quickly drinking up his tea.

"I am in love with this bit," said Marusya.

"Much obliged," said the doctor. "That's enough for me."

He took one last gulp, then stood up and reached for his hat, without manifesting the slightest desire to listen to the rest of the waltz. The old princess leapt to her feet. Embarrassed and hurt, Marusya closed the piano lid.

"Are you already leaving?" asked the old princess with a deep frown. "Wouldn't you like something else? I hope, doctor... You know the way here now. One evening maybe... Don't forget us..."

The doctor nodded twice, pressed the young princess's extended hand awkwardly, and walked silently towards his fur coat.

"Ice! A lump of wood!" the old princess began saying once the doctor was gone. "It's terrible! He is so wooden he can't even laugh! You wasted your time playing for him, Marie! It was as though he stayed just for the tea! Drank up and left!"

"But how clever he is, Maman! Very clever! Who is there for him to talk to in our house? I'm uneducated, Georges is reticent and never says a word... Are we really capable of conducting an intelligent conversation? No!"

"There's your plebeian! There's Nikifor's nephew for you!" said Yegorushka, drinking the cream from the jugs. "How about that? Rational, impartial, subjective... It just pours out of him, the scoundrel! Some plebeian! And what a carriage! Just look at it! Very chic!"

And all three looked through the window at the carriage in which the famous man in his bear-fur coat was seating himself. The old princess went puce with envy, while Yegorushka gave a suggestive wink and whistled. Marusya did not see the carriage. She had no time to look at it: she was studying the doctor, who had made the deepest of impressions on her. Who is not affected by novelty?

And Toporkov was too much of a novelty for Marusya...

The first snow fell, followed by the second and the third, and then winter set in for good with its crackling frosts, its snowdrifts and icicles. I do not like winter and do not believe people who say they do. It is cold outside, smoky inside, and wet inside your galoshes. Stern as a mother-in-law one moment, lachrymose as an old maid the next, with its enchanting moonlit nights, troikas, hunting, concerts and balls, winter palls quickly and drags on too long, wrecking the life of many a homeless consumptive.

Life in the Priklonsky household followed its usual routine. Yegorushka and Marusya had already fully recovered, and even their mother no longer regarded them as ill. Just as before, their circumstances showed no sign of improvement. Things got worse and worse, and there was less and less money... The old princess pawned and re-pawned all her jewellery, family heirlooms as well as things she had herself bought. In the shop where Nikifor was sent to pick up various small items on credit, he continued to blab that the masters owed him three hundred roubles, and showed no sign of paying up. The cook blabbed the same thing, and the shopkeeper gave him his old boots out of compassion. Furov became even more insistent. He would not agree to any more extensions and said outrageous things to the old princess when she begged him to postpone the protest of the promissory note. Spurred on by Furov, other creditors started making a racket. Every morning the old princess had to open her door to notaries, court bailiffs, and creditors. It seemed that they were competing to launch bankruptcy proceedings.

The old princess's pillow continued to be permanently wet with tears.

During the day the old princess could keep a grip on herself, but after dark she gave free reign to her tears and cried all night, until morning came. One did not need to look far to find a reason for her weeping. The reasons were glaringly obvious in their vivid clarity and tangibility. Poverty, constant insults to her pride, and insults by... whom? Petty, low-class people, various Furovs, cooks, shopkeepers. Her favourite things went to the pawnbroker, and parting with them caused the old princess deep anguish. Yegorushka continued to lead a dissolute life, Marusya's future was still not settled... Were these not enough reasons to cry? The future was shrouded in fog, but the old princess could see ominous phantoms even through the fog. This future promised nothing good. They feared it rather than looking forward to it...

There was less and less money, but Yegorushka caroused more and more; he caroused unrelentingly and with a vengeance, as though he wanted to make up for the time lost during his illness. He drank away everything he owned and did not own, his things and other people's. He was utterly brazen and shameless in his debauchery. He would not hesitate to ask the first person he met for money. He had a habit of sitting down and playing cards without a single penny in his pocket, and did not consider it a sin to drink and gorge himself at others' expense, or go for a joy ride in someone else's cab and not pay the cabbie. He had changed very little: he used to get angry when people laughed at him before, but now he just got a little disconcerted when he was thrown or escorted out.

Only Marusya had changed. She had realised something, and what she had realised was truly dreadful. She was becoming disillusioned with her brother. For some reason she had suddenly begun to suspect that he did not resemble a man whose talents were unrecognised or misunderstood, and that he was in fact simply the most ordinary of men, the same as everybody else, if anything, even worse... She had stopped believing in that hopeless love of his. It was a terrible realisation! Sitting for hours on end at the window and staring aimlessly at the street, she imagined her brother's face, and strained to detect something graceful in it, that would not cause disappointment, but she failed to detect anything in this colourless face except a shallow, worthless man! Alongside this face came flitting into her mind the faces of his comrades, guests, consoling old women, suitors, and the tearful face of the old princess herself, dull with grief, and Marusya's poor heart was overcome with anguish. How vulgar, bland and dull, how stupid, boring and tedious it was around these familiar, beloved, but pathetic people!

Sorrow gripped her heart, and a single passionate, heretical desire took her breath away... There were moments when she passionately wanted to go away, but where? Naturally to a place where people did not live in fear of poverty or indulge in debauchery, but worked, and did not waste entire days chattering with stupid old women and drunken fools... And in Marusya's imagination one decent, sensible face stood out from the rest; in this face she read intelligence, a mass of learning, and weariness. It was impossible to forget this face. She saw it every day and in the most happy of circumstances, at just those times when its owner was working or gave the impression of working.

Every day Doctor Toporkov flew past the Priklonsky house in his gorgeous sleigh with its bearskin rug and fat coachman. He had a great many patients. He made home visits from early in the morning to late at night, and in the course of the day managed to drive down every street and lane. He sat in the sleigh just as he did in an armchair: pompously, holding his head and shoulders straight, never looking to the side. Nothing was visible behind the fluffy collar of his bear-fur coat except his smooth white forehead and gold-rimmed spectacles, but even that sufficed for Marusya. It seemed to her that there were cold, proud, and scornful rays emanating from the eyes of this benefactor of humanity through his spectacles.

"This man has the right to scorn!" she thought. "He is wise! And what a gorgeous sleigh, what marvellous horses! And he's a former serf! You need great strength of character to be born a lackey and turn yourself into someone as unapproachable as he is!"

It was only Marusya who remembered the doctor; the others were beginning to forget him, and would have soon completely forgotten him if he had not resurfaced. And he resurfaced in the most delicate of circumstances.

The day after Christmas, at noon, when the Priklonskys were at home, a timid tinkling of the bell could be heard in the entrance hall. Nikifor opened the door.

"Is the dear princess at ho-o-o-me?" came a feeble old voice from the entrance hall, and without waiting for an answer, a little old woman crept into the drawing room.

"Good day, dear Princess, your excellency... benefactress! How do you do?"

"What can I do for you?" asked the old princess, looking curiously at the old woman.

Yegorushka sniggered into his fist. To him, the head of the old lady looked like a small overripe melon, with its tendril sticking up.

"Don't you recognise me, dear? Can you have forgotten? Have you forgotten Prokhorovna? I delivered your little prince!"

And the old woman crept up to Yegorushka and gave him a quick peck on the chest and on his hand.

"I don't understand," mumbled Yegorushka angrily, wiping his hand on his frock coat. "That old devil Nikifor will let in any kind of riff-ra..."

"What can I do for you?" repeated the old princess, and it seemed to her that the old woman smelled strongly of cheap olive oil.

The old woman settled into an armchair, and after endless preliminaries, smirking and playing coy (matchmakers always act coyly), she announced that the old princess had "goods" to sell, and she, the old woman, had a "buyer." Marusya flushed. Yegorushka gave a snort and went up to the old woman, his curiosity piqued.

"That's strange," said the old princess. "So you've come to matchmake? Congratulations, Marie, you have a suitor! And who is he, if I may ask?"

The old woman huffed and puffed, reached behind her lapel and drew out a red calico scarf. Undoing the knots, she shook the scarf over the table, and out tumbled a thimble and a photograph.

Everyone's noses wrinkled; the red scarf with yellow flowers on it smelled of tobacco.

The old princess took the photograph and lifted it listlessly to her eyes.

"He is handsome, dearie!" the matchmaker began commenting on the image. "He is wealthy, noble... A marvellous person, he doesn't drink..."

The old princess flushed and handed the photograph to Marusya, who paled.

"That's strange," said the old princess. "If the doctor is keen, I believe he could himself have... An intermediary is the last thing we need here!.. He's an educated man, and now... Did he send you?"

"Yes, he did... He really took a liking to you... A fine family."

Marusya suddenly squealed and ran headlong from the drawing room, clutching the photograph.

"That's strange," continued the old princess. "Surprising... I don't even know what to tell you... I would never have expected this from the doctor... Why did you take the trouble? He could have come himself... it's even hurtful... Who does he take us for? We aren't some kind of merchants... And even the merchants have changed their way of life now."

"Odd fellow!" Yegorushka mumbled, looking disdainfully at the old woman's little head.

The retired hussar would have given a lot to be able to give her a good flick on the side of the head! Like a big dog who detests cats, he did not like old ladies, and he felt a purely canine thrill at the sight of a head shaped like a melon.

"Well, dearie?" said the matchmaker, sighing. "He is not of a princely stock, but I can say, dear princess, that... You are our benefactors, after all. Oh, our sins are many! Can you really say he is not noble? He had all kinds of education, and he's rich, and the Lord has bestowed all kinds of luxury on him, may the Holy Mother of God be thanked... And if you want him to come here, then by all means... He will pay his respects. Why shouldn't he come? He can certainly come..."

And taking the old princess by the shoulder, the old woman drew her close and whispered into her ear:

"He's asking for sixty thousand... Only to be expected! A wife is one thing, but money is another. You know that yourself... I will not take a wife without a dowry, he says, because she should have all kinds of pleasures living with me... She's got to have her own capital..."

The old princess turned crimson and rose from her chair, rustling her heavy dress.

"Would you please convey to the doctor that we are extremely surprised," she said. "Offended... That's just not how it's done. I have nothing more to say to you... Why are you so silent, Georges? She should leave! There is a limit to anyone's patience!"

After the matchmaker's departure, the old princess clutched her head, sank onto the sofa and groaned:

"So this is what's become of us!" she wailed. "My goodness! Some two-bit quack, a piece of trash, and yesterday's lackey is putting a proposal to us! Noble!.. Noble! Ha! Ha! What sort of nobility is that, if you please? He sent a matchmaker! If only your father were here! He wouldn't have stood for this! The vulgar fool! What a lout!"

What upset the old princess most was not that some plebeian was courting her daughter, but that he had asked for sixty thousand that she did not have. She was insulted by the slightest hint at her poverty. She wept and wailed until late in the evening and woke twice during the night to cry.

But no one was more affected by the matchmaker's visit than Marusya. The poor girl was overcome with a high fever. Trembling all over, she collapsed into bed, hid her burning head under the pillow and, as much as her strength permitted, began to consider the question:

"Can it really be true?!"

The question was baffling. Marusya did not even know how to answer it for herself. It expressed her astonishment, her embarrassment, and also her secret joy, which for some reason she was ashamed to admit, and even wanted to conceal from herself.

"Can it really be true?! That he, Toporkov... It can't be! There is something amiss! The old woman must have got it wrong!"

But at the same time, dreams—the sweetest, most cherished and enchanted dreams, which make the heart skip a beat and set the mind on fire— began to stir in her mind, and an inexplicable rapture overcame her entire small being. He, Toporkov, wanted to make her his wife, and he was, after all, so dignified, so handsome, so smart! He had devoted his life to humanity and... rode in such a gorgeous sleigh!

"Can it really be true?!"

"I can learn to love him!" Marusya decided towards evening. "Oh yes, I accept! I am free of all prejudices and I will follow this serf to the very ends of the earth! If Mother dares to say a single word, I'll leave her! I accept!"

As for the other, less important questions, she had no time to consider them. None at all! Why the need for a matchmaker? When had *he* fallen in love with *her*, and why? Why was he not coming round himself, if he loved her? Why should she care about these and many other questions? She was stunned, surprised... happy... and it was enough for her.

"I accept!" she whispered, trying to call up in her imagination *his* face, with the gold-rimmed spectacles, and the intelligent, serious, and tired eyes looking through them.

"Let him come! I accept."

While Marusya tossed and turned in bed, feeling happiness consuming her entire being, the matchmaker was visiting merchants' houses and handing out the doctor's photograph wherever she went. As she proceeded from one wealthy home to the next, she sought goods to whom she could recommend the "noble" buyer. Toporkov had not sent her specially to the Priklonskys. He had told her "go where you want." He felt indifferent about getting married, while realising that it was a necessity: he did not care at all where the match-maker went... He just needed... sixty thousand. Sixty thousand, no less! The owners of the house he wanted to buy would not sell it to him any cheaper. And there was nowhere he could borrow such a large sum; no one would agree to a mortgage. The only option left was to marry for money, and that is what he was doing. So Marusya was truly not the slightest bit responsible for his desire to entangle himself in Hymen's bonds!

After midnight Yegorushka slipped quietly into Marusya's bedroom. Marusya had already undressed and was trying to fall asleep. Her unexpected happiness had exhausted her: she wanted to find some way to calm the in-cessant beating of her heart, which she felt everyone in the house could hear. Every wrinkle of Yegorushka's face concealed a thousand secrets. He coughed mysteriously, gave Marusya a meaningful look, then sat down on her legs and leaned slightly towards her ear, implying he had something important and se-cret to tell her.

"Do you know what I would say to you, Masha?" he began quietly. "I'll be frank with you... My view... Because I do after all care about your happiness. Are you asleep? I care about your happiness... Marry him... marry Toporkov! Don't beat about the bush; just go ahead and marry him... and be done with it! He's a proper person in all respects... And rich, too. His low-class origins don't matter. Forget that."

Marusya squeezed her shut eyes tighter. She was ashamed. At the same time she was pleased that her brother liked Toporkov.

"But he is rich! You at least won't go hungry. And you could starve to death sitting around here waiting for some prince or count... We don't have a kopeck after all! Zero! Nothing at all! Hey, are you asleep? Eh? Is your silence a sign of consent?"

Marusya smiled. Yegorushka laughed, and kissed her hand firmly, for the first time in his life.

"So marry him... He's an educated man. And it will be so good for us! The old woman will stop wailing!"

And Yegorushka lost himself in dreams. After a while, he shook his head and said:

"But there's one thing I don't understand... Why the hell did he send this matchmaker? Why didn't he come himself? Something isn't right here... He is not the kind of man who sends a matchmaker."

"That's true," Marusya thought, shuddering for some reason. "Something's really not right here... It's stupid to send the matchmaker. What does it mean in fact?"

Yegorushka, whose problem-solving capacity was normally low, hit the nail on the head this time:

"Actually, he doesn't have the time to traipse around himself. He's busy all day, running like a madman from one patient to the next."

Marusya calmed down, but not for long. Yegorushka sat silently for a few minutes, then said:

"And here's what else I don't get: he ordered that hag to say that the dowry can't be under sixty thousand. Did you hear that? 'Otherwise, it's not possible,' he said.'"

Marusya suddenly opened her eyes, shuddered all over, and sat up abruptly in bed, neglecting even to cover her shoulders with the blanket. Her eyes flashed and her cheeks burned.

"Is that what the old woman says?" she asked, tugging at Yegorushka's arm. "Tell her that it's a lie! These people, I mean, people like him...wouldn't say that kind of thing. Him... and money?! Ha ha! Only people who do not know how proud, honourable and unmercenary he is could suspect something as low as that. Yes! He's an absolutely marvellous person! They don't want to understand him!"

"I think so too," said Yegorushka. "The old woman lied. She must have wanted to worm her way into his favour. Picked up the habit from all those merchants!"

Marusya's little head nodded in agreement and ducked under the pillow. Yegorushka stood up and stretched.

"Mother is crying," he said. "Well, we will just ignore her. So, you agree? That's excellent. No point in beating about the bush. A doctor's wife... Ha ha! A doctor's wife!"

Yegorushka slapped the sole of Marusya's foot and left her bedroom, very pleased with himself. As he prepared for bed, he composed in his head a long list of guests to invite to the wedding.

"We'll have to get the champagne from Aboltukhov," he thought, as he drifted off to sleep. "And hors d'oeuvres from Korchatov... He has fresh caviar. And lobster, of course..."

The next morning, dressed simply but elegantly, and with a hint of coquetry, Marusya sat at the window waiting. At eleven o'clock Toporkov flew past but did not call. After lunch he again passed by with his black horses, right under the windows, but not only did he not stop, he did not even look at the window, where Marusya was sitting with a pink ribbon in her hair.

"He's too busy," thought Marusya, admiring him. "He'll come on Sunday..."

But he did not come on Sunday either. Nor did he come a month later, or two months later, or three... Of course he was not even thinking about the Priklonskys, but Marusya was waiting, and wasting away from anticipation... Cats—not ordinary ones, but ones with long yellow claws—scratched at her heart.

"Why doesn't he come?" she wondered. "Why? Oh... I know... He's offended that... Why is he offended?... It must be because of Maman, she was so rude to the old matchmaker. He must think that I can't love him..."

"The swine!" muttered Yegorushka, who had already gone to Aboltukhov's ten times, and asked him about ordering the very best champagne.

After Easter, which came at the end of March, Marusya stopped waiting.

One day Yegorushka came into her bedroom and, chortling maliciously, informed her that her "fiancé" had married some merchant girl...

"We are honoured to congratulate you, Sir! Deeply honoured! Ha ha ha!"

This news was too cruel a blow for my little heroine.

Her spirits fell, and she was despair and anguish incarnate, not just for days, but months. She pulled the pink ribbon from her hair and began to loathe life. But how biased and unfair feelings are! Even here Marusya found a justification for *his* behaviour. It was not for nothing that she had read novels in which people marry out of pure spite, so as to wound and injure the people they love.

"He married that fool to spite me," thought Marusya. "Oh, how wrong we were to be so rude about his matchmaking! People like him do not forget an insult!"

The healthy rosy colour faded from her cheeks, her lips forgot how to form a smile, her brain stopped dreaming about the future—Marusya became befuddled! She felt that the meaning of her life had perished with Toporkov.

What good was life to her now, if she was to be surrounded by fools, idlers, and rakes! She became depressed. Not noticing anything around her, or paying attention to anything, and heeding nothing, she began to lead the boring, drab life our unmarried women, young and old, are so prone to... She did not notice her suitors, of whom there were many, or her relatives and acquaintances. She regarded her bad circumstances with indifference and apathy. She did not even notice when the bank sold the Priklonskys' house, with all its historic, cherished heirlooms, and she had to move to a plain, humble new apartment, in petty bourgeois style. It was a long, heavy slumber, but not devoid of dreams. She dreamed of Toporkov in all possible aspects: in his sleigh, in his fur coat, without his fur coat, sitting, grandly striding forth. Her whole life took place in a dream.

But then thunder struck, and the dreams flew away from her blue eyes and blond eyelashes... Unable to cope with their bankruptcy, the old princess, Marusya's mother, fell ill in the new apartment and died, leaving nothing to her offspring beyond her blessing and some dresses. Her death was a terrible blow for the young princess. Her dreams flew away in order to give way to sorrow.

III

Autumn set in, as damp and muddy as the previous year.

It was a grey, drizzly morning outside. Dark-grey clouds, smeared as if with mud, completely shrouded the sky, their stillness inducing a feeling of melancholy. It seemed that the sun did not exist; it had not cast a single glance on the earth for an entire week, as though fearing to soil its rays in the slush...

Raindrops drummed against the windows with a particular force, the wind sobbed in the stovepipes and howled like a dog which has lost his master... There was not a single face evident on which one could not read desperate boredom.

The most desperate boredom was better than the impenetrable sadness which showed on Marusya's face that morning. Trudging through the slush, my heroine was slowly making her way to Doctor Toporkov's. Why was she going to see him?

"I am going to be treated!" she thought.

But do not believe her, reader! There is a reason why struggle can be seen in her face.

The young princess went up to Toporkov's house and with a sinking heart rang the bell timidly. A moment later, steps could be heard behind the door. Marusya felt her legs turning to ice and buckling under her. The bolt clicked and Marusya saw in front of her the inquisitive face of a pretty maid.

"Is the doctor at home?"

"We are not receiving patients today. Tomorrow!" the maid answered, and she stepped backwards, shivering from the blast of cold damp air. The door slammed right in front of Marusya's nose and shook before being loudly locked.

Flustered, the princess began trudging home lethargically. What awaited her at home was a spectacle—free, but irksome and all too familiar. A far from princely spectacle!

In the small drawing room, on a sofa reupholstered in new glossy chintz, sat Prince Yegorushka. He was sitting Turkish style, with his legs crossed. Beside him on the floor lolled his lady friend Kaleriya Ivanovna. They were playing the card game "Noses"* and drinking. The prince was drinking beer, his Dulcinea was drinking Madeira. Along with the right to hit their opponent on the nose, the winner also received a twenty-kopeck coin. As a lady, Kaleriya Ivanovna was granted a small concession: she could pay with a kiss instead of a coin. They both found indescribable pleasure in the game. They rocked with laughter, pinched each other, and constantly leapt up and chased each other around the room. Yegorushka was overcome with childlike glee when he won. He was delighted with the teasing way with which Kaleriya Ivanovna gave away her kiss when she lost.

Kaleriya Ivanovna, a tall, thin brunette with intimidating black eyebrows and protruding crab-like eyes, visited Yegorushka every day. She came to the Priklonskys sometime after nine in the morning, drank tea and ate lunch and dinner with them, and left after midnight. Yegorushka assured his sister that Kaleriya Ivanovna was a singer, and that she was a most respectable lady, etc.

"You should talk to her!" Yegorushka tried to persuade his sister. "She's awfully clever! Really!"

In my opinion, Nikifor was more correct when he called Kaleriya Ivanovna a trollop, and gave her the name of "Cavalry Ivanovna." He detested her with every fibre of his being and could not stand having to serve her. He sensed the truth, and the devoted old servant's instinct told him that this woman had no business associating with his masters... Kaleriya Ivanovna was vapid and dull-witted, but this did not prevent her from leaving the Priklon-sky apartment every day with a full stomach, her winnings in her pocket, and the certainty that they could not do without her. She was the wife of the billiards marker at the club, of all things, which did not prevent her from ruling the roost in the Priklonsky household. She was given an inch and took a mile.

Marusya lived on a pension that she inherited from her father. It was larger than the usual general's pension, but Marusya's portion was meagre. But even this amount would have been sufficient for a moderate existence if Yegorushka had not had so many whims.

Having no desire, or indeed ability, to work, he did not want to believe that he was poor, and he lost his temper if he was forced to reconcile himself with his circumstances and moderate his whims as much as possible.

"Kaleriya Ivanovna doesn't care for veal," he would say to Marusya. "She needs to have roast chicken. The devil only knows what you're doing! You try to manage the household, but you are incapable! Make sure that by tomorrow there's no sign of that rubbishy veal! We'll starve the woman to death!"

Marusya tried gently to object, but bought chicken so as not to make things worse.

"Why was there no roast today?" Yegorushka shouted sometimes.

"Because we had chicken yesterday," Marusya would answer.

But Yegorushka had little idea of a household budget, and no desire to learn. Over lunch he insistently demanded beer for himself and wine for Kaleriya Ivanovna.

"How can we have a decent lunch without wine?" he would ask Marusya, shrugging his shoulders, amazed at the extent of human stupidity. "Nikifor! Make sure we have wine! It's your job to attend to that! And Masha, you ought to be ashamed of yourself! I can't be expected to run the household! How you like exasperating me!"

He was an unbridled sybarite! And before long, Kaleriya Ivanovna came to his aid.

"Is there any wine for the prince?" she would ask when they were setting the table for lunch. "And where's the beer? Shouldn't someone be sent out for beer? Princess, give the man some money for beer! Do you have any change?"

The princess would say that she did, and give her last coins. Yegorush-ka and Kaleriya ate and drank, and did not see Marusya's watch, rings, and earrings disappear into the pawnbroker's shop one item after the other, or see her expensive dresses being sold to the rag dealers.

They did not see or hear the muttering and grumbling with which old Nikifor unlocked his little chest when Marusya borrowed money from him for the next day's dinner. None of this was any concern to these vulgar, dull-minded people, the prince and his philistine companion!

The next morning, after nine, Marusya set off to Toporkov's. The same pretty maid opened the door. As she took the princess into the entrance hall and helped her off with her coat, the maid sighed and said:

"You do know, don't you, miss? The doctor will take no less than five roubles for a consultation. Keep that in mind."

"Why is she telling me this?" Marusya thought. "What a nerve! The poor man doesn't even know what a rude maid he has!"

But at the same time she felt a pang in her heart: all she had in her pocket was three roubles. He would not send her away on account of two roubles, would he?

From the entrance hall Marusya proceeded to the waiting room, which was already full of patients. The majority of those seeking to be cured were ladies of course. They had occupied all the furniture in the room and sat down in groups, chattering to one another. The most lively conversations were underway. They talked about everything and everyone: the weather, their illnesses, the doctor, their children... They all talked loudly and laughed as though they were at home. Some of them knitted or embroidered while awaiting their turn. No one in the waiting room was dressed simply or poorly. Toporkov saw patients in the next room. They went in to see him in order. They entered with pale, serious faces and a slight tremble, but came out red-faced, sweating, and as elated as if they had taken confession and been relieved of some heavy burden. Toporkov spent no more than ten minutes with each patient. Their illnesses were evidently not serious.

"It all looks like quackery to me!" Marusya would have thought had she not been preoccupied with her own thoughts.

She was the last patient. When she entered the doctor's consulting room, which was crammed with books bearing German and French titles on their covers, she shivered like a chicken which has been plunged into cold water. *He* stood in the middle of the room with his left hand resting on the desk.

"He's so handsome!" was the first thought that flashed into his patient's mind.

Toporkov never put on airs, and he was scarcely capable of doing so, but all the poses he struck had a particularly majestic quality. The pose in which Marusya found him reminded her of the poses struck by majestic models for artists painting great military commanders. Near the hand resting on the desk was a cluster of five- and ten-rouble notes just received from his female patients. Here too, neatly arranged, lay his medical instruments, devices and tubes—all far too incomprehensible and "erudite" for Marusya. Together with the consulting room with its luxurious furnishings, they completed the majestic picture. Marusya closed the door behind her and hesitated... Toporkov gestured towards a chair. My heroine walked softly up to the chair and sat down. Toporkov swayed majestically, sat down on another chair vis-à-vis, and fixed his eyes inquisitively on Marusya's face.

"He hasn't recognised me!" Marusya thought. "Otherwise he would have said something... My God, why isn't he saying anything? How do I start?"

"Well, madam?" Toporkov mumbled.

"It's a cough," whispered Marusya, and she coughed twice, as if to confirm what she said.

"Have you had it for a long time?"

"A couple of months now... It's worse at night."

"Hm... Do you have a fever?"

"No, I don't think so..."

"I have treated you before, haven't I? What did you have the last time?"

"Pneumonia."

"Hm... Yes, I remember... Your name is Priklonskaya, I believe?"

"Yes... My brother was also sick back then."

"Take this powder... before bed... avoid draughts..." Toporkov quickly jotted down a prescription, stood up and adopted his previous pose. Marusya also stood up.

"Is that all?"

"Yes."

Toporkov fixed his eyes on her. He looked first at her, and then at the door. He was busy and was waiting for her to go. But she was standing there looking at him in awe, waiting for him to say something. How handsome he was! A minute passed in silence. Finally she gave a start, read a yawn on his lips and an expectant look in his eyes, handed him a three-rouble note and turned toward the door. The doctor tossed the money on to the table and closed the door behind her.

As she walked home from the doctor, Marusya fumed:

"Why didn't I say anything to him? Why? I'm a coward, that's why! It all turned out rather ridiculously... I just wasted his time. Why did I hold that wretched money in my hands, as if to show off? Money is such a prickly subject... God help me! One can offend people! Payments should be made inconspicuously. So why didn't I say anything?... He would have told me, explained... It would have been clear why the matchmaker came..."

When she got home, Marusya got into bed and hid her head under the pillow, which is what she always did when she was feeling upset. But she was unable to calm down. Yegorushka came into her room and began stomping noisily from corner to corner, his boots squeaking.

There was a mysterious expression on his face...

"What do you want?" Marusya asked.

"Ah-ha... I thought you were asleep, and didn't want to bother you. I want to tell you something... something very pleasant. Kaleriya Ivanovna wants to move in with us. I persuaded her."

"That's impossible! *C'est impossible*! Persuaded *who*?"

"Why is it impossible? She's very nice... She'll help you with the housework. We'll put her in the corner room."

"*Maman* died in the corner room! It's impossible!"

Marusya flinched and started shaking, as though she had been stung. Red blotches appeared on her cheeks.

"It's impossible! You'll kill me if you make me live with that woman, Georges! Darling Georges, don't do it! Don't do it! My dear! I beg you!"

"What don't you like about her? I don't understand! She's a woman like any other... She is clever and lots of fun."

"I don't like her..."

"Well, I do. I love that woman, and I want her to live with me!"

Marusya burst into tears... Her pale face was distorted by despair...

"I'll die if she is going to be living here..."

Yegorushka whistled something to himself under his breath, took a few paces, and left Marusya's room. A minute later, he came back in.

"Lend me a rouble," he said.

Marusya gave him a rouble. She had to do something to lighten Yegorushka's mood; as she saw it, a terrible struggle was now taking place in his soul: love for Kaleriya versus his feeling of duty!

In the evening Kaleriya came into the princess's room.

"Why don't you like me?" asked Kaleriya, putting her arms around the princess. "I've had so much misfortune!"

Marusya wriggled out of her embrace and said:

"I have no reason to like you!"

That phrase was to cost her dearly! Having a week later moved into the room in which Maman had died, Kaleriya found it first and foremost necessary to take revenge for that phrase. She chose the crudest kind of revenge.

"Why do you put on such airs?" she asked the princess every time they sat down to dinner. "Given your poverty, you shouldn't be putting on airs, but showing respect to good people. If I had known you had such flaws, I would not have come to live with you. And why did I ever fall in love with your brother?" she added with a sigh.

Reproaches, hints, and smirks led to her laughing about Marusya's poverty. This laughter did not bother Yegorushka at all. He considered himself in debt to Kaleriya and reconciled himself to her behaviour. But Marusya's life was poisoned by the idiotic laughter of the billiard marker's wife, Yegorushka's kept woman.

Marusya spent entire evenings sitting in the kitchen, helpless, weak and indecisive, shedding tears onto Nikifor's broad palms. Nikifor blubbed along with her and poured salt on Marusya's wounds with reminiscences of the past.

"God will punish them!" he would comfort her. "You mustn't cry."

In the winter Marusya went to see Toporkov again.

When she entered his consulting room, he was sitting in the chair, as handsome and as majestic as before... This time his face looked quite exhausted... His eyes were blinking like those of a person prevented from sleeping. Without looking at Marusya, he gestured with his chin to the chair opposite. She sat down.

"There is sadness in his face," Marusya thought as she looked at him. "He must be very unhappy with his merchant wife!"

They sat for a minute in silence. Oh, how she would have enjoyed complaining to him about her life! She would tell him the kind of thing that he would not have been able to read in any of those books with their French and German inscriptions.

"A cough," she whispered.

The doctor cast a glance at her.

"Hm... Do you have a fever?"

"Yes, in the evenings..."

"Night sweats?"

"Yes..."

"Undress..."

"What do you mean?..."

Toporkov gestured impatiently at his chest. Blushing, Marusya slowly undid the buttons on her chest.

"Get undressed. Hurry up, please!.." said Toporkov, picking up his little hammer.

Marusya drew one arm from her sleeve. Toporkov walked briskly up to her and with an accustomed hand had lowered her dress to the belt in a flash.

"Unbutton your chemise!" he said, and without waiting for Marusya to comply, he unbuttoned her chemise at the neck and, to his patient's great horror, began to tap with his hammer on her emaciated white chest...

"Lower your arms... Don't interfere. I won't eat you," Toporkov mumbled, while she blushed and wished passionately for the ground to swallow her up.

After doing his tapping, Toporkov began listening. The sound in the upper part of the left lung was muffled. The sound of a rattling wheeze and laboured breathing could clearly be heard.

"Get dressed," Toporkov said, and he began to question her: what was it like in her apartment? Did she lead a healthy lifestyle and so on?

"You need to go to Samara," he said, after giving her a whole lecture about a healthy lifestyle. "You will drink fermented mare's milk there. I've finished. You may leave now..."

Marusya somehow managed to do up her buttons, awkwardly handed the learned man five roubles, stood silently for a few moments, then left the consulting room.

"He kept me in there for a whole half hour," she thought as she walked home, "and I didn't say a thing! I was silent! Why didn't I talk to him?"

As she walked home, she was thinking not about Samara, but about Doctor Toporkov. What did she care about Samara? It was true that Kaleriya Ivanovna would not be there, but then neither would Toporkov!

What good was Samara? She was fuming as she walked, and at the same time she felt triumphant: *he* had said she was sick, and now she could just go to see him without any ceremony, as often as she wanted, even every week! It was so nice in his consulting room, so comfortable! The sofa at the back of the room was particularly nice. She would have liked to sit on that sofa with him, talking about this and that, complaining, and advising him not to charge his patients so much. Obviously, he could and should charge rich patients a lot, but he ought to give a discount to poor patients.

"He doesn't understand life, and can't distinguish between the rich and the poor," Marusya thought. "I could teach him!"

A free spectacle awaited her at home on this occasion too. Yegorushka lay sprawled on the sofa in hysterics. He was sobbing, swearing, and trembling, as if in a fever. Tears poured down his drunken face.

"Kaleriya has gone!" he wailed. "She hasn't slept at home for the past two nights! She got angry!"

But Yegorushka howled in vain. Kaleriya arrived that evening, forgave him, and took him off to the club.

Yegorushka's debauchery had reached its apogee... Marusya's pension was not enough for him, and he began "working." He borrowed money from the servants, took up card-sharping, and stole money and possessions from Marusya. One time, when they were walking down the street together, he swiped from her pocket two roubles that she had saved up to buy herself a pair of shoes. One rouble he kept for himself, and with the other he bought some pears for Kaleriya. His friends abandoned him. Marusya's friends, former visitors to the Priklonsky house, now called him "His Highness the Con Man" to his face. Even the "young maidens" in the *Chateau des Fleurs* looked at him with suspicion, and laughed when he invited them to dine, having borrowed money from some new acquaintance.

Marusya saw and understood this apogee of debauchery...

Kaleriya's brazenness was also rising to a crescendo.

"Please stop going through my dresses," Marusya said to her one day.

"Your dresses aren't coming to any harm," answered Kaleriya. "But if you think I am a thief, then... by all means. I'll go."

And Yegorushka, cursing his sister, spent a whole week at Kaleriya's feet, begging her to stay.

But that kind of life cannot continue for long. Every novella has an ending, and this little novel was also drawing to a close.

Shrovetide arrived, and with it harbingers of spring. The days grew longer, melted snow dripped from the roofs, a smell of freshness wafted in from the countryside, and you could feel that spring was on its way as you breathed it in...

One Shrovetide evening, Nikifor was sitting at Marusya's bedside... Yegorushka and Kaleriya were out.

"I feel like I am on fire, Nikifor," said Marusya.

But Nikifor whimpered, and rubbed salt into her wounds by recalling the past... He talked about the old prince, the old princess, and their way of life... He described the woods where the late prince used to go hunting, the fields in which he chased hares, and Sevastopol. It was in Sevastopol that the late prince had been wounded. Nikifor had no end of stories. Marusya particularly liked his description of the estate, which had been sold to cover their debts five years earlier.

"You'd go out onto the veranda... Spring is just beginning. And my goodness! You can't tear your eyes from God's creation! The wood is still black, but it's just a picture of delight! Then there's the beautiful deep river... Your mama used to go fishing when she was young... She'd stand at the water's edge with her rod for days on end... She loved being outdoors... Nature!"

Nikifor became hoarse from all the storytelling. Marusya listened and not let him leave her. She could read everything the old servant told her about her father, her mother, and the estate in his face. She looked intently into his face as she listened, and she wanted to live, be happy, and fish in the same river where her mother used to fish... There was the river, the fields beyond the river, the dark blue woods beyond the fields, and above it all the warm sun shining gently... It is good to be alive!

"Nikifor, my friend," said Marusya, seizing his withered hand, "darling... Will you lend me five roubles tomorrow? It'll be the last time... Will you?"

"Of course I will... It's all I have. Take it, and God will provide..."

"I'll pay you back, my dear friend. Just lend me..."

The next morning, Marusya put on her best dress, tied her hair with a pink ribbon, and went to Toporkov's. Before leaving the house, she looked at herself in the mirror ten times. A new maid greeted her in Toporkov's entrance hall.

"You do know," the new maid asked Marusya while removing her coat, "that the doctor takes no less than five roubles for a consultation?..."

There was a particularly large number of female patients in the waiting room on this occasion. All the furniture was occupied. There was one man even sitting on the grand piano. The doctor started receiving at ten o'clock. At noon he took a break to do an operation, then resumed seeing patients at two. Marusya's turn finally came at four o'clock.

Not having drunk any tea, exhausted from the wait, and trembling with fever and anxiety, she did not even notice how she ended up in the chair opposite the doctor. There was a strange emptiness in her head, her mouth was dry, and there was a fog in front of her eyes. Through the fog she could see only glimpses... of his head, his hands, and the little hammer...

"Did you go to Samara?" asked the doctor. "Why didn't you go?"

She did not answer. He tapped on her chest and listened. There was now a hollowness in nearly every part of her left lung. There was also a hollow sound in the upper right lung.

"You don't need to go to Samara. Don't go anywhere," said Toporkov.

And through the fog Marusya read something like sympathy in his austere, serious face.

"I won't," she whispered.

"Tell your parents not to let you go outside. Avoid coarse food which is hard to digest..."

Toporkov began imparting advice, got carried away, and ended up giving a whole lecture.

She sat without listening to any of it, gazing at his moving lips through the fog. It seemed to her that he was talking for too long. Finally, he fell silent, stood up, and fixed his spectacles on her, waiting for her to leave.

She did not leave. She liked sitting in this nice chair, and was scared of going home, to Kaleriya.

"I'm finished," said the doctor. "You may leave."

She turned to face him and looked at him.

"Don't drive me away!" the doctor would have read in her eyes if he had any skill in deciphering facial expressions.

Large tears began to fall from her eyes, and her hands fell helplessly down the sides of the chair.

"I love you, doctor!" she whispered.

And a red glow, like the residue of a great blaze in her soul, spread over her face and neck.

"I love you!" she whispered again, and her head swung backwards and forwards twice before drooping limply, her forehead touching the desk.

And the doctor? The doctor... blushed for the first time ever in his medical practice. His eyes blinked like those of a little boy about to be punished. Not from a single one of his female patients had he ever heard such words, and spoken in such a manner! Not from a single one! Had he misheard?

His heart began to race and thump anxiously... He coughed in embarrassment.

"Mikolasha!" came a voice from the next room, and the two pink cheeks of his merchant wife could be seen in the half-open door.

The doctor made use of this summons and quickly left the consulting room. He was glad to seize on to anything in order to extricate himself from an awkward situation.

When he came into his consulting room ten minutes later, Marusya was lying on the sofa. She was lying on her back with her face upturned. One arm and a lock of hair had fallen to the floor. Marusya was unconscious. Red-faced, and with his heart pounding, Toporkov went up to her quietly and undid her laces. He tore off a hook and ripped her dress without even noticing. Out of every frill, fold and secret pocket of the dress came cascading on to the sofa *his* prescriptions, *his* visiting cards and photographs...

The doctor sprinkled water on to her face... She opened her eyes, raised herself on to one elbow and, looking at the doctor, began thinking. She was trying to find an answer to the question: where am I?

"I love you!" she groaned, recognizing the doctor.

And her eyes, full of love and entreaty, came to rest on his face. She looked like a wounded little animal.

"But what can I do?" he asked, not knowing what to do... He asked in a voice that Marusya did not recognise, which was not measured or clipped but soft and almost tender...

Her elbow buckled and her head fell back on to the sofa, but her eyes continued to look at him...

He stood before her, reading the entreaty in her eyes, and felt he was in a grave predicament. His heart throbbed in his ribcage, and something new and unfamiliar was taking place in his head... A thousand unbidden memories began swarming around his burning head. Where had these memories come from? Had they really been summoned by these eyes with their loving entreaty?

He recalled his early childhood cleaning the masters' samovars. After the samovars, and cuffs on the back of the neck, his benefactors and benefactresses in their heavy coats came floating into his mind, as well as the religious school to which he was sent because of his "voice." The parish school with its birch rods and gritty porridge was replaced by the seminary. At the seminary there was Latin, hunger, dreams, reading, a romance with the daughter of the house-keeper-priest. He recalled how he had gone against his benefactors' wishes and run away from the seminary to the university. He had fled without a kopeck to his name, in worn-out boots. How wonderful it had felt to leave everything behind! Then came hunger and cold for the sake of his studies at university... A long, hard road!

Finally, he had triumphed, digging a tunnel to life by the sweat of his brow, passing through this tunnel, and... what was at the other end? He was expert at what he did, read a lot, worked a lot, and was ready indeed to work night and day...

Toporkov cast a sideways glance at the five- and ten-rouble notes lying on his desk, recalled the ladies from whom he had just taken this money, and blushed... Could he really have taken that long hard road just for the sake of those ladies and their five-rouble notes? Yes, indeed he had...

His majestic frame shrivelled under the weight of these memories, his proud bearing vanished, and a frown spread across his smooth face.

"What on earth can I do?" he whispered again, looking at Marusya's eyes.

Those eyes made him feel ashamed.

And what if she should ask: what have you accomplished, and what have you gained through your practice?

Five- and ten-rouble notes, and nothing else! Scholarship, life, and peace of mind—everything had been sacrificed for them. And they had brought him a princely apartment, fine dining, horses—everything, in a word, that goes by the name of comfort.

Toporkov recalled his seminary "ideals" and his university dreams, and these armchairs and sofa upholstered in expensive velvet, the wall-to-wall carpeting, the candelabras, and the clock that cost three hundred roubles now seemed like terrible, disgusting filth!

He lunged forward and lifted Marusya out of the filth on which she was lying, lifted her high up, arms and legs...

"Don't lie here!" he said, now using the intimate form of address, and turned away from the sofa.

And as though in gratitude for this, an entire cascade of gorgeous flaxen hair tumbled on to his chest... Someone's eyes began to shine near his gold-framed spectacles. And what eyes! Just begging to be touched!

"Give me some tea!" she whispered, responding in kind.

The next day Toporkov was sitting with her in a first-class train carriage. He was taking her to the south of France. Strange man! He knew there was no hope of recovery, knew it as surely as he knew the fingers on his own hand, but he was taking her... He spent the whole journey tapping on her chest, listening, questioning her. He did not want to believe what his expertise told him, and was trying with all his might to extract a glimmer of hope from all his tapping and listening!

The money that he had so zealously been accumulating the day before was now being dispensed in large doses during the journey.

He would have given anything now not to hear the accursed wheezing in even one of this girl's lungs! He and she so wanted to live! The sun had risen for them, and they were awaiting daybreak... But the sun did not save them from the darkness and... flowers are not destined to bloom in the late autumn!

Princess Marusya died before she had spent even three days in the south of France.

Upon his return from France, Toporkov took up his old way of life. He continues to treat ladies and accumulate five-rouble notes. A change can be observed in him, however. Whenever he speaks to a woman, he looks to one side, into the distance... For some reason it frightens him to look at a woman's face...

Yegorushka is alive and well. He left Kaleriya and now lives at Toporkov's. The doctor brought him into his house and dotes on him. Yegorushka's chin reminds him of Marusya's chin, and for that reason he lets Yegorushka squander his five-rouble notes.

Yegorushka is very contented.

A Speech and a Strap

He gathered us into his office and, in a voice trembling with tears, which was touching, gentle, and friendly but did not permit objections, delivered a speech to us.

"I know everything," he said. "Everything! Yes! I can see through things. I noticed this, so to speak, er... er... er... spirit, this atmosphere... these winds of change a long time ago. You, Tsitsyulsky, are reading Shchedrin, and you, Spichkin, are also reading something of that sort... I know everything. You, Tuponosov,[1] are writing... er... articles, of all kinds... and behaving like a free-thinker. Gentlemen! I'm asking you! I'm asking you not as your superior, but as a human being... It just won't do in our times. This liberalism has got to go."*

He spoke in this manner for a very long time. He had figured us all out, he had figured the current trend; he praised the sciences and the arts, with a proviso about limits and boundaries which science must never exceed, and he mentioned maternal love... We turned pale, we blushed, and we listened. Our soul was cleansed by his words. We felt like dying from remorse. We felt like kissing him, falling prostrate... sobbing... I looked at the archivist's back, and it seemed to me that this back was not crying only because it was afraid of disturbing the general silence.

"Go!" he concluded. "I've forgotten everything! I'm not vindictive... I... I... Gentlemen! History tells us... You don't believe me, so believe in history... History tells us..."

But alas! We did not find out what history tells us. His voice began to tremble, tears glistened in his eyes, and his glasses misted up. At that very moment we heard sobbing: it was Tsitsyulsky weeping. Spichkin turned as red as

---

1   Spichkin and Tuponosov are genuine but deliberately chosen Russian surnames derived from the words for "match" (*spichka*), and "blunt nose" (*tupoi nos*). Like the excessively sybillant Tsitsyulsky, which is awkward to pronounce, Tryokhkapitansky, which appears later, is an invented name derived from "of three" (*tryokh*), and the adjectival form of "captain" (*kapitansky*).

a boiled lobster. We reached into our pockets for our handkerchiefs. His little eyes blinked and he too reached for his handkerchief.

"Go!" he began to babble in a tearful voice. "Leave me! Leave... me... Mmm..."

But alas! You need only to remove a small screw from a clock or throw the tiniest grain of sand into it, and the clock will stop. The impression produced by the speech vanished like a puff of smoke, right on the threshold of its moment of crowning glory. The apotheosis did not come off... and thanks to what? A trifle!

He reached into his back pocket and pulled out some kind of little strap along with his handkerchief. Unintentionally, of course. The strap, which was small, grubby and stiff, twisted in the air like a snake and fell at the archivist's feet. The archivist picked it up with both hands and, with a respectful shudder from head to toe, placed it on the table.

"It's a strap," he whispered.

Tsitsyulsky smiled. Noticing his smile, I myself involuntarily snorted into my hand... like an idiot, like a little boy! Behind me, Spichkin snorted too, behind him, Tryokhkapitansky—and it was all over. The whole edifice collapsed.

"What are you laughing at?" I heard a thunderous voice.

Holy Moses! I look up: *his* eyes are gazing at me, at me alone... staring straight at me!"

"Where do you think you are? Eh? In a tavern? Eh? You forget yourself! Hand in your resignation! I don't need any liberals."

An Unfortunate Run-In

"I'm sleepy!" I thought as I sat in the bank. "When I get home I'm going to collapse into bed."

"What bliss!" I whispered standing in front of my bed, having had a quick dinner. "It's good to be alive! Excellent, in fact!"

Smiling endlessly, stretching, and lounging about in bed like a cat in the sun, I closed my eyes and began to drop off. Small particles began to dart about inside my closed eyes; fog began to whirl around my head, wings began to beat, pieces of fluff from my head began to float towards the heavens... cotton wool from the heavens began to crawl into my head... It was all so immense, soft, fluffy, and foggy. Tiny little people started to run around in the fog. They ran, span around, and disappeared beyond the fog... When the last little person vanished and Morpheus's job was almost done, I gave a start.

"Ivan Osipych, come here!" someone barked.

I opened my eyes. In the room next door someone had knocked then uncorked a bottle. I turned on to my other side and covered my head with a blanket.

"I loved you, and the love may perhaps still..."* a baritone struck up in the room next door.

"Why don't you get yourself a piano?" another voice asked.

"Swines," I muttered. "They won't let me sleep!"

Another bottle was uncorked and there was a clatter of dishes. Someone started walking about, jangling their spurs. A door slammed.

"Timofey, how long are you going to be with the samovar? Get a move on, my friend! We need more plates! Well, gentlemen? One little shot... In accordance with Christian tradition. Mademoiselle-tarantelle, mutton chops, *je vous prie!*"[1]

A party started in the room next door. I hid my head under the pillow.

"Timofey! If a tall blond man in a bearskin coat turns up, tell him we are in here..."

---

1   *"je vous prie"*: "I beg you" (French).

I cursed, jumped up, and knocked on the wall. They quietened down in the room next door. I shut my eyes. Again the particles began moving, the fluff, the cotton wool... But—alas!—within a minute they had begun shouting again.

"Gentlemen!" I shouted in an imploring voice. "This is plain rudeness! I have asked you! I'm not well and I want to sleep."

"You talking to us?"

"Yes."

"What do you want?"

"Stop shouting, please! I want to sleep!"

"Sleep then, no one is stopping you; and if you are not well, go to a doctor!"

The baritone struck up: 'Knights have love and honour...'

"This is so stupid!" I said. "Very stupid! It's even mean."

"Stop arguing please!" an elderly voice was heard from the other side of the wall.

"Amazing! Look at the lord and commander we've got here! A hotshot! So, who are you?"

"Stop ar-guing!!!"

"Peasants! They knock back the vodka and yell!"

"Stop ar-gu-ing!!!" the elderly, hoarse voice repeated about ten times.

I tossed and turned in bed. The thought that I could not sleep because of idle revellers was making me more and more angry... They launched into energetic dancing...

"If you don't shut up," I shouted, breathless with rage, "I will send for the police! Hey boy!! Timofey!"

"Stop arguing!!!" the elderly voice shouted once again.

I jumped up and ran next door like a lunatic. I was determined to get my way.

They were having a party... Bottles stood on the table. Sitting at the table were people with bulging, crab-like eyes. At the back of the room, a bald old man was reclining on a sofa... On his chest rested the head of a well-known blonde lady of the night. He was looking at my wall and rattling off:

"Stop arguing!!"

I opened my mouth to start cursing, when... oh, horror!!!

I realised the old man was the director of the bank where I work. Sleep, rage, and bluster left me in a flash... I ran out of the room.

For a whole month the director did not look at me or address a single word to me... We avoided each other. A month later, he sidled up to my desk and said with his head bowed, staring at the floor:

"I was presuming... I was hoping that you would yourself take the initiative... But I see that you have no intention... Hm... Now, don't you worry. You can even sit down... I was presuming that... It is impossible for the two of us to work together... Your behaviour in Bultykhin's[2] rooms... You gave my niece such a fright... You do understand... Hand over your business to Ivan Nikitich...'

And he raised his head and walked away from me...

I was done for.

---

2   The landlord Bultykhin's name, which is authentic, contains the exclamation "splash!" (*bultykh*).

An Unsuccessful Visit

A man about town charges into a house he has never been to before. He has come to pay a visit... In the entrance hall he encounters a young girl of about sixteen in a calico frock and white pinafore.

"Are your lot at home?" he asks the young girl casually.

"They are."

"Mmm... You're a peach! And is the mistress at home?"

"She is," says the young girl, blushing for some reason.

"Mmm. You're a sly one, aren't you! Saucy baggage! Where should I put my hat?"

"Wherever you like. Let me go! This is a bit strange..."

"But why are you blushing? Come on! I won't eat you..."

And the man about town swats the girl on the waist with his glove.

"Come on! You're not bad to look at! Quite pretty! Go and announce me!"

The girl blushes red as a poppy and runs off.

"A bit young!" the man about town concludes as he goes into the drawing room.

In the drawing room he encounters the lady of the house. They sit down and begin chatting...

About five minutes later, the girl in the pinafore crosses the room.

"My eldest daughter!" the lady of the house says, indicating the calico frock.

Cut.

Two Scandals

"Stop, damn you! If those bleating tenors don't stop singing out of tune, then I'm leaving! Redhead, look at the music! You, redhead, third from the right! I'm talking to you! If you can't sing, then why the hell do you put yourself on the stage with your god-awful croaking? From the beginning!"

Thus he bellowed, smashing the score with his conductor's baton. Much is forgiven these shaggy-haired gentlemen conductors. Indeed, there is no other option. For although he might curse and rage and tear his hair out, but he does this in the name of sacred art, which no one would dare to trifle with. He stands on guard, and were it not for him, who would prevent the dispersal of these loathsome semi-tones which time and time again distort and destroy the harmony? He protects this harmony, and in its name is willing to hang the whole world, himself included. One cannot hold this against him. If he was only intervening on his own account, well, that would be another story!

Most of his seething, bitter bile was directed at the red-haired girl standing third from the right. He was ready to devour her, bury her alive, snap her in half, and hurl her out of the window. She sang out of tune more often than anyone else, and he hated and despised this redhead more than anyone in the world. If the ground had swallowed her up, or she had died right there in front of his eyes, or if that grubby lamplighter had lit her instead of the lamps, or given her a public flogging, he would have chortled with glee.

"Oh, damn you! It's about time you realised that you know as little about music and singing as I do about whaling! I'm talking to you, redhead! Explain to her that it's an F, not an F sharp! Teach this dunce to read music! Now, sing on your own! Begin! Second violin, you and your unrosined bow can get the hell out of here!"

The eighteen-year-old girl stood there staring at the music and quivering like a vigorously plucked string. Her little face kept on flushing, like a glowing fire. Tears glistened in her eyes, ready at any second to drip on to the notes with their black pin-shaped heads. If only the silky, golden hair cascading down her shoulders and back like a waterfall could instead have hidden her face from people, she would have been happy.

Her breast was heaving under her bodice like a wave. All hell was let loose there: anguish, pangs of guilt, self-loathing, fear... The poor girl was guilt-ridden, and her conscience was tearing her insides to shreds. She was guilty before art, the conductor, her fellow singers and the orchestra, and she would most likely be guilty before the public too... If they were to boo her, they would be one hundred percent right. Her eyes were afraid to look at anyone, but she could feel everyone looking at her with hatred and contempt... Especially him! He was ready to hurl her to the ends of the earth, as far from his musical ears as possible.

"Oh God, please make me sing it right!" she thought, and there was a note of despair in her strong, wavering soprano.

He did not want to understand that note and went on cursing and tearing at his long hair. What did he care about her suffering, when there was a performance that evening?

"Abominable! This wretched girl is trying to murder me today with her bleating voice! You're not a warbler, but a washerwoman! Take the redhead's music away!"

She would have loved to sing well, and not out of tune... She did in fact know how to sing in tune, and was highly skilled. But was she to blame for the fact that her eyes did not obey her? Instead of looking at the music and following the movements of the conductor's baton, those beautiful but wayward eyes, which she would curse to her dying day, ended up staring at his eyes and hair... She liked the conductor's tousled hair and his eyes, which threw sparks at her, and were scary to look at. The poor girl was besotted with his face, which was riven by storm clouds and lightning. Was she really to blame for her feeble mind, which kept on thinking of irrelevant things that got in the way of her work, her life, and her peace of mind instead of immersing itself in the rehearsal... ?

Her eyes would be fixed on the score, but from the score they would dart to his baton, from his baton to his white tie, to his chin, to his little moustache and so forth...

"Take her music away! She is not well!" he ended up screaming. "I can't go on!"

"You're right, I'm not well," she whispered obediently, ready to make countless apologies...

She was sent home, and her place in the performance was taken by a singer who was no match for her in talent, but who was capable of adopting a critical approach to her work, of working honestly and conscientiously, without thinking about that white tie and little moustache.

Yet even at home he gave her no respite. When she arrived home from the theatre, she collapsed on her bed. Burying her head under the pillow, in the darkness of her closed eyes she could still see his face contorted with rage, and it seemed to her that he was beating her on the temples with his baton. This brute was her first love!

And the first pancake is always a flop.

The following day, her artistic comrades called to enquire after her health. It had been announced in the papers and on the billboards that she had been taken ill. The theatre manager and the director also visited, each expressing their respectful sympathy. He came too.

When not leading an orchestra or looking at his score, he is a completely different person. Then he is as polite, obliging, and respectful as a young boy. His face is lit up by the most deferential, cloying smile. Not only does he not curse, but he is even afraid of smoking or crossing legs in the presence of ladies. On those occasions it is hard to find anyone kinder or more decent.

He arrived with a concerned expression and told her that her illness was a great misfortune to art; that all of her colleagues, and he himself, would give anything to bring "notre petit rossignol"[1] back to health and well-being. Oh, these illnesses! They had deprived art of so much. The manager needed to be told that if the draught on the stage was not fixed, then they would all refuse to perform, and would all walk out. Good health was more precious than anything on Earth! And with that, he clasped her hands devotedly, heaved a great sigh, asked for permission to visit her once again, and left, cursing illnesses.

A splendid fellow! And yet when she announced that she had recovered, and reappeared on stage, he dispatched her to the depths of hell, and lightning flashed across his face again.

At heart he was a very decent man. One evening she was standing in the wings, leaning against a rosebush with wooden flowers and watching his movements. Her soul was filled with rapture at the sight of the man. He too was standing in the wings, laughing loudly as he drank champagne with Valentine and Mephistopheles.* Witty remarks were flowing from lips which were more accustomed to telling people to go to hell. Having drunk three glasses, he left the singers and walked towards the orchestra pit, where the violins and

---

1   *"notre petit rossignol"*: 'our little nightingale' (French).

cellos were already tuning up. He walked past her, smiling, beaming and waving his arms. His face glowed with satisfaction. Who would dare to say he was a bad conductor? No one! She blushed and smiled at him. Drunk, he stopped by her and said:

"I've gone soft..." he said. "My goodness! I feel so good today! Ha! Ha! You have all been so good today! You have wonderful hair! My goodness, how could I not have noticed that this nightingale has such a magnificent mane?"

He leant over and kissed her shoulder, which was covered with her hair.

"This damned wine has made me go all sentimental... My dearest nightingale, let's stop making mistakes, shall we? Let's concentrate when we sing? Why do you sing out of tune so often? You never did before, dear goldilocks!"

The conductor became completely sentimental and kissed her hand. She also started to talk...

"Please don't scold me... You see, I... I... You kill me with your scolding. I can't bear it... I swear!"

The tears welled up in her eyes. Not noticing what she was doing, she leaned on his elbow with almost all her weight.

"You simply don't realise... You are so cruel. I swear..."

He sat down on the bush and almost fell off it... To keep his balance, he grabbed her waist.

"There's the bell, my little one. Until the next interval!"

After the performance she did not go home alone. Drunk, sentimental, and giggling with happiness, *he* accompanied her home! How happy she was! Dear God! Feeling his embrace on the way she could not believe her happiness. It seemed to her that fate was playing a trick on her! But whatever the truth, the posters announced for a full week that both the conductor and his *she* were unwell... He did not leave her house for a whole week, and they both felt that the time passed in a flash. The girl only let him leave when it became awkward to hide away from the world, doing nothing.

"We must give our love some air," said the conductor on the seventh day. "I miss my orchestra."

And on the eighth day he went back to waving his baton and telling everyone to go to hell, his redhead included.

These women love to distraction. Despite consorting and living with her tormentor, my heroine did not give up her habits. As before, instead of following the score and the baton, she would look at his tie and face... At rehearsals and during performances, she sang even more out of tune than before. And how he scolded her in return! Before he could only scold her during rehearsals, but now he could do so at home too, whilst standing at her bedside. Sentimental wench! Even so much as a glance at the face of her beloved would be enough to make her lag behind by quarter of a bar, or cause her voice to falter. When she was singing, she would look down at him from the stage, and when she was not singing, she would stand in the wings, her eyes glued to his tall figure. During the interval they would meet in the dressing room, where they would both drink champagne and laugh at her admirers. And when the orchestra was playing the overture, she would stand on the stage and gaze at him through a small gap in the curtain. It was through this gap that the singers would laugh at all the bald heads in the front row and calculate the size of the box office takings based on the number of heads they could see.

It was this gap in the curtain that destroyed her happiness. A scandal was in the offing.

One Shrovetide, when the theatre was less empty than usual, they were performing *Les Huguenots.** As the conductor weaved his way through the music stands towards his podium, she was already standing by the curtain peering avidly through the gap, her heart aflutter.

He assumed a sullen, serious expression, and then started waving his baton in all directions. They began playing the overture. His handsome face was relatively serene to begin with... But then, almost halfway through the overture, lightning flashed across his right cheek and he screwed up his right eye. He heard a commotion to his right: a flute had fluffed a note, and a bassoon started coughing at the wrong time. A cough can stop you coming in at the right time. Then his left cheek reddened and started to twitch. There was so much fire and animation in this face! She gazed at him and felt she was in seventh heaven, in complete bliss.

"Damn you, cello," he muttered quickly through gritted teeth, barely audibly.

The cello knew the music but had no feeling for its soul! How could this tender, delicately resonant instrument be entrusted to people who were devoid of feeling? The conductor's face began to twitch, and his free hand clutched at his stand, as though his stand were to blame for the fact that the cellist was playing only for money, and not because his heart wanted to!

"Get off stage!" said someone nearby...

Suddenly the conductor's face lit up and beamed with happiness. He was smiling. The first violins had navigated a difficult section more than magnificently. This fills a conductor's heart with joy. And my red-haired heroine's heart was also filled with joy, as though she herself were one of the first violins, or had the heart of a conductor. Yet her heart was not a conductor's heart, even though it belonged to one. As this "red-haired she-devil" gazed at the conductor's smiling face, she also began to smile... but this was no time to be smiling. Something both supernatural and awfully stupid was about to happen...

The gap in the curtain suddenly disappeared in front of her eyes. Where had it gone? From above she could hear a noise, like the whistling of a steady wind... She felt something sliding upwards over her face... What had happened? Her eyes started searching for the gap, so that she could once again see that beloved face but, instead of the gap in the curtain, she suddenly saw a great mass of light , tall and deep... A multitude of lights and heads began to glimmer within this mass of light, and amongst these varied heads she saw the conductor's head... The conductor's head looked at her, then froze in astonishment... This astonishment then gave way to an unspeakable horror and despair... Without noticing it herself, she had taken half a step towards the footlights... Laughter was heard from the upper circle, and soon the theatre was drowned in peals of laughter and hissing. My word! *Les Huguenots* was to feature a lady in gloves, hat and dress of the very latest style!..

"Ha! Ha! Ha!"

The bald patches laughing in the front row started bobbing about... There was a great commotion... And his face became as withered and wrinkled as Aesop's! It seethed with hatred and damnation... He stamped his foot and flung down his conductor's baton, which he would not have exchanged even for a field marshal's baton. The orchestra was in disarray for a moment, then fell silent... She took a step backwards and, tottering, looked to one side... There, in the wings, pale, spiteful mugs were watching her... These beastly mugs were hissing...

"You're ruining us!" hissed the impresario...

The curtain fell slowly, uneasily, indecisively, as though it were being lowered in the wrong place... She reeled and leaned against a wall in the wings...

"You are ruining me, you depraved, insane creature... May the devil take you, you most loathsome of beings!"

Only an hour earlier, as she had been getting ready to go to the theatre, this very voice had whispered, "it's impossible not to love you, my little poppet! You are my guardian angel! Your kiss is worth all of Mohammed's paradise!" And now? She was done for, well and truly done for!

By the time order had been restored, and the furious conductor had started the overture for the second time, she was already at home. She undressed quickly and jumped under the blanket. Death is less frightening when you are lying down than it is when you're sitting or standing, and she was sure that her pangs of conscience and her anguish would kill her... She buried her head under a pillow and, began tossing and turning under the blanket, trembling, afraid to think, and choking with shame... The blanket smelt of the cigars which *he* smoked... What would he say when he came home?

He arrived after two in the morning. The conductor was drunk. He had been drowning his sorrows and rage. His steps were unsteady, and his hands and lips trembled like leaves in a breeze. Without taking off his coat or hat, he walked up to the bed and stood there silently for a minute. She held her breath.

"I see that we can sleep soundly after disgracing ourselves before the whole world!" he hissed. "We true artists can be at peace with our conscience! A true artist! Ha! Ha! You witch!"

He pulled the blanket off her and flung it towards the fireplace.

"Do you realise what you've done? You've made a mockery of me, damn you! Do you realise? Or haven't you realised that? Get up!"

He yanked her arm. She sat up on the edge of the bed and hid her face under her matted hair. Her shoulders were trembling.

"Forgive me!"

"Ha! Ha! Damn redhead!"

He tugged on her night-shirt and caught sight of her exquisite snow-white shoulder. But he was in no mood for shoulders.

"Out of my house! Get dressed! You've poisoned my whole life, you nonentity!"

She walked to the chair where her clothes were lying in a messy heap and started getting dressed. She had poisoned his life! It was vile and mean of her to poison the life of this great man! She would leave in order to put an end to her shameful, mean behaviour. There were enough people to poison lives without her doing it too...

"Get out! Right now!"

He threw her blouse into her face and ground his teeth. She finished dressing and then stood by the door. He had fallen silent. But the silence did not last long. Swaying slightly, the conductor pointed to the door. She walked into the hallway. He opened the door on to the street.

"Get out, you foul woman!"

And he grabbed hold of her small back and shoved her out...

"Farewell!" she whispered in a contrite voice, and disappeared into the darkness.

It was foggy and cold... And it was drizzling...

"Go to hell!" the conductor shouted after her and locked the door, not hearing her feet splashing through the mud. Having driven his mistress out into the freezing fog, he lay down in the warm bed and started to snore.

"Serve her right!" he exclaimed when he woke up the next morning... but he was lying! He felt sick to the depths of his musical soul, and longing for the redhead made his heart ache. For a week he staggered around as though drunk; suffering, waiting, and tormented by the uncertainty of it all. He thought she would return, and he believed that... But she never did. Poisoning the man she loved more than life itself was not on her agenda. She was struck off the theatre's books for her "improper behaviour." They could not forgive her for the scandal. She was not informed of her dismissal for no one knew where she had disappeared. They did not know anything, but presumed a great deal...

"She must have frozen to death or drowned!" the conductor supposed.

Within six months they had forgotten about her. The conductor forgot about her too. Every handsome artist has many a woman on his conscience; to remember each one would require too large a memory.

If virtuous and god-fearing people are to be believed, there is no escaping punishment for one's actions on this earth. So was the conductor punished?

Yes, he was.

Five years later, the conductor was travelling through the city of X. There was a wonderful opera house in X, and he stopped there for a day to get to know the company. He put up at the best hotel, and the morning after his arrival received a letter, which just goes to show how sought-after my long-haired hero was. In the letter they asked whether he would agree to conduct *Faust*. The conductor N had suddenly been taken ill and there was no one to pick up the baton. Might he, my hero (they asked him in the letter), be willing to take this opportunity and treat the most musical residents of the city to his artistry? My hero agreed.

He took up the baton, and "other" musicians glimpsed that face of storm clouds and lightning. There was a lot of lightning. And no wonder: there were no rehearsals, and he had to start dazzling with his artistry straight away during the performance.

The first act went well. As did the second. But during the third act there was a small scandal. Our conductor was not in the habit of looking at the stage, or anywhere else. All his attention was focused on the score.

When Marguerite, a marvellous, strong soprano began to sing her aria at the spinning wheel in the third act, he smiled with pleasure: the lady sang beautifully. But then, when this very same lady came in half a beat late, lightning flashed across his face, and he looked at the stage with hatred. But the lightning was put into checkmate! His mouth gaped in astonishment, and his eyes grew wide as saucers.

Sitting at the spinning wheel on stage was that same redhead he had once driven from a warm bed and shoved out into the dark, freezing fog. It was the redhead sitting at the spinning wheel, but she was no longer the same person he had turned out of his house, but someone different. Her face was the same, but her voice and body were not. Both were more elegant, more graceful, more confident.

The conductor's jaw dropped, and he went pale. His baton moved nervously, swung erratically in one spot, and then froze...

"It's her!" he said aloud and started to laugh.

He was overcome with surprise, delight, and boundless joy. His redhead, whom he had driven out of his house, had not disappeared, but had become a giant. What could be more warming to a conductor's heart? There was one more star in the world, whose art made one gasp with joy!

"It's her! Her!"

His baton froze, and when he tried to right the situation by waving it with a flourish, it fell from his hand and hit the floor. The first violin looked at him in surprise and reached down for the baton. The cello thought that the conductor had taken ill; he fell silent, then started again, but out of time... The sounds whirled round and spun in the air, letting out a painful screech in their attempt to escape the disorder...

Our redhead Marguerite jumped up and glared at "those drunks" who... She turned pale and ran her eyes over the conductor...

The audience, who were not in the least concerned, and had paid good money for their tickets, began to chatter and whistle...

To complete the scandal, Marguerite screamed at the whole theatre, flung her arms into the air and lurched towards the footlights... She had recognised him, and now all she could see were the storm clouds and lightning that had once again appeared on his face.

"Oh, you vile creature!" he shouted, and pounded the score with his fist.

What would Gounod have said, if he had seen them mocking his creation? Oh, Gounod would have killed the conductor, and with good reason!

For the first time in his life he had made a mistake, and for that mistake and for that scandal he would never forgive himself.

He ran out of the theatre with a bloody lower lip, ran back to his hotel room and locked the door. And there, locked in his room, he spent three days and three nights in self-contemplation and self-flagellation.

The musicians say that over the course of those three days he went completely grey and pulled out half his hair...

"I insulted her!" he now cries whenever he is drunk. "I ruined that role for her! I am no conductor!"

Why did he not say anything like that after he threw her out?

Idyll—Alack and Alas!

"My uncle is an outstanding person!" Grisha, the impoverished nephew and only heir of Captain Nasechkin, told me several times. "I love him with all my heart... Let us go and visit him, my friend! He'll be so glad!"

And tears would well up in Grisha's eyes when he spoke of his uncle. To his credit, he was not ashamed of those noble tears and cried in public! I acceded to his requests and dropped in on the captain a week ago. When I was in the entrance hall and peeped into the drawing room, I saw a most touching scene. The thin, elderly captain was sitting in the middle of the room in a large armchair, drinking tea. Grisha was standing before him on one knee, tenderly stirring his uncle's tea with a little spoon.

The pretty, little arm of Grisha's fiancée was wound around the old man's brown neck... The impoverished nephew and his fiancée were arguing over who would kiss their uncle first, and were not stinting on kisses for the old man.

"And now, my heirs, you kiss each other!" lisped Nasechkin, choking with happiness...

There was a most enviable bond between these three beings. Even I, a hard-hearted person, was overcome with happiness and envy, just looking at them...

"Yes!" said Nasechkin. "I have had a pretty good life, I can tell you! No one could ask for more. Just take the number of sturgeon I've eaten! A multitude! Take that sturgeon we ate in Skopin for instance... Hmm! It makes my mouth water even now..."

"Do tell us about it, please!" said the fiancée.

"Well, I arrive in Skopin with my thousands of roubles, my dear children, and go straight... hmm... to Rykov*... to Mr. Rykov. What a man... I say! A true gentleman! Worth his weight in gold! He received me as if I were one of his own... You might wonder what was in it for him, but... like one of his own! God's my witness! Treated us to coffee... After coffee there were snacks... The full spread... You could drink on the spot or take it away... Sturgeon...

from one corner of the table to the other... Lobsters... caviar. A veritable restaurant!"

I entered the drawing room and interrupted Nasechkin. It was on that very day that the first telegraph arrived in Moscow with news that the Skopin Bank had gone bust.

"I'm having a nice time with my dear children!" Nasechkin said to me after our initial greetings, and he turned to the children and continued in a boastful tone: "And the company there was distinguished... high-flying civil servants, clergy... monks, priests... After every shot you'd go over for a blessing... Rykov himself was covered in medals... Enough to put any general's nose out of joint... We ate the sturgeon... They served another... We ate that one too... Then there was fish soup with sterlet... pheasants...

"If it had been me, I would be now hiccupping and suffering from heartburn from all that sturgeon, and you brag about it..." I said. "Did you lose a lot because of Rykov?"

"Why do you think that I've lost anything?"

"What do you mean, why?! You know the bank has gone bust!"

"Very funny! I've heard it all before... It's not the first time they've tried to scare us..."

"So, you still don't know, old fellow? Serapion Yegorych! It's... it's... it's... Read this!"

I reached into my pocket and took out a newspaper. Nasechkin put on his glasses and started to read, smiling sceptically. The more he read, the paler and longer his face became.

"B-b-bust!" he howled, shuddering with every part of his body. "Too much for my poor little head to take in!"

Grisha went scarlet, read the newspaper, and turned pale... His trembling hand reached for his hat... His fiancée tottered on her feet...

"Friends! Are you really only finding out about this now? The whole of Moscow is already talking about it, you know. Friends! Calm down!"

An hour later I was standing in front of the captain and consoling him:

"Come on, Serapion Yegorych! So what? The money's gone, but you've got your dear children!"

"That's true... Money comes and goes... My dear children... That's right."

But alas! A week later, I ran into Grisha.

"My friend, go and see your uncle!" I said to him. "Why don't you pay him a visit? You've abandoned the old man completely!"

"He can go to hell! Fat lot of use he is to me, the old bastard! Fool! Couldn't he have found another bank?"

"Well, you should still go and see him. He's your uncle, after all!"

"Him? Ha-ha!.. You must be joking! Where did you get that idea from? He's my stepmother's cousin thrice removed! A distant relation! Very distant!"

"Well at least send your fiancée over to him!"

"Right! What on earth possessed you to produce that newspaper before the wedding?! Couldn't you have waited with your news until after the wedding?!.. She's turned her snout away now. She was also hoping for a slice of uncle's pie! Damned fool... She's all disappointed now."

Thus did I unwittingly break up a very close-knit trio... A most enviable trio!

The Baron

The baron is a short, thin, little old man of about sixty. His neck and spine form an obtuse angle that will soon become a right angle. He has a big angular head, sullen eyes, a bulbous nose, and a faintly purplish chin. His whole face betrays signs of mild cyanosis, probably due to the bottle of spirit in the cupboard which the props man rarely locks. And in addition to the house spirit, the baron sometimes helps himself to the champagne that is very often to be found in the bottoms of bottles and glasses in the dressing rooms. His cheeks and the little bags under his eyes hang and tremble like rags hung out to dry. On his bald patch there is a greenish deposit from the green lining of the fur hat with earflaps, which the baron hangs on the broken gas burner behind the third curtain when it is not on his head. His voice rasps like a cracked saucepan. And his clothes? If you laugh at these clothes that means you do not respect the authorities, which does you no credit. His buttonless frock coat with its shiny elbows and fringed lining is truly a remarkable garment. It dangles on the baron's narrow shoulders as if on a broken hanger, but... what of it? It did once clothe the brilliant body of the greatest of comic actors. The velvet waistcoat with its light blue flowers has twenty tears and an innumerable number of stains, but you cannot throw it out, if it was found in the room where the great Salvini* stayed! Who can vouch that the great tragedian himself did not wear it? What's more, it was found the day after that giant among actors departed; consequently, one can be sure that it is not a fake. The necktie that warms the baron's neck is equally remarkable. It is something to boast about, although for purely hygienic and aesthetic reasons it should have been replaced by one that was more durable and less greasy. It was cut from remnants of the great cloak that at one time graced the shoulders of Ernesto Rossi* when he conversed with the witches in *Macbeth*.

"My necktie smells of King Duncan's blood!" the baron often says, as he inspects his tie for parasites.

You can laugh at the baron's gaudy, striped trousers as much as you like. No authoritative person has ever worn them, though the actors joke that these trousers were sewn from the sail of the steamer on which Sarah Bernhardt travelled to America. They were purchased from usher No. 16.

The baron wears big galoshes, summer and winter, so that his boots remain intact, and his rheumatic feet do not catch cold in the draught that blows across the floor of his prompter's box.

The baron can be seen only in three places: the box office, the prompter's box and backstage in the men's dressing room. Outside of these places he does not exist and is hardly conceivable. He sleeps in the box office at night, while during the day he writes down the names of the people who have purchased boxes and plays checkers with the cashier. The scrofulous old cashier is the only person who listens to the baron and answers his questions. The baron carries out his sacred duties in the prompter's box; this is where he earns his daily bread. The box is painted a dazzling white only on the outside; inside its walls are covered in cobwebs, cracks and splinters. It smells of damp, smoked fish and spirit. In the intervals the baron hangs about in the men's dressing room. When they enter this dressing room for the first time, novices laugh and applaud when they see the baron. They take him for an actor.

"Bravo, bravo!" they say. "Your make-up is splendid! What a funny face you've got! And where did you get such an original costume?"

Poor baron! People refuse to believe that he has a face of his own!

In the dressing room he enjoys observing luminaries and, if there are no luminaries, he takes the liberty of inserting his own remarks, of which he has a great many, into other people's conversations. No one pays any attention to his remarks because they have bored everyone to tears and they smack of routine. In general, no one bothers to be civil with the baron. If he gets in the way and is a nuisance, they tell him to "scram!" If he speaks too softly or too loudly from his box, they tell him to go to the devil, and threaten him with a fine or retirement. He is the target of most backstage jokes and puns. You can sharpen your wits at his expense: he will not retaliate.

Twenty years have passed since they started to refer to him jokingly as "the baron," but in all these twenty years he has not once objected to this nickname.

To make him copy out a role and not pay him is also possible. Everything is possible! He smiles, begs your pardon and becomes flustered if you tread on his toe. Strike him on his wrinkled cheeks in public and I swear he will not lodge a complaint with the Justice of the Peace. Tear a piece of lining from his remarkable and much treasured frock coat, as a *jeune premier*[1] did recently, and all he will do is blink and blush. That is how downtrodden and meek he is! No one respects him. While he is alive, people put up with him, but when he dies, they will instantly forget him. He is a pitiful creature!

There was a time, however, when he nearly became a colleague and brother to the people he worshipped and loved more than life itself. (He could not help loving people who were sometimes Hamlets and sometimes Franz Moors!) He himself nearly become an actor, and probably would have become one had it not been for one ridiculous little thing that got in his way. He had a lot of talent, desire too, and in the beginning he even had patronage, but he lacked one little thing: courage. It always seemed to him that *they*—those heads that were spread among all five circles in the theatre, from top to bottom—would start laughing and booing if he were to show himself on stage. He turned pale, blushed, and became speechless with fright, when it was suggested to him that he should make his debut.

"I think I'll wait a little," he would say.

And so he waited until he grew old and penniless, and ended up, through patronage, in the prompter's box.

He became a prompter, but there is no harm in that. Now he can no longer be thrown out of the theatre for not having a ticket: he's an employee. He sits in front of the first row, sees better than everybody else and does not pay a single kopeck for his seat. It's good. He is happy and contented.

He carries out his duties superbly. Before the performance he reads through the play several times so as not to make a mistake, and when the first bell rings he is already sitting in his box and leafing through his prompt book. It would be difficult to find anyone in the whole theatre more diligent than he.

Nevertheless, he must be kicked out of the theatre.

Disturbances should not be tolerated in the theatre, and the baron sometimes creates terrible disturbances. He's a troublemaker.

When the acting on stage is particularly good, he takes his eyes off the prompt book and stops whispering. He frequently interrupts his reading with shouts of "Bravo!" "Magnificent!"—and ventures to applaud when the public does not. Once he even booed, for which he almost lost his job.

Take a look at him when he's sitting in his smelly box and whispering. He turns red, then white, gesticulates with his hands, whispers louder than he

---

1   *jeune premier*: "young male lead" (French).

should, and gasps. Sometimes he can even be heard in the corridors, where the ushers stand yawning by the coats. He even goes as far as to scold the actors from his box and give them advice.

"Raise your right hand!" he often whispers. "Your words are heated, but your face is ice! You're not right for this role! You're too young for this role! You should have seen Ernesto Rossi* in this role! Why the caricature? Oh, my goodness! He's spoilt everything with his philistine manner!"

These are the sort of things he whispers instead of whispering according to the book. It is a mistake to put up with this crank. If he had been kicked out, the public would not have had to witness the scandal that occurred recently.

The scandal consisted of the following.

They were doing *Hamlet*. The theatre was full. People listen to Shakespeare these days just as eagerly as a hundred years ago. When they do Shakespeare, the baron works himself up into a frenzy. He drinks a lot, talks a lot, and constantly rubs his temples with his fists. There is furious work going on behind those temples. Those geriatric brains are seething with mad envy, despair, hatred, dreams... He is the one who should have been playing Hamlet, even though one cannot really visualise Hamlet with a humpback, not to speak of the spirit that the props man forgets to lock up. It is he who should be Hamlet, and not these pygmies, who today play footmen, tomorrow procurer and the next day Hamlet! For forty years he has been studying this Danish prince, who all decent actors dream about, and who has brought laurels not just to Shakespeare. For forty years he has been studying, suffering, burning up with the dream... Death is not far off. It will arrive soon and take him away from the theatre forever... If only he could have had the fortune once in his life to tread the boards in the prince's doublet, near the sea, by the cliffs, a place that is nothing but wilderness,

> The very place puts toys of desperation,
> Without more motive, into every brain
> That looks so many fathoms to the sea
> And hears it roar beneath.

If even dreams can make one smoulder, then imagine the fire which would ignite the bald baron if his dream were to become reality!

On the above-mentioned evening he was ready to demolish the whole world because of his envy and fury. The role of Hamlet was given to a kid who spoke in a reedy tenor voice, but more importantly had red hair. Surely Hamlet cannot have been a redhead?

The baron sat in his box as if on hot coals. When Hamlet was offstage he was relatively calm, but whenever the red-haired, reedy-voiced tenor appeared on stage, he began to fidget, thrash about and whimper. His whispering was more like groaning than reading. His hands shook, he mixed up the pages, and he kept moving the candlesticks, either closer, or further away... He fixed his eyes on Hamlet's face and stopped whispering... He had a burning desire to pluck out every single hair from that red head. Better a bald Hamlet than a redhead! It was a complete caricature, for crying out loud!

When it came to the second act he did not whisper at all, but sniggered malevolently, swore, and hissed. Fortunately for him, the actors knew their roles well and did not notice his silence.

"Some Hamlet!" he cursed. "I must say! Ha-ha! These cadets don't know their place! They ought to be running after seamstresses, not acting on the stage! If Hamlet had such a stupid face, it's unlikely Shakespeare would have ever written his tragedy!"

When he got tired of cursing, he began coaching the red-haired actor. Through hand gestures and facial expressions, and by reading and pounding his fists on his book, he demanded the actor followed his advice. He had to save Shakespeare from being desecrated, and for Shakespeare he was prepared to do anything, even if it resulted in one hundred thousand scandals!

The red-haired Hamlet was terrible when he was in dialogue with the other actors. He would prance around like that "robustious periwig-pated fellow," about whom Hamlet says: "I would have such a fellow whipp'd." When he started to declaim, the baron could not bear it. Sighing and knocking the ceiling of the box with his bald pate, he placed his left hand on his chest, and gesticulated with his right. An old man's hoarse voice interrupted the red-haired actor and forced him to look down at the box:

> Roasted in wrath and fire,
> And thus o'ersized with coagulate gore,
> With eyes like carbuncles, the hellish Pyrrhus
> Old grandsire Priam seeks.

And leaning halfway out of the prompter's box, the baron nodded at the lead actor and added, no longer declaiming, in an offhand, lacklustre voice:

"Continue!"

The lead actor continued, but not at once. He hesitated for a moment during which a profound silence reigned in the theatre. The silence was broken by the baron himself when he knocked his head on the edge of the box as he retreated back into it. Laughter was heard.

"Bravo, drummer!" came shouts from the amphitheatre.

They thought it was the old drummer dozing in the pit who had interrupted Hamlet, not the prompter. The drummer bowed like a buffoon to the amphitheatre, and the whole theatre broke out in laughter. Audiences love theatrical mishaps, and if there were performances of mishaps rather than plays, they would pay twice as much.

The lead actor continued, and little by little silence was restored.

But the eccentric baron blushed with shame when he heard the laughter and clutched his bald head, most likely forgetting that those locks, once so admired by the beautiful ladies, were no longer there. And now, as if it were not enough that he would become the laughing stock of the entire city plus all the humorous magazines, they would kick him out of the theatre! He burned with shame and was angry with himself, but his whole body nevertheless trembled with delight: he had just declaimed on stage!

"That's not your job, you rusty old door knob," he thought. "Your job is only to prompt, unless you want them to clip you round the ears, like the lowliest servant. But it really is outrageous! The red-haired kid has no desire to act the part decently! Is this really how this bit of the play should be acted?"

And with his eyes glued to the actor, the baron again started mumbling advice. He once again could not bear it, and made the audience laugh again. The old crank was too sensitive. When the actor was speaking the final monologue of the second act, and paused briefly in order to shake his head silently, once again from the prompter's box came a voice that was full of bile, scorn, and hatred, but which was, alas!, already weak and broken by time:

> Bloody bawdy villain!
> Remorseless, treacherous, lecherous, kindless villain!

After remaining silent for about ten seconds, the baron sighed deeply and added not so loudly:

> Why, what an ass am I! This is most brave!

This would have been the voice of the real, not the red-haired, Hamlet, if there was no old age in the world. Old age ruins and hinders so much.

The poor baron! He is not the first, nor will he be the last, however.

Now he will be kicked out of the theatre. It is a necessary measure, you must agree.

A Kind Acquaintance

Men's tall boots and women's fur-trimmed ankle boots glide over the mirror-like ice. There are so many gliding feet that if they were in China, there would not be enough bamboo poles for them to hold on. The sun is shining particularly brightly, the air is particularly limpid, pretty cheeks are burning more than usual, and eyes are promising more than they should... In a word, live life to the full, people! But...

"Fat chance!" says fate in the form of a... kind acquaintance of mine.

I'm sitting on a bench under a bare tree at some distance from the ice rink, chatting with "her." She is so pretty, I could gobble her up along with her dear little hat, fur coat, and feet encased in gleaming skates. I am suffering, but I am also enjoying myself! Ah, love! But... fat chance...

Speusippus* Makarov, our department's porter, our Mercury and Argus, our delivery man and purveyor of pies, walks past us. His arms are piled high with men's and women's galoshes, which probably belong to Their Excellencies. Speusippus raises his hand to his cap, looks at me with love and tenderness, and stops right by the bench.

"It is cold, your honour... Wouldn't mind some t-t-tea, sir! Heh-heh..."

I give him twenty kopecks. This kind act touches him deeply. He blinks hard, looks around and whispers:

"Feel so sorry for you, your honour! Awfully sorry! A crying shame! As if you are my own son... You've got a heart of gold! You're so kind! So humble! The other day when *he*, his Excellency that is, lashed out at you, it made me sick at heart! Upon my soul! I thought, why did he do that to you? 'You're lazy, still wet round the ears, I'm going to kick you out, and so on...' Why? When you left his office, you didn't look yourself. Upon my soul... And I looked at you, I felt sorry... Ooh, I've always had a soft spot for civil servants!"

Turning to my companion, Speusippus adds:

"He is just terrible with papers. He isn't cut out to work with clever papers... He should have gone into trade or... the church... Upon my soul! He can't turn out even one paper properly... A lost cause! So he gets it in the neck..."

His Excellency really went for him... Wants to give him the boot... But I feel sorry for him. His honour is so kind..."

She looks into my eyes with the most appalling compassion.

"Go away, please!" I say to Speusippus, choking...

I feel even my galoshes have blushed. He has disgraced me, the scoundrel! Meanwhile, a little to one side sits her papa behind some bare bushes, listening and staring at us, to make sure I understand that until I have attained the rank of Titular Councillor* I should not even dare to think about... On the other side, behind some other bushes, her mother is strolling about, keeping a watchful eye on "her." I can feel these four eyes... and I want to die...

Revenge

It was the day of our ingénue's benefit performance.

Sometime after nine in the morning, the comedian was standing outside her door. He was listening intently and banging on the door with both of his big fists. It was vital he saw the ingénue. However tired she was, she had to crawl out from under the eiderdown at some point...

"Open up, damn it! How much longer do I have to freeze in this draught? If you knew it was minus twenty in your corridor, you wouldn't make me wait so long! Or maybe you're just heartless?"

At a quarter past ten the comic heard a deep sigh. The sigh was followed by the sound of someone leaping out of bed, and then came the shuffle of slippers.

"What do you want? Who is it?"

"It's me..."

The comedian did not need to give his name. It was easy to recognise him by his voice, which wheezed and whistled like someone with diphtheria.

"Just a minute, I'll put something on..."

Three minutes later she let him in. He entered the room, kissed the ingénue's hand and sat down on the bed.

"I'm here on business," he began, lighting up a cigar. "I only visit people on business, and leave social calls to those who lead lives of leisure. To get down to business... I'm playing the Count in your play tonight... You know that, of course?"

"I do."

"The Old Count. In Act Two I come on stage in a dressing gown. You know that as well, I trust. Is that right?"

"I do."

"Excellent. If I don't wear a dressing gown, I'll be sinning against the truth. The truth is paramount on stage, as everywhere else! But why am I telling you all this, *mademoiselle*? After all, when it comes down to it, Man was created for this alone—to seek the truth..."

"Yes, that's true..."

"And so, after everything I've told you, you can see that I must have a dressing gown. But I haven't got a dressing gown that is worthy of a count. If I appear in front of the audience in my cotton dressing gown, it will be greatly to your detriment. There will be a blemish on your benefit performance."

"Can I help you?"

"Yes. *He* left behind a splendid pale-blue dressing gown with a velvet collar and red tassels. A splendid, marvellous dressing gown!"

Our ingénue went scarlet... Her lovely eyes reddened and began twinkling and sparkling like glass beads in the sunlight.

"Lend me the dressing gown for tonight's performance..."

The ingénue began to pace about the room. Her uncombed hair tumbled in disorderly fashion over her face and shoulders... She began to move her lips and fingers...

"No, I can't!" she said...

"How strange... Ahem... May I ask why?"

"Why? Oh, for God's sake, it's obvious! Can I lend it? No!.. No! Never! *He* treated me badly, and was wrong... That's true! He behaved towards me like an utter swine... I agree with that! He abandoned me simply because I don't earn a great deal and I don't know how to fleece men! He wanted me to take money from these gentlemen and then deliver the filthy lucre to him. That's what he wanted! It's vile and disgusting! Only brazen scoundrels are capable of making such demands!"

The ingénue slumped into an armchair on which lay a freshly ironed blouse, and covered her face with her hands. Through her small dainty fingers the comedian could see shining dots, it was the window reflected in her tears...

"He robbed me!" she continued, sobbing. "Rob me, if you want, but why on earth leave me? Why? What did I do to him? What did I do to you? What?"

The comedian stood up and went over to her.

"Let's not cry," he said. "Tears are a sign of weakness. And anyway, we have consolation to hand at all times... Cheer up!.. Art is the ultimate solace!"

But the ultimate solace proved no consolation at all.

The sobbing was followed by hysterics.

"It'll pass!" the comedian said. "I'll wait."

While he waited for her to calm down, he wandered round the room, yawned and lay down on her bed. It was a woman's bed, but not as soft as the beds the ingénues sleep on in decent theatres. A spring poked him in the side, and his bald patch was tickled by feathers, the ends of which timidly peeped out of her pillow through its pink pillowcase. The edges of the bed were as cold as ice. None of these stopped his effrontery in having a nice stretch. Women's beds smell so good, damn it!

He lay there stretching, while the ingénue's shoulders heaved, convulsive groans escaped from her breast, her fingers twisted and tore her flannel bed jacket... The comedian had reminded her of the most unhappy episode of one of the unhappiest love affairs that had ever been! The hysterics went on for another ten minutes or so. Once she had recovered, the ingénue tossed back her hair, looked round the room and carried on the conversation.

It is awkward lying on a bed when a lady is speaking to you. Politeness is paramount! The actor grunted, got up and sat down.

"He behaved dishonourably towards me," the ingénue went on, "but that doesn't mean I have to let you have his dressing gown. Despite his despicable behaviour, I still love him, and the dressing gown is the only thing I have left of him. Whenever I see it, I think of him and... weep..."

"I have nothing against such commendable feelings," the comedian said. "On the contrary, in our mundane and hellishly practical times it's nice to meet a person with a heart and soul like yours. If you give me the dressing gown for one evening, you will be making a sacrifice, I agree... But, think how nice it is to make a sacrifice for art!"

And, after a moment's thought, the comedian sighed and added:

"Especially when I'll be bringing it straight back tomorrow..."

"It's out of the question!"

"But why? I'm not going to eat it. I'll bring it back! Honestly, you're such a..."

"No, no! It's out of the question!"

The ingénue began running about the room, waving her arms.

"It's out of the question! You want to deprive me of the only thing that's precious to me! I'd rather die than give it up! I still love that man!"

"I quite understand, but what I don't see, dear madam, is how you can put a dressing gown before art?... You are an artist!"

"It's out of the question! Not another word!"

The comedian went red and scratched his bald patch. After a moment's silence, he asked:

"So you won't give it to me?"

"It's out of the question!"

"Hmmm... Well... This is a collegial matter... One colleague asking another!"

The comedian sighed and went on:

"It's a shame, damn it! It's a great shame we're only colleagues on paper, and not in deed. Mind you, the discrepancy between words and deeds is very typical of our times. Just look at literature, for example! A great pity! A lack of solidarity and true collaboration is particularly damaging for us artists... So incredibly damaging! Actually, no! It just goes to show that we're not artists at all! We're servants, not artists! The stage is given to us only so we can show our bare elbows and shoulders to the audience... flirt with them... tickle the instincts of people up in the gods... So, you won't give it to me?"

"Not at any price!"

"Is that your last word?"

"Yes..."

"Charming..."

The comedian put on his hat, bowed ceremoniously and left the ingénue's room. Red as a beetroot, quivering with rage and spitting curses, he went down the street, straight to the theatre. He struck the frozen paving stones with his cane as he went. The pleasure he would have derived from skewing his lousy colleagues on that gnarled cane! Even better if he could impale the whole world on his artist's cane! If he were an astronomer, he would have been able to prove that this was the worst of all planets!

The theatre was at the end of the street, three hundred feet away from the jail. It was painted brick red all over, except for the yawning gaps that revealed that the theatre was built of wood. At one time, the theatre had been a barn for storing sacks of flour. It had been converted into a theatre for no other reason than that it was the tallest barn in town.

The comedian went to the box office. Sitting there at the grubby makeshift table was his pal, the cashier Stamm, a German who passed himself off as an Englishman. The cashier was part-blind, part-deaf and dim-witted, but that did not stop him listening with due attention to his colleagues.

The comedian entered the box office, frowned and stood in front of the cashier, crossing his arms on his chest like a boxer. He was silent for a while, then shook his head and exclaimed:

"What am I supposed to call these people, Mr. Stamm?!"

The comedian banged his fist on the table and lowered himself on to the wooden bench in indignation. An ocean, not a stream, of venomous, despairing, rabid words poured from his mouth, which was surrounded by an expanse that had not been shaved for a long time. Let the cashier if no one else offer him some sympathy! Some sentimental, sourpuss slip of a girl had failed to comply with the request of the man who kept this worthless shed going! Had refused to do a favour (let alone perform a service) for the first comic actor who had been invited to perform in a Petersburg theatre ten years ago! It was outrageous!

But it was more than cold in this miserable little theatre. It was as cold as a dog kennel. The old cashier was wise to sit there in his fur coat and felt boots. There was ice on the window, and a wind that even the North Pole would envy was blowing across the floor. The door would not close properly and its edges were white with hoarfrost. It was hellishly bad! It was even too cold to be angry.

"She'll not forget me!" said the comedian at the end of his tirade.

He put his feet up on the bench and covered them with the bottom of the fur coat he had inherited twelve years ago from an actor friend who had died of consumption. He wrapped himself up more tightly, fell silent and began breathing inside his coat.

His tongue was still but his mind was active. His mind was seeking a solution. He had to get his own back on this impertinent, disrespectful wench!

The comedian plunged his eyes inside the fur coat, but left them free to wander where they wanted... They, by the way, would not freeze. There was nothing interesting for them to see in the box office. By the wooden partition there was a table, in front of the table a bench, and on the bench sat the old cashier in his dog-fur coat and felt boots. Everything was grey, ordinary, and old. Even the dirt was old. There was a new, as yet unopened, book of tickets on the table. It was too early for customers. They would start coming in at lunchtime. Apart from the table, the bench, the tickets and a pile of paper in the corner, there was nothing else. Excruciating poverty and excruciating tedium!

Actually, my mistake: there was one luxurious item in the box office. It was lying under the table along with the scrap paper, which had not been swept away because it was simply too cold. And in any case the broom had disappeared.

Under the table was a large, dusty, torn bit of cardboard. The cashier would tread on it in his felt boots and would casually spit on it. It was this torn piece of cardboard that was the luxurious item. On it in big letters was written: "Today's performance sold out." Not once had it ever been necessary to hang it in the box office window and none of the audience could boast of ever having seen it. A fine, but spiteful piece of cardboard! What a pity there was no use for it. The public did not like it, but all the artists were in love with it!

As the comedian's eyes wandered over walls and floor, he could not miss this treasure. He was not usually very quick on the uptake, but this time he surpassed himself. Catching sight of the piece of cardboard, he slapped his forehead and exclaimed:

"Now there's an idea! Brilliant!"

He bent down and drew towards him the tale of a 'Full House'.

"Splendid! Superb! This will cost her a lot more than lending a pale-blue dressing gown with red tassels!"

Within ten minutes the piece of cardboard was hanging in the box-office window, for the first and last time in its whole existence, and... telling a lie.

It lied, but the public believed it. That evening our ingénue lay in her room, sobbing her heart out for the whole hotel to hear.

"The public don't like me!" she wailed.

The wind alone took upon itself the duty of commiserating with her. This kind wind howled in the chimney and air vents, moaning in many voices and probably sincerely. That evening, the comedian sat in an alehouse and drank beer. He drank beer, and that's all.

An Experience

(A Psychological Study)

It was New Year's Eve. I went out into the lobby.

Besides the porter, there were still a few people from our office standing there: Ivan Ivanych, Pyotr Kuzmich, Yegor Sidorych... They had all come to sign the sheet of paper which lay majestically on the table.* (The paper, however, was a cheap brand, No. 8.)

I glanced at the sheet. There were too many signatures and... what hypocrisy! What two-facedness! Where were you, scribbles, squiggles, underlinings and flourishes? The letters were all round and even and smooth, like rosy cheeks. I saw familiar names, but I did not recognise them. Had these gentlemen changed their handwriting?

I carefully dipped the pen into the inkwell, became inexplicably flustered, held my breath, and carefully wrote my name. I never usually insert the hard sign* at the end of my signature, but this time I did: once I had started it, I had to finish.

"Shall I destroy you?" I heard Pyotr Kuzmich's voice and his breathing in my ear.

"How are you going to do that?"

"I'll just destroy you. Yes. Shall I? He-he-he..."

"You mustn't laugh here, Pyotr Kuzmich. Remember where you are. Smiles are less than inappropriate. Excuse me, but I believe... This is a profanation, a show of disrespect, so to speak..."

"Shall I destroy you?"

"How are you going to do that?" I asked.

"Like this... The way von Klyauzen[1] destroyed me five years ago... He-he-he. It's very simple... I'll go and put a squiggle by your name. I'll do a flourish. He-he-he. I'll make your signature disrespectful. Shall I?"

---

1   *von Klyauzen*: comical invented faux-Baltic German name derived from *klyauza*, meaning petty slander or malicious gossip.

I went pale. My life really was in the hands of this man with a purple nose. I looked with fear and a certain respect into his malevolent eyes...

How little it takes to knock a man down!

"Or I'll drip some ink by your signature... Make a blot... Shall I?"

Silence fell. He was proud and majestic, aware of his power, with lethal poison in his hand, and I was miserable, aware of my powerlessness, and ready to be destroyed—we were both silent. He trained his eyeballs onto my pale face, and I avoided his gaze...

"I was joking," he said finally. "Don't worry."

"Thank you!" I said, full of gratitude, and shook his hand.

"I was joking... But I can, you know... Bear it in mind... Off you go... I am joking now... But the future is in God's hands..."

Philosophical Definitions of Life

Our life can be compared to lying on the top shelf in the bathhouse. It's hot, stuffy and steamy. The birch twigs do their job, the leaves stick to you, and your eyes sting from the soap. Shouts of 'more steam!' come from all directions. They lather your head and pummel all your bones. It is brilliant! (Sarah Bernhardt)

**

Our life can be compared to a torn shoe: its gaping hole is like an open mouth eternally begging for kasha, but nobody gives it any. (George Sand)

**

Our life can be compared to Prince Meshchersky, who is forever jostling, scurrying, exclaiming, groaning and waving his arms about; he is forever being born and dying, but never sees the fruits of his labours. He is forever giving birth, but everything he gives birth to is stillborn. (Buckle)*

**

Our life can be compared to a madman who takes himself into a certain quarter and writes cavils against himself. (Coquelin)*

**

Our life is like a newspaper which has already been given a second warning. (Kant)

**

Our life cannot be compared to a letter that is safe to read out loud, but it can be compared to a letter that fears it will not be delivered. (Draper)*

**

Our life is like a typesetter's drawer filled with punctuation marks. (Confucius)

***

Our life is like an old maid who does not lose hope of getting married, and to a face covered in spots and wrinkles: an ugly mug, but which takes offence when it is punched. (Orabi Pasha)*

***

Ultimately, our life can be compared to a frostbitten ear, which is not cut off only because there is a hope it will recover. (Charcot)*

Dredged up by Antosha Chekhonte from various philosophical essays.

Reluctant Cheats

(A New Year's Eve Tall Tale)

There is a party underway at Zakhar Kuzmich Dyadechkin's. They are celebrating New Year and congratulating the hostess Melanya Tikhonovna on her
name day.

There are many guests. They are all respectable, trustworthy and sober
people of good character. Not a single scoundrel. Their faces show tenderness,
pleasantness, and a feeling of their own worth. Sitting in the living room on the
large oilcloth sofa are the landlord Gusev and the shopkeeper Razmakhalov,
from whom the Dyadechkins buy goods on credit. They are discussing eligible
bachelors and daughters.

"These days," says Gusev, "it is hard to find a man who isn't a drinker and
is well-to-do... a man who works... It's hard!"

"The main thing is to have order at home, Alexey Vasilich!
You won't have that if at home you do not have that... which... order
at home."

"If there is no order at home, then... it's all so... There is a lot of modern
nonsense in this world... So how can you have order? Hmm..."

Three old women are sitting on chairs near them and hanging on their every word. Astonishment at such pearls of wisdom is written in their eyes. Godfather Gury Markovich is standing in the corner, examining the icon. There is
a lot of noise coming from the master bedroom. The young ladies and their
suitors are playing lotto in there. The stake is one kopeck. First-year schoolboy
Kolya is standing by the table crying. He wants to play lotto, but they will not
give him a place at the table. Is it his fault that he is little, and that he does not
have a kopeck?

"Stop wailing, you fool!" they admonish him. "What are you crying for?
Do you want Mama to spank you?"

"Who is that wailing? Kolka?" Mama's voice can be heard from the kitch-
en. "As if I hadn't walloped him enough, the little imp... Varvara Gurievna, give
him a yank on his ears!"

Two young ladies in pink dresses are sitting on their hosts' bed, which is covered by a faded calico eiderdown. Before them stands Kopaisky, a young fellow of about twenty-three who works for an insurance company and who, *en face*, looks very like a cat. He is courting them.

"I do not intend to marry," he says, showing off and loosening the high collar which is cutting into his neck with his fingers. "A woman is a radiant point in the men's mind, but she is capable of destroying a man. She is a malicious creature!"

"What about men? Men cannot love. They do all sorts of rude things."

"How naive you are! I am neither a cynic nor a sceptic, but I nevertheless know that a man will forever occupy pride of place when it comes to the emotions."

Pacing from corner to corner, like wolves in a cage, are Dyadechkin himself and his first-born Grisha. Their souls are on fire. They drank heavily over lunch and now are desperate for a hair of the dog that bit them... Dyadechkin goes into the kitchen where the hostess is sprinkling a tart with icing sugar.

"Malasha," says Dyadechkin. "You should serve appetisers. Something for the guests to nibble..."

"They can wait... Or you'll eat and drink everything now, and then what will I serve at midnight? You won't die of hunger. Go away... Get out from under my feet!"

"Just a little shot, Malasha... There will be more than enough to go round... May I?"

"Bother! Get out, I'm telling you! Go and sit with the guests! Why are you crowding the kitchen?"

Dyadechkin sighs deeply and leaves the kitchen. He goes to look at the clock. The hands show eight minutes after eleven. Fifty-two minutes to go until the desired moment. This is terrible! The anticipation of a drink is the hardest kind of anticipation. Better to wait five hours in the freezing cold for a train than to wait five minutes for a drink... Dyadechkin eyes the clock with loathing, paces up and down for a bit, then moves the big hand forward by five minutes... And Grisha? If Grisha isn't given something to drink right now, then he will go to the tavern and drink there. He is not prepared to die of misery...

"Mama," he says, "the guests are angry that you aren't serving refreshments! It's just rude... You're starving them to death!.. You could at least give them one shot!"

"You'll have to wait... It won't be much longer... Soon... Stop crowding the kitchen."

Grisha slams the door and goes for the hundredth time to look at the clock. The big hand is pitiless! It has barely moved.

"It's slow!" Grisha consoles himself, and with his index finger he nudges the hand forward seven minutes.

Kolya runs past the clock. He stops in front of it and starts working out the time remaining... He cannot wait for the moment when they shout "hurrah!" The motionless hand stabs him in the heart. He clambers onto a chair, looks round timidly, and snatches five minutes from eternity.

"Can you go and see *quelle heure est-il?*"[1] one of the young ladies urges Kopaisky. "I can't wait. It's the New Year, after all! New happiness!"

Kopaisky clicks his heels and rushes to the clock.

"Dammit," he mutters, gazing at the hands. "Such a long time still! I'm dying to tuck in... I will definitely kiss Katka when they shout hurrah."

Kopaisky walks away from the clock then stops... Having thought for a moment, he turns round and shortens the old year by six minutes. Dyadechkin downs two glasses of water, but... his soul is on fire! He paces backwards and forwards... From time to time, his wife chases him out of the kitchen. The bottles standing on the window ledge tear at his soul. What can he do? It is more than he can bear! Again he grasps at a last resort. The clock is at his service. He goes to the nursery where there is a clock hanging on the wall and encounters a picture which does not please his parental heart: Grisha is standing in front of the clock and moving the hand.

"W-w-what are you doing? Eh? Why did you move the hand? What a fool you are! Well? Why did you do that? Eh?"

Dyadechkin coughs, hesitates, frowns deeply, and makes a dismissive gesture with his hand.

"Why? Oh well... Go ahead and move the damn thing!" he says before pushing his son away from the clock and moving the hand himself.

There are eleven minutes to go until the New Year. Papa and Grisha go into the living room and start to lay the table.

"Malasha!" shouts Dyadechkin. "It's almost New Year!"

Melanya Tikhonovna runs in from the kitchen to verify her husband's words... She stares at the clock for a long time: her husband is not lying.

---

1   *quelle heure est-il*: 'what time is it' (French).

"What am I to do?" she whispers. "The peas for the ham aren't even cooked yet! Hmm. Bother. How can I serve them?"

After a moment's thought, Melanya Tikhonovna moves the big hand backwards with a shaking hand. The old year is handed back twenty minutes.

"They can wait!" says the hostess, running back into the kitchen.

Fortune Tellers

(New Year Scenes)

The children's old nanny is telling the fortune of Papa the quarter-master.

"There is a road," she says.

"Where does it lead?"

The nanny waves her hand in a northward direction. Papa's face grows pale.

"You are travelling," the old woman adds, "and there is a sack of money on your lap..."

Papa's face lights up.

***

A clerk is sitting at a table and staring into a mirror by the light of two candles.* He is trying to divine the height, hair colour and temperament of the man who has not yet been appointed as his new boss. He gazes into the mirror for one, two, three hours... Spots appear before his eyes, sticks jump about, feathers fly, but still there is no sign of his new boss! There is nothing to be seen at all, neither bosses, nor subordinates. Another hour passes by, a fifth... Eventually he grows tired of waiting for his new boss. He stands up, makes a dismissive gesture with his hand and sighs.

"That means the position will remain vacant," he says. "And that is not good. There is nothing worse than anarchy."

***

A young lady is standing in the yard by the gates and waiting for someone to pass by. She longs to know the name of her future intended. She hears footsteps. She flings the gates open and asks:

"What is your name?"

In answer to her question, she hears a moo and through the half-open gate she sees a large, dark head... On the head there are horns...

"That would be right," thinks the young lady. "The only difference will be his mug."

***

The editor of a daily paper sits down to divine the fate of his precious off-spring.

"Leave it!" they tell him. "Why upset yourself? Forget it."

The editor does not listen and stares at the coffee grinds.

"So many shapes," he says. "God knows what they mean... These are mittens... This looks like a hedgehog... And here is a nose... Just like my Makary's... And here's a calf...* Can't make anything out!"

***

The doctor's wife is fortune-telling in front of a mirror and sees... coffins.

"Could be two things," she thinks. "Either somebody is going to die, or my husband is going to have a lot of patients this year..."

The Distorting Mirror

(A Christmas Tale)

My wife and I entered the drawing room. It smelled of moss and damp. Millions of rats and mice scurried off in all directions when we illuminated walls which had not seen light for a whole century. As we closed the door behind us, a gust of wind rustled the reams of paper lying in the corners. The light fell on this paper, and we caught sight of ancient lettering and mediaeval illuminations. Hanging on the walls, which had turned green with age, were portraits of my ancestors. These ancestors looked haughty and stern, as if they wanted to say:

"You need a good thrashing, old fellow!"

Our footsteps echoed throughout the whole house. My cough was answered by an echo, the very same echo that had once answered my ancestors...

Meanwhile, the wind was howling and moaning. There was someone crying in the chimney, and in this weeping was the sound of despair. Large drops of rain hammered against the dark, opaque windows, and their hammering gave rise to a feeling of melancholy.

"Oh ancestors, forebears!" I said with a meaningful sigh. "If I were a writer, I would have written a long novel, looking at these portraits. For these old men and women were all young once, and they each had their own story. And what a story! Take this old woman, for instance, my great grandmother. This unattractive, ugly woman had her own fascinating tale."

"See that mirror?" I asked my wife, "the mirror hanging in the corner?"

And I pointed to a large mirror in a blackened bronze frame, hanging in the corner by the portrait of my great-grandmother.

"That mirror possesses magical properties: it ruined my great-grandmother. She paid a huge sum for it and did not part from it until the day she died. She stared into it constantly for days and nights on end, and she even stared into it when she was eating and drinking. When she went to bed she always laid it beside her on the mattress, and when she was dying she requested that it be put in her coffin. The only reason her request was not carried out was that the mirror would not fit into the coffin."

"Was she a coquette?" asked my wife.

"Let us assume she was. But surely she had other mirrors? Why did she love this particular mirror so much, and not some other one? Didn't she have any better mirrors? There's clearly a dreadful secret lurking here, my dear. It can't be otherwise. Legend has it that there is a devil sitting in this mirror, and that my great-grandmother had a weakness for devils. That's nonsense, of course, but there's no doubt that this mirror in the bronze frame possesses some mysterious power."

I brushed the dust from the mirror, looked into it, and burst out laughing. My laugh was answered by a hollow echo. The mirror was distorted, and it distorted all my features: my nose ended up on my left cheek and I now had two chins that pointed sideways.

"What strange taste my great-grandmother had!" I said.

My wife approached the mirror tentatively and also gazed into it—and, immediately, something dreadful happened. She turned white, all her limbs began to tremble, and she gave a shriek. The candlestick fell out of her hands, rolled across the floor, and the candle went out. Darkness enveloped us. At that very moment I heard something heavy fall to the floor: it was my wife who had lost consciousness.

The wind began to howl even more mournfully, rats started running about, and mice began to rustle amongst the papers. My hair stood on end and was ruffled when a shutter was torn off its window-frame and fell down with a clatter. The moon appeared in the window...

I gathered up my wife, put my arms around her and carried her out of my ancestors' house. It was the evening of the following day before she came to.

"The mirror! Give me the mirror!" she said as she regained consciousness. "Where is the mirror?"

For an entire week she did not drink, eat, or sleep, but kept asking for the mirror to be brought to her. She sobbed, pulled out her hair, tossed and turned, until finally, when the doctor said that she might die of starvation, and that her situation was very grave, I overcame my fear, went downstairs again and brought her back my great-grandmother's mirror. When she saw it, she began to laugh with joy, then she grabbed it, kissed it, and feasted her eyes upon it.

Since then, ten years have passed, and she is still staring into the mirror, unable to tear her eyes away even for a moment.

"Is that really me?" she whispers, and an expression of bliss and rapture joins the blush colouring her face. "Yes, it is me! Everything lies except this mirror! People lie, my husband lies! Oh, if only I'd seen myself before, if only I'd known what I was really like, I would never have married this man! He is not worthy of me! The finest, most noble of knights should be lying at my feet!.."

On one occasion when I was standing behind my wife, I unwittingly looked into the mirror and discovered the terrible secret. In the mirror I saw a woman of dazzling beauty, such as I had never seen in my whole life. She was a miracle of nature, a perfect balance of beauty, elegance, and love. But what was this? What had happened? Why did my unattractive, clumsy wife appear so beautiful in the mirror? Why?

The answer is that the distorting mirror had completely distorted my wife's unattractive face, and the rearrangement of her features had accidentally made it beautiful. A negative plus a negative had yielded a positive.

And now both of us, my wife and I, sit in front of the mirror, staring into it, unable to tear our eyes away for even a moment: my nose is creeping over to my left cheek and I have two chins that point sideways, but my wife's face is entrancing—and I am possessed by a mad, raving passion.

"Ha ha ha!" I laugh wildly.

And my wife whispers, barely audibly:

"How beautiful I am!"

Two Romances

I

A Doctor's Romance

If you have reached the age of maturity and completed your education, then the prescription is: *feminam unam*[1] and a dowry *quantum satis*.[2]

I followed it: I obtained a *feminam unam* (it is forbidden to obtain two) and a dowry. Even the ancients reprimanded those who did not take a dowry when they married (Ichthyosaurus, XII, 3).

I prescribed myself horses and a first-floor apartment, began to drink *vinum gallicum rubrum*[3] and bought a fur coat for 700 roubles. In short, I began to live by the *lege artis*.[4]

Her *habitus*[5] is fairly good. Her height is average. The colouring of her epidermis and mucous membranes is regular; the dermal-cellular layer is developed in a satisfactory manner. Her breast is proportional, she does not wheeze, and her breathing is vesicular. Her heartbeat is clear.

In the sphere of psychological manifestations, only one deviation is noticeable: she is chatty and shrill. As a result of her chattiness, I suffer from a hypersensitivity of the right auditory nerve. When I look at a patient's tongue, I think of my wife, and this recollection gives me heart palpitations. Wise was the philosopher who said, "*Lingua est hostis hominum amicusque diabolic et feminarum.*"[6] *Mater feminae*—the mother-in-law (from the class *Mammalia*)[7] is also afflicted with this.

---

1 *feminam unam*: "take: one female" (Latin).

2 *quantum satis*: "as much as you like" (Latin).

3 *vinum gallicum rubrum*: "French red wine" (Latin).

4 *lege artis*: "according to the law of the art" (Latin).

5 *habitus*: "a person's general constitution, especially physical build" (Latin).

6 *Lingua est hostis hominum amicusque diabolic et feminarum*: "Language is the enemy of men and the friend of the devil and women" (Latin).

7 *Mammalia*: "mammals" (Latin)

And when they are both shouting 23 hours a day, I suffer from a propensity to derangement and suicide.

According to my esteemed colleagues, nine-tenths of all women suffer from an illness that Charcot calls hypersensitivity of the speech-governing centre. Charcot suggests amputation of the tongue.

Through this operation he promises to rid mankind of a terrible ailment, but alas! Billroth, who has performed this procedure multiple times, says in his classic memoirs that afterwards women learned to speak with their fingers, which had an even worse effect on their husbands: it hypnotised them (*Memor. Acad.*, 1878). I propose a different treatment (see my dissertation). Without ruling out the amputation of the tongue suggested by Charcot and giving full faith to the words of an authoritative figure like Billroth, I propose combining this amputation with the wearing of mittens. My observations have shown that deaf-mute people who wear single-fingered mittens are speechless even when they are hungry.

II

A Reporter's Romance

A prim little nose, a delightful bust, marvellous hair, lovely eyes—not a single misprint! I copy-edited and married her.

"You will belong to me alone!" I told her at the wedding. "I categorically forbid retail distribution! Remember that!"

The day after the wedding, I already noticed a certain change in my wife. Her hair was thinner, her cheeks were not so provocatively pale, and her lashes were not so infernally black, but ginger. Her movements were not so suave, nor her words so tender. Alas! A wife is a bride half-crossed out by censorship!

In the first six months of our marriage I caught a young officer kissing her (young officers love *gratis* pleasures). I pronounced my first warning to her and strictly forbade retail distribution for the second time.

In the second six months of our marriage, she rewarded me with a bonus: she gave birth to a son. I looked at him, looked at myself in the mirror, looked at him again and told my wife:

"The plot has been ripped off, my dear! I can see it in his face! You can't fool me!"

I said this, and pronounced my second warning, with a prohibition on appearing before my eyes for the duration of three months.

But these measures did not prove effective. In the second year, my wife had not just one young officer, but several. Seeing her lack of remorse and not wishing to confide in my colleagues, I pronounced my third warning and sent her, together with the bonus, back to her hometown, under her parents' watch, where she remains to this day.

A monthly honorarium is sent to my wife's parents to cover her board.

Explanatory Notes

Letter to a Learned Neighbour

3   ***Exquse and forgive this old codger***: According to Chekhov's younger brother Mikhail, the letter parodies epistolary flourishes in the correspondence of their grandfather Yegor Mikhailovich and their devout but pompous father Pavel Yegorovich, who was far less well educated than his children. Other possible sources include a pamphlet entitled *Reply to the Letter to Learned People* published in Odessa in 1878 by Pyotr Tsitovich (1843-1913), the son of a village priest from Chernigov (Chernihiv in current-day Ukraine) who rose to become a professor of law in Odessa and held reactionary political views. The aforementioned "Letter to Learned People" which had been published earlier in the year by the Populist critic Nikolay Mikhailovsky in the progressive journal *Notes of the Fatherland*, contained a serious critique of Tsitovich's ideas about common landownership, and Chekhov was undoubtedly familiar with their polemic. Tsitovich went on in 1879 to publish a notorious attack on Chernyshevsky's radical 1863 novel *What is to be Done?*, before being appointed in 1880 as a Senator and Privy Councillor, and becoming editor of the ultra-conservative St. Petersburg daily newspaper *The Shore* (*Bereg*), which folded within the year despite being government-funded.

4   ***Joachim Shostak***: both first and second name are of Polish origin, "Shostak" in Russian being derived from the Polish "szostak," originally the name for a silver coin minted in the Polish-Lithuanian Commonwealth (the composer Dmitry Shostakovich's grandfather Szostakowicz came from a Polish Catholic background). Together with the letter writer's reference to his grandfather living "in the days of the Kingdom of Poland," and his membership of the Don Cossack army, he appears to reside in the steppe lands of southern Russia, close to Ukraine and Chekhov's native city of Taganrog. Most of current-day Ukraine became part of the Polish-Lithuanian Commonwealth when it was established in 1569.

Chase Two Hares And You Will Lose Them Both

9   *Siege of Kars*: the capture of the Ottoman city of Kars was a major victory for Russia during the Russo-Turkish War of 1877–1878.

Holiday Assignments
Completed By Boarding School Student Miss Nadya N.

14   *Recently Rusia was at war with Abroad, More Over many Turks were killed*: a poorly spelled sentence, riddled with grammatical mistakes.

    He had not even breathed a sound before the bear hurled him to the ground: a slightly reworded version of a rhyming couplet from the early nineteenth-century fable "The Peasant and the Worker" by Ivan Krylov (1769–1844), in which it is the peasant who has not breathed a sound ('Krest'yanin akhnut' ne uspel / Kak na nego medved nasel').

15   *"I read many books including by Meshchersky, Maykov, Dumas, Livanov, Turgenev and Lomonosov"*: an incongruous list, indiscriminately including amongst distinguished authors the conservative newspaper editor Prince Vladimir Meshchersky (1839–1914), author of the novel *Women of Petersburg High Society* (1876), and Fyodor Livanov, who published nonfiction works such as *Sectarians and Prisoners* (1868) and *The Life of a Village Priest* (1877).

    The young trees... wild pinks: the plagiarised sentence comes from Chapter IV of Turgenev's 1854 story "A Quiet Backwater."

16   *Chekhonte*: Chekhov's best-known early pseudonym, derived from a nickname given to him by one of his school teachers ("Chase Two Hares and You Will Lose Them Both" was the first story published under this pseudonym).

Papasha

21   *Titular Councillor. However, it should be the 8th grade in terms of my post*: Titular Councillor was the 9th grade in the imperial civil service Table of Ranks introduced by Peter the Great in 1722; Collegiate Assessor, 8th grade, was one level above. There were 14 grades in all.

My Jubilee

23 *I sowed about fifty stamps in the Cornfield, drowned a hundred in the Neva, burned dozens in Little Fire, and blew five hundred on the Dragonfly*: the narrator is referring to popular weekly magazines published in St. Petersburg from the end of the 1870s. Chekhov himself was at this point only a regular contributor to *The Dragonfly*, the illustrated comic journal which published the present story, and in which he had made his literary debut with *Letter to a Learned Neighbour* some four months earlier.

On Account of the Apples

27 *Antonovka apples*: a particularly popular Russian variety.

as Eugène Sue spent on his magnum opus The Wandering Jew: the ten-volume serial novel *Le Juif errant* by Marie-Joseph "Eugène" Sue (1804–1857) was published in 1844–45.

28 *"Dimwit, nitwit, dumb-bell, dummy lost at Rummy"*: the untranslatable Russian original, "Muzhichki, prostachki, chudachki, durachki proigralis' v durachki," with its repeated diminutive plurals (ending in "chki") literally means: "Peasants, simpletons, cranks, fools lost at [the card game] Fools"—in other words been made fools of.

his soul was partaking with a particular ardour in cold slumber: an ironic partial quotation of the line 'dusha vkushaet khladnyi son' ('[his] soul partakes cold slumber') from "The Poet" (1827), Pushkin's celebrated poem about the arrival of creative inspiration.

Before the Wedding

33 *Collegiate Registrar*: the 14th and lowest grade in the imperial civil service Table of Ranks.

Lanin champagne: inexpensive sparkling wine produced by Nikolay Lanin (1832–1895), a well-known Moscow merchant who specialised in effervescent drinks.

letter yat: vowel in the Cyrillic alphabet almost indistinguishable from 'e' which became increasingly obsolete in the nineteenth century, and was eliminated with spelling reforms introduced in 1917.

34 *magazine Entertainment*: one of the first comic magazines published in Russia. *Razvlechenie* was founded by Fyodor Miller, a Russian translator and poet of German descent, in 1859.

36 *Malthus*: Thomas Malthus (1766–1834)—English economist and demographer best known for his theory that population growth will always outrun food production.

Court Councillor: Seventh grade in the imperial civil service according to the Table of Ranks.

Titular Councillor: see notes to "Papasha."

The American Way

38 *St. Peter's Day*: celebrated on 29th of June according to the Julian calendar, St. Peter's and St. Paul's day traditionally marked the start of the summer hunting season.

Rejections Column: this is where editors of comic journals would traditionally notify authors of unsuccessful submissions.

The Dragonfly: see notes to "My Jubilee."

The Russian Newspaper: the Moscow-based *Russkaya gazeta* experienced problems with censorship, and was published intermittently between 1876 and 1881.

My favourite poets are Pushkarev and sometimes myself: Nikolay Pushkarev (1841–1906)—Russian poet and journalist whose poems often appeared in magazines which he published himself. Chekhov was on friendly terms with him.

certainly not a Jew. A Jewish wife is bound to ask "What do you charge per line? And why didn't you go to Papa? He would have taught you how to make money": Chekhov's crude caricatures here can be attributed to youthful ignorance: antisemitism was rife in the Russian empire, and became even more pronounced in the 1880s. Over the course of the decade, as he matured, Chekhov acquired a rare sensitivity to ethnic and religious minorities, which led him deliberately to place sympathetic Jewish characters from the Pale of Settlement, hitherto absent from Russian literature, at the heart of his fiction. He also formed a close friendship with the Jewish-Russian painter Isaak Levitan. The stories in this volume show that Chekhov was just as capable of producing crude caricatures of other ethnicities.

39 *Entertainment*: see notes to "Before the wedding."

39 **New Times Weekly**: literary-scientific magazine founded by Alexey Suvorin in St. Petersburg as a weekly supplement to the newspaper *New Times* (*Novoe vremya*). It was later superseded by *Historical Herald* (*Istoricheskii vestnik*).
Nana: novel by Émile Zola (1880).
The Moscow Gazette: *Moskovskie vedomosti* was Russia's largest newspaper from its foundation in 1756 until the mid-nineteenth century, when it was overtaken by St. Petersburg dailies, and became more conservative-leaning.
The Shore: see notes to "Letter to a Learned Neighbour."

Artists' Wives
(Translation from the Portuguese)

51 **Derzhavin**: Contemporary Russian readers would have been amused by Chekhov's playful reference to the poet Gavriil Derzhavin (1743–1816), who could not possibly have been a contemporary of Zola (1840–1902).
Lermantoff: thinly disguised reference, via an inaccurate foreign transliteration, to the poet Mikhail Lermontov (1814–1841), who was too young to have known Derzhavin.

52 **"To hell with all those artists," as the Ukrainians say**: "Tsur [im] i pek" is an exclamation used by Ukrainians wanting to be rid of something—Pek is a pre-Christian god of hell. Chekhov had a Ukrainian grandmother, grew up in the southern city of Taganrog hearing and speaking the language, and identified as partially Ukrainian. His word for Ukrainians, used affectionately here, is "topknots" or *khokhols* (*khokhly*), which refers to the tufts of hair Cossacks retained on their otherwise shaved heads. The Internet Encyclopaedia of Ukraine tells us that although it was a word "primarily used by Russians to denigrate Ukrainians, at times, especially in the nineteenth century, it was used by Ukrainians as a term of self-identification," which is the case here.

St. Peter's Day

53 **The 29th of June has arrived**: see notes to "The American Way."
the tarantasses: old-fashioned four-wheeled carriages on a long frame without springs, which are here each harnessed to three horses, hence the earlier reference to two "troikas" (literally a "group of three"), which are traditional Russian sleighs or carriages drawn by three horses harnessed abreast.

Avvakum: the name of a famous Old Believer archpriest, author of the first Russian autobiography, burned to death for his zealotry during Siberian exile in 1682. Later on in the story, another servant called Firs is mentioned. Both names were archaic, and very uncommon in the nineteenth century. Chekhov later gave the name of Firs to the old retainer in his last play, *The Cherry Orchard*.

54   *St. Anna's Cross*: Russian imperial decoration awarded for distinguished state service with four classes, the first of which conferred hereditary nobility, the lower three personal nobility. The retired General wears his St. Anna's Cross round his neck, denoting it is second class. Chekhov would in 1895 write *Anna Round the Neck*, a story with a punning title.

57   *The Cornfield*: see notes to "My Jubilee."

      Rejections Column: see notes to "The American Way."

58   *kurgan*: prehistoric burial mound frequently found in the southern Russian and Ukrainian steppe, mention of which, along with great bustards, confirms the story is set in the countryside outside Taganrog which Chekhov enjoyed exploring in his late teens.

Personality Types
(According to the Latest Scientific Findings)

66   *Hufeland*: the pioneering German biologist and doctor Christoph Wilhelm Hufeland (1762–1836) was author of the book *Macrobiotics, or the Art of Prolonging Life* (1805), which underwent numerous editions and was translated into many European languages.

67   *The Cornfield*: see notes to "My Jubilee":

68   *At one time, he read The Moscow Gazette, but this caused him chest pain, heart palpitations and blurred vision, so he gave it up*: this sentence was censored when the story was first published, as criticism of the newspaper and its editor Mikhail Katkov was not tolerated at this time.

      Debay and Jozan: Auguste Debay (1802–1890)—French physician and author of a book which became a much reprinted best-seller for its frank discussion of conjugal relations: *Hygiene and Marital Physiology: Natural and Medical History of the Married Man and Woman in Its Most Curious Details* (Hygiène et physiologie du mariage: Histoire naturelle et médicale de L'homme et de la femme mariés dans ses plus curieux details, 1848). Emile Jozan: French physician (1817–1892), specialist in genito-urinary pathology, and author of such works as *Practical Treatise On Diseases of the Urinary Tract* (Traité pratique des maladies des voies urinaires, 1850) and *On A Frequent and Little-Known Cause of Premature Ejaculation: A Practical Treatise on Loss of Semen for Lay People* (D'une cause fréquente et peu connue d'épuisement prématuré: traité pratique des pertes séminales à l'usage des gens du monde, 1858). The editors of Chekhov's Complete Collected Works tell us the works of Debay and Jozan were very popular in Russia in the 1870s and 1880s.

68 **Vetlyanka plague**: this refers to an outbreak of bubonic plague in the village of Vetlyanka in Astrakhan Province in 1878, which caused the deaths of 446 people out of a population of 1700, causing widespread alarm.

Luchinushka: immensely popular Russian folk song with many variations—in one of them a woman is waiting all night for her "friend" to arrive and lamenting that the birch splinter (*luchinushka*) illuminating her home is not burning brightly enough for him to see it.

69 ***A black cat crossed his path, a devil knocked him on the back of the head and he turned into a choleric-melancholic. I refer to an illustrious and immortal neighbour of the editorial office of The Spectator***: the editorial offices of the *Moscow Gazette* were also located on Strastnoy Boulevard in Moscow. The entire passage describing the "choleric-melancholic" temperament was censored (or cut before submission to the censor) owing to it being a thinly disguised satire of the newspaper's editor Mikhail Katkov. *The Spectator*: illustrated literary and comic magazine published in Moscow from 1881 until 1886, with issues at first appearing three times a week, then twice a week. This story was published in *The Spectator*.

On the Train

71 **Reval**: historic Germanic name for Tallinn, capital of current-day Estonia.

72 **Railway baron Polyakov**: the celebrated "railway king" and philanthropist of Jewish descent Samuil Polyakov (1837–1888), who was based in St. Petersburg, had by the time of his sudden death at the age of 50 built about a quarter of all the railways in imperial Russia, including the Kozlov-Voronezh-Rostov-on-Don and Kursk-Kharkov-Azov lines, on which Chekhov travelled when returning home to Taganrog.

Salon des Variétés

76 **Salon des Variétés**: a popular cabaret on Bolshaya Dmitrovka Street in Moscow. It was frequented in the summer of 1881 by Chekhov, his brother Nikolay and a couple of their distant maternal relatives, Fyodor Gundobin and Ivan Lyadov, both merchants from Shuya, Ivanovo province. Gundobin ran a successful grocery business. They all make an appearance towards the end of the sketch.

78 **Biersuppe**: a German roux-based soup made with beer.

79 **Mr. Kuznetsov himself**: Yegor Kuznetsov was the proprietor of the Salon des Variétés.

Kolya, shall we scratch our throats? Drink, Mukhtar: Kolya here is the nickname of Chekhov's brother Nikolay, while the person asking the question is Ivan Lyadov, and Mukhtar is Fyodor Gundobin. Chekhov nicknamed him "Mukhtar," since he resembled Ahmed Mukhtar Pasha, the commande er-in-chief of the Turkish army on the Caucasian front of the Russo-Turkish War (1877–1878).

Antosha Chekhonte's Classified Ads Bureau

84 **The Spectator**: see notes to "Personality Types."

Sarah Bernhardt: the legendary French actress (1844–1923) appeared in Moscow in November 1881 in twelve performances of Dumas-fils' *La Dame aux Camélias*.

85 **N. Morskoy**: pen name of the writer Nikolay Lebedev (1846–1888). The first part of his novel *Sodom* (1880) was published in the *New Times Weekly* supplement before being banned, although all four parts were published in book form in 1881. The conservative critic Nikolay Mikhailovsky discussed *Sodom* along with other recent Russian fiction about tangled relationships in a review entitled 'Pornography' published in the journal *Notes of the Fatherland* in May 1881.

Tsitovich: see notes to "Letter to a Learned Neighbour."

Evgeny Lvov: pen name of Evgeny Lvovich Kochetov (1845–1905), a journalist for the conservative newspaper *Moscow Gazette*.

Andrey Pechersky: pen name of Pavel Melnikov (1818–1883), author of *In the Forests* (V lesakh, 1871–1874) and *On the Hills* (Na gorakh, 1875–1881), lengthy and very popular linked novels about the life of Old Believer merchants in Nizhny Novgorod.

the newspaper Rus: weekly Slavophile newspaper published in Moscow between 1880–1886 by the journalist Ivan Aksakov (1823–1886).

86 **the Moscow Sheet**: one of the first Russian daily newspapers to be aimed at a mass readership, *Moskovskii listok* was founded in 1881 by its entrepreneurial editor Nikolay Pastukhov (1831–1911), a former reporter with basic education who unashamedly pursued commercial success. Printed on the cheapest paper, and particularly popular with the working classes, it focused on local news instead of international politics, transforming, in Daniel R. Brower's words "the sensational and ephemeral events of the city into a sort of daily street theatre" (*The Russian City between Tradition and Modernity, 1850–1900* [Berkeley: University of California Press, 1990], 178).

The City Is Being Abolished: a play by Viktor Krylov (1838–1906), a prolific but undistinguished playwright who wrote under the pseudonym Viktor Aleksandrov. It was published in 1882, just before Chekhov published these parodies of classified ads.

87 **the Russian Newspaper**: this Moscow-published newspaper had four joint publishers and editors in 1880. It ceased publication in October 1881, and in 1882 it produced only one issue before closing permanently.

the Winkler Museum: in addition to a museum of life size mechanical wax figures, Hugo Winkler ran a 'menagerie and monkey theatre' on Tsvetnoy Boulevard in Moscow in the 1880s. It gave four performances daily, and featured the sensation of an Indian elephant 'riding a bicycle'.

It can carry 26 ballerinas: pupils from the Imperial Ballet schools in St. Petersburg and Moscow in the nineteenth century were famously transported to and from performances in an ancient carriage.

88 **the clothes are by Ayé**: the French tailor Philippe Ayé (presuming this is the correct spelling from the transliterated Russian) on Tverskaya Street was considered the best and most stylish in Moscow. In 1876, Tolstoy spent some of his 20,000 rouble advance for *Anna Karenina* on a frock coat and a black bear fur coat made by him.

This and That
(*Letters and Telegrams*)

91 **Sarah's health**: Chekhov's spoof letters and telegrams all concern the Moscow performances of Sarah Bernhardt.

94   *Sobakevich*: invented comic name for a character in Gogol's novel *Dead Souls* (1842) derived from the word *sobaka* (dog). Chekhov later uses the name Sobakevich again in *"The Alarm Clock* Almanac." The name of the usher 'Major Kovalyov' comes from Gogol's surreal 1836 story *The Nose*.

The Sinner From Toledo
(*Translated from the Spanish*)

95   *(Translated from the Spanish)*: needless to say, Chekhov knew no Spanish, and never visited Spain, but in November 1881, a few weeks before writing this story, he made friends with the Spanish virtuoso violinist Pablo Sarasate (1844–1908) during his Moscow tour. At the end of 1881, Sarasate sent his 'friend Dr. Antonio Chekhonte' his photograph from Rome 'as a token of his gratitude to medicine'.

Supplementary Questions to the Personal Census Forms,
Suggested By Antosha Chekhonte

100   *Supplementary Questions to the personal census forms, suggested by Antosha Chekhonte*: there were fifteen questions included in the official census, conducted in Moscow between 23 January and 25 January 1882. During his work as a census taker, Chekhov thought up ten additional frivolous questions, which he published a few days later.

      Which columnist is most to your liking? Suvorin? Bukva? Amicus? Lukin? Julius Schreier or?: Alexey Suvorin—editor of *New Times*; Bukva—pseudonym used by *Dragonfly* editor Ippolit Vasilevsky for his Sunday articles in *Stock Exchange Gazette* (*Birzhevye vedomosti*); Amicus—pseudonym of Pyotr Monteverde, who became editor of *The Petersburg Newspaper* in 1881; Aleksandr Lukin—regular Moscow columnist for *The News* (*Novosti*); Julius Schreier—columnist and former editor of *The News*.

      Are you a Joseph or a Caligula? A Susanna or a Nana? Chekhov resorts to extremes by asking male respondents to identify with either with meek biblical figures of Joseph or the tyrannical Roman emperor Caligula, while females are asked to identify either with the chaste Susanna or the courtesan Nana, the eponymous heroine of Zola's novel.

At the Wolf Baiting

101   Chekhov was one of several writers who condemned the hunting of wolves which took place in Khodynskoe Field in the north of Moscow in January 1882. Due to the outcry, by the following year it had ceased to be a public spectacle.

Comic Advertisements and Notices
(Reported by Antosha Chekhonte)

106   **Dentist Gewalter**: A dentist called Grigory Valter actually did place several announcements in the *Moscow Sheet* in 1882. He wanted to distinguish himself from another dentist called Alexander Valter, with whom patients were confusing him.

   Leukhin's Bookshop: the names of the books which Sergey Leukhin advertised as being on sale in his Moscow bookshop often sounded comical even before Chekhov subjected them to parody.

107   **News and Stock Exchange Gazette**: in 1880 the journalist and dramatist Osip Notovich (1849–1914) combined the *News* and the *Stock Exchange Gazette*, which became an influential daily newspaper.

   Minute's editorial office: the commercial daily newspaper the *Minute*, which launched in St. Petersburg in 1880 was edited by Ivan Batalin (1844–1918).

108   **Barrister Smirnov**: the fist fight between the lawyer M. N. Smirnov and one of his colleagues filled many column inches in the Moscow press in 1882.

   Nana Sukhorovskaya: comical combination of the first name of the courtesan Anna 'Nana' Coupeau, the heroine of Zola's provocative novel, published in 1880, with the surname of the painter Martsely Sukhorovsky (1840–1908). The recumbent and seductive nude portrait he painted of Zola's scandalous character brought him both fame, fortune and notoriety. Seen as pornographic in conservative quarters, it was exhibited with great success in towns across Russia and also in Europe and America, where it was billed as the 'world's greatest picture' and sold for the highest sum ever paid for a Russian painting before 1917. It was first exhibited in Moscow in February 1882 (just before the publication of Chekhov's comic advertisements), in a separate gallery on Petrovskie Linii Street, for the exorbitant entrance fee of 50 kopecks.

   Journalist Molchanov: Alexander Molchanov (1847–1916) was a foreign correspondent for *New Times*.

One hundred and forty-five lawyers, for Taganrog: a reference to the impending trial of the Greek-Russian millionaire merchant Mark Valiano (Marinos Vallianos, 1808–1906), who in the 1840s had set up a highly lucrative grain trade and shipping business with his brothers Panayis and Andreas in Chekhov's native city. He was arrested by the Russian government in 1882 for wide-scale corruption and non-payment of taxes.

To be wept by Mr. Ivanov-Kozelsky: stage name of the actor born Mitrofan Ivanov (1850–1898), who came from a peasant family in Kiev province. His greatest role, which he worked on throughout his career, was that of Hamlet. He first performed in St. Petersburg and Moscow in 1880.

To be declaimed with indignation by Averkiev: the St. Petersburg-based dramatist, poet and critic Dmitry Averkiev (1836–1905), author of historical plays, as well as the libretto to Serov's opera *Rogneda*, came from a merchant background in Krasnodar and tended to write in an elevated rhetorical style.

To be fizzed by the editor Mr. Lanin: as well as producing sparkling wine, in 1880 Nikolay Lanin took over the newly established daily newspaper the *Russian Courier*, and became its editor the following year.

To be sung by Mme Brenko: stage name of the enterprising actress Anna Chelishcheva (1848–1934). Via various circumnavigations she managed to open Moscow's first privately run theatre in 1880, two years before Alexander III abolished the Imperial Theatres monopoly and made it legally possible to do so. The Pushkin Theatre, so called due to its location near to Pushkin Square, was artistically ambitious—Ivanov-Kozelsky starred in its noted production of *Hamlet*. Financial problems caused it to close half way through its second season, however, as reported in the *Moscow Sheet* on 7 February 1882, just before Chekhov's parody went to press. He alludes to its insolvency in the next item of his spoof recital programme.

109 *to be performed Mr. Shostakovsky*: Pyotr Shostakovsky (1851–1916) was a pianist of Polish descent (his father's name was Adam) who was probably born Piotr Szostakowski. He grew up in current-day Latvia and studied at the St. Petersburg Conservatoire and with Liszt in Weimar, before settling in Moscow. In addition to giving popular recitals, he opened a music school in 1878.

The Mad Mathematician's Maths Test

110 *Autolimedes*: invented name.

Forgotten!!

114 ***Liszt, Rhapsody Number Two***: Chekhov and his brother Nikolay later became
enraptured with Liszt's famous Hungarian Rhapsody no. 2 in C sharp minor
of 1847 after hearing Pyotr Shostakovsky perform it at the All-Russian Exhibition in Moscow which opened in May 1882.

Life in Questions and Exclamations

115 ***Krylov's fable Demyan's Fish Soup:*** this famous fable by Ivan Krylov, in which
the peasant Demyan plies his neighbour Foka with too much fish soup against
his will, gave rise to the phrase 'Demyan's fish soup' denoting a situation in
which one is foisted with something burdensome and excessive against one's
will.

116 ***George Born***: pseudonym of the German historical novelist Karl George Füll-
born (1837–1902) whose *Eugenia, or the Secrets of the Tuileries* (Eugenia oder
die Geheimnisse der Tuileries, 1872), was published in Russian translation in
1882, just when Chekhov was writing this story.

    Strelna... Yar: popular restaurants famed for their gypsy music, both located on
the northern outskirts of Moscow on the Peterburgskoe Shosse, the main road
to the capital.

117 ***The Jester***: the satirical weekly "artistic magazine with cartoons" was founded in
Saint Petersburg in 1879 by the artist Dmitry Esipov.

Confession, Or Olya, Zhenya, Zoya
(A Letter)

120 ***fair-minded as Aristides, and as strict as Cato***: the Athenian general Aristides
was nicknamed 'the Just' (530–468 BCE); the Roman senator and historian
Marcus Portius Cato, Cato the Elder (234–149 BCE) was known for his public morality and discipline.

121 ***Khokhlov, Kochetova, Bartsal, Usatov, Korsov...***: Pavel Khokhlov (1854–
1919)—baritone soloist at the Bolshoi Theatre, 1879–1900; Zoya Kochetova
(1857–1892)—soprano soloist at the Bolshoi Theatre, 1880–1883; Anton
Bartsal—Czech-born tenor soloist at the Bolshoi Theatre 1878–1902; Dmitry Usatov (1847–1913)—tenor soloist at the Bolshoi Theatre, 1880–1889;

Bogomir Korsov, born Gottfried Gering—baritone soloist at the Bolshoi Theatre, 1882–1905.

124 **Brother writers, something fatal lies in our destiny!**: famous line from Nikolay Nekrasov's 1855 poem "In the hospital."

The Greeting of Spring

125 **Zephyrus has taken over from Boreas**: reference to two of the Greek wind gods, Zephyrus being the bringer of spring breezes from the west, and Boreas ushering in cold winter air from the north.

126 **Jews**: Chekhov uses here the pejorative term 'zhid'. Post-Emancipation industrialisation was accompanied by an increase in antisemitism at all levels of Russian society from the late 1870s onwards, as reflected in Dostoevsky's *Writer's Diary* (1876–1881) and Tolstoy's novel *Anna Karenina* (1878). The crude ethnic stereotyping in Chekhov's writing gradually disappeared as he matured, particularly after he developed a close friendship with the Russian-Jewish painter Isaak Levitan. Russian antisemitism persisted after the abolition of the Pale of Settlement in 1917, and it is striking but perhaps not surprising that Chekhov's use of the term 'zhid' in his juvenilia receives no comment in the annotations to the Soviet edition of his Complete Collected Works, published between 1974 and 1983.

kulaks: in Chekhov's time "kulaks" were entrepreneurial and well-to-do peasants in the post-Emancipation era who often became notorious money-lenders.

cachucha: lively Spanish dance in triple time accompanied by castanets.

127 **Berdichev, Zhitomir, Rostov, and Poltava**: provincial towns located in the Pale of Settlement. This was the area established by Catherine II in 1791 in the most westerly region of the Russian Empire where her newly acquired Jewish subjects were obliged to reside following the Partitions of Poland. Berdichev, Zhitomir and Poltava are all located in current-day Ukraine; Rostov-on-Don (and nearby Taganrog, Chekhov's home town) officially ceased to be part of the Pale of Settlement in 1888.

Alarm Clock Almanac
For March–April 1882

128 **Kasha**: cooked grain, usually buckwheat.

Autolimides II... Dodon IV: while Autolimides is an invented name first used by Chekhov in his earlier *Comic Advertisements,* 'Dodon' is the name of a frequently incompetent Tsar in Russian fairy tales, and in Pushkin's story *The Golden Cockerel* (1835).

Prince Meshchersky: in addition to his satirical high society novels Prince Vladimir Meshchersky (1839–1914) was the editor of the conservative St. Petersburg weekly journal the *Citizen* which he founded in 1872. It was subsidised by the Tsarist government and began to appear twice-weekly in 1882.

129 ***"Little Russian"***: archaic appellation for the part of Ukraine which became part of the Russian Empire. Originally an innocuous Byzantine ecclesiastical term now perceived as pejorative, it was re-introduced in the seventeenth century when the Cossack Hetmanate came under Russian protection in 1654, and came to denote most of modern-day Ukraine after Catherine II abolished the Cossack Hetmanate in 1764.

Pan Twardowski died in the "Rome" inn: reference to the hero of a famous Polish equivalent to the Faust legend. In it a sixteenth-century sorcerer is lured by the devil to a tavern called "Rome," the city where he has agreed to give up his soul. The editors of Chekhov's Complete Collected Works err in believing the reference could be to Verstovsky's by then obscure 1828 opera *Pan Twardowski.* Chekhov was familiar with the story via a re-telling first published in Moscow in a cheap popular edition in 1868 and reprinted dozens of times. He knew and admired the author Mikhail Evstigneev (1832–1885), whom he met in 1882, and failed to persuade him to write his autobiography before his untimely death from alcoholism. The illegitimate son of a lower-class townsman and a former serf, "Misha Evstigneev," as he invariably signed his books, led a peripatetic life working in the leather and fur dying trade before writing more than 150 books in many different genres, often illustrating them himself, with the express aim of entertaining his mass-market readership, who bought them at fairs all over Russia.

an impostor will appear, claiming to be Hamlet: Pyotr Veinberg (1831–1908) had just published someone else's poem under the pseudonym "Hamlet" in *The Dragonfly* in March 1882.

Alexander Philipovich of Macedon: Chekhov gives Alexander the Great a Russian-style patronymic (he succeeded his father Philip II in 336 BCE). Bucephalus was his favourite horse.

130 ***Gladstone will dine with the king of the Ashanti***: After beginning his second term as British Prime Minister in 1880, William Gladstone (1809–1898), who

opposed the Conquest of Africa, sought more peaceful relations with the Ashanti Empire, with which Britain had already fought several wars in the nineteenth century. It was nevertheless later colonised in 1901, and since 1957 has been part of Ghana.

Maly Theatre: the Imperial Maly Theatre (literally 'Small Theatre'), situated in the same square as the Bolshoi ('Big') Theatre, was the main stage for drama in prerevolutionary Moscow.

131 *demure Theodelinda*: born a Bavarian princess, in 588 Theodelinda (c. 570–628 AD) was married for the first time to Authari, King of the Lombards, who died two years later.

Mr. Stalinsky: Yevgeny Stalinsky was editor and publisher of the newspaper *Kharkov*, which he founded in 1877. In 1880, its final year, he published an issue dated 30 February. Three years later (in *Fragments of Moscow Life*, 13 August 1883), Chekhov described him as someone who wore an old-fashioned top hat, wrote poetry and loved philosophising.

132 *Menelaus made the acquaintance of both Ajaxes*: Menelaus was the brother of Agamemnon, King of Sparta, and husband of Helen, whose abduction by Paris provoked the Trojan Wars. Ajax the Great, hero of the Trojan Wars, was the son of Telamon, King of Selamis. Ajax The Lesser, another Greek hero, was the son of Oileus, King of Locris.

Pyotr Boborykin: the prolific novelist, dramatist, essayist, critic, editor, and philosopher Pyotr Boborykin (1836–1921) had long been a figure of public ridicule by the time Chekhov began publishing the four instalments of his "*Alarm Clock* Almanac" in March 1882. A second-rate writer with an over-inflated sense of his own importance, he was particularly notorious for his interminable, turgid novels, which had been the target of widespread satire since the early 1860s. His birthday was in fact on the 15th not the 16th of August.

"*A collision between a comet and Mr. Lentovsky*": the actor, director and impresario Mikhail Lentovsky (1843–1906), originally from Saratov, was a colourful and extravagant figure in Moscow theatrical life in the 1880s when restrictions on privately run theatrical ventures were finally removed. In 1878 he began renting the "Hermitage" pleasure garden in northern central Moscow and opened the city's first operetta theatre there. Its great popularity, coupled with his love of grandiose and unusual scenic effects, led him in 1880 to install gas lighting and start rebuilding, with assistance from Chekhov's artist brother Nikolay. The opening of the "Fantastic Theatre" in July 1882 during the All-Russia Exhibition was the subject of one of Chekhov's earliest pieces of journalism, written a few months after completing his *"Alarm Clock Almanac."*

133 ***Madame Olga Molokhovets' Classic Russian Cooking***: Elena Molokhovets (1831–1918) was author of the classic cookbook *Gift To Young Housewives*, first published in 1861 and reprinted many times.

Messrs. Potekhin, Suvorin and the folk hero Alyosha-Popovich: the writers Potekhin (1829–1908) and Suvorin (1834–1912), shared the same first name: Alexey. Chekhov achieves a comic effect by aligning them with the diminutively named folk hero Alyosha-Popovich ("Alexey, son of the priest"), a mythical knight who features in Russia's medieval epic ballads.

Bloch will experience pangs of guilt: After the banking operation set up in Moscow by Sigismund Bloch in 1871 collapsed in 1881, its founder fled his creditors and went abroad, causing some desperate bankrupted investors to commit suicide, as reported on in the press. When Bloch returned to Russia in 1882, he was immediately sent to debtors' prison.

Baker Filippov: Ivan Filippov (1824–1878), granted the imperial warrant in 1855, became the most famous baker in Russia, and was the founder of a dynasty which continued to expand the family business after his death. By the time that Chekhov was writing, the Filippov Bakery had branches both in Moscow and St. Petersburg, with hundreds of employees.

134 ***The Murder of Coverley***: Russian name for the five-act French melodrama *L'Affaire Coverley* by Adrien Barbusse and Henri Crisafulli, which was translated by Nikolay Kireev (1843–1882) soon after it was written in 1875. It was successfully staged in provincial theatres in Russia, including in Taganrog, where it became a firm favourite with the adolescent Chekhov. The play begins with Arthur Gordon murdering Sir Roger Coverley on a steamship which sinks in the Pacific, and ends with him going mad and dying, after his accomplice and cousin has been sensationally run over by a whistling steam train appearing to roar out of a tunnel from the depths of the stage straight towards the audience, who are dazzled by its headlights. Chekhov deployed the same device of an advancing train in the second act of his unwieldy first play *Platonov*, which he wrote in 1878.

not your aunt: part of the Russian proverb "hunger is not your aunt; it will not bring you a pie."

the Salamonsky circus: a famous circus founded in Moscow in 1880 by the circus acrobat and rider Albert Salamonsky (1839–1913).

134 *Mr. Lokhvitsky's birthday*: Alexander Lokhvitsky (1830–1884) was a scholar and teacher of law in St. Petersburg. After the 1864 judicial reforms and the introduction of public trials, he became a prominent and controversial criminal defence barrister and moved to Moscow where he became renowned, according to his daughter, the popular writer Nadezhda Teffi, for his oratory and wit.

135 *concert at the Assembly Hall of the Nobility*: The Assembly of the Nobility was a self-governing organisation in each province instituted in 1766 which concerned itself both with the noble class and local administrative affairs. Its headquarters in central Moscow, the late eighteenth-century House of Unions, was a venue famous for balls and other social occasions attended by the nobility.

136 *Kind Soul*: humorous magazine with cartoons which began appearing in 1882 as a weekly supplement to the *Citizen*, the newspaper published by Prince Meshchersky (in Russian: *Dobryak*).

   Rus editorial offices: see notes to "Anton Chekhov's Classified Ads Bureau."

   kvass: low-alcohol drink made from fermented black bread.

   Strelna restaurant: see notes to "Life in Questions and Exclamations."

   Misha Evstigneev's birthday: see earlier note about Pan Twardowski.

137 *Donetsk Coal Mining Railway*: dense cluster of new railway lines built by Savva Mamontov between 1875 and 1880, linking mining villages to the port of Mariupol for the export of Donbas coal. Chekhov was familiar with this network, which was located immediately to the north of Taganrog, and intersected with the main line to Kharkov.

   the arch-oddball I. N. Pavlov: the Moscow-based journalist, teacher and critic Ippolit Pavlov (1839–1882) contributed to various conservative and Slavophile newspapers and journals, and in 1880 edited the short-lived weekly *Horizon* (*Krugozor*), which was vicious in its criticism of contemporary realist writers such as Zola, Saltykov-Shchedrin and Boborykin. Pavlov took the same stance in lectures he gave on modern Russian literature in Moscow in 1882.

   apart from Prince Meshchersky and Prince Batalin: allusion to the small number of subscribers to Meshchersky's the *Citizen* and Batalin's *The Minute*.

   Messrs. Sadovsky, Musil and Pravdin: Mikhail Sadovsky, Nikolay Musil and Osip Pravdin were all well-known actors at the Imperial Maly Theatre in Moscow in 1882.

138 *kulich and paskha*: rich Orthodox celebratory foods forbidden during Lent. "Kulich" is a sweet yeast bread made with butter, eggs and raisins traditionally baked in a cylindrical tin. "Paskha" (the Russian word for "Easter") is made in a pyramid-shaped mould with milk, eggs and curd cheese, and then decorated

with dried fruits and the Russian letters 'X B,' standing for *Khristos Voskrese*— Christ has Risen.

the poet Khrushchov-Sokolnikov: the son of a wealthy Tula landowner and a prolific novelist, Gavriil Khrushchov-Sokolnikov (1845–1890) also founded and edited a journal, published poetry under dozens of pseudonyms, and established a successful photographer's studio. Chekhov knew him quite well as a fellow contributor to magazines, but they were not friends. By the time he came to be writing his "*Alarm Clock* Almanac" in the spring of 1882, his elder brother Alexander had formed an ill-fated relationship with Khrushchov-Sokolnikov's ex-wife Anna, who also worked as an editorial secretary at *The Spectator*, which at that time employed four of the Chekhov brothers in varying capacities. She was his elder by eight years, suffered from tuberculosis, already had two children, and had been banned by the church from remarrying under the terms of the divorce she had been granted in 1877. When she became pregnant with the first of their three illegitimate children in the summer of 1882, she and Alexander moved to Taganrog, where he could only find a lowly job in the customs office, having dropped out of university. Chekhov shared his parents' disapproval.

140   **the poet M. Yaron**: the son of an Odessa vet, Mark Yaron (1863–1893) became a poet and newspaper reporter for the Moscow boulevard press disliked by Chekhov. An inveterate gambler, he later married the opera singer Eleonora Melodist and translated librettos.

the Russian Satirical Sheet will go under: illustrated comic weekly founded in Moscow in January 1882 by Nikolay Polushin. It ceased publication after only twelve issues in April 1882 (just as Chekhov was compiling the entries for his Almanac), resuming only in February the following year.

Kifa Mokievich: character in Gogol's *Dead Souls* (1842) preoccupied with pondering the meaning of the world.

Krechinsky: the title character, a gambler and conman, in Alexander Sukhovo-Kobylin's play *Krechinsky's Wedding* (1854), which was partly written in prison while the author was under suspicion for the murder of his mistress.

Khlestakov: central character in Gogol's play *The Government Inspector* (1836)— a petty official from St. Petersburg defined by the author as the "incarnation of lying and deception."

New Times: influential and initially liberal newspaper founded in St. Petersburg in 1868. Its politics became increasingly right-wing after Alexey Suvorin became proprietor and editor-in-chief in 1876. A prolific writer and publisher who pioneered inexpensive mass-market editions, and opened a nationwide chain of bookshops, Suvorin was the first person to publish Chekhov's stories under his own name in 1886. The two became close friends, but fell out finally in the late 1890s over the Dreyfuss case, and the anti-Semitic stance espoused by both Suvorin and his newspaper.

Sinichkin: popular five-act vaudeville *Lev Gurych Sinichkin, or the Professional Debutante'*—an authorised translation by Dmitry Lensky of the 1837 play *Le Père de la débutante* by Jean-François Bayard and Emmanuel Théaulon, first performed in Moscow in 1839.

Kühner composed his Latin Grammar: the German classical scholar Raphael Kühner (1802–1878) published his widely reprinted *Elementargrammatik der lateinischen Sprache* in 1849—it was a textbook Chekhov was himself familiar with from his Taganrog schooldays.

141 **Ephialtes betrayed his homeland to the Persians**: Ephialtes of Trachis, son of Eurydemus of Malis, betrayed King Leonidas I and the allied Greek forces in the Battle of Thermopylae in 480 BC in exchange for a reward from the Persian King Xerxes I.

Tsitovich learned to write: see notes to "Letter to a Learned Neighbour."

Mr. Batalin: the poet Alexander Batalin (1787–1846) came from an impoverished noble background in Kaluga, where he worked for over thirty years as a minor official.

Boborykin and Markevich are great writers: the right-wing civil servant, novelist and critic Boleslav Markevich (1822–1884) was of noble Polish descent. Like Boborykin (see earlier note), he lived and worked in St. Petersburg and was equally despised by Chekhov.

Lokhvitsky has died: the lawyer Alexander Lokhitvsky (see earlier note) in fact died two years later in 1884 at the age of 54.

Arifa: Arifa, Pearl of Aden: ballet with music by the Warsaw-born composer Yuly Gerber (1831–1883) first staged at the Bolshoi Theatre in Moscow in February 1881.

Madame Menter: the celebrated German virtuoso pianist Sophie Menter (1846–1918) was a favourite pupil of Franz Liszt, and enjoyed a distinguished international career. From 1883 to 1886 she taught at the Saint Petersburg Conservatoire.

The Maiden of Hell: four-act "fantastic" ballet with music by "Nefkur," first staged at the Bolshoi Theatre in November 1879.

142 ***Ivan Ivanovich quarrelled with Ivan Nikiforovich***: characters in Nikolay Gogol's humorous story "The Tale of How Ivan Ivanovich Quarrelled with Ivan Niki-forovich", first published in 1834.

Akaky Akakievich: the hapless main character in Nikolay Gogol's tragi-comic story "The Overcoat" (1842)—the overcoat he saves up for is stolen from him on the first evening he wears it.

Name days: the editor of Current News Mr. Gilyarov and the late N. I. Krylov: the Slavophile theologian, former censor and journalist Nikita Gilyarov-Pla-tonov (1834–1887) became the founding editor of Moscow's first daily news-paper *Current News* in 1867. Aimed at a less well-educated mass readership while never becoming "tabloid," the paper flourished until the arrival in 1881 of the more openly commercial *Moscow Sheet*, set up by its ambitious former contributor Nikolay Pastukhov. Nikita Krylov (1807–1879), who also served as a censor, from 1839–1844, was a distinguished professor of law at Moscow University.

The Battle between the Russians and the Kabardians: a spoof name for a por-tentous new drama by Dmitry Averkiev taken from the title of an 1840 novel by Nikolay Zryakhov (1782 or 1786–1846).

Agafya Fedoseyevna: a character in Gogol's 1835 story "The Tale of How Ivan Ivanovich Quarrelled with Ivan Nikiforovich" who likes gossiping, swearing and eating boiled beetroot every morning.

Nikolay Rubinstein: the Russian pianist, conductor and teacher Nikolay Rubin-stein (1835-1881) became the first director of the Moscow Conservatoire in 1864. Tchaikovsky, one of the first teachers to be hired, became a close friend and mourned his untimely death from tuberculosis at the age of 45.

Agafopod Yedinitsyn (author of Rockets of Five Feelings): pseudonym of Alex-ander Chekhov (1855–1913), Anton Chekhov's elder brother.

Pythagorean "Trousers": when learning the Pythagorean theorem, Russian schoolchildren used to memorise a rhyming couplet: "Pythagoras' trousers / on all sides are equal" (Pifagorovy shtany / na vse storony ravny).

143 ***King Alivemelekh of Nicomedia***: a parodic name, similar to the Biblical Abi-melech.

Pulkheriya Ivanovna: a character in Nikolay Gogol's 1835 story "Old World Landowners," a modern Ukrainian-Russian retelling of the Philemon and Bau-cis in Ovid's *Metamorphoses*.

The artist of arts Mr. Yukhantsev: reference to Konstantin Yukhantsev, a ca-shier who between 1873 and 1878 stole over two million roubles from the

St. Petersburg branch of the Society of Mutual Land Credit (which had been set up to provide financial support for impoverished landowners following the abolition of serfdom in 1861). The scandalous case reached the courts in 1879. Chekhov could have never imagined when he was compiling his *"Alarm Clock Almanac"* in 1882 that eight years later he would meet the exiled Yukhantsev in Krasnoyarsk, during his three-month journey to conduct a census of the penal colony on the island of Sakhalin.

lead article in the Current: reference to the Moscow daily *Current News*, edited by Nikita Gilyarov-Platonov—see earlier note.

144 **Africans and Zenos**: allusion to the third-century north African martyr St. Zeno who suffered for Christ during the reign of the Roman Emperor Decius. He is known in the Orthodox Church as "Zeno the African (Carthaginian)" (*Zeno Afrikanskii (Karfagenskii)*), to distinguish him from other saints named Zeno.

Ponson du Terrail... 1,000,005 Francs will be handed out: Pierre Alexis, Viscount of Ponson du Terrail (1829–1871) was a hugely successful French writer. He is best-known for nine sensational adventure novels featuring the lawless character Rocambole (1857–1871) which appeared in Russian translation in the late 1860s. A notorious Moscow-based criminal association active across Russia between 1871 and 1875 took its name from the second in the series *The Jack of Hearts Club* (*Le Club des Valets du Coeur*, 1858), and even modelled its extravagant acts of theft, deception and forgery on those recounted in the novel. Chekhov was no doubt familiar with the new Russian edition of *The Jack of Hearts Club*, which was published in Moscow in 1878, the year after forty five mostly well-educated swindlers were finally brought to trial in a case which attracted international attention. In 1882, the same year in which Chekhov published his *"Alarm Clock Almanac,"* he wrote three chapters of an unfinished parodic novel entitled *The Secrets of a Hundred and Forty-Four Catastrophes, or the Russian Rocambole (A Most Enormous Novel in Condensed Form. Translation from the French)*.

'Beelzebub will pop up out of Carl Heymann's sleeve': The German virtuoso pianist Carl Heymann (1854–1922) performed in Moscow in March 1882.

Green Point
(A Small Novel)

146 **artist Chekhov**: reference to the author's brother, the artist Nikolay Chekhov (1858–1889), who provided a colour illustration for this story when it was

first published. This is the first of several other references in this story to real people, whose names have been preserved. The Georgian-sounding names (Mikshadze, Chaikhidzev) appear to have been invented by Chekhov.

retired first lieutenant-artilleryman Yegorov: the friendship Yevgraf Yegorov formed with the Chekhov brothers in the early 1880s soured when his romantic overtures to their sister Maria were discouraged by the family. That would quickly be forgotten when Chekhov renewed their acquaintance towards the end of 1891, inspired by Yegorov's vigorous contribution to the famine relief effort as land captain in Nizhny Novgorod province.

the medical student Korobov with his wife Yekaterina Ivanovna: Nikolay Korobov (1860–1919) was a fellow medical student with Chekhov and was one of three lodgers in the family's dank basement flat when he first arrived in August 1879 from distant Vyatka (current-day Kirov, 600 miles north-east of Moscow). Employed as a doctor at the same Moscow hospital throughout his career, he became Chekhov's lifelong friend, and is the dedicatee of the story "Late-Blooming Flowers" in this volume. His wife was indeed called Yekaterina Ivanovna.

The Great Menaion Reader: the first Russian "Cheti Minei" (from the Greek *Menaion*, meaning month), a compendium of Orthodox saints' lives, homilies and other doctrinal texts consisting of twelve volumes for each month of the year, was put together in the sixteenth century by Metropolitan Makary.

148 *Lomonosov*: Mikhail Lomonosov (1711–1765), Russian polymath, scientist and writer.

Tiflis: the pre-1936 name for Tbilisi, the capital of Georgia.

Yekaterinoslav: city founded in 1787 by Grigory Potemkin in honour of Catherine the Great which is modern-day Dnipro in Ukraine.

"The Rendezvous did Take Place, But…"

162 *Tryokhgornoe*: a famous Russian brewery founded in Moscow in 1875.

The Correspondent

164 *Chernyaevsky March*: after largely serving with distinction in the Imperial Russian army during its conquest of Central Asia and then in 1871 founding the conservative St. Petersburg-based newspaper *Russian World* (*Russkii mir*), Mikhail Chernyaev (1828–1898) was appointed Commander-in-Chief of the

Serbian army at the outbreak of the Serbo-Turkish War in 1876. He became a famous symbol of the Pan-Slavist cause, to which he had dedicated his energies.

168 *"Blessed is he who in his youth was young!"*: a quotation from chapter 8, stanza 10 of Pushkin's *Eugene Onegin* ("blazhen, kto smolodu byl molod!").

170 *The Voice*: the important liberal St. Petersburg newspaper the *Voice (Golos)* was founded by Andrey Krayevsky (1810–1889) during the age of reforms in 1863 and closed in 1883 rather than submit to the stricter censorship rules imposed during the reactionary reign of Alexander III. It campaigned for universal state education and earned a reputation in the 1870s for exposing corruption.

The Courier: see notes to "Comic Advertisements and Notices".

"for those who lost their lives at Plevna": the Russian army suffered heavy losses in three battles before its victorious five-month Siege of Plevna (the northern Bulgarian city of Pleven), which became a vital turning point in the Russo-Turkish War in 1877–1878.

171 *Game of Preference*: a trick-taking card game for three players with an originally French name (*Préférence*) but Central and East European origins. It became extremely popular in nineteenth-century Russia, where it was known as *preferans*.

The Northern Bee: a semi-official newspaper founded in St. Petersburg in 1825 by Faddei Bulgarin and Nikolay Grech, the *Northern Bee* (*Severnaya Pchela*) became known as an unofficial organ of the notorious Third Department (the Tsarist secret police). It closed in 1864.

Son of the Fatherland: the St. Petersburg newspaper *Son of the Fatherland* (*Syn otechestva*), founded by Albert Starchevsky, appeared between 1862 and 1905 and was Russia's first newspaper aimed at a mass readership.

Belinsky: Russia's first professional literary critic, Vissarion Belinsky (1811–1848) was editor of two major literary journals, *Notes of the Fatherland* (Otechestvennye zapiski) and *The Contemporary* (Sovremennik), before his premature death from tuberculosis. He was an ardent Westernizer and campaigner for social justice.

Bulgarin: Thaddeus (Faddey) Bulgarin (1789-1859), Russian journalist, writer and publisher of Polish descent, who served under Napoleon in the Patriotic War 1812 and later worked for the Tsarist Secret Police.

Rural Aesculapiuses

180 *Asclepius / Aesculapius* was the Greco-Roman god of medicine and healing.

The zemstvo surgery: the zemstvo, introduced in 1864 as part of Alexander II's reforms, was an elected provincial council which provided limited self-government. The pioneering public health programme of zemstvo medicine, implemented the following year, funded the building of the first clinics and hospitals in rural areas, employed idealistic young doctors, and offered free medical care. In so doing, it gradually revolutionised Russia's primitive health care provision, whereby there had been usually one doctor for tens of thousands of patients, and peasants were treated by poorly educated orderlies, as in this story. Chekhov would become an active supporter of zemstvo medicine when he qualified as a doctor.

A Lost Opportunity
(*A Vaudeville Incident*)

186 **Sokolniki**: a wooded area with a large park in north-east Moscow created by Tsar Alexey Mikhailovich in the seventeenth century as a home for his falconers (*sokol* is the Russian word for falcon). In the late nineteenth century it became a popular destination for Muscovites wanting to get out of the city.

Flying Islands

191 **yacht Katavasia**: the Ancient Greek word *katabasis* (literally: descent) denotes a journey to the Underworld, or a literary work describing one which culminates in an ascent (anabasis). In the Eastern Orthodox Church, *katavasia* or *katabasia* is a type of hymn where the two choirs descend from their stalls and sing together in the middle of the church (as Chekhov did when he was a chorister). The word in Russian also means turmoil or mayhem.

195 **Meshchersky**: see notes to "Holiday Assignments."

A Rotten Story
(*Something Vaguely Novelistic*)

200 **Rakhvael**: Lyolya's poorly educated father Timofey Aslovsky mispronounces the name of the celebrated Renaissance painter Raphael.

201 **The Jester**: see notes to "Life in Questions and Exclamations."

203 **Afanasy Fet**: the distinguished lyrical poet Afanasy Fet (1820–1892) was also a translator of German and Latin literature and philosophy.

The Twenty-Ninth of June
(The Tale of a Hunter Who Could Never Hit His Target)

207   **The Twenty-Ninth of June**: Like "St. Peter's Day" earlier in this volume but exactly a year later in 1882, this story was published on 29 June, on the day marking the official beginning of the hunting season.

210   **La Fille de Madame Angot**: "Madame Angot's Daughter" was a popular French comic opera written by Charles Lecocq in 1872, and undoubtedly performed at the theatre in Taganrog when Chekhov was growing up.

      as foolish as forty thousand brothers: a humorous allusion to the Russian translation of Hamlet's words in Act 5, Scene 1 of Shakespeare's play: "I loved Ophelia. Forty thousand brothers could not with all their quantity of love make up my sum." The phrase "Forty thousand brothers" crops up several times in Chekhov's early prose, including *A Hollow Victory*, which appears later in this volume.

Which of the Three?
(An Old, Yet Eternally New Tale)

215   **State Councillors:** the fifth grade in the Table of Ranks equivalent to Brigadier in the army.

217   **"The Marksman"**: reference to a light-hearted Russian version of the Czech folk song "Šly panenky silnicí" ("The girls walked down the road"). The song became wildly popular in Russia in the late 1870s, not least due to the jaunty, syncopated dance rhythms of its rhyming couplets, and is used ironically by Chekhov here, since its story of a hunter marrying one of the girls he encounters one day and living happily ever after is in direct contrast to Baron Vladimir von Strahl's rejection of Nadya's proposal of marriage. The song is mentioned in two other early stories by Chekhov, including "The Fair," written two weeks later, which appears later in this volume.

He and She

221   **Marguerite**: the leading soprano role in Gounod's 1859 opera *Faust*.

223   **kvass:** see notes to "The *Alarm Clock* Almanac."

224   **Patti**: due to popular demand, the renowned Italian coloratura soprano Adelina Patti (1843–1919), said to be the second most famous woman in the world

after Queen Victoria, and the highest paid, repeatedly returned to Russia on tour in the 1870s, where she formed numerous friendships amongst the aristocracy and creative elite.

The Fair

231 ***"I'm not Straitanoff—I'm Ivan Fedoseyev."***: Chekhov introduces an untranslatable play on words in this exchange. In the original story, the instruction "Stoi rovno!" ("stand up straight!"), with the stress in "rovno" falling on the first syllable, and the second pronounced as "na," receives the response "Ya ne Marya Petrovna, a Ivan Fedoseyev" (I'm not Marya Petrovna but Ivan Fedoseyev"). An equivalent has been found in English.

232 ***Grachovka***: street in a deprived area of northern Moscow where Chekhov lived when he first arrived in Moscow in 1879, now known as Trubnaya Street.

The Mistress

235 ***trying not to emphasise the penultimate one***: Russian readers would have immediately recognised the estate manager Rzhevetsky as a Pole on the basis of his first name, patronymic and surname (which would be spelled Rzewecki in Polish), and this reference to the paroxytonic stress common in the Polish language further confirms his nationality.

237 ***kvass:*** see notes to "The *Alarm Clock* Almanac."

238 ***kurgans:*** see notes to "St. Peter's Day."

252 ***Kuban***: historic region adjacent to the Don steppe in the North Caucasus region of southern Russia surrounding the Kuban river, with access to the Sea of Azov and the Black Sea. After Catherine the Great annexed Crimea in 1783, the Kuban river became the Russian frontier.

A Hollow Victory
(A Story)

255 ***Ilka Dog Teeth***: the heroine's first name would probably have reminded Russian readers of the soprano Etelka Gerster (1855–1920), the "Hungarian nightingale," who made her debut in 1876, sang with the Italian Imperial Opera in St Petersburg at the end of the 1870s, and performed in Moscow in 1882. "Dog Teeth" ("Sobach'i Zubki") is her unusual nickname. Chekhov seems to

have derived the supposedly Austro-Hungarian "Zwiebusch" (transliterated as "Zvibush" in Cyrillic) from the name of a residential area in Brandenburg, Germany.

Hungarian steppe: Chekhov had placed a bet with Alexander Kurepin, editor of *The Alarm Clock*, that he could write a story which readers would think was by the Hungarian novelist Mór Jókai (1825–1904), if it was published without attribution. Despite his ignorance about Hungary, Chekhov won the bet, and this lengthy story appeared over nine successive instalments of the popular weekly magazine between the middle of June and the end of August 1882. Although it bears no resemblance to the popular Russian translations of Jokai's novels, which began to appear at the end of the 1870s, numerous readers wrote to the magazine to ask if Jokai was the author. The editor made various cuts, reserved the right to cease publication at a time of his choosing, and at the end of July 1882, after six instalments, began exhorting Chekhov to bring the story to a conclusion. Chekhov was in the end given column inches in three more issues, but still did not provide a satisfactory denouement.

265 *Godefroy de Bouillon* (1060–1100), son of Eustace II, Count of Boulogne, leader of the First Crusade in 1096 and first ruler of the Kingdom of Jerusalem in 1099.

272 *Lucullan feasts*: the Roman General Licinius Lucullus (118–57 BCE) established such a reputation for lavish banquets that his name has become synonymous with luxurious gastronomy.

281 *Erlking*: an elf-king or a malevolent spirit in Germanic folklore who lives in the forest and stalks and kills children—an omen of death.

288 *Billroth*: the German surgeon Theodor Billroth (1829–1894) is regarded as the founder of modern abdominal surgery.

293 *Boccaccio*: three-act operetta by the Austrian composer Franz von Suppè first performed in 1879.

Live Goods

332 *to F. F. Popudoglo*: Chekhov shared a merchant background with the writer Fyodor Popudoglo (1846–1883), a fellow contributor to *The Alarm Clock*, and they became friends. In 1882 he was already ill from the cancer of the rectum from which he would die the following year, and which Chekhov correctly diagnosed when he began treating him.

335 **The Assembly**: see notes to *"The Alarm Clock* Almanac" concerning the Assembly of the Nobility.

339 **Russian troikas**: see notes to "St. Peter's Day."

342 **ancient kurgans**: see notes to "St. Peter's Day."

351 **Order of St. Stanislav**: an order originating in Poland which was included in the Russian honours system in 1832 and occupied its lowest rank. Divided into three classes, only the first of which bestowed hereditary nobility, it was awarded for military or civilian distinction, or for charitable work, and took the form of a cross worn across the shoulder, round the neck or in the buttonhole. The Order of Saint Stanislav, Third Class was routinely awarded to all government employees of merit in the Table of Ranks, such as Liza's civil servant husband Ivan Petrovich. Chekhov himself would be awarded the Order of Saint Stanislav, Third Class in December 1899, for his services to education, but shrank from all associations with the establishment, and never mentioned it.

Late-Blooming Flowers

364 **Korobov:** see notes to "Green Point".

389 **card game "Noses"**: the old Russian card game "Noski" takes its name from the plural of the diminutive for "nose" (*nosik*). The loser, when there is no money available for stakes, is hit on the nose with three cards by each of the other players. The number of times the loser is hit on the nose is determined by the last card drawn from a shuffled deck at the end of the game and a pre-arranged calculation, the highest being 11 in the case of it being an ace. The loser attempts to protect their face by holding several cards in front of it in both hands and leaving only their nose protruding.

A Speech And A Strap

402 **This liberalism has got to go**: the archivist is warning his colleagues of the supposed dangers of reading the satirical writer Saltykov-Shchedrin in the new conservative regime of increased censorship under Alexander III after he became Tsar in 1881. Chekhov's irony was not appreciated by the censor, and his story was forbidden from being published in November 1882. This was despite Nikolay Leikin, the editor of the comic magazine *Fragments* (*Oskolki*), making a special request that the story be discussed at the censorship

committee meeting. Noticing that the censorship was slightly less strict two years later, Leikin re-submitted the story, and this time was successful, hence its publication in 1884.

An Unfortunate Run-In

404 *I loved you, and the love may perhaps still...*: the opening line of a famous lyric poem by Pushkin written in 1829. Of the three song settings, by Alexander Dargomyzhsky (1813–1869) in 1832, Alexander Alabiev (1787–1851) in 1834, and Boris Sheremetiev (1822–1906) in 1859, the last is by far the most popular. Sheremetiev's best-known composition, it is undoubtedly the song Chekhov has in mind.

Two Scandals

410 *Valentine and Mephistopheles*: characters in Gounod's 1859 opera *Faust*, loosely based on the first part of Goethe's 1808 play *Faust: A Tragedy*.

412 *Les Huguenots*: spectacular grand opera by Giacomo Meyerbeer composed in 1836, and a mainstay of the prerevolutionary repertoire in both St. Petersburg and Moscow.

Idyll—Alack And Alas!

418 *Rykov... Skopin Bank*: reference to Russia's first pyramid scheme, which led to six thousand investors losing a total of twelve million roubles, as in the case of Captain Nasechkin in Chekhov's story, written very soon after the scandal was exposed. Ivan Rykov (1831–1897) had been director of the recently established Skopin Municipal Bank in Ryazan province for five years when he first began cooking the books in 1868 in order to cover up an initial deficit of 54,000 roubles. As well as submitting false reports to the Ministry of Finance, bribing the local administration and selling shares in a non-existent mining company, he was soon advertising an improbable 7.5% interest rate which lured credulous new investors from all over Russia, including civil servants, teachers, priests and army officers. Local whistleblowers waited six years for the Ryazan governor to respond to their request for an investigation, only for it to be turned down in 1874 on the grounds that it was incorrectly submitted. When their appeal to the Ministry of Justice was also turned down four years

later on a technicality, they resolved to approach the press, but as Rykov had bribed the postmaster into intercepting undesirable correspondence, it was not until late 1882 that the first revelations began to appear in the *Russian Courier* newspaper in Moscow, leading instantly to the bank's collapse and Rykov's arrest. Chekhov was fascinated, and reported on the case for the *Petersburg Newspaper* when Rykov was brought to trial in 1884 and exiled to Siberia.

The Baron

421 **Salvini**: the celebrated Italian actor Tommaso Salvini (1829–1915) brought his company on tour to Russia during the Lent season of 1882, and his performances in Moscow as Othello, his signature role, had a huge impact on the future director Konstantin Stanislavsky, then still a teenager.

Ernesto Rossi: the equally celebrated actor Ernesto Rossi (1827–1896), Salvini's great rival, undertook five tours to Russia, beginning in 1877, and was also admired for his Shakespearean roles, particularly Hamlet and Macbeth.

A Kind Acquaintance

428 **Speusippus**: Chekhov gives the porter the improbable first name of "Spevsip," the Russian form of Speusippus, who was an ancient Greek philosopher like his uncle Plato.

Titular Counsilor: see notes to "Papasha."

An Experience
(A Psychological Study)

436 **the sheet of paper which lay majestically on the table**: it was the custom in imperial Russia for all civil servants to sign a seasonal greeting to their superior at New Year.

insert the hard sign: in the prerevolutionary Russian orthography, the hard sign, called "yer" and written "ъ," was usually added to the end of a word following a non-palatal consonant, despite having no effect on pronunciation. This practice was discontinued in the spelling reform of 1918.

Philosophical Definitions of Life

438 **Buckle**: a translation of the monumental *History of Civilisation in England* by Henry Thomas Buckle (1821–1862) was published in St. Petersburg in 1863, six years after its original British publication, and became very popular amongst Russian university students. Held in as high regard by such figures as Darwin, Kant, Marx and Feuerbach during his lifetime for attempting to discover scientific laws behind historical progress, Buckle is today best known for his victory in the first chess tournament in London in 1849.

    Coquelin: one of the greatest actors of his age, Benoît-Constant Coquelin (1841–1909), was known as Coquelin The Elder (to distinguish him from his younger brother, also an actor). A full member of the Comédie-Française since the age of 23, he came on tour to Russia for the first time at the end of 1882, and performed in Moscow at the Bolshoi Theatre.

    Draper: the celebrated English-born American scientist John William Draper (1811–1882) taught chemistry and botany from 1839 at New York University where he founded its medical school, created the first detailed photograph of the moon in 1840 and the first daguerreotype portrait. In Russia he became best-known for his writings, including his *History of the Intellectual Development of Europe* (1862), translated in 1866, and particularly his *History of the Conflict Between Religion and Science* (1874), translated in 1876.

439 **Orabi Pasha**: the first Egyptian political and military leader to come from a peasant background, Ahmed 'Urabi, or Orabi Pasha (1841–1911) led a revolt in February 1882 against foreign control and absolutist rule which resulted in him serving as Prime Minister from July to September, when a large-scale British intervention led to his surrender. His trial and subsequent exile to Ceylon in December 1882, just when Chekhov was writing his philosophical definitions, were extensively covered in the Russian press.

    Charcot: the legendary French physician Jean-Martin Charcot (1825–1893) was appointed Professor of Anatomical Pathology at the University of Paris in 1872, and became an influential figure in the development of psychotherapy, founding a pioneering neurological clinic at the Salpêtrière Hospital in 1882, where he carried out influential work on hypnosis and hysteria.

Fortune Tellers
(New Year Scenes)

444 ***staring into a mirror by the light of two candles***: this was a customary form of divination practised in prerevolutionary Russia at yuletide between Christmas and Epiphany, mostly by young women hoping to see the face of their future bridegroom.

445 ***mittens... hedgehog... Makary's... calf...***: the divination contains untranslatable comic allusions to two familiar phrases respectively denoting harsh treatment and political exile to Siberia, which Chekhov's Russian readers would have immediately grasped. The expression to rule with "hedgehog mittens," meaning to rule with a rod of iron, derives from the old Russian practice of wearing unlined leather mittens as protection when holding hedgehogs. The vaguely ominous phrase "there, where [even] Makary has not driven cattle", meaning very far away (in other words, Siberia), has two possible meanings. It can be an ironic reference to the most downtrodden Russian peasants, who were never able to afford having their own cattle, or indeed any animals, or it can refer to the arduous task of their being obliged to drive other people's cattle to very remote pastures. Makary had become a generic name for a particularly poor, unlucky peasant since the times of Peter the Great, who once encountered three peasants in a row in Ryazan with that name.

Original Publication Dates

1. ... v, "Letter to a Learned Neighbour" ["Pis'mo k uchenomu sosedu"], *Strekoza*, 9 March 1880.
2. Antosha, "What Does One Usually Encounter in Novels, Tales, Etc.?" ["Chto chasche vsego vstrechaetsya v romanakh, povestyakh i t.p.?"], *Strekoza*, 9 March 1880.
3. Chekhonte, "Chase Two Hares and You Will Lose Them Both" ["Za dvumya zaitsami pogonishsya, ni odnogo ne poimaesh'"], *Strekoza*, 11 May 1880.
4. Chekhonte, "Holiday Assignments" ["Kanikulyarnye raboty institutki Naden'ki N."], *Strekoza*, 15 June 1880.
5. An. Ch., "Papasha" ["Papasha"], *Strekoza*, 29 June 1880.
6. "Prosaic Poet" ["Prozaicheskii poet"], " My Jubilee" ["Moi yubilei"], *Strekoza*, 6 July 1880.
7. Antosha Ch., "One Thousand and One Passions, Or a Terrible Night (A Novel in One Chapter with an Epilogue)" ["Tysyacha odna strast', ili Strashnaya noch' (Roman v odnoi chasti s epilogom)"], *Strekoza*, 27 July 1880.
8. Chekhonte, "On Account of the Apples" ["Za yablochki"], *Strekoza*, 17 August 1880.
9. Antosha Chekhonte, "Before the Wedding" ["Pered svad'boi"], *Strekoza*, 12 October 1880.
10. Antosha Ch., "The American Way" ["Po-amerikanski"], *Strekoza*, 7 December 1880.
11. Antosha Chekhonte, "Artists' Wives (Translation... from the Portuguese)" ["Zheny artistov: (Perevod... s portugal'skogo)"], *Minuta*, 7 December 1880.
12. Antosha Chekhonte, "St. Peter's Day" ["Petrov den'"], *Budil'nik*, 29 June 1881.
13. Antosha Ch***, "Personality Types (According to the Latest Scientific Findings)" ["Temperamenty: Po poslednim vyvodom nauki)"], *Zritel'*, 17 September 1881.
14. Antosha Ch., "On the Train" ["V vagone"], *Zritel'*, 29 September 1881.
15. Antosha Ch., "Salon De Variété" ["Salon de var'ete"], *Zritel'*, 4 October 1881.
16. Antosha Chekhonte, "The Trial" ["Sud"], *Zritel'*, 23 October 1881.
17. Antosha Chekhonte, "Antosha Chekhonte's Notifications Office" ["Kontora ob'yavlenii Antoshi Ch."], *Zritel'*, 24 October 1881.
18. Antosha Ch., "This and That (Poetry and Prose)" ["I to i se (Poeziya i proza)"], *Zritel'*, 29 October 1881.
19. Antosha Ch., "This and That (Letters and Telegrams)" ["I to i se (Pis'ma i tele-grammy)"], *Zritel'*, 6 December 1881.
20. Antosha Ch., "The Sinner from Toledo (Translated from the Spanish)" ["Gresh-nik iz Toledo: (Perevod s ispanskogo)"], *Zritel'*, 23 December 1881.
21. Antosha Chekhonte, "Supplementary Questions to the Personal Census Forms, Suggested by Antosha Chekhonte" ["Dopolnitel'nye voprosy k lichnym kartam

statisticheskoi perepisi, predlagaemye Antoshei Chekhonte"], *Budil'nik*, 29 January 1882.

22. Antosha Ch., "At the Wolf-Baiting" ["Na vol'chei sadke"], *Literaturnoe prilozhenie zhurnala "Moskva,"* 3 February 1882.

23. Antosha Chekhonte, "Comic Advertisements and Notices (Reported by Antosha Chekhonte)" ["Komicheskie reklamy i ob'yavlenia (Soobshchil Antosha Chekhonte)"], *Budil'nik*, 12 February 1882.

24. Antosha Chekhonte, "The Mad Mathematician's Math Test" ["Zadachi sumass-hedshego matematika"], *Budil'nik*, 20 February 1882.

25. The Man without a Spleen [Chelovek bez selezenki], "Forgotten!!" ["Zabyl!!"], *Moskva*, 25 February 1882.

26. Antosha Chekhonte, "Life in Questions and Exclamations" ["Zhizn' v voprosakh i vosklitsaniyakh"], *Budil'nik*, 25 February 1882.

27. Mr. B-v [G. B-v], "Confession, or Olya, Zhenya, Zoya (A Letter)" ["Ispoved', ili Olya, Zhenya, Zoya: (Pis'mo)"], *Budil'nik*, 20 March 1882.

28. The Man without a Spleen [Chelovek bez selezenki], "The Greeting of Spring (A Treatise)" ["Vstrecha vesny: (Rassuzhdenie)"], *Moskva*, 23 March 1882.

29. Antosha Chekhonte, "Alarm Clock Almanac 1882" ["Kalendar' 'Budil'ni-ka' na 1882 god"], *Budil'nik*, Nos. March–April 10-14 1882; No. 14 signed Mr. Baldastov.

30. Antosha Chekhonte, "Green Point (A Small Novel)" ["Zelenaya kosa (Malen'kii roman)"], *Literaturnoe prilozhenie zhurnala "Moskva,"* 23, 30 April 1882.

31. Antosha Chekhonte, "The Rendezvous Did Take Place, But..." ["Svidanie khotya i sostoyalos', no..."], *Moskva*, 7 May 1882.

32. Antosha Chekhonte, "The Correspondent" ["Korrespondent"], *Budil'nik*, 20, 27 May 1882.

33. Antosha Ch., "Rural Aesculapiuses" ["Sel'skie eskulapy"], *Svet i Teni*, 18 June 1882.

34. Antosha Chekhonte, "A Lost Opportunity (A Vaudeville Incident)" ["Propash-chee delo: (Vodevil'noe proisshestvie)"], *Sputnik*, 22 June 1882.

35. A. Chekhonte, "Flying Islands (Written by Jules Verne. Translated by A. Chekhonte)" ["Letayushchie ostrova: (Soch. Zhyulya Verna. Perevod A. Chekhonte)"], *Budil'nik*, 21 May 1883.

36. Antosha Chekhonte, "A Rotten Story (Something Vaguely Novelistic)" ["Skvernaya istoriya: (Nechto romanoobraznoe)"], *Svet i Teni*, 26 June, 4 July 1882.

37. Antosha Chekhonte, "The Twenty-Ninth of June (The Tale of a Hunter Who Could Never Hit His Target)" ["Dvadtsat' devyatoe iyunya: (Rasskaz okhotnika, nikogda v tsel' ne popadavshchego)"], *Sputnik*, 29 June 1882.

38. Antosha Chekhonte, "Which of the Three? (An Old, yet Eternally New Tale)" ["Kotoryi iz trekh?: (Staraya, no vechno novaya istoriya)"], *Sputnik*, 13 July 1882.

39. A. Chekhonte, "He And She" ["On i ona"], *Mirskoi Tolk*, 23 July 1882.

40. Antosha Chekhonte, "The Fair" ["Yarmarka"], *Moskva*, 25 July 1882.

41. Antosha Chekhonte, "The Mistress" ["Barynya"], *Moskva*, 30 July, 7 August, 17 August, 1882.
42. A. Chekhonte, "A Hollow Victory (A Short Story)" ["Nenuzhnaya pobeda (Rasskaz)"], *Budil'nik*, 18 June, 25 June, 2 July, 9 July, 23 July, 30 July, 6 August, 13 August, 20 August, 27 August 1882.
43. A. Chekhonte, "Live Goods" ["Zhivoi Tovar"], *Mirskoi Tolk*, 6 August, 14 August, 22 August, 27 August 1882.
44. A. Chekhonte, "Late-Blooming Flowers" ["Tsvety zapozdalye"], *Mirskoi Tolk*, 10 October , 17 October, 23 October, and 11 November 1882.
45. A. Chekhonte, "A Speech and a Strap" ["Rech' i remeshok"], *Oskolki*, 24 November 1884.
46. Antosha Chekhonte, "An Unfortunate Run-In' ["Narvalsya"], *Oskolki*, 20 November, 1882.
47. The Man Without a Spleen ["Chelovek bez selezenki"], "An Unsuccessful Visit" ["Neudachnyi visit"], *Oskolki*, 27 November 1882.
48. A. Chekhonte, "Two Scandals" ["Dva skandala"], *Mirskoi Tolk*, 16 December 1882.
49. Antosha Chekhonte, "Idyll—Alack and Alas!" ["Idilliya—uvy i akh!"], *Oskolki*, 18 December 1882.
50. A. Chekhonte, "The Baron" ["Baron"], *Mirskoi Tolk*, 20 December 1882.
51. The Man Without a Spleen ["Chelovek bez selezenki"], "A Kind Acquaintance" [Dobryi znakomyi], *Oskolki*, 25 December 1882.
52. A. Chekhonte, "Revenge" ["Mest'"], *Mirskoi Tolk*, 31 December 1882.
53. Antosha Chekhonte, "An Experience (A Psychological Study)" ["Perezhitoe (Psikhologicheskyi etyud)"], *Zritel'*, no 1 (1883)
54. Antosha Chekhonte, "Philosophical Definitions of Life" ["Filosofskie opredeleniya zhizni"], *Zritel'*, no 1 (1883)
55. The Man Without a Spleen [Chelovek bez selezenki], "Reluctant Cheats (A New Year's Eve Tall Tale)" ["Moshenniki ponevole: (Novogodniya pobrekhushka)"], *Zritel'*, no 1 (1883)
56. The Man Without a Spleen [Chelovek bez selezenki], "Fortune Tellers (New Year Scenes)" ["Gadal'shchiki i gadal'schitsy: (Podnovogodnie kartinki)"], *Zritel'*, no 1 (1883)
57. A. Chekhonte, "The Distorting Mirror (A Christmas Tale)" ["Krivoe zerkalo: (Svyatochnyi rasskaz)"], *Zritel'*, 5 January1883.
58. The Man Without a Spleen ["Chelovek bez selezenki"], "Two Romances" ["Dva romana"], *Oskolki*, 8 January 1883.

www.ingramcontent.com/pod-product-compliance
Lightning Source LLC
Chambersburg PA
CBHW020605040726
47498CB00003B/646